THE STARGODS
TRILOGY

IRENE RADFORD

THE STARGODS TRILOGY

THE HIDDEN DRAGON

✦—•—✦—•—✦

THE DRAGON CIRCLE

✦—•—✦—•—✦

THE DRAGON'S REVENGE

DAW BOOKS, INC.

DONALD A. WOLLHEIM, FOUNDER

375 Hudson Street, New York, NY 10014

ELIZABETH R. WOLLHEIM

SHEILA E. GILBERT

PUBLISHERS

www.dawbooks.com

First Printing, January 2015

1 2 3 4 5 6 7 8 9

DAW TRADEMARK REGISTERED
U.S. PAT. AND TM. OFF. AND FOREIGN COUNTRIES
—MARCA REGISTRADA
HECHO EN U.S.A.

PRINTED IN THE U.S.A.

INTRODUCTION

I CONFESS, *The Glass Dragon: The Dragon Nimbus #1* was supposed to be my therapy book. I threw in every pun and trope I found fun, because I could. Then, when my critique group started making noises about that book being the best thing I had ever written, and my newly acquired agent started hounding me to finish it . . . I had to think seriously about my world building.

Part of me wanted to skip the religion aspect. It's hard thinking up a new religion. This was therapy, not work. I didn't want to offend people. Blah, blah, blah.

When I finished grumbling and looked at what I had cobbled together so far, I realized that I'd thrown in references to "The Stargods," whispered in great awe. Well, that was between my brother and me: Captain Kirk violating the Prime Directive once again. Just another trope to make the book fun for me to write.

Was that all it was?

Maybe not.

So I went looking in my lizard brain for what it had told me ages before about what the book needed. I found three outlaw brothers, space jockeys, one-step ahead of the law, who crash land on a planet where dragons are real and magic works. They use their technology for some necessary "miracles" and are proclaimed as the Stargods.

Then they have to live up to it. And keep the law from finding them and their pristine world.

Eventually the time came when I couldn't move the *Dragon Nimbus* and *Dragon Nimbus History* books forward until I fleshed out the story of how the scoundrels became the Stargods. As usual, my "Aha!" moment evolved into three books, rather than a short story or chapter.

I hope you have as much fun reading these adventures as I had writing them. Some of my all-time favorite characters sprang from these books. I wonder if they have more stories hidden up their sleeves—along with an extra ace or a tiny derringer . . .

—Irene Radford
Welches, Oregon

THE HIDDEN DRAGON

This book is dedicated to all my loyal readers.
I love you all.

ACKNOWLEDGMENTS

First off, I need to thank Beth Gilligan, Lea Day, and Karen Lewis for all their help and advice in getting me to finish this book when all I wanted to do was whine and complain.

The final draft would not have happened if Dr. Ken Wharton, PhD, had not redesigned my spaceship just so I could trash it. Thank you once again, Ken, and good luck with your own career as an SF author.

Of course, my agent, Carol McCleary of the Wilshire Literary Agency, always inspires me with advice, sympathy, and kicks where I need them most.

Sheila E. Gilbert, editor extraordinaire for DAW Books, gets virtual hugs from all the way across the country for her help and dedication to making my work the best book I can possibly turn out.

Thank you one and all,

    Irene Radford

CHAPTER 1

✦━━·━━✦━━·━━✦

"**H**OLY MOTHER OF GOD!" Kim O'Hara's stomach somersaulted repeatedly. His balance skittered in several directions.

Reality blurred.

Then the saucer-shaped *Sirius* dropped back into normal space from an unplanned jump. Kim said a brief silent prayer of thanks and wonder—all his body parts seemed intact and functioning.

An inner awareness of his two brothers reassured Kim that all three O'Haras had made it through the jump intact. He didn't need to see them, merely feel them breathing beside him on the circular bridge of the family cargo vessel.

"All present and functioning," the computer's voice, sounding as much like his mother as artificial vocal cords could, reported Kim's own observation.

"Thank you, Mum, but I'm busy!" Loki, the oldest brother, replied as he slapped the mute. None of the brothers would speak so rudely to Mum in person, but she wasn't on this frantic journey and the computer obeyed them.

No two FTL jumps were alike. Some happened so fast Kim barely felt them. Others lasted as long as a dream with detailed images fixed in his brain afterward. A very few offered glimpses into some Wonderland where dragons were real and magic worked. Some just hurt. This last one seemed a mixture of all three types.

He was anxious to find out where the miracle of crystal drives and technology had taken them. He extended his prayer that they had managed to leave the pursuing IMPs behind. Three jumps and thousands of light-years had passed since the law had first ordered them to stand down and prepare to be boarded.

Kim and his brothers couldn't afford to let the Imperial Military Police confiscate their cargo of Nautilus pearls. They needed the money from the contraband.

Mum would never forgive them if they let the cargo go.

Kim surveyed the sensor board. He scrunched his eyes and forehead trying to read and decipher the numbers too rapidly.

"Uh, Loki," Kim asked his oldest brother, "where'd you dump us? There's an IMP vessel directly in front of us. Two million klicks to firing range."

Loki slammed his fist into his pilot's console. The *Sirius* jerked half a degree to starboard.

"A different ship?" Konner, the middle brother, asked. He unlocked his chair from jump safety protocols and slid it between engineering and the crystal networks stations. He played with the nitrogen feed to the driver crystals. None of the numbers on his console changed.

Magnetic monopoles could only shoot out so many electrons no matter how much nitrogen you fed them.

"The . . . Shite! It's the *Valiant*, the same friggin' ship that's been on our tail since the first jump out of Nautilus." Kim wanted to hit something, too. Didn't dare. The weapons interface was directly under his left hand.

"That captain is outthinking us. Anticipating our actions and our knee-jerk reactions." Loki made arcane gestures over his helm interface.

Kim's sensors showed the *Sirius* rotating and diving away from the previous plane of reference. The *Valiant* followed, rapidly closing on their tail.

"How'd the IMP get here first?" Loki muttered on a deep exhale. He continued evasive maneuvers. Thrusters screamed each time he shifted away from the current horizontal so that the ring of directional crystals on the circumference of the saucer-shaped ship could find a new "forward."

The *Valiant*, an efficient teardrop shape with a full globe of directional crystals, matched them, barely a femtosecond behind.

"We didn't know where we were running to until we jumped," Loki muttered.

"Could be a 'her' at the helm." Konner fussed with his interfaces. "Someone like Mum, who can outthink us."

All three brothers shuddered.

"Wonder if the law co-opted Katie to work for them?" Konner found his readouts more interesting than risking eye contact with Loki.

Kim looked away, too. He chewed his lip trying to suppress a laugh. Nothing riled Loki like the possibility of running into the sister who had been missing from the family for nearly as long as Kim could remember.

"Not a chance *your* sister commands that ship," Loki sneered. He kept up his squiggling path out of firing range from the *Valiant*. "No O'Hara, let alone Mari Kathleen, ever worked *for* the law."

Out of six available jump points Kim had selected one at random. Loki had told him to jump without planning. The pursuing captain had learned Loki's tactics well and anticipated them, but how had the IMP captain guessed Kim's jump point and gotten here first?

"*Valiant* closing. Firing range in five hundred thousand klicks," Kim announced.

The pursuing ship was catching up at an awesome rate. Kim played with his sensors. Sometimes jump distorted the sensitive instruments, tricking them into believing dragons lived in jump space and ships dissolved into nothing.

Fine tuning only verified the speed of the ship on their tail. There was something different about this vessel, something special and so top secret none of the underground networks had predicted it. Unlike Kim's brother, Konner, the engineering genius of the family, IMP engineers didn't tinker with their ships outside of base protocols. And the brothers would have heard if a new vessel—no matter how top secret—had been launched, even if they didn't know the exact technology aboard.

"What has this IMP got that he's gaining on us? We should have lost them at the last jump point," Kim said, puzzled by the configuration showing on his sensor read-outs.

A surge of adrenaline sent Kim's hands flying over his weapons array even as he began to doubt the effectiveness of his ancient laser cannon.

"One more run," Mum had promised. "Just one more score and we'll have money enough to find Katie."

When Mum reunited the family, then each of the brothers would be free to follow their own private daydreams. They could put the smuggling business and its inherent dangers behind them.

"Can't you get any more speed out of this hangar queen, Konner?" Loki shouted. "I thought your last round of modifications were supposed to help us outrun the IMPs, not slow us down!" He looped their flight path onto a new vector, passing across the *Valiant*'s bridge.

"I'm trying," Konner grumbled, sounding equally distracted—unusual for the calm mechanic, the middle brother, the placater. "We're already five percent over my expectations for the modifications and twenty percent over specified optimum for this drive." His eyes glazed a little. Kim recognized the trance his brother used while computing figures in his head. A femto later, Konner laid his palm flat upon his terminal. He touched no particular interface. Kim wondered if he actually stretched his senses and grabbed hold of all of the controls at once. His flesh seemed to merge with the flashing lights and bouncing graphs.

The *Sirius* shuddered and whined.

"IMP coming up hard on our heels," Kim said again. "One hundred thousand klicks to firing range and closing." He closed his eyes a moment and entered a new firing sequence.

IMP weapons only fired one at a time, each blast requiring all the power they could generate. For some unknown reason, gunnery sergeants always seemed to fire the first warning shot from the port side. A few femtos later, their power would rebuild for the second killing blast from starboard. A single heartbeat of vulnerability between the two.

But this guy was different. Kim set coordinates for a first shot to his pursuers' port side. They'd dodge the required warning shot—most likely from starboard this time. Then he'd take out the port gun before it could sweep through the bridge of the *Sirius*—the easiest path to the king stone at the heart of the crystal drive.

"We'll dodge the warning shot, Kim. It'll come from the starboard. Be ready to blast their port weapons array before it can recharge," Loki ordered.

Kim half smiled. As usual, Loki had voiced Kim's suggestion before he'd fully thought it through.

"We need more speed, Konner!" Loki yelled.

"Or a miracle," Kim muttered to himself. "I promised Mum this one last run and, by St. Bridget, we're going to survive with our cargo intact! I don't want to be on the receiving end of her tongue-lashing." *Or be the author of her disappointment.*

"Environmental's running at half power, laser cannon at twenty-five percent," Konner reported. "We cut the artificial gravity an hour ago to save power and increase response time to the directionals! Everything we've got is going into the driver crystals for speed. But we're running low on nitrogen. Magnetic monopoles don't shoot out energy without fuel. I've only got one last miracle in my arsenal."

"Not again, Konner. That never works," Loki muttered. He shook his head without taking his eyes off his instruments.

Konner sighed, ignoring his brother's comment. He rose from his place at the engineer's station with elaborate care. Every movement had to be precise with an equally precise counteraction in null g.

Loki buried his head in his hands. The ship flew straight. The IMP veered. For once, the other captain had guessed wrong.

Konner opened the bulkhead and looked in dismay over his connections to the crystal network. "It's our only option."

He kicked the interface panel on the bulkhead. Vibrations rippled around the deck. Lights flickered across all three terminals.

The temporary gravity of acceleration snapped Kim's head back into the pressure-absorbent neck rest of his chair.

"I'll be danged. We just boosted our speed another three percent," Loki gaped at his display for a split femto, then fed a new configuration to the computer. He tipped the ship to starboard, raising the port side. A bolt of energy slid beneath them.

The teardrop-shaped *Valiant* recoiled. Why? Laser cannon didn't work that way. Not like the ancient explosive weapons of planet-bound sailing ships.

What about an ion cannon? Last Kim had heard, that weapon was still only a theory.

The *Valiant*'s flinch presented Kim a clear shot at the bridge. He could take them out with one extended blast.

The entire bridge crew would die.

He couldn't do it.

"Warning shot clear. No damage," Kim announced with relief.

"Just," Konner sighed.

Kim's hand hovered over the cannon trigger. He had to fire, had to take the chance he'd only disable the ship, not be responsible for the deaths of other sentient beings.

Loki continued jerking the ship through an unorthodox series of flips and twists. Difficult to lock on target with neither ship following a set course. Kim lost his clear shot to the bridge. He'd take the next target he could latch onto.

There! He locked targeting onto the forward crystal array compartment. "Returning fire!" Kim poised his hand over the trigger.

"Not yet!" Konner shouted. He kicked the interface once more. A little jolt of power surged them forward. Temporary gravity reasserted itself.

The IMPs fell behind ever so slightly.

"Guess their superior technology isn't a match for O'Hara modifications," Konner chortled as he made a micron adjustment to something. He reared up from the bulkhead frowning.

"Find a new jump point quick, before this burst of speed fizzles!" Konner shouted, clinging to the ports behind the bulkhead as if he added his own energy to the crystal drive.

"Nothing on the charts except back the way we came, but I'll take it," Loki said around a huge smile. "They'll never expect us to go there."

"Worth a try," Konner agreed.

The gravity faded as they ceased acceleration and cruised.

The *Sirius* shuddered again, and Kim's screens went dark.

"What the . . . ?" Konner stared at his blank screen.

"St. Hildy Wonstead's tits! They've knocked out our sensor array with . . . with I don't know what." Loki followed with a string of more colorful curses. His face flushed with anger as he tried desperately to coax some kind of signal back into his nav port. "I should have anticipated this. I should have known."

Kim's face went numb. His fingertips lost feeling. More than just the mechanical sensors had shut down. One by one, he lost each of his own perceptions. He tried to open his mouth, alert his brothers. He couldn't hear himself speak, couldn't feel his mouth moving.

Not now. I don't need a vision now. I need reality.

He drifted in absolute darkness. Only his mind existed. Only his thoughts had meaning.

A string of flames streaked across his inner vision followed by images of the *Sirius* tumbling, tumbling into an alien atmosphere. A huge winged creature flew straight at them, blasting flames.

The ship rocked, seeking stabilization. Towering trees with exotic leaves, mottled pink and green, fat with vital oils, reached up to cradle the ship. Not the circular *Sirius,* their snub-nosed, winged shuttle *Rover.*

As abruptly as the vision came to him, it departed. An acrid/sweet taste lingered on his tongue.

"There's a solar system at the end of an uncharted jump with an Earth-class planet. We can hide there." He had to report the words the vision dragged out of him, whether he understood them or not.

He didn't mention the dragon. It could be symbolic. It could be real. He wouldn't know until he encountered the flames.

CHAPTER 2

"STOP DAYDREAMING, Kim," Loki sneered at his baby brother. "Whoever heard of anyone coming back from an uncharted jump? King stones are limited in their range. Beyond a certain point they can't communicate with their mother stone."

"Unproven," Konner muttered. "In theory a king stone should be able to trace the web of transactional gravitons anywhere in the universe."

"The planet exists. I know it like you knew the IMP's firing pattern," Kim insisted.

"I'll believe it when I see it," Loki muttered, then decided to ignore both his brothers. They had their areas of expertise, but at the moment they were both wrong. He didn't need Kim seeing things that weren't there or Konner communing with inanimate crystals.

Loki's own flashes of insight into other people's minds (really nothing more than good guesses. Really.) were disconcerting enough. He couldn't listen to them. Not now. Not when they had a cargo that might finally give them enough hard cash to bribe the right officials to regain their citizenship and maybe even their confiscated shipping business. Mum would need that kind of respectable base to find the missing Katie. Without citizenship, bribing the right official in charge of the right database was useless.

This run had to succeed, IMPs or no IMPs on their tail.

His fiancée, Cyndi, wouldn't wait much longer for him to buy back his citizenship. Her father had insisted she marry that drooling idiot of a diplomat's son over a year ago. How long could a woman stall?

"Port sensor coming back on line," Konner said, eyes closed. He spread his hands flat on his terminal, not touching any specific controls, just interpreting changes that somehow matched the electrical magnetic energy of his own brain synapses—at least that was the latest scientific theory for "genius engineers."

The computer could have reported the same information. If Loki had released the mute. But frankly he needed silence on the bridge when Mum was gone. He had no excuse to sneer at his mother's voice, so he took out his anxiety on Konner, the nearest target.

"The greatest mechanic in the galaxy and you have to *become one with your ship*," he muttered. But Konner often sensed hidden things about the ship that the computer could not report, like a micron clog in the nitrogen feed or a less than .01 degree extra arc in fiber optic cables—enough to interfere with the optimum running of the ship but not enough to cause problems.

Instinctively Loki zigzagged the *Sirius* through another weird series of maneuvers. A laser cannon blast jolted past them.

"Close call, Loki." Kim breathed through his teeth. He looked pale and uncertain. That must have been some vision the kid had experienced. Should he turn Mum's voice back on to soothe him?

Nah. Silence was a better healer. Even for the baby of the family.

"Dammit, we just lost two crystals, right next to each other." Konner bolted for the passageway. "They're cracked! *Cracked!* The inertia dampening field is compromised. How can I fix the ship if you two steer like maniacs and drive us *into* weapons fire? Spin the saucer. It's the only way to compensate. I'll bypass the damaged crystals to give you a full range of inertia dampening."

"Kim, just find us a jump and that flaming planet," Loki growled. He hated it when his brothers were more right than he.

"Interesting choice of words." Kim smiled. But it looked more like a grimace. He read his sensor output like a second language—maybe as fluently as if it were his mother tongue.

"Just find us a place to hide before Konner fuses to his precious ship and those IMPs get any—"

His words were cut off as the ship tumbled wildly, like an astro compass on a black hole horizon. Gravity returned with the centrifugal force. The nav port blanked out again. Loki jammed combination after combination into the interface. His fingers flew across the lightboard. Nothing responded. The *Sirius* continued out of control, throwing them in ever wilder directions.

The jump bolts anchoring the chairs in place along the circular slide track strained with ominous groans.

Sudden weight tugged at Loki's facial muscles and fused his hands to his terminal. Another spin. More weight.

"Stay put, Kim. Don't release your bolts or seat harness." Panic put an edge in Loki's voice he didn't like. He should remain calm. In control. Like Mum. Always in control.

Kim stretched to unlock Konner's engineering terminal to feed into his own. He couldn't reach it while strapped in. He flipped the belt open and reached again. Easier to relock the harness than the jump bolts in an emergency.

"Kim, I told you . . ." Loki didn't dare spare his brother any more attention. The IMP fired again.

Kim's fingers brushed the engineering console and unlocked the data. The ship jerked. Kim flew across the bridge, landing headfirst against the bulkhead Konner had left open. He moaned once and went limp. Blood trickled from his temple.

"Kim!" Loki shouted in despair. "Don't die on me. Please, don't die."

"Konner, get back here!" Loki's voice boomed in Konner's ears over the intership system.

"Not if you want control of this 'hangar queen'!" Konner grabbed the first handhold in the rabbit hole, the conduit that ran the circumference of the saucer. Perhaps Loki had done right in not spinning the saucer. The centrifugal force would make Konner's job all the more difficult. The limited space was designed for maintenance, not rapid emergency repairs. Shortsighted of the New Detroit builders. Circular merchant ships with most of their interior dedicated to cargo hold weren't supposed to need rapid getaways and repairs from laser cannon fire. That was for IMP vessels with their trademark teardrop shape and the torpedo-shaped military courier vessels that smugglers usually modified for their own use.

Konner half smiled to himself. New Detroit wouldn't recognize most of the modifications he had made to the *Sirius*.

He briefly contemplated selling his modifications to Melinda. Maybe then his ex-wife would allow him docking privileges on her planet—let him see their son. Money drove Melinda. Money had caused their bitter divorce and her cheating him out of the settlement in their prenup. How much more money could she make with decently modified ships? Would she reward Konner, or cheat him again?

Above and below him, the red directional crystals, each a half meter in length with sharp points on six faces, glowed slightly from the energy pulses fed them from the twelve green drivers at the center of the ship. Each magnetic monopole driver fed twelve of the directionals.

He heard a nervous chattering sound in the back of his head, like a muted conversation on the other side of the bulkhead. Today the voices of the supposedly inanimate crystals seemed strident, unharmonious instead of the quiet shushing he needed from them. The crystals "knew" that one or more of their number was ailing. Without the complete set, their symmetry and therefore their reach toward sentience was broken as well as their ability to block (or merge with) the web of transactional gravitons that held the universe together and at the same time conspired to keep everything in its proper place. Somehow, the crystals blocked the inertia of the universe, allowing the ship to travel.

A deep moan cut through the background noise. Then absolute silence left Konner's ears ringing.

The chatter started up again on an even shaper note, edging toward hysteria. His crystals were in trouble. Not just one or two, but all one hundred-forty-four directionals, and twelve drivers. Their lack of symmetry put a terrible strain on the two-meter-high king stone that anchored to a mother crystal at the factory in Earth orbit and used the TG web for sub-light communications.

Without the king stone "anchoring" them, they couldn't find their way home after faster-than-light jumps.

He climbed through the rabbit hole using the small anchor loops on the interior bulkhead as a ladder instead of propelling himself. With the erratic course Loki flew, Konner could end up smashing into a crystal or dropping back the way he had come.

"I'm coming," he whispered. Most good engineers recognized the life within the crystals and their semi-sentience. His brothers might scoff at communing with the ship, but the crystals told him everything about the Sirius. He knew every sound she made, felt every vibration and change of course in his gut. He couldn't let the law destroy his ship before he had a chance to teach his son—a son neither of his brothers knew he had—everything about the Sirius.

"I'm coming," he whispered to both his crystals and his son.

Another wild tumble and the gravity increase broke his hold on the loops. He bounced off the bulkhead with the next flip. Then he slammed into the red crystals. The sharp point of one rammed into his ribs.

Warm blood trickled down his back. Sharp, burning pain followed. Damn. The crystals had cut him. Who knew what stray and possibly toxic electrons they pumped into his system? He needed to work fast and get a pressure bandage on it right away. Before Kim found a jump.

"Konner, I need you!" Loki's voice came through the silence. "Kimmer . . . Kim is hurt."

Must be bad if his brother used Kim's full name. Mum, Margaret Kristine, might be enamored of all of them having the same initials—Mathew Kameron (Loki), Martin Konner, and Mark Kimmer, not to mention the missing Mari Kathleen—but everyone else got confused.

"Do you want control of this ship back or not, Loki?" Konner shouted. The cut on his back burned sharply with the effort of speaking, and breathing, and hauling himself through the conduit.

"I can't get back to our last jump. IMP's blocking the path. Gotta jump blind."

"No, Mathew Kameron O'Hara. Loki. Don't jump! I'm bleeding. Kim's hurt. The inertia dampening field is compromised. A jump will kill us."

"Would you rather die in jump or in prison?"

Reality blurred.

CHAPTER 3

K IM'S ENTIRE BODY ached. Especially his head. It felt as if he had gotten stuck in the inner workings of the *Sirius*. He couldn't hurt more if crystals gouged his eyes and sanitation pumps pounded his skull. He dared not let his stomach turn itself inside out. The pumps might throw it back inside him. Instead he tried to find the core of the pain, isolate it, and then figure out why he tasted blood.

His fingers found a bloody mess along one side of his head. Another inside his mouth where he'd bitten it. He stared at the red dripping from his fingers for several moments trying to decide what to do.

He clamped his eyes shut again. He felt like a Denobian muscle-cat hiding from the mice it was supposed to catch. Of course the muscle-cats were the size of Earth lions with fifteen-centimeter fangs and would tackle any living creature up to twice their size. But they practiced invisibility when confronted with a Denobian mouse about half the size of one of their fangs.

Kim wanted to shrink away from the pain, become invisible to it. Easier than dealing with it. But the ship's warning klaxon, which signaled the *Sirius* was about to jump, screamed through his nervous system. He couldn't think. Couldn't remember why he curled in a painful heap against the bulkhead.

He opened his eyes. The familiar images of the ship's circular bridge looked fuzzy. What should be close to him appeared distant and vague while equipment on the opposite side from him remained detailed and sharply focused. He blinked. The blurring remained. Instinctively he clamped his hand over the wound on his head, careful to keep his fingers pressed tightly together and over the wound.

The klaxon paused, then started up on a louder, sharper command to prepare. Automated systems took over. Humans couldn't compute jump navigation fast enough. Once the sequence was engaged, no one could abort the alarms or the jump. Within a star system most pilots commanded their vessels manually. What lay between the stars remained unknown.

Kim curled tighter into a fetal ball, chin tucked tightly against his chest. He couldn't do anything until the ship finished rearranging time and space at some distant point.

"St. Bridget! Let the computer put me back together right, with my blood circulating in my veins and not in the ship's sanitary system," he pleaded. "Please, St. Jude of lost causes and lost wanderers, add a wee bit of boost to this prayer."

If he had cashed in his ace before this last run, he'd be safe on some nice bush planet growing watercress or cucumbers (both exotic cash crops) instead of bleeding all over space. But Mum had taken him aside before this run and made promises. Once they found his missing sister, Katie, Mum promised him a farm and no more black market runs. No more hiding. No more . . . Any sane male knew better than to argue with a woman of Irish Catholic heritage.

Besides Mum always kept her promises. He and his brothers had a responsibility to keep their promises to her.

The klaxon stopped beating at his headache. His awareness of his body and his pain ceased. Only his mind existed, and he wasn't sure sanity remained. He counted the seconds, willing his heart to keep beating as the ship phased from real space to jump space. He sensed his molecules streaking through the space/time continuum faster than light, faster than thought.

Hold on, a disembodied voice ordered. It reverberated deeply, like it had to travel out from the center of the galaxy to reach his mind. *We'll keep your identity intact no matter where you end up, or in which body.*

Not a completely reassuring thought. He wanted his own body with his own mind inside it.

"One hundred eighteen, one nineteen, one twenty." Kim counted. If he counted, he didn't think. If he didn't think, he just might come out of this whole and sane.

Unlikely, his hindbrain reminded him. That unevolved lizard part of him gibbered in fear, wanting to jump up and run screaming through the ship. He needed to bury his head in Mum's lap, as he had when he was six and had his first skirmish with the law. Twenty years on the run. One year too many.

He had to stay put. Had to count. "One twenty-five, one twenty-six."

Soft communication bells filtered through to him. He kept counting. "One thirty-eight, one thirty-nine, one forty."

"Kim?" Someone shook his shoulder.

"Wha—aa—aht?" He risked peeking beneath his arm. Loki crouched beside him, fingers pressed tightly against Kim's neck pulse point.

"You're alive. Are you whole?" Loki whispered.

"I think so." Kim had trouble forming words around his swollen mouth.

He felt a tremendous sigh of relief from that strange disembodied voice that spoke to him during jumps. Only then did he have the time to wonder who or what existed in the surreal space between here and there.

"Your head isn't bleeding as much, thank God. I need your help." Loki sounded worried, calm but worried.

"Help," Kim muttered, not certain he could *do* anything at the moment. But he needed to explore those voices, needed to satisfy his curiosity and sense of wonder.

"Can you sit up? I found your planet. But . . ."

The klaxon blared again. Kim ducked his head, trying to muffle his ears and endure yet another jump.

"Shite!" Loki dove back to the pilot's console through null g. "That's the proximity alarm. We jumped into the middle of a damned asteroid belt!"

They had found an uncharted planet! Kim's mind raced with possibilities. Mum and Katie and pearls be damned.

"IMPs?" Kim dragged himself back to his own chair, trying desperately to balance action and reaction. He didn't have Konner's grace and precision.

"I think we left the IMPs behind. This jump was wild."

"Hope the computer remembers the coordinates so we can get home, in case the king stone can't reach the mother stone from this far out." Kim slid into his chair. He pulled up engineering as well as his own sensors and weapons. He blasted three small chunks of ice and rock in quick succession. The next speeding planetoid headed their way was big enough for Loki to steer around.

"Where's Konner?" Kim asked, wishing he didn't have to divert his concentration. Those asteroids were thick and fast. They flew at the *Sirius* almost as if they were directed. Impossible!

There were just too damn many of them to fight a path through.

"Konner's still in the rabbit hole. I hope."

"What do you mean 'you hope.'" Kim nearly came out of his chair in protest. "You could have killed both Konner and me with that wild jump. You didn't even check or ask if he was in a position to survive it?"

"Look, little brother, I know what I'm doing. Getting all three of us, this ship, and our cargo home safely is my responsibility." Loki stood up. "I'm the one Mum will blame if anything goes wrong. And, frankly, I'm not eager to incur that woman's wrath!"

The klaxon blared. They both whirled back to their stations, bitterness forgotten.

One quick cannon blast, barely aimed, merely tore a few chunks of mass off the rock hurtling toward them. Kim took a deep breath and found a target closer to the center of the asteroid. It absorbed the energy. A third shot had no more effect upon it either.

"Holy Mother of God. That thing's as big as a moon!" Loki stared at the looming asteroid.

"Steer, damn it! Get us away from that thing," Kim ordered.

"Crystals balanced. You can steer, Loki," Konner gasped over the intercom. "I'm rerouting sensors for a full view. Focus will be fuzzy in places, though."

"Konner, you okay?" Kim asked.

Loki fired thrusters and put the *Sirius* into a dive below the chunk of rock big enough to create its own gravity field—a weak one, but strong enough to make the ship shudder as it strained to pull away.

With a jerk and a popping sound, the ship slid beneath the mountain of rock.

"Dammit!" Konner yelled over the intercom. "We just lost a thruster! How you gonna rotate to new horizontals if you aren't more careful with *my* ship?"

"Do you need help, Konner?" Loki asked, dodging between two obstacles.

"No." A long silence.

Kim concentrated on eliminating the obstacles in their path. If he thought about the loss of thrusters that allowed rotation so the ring of directional crystals could forge a path through the inertia field, he might just give up.

"Secondary thrusters on-line. But go careful. They aren't as powerful and have a delayed reaction," Konner sighed over the intercom.

"What about you, Konner?" Kim asked. "Are you okay?"

"As long as you keep the gravity off, I think I can climb out of the rabbit hole. Don't know after that." Konner's breathing sounded heavy, his words slurred.

"He's hurt. Hurt bad. I'm going after him." Kim started away from his station.

"Not yet," Loki ordered. "I need you on those sensors and cannons. Can't dodge 'em all, especially with a backup thruster. Heaven help us if we lose another." The ship jerked upward suddenly as he avoided yet another asteroid.

Reluctantly, Kim sat down again. His little bush farm with a tidy house where he could celebrate changing seasons seemed farther away than ever. He scanned the asteroid belt looking desperately for a path through the mess.

"Incoming!" he screamed. "Hang on, Konner!"

Loki ran through complex patterns on the helm. Six asteroids passed them. A seventh struck them aport. The *Sirius* careened in a new direction.

"Port hold breached," Kim reported as if instructing a class in arcane history.

"Another thruster gone!" Konner yelled.

Loki's hands shook, and his eyes wanted to clamp shut. If only he could curl up and sleep until this all went away. But he couldn't. He was the oldest and the captain. He had to find a place to land and repair the ship—with both his brothers intact. Damn the cargo.

Good-bye, Cyndi, he whispered with his mind. He couldn't plan on getting home in time to prevent her marriage to another man. He dared not hope that this run would be his last or be profitable enough to bribe back his citizenship.

"Is—Konner—" Loki's voice came out a strangled gasp. He swallowed heavily around a large lump in his throat. No sense in panicking the boys by showing his own fear. "Is Konner in the port or starboard rabbit hole?" This time his words sounded normal, authoritative.

"Starboard." Kim heaved a sigh of relief as he checked the engineering sensors.

"Konner?" Both brothers asked through the communication system.

"Hanging on," came the weak reply. "Can you park this damn hangar queen someplace?"

"Working on it," Loki replied. With his jaw set in a stubborn clench, he rummaged beneath his console. His hand curled around a heavy shaft with a knob on one end and sensor slots on the other. He flipped open a port at his knee, then jammed the rod into it. The joystick rested comfortably against his palm. He flipped another switch and the viewscreen morphed from tactical displays to real time images—mostly points of light against a black velvet background. "I've had enough of letting the computer make decisions. I want control!"

"Loki, no," Kim said wearily. "The joystick is archaic. It can't interface with . . ."

"I damn well interface with it!" Loki shouted.

As Loki shifted the stick up and down, right and left, the ship responded seamlessly. No delay while the computer thought about it, no questions, just himself and the ship working together. The way it should be.

"One gas giant planet and three frozen rocks in the outer system," Kim reported. "We seem to be clear of the asteroids, for a moment. Fourth planet from the sun is Earth-class with atmosphere, landmasses, and water. Smaller gas ball and two boiling rocks between it and the sun."

"Found us a place to land, Konner. Let's hope there's a doctor and a space-dock down there," Loki reassured his brothers and himself.

"Fat chance, big brother." Konner crawled up the passageway. The back of his red shirt was dark and moist. Blood? "We don't know where we are and what, if anything, lives on that planet."

Kim rested his head in his hands. Blood, as brightly red as Konner's shirt, trickled from the rapidly bruising gash at his temple.

Loki felt faint for a moment. He'd failed to protect his younger brothers. He'd been thinking about Cyndi—not his mission. Damn!

CHAPTER 4

KONNER HAULED HIMSELF into his chair and took over the engineering data feed. Kim didn't look too good. His face was as pale as his collarless shirt. A slight flush rested on his high cheekbones in stark contrast to his pallor.

"You look like shit, little brother," he whispered.

"So do you. How much blood have you lost?" Kim slurred his words. His lower lip looked swollen into his left cheek and jaw. The beginning of a bruise darkened half his face from temple to chin.

"I've lost more blood than I want to think about. Too much," Konner replied tersely. "What about you?"

"Leprechauns playing horseshoes in my head—and the shoes belong to draft horses, not tiny fairy ponies—and all I want to do is sleep." Kim rubbed his face hard with his fingertips.

"Concussion. You won't be much good for much longer."

"I'll manage. Loki is whole and hale and surly as ever," Kim added sotto voce.

"Crystals stable for the moment," Konner said loudly enough to break through Loki's delighted concentration. He loved that joystick. "But they won't take another jump. Don't know how long they'll stand interplanetary speed either. Some crystals are cracked. Some just dead. Three of the twelve thrusters are gone." He heaved a deep sigh. The chatter of the crystals in the back of his head had turned to a mournful dirge about the time he awoke after the jump. He wondered how the computers had managed to keep him intact while spreading their molecules across the space/time continuum. Maybe he had Kim's blood in his veins and his was in Kim. Lucky they were the same type with most of the same antigens.

"Pooling my sensors with yours, Kim," Konner said tightly. Every breath made his wound seep and his ribs burn. But it was time to get back to work and find a safe haven to repair and recover.

Together they compiled data on their destination, a point of greenish light in the distance. Kim seemed to absorb the information through his fingertips. Konner gave up reading the numbers, concentrating on using Kim's interpretations to keep a balance of energies flowing through the ship.

Loki jockeyed around the missing and damaged thrusters, flying seamlessly.

Slowly they drew closer to the enticing green light. They all stared for long moments at the awesome green planet growing to fill the viewscreen. Konner didn't have the energy to break the silence with more than an occasional grunt. Kim seemed to pass in and out of consciousness but remained upright in his seat. The bleeding at his temple became sluggish, nearly stopped. Scalp wounds always bled heavily at first, not a true indication of the depth of the hurt. Loki hummed happily as he steered the *Sirius* closer and closer to the planet.

"Computer coming through with our coordinates," Loki announced. "Can you figure out where we are, Konner?"

"The back of beyond," he replied after a cursory comparison of the numbers with the known starcharts. "About three sectors off the normal shipping lanes. Only cursory surveys from far distances before this. This star isn't on the maps. No one has recorded actually *being* here before."

"Uncharted territory," Loki breathed. The light of greed flitted across his face. "Big bonus from the GTE for discovering new bush worlds. We'd have to use a fence to collect the money, but, even less his percentage, this is big money. We can be legitimate citizens again! I'll sue that damn IMP for unwarranted damage to private property when I get my papers back. Someone's going to pay for hurting my ship and my brothers."

"Money only comes if we can get something to grow here. The GTE needs food more than it needs pearls or more IMPs. Food: that's the only reason for finding new bush worlds."

"This place is very green and lush," Kim breathed. "Lots and lots of organics in the readings. Just don't know if the soil and light spectrum are compatible with anything humans can eat."

"I'm cutting off communications between our king stone and the mother crystal."

Loki rolled his eyes like he didn't truly believe the action necessary.

Konner wanted reassurance they wouldn't be followed. "That IMP had time to read our comm signature and trace registration. When they discovered it's all forged they *will* follow if they can." Konner made the necessary adjustments, apologizing to the crystals in his head for the instant loneliness they must feel. They wouldn't need a connection to the crystals' home until time to leave the star system. Then the king stone would work with the ship's computers and the TG web to guide them back into charted space. For now the crystals were alone, just as Konner and his brothers were.

"Putting us into tight survey orbit," Loki said around a huge smile.

With each passing femto the planet glowed greener and more enticing.

"Unmapped star *MKO*. The computer has assigned a name with the family initials. It's a little bigger than Sol, redder, too. Atmospheric readings on the planet not coming through yet." Konner interpreted the numbers while Kim rubbed his eyes. "Our planet is a little farther away from solar radiation than Earth, but temperature compensated by increased size. Probably a younger system than Earth by a millennium or six."

"MKO-IV could be more landmass than water, judging by the green. Earth looks blue from orbit because of all the water," Kim added. "That doesn't look good for agriculture. Not enough moisture to generate rain, presuming we can breathe what's down there."

"You aren't thinking straight, Kim." Loki flicked Kim a concerned glance. "If that were the case, wouldn't our planet look more brown—as in desert?" Loki added. His eyes returned to the viewscreen. "I think I'm in love. A pristine planet ready for us to exploit."

"Still, we'd better activate breathing adapters now. Let them warm up before we try breathing that air." Konner pressed the implant alongside his Adam's apple. Kim did the same. The artificial filters would separate out the varying elements in the atmosphere then recombine them into either breathable or inert components. Truly nasty toxins, viruses, and bacteria wouldn't make it past the filter.

Unfortunately the adapters only worked for short periods before they needed cleaning and recharging.

Loki didn't bother with his adapter. "I believe in my planet, brothers." He grinned at them.

"Single moon. No sign of man-made satellites," Konner continued his toneless litany. The numbers kept him from thinking about the burning pain radiating from the stab wound around his ribs and the warm stream of blood that continued to trickle down his back. The rest of him was cold. He needed a stiff drink and a warm fire.

And his mother. Mum would know how to fix him up. Mum would have kept Loki from jumping wildly into the unknown with two men bleeding. Protocol demanded that all open wounds be pressure bandaged or in a stasis field during jump.

"No pollution indicating industrialization," Kim added. "This doesn't look good for doctors and spacedocks. Atmosphere coming through as dominantly oxygen. Nitrogen and helium present. We can replenish the nitrogen fuel tanks. A little ammonia, but not enough to hurt us. Turn on your damn adapter, Loki, at least until we know there are no nasty bugs in the air."

"Don't worry about that. I'll find a way to fix both of you and the ship, just find me a place to land," Loki insisted.

"You can't fix everything, Mathew Kameron O'Hara," Konner whispered.

"Well, I'll give it my best shot, Martin Konner O'Hara."

"I'm getting strange readings," Kim said. A puzzled frown added a little color to his wan face. "Sensors are picking up an odd mixture of familiar and alien DNA in the plant life."

"Let me look at that!" Konner slid his chair along the track so he could look over Kim's shoulder—as if his brother's readings might be different from his own. He peered long and hard at the anomalies.

"My God, this place has been partially terraformed. Maybe we're saved after all. A lost Earth colony. Humans, that means doctors and medicines at least, if not spacedocks."

"Bigger bonus for lost colonies than for pristine worlds." Loki bounded over to the console to see for himself.

"Wait a minute, brothers. Partially terraformed. That means they started adapting the landscape to Terran biology and then abandoned the project before it took over completely. Something made the colonists flee this place before they finished." Kim added cautiously, "We could be looking at some really poisonous and dangerous flora *and* fauna."

"What could make Terrans abandon a bush colony?" Konner asked his younger brother. Kim was the scholar, the historian in a family of addicted readers. Konner absorbed engineering texts. Loki tended toward adventure fiction and detailed reports of explorers. But Kim read everything from classic literature to history to religion and spiritualism. He'd earned the equivalent of three doctorates—of course the universities were unaccredited since Kim didn't have citizenship to get into a real institute of higher learning. Surely he'd put together a reasonable scenario based on this data.

"I think we've found the home of dragons," Kim whispered, staring blankly at the planet that now filled their viewscreen.

"There is no such thing as dragons. Just some oversized lizards here and there. A few even fly," Konner scoffed. "Dragons aren't aerodynamically capable of flight."

"Maybe, maybe not. Bumblebees aren't supposed to be able to fly, but they do, even on heavy gravity worlds. Let's get the shuttle and go look. I know there are dragons there." Kim was out of his chair and halfway down the passageway in one bound.

"There's no such thing as dragons!" Konner and Loki shouted after him.

CHAPTER 5

"IT'S A LONG TRIP DIRTSIDE, can't we do this on the way?" Kim wiggled under Loki's heavy-handed application of Bruise Leech®. The gadget used electromagnetic and ultrasound waves to speed healing while it drained off the excess accumulated blood around a wound. If the thing worked under Loki's very ungentle administration, his face should lose discoloration and swelling within the hour.

Konner's stab wound didn't look quite so easy to fix. Kim had hooked up an IV with a blood transfusion and additional saline to rehydrate him. Supplies of both were running low. He just hoped they wouldn't need them again until they could resupply.

"Mum will have my hide when she reads the log of this run," Loki grunted. "I'm not allowing you two to go anywhere until I fix you."

"At least let Konner and me fix each other up." Kim grabbed the palm-sized unit away from his brother. "You're likely to cause more damage than you fix."

"You two fight about it, I've got a ship to fix." Konner rose stiffly from the crash couch in the living quarters. He paused halfway up, clutching his right side.

"You aren't going anywhere." Kim pushed him back down. He double-checked the IV to make sure Konner hadn't loosened it.

For once Konner didn't protest. He must really be hurting. Weak, too. Kim added a second transfusion to the mix.

"Maybe I should take the *Rover* dirtside alone while you two recover and figure out the extent of the damage. I'll scout the crashed colony ship and the satellites. If we're going to find spare parts, it will be there. Konner can work on the drive system and you, Kim, can continue looking for people from a survey orbit." Loki edged toward the hatch.

"You aren't going down there without me," Kim protested. He stood in the hatchway, hands on hips, feet spread. Loki could easily knock him down, if he really wanted to.

"Fine, then. We all go together. But not until both of you are in better shape." Loki glared at Kim for several long moments. Then he grabbed a larger ultrasound from the emergency kit and started examining Konner. The middle brother yelled in protest at the unnecessary pressure Loki applied.

To Kim's half-trained eye, the readout looked good. He couldn't see any internal organ damage or broken bones. Just a lot of bruised and torn tissue. Too much for the Bruise Leech® to handle, and too deep to just hold everything together with surgical glue.

"This is beyond me," Kim muttered, shaking his head. He grabbed the US unit away from Loki. "I can start the healing process with the Leech and patch you up, but it's going to take time before you are up to par."

"Just glue me back together enough to let me get into the guts of my engines," Konner returned. Fierceness glazed his eyes.

"Maybe we should go down to the surface, do a couple more survey orbits on the way," Loki suggested. "The longer we keep Konner quiet, the better chance he'll have to heal properly. Another IV won't hurt him either."

"I agree," Kim replied. He felt strange actually agreeing with Loki. "We need to know why the colony ship and five communications satellites are now corroding away to useless scrap." He applied the Bruise Leech® to Konner's open wound.

"That will wait," Konner protested. He batted the Leech away and tried to stand up again.

Kim held him in place with one hand while he pressed the gadget against the open wound. "This is going to hurt whether I do it gentle or hard. Keep protesting and it gets harder," he threatened.

He and Konner locked gazes for several long moments. Finally Konner looked away and settled back against the crash couch.

"Let's make a list of what we need." Loki pulled out an electronic clipboard. "Nitrogen first. Can't go anywhere without more fuel."

"We'll need to clone three crystals from shards and submerge six others in the bath to let them grow repairs," Konner said around a grimace. "I checked the crystal bath starter kits. The omniscium has become unstable. The ones we bought in Nautilus must have been outdated and repackaged to look new. We were cheated."

Something about the way Konner said the word "cheated" alerted Kim. Before he could puzzle out the hidden meaning beneath the word, Konner continued.

"The key ingredient to the crystal bath might as well be missing. We've got to find more."

"Omniscium? That's pretty rare, Konner." Kim voiced his musing out loud. "And until it crystallizes, it goes inert pretty quickly."

"That's why it's rare enough to be the only thing in known space more valuable than food," Konner admitted. "It doesn't occur naturally on Earth, and rarely on solid planets. It's found most often in gas giants. We haven't the equipment to mine something that volatile. We can only pray there is more than a trace on this bloody planet."

"Readings indicate omniscium occurs naturally here," Kim reassured him.

"I've heard that one before," Konner snorted.

"Presuming we can find the right mix for the crystal bath, we should be out of here in three standard months. If we send a sub-light message to Mum now, she'll get it about the time we break orbit," Kim added.

"And risk the IMPs picking it up and tracing it back to us? No way," Loki insisted.

Konner ignored Loki's protests and grabbed Kim's reader off his belt. "Lots of copper and copper sulfate embedded in everything. That will taint the solution. I'll need extra filters and a real still to separate out the components. With the colony ship and the satellites gone, we have no idea if there's a civilization with what we need down there. The colony ship's probably been cannibalized."

He paused for breath while he read the survey reports. "Hey, that hurts!" Konner clamped his hand over Kim's wrist, keeping him from pressing any harder with the Leech.

Kim let up some of his pressure. When Konner relaxed again, he began working it over the wound. A lot of smaller blood vessels were rejoining, and the muscle tissue looked less shredded. The Leech would die of old age before they finished, though.

"We're stuck here for at least three standard months," Kim sighed, feigning disappointment. Excitement began to bubble up within him. Three whole months to explore a new planet. Oh! the discoveries waiting for him. "You don't have to go dirtside, Konner, until you're healed."

"What about the thrusters?" Loki asked. "I can't rebuild one."

"We need whole new units. The asteroids sheered them off." Konner revived enough to take an interest in the readings on the Leech. "Aren't you done yet?"

Kim shook his head and kept working the Leech. It was getting sluggish, bloated with the excess blood and serum that it drained off.

"Anything else?" Loki asked.

"Won't know more about repairs until baby brother here lets me get off this friggin' bed and go look. But those are the big things. The essentials. Anything else, I can probably cobble together replacements. You couldn't blind jump into a civilized system, could you, Kim?"

"If we'd jumped into a civilized system, or even into a bush colony, the IMPs would have us in custody now and we'd be making the dreaded call to Mum."

All three brothers stared at each other in silence.

"Okay, so we have to make the best of a bad situation." Loki rubbed his hands together. "Let's load *Rover* with supplies and get going."

"First stop is the colony ship," Kim called to Loki's retreating back. "I want their data files."

"I want their thrusters," Konner added.

"I want . . . it all." Loki's eyes gleamed with greed.

"Can we slow down a bit, brothers?" Kim asked suddenly. His head buzzed the way it did so often as they came out of jump. "I'm getting a bad feeling about this."

"Okay, we'll be as cautious as if Mum were here." Loki slapped Kim's back.

Somehow Kim didn't think Loki intended to follow through with that statement. And Konner groaned as he aimed for the loading bay and their shuttle. Kim threw as much of the emergency kit as he could into his carryall. He wanted to be able to stay a good long time once they landed.

• —◆— •

"Trash." Kim kicked at the canted hulk of the colony ship. The magnetic boots of his SealedSuit clanked against the ceramic/titanium alloy. Flakes of the nearly indestructible hull drifted to the ground. One saucer edge rested in the reddish desert sand. The opposite side stood hundreds of meters in the air. The central hub with the loading bay doors was partially buried.

"Not enough moisture in this desert to cause this much corrosion," Konner mused. He, too, kicked at the looming hulk. Then he ran a sensor over the patch of raw alloy exposed by their mistreatment. "I'm getting organic readings. Mostly dead and mummified. Looks like that layer of diatomaceous plants in the upper atmosphere ate the ship until the lack of moisture mummified them. Those plants are the only reason I can figure why the planet looks green from orbit and why this ship is such a mess."

"We'd better give the *Rover* a bath as soon as we leave this area," Kim muttered.

He walked over to one of the downed satellites, about one half a kilometer from the colony ship. It showed the same pattern of decay.

"With all the copper sulfate embedded in all the organics, fire is going to burn green here," Kim said, returning to Konner's side. Scorch marks on the tilted hull evoked many horrible images of the ship's last moments.

"I've breached the loading bay doors," Loki called from the other side of the ship. Kim and Konner trekked under the vast saucer—one hundred times the size of the *Sirius*—to the central hub.

They climbed over a pile of boulders—many as high as their shoulders—to reach the exposed bay. Konner had to take it slow. Kim helped him over the roughest spots. Loki bounded ahead, barely waiting for them to catch up.

Together the three turned on their helmet lights and sidled into the wreckage. Loki had only pushed the bay doors open as far as necessary to accommodate their bodies. Inertia, debris, decay, and some serious dents from the strewn boulders conspired to keep those doors shut.

Kim kept a close eye on Konner. He walked steadily but slowly, partly due to the bulkiness of their SealedSuits, partly due to conservation of energy. Would a StimPatch help or hinder the healing process? Maybe later, when Konner showed signs of gross fatigue.

Their footsteps echoed hollowly as they made their way to the first hold. The resounding booms sounded vaguely like the belling voices that spoke to Kim during jump. He wondered if the noise would wake the ghosts of the departed passengers and crew.

"Foolishness," he admonished himself.

"What?" Loki asked, tearing himself away from his fascination with the first hatch they encountered.

"Nothing more important than my imagination." Kim shook his head trying to clear it. Bad idea. The helmet of his SealedSuit limited his movements.

"Empty." Loki played his portable torch over the bulkheads of the first cargo bay. Shadows danced eerily.

"I hate ghost ships," Kim muttered to himself, careful to keep his suit speakers on mute.

"We'd expect the colonists to take all their supplies," Konner replied. He moved deliberately toward the inclined passageway to the ship's interior. "We don't need cargo so much as mechanicals."

Hold after hold proved as empty as the first. Then they reached the cabins. Departing passengers and crew had left behind a little more evidence of their presence here. A dirty sock, a broken comb, a worn-out sonic dental brush. Nothing more useful. Mattresses, sheets, and blankets, mirrors, even the framework for the stacked beds had been stripped away. Kim paused to run his fingers over each of the few remaining items. Lives had touched them. He wondered who. His imagination tried to create a connection between those people and himself. He failed. Not enough data.

Closer to the center of the giant saucer ship they found the crew quarters. Smaller cabins, more utilitarian. Here there was more evidence of life, and a more hasty departure. The beds remained intact, as did the woven metal blankets. Sheets and mattresses had deteriorated to shredded strands. They looked intact until he touched one. It crumbled to dust. Not even mice lived in this desert to cart away the fibers to make nests of the detritus.

"Here's why they left." Konner's voice sounded sad and distant over the helmet speakers.

Kim hurried to catch up to his brothers. Loki and Konner stared at the shattered king stone. Once bright shards of blue crystal littered the drive compartment. No glimmer of life shone beneath the layers of thick dust. Dark streaks in the dust showed Kim the obvious cracks in every one of the green driver crystals. Even the net that kept the stones bathed in energy-producing nitrogen had shredded.

Konner hurried away as if an urgent errand propelled him.

"Halt," Loki commanded.

Kim froze in his tracks as did Konner. They'd flown together too many years to disobey a direct command from the pilot, the captain of their ship. Survival often rested on instant obedience.

"Think, Konner," Kim pleaded when the shock of obedience began to fade. "The crystals are grown as a family, all at the same time in connected baths. When the king stone shattered, all the others went dead. That's the way it always happens."

"But . . . some of them are still alive. I can hear them." Konner took three steps along the passageway.

"What good will reviving them do?" Kim asked. "Without the rest of the family, they have no purpose, they'll drift in limbo aboard our ship as well as here."

Konner hesitated.

"They *will not* interface with your beloved crystals. No one can regrow a king stone and twelve drivers from this mess of shards," Loki said, maintaining his authoritative voice. "Tend to your living family of crystals, not a shattered and scattered one."

"He's right, Konner," Kim added. "Give them the dignity and solace of staying near the remains of their family. Leave them and scout the rest of the ship with us. We might be able to salvage the thrusters."

Head hanging, Konner pivoted and started back the way they had come. "I'll collect the thrusters and meet you at the *Rover*." Silently he retreated.

"Kim, go with him. He's still weak from the wound and blood loss." This time Loki's voice sounded concerned, more hesitant.

"I think we all need StimPatches. This place is depressing." Kim turned to follow his brother.

"Kim?" Loki asked. A tinge of his usual brightness colored his tone. "Can we shed the suits? I want to breathe real air again, feel the wind on my skin, hold dirt in my hands."

"My readings say the air is breathable. Make sure you use your adapter."

Kim reached to press the chip beside his brother's Adam's apple the moment he lifted the helmet off.

"That's better." Loki shook his head, and short-cropped red hair sprang free of the inner hood. He breathed deeply.

Suddenly Kim experienced the terrible confinement of their survival suits. He broke the seal on his helmet and gulped in the hot dry air. It smelled fresh and alive despite the emptiness all around them.

"We've been breathing canned air and eating tanked food too long. Let's go explore," he said.

"Yeah, we won't find anything useful here. The place has been stripped." Even so, Loki poked his nose into the bridge.

Gaping holes greeted them at each of the consoles.

"Guess we're on our own. No help from the original crew logs," Kim said. Excitement bubbled. "A whole new world to explore."

They both stared off into space. Kim didn't need words to know what his brother thought. *Adventure. Wealth. Excitement.*

"Three thousand people came to this planet. Surely some of them survived, propagated. Their descendants have to be somewhere. We have to find them," Kim decided.

"Yes. And if they don't have a tech civilization, then we'll make do with what we find, Kim. We always do. And we always learn something new from our adventures." Loki slapped Kim on the back. "Mum can wait a little while longer for the pearls in our hold."

They practically skipped with glee on the way out. Thoughts of Mum and a missing sister and a bush farm didn't seem important right now.

CHAPTER 6

HESTIIA STALKED QUIETLY along the game trail, careful to place her bare feet atop the tracks of the deer. She needed to walk in the animal's path, feel and observe what it experienced. Only when she became one with her prey could she hope to hunt it with the dignity and honor it deserved.

The steady drip of rain on the leaf canopy masked the tiny sounds of her breathing and her footsteps. The quiver of arrows lay snugly across her back and did not bounce or rattle. She kept her tightly strung bow free of the overhanging branches and underlying saber ferns.

She had discarded her buskins and jacket hours ago. The exertions of the hunt kept her warm in the untypical cold rain. The freedom of bare skin helped her merge with the forest and with her prey.

In her thoughts she recited the legends of women who had hunted in ancient times. She imagined herself as one of the strong women who spoke equally with the men in council and carried swords of light.

With a sigh she released the heroic images in her head. Women hunted no longer and no one had ever truly carried a sword made of light. High Priest Hanassa had declared the old legends untrue. They could no longer be told around the evening fires. Since he had become High Priest ten years ago, women were forbidden to touch anything that resembled a weapon; women were forbidden to speak in or attend Council.

That did not keep the women from repeating the stories in private, making certain their daughters and granddaughters knew about their ancestors. Nor did Hanassa's decree stop Hestiia from hunting to feed the desperately hungry women and children of her village.

She shuddered in revulsion at the thought of Hanassa and what he would do to her if he discovered she hunted, if she defied him in any way. He always seemed to stand next to her, breathing heavily upon her neck, whispering invitations to his bed. When her father looked elsewhere—purposefully?—Hanassa pressed his body against her and stroked her breasts.

At least Hanassa had not yet been able to banish the custom of requiring a free woman's consent before taking her. She hated to think what would happen to her if the men allowed the High Priest to end that law with a sweep of his staff as he had so many others.

Women now kept silent in fear for their lives.

Above her, Gentian circled on hawkish wings, chirping encouragement and an occasional direction to her. She silently bid him to be quiet. He circled higher into the cloud cover.

Her stomach gnawed at her backbone, reminding her she had not eaten this day or the last. A hunter's eye sharpened with hunger, and reflexes quickened.

Her brother, Yaakke, had told her that when he and the other warriors stayed home from war for more than a day.

The winter had been hard, keeping the men home from war, devouring the village stores, and squandering the last of the livestock for their feasts. Last year's crops had been meager. This year's crops barely planted, and already rotted under the steady rain. Rain that should have dried up a moon ago. The village had slaughtered all of the cows, woolies, and oinkers they could afford to and still have breeding stock this spring.

A shift in the pattern of green and brown made her freeze in place. She barely breathed, waiting.

The deer, a young doe standing nearly as tall as Hestiia's shoulder, reached up its head to nibble the tender leaf buds of an alder tree. It flicked and rotated its ears seeking any sign of danger. But Hestiia was downwind of the animal and determined to move slowly and naturally. She watched its great vein pulse in the long neck. Then, slowly, she brought the bow into position and withdrew a single arrow from her quiver. Each time the deer looked about, alert to some subtle change in scent or sound, Hestiia ceased all movement. Each time the animal resumed eating, she approached a little closer.

At last she had the arrow nocked. Her shoulder muscles screamed in protest as she pulled the bowstring back to her ear. Her hunger and her need to succeed overrode the pain. The deer's heart was in her sights.

A wild roar filled the heavens, louder than thunder. The ground shook, the forest swayed in the sudden wind.

The deer bolted.

Hestiia tossed aside her weapons and crouched on the ground, hiding her head beneath her arms. "Simurgh, spare me. I only wanted to feed my family. Please, oh, great winged god, master of the skies and the land and all its peoples, forgive me this transgression."

Heat blasted her face and the light of a thousand fires glowed through her closed eyelids. Never had the heavens released such a violent thunderstorm—if that was what assailed her.

Gentian gibbered in fear in the back of her mind. She had not a thought to spare for him and his fears. Words of supplication poured from her mouth.

The heat grew, the light intensified, the roaring came closer. Fear overfilled her bladder. She huddled into herself more tightly.

Lumbird bumps crawled across her skin from sudden chill. Her bare nipples puckered into tight buds. She needed to be up and moving or retrieve her jacket and buskins.

But she dared not move far or fast until she knew what attacked her.

At last the mighty roar died away. But her ears continued to echo with the unholy noise.

A gentle thud sounded beside her right ear. Gentian nuzzled her with soft cat whiskers and a plaintive "Merow?"

The flywacket radiated fear. Hestiia risked bringing her hand away from the back of her neck to scratch his ears and stroke his neck. He replied by crawling beneath her. His bulk would not fit.

"Merow," he said again.

She received the impression that the danger had abated a little—not removed entirely but far enough away for her to rise and flee. Or did Gentian suggest investigating from deep cover? Sometimes Gentian's communications were not clear.

She often believed that he merely reflected her own emotions. Curiosity was her fault, not the flywacket's.

A quick glance around her hiding place told her that no monster hovered within sight. Gentian's nose told her nothing unusual lurked in the immediate environs.

Hestiia crawled to a sitting position and gathered Gentian into her arms. He filled her lap and his hind legs spilled over onto the ground. He purred lightly as he tucked his black hawk wings out of sight beneath the extra flap of black skin and fur. To the casual observer he appeared nothing more special than a very large black cat. His body warmed her enough that she could think clearly and observe.

Gradually Gentian's senses became Hestiia's. She picked out the individual scent components of dirt, rotting leaves, growing saber ferns, fresh alder buds, salty moisture moving in from the Great Bay, the brackish water surrounding the river island where she sat, and then something entirely different: hot metal similar to the scents around the blacksmith forge where bronze weapons and shields and tools miraculously formed out of burning sea coal and melting rocks—when they still had a blacksmith in the village.

And something else. It smelled almost, but not quite, of pottery firing in the kiln.

This was something powerful, dangerous, and alien.

Hestiia draped the flywacket across her shoulders and stood up. She had no fear that his talon-long claws would scratch her skin. Gentian's senses continued to augment her own as she crept toward the source of the strange scent. Through his ears she heard a faint click, rhythmic, predictable, lulling.

She followed the swath of destruction left by whatever had invaded the solitude of this remote river island. Charred wood, broken underbrush, and dead birds littered the path. She picked up one of the larger birds, pulled the feathers away from the charred skin, and gnawed at the scant meat. Not enough to satisfy her greedy stomach. As she reached for a second bird, a prayer of forgiveness for the wanton destruction of the forest and wildlife spilled from her heart.

She filled her game bag with more roasted birds. Not enough meat to feed the entire village, but perhaps enough to make a vegetable stew heartier.

She barked her shins on the outflung branches of a downed silver blood-wood tree. Pain, sharp and hot where the toxic bark burned her skin, stopped her in mid-step. The tree's blood-red, heart-shaped leaves had already withered and faded. Gentian crept forward over the tree, through the underbrush to a hidden spot within sight of . . . of . . . Neither she nor Gentian had ever seen anything like the shiny . . . whatever it was . . . longer and taller than the chief's longhouse. Nearly as massive as Hanassa's temple.

She needed a closer look. Perhaps she could recognize something that Gentian did not understand. The downed tree rustled with her passing. Loose vines snagged at her naked skin. She moved more slowly as she slid silently through the foliage and branches. At last she came to a newly made clearing and dropped behind a screen of brambleberry bushes and ferns.

Perhaps one hundred paces separated her from the beast.

Gentian hopped down, investigating the scene with his nose from behind her.

"Simurgh, spare me," Hestiia gasped. "It has wings like the god. It stares at me as does Simurgh. But with three eyes that reflect the sunshine, not two that absorb all light."

Gentian nudged her ankle. When she continued to ignore him, the flywacket nipped her with his sharp teeth.

"Ouch! What ails you?" Finally she looked at her pet.

"Not Simurgh," she muttered the words he gave her. "Wrong color. You are right, Gentian. Simurgh is nearly invisible with red marking his horns, wing veins, and talons. Red the color of blood. This monster is white and silver all over. And it does not smell of carrion."

Gentian agreed.

"But if this demon be not Simurgh, then what is it?"

The beast hummed quietly. Hestiia dropped to her knees once more. She resisted the urge to bury her head in her arms.

Gentian crept forward two cautious steps, nose and ears working. He jumped backward, hind legs scratching her thighs below her leather sarong as a portion of the silver-and-white beast's belly gaped.

Hestiia crossed her wrists and flapped them three times in ward against the evil that she had stumbled upon while committing the sin of hunting with men's weapons.

A man appeared in the belly opening. A whole man not the bits and pieces of the monster's last meal. His red hair shone in the sunlight like copper offered to the sacred fires on Simurgh's sacrificial altar. He seemed tall, but she could not be sure until he stepped away from the monster and stood next to something familiar for comparison. His fire-green tunic stood out in sharp contrast to his black leggings. Neither his garments, nor his black boots were fashioned in the manner or materials of her people, or any of the other people she knew of under Simurgh's dominion.

She envied him his boots, much more substantial than her soft-soled buskins. His long-sleeved shirt would go a long way toward warming her chest, back, and shoulders. She began to shiver in the cold rain.

Rather than think about her discomfort, she returned to observing the man. His hair thinned like an old man's and did not grow past his earlobes, but his face was clear of beard as a young boy's would be.

The man turned his head and spoke into the belly of the silver monster. He dashed rain out of his eyes repeatedly. His posture showed extreme annoyance at the drips, as if he could affect a force of nature.

He spoke again. Some of the words were almost familiar. Most passed Hestiia's ears as meaningless noise.

Possibly something about smelling the rain?

Then miracle on top of miracles, a set of steps grew from the gap in the beast's belly. The man skipped lightly down those stairs, making no more noise than Hestiia had made while tracking the deer.

Another man appeared in the opening, a younger near replica of the first. He wore a tunic as creamy white beneath splotches of grime as doeskin bleached many days in the sunlight—like Hestiia's sarong. Hestiia spotted other subtle differences between the men, including a faded bruise at the younger one's left temple. This second one was taller, slighter, with darker hair, the color of cooled bronze. The two appeared near enough in age and visage that they must have sprung from the same womb. Gentian confirmed that their scents nearly matched each other as only brothers or father and son could. The second man spoke to his brother in query using the same rapid tongue filled with sharp sounds and abrupt ends.

Hestiia tried tasting a few of the syllables. They were so close to something familiar she could almost shape them into words, but not quite. She worried at the sounds for a bit, then cast them aside. The memory of where and when she had heard something similar would jump out at her when she least expected it.

The first man replied to his brother in harsh tones that did not entirely cover an excited laugh. The high color on his cheeks spread across his entire face

Then Hestiia reeled, her vision seeming doubled and out of focus as a third man appeared in the opening. He, too, must be close kin to the others. Paler of face and hair than either of the first two and probably between them in age, he stood a bit shorter and broader. His tunic was the color of tartberries. He moved stiffly, holding his side with one hand. She caught the sharp smell of a fever sweat on his skin.

"Was he sacrificed to this god and his brothers placated it somehow? Before the beast ate him? They must be magicians of the highest order, higher than even our priests!" she murmured to Gentian.

The flywacket exhaled sharply, almost a snort of disagreement.

"See how they use their left hands to emphasize their words? That is a true sign of a magician."

The cat snorted again and ruffled his wings. He knew true magic when he saw it. He possessed some of it himself.

Hestiia crept a little closer. Gentian remained huddled in place.

"Hush."

That word came from the tallest brother, the young one, and sounded very like her own command for quiet.

The stream of words that followed meant nothing more than the rise in inflection that indicated a question. He held up his hand to signal silence between his two brothers.

Hestiia froze in place, barely daring to breathe. Had they heard her soft murmur to the flywacket?

"Over there." The first brother, shortest of the three, pointed toward Hestiia's hiding place. He seemed to peer through the screening shrubbery to stare directly into her heart.

His accent was strange, rapid and clipped, but the words were familiar.

She crouched even lower, praying that the thick undergrowth would shield her from view.

The oldest brother stomped toward Hestiia, swinging his head back and forth. His nostrils flared. He reached for something fastened to his belt. A small black rock with perfectly straight edges and sharp corners fit snugly into his palm. He held the rock up, arm stiff, elbow locked, and shouted something in belligerent tones.

A compulsion overtook Hestiia. She stood, removing her broadbrimmed rain hat. The saber ferns and shrubs reached only to her waist. Her entire body chilled and bumped, and her hands trembled in fear. She could not run, could not hide. Simurgh had chosen to punish her for her sin of hunting. Was Hanassa right that only men could handle weapons and hunt?

The strange men shifted their gazes from someplace beyond Hestiia's shoulder to directly at her. Their mouths dropped open. They uttered incomprehensible sounds. Their eyes remained fixed upon her . . . upon her breasts.

She stiffened her spine and threw back her shoulders. She was young, fertile, and not promised to any man. Only when she belonged to a husband would she hide her pride from the gaze of all others.

The middle brother recovered first. "Not her," he said sharply, nudging his brothers' shoulders. "She," something, something, "noise."

She could not have made that much noise. The words filtered into her mind slowly. They were oddly accented but understandable if Hestiia thought about them after the rapid bursts had settled in her mind.

"Over there." The eldest of the three pointed his black rock beyond Hestiia and slightly to her right.

She shifted her attention to the now audible crashing through the woods. Stupid of her. The visitors with their alien dragon had so enthralled her she had not listened to her surroundings. An enemy or a wild tusker could easily have killed her while she gaped at the newcomers.

Danger still did not alarm her. Her gaze kept returning to the youngest brother. His bluer than blue eyes moved to her face but never left her entirely. She found the steadfastness and intensity of his stare unsettling, like hundreds of butterfly wings caressing her skin.

And she could not look away from him.

No man had ever looked at her with such longing and wonder—Hanassa only looked at her with greed and lust. No man had excited her as this one did. She wanted to oil her skin and perfume her hair to entice him further. The hunger left her empty belly and invaded her breasts, her nether regions, her fingertips. She wanted . . .

The angry shouts and thrashing bushes off to her right finally broke the youngest man's fixed attention upon her. He and the middle brother both lifted little black rocks from their belts.

"Intruders!" Yaaccob, her father, yelled, crashing through the forest, two dozen men at his back.

"Kill them!"

"They seek to enslave us."

And then her father's voice lifted above the melee. "Circle them. No one leaves the clearing alive."

CHAPTER 7

KIM'S HAND SHOOK. A dozen or more howling primitives clad in skins and furs, with altogether too much facial hair, descended upon the clearing and the shuttle. They paid no attention to the constant drizzle that blurred his vision, chilled his body, and numbed his fingers. He searched his attackers' eyes for signs of intelligence. An intelligent man could be persuaded, shown more beneficial courses of action. He would not shoot a man. Never again.

Stunners had been designed to fell a person without killing them. He knew how to kill a man with the basic weapon of the Galactic Terran Empire. He would not take a chance that his blast became lethal.

Insane howls erupted from the dozen or more throats. The four men in the front poised their spears above and behind their ears for long casts.

Loki loosed a short burst of energy from his stunner at the leader of the mob. The man crumpled. His companions launched their primitive missiles.

"Shit!" All three brothers ducked and retreated. The shuttle's steps offered little or no protection from the attackers or the water-soaked air. The wheel struts beneath the long body and stubby wings provided little more shelter.

"Get inside, Konner," Kim directed. His brother was still weak and only partially healed, still vulnerable. Maybe they should have left him aboard the *Sirius* where he could rest and recover.

But he wouldn't have rested. He'd have exhausted himself tinkering with his ship, cobbling together repairs out of nothing.

"You get inside, too, baby brother," Loki ordered. "I'll watch your back."

"What about the girl?" Kim couldn't help shooting a glance at the dark-haired beauty, with her dark tan and huge brown eyes.

"She was bait. And we fell for it!" Loki loosed another blast at a warrior running toward them with a knife.

That man crumpled, too. His blade looked a foot long, wickedly sharp, and very lethal.

"I hope you've got that thing set low." Kim stared at the two fallen men. A cold knot twisted in his stomach at the thought of taking a life. Civilized worlds did not even countenance the death of an animal for food.

"They're bushies. We don't even know if they are sentient. Who can tell under all that hair?" Loki pushed Kim toward the hatch. "Get inside until we decide how to handle this."

"If you haven't forgotten, Loki, we're bushies, too," Kim dropped into his lecturing voice rather than let his anger at Loki rise to the surface. "We are reviled and denigrated by the civils back home because we choose not to live on domed planets, existing solely on canned air and tanked food. We even allow ourselves to get *wet* in the weather."

"You know what I mean. Now get inside before they actually hit one of us with those bronze blades."

As Loki spoke, another spear whizzed past Kim's ear. Too close for comfort. He dove into the hatch.

Konner hauled him off the steps, then groaned and collapsed against the bulkhead.

"We've got to get you bandaged up better." Kim crawled toward the middle brother.

"I need stitches," Konner gasped. He took his hand away from his back. It came up red and sticky. "I guess the Leech and glue aren't enough."

"Stitches will leave a scar, Konner," Kim warned.

"Then I'll visit a plastic surgeon when we get home. Just do it." Konner blanched again.

"By St. Bridget, those men are stubborn!" Loki jumped into the ship and slapped the hatch switch. The iris slid closed slowly as it had been designed to do. Two spears flew inside before it latched.

Kim crouched over Konner, protecting his vulnerable back from further injury.

"They have hard heads, too," Loki continued. "The first one I downed is up already and roaring mad." He looked more happy than worried. Loki was always the first to wade into a fight, fists flying, and usually the last one standing.

"Did it ever occur to you, that maybe we should have tried to communicate with them first?" Kim asked.

"You want to talk while they cleave your head in two with one of their bloody war axes?"

"There's the girl. We might have been able to talk to the girl," Kim insisted.

"Stop obsessing about the girl. They sent her to distract us with those magnificent bare boobs and her endlessly long legs." Loki gazed off into the distance with a slight smile on his face. "Did you notice her skin is a uniform tawny shade? Wonder if it's natural pigmentation or near permanent sun exposure?" His eyes glazed as he continued his lustful reverie.

"He's right," Konner admitted. "The girl is one of them. We have to find a new strategy for getting repairs to *Sirius* so we can go home. The thrusters we salvaged from the colony ship are useless. Between damage from reentry and landing and the corrosion, there isn't even enough metal left to reforge into new units."

"Are we ready to face Mum and her grand family reunion?" Kim lifted one eyebrow to his brothers.

They all looked at each other guiltily. They'd delayed overlong on Nautilus rather than deal with Mum and her schemes. The delay had allowed the law to catch up with them.

"Kim's right," Loki replied. He sat down heavily, his posture broadcasting discouragement. "We have no idea if Mum can truly find Katie this time. For twenty years, every scheme has failed, or she's conspired to wait for more money. Sometimes I wonder if she truly wants to find her daughter. Manipulating us is more fun."

"Mum cares about us, Loki! She's committed to keeping her family safe and together. We have a responsibility to help her."

Loki scowled at him.

"Whatever. We can't go home until we regrow some crystals and make new thrusters," Konner intervened. "We need to find the descendants of the original colonists."

"What if these are the descendants?" Kim whispered. "What if they've forgotten all their technology? What if this primitive bronze age culture is all that's left?"

Silence.

After a moment Loki's face brightened. "Then we have a nearly pristine world ready for exploitation. Wonder if the locals have evolved to farming yet? Imagine it, brothers. If they can be taught to grow a surplus of food, we have a protected supply no one else can find, for the most valuable commodity among the civilized worlds. Fresh food!"

Each of the three brothers stared off into the distance with his own private daydreams. Kim wondered what his brothers dreamed about, what Mum had promised them at the end of this run.

"We have to talk to them first!" Kim reminded them.

"Yeah, I guess we do." Loki shook himself as if needing the physical action to release his vision of the future. "Well, you're the scholar in the family, Kim. How do we do that?"

"Hell if I know!" Kim clambered to his feet and stared out one of the ports. His head ached and his eyes didn't want to focus. At least the wound in his temple had nearly healed. He needed another session with the Leech to stimulate healing the concussion. He wished he could say the same for Konner's bloody back. They would have to tend to it before he did anything else.

He reached for a med kit and fished out a needle and specially treated spider silk thread that would gradually dissolve as the wound healed. Konner handed him a Sterile Field Generator.

"Where's the NumbSkin?" Kim asked. His mind spun and refused to settle. He had to concentrate on one thing and one thing only until he knew how to proceed.

Loki handed him the attachment to the SFG that would temporarily paralyze Konner's nerve endings around the wound.

Layer by layer, Kim worked the spider silk through the rent tissue. He concentrated on each stitch, making it as uniform in length and tension as he could. A blue haze surrounded his vision, blocking out interference and distractions. Before he realized how much time had passed, he'd stitched the wound closed. He should have done this aboard the *Sirius*, but Konner had responded so well to the Leech, Kim thought the wound would close on its own. As he knotted the last thread, a dull and throbbing chant filtered through to his ears.

The primitives paced around the shuttle shouting repetitive phrases and waving their spears. Their movements took on the rhythm of a ritualistic dance.

He didn't understand a single word they said. But two syllables seemed to repeat over and over. "Si-murgh." Or was it "Shea—murg—ah?"

"What could that possibly mean?" He shook his head as he fixed up another transfusion for Konner. Then he made his way to the cockpit and all of the computers. Maybe he could start a language database from sound bites. Maybe he could find a DNA sample somewhere and see if they were human or merely humanoid. The girl certainly seemed human enough. But who could tell about the men with all that hair on their heads, and faces. He'd almost bet that their chests, arms, and legs also sprouted thick pelts.

"If they are human, descendants of the colonists, wouldn't their language be derivative of one of our languages?" Konner asked. He remained slumped against the bulkhead. His normally pale skin had already regained some color. Good. That was the last plasma bag, and they'd depleted the IV saline drastically.

"I'll get Konner into bed," Loki said quietly. "Any ideas how to talk to those . . . whatever they are?"

"Ideas only." Kim accessed a library file. But his eyes kept straying to the viewscreens. The men continued their chanting dance. The girl had disappeared.

If only he could think straight, he could figure this out. The lingering headache from his previous wound blurred his vision. He kept seeing wings on the black cat that paralleled the men's path just outside their circuit of the shuttle.

"Give Konner something to eat, with lots of liquid," he reminded Loki.

"What about you, Kim? You haven't eaten in hours and you lost some blood, too." Loki prodded his shoulder.

"Soon," Kim promised, barely hearing what Loki said or how he replied.

The computer hummed to itself for several more moments. Then Mum's voice came on-line. "Simurgh: a monstrous bird of Persian myth, with the power of reasoning and speech. A demigod of ancient Persia. Little is known of the cult. A few images survive in archaeological ruins that have strong links to dragons and griffins of other mythology." The artificial voice spoke without the inflection or the musical lilt that suggested laughter just behind the words that Kim associated with Mum.

"One word could be coincidence. Anything else match?" Kim asked the machine. Memories of his vision about dragons and the "coincidence" of a word suggesting a dragon brought excitement to his blood. He forgot the headache.

The computer pronounced three more words and then the modern equivalents: Sacrifice, hunt, and fire.

The artificial voice nearly snorted in disapproval of what the brothers had stumbled into.

He turned off the computer's voice, content to read in silence.

"I think we're on to something," he called back to his brother. By the time Loki poked his head into the cockpit, the computer had deciphered the entire repetitive chant.

"Great winged god, Simurgh, bless this sacrifice. We build the fires high to honor you with the first kill of our hunt." The words scrolled across the screen.

Hunt, fire, sacrifice. "Looks like they want us for dinner," Kim said.

CHAPTER 8

"PAPA, you cannot burn this dragon! It is a god, as Simurgh is a god."
Hestiia tugged at the branches of the sacred Tambootie tree her father carried toward the great white-and-silver beast.

"Thus sayeth the great winged god, Simurgh: 'This is a false god and must be destroyed.'" High Priest Hanassa pulled her out of her father's path. His hand lingered just below her breasts.

He held up his long staff, decorated with a small animal skull, beads, feathers, and bits of bone. When all eyes fixed upon the icons, the priest shook it with angry authority. The blood-red jewels in the eyes of the skull glowed lightly in the tree-filtered sunlight.

Then he shook his head, and his elaborate headdress rattled in time with the staff.

Hestiia pointedly removed his free hand from her body.

The dozen warriors proffered their gathered wood to the priest, and therefore to their god, and bowed.

"How do you know what the god demands?" Hestiia challenged the priest in quiet whispers only he could hear. If she had spoken aloud, he would have had to punish her to maintain his honor.

His bushy, silver-blond eyebrows drew together into a single line above small, pale blue eyes that saw altogether too much.

He stared deep into her eyes. She could not look away. She saw herself reflected in his pale blue irises; her body nude and inviting.

Gentian squawked an irritating note into the back of her mind.

She wrenched her gaze away from Hanassa, refusing his invitation to mate. As first wife to the High Priest she would have great honor and luxury among the villagers. But the cost of such privilege was too great. Hanassa was not known to be a gentle man, especially among the women that had borne him children. Children he refused to acknowledge or support.

Such a crime from another man would bring condemnation and exile. But Hanassa had declared himself above the law.

"How dare you challenge a priest!" Her father backhanded her across the cheek and jaw.

The ground met Hestiia's butt before she realized her face and neck hurt. How had her father heard her? She did not think she had spoken loudly enough for any to eavesdrop. Carefully, she rubbed the sharpest pain beside her jaw. A trickle of blood touched her tongue where she had bitten her lip. Tears blurred her eyes.

"Those men inside the white dragon have done nothing to earn the rite of sacrifice," she said around her swelling cheek.

"Yaaccob, do not dignify this child's words with a retort," Hanassa admonished Hestiia's father.

Yaaccob looked as if he would protest Hanassa's interference. Then he froze for several long moments, staring into the High Priest's eyes.

Hestiia counted her heartbeats. Twenty-five, thirty. The silence dragged on and on as if Yaaccob struggled against Hanassa's control.

Before Hanassa had become High Priest, Hestiia had followed her father everywhere. She had learned the rudiments of archery as well as swordplay. She had listened to the men plan raids and hunts. The bond between them was strong. Yaaccob would not allow Hanassa to harm his beloved daughter.

Or would he? Hanassa inflicted fear into the hearts of many mighty warriors.

At last, the two men turned their backs to her and resumed piling wood around the white beast. Hanassa smiled at her with arrogance and determination.

Accept me as your mate this day, or die.

Hestiia shook her head to clear it of the words she imagined he thought.

She bit her lip to keep herself from screaming in fear. Maybe she should just leave the clearing before Hanassa thought up a new plan.

Continuing to smile, the high priest raised his staff of office once more, letting the jewels catch a bright ray of sunshine. With his left hand he pointed at the brush beneath the beast's belly.

"It will not burn," Hestiia murmured. "'Tis too green and wet." But it would produce a great deal of smoke. Enough to choke the three red-haired men.

And much of the wood was from the Tambootie tree. The smoke would poison their lungs and give them visions of the death Simurgh would inflict upon them. The priest and her father would wait safely upwind of the fire.

Hestiia struggled to her feet, her balance off and her face throbbing. She began edging toward the cover of deep woods. Nothing seemed right about

this sacrifice. But how could she challenge both the High Priest and her father, the most powerful war chieftain in the entire land?

"Yaaccob!" Nimmrodd, one of the warriors stomped through the woods,
Hestiia's bow in one hand and a quiver of arrows in the other.

"Here is the bow and quiver I reported stolen by demons last moon. I say
this worthless female has brought Simurgh's displeasure upon all our people
by taking weapons and attempting the hunt!" Nimmrodd spat onto the
ground at Hestiia's feet.

She froze in place.

"Is this true, woman?" Yaaccob thrust his face into Hestiia's. His breath
smelled of fresh meat, woodsmoke, and the Tambootie.

Her stomach growled, reminding her that two small songbirds had provided her only meal in two days. Nor had any of the women and children
eaten more than a few handfuls of rotting grains in that time. Yaaccob and his
warriors had eaten well this morning.

Hestiia drew herself up to her full height. The top of her head barely
reached her father's shoulder. But she had seen Pryth, the old wisewoman of
the village challenge the High Priest as well as enemy warriors with only her
posture, her pride, and her dignity as protection.

Suddenly she knew that someone had to challenge Hanassa's authority.
Yaaccob would not have the courage to bring change to their village unless
she showed him the way. Her brother Yaakke would follow her lead. How
many of the other men would?

"What if I did steal the weapons? What if I sought to bring home meat to
the hungry children of our village. How will the boys grow to become warriors if you do not feed them? How can they serve you or Simurgh if they die
of hunger and plague before they have a chance to prove themselves worthy
of manhood initiation?"

Frantic whispers broke out among the warriors.

Hanassa silenced them with a single rattle of his staff and headdress. "If
Simurgh chooses them to die, we may not question." The bones and stone
beads of his staff continued to rattle at each word for emphasis.

"This worthless female chose to break one of our most sacred laws." Nimmrodd narrowed his eyes and licked his lips.

Hanassa caught her eye. She had only to go to him and he would protect
her from Nimmrodd, her father, *and* Simurgh. But not from himself.

Hestiia shivered. At least if they punished her for her sin, her death and the
end of pain would come quickly. The other women and children would
slowly starve to death if Hanassa had his way.

But then who would he command if there were no more women to give
birth, no more children to replace warriors killed in battle?

She turned her face away from the priest. Surely he must realize the insanity of his current path.

"She must burn." Hanassa licked his lips in anticipation. Almost as if he derived a peculiar satisfaction in watching others writhe in pain.

Chills ran up Hestiia's spine. Chills that had nothing to do with the cold wind coming off the Great Bay.

She looked to her father with imploring eyes. If anyone could override the judgment of the priest, it was the war chieftain, the ruler in Simurgh's name.

Yaaccob turned his back on his only daughter. His shoulders slumped in defeat, and he hung his head. But he did not defy the priest.

"Tie her to the silver beast. She burns with the invaders and their usurping dragon," Hanassa pronounced.

"No!" The word barely escaped Hestiia's mouth.

Heavy hands clamped around her upper arms. She struggled to free herself from the grim-faced warriors, kicking at their legs, balling her fists, and jerking her arms as best she could.

They merely held her tighter and lifted her higher so that she had no leverage.

"No!" her brother Yaakke shouted, pelting into the clearing. "Father, you cannot. She is your daughter, my sister!" Yaakke pushed the man on Hestiia's right. The warrior stumbled but did not let go.

Hestiia used the moment of his imbalance to strike out with her foot. She connected with the man's groin. He doubled over, groaning. Yaakke attacked the second guard. He ducked.

Shrieking, Gentian dove into the fray. Talons extended, he raked Hanassa's arm. The priest shrieked louder than the flywacket as he dropped his staff. He batted at the animal with both hands as Gentian snatched away the elaborate headdress.

Hanassa's unnaturally pale hair and skin was exposed to all. His pale blue eyes that faded into lavender at the edges narrowed, and his jaw clenched.

"Burn them both!" he proclaimed.

Taneeo, the apprentice priest retrieved the headdress and staff. He offered them to his master with eyes averted.

"Look at Hanassa!" Hestiia called at the top of her lungs. She had nothing left to lose by her defiance. If she could make these men think about Hanassa's orders, and how many changes Hanassa had made in their lives, perhaps she had a chance. "He is not one of us. Look at how different he looks from the rest of us with his white hair and pale skin and his uncanny eyes."

The warriors hesitated a moment in indecision. None of them looked directly at Hanassa, more afraid of him than of his alien coloring.

Gentian launched himself toward Hestiia's attackers in that one brief silent moment. Hanassa caught his left wing with the staff. The flywacket faltered and crashed to the ground. A warrior kicked him aside.

Yaakke tackled the man, both of them rolling toward the piles of brush.

"Gentian!" Hestiia tried in vain to reach her heart-cat. He mewled and whimpered. Hestiia's heart nearly broke because she could not go to her friend and comfort him.

Two more men moved closer. One grabbed Hestiia from behind, wary of her long legs and vicious kicks. The second slammed his fist into Yaakke's jaw.

In moments, the warriors had bound Hestiia's wrists and ankles with leather thongs. Then they wound a third strap around her throat and fastened it to the metal legs of the white-and-silver dragon.

They dragged Yaakke away, none too gently. He would be disciplined later. His warrior skills were too valuable to allow him to die in sacrifice.

"Someone help me," Hestiia cried over and over. But she knew no one would listen. According to Hanassa, women had no value to Simurgh except to bear more children to sacrifice to him. Simurgh valued only proven warriors who gave him blood and death.

Neither Hanassa nor Simurgh would be happy until all humans had died.

"I can save you," Hanassa whispered into her ear as he checked the tightness of the thongs. "Give yourself to me, and no one will ever hurt you again. You will be above the law—as am I."

"No one should be above the law." She spat in his face.

"Simurgh, light your holy fire! Cleanse us of this woman's taint!" Hanassa bellowed as he pointed his staff at the brush piled high around her.

Sunlight hit the red crystals. A shaft of light, not unlike the bolts streaming from the black rocks carried by the strangers, shot from the crystal to the piles of brush. Smoke rose in choking billows.

CHAPTER 9

EXTERIOR SENSORS on the shuttle fed scene after scene to Kim's screens. Warriors wrestling with the girl and her erstwhile savior. Piles of brush around the shuttle's struts. The girl screaming invective at the men. Only when the fanatic in the headdress slammed his staff into her jaw did she cease her protests. And then the fire, and the smoke. He stared at each image in horror. His heart beat faster and his face felt cold and clammy.

Not again. He couldn't be casual about the loss of a life. Not again. Never again.

"We've got to save her!" Kim hastened to the hatch. He raised his hand to slap the iris open.

Loki stopped his hand with an iron grip. "Stop and think a minute, Kim. They outnumber us four to one. We can't get them all fast enough with our stunners. They have very sharp weapons, and they want our blood. Do you want to break out the needle rifle?"

They only had one lethal weapon aboard. Ancient and illegal. One last resort when all alternatives failed.

"We can't just leave her," Kim protested. He smelled smoke. They'd left the vents open as soon as they discovered the local air breathable. Vents saved a lot of energy and oxygen resources. Now he slapped them closed without a second thought. Smoke and fire, the worst enemies imaginable aboard a vessel.

His ears felt stuffed, and his nose burned with the artificial atmosphere of the ship.

He'd swallowed a great gulp of smoke-laden air. Already his chest tightened and his head threatened to detach from his neck. What kind of hallucinogen had they added to the bonfire?

"He's right, Loki," Konner said. "We can't let that fire burn. It will damage our hull, our only hope of returning to the *Sirius* with any kind of wealth or even raw material for repairs."

"I won't endanger you two any more than I already have," Loki insisted. "Mum will . . ."

"Mum is very far away and doesn't know half the things we get into," Konner reminded them.

"Sonics," Kim said. He returned to the cockpit.

"Sonics are dangerous. And illegal!" Konner shouted.

"Who's going to tell?" Loki asked. "I don't see any IMPs lurking behind those bushes."

"Legality didn't bother either of you when you installed them," Kim reminded them both. "I swear, sometimes you two object just because *I* propose it." If Kim announced that he had earned citizenship, Loki would probably retort that legal status was worthless, just to counter his brother.

"I installed the sonics to be used against IMPs and customs agents. Your precious bushies won't have lost any of their natural hearing due to noise pollution. The sonics might even kill them," Konner continued protesting.

"Just a short blast. Enough to knock 'em out. We grab the girl and take off, find another place to land."

"Just a short blast," Loki confirmed. "No more than five seconds."

Konner nodded in reluctant agreement.

Closing his eyes and gritting his teeth, Kim touched the yellow icon in the upper right-hand quadrant of his display—a place he would not accidentally brush against. He counted slowly to five.

A muffled tingle in his ears told him the illegal weapon worked. Outside, all the warriors clutched their heads, reeled slightly, and collapsed in place. He couldn't see the girl—the sensor closest to her was obscured by some dark shadow, possibly smoke. He couldn't judge how the high-pitched blast affected her.

But the weird flying cat sat up and stared at the nose of the shuttle with curiosity and a strange alertness. It opened its mouth as if squeaking a question at the ship.

Kim slapped off the sonics. Only the cat stirred outside.

"Quick, grab the girl before they wake up!"

Konner opened the hatch.

◆

What strange creature is this that rests in the center of the center island amongst a braided chain of land and river delta? Why can I not scent its last meal on its breath and its last resting place on its belly and claws?

And yet I can hear it call to me in my own language.

A strange portent tugs at my mind and adds weight to my wings. This creature that flew out of the sky like one of mine own, but is not one of mine own, brings change to us all. This creature must be watched with vigilance. I shall set others to that task. Others with more mature eyes than mine. More maturity, but less initiative.

The initiative belongs to me, Iianthe, the only purple-tip within the nimbus.

As the steps extruded from the belly of the shuttle, Konner surveyed the battlefield around him. Only the flying cat stirred. The blacker-than-black critter seemed to absorb all of the light from the sun, the fire, and any other source. Kind of like a black hole.

And like a black hole, the beast seemed to grow.

"Just bristling fur," Loki reassured him, his eyes riveted to the animal.

Konner hadn't spoken. He should be used to Loki anticipating his statements and actions. With that weird cat staring at him, his brother's prescience sent chills up his spine.

Maybe he only imagined the cat and Loki's mind reading. Weakness from the bandaged wound on his back must be playing havoc with his brain synapses. The stitches holding him together felt tight to the point of ripping. He slowed his movements and shifted his posture to favor that side.

Loki slipped on a glistening amphibian lurking beneath the leaf litter. He let out a string of curses as he fought for balance.

Konner stepped more carefully, aware of dozens of frog eyes watching him.

"Forget the cat. We've got to grab the girl and lift off before the men recover," Kim called from the doorway. He scanned the clearing, stunner at the ready.

"What if the cat attacks us trying to defend the girl? You saw what he did to the warrior. There isn't a lot left of his face." Loki hesitated. Loki never hesitated. He always rushed into things.

"Throw a bag over the cat, Kim, and bring it inside. I'll free the girl." Konner unsheathed the little throwing knife he kept inside his ankle boot. The blade was only two inches long but as sharp as a sonic cutter. He'd make short work of a simple leather thong.

Unless, Konner thought, the leather was made from a beast with a hide stronger than the finest alloys available to the GTE. This planet was proving so bizarre he almost expected it.

He kicked the smoking brush away from the strut where the girl was tethered. Three frogs jumped away from the smoldering wood. It hadn't burned well. The constant drizzle kept the wood too wet. But it smoked a lot. He couldn't avoid the thick roiling clouds of smoke. His vision split, then doubled. He thought he saw layered halos around every object, animate and inanimate.

Each layer took on a different symbolic hue. He checked his breathing adapter. Damn, the thing was clogged already. The vertigo persisted.

"Shite!" Loki yelled as the cat scratched him through the woven metallic threads of the blanket he threw over the beast. "Claws like—each one is as long and sharp as your knife. And he's got fangs. Dozens of them. I hope they aren't venomous."

The cat exploded outward, wings fully extended and legs splayed for maximum traction on the ground. Only its head and back stayed beneath the blanket.

Loki threw his entire weight onto the beast, scrambling to tuck the covering around the exposed extremities.

"Hurry with the girl, Konner. Sensors show this smoke reaching toxic levels," Kim urged, attacking the thongs with his own knife. His neck pulsed where the adapter worked overtime.

Or maybe it didn't work at all against this particular toxin. Kim's eyes looked a little glazed, and he kept pausing in his attack on the leather.

Konner turned his attention to the neck thong on the unconscious girl. "Shite!" he echoed his brother's curse as he surveyed the tight knot on the thong. "The leather's wet from all this rain. It's shrinking under the heat of the fire. It's strangling her." The leather was so tight around her neck now, he didn't think he could slip his knife blade between it and her vulnerable skin without slicing a major artery. He didn't have time to go back into the shuttle for a laser or sonic cutter. Didn't want to chance the tools would damage the *Rover*.

He worked on the strap attached to the shuttle's wheel strut.

The strap resisted cutting, as if it had titanium threads strung through it. Konner's knife quickly dulled.

Behind him he heard the groans of men awakening.

"Hurry, Konner," Kim said as he helped Loki with the burden of the still struggling cat. He'd cast aside his own knife, completely dull now.

"Mum always said: 'The hurrier I go, the behinder I get,'" Konner muttered.

With the cat inside, Kim bolted down the steps. He retrieved one of the bronze knives from a fallen warrior and began worrying the knots that bound the girl's wrists. The weapon had been forged all of a piece, a seamless blade and hilt with no weak points to break unexpectedly.

"If the leather dulls a titanium alloy, why do you think bronze will work?"

"Their leather, their weapons."

"Try this." Loki tossed Kim a portable sonic cutter.

Konner concentrated on the knot at the strut. It seemed a little looser than the one near her throat.

"She's turning blue around the mouth and nostrils!" Kim nearly shouldered his brother aside in his anxiety to free the girl. He sliced through her ankle bonds effortlessly. But the cutter whined and sputtered immediately afterward. It didn't like the dripping atmosphere. Konner returned to worrying the knot with his knife as a probe. His fingers slipped. The knife refused to wedge between layers.

Rustling in the brush around him, and questioning grumbles alerted him to the stirring warriors.

"Dammit! Loosen up," he screamed at the knot. He could almost see the thing opening in his mind.

Miraculously, it loosened with his next thrust. He didn't question his luck or the timing.

Neither did Kim. He flung the girl over his shoulder, and bolted up the steps into the shuttle.

Konner stumbled after them, holding his hands to his aching lower back and ribs.

"If I didn't need three new thrusters and a batch of omniscium I'd return to the *Sirius* right now. I wasn't meant to live dirtside for long."

Loki wrapped the woven metal blanket tighter around the squirming, thrashing, volatile bundle of the winged cat and flung it into the corner of the lounge at the center of the shuttle. Padded chairs offered comfortable seating during long flights for passengers or relief crews. The two couches on opposite sides stretched long enough for two brothers to nap. A separate sleeping cabin and head separated the cabin from the hold and rockets. (Konner already had the compressors in the hold distilling nitrogen out of the local atmosphere and running the liquid into fuel cells.) He folded down the table across the wedge-shaped end piece to help confine the reluctant passenger. Already one blacker-than-black wing protruded from the edge of the blanket. A long claw worked at a small puncture hole in the woven metal.

How had a simple cat's talon penetrated the fabric that was supposed to be strong enough to withstand weapon blasts, polar winters, and torn metal or ceramic should the shuttle crash?

"Keep that beast from tearing the place apart. I'm going to find another landing place," Loki threw over his shoulder at his brothers.

He guessed that the fanatic with the long staff and wild headdress of feathers and bones plotted revenge for losing his sacrifice.

The warrior leader had already roused and was shouting at his men.

"You deal with the critter. I'm trying to keep the girl alive," Kim retorted as he eased the leather thong away from the girl's throat. Her nostrils and lips looked a little too blue.

"I can't fly this thing with that cat on the rampage. Not that it's anything like a normal cat." It had to weigh twelve kilos at least.

"You want to explain to our baby brother if I lose the girl while babysitting your cat?" Konner's voice took on a hint of a smile despite the sternness of his expression. He pulled bandages and oxygen from the first aid kit.

"Mark Kimmer O'Hara does seem a bit smitten." Loki smiled, too. He kept his back to his youngest brother, deliberately taunting him out of his near panic over the girl.

"Never seen our little boy so passionate about anything but his books," Konner replied, also ignoring Kim's grunts of dismay.

"About time, too." Loki and Konner shared a knowing smile. "Okay. Get the girl breathing again. Maybe she can control that animal. Wonder if Mum would like a flying cat as a souvenir of *our* planet?"

"It's not *our* planet yet, Loki. We just got chased out of our first landing site. Who knows if we'll be able to tame the natives long enough to exploit the agriculture and natural resources." Konner sat back on his heels.

Kim finished with the knot of wet leather and peeled away the thong.

"Not a girl anymore," Loki muttered. He couldn't keep thinking of their captive/rescue/hostage as a mere girl; not with tits as well-formed as hers. She'd achieved womanhood. Briefly, he played with the idea of winning her heart. Cyndi was a lost cause. He hadn't seen her in two Terran years. He had to accept that her father had forced her marriage to another. The look on Kim's face changed his mind. The boy would never forgive him if he stole the girl.

If he came home wealthy enough, Cyndi could always file for divorce from the whining diplomatic idiot.

"Come with me, Kim." Loki hauled his brother away from their guest by the collar of his shirt. "You need to prepare for liftoff. Let Konner handle the girl. His head is cooler right now. You and I, baby brother, are going to look for a new base of operations."

This one had held such promise until the attack. Near a village on the mainland with evidence of plowed fields, but on an island far enough removed—they thought—to keep their technology secret. And, well, such was life.

He whistled a jaunty tune as he sat in the pilot's chair. Nothing like a new adventure to wipe out painful memories of IMPs on his tail, a damaged mother ship, and too-vague jump coordinates. He'd return to Cyndi eventually. They had the kind of love that would not die from a minor separation.

Minor? Something questioned in the back of his mind. *You haven't seen her in two years and that was only one hurried kiss and a few desperate whispers behind a potted palm.*

"Uh, Loki," Kim said quietly.

"What?" Loki kept his eyes on his mapping software, looking for another opening in the near endless forests that wasn't on top of a plowed field and primitive habitation. *St. Bridget,* the wealth contained in those trees. He wondered if acorns could be made into some kind of nut butter. His mouth watered at the thought. Real nut butter, not the thin goo of tanked plant matter. And fresh baked bread made from real flour, leavened with real yeast rather than flat and thin like the cracker bread pasted together with some kind of synthetic fiber. Ship's rations rarely spread beyond that staple diet.

He'd give Cyndi an entire tub of nut butter as a wedding gift.

A loud rumbling sounded like his stomach craving some of that nut butter. Come to think of it, he was hungry. Something sweet, like chocolate, would taste very good right now. Food might anchor his head. He felt as if he were drifting with his thoughts. He half expected Cyndi to come walking through the curtain that separated the cockpit from the lounge.

"Uh, Loki, I think you'd better look at this," Kim called.

"Now what?" Loki looked up from his screen. Something in his brother's tone alerted him to potential danger. Kim was excitable and prone to exaggeration, but he usually had *some* basis for his panic.

Loki's head did not want to look up. Sleep sounded very good, almost as good as food.

Kim just pointed out the window at the real-time view. His mouth hung agape, and his eyes widened in disbelief.

Loki threw a quick glance, then let his attention return to the screen.

What he saw finally registered in his mind.

"Tell me this is a nightmare born of too much whiskey," he pleaded.

"I don't think so."

"How do you know."

"I'm wide awake, and I don't drink. At least not as much as you do. But it might be a hallucination from the smoke."

"I didn't breathe much of it. My adapter is still working. And people don't usually share hallucinations."

"But we share thoughts. A lot." Kim gulped. His pointing finger shook.

"Then maybe that really is a nearly invisible dragon perched on the shuttle's nose."

CHAPTER 10

◆—•—◆—•—◆

GENTIAN'S ALMOST AUDIBLE chitters pulled Hestiia out of the deep blackness. Images of green flame and roiling smoke clung to her mind. Her throat felt as if Hanassa's ritual knife had sliced through to her spine. Each breath or swallow burned all the way to her toes. She retreated back to the black nothingness.

The flywacket became insistent.

Hestiia opened one eye to see what upset her heart-cat so.

Gentian's predicament became obvious immediately. Someone had thrown a blanket over him, robbing him of essential light. Only wingtips and claws showed through the shiny fabric. What wonders had created such a blanket? It glittered like the hide of the white-and-silver dragon, but folded and draped like the finest woven wool.

Without thought, Hestiia rolled to her knees. She had to save the fly-wacket. Without light, he would wither away to a shrunken husk.

She also wanted to touch that blanket and figure out how to make one.

A strange mask covered her nose and mouth. No wonder she could not breathe. Carefully she pushed the thing atop her head. Masks contained great spiritual power. She dared not risk damaging this one.

"Wait," a male voice said. He sounded very much like one of the three men from the strange dragon.

That one word held true meaning for her. But she could not wait. Gentian needed her.

"You are barely breathing. You cannot move around yet." The words were spoken too quickly to hear. By the time she thought about them, she had crawled halfway to the flywacket.

The man tried to push the mask back over her nose. She shoved him away, determined to reach Gentian. Just a few arms' lengths away. Too much trouble to haul herself upright on weak and aching legs.

Gentian's chitters became meaningless mews. The tears in the shiny cloth revealed the damage he had inflicted when angry. He was beyond angry now, reduced to helplessness. How humiliating for the proud beast.

"Konner, get up here," came a hoarse cry from some other region inside . . . inside where?

Hestiia grew hunted-still.

A background hum registered in her mind, a constant irritation to her hearing. Her skin crawled from the noise, sensed more than heard. The added stress of the noise must be tearing at Gentian's sanity, as it did hers.

"Blanket first. Then we escape this noise and drive a spear through the guts of this beast to silence it." She reached to pull the blanket off Gentian.

A strong fist closed over her wrist a mere finger's length from saving the flywacket. "No way," the man said. At least, she thought that was what he said. The words came fast and clipped, like he chopped out half of the middle. He said more, but she did not understand the words.

His grip forced her hand back to the ground. Gentian mewled again, more desperate sounding this time.

"Konner, what is keeping you?" The voice from elsewhere sounded strangled, on the edge of panic. But each word came through clearly, precise and spoken at normal speed.

The man—Hestiia thought Konner might be a name or title applied to him—hauled Hestiia to her feet. "You are coming with me."

The strength of his grip on her wrist propelled her in his wake. She stumbled to her knees, making sure her left foot snagged the slippery blanket covering Gentian. As the man pulled her up again, the blanket shrugged off of the flywacket.

A satisfied squeaky sigh in the back of her mind told her she had uncovered enough of her companion for him to work free of the strange fabric. Feigning meekness, Hestiia followed her captor. Men always expected meekness from their women.

True, the strange men living inside the stranger dragon had saved her from death—a death she knew she courted in her defiance of Hanassa. Their rough treatment of her now, and their lack of respect for Gentian, told her that they were not necessarily friends to her or to her kin. She must bide her time and wait for the best opportunity to escape.

(Do not leave me behind, my friend!) Gentian squeaked in her mind.

Hestiia stopped short, resisting the man's compulsion to move forward through a curtain made of the same wonderous and shiny fabric as the blanket. Gentian had shared emotions with her, as well as physical perceptions, but never coherent thoughts. The danger from these men must be truly terrible for him to speak so openly.

"Now what is stopping you?" Konner, the pale and broad-shouldered middle brother, heaved a tremendous sigh as he tugged on her wrist.

Hestiia shrugged and followed him once more. The fabric parted at his touch and they entered a bizarre temple of a room filled with flashing lights without smoke or flame and furniture of twisted contours.

Women's tales told of hallowed temples of old like this. Only the most holy of the ancients should enter this room and live!

The likes of Hanassa who profaned all of the old legends would defile this place with his breath. No wonder the strangers had rescued her. They followed the old ways and recognized Hanassa as an enemy. "The enemy of my enemy is my friend," Pryth, the village wisewoman, had told Hestiia. And so the strangers had befriended her.

A glimmer of hope sprang to life deep within Hestiia. She had prayed for a means to end Hanassa's tyranny. The gods had answered by sending these three brothers.

Happily, she memorized every detail of this temple. Strange lights, stranger smells, textures that defied definition. But the strangest sight of all was the silver-and-purple god perched outside the clear eyes of this dragon where the men lived.

She fell to her knees, panic and awe choking her. None of the prayers of obedience and subservience sprang to her lips. She could only prostrate herself and hope that Simurgh's messenger would recognize her as one of the faithful.

The moment the girl went down in an attitude of supplication, Kim finally dared shift his eyes from the impossible beast outside the viewscreen to his sensor array.

"Is that what I think it is?" Konner asked. His wide blue eyes, that usually flitted here and there absorbing details as easily as he breathed, remained fixed upon the creature.

"If we all see the same thing, it can't be a hallucination. Sensors don't read anything. It has to be a holographic projection," Kim replied.

"From where?" Loki asked. "There's nothing remotely mechanical on this whole frigging planet. Barely even any metallurgy. By all our surveys and observations we landed in the middle of a bronze age culture."

"Something hidden underground?" Kim offered. He shook his head, trying to make his eyes agree with the sensors he trusted.

"I'd have picked up vibrations, or energy surges, or something. We'd have found anything mechanical right down to bedrock," Konner insisted.

"All the science in known space agrees that dragons cannot exist," Loki stammered. "But I see one. Right there on the shuttle nose."

"Four centuries ago, faster-than-light travel belonged to science fiction, it broke every rule of known physics. And look at us now. All the science in known space today says a flying pussycat can't exist," Kim retaliated. "But there is a black one strutting into the cockpit right now as if he owned it." Sure enough, the black critter sniffed each of them before jumping onto the pilot's console with only a little extension of his wings. He perched on the narrow ledge between the controls and the viewscreen and peered out at the crystalline dragon outlined in royal purple.

"A telepathic illusion, then. That's what it has to be." Kim finally came up with an explanation that satisfied his education and his senses. He'd never had one of his symbolic visions come to life before.

"Never been a *documented* case of true telepathy." Loki lowered his eyes to his hands and bit his lip.

His posture told Kim that his oldest brother lied, but he knew the statement for truth. Every supposed psychic had been exposed as a hoax—at least the ones who publicly claimed an extrasensory talent had been exposed. Who knew about the secret ones like himself. How else could he explain the flashes of vision he experienced? He had *seen* this dragon hours ago, millions of light-klicks away. It was supposed to symbolize something, though, not come to life and return his stare so levelly.

Then the winged cat began to squeak and chirp. The sounds were alien. A sense of their meaning tickled the back of Kim's mind. Questions. The cat asked the dragon questions.

And the dragon replied! Silently.

Kim's entire body trembled with shock, surprise, wariness, and . . . and curiosity. He somehow shared the conversation between the two creatures.

"Let's look at this situation scientifically," Konner said quietly. His fingers itched to caress the crystal-and-purple creature sitting on the nose of the shuttle. They'd not lift off until their dragon departed. Too much weight. "Weight. The thing has weight. We can see the shuttle nose slightly depressed. We can see the thing for that matter. Just because we can't measure it yet, doesn't mean it doesn't exist."

"I wouldn't bet on that," Loki replied.

Loki always made decisions and took action. His uncertainty—staring at the unknown, not moving, mouth agape—seemed strange and even bewildering.

"We have to believe it exists. I can hear it speaking to the cat," Kim said flatly. He, too, stared at the dragon rather than studying his instruments. The instruments that guided them through space, maintained the life-support systems, and warned them of danger. Lifesaving instruments.

"Gentian is a flywacket, not a mere cat," the girl corrected them in her slow, drawling accent.

"Flywacket?" Kim broke free of his enthrallment long enough to do something with his library files. "No such word. Computer suggests a variation of 'pywacket' a witch's familiar."

"A flying pywacket," Loki confirmed. "A flywacket. What else would you call it? She's a witch. The cat's a pywacket." He giggled nervously, bordering on hysteria.

Just then the flywacket spread its wings, chittering a wild discordant reply to the dragon. Light streamed through the feathers and membranes, showing more of the bone structure than was usually visible. The dragon also spread its wide membrane-covered wings, translucent at the center, veined and tipped with royal purple. The talons at the elbow joints mimicked the very sharp and very long claws of the cat that had penetrated and torn the metallic blanket.

"Look at the wings," Konner ordered his brothers. "Look at both their wings." He kept his words slow and deliberate so that the girl could understand him.

"Bat wings and hawk wings," Loki said. He shrugged and continued staring at the dragon.

"But the flywacket's wings aren't shaped exactly like a hawk's." Kim excitedly shifted his gaze back and forth between the two animals and his library texts. "Bird wings are different from a bat's. The dragon wings—or bat wings—show the same bone structure as the flywacket's."

"Somehow, those two critters are related," Konner confirmed.

"Of course they are related," the girl huffed, rising slightly from her crouch. (Why did it take her twice as long to pronounce each word, twisting the syllables to impossible contortions?) She seemed less afraid and more authoritative. "There can only be one purple-tipped dragon at a time, yet they are always born twins. One of them must take another form. They become flywackets to guide us, teach us. A flywacket shows us the path of wisdom laid down by the ancients. The great winged god Simurgh has honored my generation with a flywacket, signifying great challenge and great change."

Her words scrawled across one of Kim's screens, aiding in translation. She pronounced the god's name "Shea—mur—gh—ah," with long, drawn out vowels as if she had all the time in the world to say each word. Perhaps the locals had time since they probably had no timekeeping devices other than the passage of sun and moon across the heavens.

Good thing Loki had parked the *Sirius* on the other side of the planet so the locals wouldn't notice a new "star" in the heavens. But having the ship over the horizon would hinder communications. They could access the primary computer only twice a day, at sunset and sunrise. And they had no uplink for surface communications more than one hundred meters beyond the *Rover*. If they had to leave the shuttle and got separated . . .

"Is Simurgh a dragon?" Kim asked.

Konner remembered legends of old Ireland that Mum had drilled into them all from earliest childhood.

"Never say that!" The girl immediately prostrated herself again. A stream of odd syllables followed her protest. Even the computer couldn't translate them.

The dragon leaned over, peering into the viewscreen.

"He almost looks concerned," Loki giggled nervously.

"This has gone on long enough. We've got to get that thing off our nose so we can take off." Konner ran some calculations at his console. He frowned, not liking the figures. "That dragon weighs entirely too much. The landing gear has already sunk into the sandy soil of the river island. Wet, sandy soil. The rain is digging us deeper."

"Try rocking the ship," Loki suggested, coming out of his stupor.

"You run the danger of that thing flaming us," Kim added. "I saw it belching fire at us in a waking dream."

"Don't go all psychic wonky on us, baby brother," Konner warned.

"My dreams have never been wrong. And this one was more vivid than any I can remember." Kim crouched down beside the girl. Gently, he eased her to a sitting position. "Do you have a name?" he asked, enunciating every word carefully, almost as slowly as she did.

"I was named Hestiia three days after my birth, when the great winged god Simurgh declared that I would survive." Her voice came out barely above a whisper.

"Library says the name Hestia is ancient Persian for star. Mythological goddess of the home," Kim reported. "I guess that's appropriate. Considering we came from the stars to find a goddess." The edge of hysteria crept into his own voice. Time to take action and stop talking.

"Rock the ship side to side, Loki. Kim, belt yourself and the g . . . Hestiia in tight. This could get rough," Konner announced.

Both brothers leaped to action. The shuttle listed to the left and then the right. The dragon spread its wings for balance and gripped the nose of the craft with long talons.

The screech of those talons on the ceramic alloy set Konner's teeth on edge. His brothers grimaced as well.

Then the flywacket—Hestiia had called it Gentian—also spread its wings and gripped the console edge with wickedly long claws. Both animals screeched louder than the scratchings.

Konner winced.

"Enough! You," Konner stood and pointed at the dragon, "get off my ship!" Blue sparks almost flared from his fingertip.

The dragon slid backward to the very edge of the craft. It looked surprised and spread its wings farther, then gripped even tighter with its talons.

Konner stared at his finger. A tiny flamelet of blue lingered on the tip. He hadn't shoved the thing by just pointing at it. He couldn't. It must weigh a couple of metric tons at least.

"What did I do?" he breathed.

(Stay.) The word formed inside Konner's head with remarkable clarity. Deep and melodic, the voice resonated along his spine.

He clung to the edge of his console. All of his perceptions tilted along with reality.

(Please?)

CHAPTER 11

✦ —— · —✦— · —— ✦

HANASSA GROANED. His head hurt. But the piercing noise that had rendered his frail human body unconscious had ceased. He rolled to his right side and groaned again. His stomach rolled with him. Fiercely, he clamped down on the bile that burned the back of his throat.

"I will not give in to this weakness," he said to himself through clenched teeth. "I am above this frailty."

Muscle by muscle, the High Priest's body came under his control once more. He shifted position to his knees, slowly, making certain no part of him rebelled, especially his stomach. From knees to feet took more care, but at last he stood upright. The sight of more than a dozen warriors sprawled on the ground around him made him snort with disgust. Why had he not sacrificed them years ago? They were too weak to fulfill his plans.

He shifted his gaze to the strange dragon creature that had invaded their land.

It smelled wrong. He could detect no trace of dragon musk, of fresh kill, or of the Tambootie leaves dragons regularly ate. But it did smell hot, just like a dragon preparing to flame its kill or an enemy.

And what was that low-level hum? Just below hearing, felt more than understood.

He stepped over the retching body of one of the warriors—*Yaakke,* he thought—to get a closer look at the beast. The red crystals on his staff focused the light for a better view of details. Peculiar scales, much bigger than the behemoth fish that lurked just outside the shallows of the Great Bay. He thumped one with his fist and found it harder and less pliable than expected. The hide absorbed the sound of his blow as if he had never touched the thing.

"I will know your secrets, white dragon with no defining colors on your wing veins or talons. Your horns are few and spindly. They carry the silver color of a juvenile, and yet you mass more than a full-sized male dragon," he whispered to the creature.

(You will never pry out the secrets of this one. I will make certain of that. You are forever forbidden to delve into the lives of dragons.) The dreaded voice of the nimbus pounded into Hanassa's brain. *(You made that choice when you sent your first innocent to the sacrificial altar.)*

Involuntarily, Hanassa stepped back, away from the voice of his enemy. He trod heavily on a foot. "Get out of my way," he snarled at his victim.

"Master, I cannot," Taneeo, his apprentice, said.

"You cannot?" Hanassa whirled to face the impudent boy, staff raised for a punishing blow. He trapped the boy's gaze with his own, needing him to cower in subservience and fear.

"Why did I take you on, brat? You are as stupid as your mother."

"Now I can cease to impede your retreat, Master. You have removed your foot from atop mine." Taneeo took one respectful step to the right. But he did not bow his head and dared maintain eye contact.

"Impudent apprentice." Hanassa lowered his staff. Secretly, he liked the boy for his courage. He would make a fine priest someday. But he would never become High Priest. Mostly because Hanassa had no intention of dying any time soon. His spirit would long outlast this body. Perhaps this youngster's body would serve him when the time came to cast off the limitations of mortality.

"My Lord Priest," Taneeo said. "I believe something at the front of this foreign beast requires your attention."

"What?"

"Please look, sir." Taneeo half bowed with his right arm extended in the direction he wished his master to look.

Hanassa set his face in his most formidable scowl. If any of the warriors dared scuttle away from this conflict, he would send them all to the fires. Or, better yet, he would slit their throats upon the altar. Blood to give Hanassa power. Blood to frighten the common folk of Coronnan. All of them. Not just Yaaccob's village.

"Please look carefully, Master," Taneeo implored.

Hanassa wrenched his gaze from the fallen warriors to the front end of the invading dragon. The only purple-tipped dragon in the nimbus rose up on his hind legs, wings spread in an intimidating display.

"Iianthe," Hanassa hissed, not at all impressed. Silver glossed the wing membranes and fur. The purple-tipped dragon had barely begun his fourth decade, nor had he reached his full adult mass. And he would not for another fifty years.

"I will kill you now!" Before it matured any further. "Then my proper

destiny shall fall upon my shoulders once more." Hanassa charged forward at
the hulking dragon. He flung his staff at the gaping maw of his nemesis.

"Master!" Taneeo cried in ourrage. "The dragons are the special messengers of Simurgh. We must protect them at all costs." He clung to the staff
with all of his weight.

"I am the High Priest of Simurgh. I *am* Simurgh. I shall kill this particular
dragon that plagues me."

"No, Master. You may not kill a dragon." The boy crossed his wrists, right
over left and flapped his hands. Then he hastily searched the skies for signs of
a vengeful god swooping down to flame them all.

"And just who is to stop me?" Simurgh remained out of sight, just as
Hanassa knew he would. He glared at his apprentice, suddenly aware that
Taneeo had grown to manhood, stood tall with broad shoulders and a spreading middle. Too much good food. Priests always received the best of the harvest and the hunt. "You? You have not a muscle on you, only fat. I have been
feeding you too well. All the more fat to fuel the sacrificial fires."

"No, Master, I shall not stop you alone. But all of these warriors are now
awake and have heard you blaspheme a dragon. They will stop you from killing one protected by Simurgh."

Sure enough fifteen fully grown, well-muscled warriors now stood between Hanassa and the purple-tipped dragon. All of them had weapons at the
ready and grim determination on their faces.

*(Even you may not flaunt the law, Hanassa. I stay with a purpose. Retreat with
your men. Now.)* Iianthe commanded.

"Did I just see a minor rebellion out there?" Kim asked no one in particular.

"Taneeo is a very strong magician. He will be a great priest when he passes
his final trials," Hestiia said. A note of pride crept into her voice. As her
shoulders settled back, assuming a posture to match her tone, her breasts
firmed and thrust slightly forward.

Kim gulped, all too aware of her femininity. "Someone give her a shirt or
something," he pleaded with his brothers, never taking his eyes off Hestiia.

Konner draped the metallic blanket the flywacket had discarded over the
girl's shoulders. She held it tight, snuggling into the sudden warmth the fibers
produced.

"So warm," she said in wonderment, stroking the silky smooth surface.
She snuggled into the blanket, looking tousled and sleepy and absolutely
adorable. "What magic is this cloth?"

"Not magic. Just woven metal. It absorbs your warmth and reflects it back
to you," Kim explained. He needed the science to keep his head and his emotions on straight.

"Magic!" she whispered.

"Whatever," Loki interrupted. "Just tell me why the men stood up to the priest when they seemed willing to die for him." Wisely, he kept his words slow, even, and deliberate so she could understand him.

"Even Hanassa may not break the law," she replied. " 'Tis the only reason Taneeo would dare confront the High Priest, the only reason the warriors would question his judgement."

"And what law did High Priest Hanassa try to break?" Konner asked.

Kim's curiosity flared. He needed to know more about this primitive culture. The format for a scientific paper on them began circling his head. A lifetime pursuit of the anthropological implications of these people—obviously descended from a technological Earth-based community.

But what about Mum and the family reunion they all wanted so desperately? They had to go home as soon as they made repairs.

Three standard months for the crystals to regenerate. He had three months to study these people and collect data. A doctoral dissertation at least. An honest degree from a real university.

Only three standard months. A lifetime would not be long enough to study this planet, this culture, this young woman.

His dream of a farm with a snug cottage and the right to watch and celebrate the changing seasons shifted a bit, became more primitive, more alluring.

"Perhaps Hanassa threatened the dragon when he ran forward? 'Tis forbidden to challenge one of Simurgh's special messengers." Hestiia bowed her head toward the creature still perched outside the viewscreen.

"Interesting that these people can separate the law from the instrument of the law. A very advanced concept in a primitive culture," Kim mused.

"We are not primitive!" Hestiia announced indignantly. "We do not live in caves and eat . . . bugs like the peoples over the mountains toward the sunset."

"Interesting." All three brothers remarked with slightly raised eyebrows.

Hestiia's eyes took on a frantic look as she shifted her gaze rapidly from brother to brother. Then she forsook holding the blanket in order to cross her wrists, right over left, and flap them rapidly. "Do not curse me with your magic," she pleaded, continuing the flapping gesture.

The blanket slipped, revealing most of her breasts again.

Konner repositioned it around her shoulders, carefully keeping his eyes averted.

"The work of a lifetime," Kim said quietly.

"These are dangerous people, Kim, with unknown motives," Loki reminded him.

"Maybe we'd best just send this dragon elsewhere and go back to the *Sirius*," Konner threw in. "Before someone else tries to kill us."

"Then maybe we'd best discover their motives." Kim decided he wasn't going back to the *Sirius* yet. Finding Katie was obviously important to Mum. But to Kim and his brothers? Kim could barely remember Katie. How real was she to any of them? If she lived. Perhaps Mum was wrong.

That thought shook him to his bones.

"Motives. That's the best idea I've heard all day," Loki said. "We can still salvage something out of this operation." Possibilities opened before him. "We know they have some kind of primitive metallurgy—bronze tools. That's a start toward our repairs. Do your people plant crops and harvest them?" He asked the last question of Hestiia, keeping his words slow and precise. "Do you domesticate animals and keep them for food, and transport?"

"Of course," she nearly snorted.

"You are not as primitive as the people living across the mountains toward the sunset," he reassured her. "Mountains, mines. Bet we can find iron in them thar hills." He couldn't help grinning foolishly. "We'll buy back our citizenship yet."

"And clay on the riverbanks for ceramics," Konner jumped in enthusiastically. "I should be able to cobble together a primitive forge to smelt the iron and ceramics together. Both are industries well established by medieval times. I'll be able to repair the hull breach. Steel will do for the thrusters. We just might get off this planet within six months—eight at the very latest—and I can make a very important appointment."

Loki raised an eyebrow in question. Konner just returned his stare in mute stubbornness.

Well, well, well, so Konner the engineer had a life beyond his drive crystals and interfaces. Would miracles never cease?

"But we need to study these people. Disturbing their bronze-age technology and attitudes will destroy a wealth of information about our own history and anthropology," Kim protested. As he always protested.

"We are talking about survival, baby brother," Loki insisted, grabbing Kim's shoulder and squeezing tightly. He needed to impart the urgency behind his plans. Kim couldn't be allowed to go off on some scholarly space ghost chase. "We haven't time for romantic notions of the inherent nobility of primitive man, Kim. We have to get our cargo back to civilization and organize Mum's plans. She can't find Katie on her own."

"I . . . ah . . . Can't you go off on your own and smelt your iron alloys and search out the omniscium by yourself while I study these people undisturbed? We've got a little time until the crystals are ready."

"No." Both older brothers replied. "We won't have communication in an emergency."

Then Loki asserted his authority as the eldest, as the captain. "We're in this together, Kim. We've already disturbed them by landing. Make notes of how these people react to change. That should tell you more than years of distant observation."

"I . . ." Kim hesitated just long enough for Loki to know he had struck a chord with the quiet scholar.

"Good. Now then, we need first-hand observation to see what resources are at hand." Loki rubbed his hands together, eager to get started. "We'll make Mum proud of us."

"We'll talk about Mum and Katie later," Kim grumbled. "I'll take Hestiia and Gentian back to the village. And . . ." He buried his face in his hands, pressing hard against his temples. "Ohhh," he moaned, and his knees buckled.

Hestiia caught his arm, partially holding him up. "Help him, please," she pleaded. But her gaze remained fixed on the dragon outside the window rather than on the brothers.

Or rather where the dragon had been. The beast no longer laid claim to the nose of the shuttle as a perch.

"Must be the concussion," Konner said as he helped Hestiia lay Kim flat on the deck without banging his vulnerable head.

"Blood, axes, flames. An execution. Blood on the fire. Always more blood," Kim ranted as he thrashed back and forth beneath Konner's firm grip.

Hestiia bit into her fist. The flywacket jumped from the console onto Kim's chest, anchoring him.

Loki's face went cold. "Kim's visions are never wrong." What had he led his brothers into?

CHAPTER 12

✦━─·──✦──·─━✦

KIM LOCKED THE SHUTTLE doors with slow precision. His head still throbbed and his hands shook. This last vision had left him drained and aching. His eyes did not want to focus. The lingering smell of smoke in the clearing threatened to send him back into strange realms.

He clenched his eyes shut a moment to clear them of the colored afterimages he saw around every object. Organics tended to have more brightly colored auras, but even rocks appeared alive and pulsing to his new ClearSight. (What else could he call this?) He could almost taste the texture of everything he saw. He felt as if he'd plunged into a jump without the protection of a ship and crystal force fields. The hallucinogens in the smoke seemed to have sensitized him to this planet far more than months of cool observations could have.

Both his brothers had been affected by the smoke as well. But not as severely. Exposure seemed to have enlivened Loki, and speeded Konner's healing. So they had decided to escort Hestiia back to her village, leaving Kim to recover from the vision. He didn't trust Loki to maintain a discreet distance from the natives. Nor did he trust Konner to curb his enthusiasm for beginning repairs to his beloved *Sirius* immediately—without waiting for cooperation or even permission to use the primitive forge.

Kim had a feeling this entire enterprise would prove much more difficult than either Konner or Loki imagined. His visions didn't lie, and they always showed disaster. Just once he'd like a vision of happily ever after. Like his snug cottage with Hestiia and a dozen miniature versions of her filling their lives.

The flywacket sat on a nearby hummock watching him with undisguised curiosity. Raindrops glistened on his black fur. Rain dripped from the trees. Two frogs hopped out of his path.

"Does it ever stop raining, Gentian?"

The cat stared at him, blinking the rain out of his eyes.

"You agree with me don't you, Gentian? Danger awaits us in unexpected places," Kim said to the beast. Strangely enough, he had a feeling the cat replied in the positive.

"Is that why you elected to remain with me rather than following Hestiia?"

The cat scratched an ear with a hind foot.

"Are you here to protect me, or guide me to the village?" Kim kept talking to Gentian even though he knew he'd get no reply. He just needed to talk to someone, relieve the eerie silence of this place.

(You need me.)

"This place is getting to me. You didn't really talk to me." Kim stared Gentian in the eyes. The cat did not look away. Somehow the animal's steady gaze confirmed what Kim had heard.

"It's spooky the way Konner made that dragon move just by pointing at it, and Loki seems to know what everyone is thinking. And now a flying cat talks to me."

(And your visions are more frequent and more powerful.)

"Who said that?" Kim whirled around looking anxiously into every shadow for an unseen lurker. It couldn't be Gentian. It just couldn't.

He saw only shadows and the flywacket industriously cleansing the base of his tail with a long pink tongue.

"Is your tongue forked like a dragon's?" Kim moved closer, not at all certain why.

Gentian resumed his upright sitting posture, ears cocked to alertness. He looked like nothing more than the fat cat Mum had kept at the homestead of Kim's earliest memories.

Then the planetary governor got greedy. He confiscated the family shipping business and outlawed the O'Hara clan for resisting his takeover. The ordinary tabby cat had disappeared in the explosion of the homestead and the family's hasty retreat. So had Kim's older sister, Katie. He hoped Katie and the cat had escaped together, helped each other as Gentian seemed to help Hestiia. And now the flywacket wanted to help him.

Kim had the feeling that Gentian bristled at being compared to an ordinary tabby—an ordinary *anything*. His lustrous fur was as black as empty space; so black he seemed to absorb all light and energy—like a black hole.

"Let's go watch the watchers." Kim set off on the faint trail his brothers had left. He shrugged off the odd notions. Psychic powers had been disproved time and again. He indulged in fancies. Probably he had an undiagnosed case of epilepsy or something just as mundane.

(Would your healers have missed such a disease when you were born?)

Again Kim whirled around, looking for the person who answered his thoughts with words. He saw only the black cat trotting at his heels like a well-trained dog.

"Cats aren't supposed to be trainable or obedient," he accused Gentian.

Gentian passed him and kept walking soundlessly through the forest. He obviously knew the way.

Kim's boots squished in the damp leaf litter. His passage wasn't nearly as silent as Gentian's. He wanted to move about the world strictly as an observer, and leave no trace of his passing. Somehow he didn't think he'd be allowed that luxury for long.

"Does it ever stop raining around here, Gentian?" he asked again.

The cat shrugged. As much as any cat could manipulate its shoulders to express a comment.

They walked though dense forest. Raindrops plopped from the branches above to the path below. Frogs croaked. Birds called to each other. Frogs croaked. Insects buzzed and whirred. Frogs croaked. Ferns and undergrowth rustled.

He had to stop periodically and turn in a circle, taking in as much detail as his limited senses could absorb.

"This place isn't nearly as silent as I supposed it would be," Kim commented to himself as much as to the flywacket. At his words, the noise ceased. He froze in the eerie silence, unsure what was wrong. A hush of waiting hung heavily in the air for many moments. He held his breath. After a few moments the cacophony resumed. Kim walked on, feasting on the forest details.

The needled trees had a decidedly blue tinge. "Ever-blues," he decided. "I'll name them everblues."

Gentian snorted.

"All right, so that's an obvious name. I still like it."

The cat almost rolled his eyes, but kept walking, following a path only he could see.

Cursory examination showed the trees to be probably all the same species. Native or a crossbreed with Terran flora?

They entered a deeper, darker section of woods. The critter voices faded.

The tree canopy wove together as densely as a blanket. Little light penetrated, and undergrowth was sparse. The sight of all those ghostly trunks rising like so many columns in an empty temple made his skin crawl.

The noise of his passage seemed almost a sacrilege. He'd felt like this once before, in Mum's church. Filled with candles and greenery on Christmas Eve on some bush world he could no longer name. They'd stayed only a few moments to light yet one more candle in missing Katie's name and kneel in silent prayer. Then other worshipers had come in and shattered the sense of unity and belonging.

Later adventures crowded his memories with nightmares. Every shadowed tree could hide armed troops, vengeful ghosts, or even the emperor himself.

And then the towering everblues ended quite suddenly, replaced by smaller, less dense hardwoods. Most were just coming into leaf. Their bark and silhouettes looked almost familiar. "This is where the terraforming ended," he muttered. "Wonder why the original colonists bothered with new growth. They could just as easily use the native trees."

His mind and ears remained empty of answers.

A few steps farther and the trees gave way to low shrubbery and a steep bank down to a creek surrounded by squishy mudflats. Kim followed a near path of footsteps down. Then he lost track of his brothers' passage. A series of stones had been placed in a straight line across the flats. The gentle flow of water in the three channels gradually rose, lapping at the stones.

"The tide must be coming in, Gentian. Guess we'd better hurry before we need a boat to get across."

The flywacket looked at him with disdain, spread his wings, and leaped into the air. Three flaps of his extra appendages put him on the opposite embankment. He settled in to wait for Kim's less graceful crossing.

"Don't look so disapproving," Kim called to the cat as he wavered dangerously on one foot, arms flailing. "My balance isn't up to par after that vision." He exhaled gratefully as he finally brought his left foot down on the next rock. Three deep breaths helped him regain his mental and physical equilibrium.

Gentian opened his mouth and perked his ears in a close approximation of a laugh.

"Shut up." Kim glared at him as he took three more steps. His confidence returned. Six more steps on the evenly placed stones. Then two more. He almost flew to the last stone only to miss it entirely.

He sank up to his knee in mud.

The cat fluttered his wings and shifted his hindquarters.

"May the fleas of ten thousand Silasian hyenas infest your hide," he cursed.

Gentian scratched behind his ear with his hind foot. His eyes crossed, and his whiskers twitched in consternation.

"Yeah, well you deserve it. Laughing at a mere man just because he can't fly," Kim said as he hauled himself out of the thick goo, getting more on his hands, shirt, jacket, trousers, face, and hair. Finally he plunked himself down beside the flywacket.

The rain increased. He shivered with new chill. At least the downpour washed his face and hands clean of mud. His boots were probably ruined.

Gentian tucked his wings away and curled up next to Kim. A low rumble rippled across his chest. Peace invaded Kim, and he breathed easier.

"Thanks, Gentian," he said and scratched the cat's ears.

The flywacket purred louder and leaned against Kim with his entire weight. Kim found himself listing as he supported the cat. "I'm going to have to revise my estimate of your weight upward." He shoved the cat upright. "Enough. We have to get moving."

Gentian moved out at a smart trot. The next obstacle widened and deepened into a full branch of the river spanned by a rickety rope and plank bridge. Several planks were missing. The rope supports were gray with age and neglect. In places they looked frayed and frail.

Taking a deep breath, Kim placed one foot on the unsteady surface while clinging to the nearest tree. The bridge swayed. The supporting ropes bowed. Kim jerked his foot off the plank. The bridge continued to sway.

"I don't like this, Gentian." He scanned the riverbank leading down to the water. Very steep and a good ten meters below. "Did Loki and Konner use this bridge?"

Gentian didn't comment. Kim couldn't find evidence of footprints in the embankment.

He took another deep breath and looked straight ahead. "If I don't look down, this won't be so scary." Two steps across and he revised that statement. The bridge developed a rhythm of back and forth, up and down, that undermined his balance.

"Okay, what's one more soaking? The water should be deep enough below me to keep me from breaking my neck." He practically ran across. Miraculously the bridge remained intact.

Kim crossed another plank bridge at the next span of river. This one, thankfully, was shorter and a little sturdier. Then he met a causeway. Jagged and uneven, it presented solid ground. Kim picked his way across with care but little concern. Rocks he could handle, rickety bridges scared him. At last he set foot on the mainland. He immediately noted the differences in the rising ground and evidence of human hands in the clearing of fields, an occasional hut (which they skirted) and even a few curls of smoke from friendly fires.

Kim longed to seek shelter from the incessant drizzle, but Gentian kept trotting on with determination. Every time Kim paused, the flywacket wove intricate figures around and through his legs, purring deeply and butting his head against Kim's legs. A sense of urgency pushed Kim to keep going when he'd rather just sit and sleep a few moments.

After nearly an hour of walking, he spied a cluster of rooftops in the distance. More than huts, these habitations seemed to be substantial houses made of planed logs, roofed with dense thatch. Stout stone chimneys with real mortar rose above each rooftree.

Almost one hundred houses, he guessed. They clustered around communal fire pits in loose circles, a dozen or so to a fire. A few chicken crossbreeds pecked at the damp earth. Three piglike creatures with long curved tusks rooted around the edges of a dying fire. No other sign of life greeted him.

All remained eerily silent.

At the northern end stood a house slightly larger and more substantial than all the rest. At the southern end of the small town, a great stone building rose two full stories above the other rooftops. Massive wooden pillars, carved with many winged dragons and stained blood red, supported a wood-shingled roof.

"A temple?" he breathed. It was darker and scarier than the ghostly tree trunks parading endlessly away from him on the islands.

In the open space before the temple, High Priest Hanassa stood with his staff raised and his eyes fixed upon the sky. A myriad of dragon figures peered back at Kim from the carved pillars. They seemed to warn him that he could never truly hide from Simurgh or his High Priest. Hanassa shook the staff so that it rattled almost as loudly as his voice. He chanted some strange litany that jarred Kim's teeth with atonal resonance.

Around the priest the warriors gathered, all on their knees; all with heads bowed and their bronze weapons set before them.

Gentian tugged on his pant leg. Kim looked down at the creature. The flywacket crouched low as it crept around the perimeter of the village. Kim mimicked him. When they had cleared the habitations, low barns, and animal pens—the horses just didn't look right, but the sheep were familiar, if a bit big, with more dense wool than he'd ever seen—Gentian led the way back into the village by way of an alley that must be the path to the midden. Kim pinched his nose closed with his fingers and breathed shallowly through his mouth. Even the adapter couldn't filter out that stench.

The flywacket paused at the corner of a house, keeping low and well within the shadows. Kim took the hint and copied his posture.

The women cowered in the doorways to the huts they passed—many more women than huts. They kept their few children close beside them. The ragged and dirty tykes stared wide-eyed with terror at the scene before them. No one seemed to hold an infant.

"Simurgh has spoken. A sacrifice is demanded for our failure to capture the strange dragon that has invaded us. Simurgh has spoken!" Hanassa lowered his gaze to the men around him. Then he shifted to stare at the women.

Most of them stepped back, deeper into the shadows of their windowless houses, dragging their children with them.

"Bring ten slaves to the altar. Prepare the fires!" Hanassa announced. At last he lowered his staff and planted the end in the ground beside him.

The warriors rose, each heaving a sigh of relief. Many rubbed the backs of their necks as if checking to make sure their heads remained intact.

"Where are Loki and Konner?" Kim whispered to the flywacket. His stomach churned in apprehension.

Gentian did not look overly concerned.

"I take it Hestiia is safe at least."

Gentian looked at him as if he were stupid to even ask.

"But where are they?"

As if in answer to his question, the shadow at another house corner off to his left shifted. He caught a glimpse of Konner's red sleeve hauling Loki back under cover.

Gentian darted from shadow to shadow. Kim followed the flywacket, as he had been doing all afternoon. Luckily, the villagers seemed to have their attention glued to the commands of the High Priest and the ten men and women, all wearing heavy metal rings around their necks, being herded together. The captive men wore only loincloths. The women wore sarongs similar to Hestiia's, but shorter and less full, that left one entire leg bare. He doubted they wore any undergarments at all.

Most of the slaves had long red weals on their backs.

"We've got to end this," Kim hissed as soon as he reached his brothers. He waved to indicate the entire hideous scene. "Slavery is an abomination."

"Slavery is a sign of wealth," Hestiia replied. But she kept her head down and refused to look any of the men in the eye.

"I bet your people consider themselves the richest of all the tribes," Loki spat.

"We are the strongest. Our warriors win every battle and bring home many slaves. None of the others dare attack us. As long as I have lived, none of the Coros have ever been taken as slaves," she defended the village.

"Coros? What does that mean?" Kim asked. The word bounced around his head a dozen times without coming up with anything resembling a definition.

"Coros are Coros. We have always been Coros." Hestiia shrugged matter-of-factly.

"But what does the word signify?"

"The people of Coron."

"Maybe that was the name of one of the original colonists—their first leader perhaps." Kim consulted his reader.

"We haven't time for word games, Kim," Loki insisted. "We've got to do something about those slaves before Hanassa kills them all."

"But the slaves must be sacrificed to placate Simurgh," Hestiia gasped.

"And I say that Simurgh is a crock. Has anyone ever seen him? Has anyone ever talked to him?"

"Hanassa," she said quietly. But her eyes gleamed with harsh emotions.

Kim suddenly knew that she did not believe Hanassa.

"My point exactly. He's as much a charlatan as your god."

"But he is the High Priest. He has much power. We must obey. His trials of initiation and spirit quest must open his mind to the god. No one else has survived the Tambootie smoke."

"No one else has his audacity," Konner snorted.

"Where is the altar?" Loki asked. A sneaky smile spread across his face.

"You've got a plan, big brother," Kim smiled.

"Don't I always?"

"Most of the time."

"Take us to this altar, Hestiia. It's time we end this abomination." Loki drew his stunner from his belt.

"Even the GTE doesn't permit slaves, the death penalty, or blood sacrifice. Hell, they don't even permit a blood diet! Even when I was in jail, restrained by force bracelets and guards at every step, I had more rights than those poor souls." Kim shook his head, saddened by the state these humans had sunk to. Was this a statement about humanity in general or just the cruelty of one society?

"Sometimes one has to counter violence with more violence." Konner drew his stunner as well. "We'll end this, no matter the cost."

"It ends here and now. No matter what." Kim swallowed the lump in his throat. *Not again, God,* he prayed. *Please don't make me kill a man again.*

CHAPTER 13

✦ —— · —— ✦ —— · —— ✦

HESTIIA REARRANGED the silvery blanket, draping it over one shoulder and knotting it at her waist. She gathered her dignity with the blanket. Before she confronted Hanassa and her father again she must have all of her thoughts and arguments in order.

Clearly, she now belonged to these three strange brothers. They relied upon her knowledge, included her in their plans, and protected her from the predatory males in the village.

They had asked her to cover her breasts.

She was their wife.

She had never thought about having three husbands before. The idea did not seem unpleasant. They would work out the details of it later.

She suppressed a giggle. Men often took more than one wife, but only if they could afford to feed and clothe all of them with equal honor. Did three men sharing one woman make her the wealthy spouse? Or speak of their impoverishment?

She could not imagine these three men as poor. They possessed such wonders in their woven clothing, their closeness to the gods, and their weapons.

Their weapons. The ones they pulled out now and twisted and tugged in odd ways.

"Full setting," Loki, the eldest and therefore her number one husband, said grimly.

"We are not going to kill people with these," Kim, the youngest brother, replied with a warning note in his voice.

"Only if our victim is that bastard Hanassa," Konner stated firmly.

Hestiia shied away from the violent undertones in her husbands' voices.

"What do you plan to do?" She eyed the curious black rock weapons with wonder and a touch of fear. She had seen the magic light shoot out of those rocks and knock down mighty warriors. With their blood lust up, the warriors should have continued their charge even with mortal wounds to belly or heart. Surely the white-and-silver dragon that sheltered them in its belly was a mightier god than Simurgh.

Perhaps they were gods themselves and had tamed the white dragon.

"You will remove Hanassa from us?" She stood proudly, ready to lead her men to victory—a place no woman in recent history had held. But some of the old legends—the ones Hanassa had forbidden—claimed that long ago women had marched beside their men into battle. Some of them may have led the men.

"Did you sacrifice slaves before Hanassa became your High Priest?" Kim asked. He alone among the three husbands lowered his black rock weapon so that he no longer pointed it ominously ahead of him.

"Only at the Winter Solstice, to make Simurgh give us back the sun. And the sacrifice had to be willing. We did not force fearful and reluctant ones into their next existence," Hestiia replied, trying to remember a time before Hanassa had ruled the Coros. He had aided her father and his warriors in conquering the nearest villages when she was but a child. The old priest had died shortly thereafter—his heart had given out long before his time—and Hanassa had taken his place. Since that day, Hanassa and Yaaccob had conquered all of the far-flung villages of the Coros. Each village sent tribute to Hanassa and Simurgh at the Autumnal Equinox. They all sent slaves and honored villagers to the sacrificial altar.

No one dared challenge Hanassa and Yaaccob now.

"How often does Hanassa demand sacrifices?" Loki raised one eyebrow in an intrigued gesture.

"Hanassa calls for sacrifice whenever the whim takes him. Whenever he gets greedy for blood, or for power." She voiced the thoughts she had kept deep inside her for many moons; thoughts that would send her to the fires if Hanassa heard them.

"How do you keep enough slaves to feed his blood lust?" Konner shook his head in dismay.

"Our warriors must go forth and conquer villages farther and farther away." Hestiia hung her head lest she show her anger at how often the men deserted her village, leaving the women and children cold and hungry—and defenseless.

"And I bet Hanassa becomes the High Priest over all those villages, too. Sounds like he's setting up a petty kingdom based upon blood and tyranny," Kim spat.

"Consolidating power. Taking the first steps toward a national identity," Loki replied.

Kim glared at his older brother.

Hestiia shied away from the violence in his expression. Violence akin to Hanassa's blood lust. At the same time she warmed toward his attitude. He seemed ready to focus that violence upon Hanassa to save the lives of the slaves—slaves who had once been proud warriors and innocent women.

Hanassa did not usually order the sacrifice of children—unless they were sickly or defective. Did children not possess enough blood to satisfy Simurgh? Or himself?

Hestiia took three steps, skirting the village to follow the procession up to the altar in the hills in the direction of the sunrise. Raised voices back in the village halted her.

"I thought them all gone. Hanassa requires everyone to attend him at the altar." She whirled around to see who dared violate the High Priest's orders.

Taneeo, the apprentice priest, as pale of skin and hair as Hanassa, hung onto the arm of Pryth, the village healer and wisewoman. Everyone knew that Hanassa had sired Taneeo on an unwilling woman. Hanassa refused to acknowledge the kinship.

"Unhand me, you overfed beardless whelp!" The stout woman pried the young man's fingers from her arm. Her Rover heritage was still evident in her swarthy wrinkled skin, despite the grayness of age in her hair, eyebrows, and the thin film of hair on her upper lip.

"You must not interfere, Lady," Taneeo protested.

"I cannot *not* interfere, young man." She fixed her piercing black eyes upon him until he dipped his head in submission.

"Hanassa will not allow you to substitute yourself for one of the slaves. He will just add you to the number of sacrifices!" Taneeo murmured.

"No," Hestiia whispered. Her feet seemed rooted to the ground. She could not move, could not think. But her stomach and hands shook with terror.

"And perhaps my death will teach you idiots once and for all that Hanassa does not obey the orders of Simurgh. He merely makes up ritual and sacrifice on his own whims."

"We need your wisdom, Lady. Please do not do this." Taneeo pleaded, maintaining his firm grasp on the old woman's arm.

Hestiia needed to add her own protests to that of the apprentice priest. Pryth had taught her most of what she knew about being a woman, about her people's special relationship with the land, and with the dragons. Without Pryth's teaching, she would never have found the courage to accept Gentian as her heart-cat when it deserted Hanassa's home.

"I shall die this day, Taneeo, by Simurgh's hand or Hanassa's. But I cannot allow this abomination to continue." Pryth folded her arms beneath her substantial bosom. Nothing would stop her.

Except, perhaps, if Hestiia offered herself as a substitute for the slaves. The daughter of a Chieftain was much more important to the god than mere slaves.

She could not do it. She had narrowly escaped death once already today. She could not die yet.

My agents seek trouble. Trouble I cannot subdue. Do I dare risk them? Do I dare interfere?

'Tis Gentian's fate to interfere. I fear he is too timid for aught but subtle hints. He should never have accepted the role of mentor and counselor. He failed with Hanassa and found a new companion with Hestiia. If he fails again, the destiny of dragons and humans will forever be altered.

Trouble will find my chosen ones no matter what I do. Their fate is beyond my limited means to alter. I can only watch and wait to determine if they are worthy of the next step in my plans.

A heavy wave of sleepiness washed over Kim. What had they got into this time? He should do something. But what? Something nagged at the back of his mind but would not materialize. Something about the hallucinogenic smoke and his special talents. Visions would not stop this madness. He needed action.

Loki with his ability to second-guess people, or Konner's easy manipulation of inanimate objects had a better chance of success.

But the smoke, and the auras he saw . . . what?

"No one will be sacrificed this day, Hestiia," Loki reassured the girl.

Kim was glad his brothers urged her along the path. He no longer had the energy to make decisions. He could only follow. As he had always followed, the youngest and therefore the one with the least valuable opinion.

When this was all over with, Kim knew he must strike out on his own, leave his brothers, and desert Mum and all of her schemes.

But he had a responsibility to help Mum this one last time.

"Let's get this over with," Konner muttered. "I've a date I can't break in less than a year. I want my ship repaired and off this planet long before then."

"What about Mum and Katie?" Kim asked, not certain he wanted to hear the answer.

"I'll deal with Mum in my own way when the time comes," Konner replied firmly.

Kim recognized that his brother had an agenda separate from Mum. What about Loki? Did he plan on going his own way before or after Mum's family reunion?

The path wound upward. Off to their right the louder procession of warriors, villagers, and slaves, led by the High Priest, turned their grim errand into a parade along a broader path through the endless forest and endless rain.

The narrow animal trail Hestiia trod doubled back on itself several times. They followed the contours of the landscape, skirting depressions, rises, and yet more trees. They crossed at least three creeks. Frogs croaked at them along the entire route. Kim's feet hurt. Blisters rose on his heels and the balls of his feet. His boots were ruined from their previous soaking and now this tramp through the wilderness. He and his brothers would have to devise something sturdier and waterproof to cover their feet. Or learn to go barefoot like their guide.

Hestiia placed her bare feet carefully, making no noise and barely disturbing the dirt. Kim and his brothers were not so delicate in their passage. Even he could follow the trail they left behind like his sensors could follow a trail of engine emissions across trackless space.

They had a lot to learn about living on this planet before they could hope to bring these people back into civilization. They had to improve agriculture, industry, government, economics, sanitation, medicine, etc., etc., etc. And religion. The cult of Simurgh and human sacrifice had to go.

Did Loki realize how big a job they had ahead of them? Dreams and plans were one thing, executing them another.

This scheme would keep them from helping Mum. They had to go home as soon as they could.

But he wanted to stay here, study, and help these people.

At last the path emerged into a wide clearing. They stopped at the edge of a line of trees at the top of the clearing. Trees on three sides. A small cliff soared sharply upward, bounded the open place at the top of the slope. A gentle cascade of water chuckled down the cliff. The processional way ended at the shrub line on the downslope.

A huge flattened stone dominated the landscape fifteen meters directly in front of them. It rested near the tallest trees at the base of the waterfall so that the people could gather in "front" of it. From the weathering on the rock and the depth of turf edging the thing, Kim guessed it had been here a long time, possibly left during glaciations aeons ago.

Piles of brush and firewood rested near the altar. Scorch marks climbed the rock on all sides. Many fires had been lit around the base. Too many.

Hanassa entered the clearing, holding his staff high above his head like some perverted parody of a drum major. A carved mask shaped like the muzzle of a dragon, complete with red twisted unicorn horn, covered his face and most of his head. In his right hand he hefted a flaming torch. The priest directed the warriors to bring forth the prisoners. The women scuttled around, piling the kindling and firewood around the altar.

Each of the intended victims grew paler, their eyes wide and staring. No placating drugs for them, like ancient Earth cultures who prized "willing" victims. These people knew their fate and dreaded it. The stink of their fear wafted across the clearing as pungent as the now extinct skunk.

Hanassa licked his lips in almost sexual satisfaction.

The old woman, Hestiia had called her Pryth, stalked into the clearing with the apprentice priest at her heels. She held her shoulders back and her head high.

"Free the slaves," she ordered in a clear voice that carried to every ear in and around the clearing.

"Slaves are the natural booty of victory," the chieftain protested. He placed himself between Hanassa and the seething woman. "They knew their fate the moment their chieftain fell under my sword." He kept looking over his shoulder at Hanassa for confirmation, or a backbone.

"We need their deaths in order to survive. Without blood sacrifice in honor of Simurgh, the god will desert us. We shall become weak and fall victim in the next war. Then all of you will die as these slaves die!" Hanassa roared.

The crowd edged away from him. No one risked eye contact with anyone else.

"Release the slaves and place me upon your filthy altar then, Hanassa. Give my blood to Simurgh in their stead." The older woman stalked forward. She and Hanassa stood alone in the center of the clearing.

The entire crowd gasped at the old woman's audacity as they edge farther away.

"You?" Hanassa sneered. "You are not worthy. A Rover." He spat at Pryth's feet.

"I have been one of the Coros for fifty years, since the day I married Yaac-cob's uncle. Five of your warriors are my grandchildren," she defended herself. "My place in council was bestowed upon me by your predecessor. I did not approve you as High Priest. You stole the position by intimidation and bribery." She spat at Hanassa's feet.

"Women are not worthy of sitting in council!" Hanassa retorted. "Women are weak. Women speak lies. Your death will satisfy me truly. I add you to the ten." Two warriors rushed to bind the woman's arms behind her back.

"It is as she predicted," Hestiia sobbed. "I must do something." She dashed forward.

"No." Kim held her back. He would not risk this young woman's life.

Then Kim saw the indentations atop the "altar." Were they natural, or had many generations of sacrificial victims lying on it made it conform to the human frame.

Suddenly Kim's knees threatened to give way. His face grew very hot and his hands so cold he didn't think he could hold onto his stunner any longer.

Hundreds, probably thousands, of people had lain upon that altar and known that death, long and horrible, awaited them. Echoes of their terror burned through him.

He saw them die. Sharp images flooded his mind's eye. He shared the agony with them. They told him the first step in a plan to end Hanassa's tyranny.

Anger boiled up, replacing his weakness.

Ruthlessly Kim aimed his stunner directly at the flat rock.

"No more. No one else shall die here!" He pressed the firing button. "I shall not be a party to death again. Never again."

Loki and Konner moved out to surround the rock and followed suit. Their faces looked as grim and as determined as Kim felt.

The altar pulsed red and blue under the sustained assault of energy from three stunners set at maximum. The rocks and trees vibrated with a loud hum that resonated with the weapons. Cracks appeared in the rock.

The people cried out in fear and retreated to the trees. They huddled together crying and beseeching their god for aid. But they did not leave.

The altar groaned.

The land vibrated under Kim's thin boots.

Hestiia knelt with her face and hands turned upward. A smile of satisfaction crossed her face.

With a roar and a cracking explosion, the altar blew apart.

A hundred throats screamed in terror.

A rain of shards descended upon them all, ripping and tearing at flesh, more deadly and indiscriminate than a warrior's bronze sword.

CHAPTER 14

K ONNER DOVE BEHIND a clump of bushes. "St. Bridget, send those missiles the other way!" he prayed as he ducked his head and covered it as best he could with both his arms. Nearly forgotten childhood prayers sprang to his lips as he waited for the inevitable pain and gush of blood that must follow the rock explosion.

With his eyes scrunched closed, he visualized the bits and pieces of rock descending in a wide arc well away from the hundred and more people scattered around the clearing. Again and again he re-created the image in his head of the shards suspended in the air until they could be pushed *elsewhere* before falling. As an afterthought he visualized the shards that had already fallen, rising up to join their fellows.

Nothing happened.

He counted to one hundred. Twice. Still no pain slashed his back or arms. He listened carefully. If any of the rock fragments landed, they made no discernible noise.

Carefully, he looked up. So did a number of other people. Their screams of terror turned to gasps of awe. They pointed and urged their companions to look as well.

All of the rock fragments hung in the air a good three meters above the ground. They littered the air over the entire clearing in a complex pattern that reminded Konner of the nomenclature of a crystal interface. The purple dragon hovered near the tops of the trees—the bizarre ones with the mottled leaves of pink and green, fat with oils. The breeze generated by fanning dragon wings pushed the suspended rock shards away, up into the hills behind the clearing.

"This isn't happening," Konner told himself. "The laws of gravity apply everywhere in known space. And there are no such things as dragons."

"But we aren't in known space any longer." Kim grinned at him. He showed his teeth in a feral expression that frightened Konner.

Without much more prodding, Kim would go bush, forsaking the benefits of civilization. Putting aside the dreams of citizenship and a reunited family that had sustained them all for so long. Konner needed citizenship. Legal status in the GTE would go a long way toward convincing lawyers and judges that Melinda should relinquish custody of her son to Konner.

Mum could go searching for her daughter. Konner knew where his son lived and planned on bringing him into the family as well.

A collective sigh of relief alerted Konner to a change. He searched the clearing again for the next source of danger. Kim still huddled on the ground with his arm draped around Hestiia. Maybe Kim had found the family he craved.

A number of the locals had sunk to their knees and touched their foreheads to the ground, arms stretched forward. They all directed their awe and respect toward the three O'Hara brothers.

A lump of confusion lodged in Konner's throat.

"What?"

Suddenly Loki's face went blank. Then he shook himself free of whatever enthralled him.

"Watch out for Hanassa! Quick, he's going to kill us." Loki whirled to face a clump of trees on the far side of the clearing.

"Evil sorcerers! Dragon spawn turned against Simurgh!" Hanassa charged forward screaming his outrage. No longer masked, but still carrying his staff, he launched himself at Loki and Konner.

Deliberately, Loki raised his stunner and pointed it at the irate priest. A look of horror crossed his face. "Empty. It's tapped out. Shoot him, Konner. Shoot him before he kills us."

Konner raised his own weapon. It, too, lay inert. Empty.

"Kim!" Both brothers shouted for assistance.

The youngest brother swiveled to his knees, aiming and firing at the same time. A few sparks of energy dribbled from his weapon. "Used it all up on the altar." His face turned paler yet.

"Weapons. We need weapons." Loki turned in a quick circle, eyes searching.

Konner stepped in front of his brother and into Hanassa. They crashed together. The skull atop Hanassa's staff slammed into his gut. Air rushed out of his lungs in a sharp gasp. He couldn't get it back. His chest felt frozen. The stitches in his back strained, but did not break. He dropped to his knees.

Hanassa reached for his throat. Loki blocked the priest with a quick uppercut to his jaw. Konner stuck out one leg to trip Hanassa. He staggered briefly, regained his balance, and surged forward once more, swinging the staff like a giant club.

Loki surged forward beneath the staff with its weight of crystal and dangling stone beads and sharpened bones. Hanassa dodged left. Loki twisted and caught him with his shoulder.

But Hanassa was faster. He brought the staff around. The weight of it added impetus to his swing at Loki's head.

"No!" Konner screamed. He launched himself at the staff. His fingertips brushed the wood. Not enough to deflect the blow.

If only they'd had weapons.

Konner wished Hanassa's own bronze knife would stab in him in the back. He could almost see it happening.

Hanassa opened his mouth in surprise. No sound passed his lips. His fingers spasmed open. The staff fell to the ground.

Loki scuttled backward.

Hanassa collapsed, his own knife sticking out of his back.

"By St. Jethro Mulligan's necrotic toe, how did that happen?" Kim inched cautiously toward his brothers and their fallen foe.

"St. Jethro Mulligan?" Loki raised one eyebrow in question, all the while avoiding looking at the body at his feet.

"In all of Mum's lexicon, I couldn't think of anyone else." Kim shrugged, grateful for the light tone. He didn't think the levity would last more than a few seconds. Very soon his brothers would realize they had killed a man. Not just an animal, but a *MAN*.

His knees began to tremble and dieflyn imps used his stomach as a trampoline. Blackness edged toward the center of his vision. His mind tried very hard to detach from his body.

"Is . . ." Konner swallowed heavily. "Is he dead?" His eyes remained riveted upon Hanassa's back and the bronze knife with the staghorn hilt.

Kim knelt beside the High Priest. He didn't see any signs of breathing, shallow or otherwise. Hesitantly, he stretched his fingers toward the man's neck, certain that at any moment he would jerk upright and attack them once more. Hanassa remained immobile. His skin was still warm.

"I can't find a pulse," Kim said on a long exhale. He could not be sure about that. Hanassa's bones seemed bigger than his frame suggested. The soft tissue of the neck where he should find a pulse almost seemed encased by bone. He concentrated on the science of the skeletal structure, of pulse points and joints. He looked for things that could be measured. If he stopped for even a moment, he'd realize what he and his brothers had done. So he continued seeking some elusive flutter beneath the skin that would indicate life lingered.

The incessant rain beat a tattoo upon the fallen man's back, masking any sign of a pulse.

"I . . . I didn't sense a soul passing," Loki said quietly. "Mum always said we'd know, we'd share the moment of transition if we ever took a life."

Mum had been right about that. But Kim couldn't bring himself to say so. Had he sensed Hanassa's soul passing? He didn't know. He hadn't wielded the knife.

"Mum also told us the monster under the bed would grab us if we got out of bed in the middle of the night. Can't tell you how many times I almost wet the bed out of fear of that monster," Konner reiterated.

"But how did this happen?" Kim wanted to shrug off the childhood superstitions but couldn't quite.

Neither of his brothers replied. Neither did they look him in the eye. They knew something.

"Masters?" one of the slaves approached them. He shuffled his feet nervously and kept his eyes lowered, his posture meek. "How may we serve you?"

"We are no man's masters," Kim said, raising his face to the man rather than the grisly death at his feet.

All ten of the slaves looked to each other in confusion.

"But what are we to do, Masters?"

"Whatever you want. You are free to go. Go home." Loki shrugged. His face and posture radiated confusion.

Gasps of horror escaped every native throat in the clearing.

"You freed us from death only to humiliate us in life. Death is preferable!"

"No, no, of course not." Konner stepped up next to Kim to face the bewildered throng. "You are no longer slaves. Go back to doing whatever you did before you became slaves," he tried to explain.

"I don't think they can do that," Kim said, rising to stand beside his brothers.

"Why is that, know-it-all-brother?" Loki sneered at Kim.

Kim ignored the jibe. "These people are warriors. They lost the war. Slavery was their punishment for losing. Being obedient slaves is the only way to redeem their honor."

"Since when did you become the expert?" Konner jumped in.

"He speaks correctly," Hestiia said. She came to Kim's side and took his arm. The metallic blanket flowed around her like a royal mantle. "These people have no place to go except to become your slaves. They are yours by right of conquest."

"But what do we do with them?" Loki asked. His eyes searched the clearing. None of the natives, including the slaves, would look at him.

"We need a work force to help produce a surplus of food and help us make repairs." Konner grinned. Speculation gleamed in his eyes like mischief.

"For that we need land," Kim added, trying to be practical while Hestiia's closeness robbed him of concentration on anything but her. He wondered what her father thought of her live presence in the company of three virile men after he'd tried to sacrifice her.

"We need a lot of things," Loki mused. "Very well, these people now work for us. But they work honestly, receiving a day's wage for a day's work."

Smiles and nods from all ten of the slaves.

"Um . . . Loki, what do these people consider a day's wage? Do they have coins? If I remember my reading correctly, and I always do, this should be strictly a barter economy, almost communal within the village, reserving surpluses for trade with neighboring communities for things they don't have or don't produce as skillfully." Kim's head spun with details. Where would they get seeds and livestock and plows and . . . and housing?

What had they got themselves into?

They didn't have time for this. They had to get home. They had a responsibility to Mum.

They also had responsibilities to these people.

"Do you challenge me for the rights of this village?" The headman, Hestiia's father, stepped forward, hand on the hilt of his bronze sword. This weapon was all one piece, hilt and blade, unlike the knife that had killed Hanassa.

"Uh, no," Loki replied, eyeing the sharpness of the inch or so of blade that Yaaccob pulled out of the leather and wood sheath.

"We will find our own settlement," Hestiia faced her father with pride and resolution.

Kim had come to expect her forthrightness. But wasn't that out of place? The men had tried to execute her without trial for the sin of handling a weapon. He thought women subservient in this type of culture.

"You will return to the village for trial for your crime of handling weapons, daughter." Yaaccob released his sword and raised his hand as if to strike Hestiia.

Kim pushed her behind him, ready to deflect the blow. Somehow.

"You no longer have the right!" Hestiia spat at him.

"The right! You are my daughter. I am War Chieftain."

"I have husbands now. I answer to them and their laws. Not to you. Never again to you."

"Husbands?" Kim asked. He heard his question echoed by each of his brothers, by Yaaccob and his son Yaakke.

"Which man claims you without requesting permission to court you. Which man claims you without offering bride-price?" Yaaccob looked at each of the three brothers. Anger flooded his face with high color. His eyes narrowed, and his lips pursed. The blade inched farther out of the sheath.

Something apprehensive and excited sank into Kim's belly. He had a strange feeling about this. Husbands? She'd definitely used the plural.

"All three of them," Hestiia announced proudly. "I am mate and partner to all three of the gods who came to us from the stars."

CHAPTER 15

◆——·——◆——·——◆

"**I**MPOSSIBLE!" Yaaccob exploded. He raised his fist to backhand Hestiia.

She refused to cringe.

Each of her three husbands moved to intercept the blow.

"Who is to say what is impossible?" Hestiia replied, peering from behind Kim's back. She kept her tone mild. Revealing her own anger and resentment toward the man who had sired her, had controlled every aspect of her life for eighteen summers, would only complicate matters. She would not allow him to block this new enterprise of her husbands.

"No one woman has more than one living husband."

"The Stargods have all chosen me. Who am I to question the gods?" She looked up at her father through her lashes, feigning meekness. He always responded when she pretended vulnerability.

"Stargods? Bah!"

"Spare us, O gods from the sky who rode down on a white-and-silver dragon," the kneeling villagers chanted, almost as if the ritual words had come from antiquity.

Yaaccob glared at his people for a long moment. They continued kneeling to Hestiia's three husbands.

"No one has ever started a new village while the old one thrives," Yaaccob reminded them all with massive contempt, completely ignoring the worshipful attitude of the others. "These slaves belong to *my* village, *my* warriors. I refuse you permission to separate. I do not recognize your victory over *me* to claim these slaves."

"Are you going to stand in our way?" Loki asked, raising his black rock weapon.

Yaaccob lowered his fist, but did not retreat from the implied threat.

"It is about time we begin a new tradition." Kim raised his voice to include all of the villagers.

"A new tradition that puts an end to slavery for all time," Konner added.

"Who will plow the fields and chop the firewood? How are we to live, to prosper?" Yaakke asked, more curious than angry. Hestiia's brother moved up to stand beside their father. The two men stood shoulder to shoulder, matched in height, breadth, and stubbornness.

Hestiia was proud that her brother could look beyond the past to find something better in the future.

"We will all survive by trade, by alliance, by honoring life more than wealth," Kim stepped forward, empty hands displayed as a sign of his good intentions. "There are times when sacrifice is required. But it means nothing unless it is made willingly for the benefit of all. Murdering innocents just to feed one man's bloodlust helps no one, appeases no god worth worshiping."

Frightened murmurs broke out among the villagers. Hestiia's insides fluttered as well. These men, her *husbands,* wanted to change the ways of her people. Change was good. She wanted change. The presence of the flywacket foretold it. But this much change all at once?

Her sense of up and down, right and left, spun wildly, righted and reoriented with Kim, Konner, and Loki at the center.

"Who then shall we worship, mighty lords from the sky?" Pryth asked. The old wisewoman never relaxed her challenging stance with her arms folded beneath her impressive bosom, shoulders back, chin lifted. Her gaze met each of the three men, demanding they answer the question.

"We shall worship the gods who came from the stars!" Hestiia announced. Even as she spoke, she dropped to her knees and bowed before the three men who claimed her life and her love.

"Will you get up!" Kim grabbed her arm and hauled her to her feet. "This is embarrassing."

"But useful, little brother," Loki replied. "Just think of it. On this world we are gods. Everything we want or need will be given to us without question."

"Uh, I'm not sure we want to get into this, Loki," Konner said, biting his lip. "We might never get off this planet."

"Do not speak of leaving us," Hestiia cried. "You have just given us hope of life and freedom and prosperity. Why would you desert us?"

"Do not question your betters, daughter," Yaaccob sneered.

"No one is anyone's 'better.'" Kim shoved Hestiia behind him. She stumbled, flailed for balance. Konner caught her and steadied her.

A special warmth replaced the apprehension in her belly. Her husbands would protect her. Together, they would guide the Coros through the years of change. She would make the gods see that they had to stay. Their place in history was here with the Coros.

And she would never obey the cruel whims of her father again. Nor those of the High Priest who took everything and gave back nothing.

•——◆——•

Error compounded upon error. I sought to help these frail mortals and they turn their victory into a . . . I do not know what to call this turn of events. Only do I know that they ignore their biggest threat. How can I alert them?

Not enough that they supplant the long dead rogue dragon, Simurgh. Not enough that they make the people question another rogue, Hanassa. They must end Hanassa's reign of terror, not merely question it. I must show them their mistakes. But will they listen?

•——◆——•

Hanassa bit his lip against the pain. In his back, down his legs, spreading out along his arms. He must not cry out. To reveal that he lived would only bring death, swift and certain. If not from the interlopers who sought to steal his power and his followers, then from those followers themselves. Once freed of their fear of him, they would not hesitate to complete the murder begun by the strangers.

Gods descended from the stars? Bah! Charlatans and fools. In the end they would not stand against Hanassa.

With Simurgh as his tool, he had power. He must triumph.

Careful not to move, Hanassa waited as only one of his heritage could wait. The knife in his back had done much damage, but his unique backbone had deflected the blade. He would need time and care to heal before he sought to right wrongs done against himself this day.

The Rover woman, Pryth joined the parade of slaves and malcontents on the game trail with the false gods. Good. Let the old bat pester them for a while. She could find fault in any action or thought. She claimed that her Rover heritage allowed her to see the future. A future without Hanassa and Simurgh ruling the land? Bah! No one could see the future, not even the dragons. Pryth just made good guesses. But Hanassa made better ones.

While he waited for the three brothers to make a mistake—and Hanassa would ensure that the mistake was fatal—he would gather more followers. Not everyone trusted the strangers. Even now Yaaccob and some of his warriors hung back, refused to take a chance on the new gods from the stars.

The clearing of a new village and farmland would take much work. Even the miracles the brothers brought with them would require many seasons. They would need many more seasons to teach the slaves the skills necessary to survival.

And when they failed, Hestiia would come to him willingly. Strong women, defiant women, needed stronger men to satisfy them and keep them from harming themselves and those around them. Soon she would realize her foolishness and accept the strongest man in ten villages as her husband: Hanassa.

In the meantime, every time they tried to plow or plant or remove weeds, they would fall victim to the curses that lay buried in the soil. That was why he allowed only women and slaves to plow and plant among the Coros. Better to keep the warriors healthy and ready to defend the village against raiders.

Wise warbands waited for a village to show signs of weakness among the men before attacking.

How long would the Coros believe in these new Stargods when they failed to protect them from the plagues? Even Hanassa could not protect them from the demons planted by human ancestors many generations ago.

The so-called Stargods would protect Hestiia and forbid her to plow. She must survive to return to Hanassa.

"Time is on my side," he whispered as the last villager trooped down the processional path. "I have no deadlines to draw me elsewhere. Hestiia is young yet. She will thrive to bear me many sons."

Loki looked over the motley array of barely clad slaves, women, children, and half-grown boys who looked at him with adoration. Suddenly his grand scheme of transforming this primitive bush planet into a prosperous agricultural paradise seemed more daunting than it had during the rush of adrenaline after the fight with Hanassa.

"Um . . . is anyone going to bury the bastard back in the clearing?" he whispered to his brothers.

The bulk of his followers held back, giving him a semblance of privacy. A semblance only. He was certain they heard and understood every word he said—even with their oozingly slow speech patterns.

"His body will be allowed to rot without honor, food for carrion birds and beasts," Hestiia spat. "As he forced the same dishonor upon his sacrificial victims."

Loki felt the weight of his brothers' stares.

"Mum wouldn't like that," Konner said quietly. "She believes in honoring our enemies in defeat, no matter how heinous the crime." He, too, kept looking at the crowd behind them.

"Mum won't like hearing that we set ourselves up as gods either," Kim added. "We have a responsibility to be honest with them."

"And who is going to tell Mum what we've been up to?" Loki stopped short on the path down the hill. The time had come to separate his younger brothers from their fantasy that Mum was infallible, that Mum loved them all equally, that Mum was anything but a plotter and schemer with her own agenda.

Konner and Kim nearly plowed into him. But Hestiia didn't. She seemed to anticipate his moves even before he thought them through.

Just like Mum. Nimble nebulae! What had they let themselves in for?

"Doesn't matter if we tell Mum or not. She always finds out." Kim shook his head.

"It's almost like she reads our minds." Konner continued walking.

"Reads our minds." The memory of the fight with Hanassa played across Loki's inner vision. "I knew he was going to attack and from where before he charged, before he was in sight." He gulped heavily.

What was it about this place? Dragons and mind reading. Bloody sacrifices and flying cats.

Maybe it was all just a nightmare. Pretty soon he'd wake up and Mum would call him to breakfast.

If it was all a dream, then why did his feet hurt? His thin ship boots weren't meant for trekking around a wilderness. Come to think of it, the backs of his legs also ached abominably. All this hill climbing. And descending played havoc as well on muscles that had grown used to fixed workouts in the heavy grav section of the outer cargo holds.

"What if we set it up so that Mum is the Goddess and we but her messengers?" he asked his brothers. "Mum would like being the Goddess." So would Cyndi. Maybe after he had bought his citizenship, he'd bring her back here for a honeymoon. The daughter of a planetary governor was used to being waited on hand and foot. Being named a goddess was only a small step above that.

"Mum is Catholic from a long line of Irish Catholics," Kim reminded him. "She won't like any of this."

But Cyndi sure would. She didn't believe in anything but herself and her ability to solve all the problems of the universe. Just like Loki.

If that was so, then why hadn't she convinced her father to issue a pardon for Loki?

"A woman can only give birth to gods. She cannot be one," Hestiia protested. At least she did not look as appalled as some of the followers.

Loki shrugged. He'd had enough of this conversation. He needed to find a place to sit down and maybe a long cool beer before he could decide anything. "Any ideas where we should set up this new community?" he asked his brothers in a barely audible whisper. He thought they should maintain a guise of dignity and omniscience if they were to be hailed as gods.

All three brothers looked to Hestiia for ideas. Almost as if they deferred to her. Almost as if she had the right to advise them, as a wife would.

That was another piece of nonsense Loki was too tired to deal with.

"You are the gods. You should know these things," she said succinctly. Her face remained a blank mask, giving no clue to her thoughts.

Loki wanted to probe deeper into her mind, as if he really could read her thoughts and ideas, her motivations and plans. Save a lot of time and disagreement.

But that talent, if he truly had it, seemed to have deserted him.

"I want to look at the survey charts first," Kim replied in his musing academic voice while he stared vacantly off into the distance. "We need to look for a deep soil cover; open grassland would be best. If the local cereals have enough protein, we can salvage the seeds out of the grasses we cut before plowing."

"Well, then, maybe we should just go back to the shuttle and lay some plans." Loki thought longingly of that cold beer and a place to prop up his aching feet. How many kilometers away was the *Rover*?

They'd emerged from the tree line and now overlooked the village from the first of the rolling hills.

"The sun will set shortly," Hestiia reminded them.

Was that a superior smirk on her face?

Loki studied the western horizon. Sure enough, the sun dipped mighty close to the blue smudge in the distance that must be foothills.

"Can we make it back to the shuttle in an hour? There should be a fairly lengthy twilight this far south of the equator." The big question was whether his feet would last another hour.

"I know a shortcut." Hestiia tripped ahead of them. Kim kept close to her heels.

Maybe that was the solution to the "marriage" problem. Let her think she was married to the youngest brother. The kid needed someone to care about other than his books and his sensors. That would leave Loki and Konner free to . . . free to do what? He had no idea what they should do now to bring about his dreams of wealth and citizenship.

"Now I wish I'd paid attention as a kid to some of the things Mum tried to teach us about surviving on a bush planet."

CHAPTER 16

◆ — · — ◆ — · — ◆

KIM STRETCHED HIS BACK as much as he could, perched on a rock with his feet pointed toward the campfire. He had trouble accepting that the dancing flames were *green*. They should be red/orange/yellow. Konner had said something about copper sulfate permeating the soil and all of the organics. Whatever. It still looked weird.

The flames heated the worn soles of his boots. Not good. He needed to soak his feet in cold water after the long walks today over uncertain terrain. Moving slowly, so as not to jar the weary muscles in his back, he bent forward and loosened the adhesive flaps across his instep and ankle. Just the release of that little pressure helped.

He noticed Konner and Loki doing the same. Kim watched a moment, waiting to see if either of his brothers took the initiative to remove his boots. Loki kicked off the black faux leather followed immediately by Konner. Kim was only a heartbeat behind. Almost as if his oldest brother had made the decision for him.

Another time, when he wasn't so tired, Kim would fight the notion of his brother in control of another's thoughts. Tonight he'd just mull it over while he savored the smell of roasting vegetables and venison as Pryth told her stories.

Every person gathered around this fire knew what had transpired today. They'd all been a part of it. Yet they still listened eagerly while the old woman retold the events, embellished only a little. For the most part she gave an accurate rendition of the rescue of the slaves, of the destruction of the altar and the defeat of Hanassa. But it sounded so much better coming from her than the bare facts laid out in the ship's log and Kim's personal journal.

Kim enjoyed a luxurious moment of speculation. Would generations to come listen as eagerly, with bated breath, to the same story, told in the same words, perhaps set to music, as they sat around a hearth waiting for the evening meal to cook?

His vision rocked. Stone walls seemed to form out of mist. The refugees gathered together here morphed into different people. They wore tunics and tight-fitting breeches of fine cloth. The fire crackled in a fireplace with a wide mantel and a soaring chimney. Pryth became a wandering minstrel clad in bright colors, strumming a stringed instrument. And she/he told this same story with wonder. The audience gasped in awe. Then they whispered among themselves with confidence and pride. They were the descendants of that first ragged band of followers who had ended slavery forever in their enlightened kingdom.

Then the ghostly images, superimposed upon reality, vanished. The ragged band of followers huddled together around the fire for warmth, waiting for food. Their backs sprouted goose bumps—no, lumbird bumps; the locals didn't have geese—where the fire did not warm them. Their shoulders drooped in exhaustion. The slave collars weighed heavily upon them, mute symbols of what they hoped to escape. Tomorrow Konner had promised to take one of his high-tech cutters to the bronze bands and truly free them.

These refugees had come away from the old village with nothing more than the few tattered clothes they could claim as their own. (Kim suspected that more than a few bronze tools and pottery vessels had also come away with the former slaves, but until he saw them, he could not be sure.) Still these people—his people—listened to Pryth, unaware they had just been elevated to the stuff of legends.

The story ended with the triumphal march away from the shattered altar. Pryth led a reenactment of the parade around and around the circle of the campfire. Gentian swooped around with them, chattering his own song of victory. The green flames splattered wild shadows across swinging arms and bare torsos.

Kim's vision split again and he saw the faces of generations of descendants in those shadows. When his eyes cleared, Hestiia stood in front of him proffering a bark trencher piled with freshly roasted venison, yammat flower bulbs that grew in the local wetlands, baked in the coals, and fresh water greens, similar to spinach in color and texture but not quite the same, dressed with the fat from the carcass. How much in material goods did these folk need when they could hunt and gather a feast like this?

His mouth watered and his stomach growled. He wanted to gulp down every morsel Hestiia offered him. But he knew he couldn't. Decades of conventions from civilized worlds had been beaten into him. Blood diets were unhealthy, cruel, and barbaric. His stomach would bolt if he ate the meat or fat from an animal that had once lived.

Konner and Loki dug into their meals with hearty appetite.

"Careful, brothers, we've eaten nothing but tanked food for too long. If you eat all that meat, you'll spend the night in the head throwing it back out from both ends," Kim warned.

Loki ignored him. Like his namesake from ancient Terran legend, he always plunged into each adventure without caution.

"A few bites until you become used to this new diet," Kim insisted. "I figure two weeks to acclimatize our stomachs."

"Leave it to Kim to come up with a precise timetable," Loki scoffed as he bit into a hunk of meat.

His throat froze in the act of swallowing.

"Chew, big brother. Chew it first, nice and slow." Konner slapped Loki on the back. His cheeks bulged as his jaw began working at the tender morsel.

"This stuff is so tender it falls apart," Konner added on a soft purr. He slipped a sliver of meat into his mouth and began to chew. His eyes closed in bliss.

Kim pushed the meat aside. He used to enjoy a blood diet on bush worlds. But since . . . for the past two years he'd declined the indulgence his brothers savored.

"I could get used to this," Loki murmured, chasing the meat down with some of the starchy bulb and greens. "Even the emperor doesn't eat this well. I know at least a dozen wealthy nobles who will pay a fortune for a secret banquet of this wonderful food—of course, they will never admit in public that they indulged in a blood meal even for one night. That would be 'uncivilized.'" He laughed heartily.

"Wonder if we can make flour with these bulbs." Kim's mind continued to work. Strange how an influx of natural food, even just a few bites, revived his thought processes.

Yes, he could get very used to this diet even without the meat.

Hours later, when the fire had died down, the former slaves had broken into small groups laying down fresh ferns for their beds. Kim tossed them as many of the blankets from the *Rover* as he could find. Then the three brothers retreated to the shuttle. Kim leaned back against the couch in the lounge. Slowly he lifted his aching feet to the table in front of him. Mum would never allow feet on the table, especially bare ones. But these were extraordinary circumstances, and Mum wasn't here to yell at him. Or at his brothers as they, too, eased the weight off their blisters.

They had walked miles today over rough terrain. They'd endured trauma and injury, running from the law and landing here—wherever here was.

"I'll dig out those survey charts in a minute," Kim mumbled, closing his eyes and resting his head on the ergonomically designed pillows.

"You need to soak your feet." Hestiia clicked her tongue in disapproval. "I would think that gods would have more sense than to walk even the short distance to the village and the altar without better footwear, or none at all. What use are these—these flimsy foot coverings?" She sounded just like Mum as she lifted one discarded boot. Her nose almost curled in disgust at the smell.

All three brothers cringed. Nothing like a strong woman with men to manage to make the entire world tremble.

"I think there are washbasins in the cupboard beneath that console," Loki pointed lazily to the almost invisible crack in the bulkhead.

"I shall fetch water from the river. I presume you three have enough brains among you to light a fire to warm it?" Hestiia poked and prodded the crack for several moments before finding the release pressure points.

Kim's estimation of her intelligence rose another notch. His brothers seemed more interested in admiring her trim little backside as she bent and twisted while she figured out the puzzle of the cupboard. Resentment rose in Kim like a hot flash of energy. Gone was the pain in his feet, calves, and thighs. Gone was the sleepiness from a full stomach and a long day of problem compounded upon problem. He wanted only to reach out and strangle both men.

At the same time, Hestiia's slender back and long legs enticed him to crane his neck for a better look.

The object of his admiration rose gracefully, supporting three cerama/ metal bowls of varying sizes. "Are these the basins you suggested?" She eyed them skeptically. The smallest vessel only had room enough for one foot at a time.

"Those will have to do until we can make more out of native materials," Kim answered.

Hestiia left, making a "huff" sound as she slapped the exit iris. Kim wondered briefly if she knew that she could open the hatch with a touch from one finger or if she figured one had to slap it hard because she had only seen Kim and his brothers do so.

"We could have told her about the tap in the galley, or the one in the head," Konner said half-heartedly.

"But if we did, we'd never have a moment's privacy from her," Loki replied. He roused a little, sitting up straighter, but keeping his feet firmly planted on the table.

"I sense some unease in your posture, big brother," Kim said around a yawn. Even though he knew he should pay close attention, he just . . . couldn't.

"Didn't any of you pay any attention to Hestiia's little announcement back in the clearing?" Loki asked. This time he did plop his feet down. Immediately, he winced and lifted them back to his lap for a massage.

"You mean the fact that she considers herself married to all three of us?" Konner asked. He opened one eye, watched Loki fuss with his feet, and decided to do the same with his own.

"Are we going to take her seriously?" Loki asked.

"I think we have to," Kim replied. Did he truly want to? He couldn't think beyond the moment to figure out how they should handle this. "She told her father, and he seemed to accept it. Everyone else in the village as well. If we refuse her now, she will be humiliated and we will lose some of our authority over these people."

"I think you are right, baby brother," Konner agreed. "If Mum could only see us now."

"But if we accept Hestiia as our wife, what are we going to do with her. We can't exactly take her home to visit Mum!"

"Heaven forbid! *One* girl among the three of us. She'd rip us to shreds with her tongue and then start in on Hestiia," Kim said around a smile. In his mind's eye he could envision Hestiia giving back to Margaret Kristine O'Hara as fiercely as she got.

His brothers nodded grimly. Silence hung heavily in the shuttle.

"So what do we do with her? We can't exactly all share a conjugal bed." A flush crept up Kim's neck to his cheeks. He looked away rather than let his brothers see him blush.

"Ahem," Konner coughed heavily, also embarrassed. "Do we have to do anything other than let her wait on us and give us advice about farming and such?"

"We need to talk to her, let her know what she should and should not expect of us. Just because the marriage isn't valid in the GTE doesn't mean it's not valid here." Kim pounded the table. He wasn't sure why, but it seemed to get their attention.

"Before we can talk to her, we need to come to an agreement among ourselves," Loki insisted.

"Agreed," Kim replied. "Are we agreed that none of us shares a bed with her?"

"Yes," Konner said with a sigh of relief.

"Yes," Loki said quietly. He almost sounded disappointed.

"Okay, then. We need to list our assets and requirements before I go looking for a new location for our village." Kim dug out an electronic slate to doodle on while they talked. He wanted to devise a force field around Hestiia's assigned bed in the back of the shuttle to make sure his brothers lived up to their agreement.

"Uh, how long is this enterprise going to take?" Konner asked.

"Which one?" Loki replied around a yawn. "Kim should have his list in a few moments and then you and I can grab some shut-eye while he searches."

"No. I mean this farming business. I need a forge, and I need to do some mining. We've got to repair the *Sirius*. That's our first priority."

"Our first priority is the safety and well-being of *our* followers," Kim insisted. "I'll go along with this godhood business, but only if both of you acknowledge the responsibilities that go along with it!"

"I have to repair the ship. I have an appointment I won't miss!" Konner's voice rose.

"We have to return to Mum with a big ticket cargo. We need money to regain our citizenship." Loki shouted louder than Konner.

"None of that is important if we leave here before we finish what we started. We can't abandon these people to fall back into blood slavery and blood sacrifice," Kim's quiet words sliced through their arguments. All of a sudden, Mum and her family reunion didn't seem so very important.

He almost crossed himself at that horrendous thought. They had to get back to Mum—and soon.

"We'll see about that, baby brother." Konner and Loki stomped out of the shuttle.

CHAPTER 17

"WHAT STRANGE VISION is this?" Hestiia gasped. The moving images of green forests, grassy plains, and blue/green waters all seen from *above* made her senses spin. She grabbed hold of the back of Lord Kim's throne. The temple room seemed to spin around her. "How can this be? The sun has set, your dragon remains on the ground, and yet we fly through the daylight looking *down* upon the land."

Abruptly, she sat on the floor. Her fine dinner of venison and roots threatened to come up. She must not waste the sacrifice of the animal's life her brother Yaakke had hunted. Two deep gulps of air, keeping her eyes closed and her head lowered, settled the food.

"Uh, there is no easy way to explain this, Hestiia," Lord Kim said. His expression softened, and his voice was kind as he shifted his gaze from the incredible vision to her.

"Magic." She stood up, resolved to accept the talents of her husbands as a part of her life.

Behind her, Gentian huffed. When she looked at him for an explanation, he abruptly began cleaning the base of his tail with one foot stuck upward at a derisive angle.

The vision shifted. Hestiia realized Lord Kim had been following the river, searching both sides of it for a suitable site for the new village. Red lights flashed arcane symbols beside the view. He shook his head and moved on.

"What do you search for?" Hestiia asked, puzzled. Now that she realized the dragon was giving memories of a flight to Lord Kim, her stomach settled and she could concentrate on the dream images.

"A site for us to settle," he said, still shaking his head.

"What about there?" Hestiia pointed to a grassy area that curved with the river. The waters took on the deep blue hue of depth. "Good fishing. No trees to clear for plowing. That small lake will draw game for hunting until we can capture and breed wild tuskers and woolies." She shrugged at the obvious.

"That lake is surrounded by swamp that will trap animals in mud."

"The mud will dry when the winter rains cease. In all my summers this is the first season that swamps have lingered past the Equinox. When the mud dries, birds will nest in the reeds beside the lake. We will have eggs."

"The soil is too thin, and the reason there is no timber is because it is a swampy flood plain. The river will wash away the village and our crops." Lord Kim moved on with his search.

"No place is perfect. If the soil is too thin, you add compost. Villages always have compost."

"Night soil holds all the diseases that humans have and puts them back into the soil. Livestock manure maybe, once we find some livestock. But human waste must be buried at a goodly distance from the village."

"Diseases are the curse of the gods. Surely you can remove them. You are gods."

"It is not that simple, Hestiia. Some things are beyond our powers." Lord Kim turned back to the dragon memories. The grasslands spotted with game gave way to rolling hills and then steep mountains with sharp ravines.

"Turn back, husband, please. You do not wish to settle there." Her eyes remained fixed upon the barren sight.

"No, not in the mountains. Wrong climate for farming. But we will need to seek out mines there for metals."

"If you must dig in the mountains, please stay on the sunrise side of them. Please," Hestiia begged. Worry began to tie her belly in knots and upset her meal once more. Too many nightmare stories had been told around the fires on wintry evenings about the evils on the sunset side of those mountains.

Pryth was the only person ever known among the Coros to cross those mountains and live. Before she married a Coros man, she had wandered the world with her Rover clan. She reported unbelievable things—even lands beyond the Great Bay!

"Why must we stay away from the far west—er—the sunset side of the mountains?" Lord Kim asked. He held her gaze. The deep blue of his eyes seemed to beg for explanation.

"Evil dwells over there. The mountains are the only barrier that keeps evil from spilling over to our lands." She crossed her hands and flapped them in the age-old ward against Simurgh and his horde of demons.

"What could be more evil than Simurgh and Hanassa demanding unwilling human sacrifice?"

"Cannibals." Hestiia flapped her hands again and shuddered.

"I thought you said those people live in caves and eat bugs."

"When they cannot capture their enemies and eat them."

"Cannibalism has been proved a myth among sentient races by anthropologists in the latest anthropological studies," Lord Loki said dismissively. He wandered into the temple yawning and looking years younger than he had before his meal and rest. He also looked more handsome than ever.

Hestiia's apprehension was replaced by a fluttering warm feeling deep inside her. Night had come. Soon she would take up her wifely duties with her husbands. All of them were handsome powerful men. She guessed that Loki would join her in her bed first since he was the eldest. She almost wished Kim would be the first. But as the youngest he would most likely be the last. The one she would fall asleep beside and wake up with in the morning.

Yes. That would be the most satisfying way to proceed. Should she suggest that the time had come? Perhaps they would order her to bed when their need overcame their fascination with the dragon memories playing across the temple.

"Have the anthropologists proved cannibalism a myth because it is a myth or because they wanted it to be that way?" Lord Konner asked.

His words meant little to Hestiia. She concentrated on deciphering the arcane symbols beside the imagery rather than puzzling out the equally arcane conversation.

"Whatever," Lord Loki said, taking his throne. "What have you found, Kim?"

"The best soil, geology, and flood control are west of the mountains. We should also have better access to mineral deposits and rudimentary mines on that side. But it's a long way away from here. We don't have enough room or thrust or fuel to transport all our people there in one trip or even three. And I don't think we could convince any of them to walk there, given Hestiia's folklore about the inhabitants." Lord Kim continued to tap an interesting tattoo against the tiny altar where the visions continued to play.

"What's the second-best alternative?" Loki leaned over to look at the images as well.

Konner sat between them. He played a different tattoo, and suddenly the dragon memories repeated themselves at all three altars before the three thrones.

Hestiia had to look away or fall to the floor with dizziness. Her head might have accepted her husbands' magic as a fact, but her eyes still failed to comprehend it all.

"Next best place is right here on the river delta," Lord Kim said almost smugly.

"Aren't we too close to the river?" Konner asked. "Tidal influences. Storms, flood. Are you sure?"

"Geologically, over half of the bigger islands are as stable as the mainland. The small aits are temporary and disappear at will. Most of the permanent islands are high enough to be above the ten-year flood plain. The river silt is rich in nutrients from the hinterland. Lots of fresh water and game to supplement farming—but not for long. We'll need livestock soon."

"But we are too close to my father's village!" Hestiia protested. "This is their prime hunting ground. He will see this as a challenge to his authority and his manhood. He will attack, and soon, with every warrior, priest, and magician he can find."

"We have men and weapons." Loki shrugged as if the threat were truly unimportant.

"Your weapons are depleted. You have slaves who are forbidden to fight. My brother Yaakke and three half-grown boys who are too weak to train to become warriors are your only defense. We cannot settle here."

"If Yaaccob does not like our presence on these islands, then we launch a preemptive strike." Loki shrugged again. "Hit them hard when they least expect it. They'll leave us in peace once we hurt them badly." Couldn't his brothers see the simple solution?

"We are supposed to be teaching these people the value of civilization and peace, not hitting them over the head and enslaving them all over again." Kim stood up, clenching his fists.

"Surely there are other spots to start a village on this planet." Konner, always the peacemaker, stepped between them. "Now then, let's look at the surveys again. We don't need the perfect spot. Just a good one." Konner sat at his console and began scrolling through the surveys.

Loki continued to keep his attention focused on his youngest brother. Kim seemed about ready to explode. Maybe Loki and Konner should let the boy bed Hestiia and work off some of the frustration boiling within him.

"I can see that the three of you vie for dominance," Hestiia said. She dropped her face, allowing her mass of dark curls to hide her blushes. "I shall wait in the bed for the one who wins first rights." She turned and made a hasty exit.

A wave of guilt washed away Loki's irritation. He reached to detain the woman. "Hestiia, it's not like that." But it was. Up until that moment he had planned to sneak into her bed as soon as his brothers fell asleep.

She stared up at him. Her face revealed her relief as well as her disbelief.

About time you acted with dignity, like the god you want to be, Mum's voice snorted derisively directly into his mind. Her words were so clear she might have been standing right next to him, whispering into his ear.

He suppressed the urge to look around for evidence of the flame-haired woman who stood only as tall as the middle of his chest but sent chills of terror up his spine.

When his mother was angry, her bright hair crackled around her head like flames shooting from the core of a fire. The reminder didn't really take away the imagery of his mother, anger written in her posture, her voice, and her eyes. "Flames on this world are green. All the copper permeating the soil, drawn up into the wood by groundwater, burns green," he whispered to himself. "Flames here are as green as my sister's eyes."

"You spoke, my husband?" Hestiia asked politely.

"Someone explain it all to her," Loki shouted over his shoulder as he exited the cockpit and then the shuttle. He needed to put as much distance as possible between himself and his scruples. At this rate they'd never make a profit off this planet and he'd never marry Cyndi. The woman he loved.

Right?

His head echoed emptily.

Right! he insisted into the silence. He loved Cyndi with every fiber of his being. He'd agreed to this final run simply so he could finally have the means to be with Cyndi legally. He wouldn't subject her to a life on the run.

He loved her.

He nearly put his fist through the bulkhead trying to get the hatch open.

CHAPTER 18

✦━━━・━━━✦━━━・━━━✦

KIM SWALLOWED HARD and opened his mouth to explain. St. Bridget! How did he begin to tell this sweet young woman that she would sleep alone tonight and every night hence?

"Um . . . Hestiia, in our culture, our marriage to you is not valid."

She cocked her head to one side and narrowed her eyes. Confusion clouded her eyes.

"Among our people, there is more to a marriage ceremony than asking a woman to cover her naked body," Konner added dispassionately. He kept his eyes on the scrolling images before him.

"Then what must we do?" Hestiia asked innocently.

Kim immediately felt his face heat up.

He slowed his speech and enunciated every word carefully, so she would understand. "Uh . . . there is a ceremony performed before a priest, or a judge. The consent of both families, and um . . . only one bride and one groom. Multiple partners in a marriage is illegal." Kim tried to follow his brother's example and avoid looking at her.

But she was so sweet. So innocent.

His eyes kept straying back to her face.

"I am disgraced." Hestiia hung her head. Her shoulders slumped and . . . and a tear streaked down her cheek.

"No. No, never that, Hestiia." Kim immediately gathered her into his arms. "We will not put you aside. You will stay with us. But until some things are settled, none of us will . . . uh . . . consummate the marriage."

"But if I do not quicken with child, I will be equally disgraced. Now that we are free of Hanassa and his demand for sacrifices, we women should begin bearing children again. In plenty." She continued to sob, burying her face in her hands. At the same time she seemed to snuggle closer yet to Kim.

"Bear children again?" Konner asked, finally looking up from the surveys.

Hestiia's face colored deeply. "We . . . ah . . . took measures to keep from quickening ever since Hanassa became our High Priest. What is the sense in bringing new life to the village if Simurgh only snatches it away again at the slightest whim?"

Kim ground his teeth. Another reason for banishing the lingering guilt that he and his brothers had taken a life, even in self-defense.

"Surely we have some time before . . . before the women would notice you do not . . . quicken?"

"The space of three, perhaps four moons," she gulped.

"Enough time to get some fields cleared and crops planted," Konner said decisively and stood. "I need to be gone by then, with or without my brothers."

"Konner . . ." Kim stared at his brother in warning. "We have responsibilities."

"Yes. And not all of them are on this planet. Remember Mum and Katie as well as my own appointment."

Silence stretched between them. Konner obviously did not want to reveal his reasons. Kim didn't know how to counter him.

"I found us a village site," Konner finally said. "Upriver about three miles. Nice bend in the river, deep water for fishing. Grassy plains where big game graze and an acceptable flood plain that replenishes the soil every year. I'm a little bothered by the wetlands, but if we have to, we can drain them into the river, skirting our fields."

Kim looked over his shoulder to the survey screen. The site Konner had selected was the same one he had rejected when Hestiia had recommended it not too long ago.

Hanassa sat with his back braced against a silver bloodwood tree. The rough ridges in the pale bark fit his unique spinal structure as if made to match. The mildly poisonous bark did not bother him. His body absorbed the toxins and put them to use keeping infection at bay. If he kept very straight and very still, nothing hurt. For a time. He focused all his energy into maintaining every muscle in his body until he almost heard the sap rising in his tree, almost felt the worms digging their endless tunnels through the dirt beneath his rump.

The rain dripped from the heart-shaped red leaves above him. He felt the tiny vibrations as each drop hit the ground. He was as much the rain as he was the tree and the land.

Eventually, his back became so accustomed to the tree he felt merged with the silver bark and inner layers of bloodwood. His tree. It matched his silver hair and pale skin on the outside and the blood that coursed through his veins on the inside. No mere human could tolerate this prolonged contact with the tree bark.

If only he could absorb Hestiia as easily as he did this tree. Take her under his control, make use of her strength. She was like this tree, beautiful to look at, with an acid tongue. He could use her to control more men, add to his power.

Later. He would dream of Hestiia standing just behind his shoulder later.

Now he was ready to greet the dawn, and his visitor.

A green bird chirped a question at the growing light.

Hanassa answered it with a low, plaintive whistle, a seduction.

The little creature fluttered down from its perch deep among the red heart-shaped leaves. It flapped around Hanassa a moment, then settled uncertainly on his wrist. It chirped again.

He whistled back a more positive note. Would that Hestiia responded to his seduction as easily as this bird.

The light grew.

The bird fluttered its wings and rustled its breast feathers in satisfaction. Every dawn for the past six mornings he and the bird had carried on the same conversation. But this was the first time the bird had actually lit within reach of Hanassa's strong left hand.

Just as the sun shot a first red arrow of brightness above the horizon, Hanassa grasped and broke the bird's neck in a movement so swift, his weak human eyes could not follow.

But his predator instincts knew the precise moment of death and gloried in it. A measure of his pain and perpetual fatigue eased.

A tiny fraction of the strength he needed to regain control of his people filled him. And when he mastered the Coros once more, Hestiia must come to him, attracted to his power as a moth to a flame.

"Thank you for becoming my breakfast," he said to the inert bird's carcass.

A tiny sound, one twig brushing against another, disturbed his reverie.

Hanassa rested his head against the rough silver bark once more. He allowed the tree's ponderous progress through life to absorb his being once more. The dead green bird blended with the thick grass.

Hanassa watched Taneeo plod into the clearing, as he had every morning since the Stargods had destroyed the altar. Patiently, the apprentice priest circled the bare ground where the altar had stood. He knelt and plucked a weed that dared intrude upon the sacred space. Then he resumed his circle.

Hanassa did not know why the boy returned here so faithfully each day. But the time had come to make his presence known. He was strong enough to maintain the myth of his immortality. No sense letting Taneeo develop a sense of superiority or that Hanassa should be beholden to him for anything. If Taneeo had discovered him earlier, then the apprentice would have been obligated to nurse him back to health. Hanassa would have owed his life to the boy.

But the boy owed his life to Hanassa. Hanassa had sired him. He could use that obligation if necessary. So far, obedience to Simurgh seemed enough motivation to keep the boy disciplined.

"Apprentice," he hissed quietly.

Taneeo jerked his head up. He stood hunted-still. Only his eyes moved as they searched the clearing. His gaze passed Hanassa, then returned with a jerk.

"Master?" He dropped to his knees, hands held before him in an attitude of prayer, or a plea for forgiveness. "You live!"

"'Twill take more than the false gods from the stars to kill me," Hanassa said quietly. "But you must tell no one yet that I live. I plan my return for the most advantageous moment. A moment when no one will be able to deny the superiority of Simurgh and his High Priest." He paused to let those words sink in. And for breath.

"Do I have your word of honor?"

Not that the boy had much honor yet. He had yet to kill a man in battle. Yet to bed a woman. Hanassa had sired Taneeo when he was two full years younger than Taneeo was now. He had sired many brats, but no others with his own pale coloring. The children Hestiia must bear him would be pale. He knew it in his heart.

"What must I do, Master?" Taneeo kept his eyes downcast.

Hanassa stared at the boy, willing him to look up. He never trusted his apprentice unless he could look directly into his eyes and know that he obeyed without reservation. When Taneeo would not meet his gaze, he suspected the boy planned devious plots to depose the High Priest. Possibly to defect to the Stargods.

That was what Hanassa would do.

"You must build a fire for me. Then bring me food."

"I found your staff and headdress."

"I know. Why did you not assume possession of them and make yourself the High Priest?" This son of his must have some intelligence and ambition. Otherwise he was useless.

"Because I am not ready—or worthy—to lead our people." Taneeo blushed guiltily.

More likely, Yaaccob had put the boy in his place and taken over priestly as well as chieftain duties among the Coros. Taneeo was not yet strong enough to stand up to a seasoned warrior greedy for power.

"W . . . will y . . . you come back to us, Master?"

"Not for a time. The Stargods injured me. They cannot kill me, but they can do me harm. I must complete a quest to replenish myself. My destiny lies—lies to the south. I must go there to find it. Then I will return. Stronger, wiser, in closer communion with Simurgh."

To the south. Yes, to the south. Something there called to him. Had called to him for some time now. He just had not chosen to acknowledge it until now.

"The people question every decision Yaaccob makes. They question me, and they question Simurgh. They want to know about the Stargods. I have many questions about them myself. You must not stay away too long, Master, lest we stray from the path Simurgh has set for us."

The path that I have set for you. Hanassa grimaced. *Simurgh was nothing but another dragon who developed a taste for human flesh. So the people began sacrificing to him out of fear. Eventually they made him a god.*

Good that the people questioned Yaaccob. So much easier to manipulate the warrior if his people doubted him. But he did not like the news that the people already questioned Simurgh. The god was a powerful tool to control mere humans. Eventually, Hanassa would have enough power that he no longer needed the god, no longer needed the people for anything but their deaths.

"I must go away for a time. A spirit quest," Hanassa explained to Taneeo very carefully. "Simurgh will guide me in how to deal with these interlopers." While away, he would find a way to bring Hestiia back to him. She was the only one among all the Coros he would not kill. Her death would give him much power. Her life would give him more.

"I shall prepare for the journey, Master."

"No. I must go alone. When the time comes for you to assume your priestly duties, you must journey on your own quest alone."

"Then what must I do while you are gone?" At last Taneeo looked into Hanassa's eyes.

At last. Hanassa captured the youth's gaze with his own. He stared into the depths of his apprentice's soul, claimed it and compelled him to listen and obey.

"While I am gone, you must observe the Stargods. Watch everything they do, very carefully. You must know everything they do and everything they preach. Knowledge is power, my boy."

"I must watch," Taneeo recited in a monotone. His gaze remained fixed upon Hanassa.

"You must devise ways to separate Hestiia from their ranks. I will not have her tainted by strangers."

"How must I do that, Master?" Taneeo's voice and face remained devoid of expression.

"You will know what to do when the opportunity presents itself."

"I will know."

"You must watch and listen closely. But do not believe them. *Never believe them*. They are tricksters. They twist the truth to their advantage. But you and I know that only Simurgh rules the skies of this land. You and I have survived the trial by smoke of the Tambootie tree. We have seen the truth."

"We have seen the truth."

"Simurgh has ordained that warriors rule, the conquered must be slaves, slaves must be sacrificed to Simurgh. If we do not have slaves, then we must sacrifice our wives and children. Only then will Simurgh chase away the summer storms so that our crops will grow. Only then will Simurgh banish the plagues that come with the rain. Only when we sacrifice to him will Simurgh give us victory over our enemies."

"Victory over our enemies."

"And then I shall become a god." *And Hestiia my only worshiper, for all the others will die by my hand.*

CHAPTER 19

$\blacklozenge \!\!-\!\!\cdot\!\!-\!\!\blacklozenge\!\!-\!\!\cdot\!\!-\!\!\blacklozenge$

"**O**UR FIRST PRIORITY is housing," Konner said as he inspected the bronze collar on Raaskan, the burliest and healthiest of the former slaves. "I'm tired of being wet all the time."

Raaskan surveyed the new village site rather than look at the laser cutter Konner held. "Eighteen of us," Raaskan said. "We should, with your permission and approval, my Lord Konner, start with two dwellings, one for the women, here, and one for the men over there." He pointed to opposite sides of the level area adjacent to the river.

"Ten-year flood plain?" Kim asked. "We want the fields close to the river and the permanent houses on higher ground."

"One flood in ten years outweighs the hard work of hauling water?" Poolie, Raaskan's mate asked. "Fine for you men, but what about the women who have to carry that water!" She seemed to have found a voice along with her freedom, offering advice and criticism at every turn.

"Build the houses close to the river, for St. Bridget's sake!" Loki yelled. "Stop arguing and just do it."

Kim closed his mouth and concentrated his gaze on Hestiia as she paced out the distance between the proposed houses. A distance of at least twenty-five meters. Far enough apart to give both genders a sense of privacy, but close enough to mingle in the common ground at the center.

"What we need first is food!" Loki insisted. "After that walk in the rain, I'm starving."

"The rain is precisely the reason we need shelter first. We have to protect our readers, stunners, and laser cutters from the elements," Kim championed Konner's stand.

Leave it to Kim to think of his readers before his own sopping body.

"We've parked the shuttle two kilometers from here in deep camouflage. Do you want to trek that far every time you want a reference or a piece of equipment?" Kim continued his retort to Loki.

Konner had worked hard to make the camouflage effective with the noise of the compressors distilling nitrogen day and night alerting any passersby to the presence of something alien.

He concentrated on the task in his hands. He needed to get the collars off. The former slaves wanted their dignity restored. The collars represented all that had been stolen from them by Hanassa and the raiders. Konner wanted the bronze. Easier to melt this down and reforge it as simple tools than to start from scratch building a forge, reducing trees to charcoal, and mining iron. That must all come later. But not too much later. He would not take a chance on missing the court date. He had one chance to gain custody of his son, on the boy's fourteenth birthday. Konner refused to leave the boy with his cold, selfish, power-hungry, unscrupulous, cruel mother any longer than necessary.

"Let me know if this gets too hot," he said quietly to Raaskan.

The big man nodded. "You have restored to me my honor as a warrior. I will not flinch."

"Go ahead and flinch. That will tell me if I'm close to damaging you." Konner gritted his teeth and set the cutter at the narrowest beam. He held it a scant five centimeters from the thick metal and began cutting.

"Perhaps if you cut through in layers, avoiding the skin until there is only a thin bit of metal left," Kim mused.

Konner shut out the noise of the villagers as they bustled about, marking the various sites in their new home. Closer and closer he brought the cutter. The bronze glowed red. Heat flushed Raaskan's neck, shoulder, and jaw. His rigid posture told Konner of his fear as well as his courage. He did not flinch.

"Stop hesitating," Loki suggested. "Just cut the damn thing. Quick and sure like you would cut away laser cannon damage aboard the *Sirius*."

"Not that easy." Konner drew the cutter up and down with precise strokes, keeping the beam of light on the metal.

Quicker than he thought possible, the bronze parted. Raaskan reached up and yanked the collar apart wide enough to remove it. Then he flung it toward the central fire pit.

Konner breathed a sigh of relief when it did not roll into the fire. He could retrieve it later.

"Thank you, Lord Konner." Raaskan breathed deeply. "I have not felt so well in over a year." He rubbed the ring of raw skin around his neck.

"Please, Lord. Remove mine next." Poolie stepped into her husband's place beside Konner. "I would be as free as my mate."

"I'll do everyone, Poolie. Now that I know how, I don't fear I'll hurt you. Much."

"Can we do something to keep these frogs from getting into everything, Kim?" Loki asked sheepishly. He kicked at the grassy growth. Two frogs leaped away from him into a puddle, then down the embankment to the muddy river.

"We build up a stone foundation, then . . . then . . ." Konner hesitated. What came next? They did not have any plasti-foam, no molds, none of the standard construction materials Konner was familiar with.

"Uh . . . why don't we ask them?" Kim pointed to the scantily clad men collecting rocks and stacking them neatly together to form the beginnings of a low wall precisely where Konner had indicated the men's quarters should be. Inside the dimensions of the structure, the women began beating down the grasses by the simple expedient of stomping on them.

Loki shrugged and leaned over to pick up a rock. He added it to the growing foundation. The former slave beside him, quickly repositioned it so that it fit snugly.

"How high do we build the foundation, Raaskan?" Konner asked. The man had wasted no time in getting to work.

"This high." Raaskan indicated a spot near his knee. Poolie scampered to join him the moment she was free of her collar. Konner smiled at the way their hands often met and the fond gazes they exchanged. Tonight they would be husband and wife again. Their lives as slaves had probably kept them apart. Possibly Poolie had been used by her owners.

Konner shuddered at the abuse the locals heaped upon each other. He couldn't wait to get back to civilization.

But were Melinda, his ex-wife, and other wealthy and noble citizens of the GTE any less cruel?

Loki moved off, stooping to pick up rocks as he went.

"When the foundation is high enough, what do you suggest we build the walls with? Uh . . . which trees make the best walls." Konner made a wild guess that the abundance of trees nearby might provide a solution. Wasting precious wood on walls when it could be sold for a fortune to make small decorative objects back home grated on his sensibilities.

"Not the everblues. The wood is too soft. The silver bloodwood is best but too rare now. We reserve it for temples." Raaskan continued fitting rocks together, never pausing while he talked. "The bark of the silver bloodwood is toxic and must be disposed of carefully, or it will damage all that it touches."

"A hardwood—from deciduous trees," Kim interjected. "I've identified oak and alder from old Earth references and terraforming manuals. We can cut them with the laser cutters. But we'll have to recharge them about every third tree."

"Then how do we plane them, make boards, and nails to hold them together?" Konner's mind designed and rejected four plans for planing in the space of three heartbeats. The most efficient would be a pit with the log slung across the top. Men below with tools . . . what kind of tools? Made from iron . . . which they did not have and had no way of forging. Would bronze take a keen enough edge to use as saws and planes?

"Planes? Nails? Why do you not just stack the logs?" Raaskan asked. He picked up a handful of twigs and thick grass stalks, laid two parallel, then stacked two more across on the opposite parallel. The next two he placed atop the first two.

"And we fill the chinks with mud!" Konner shouted triumphantly.

"Turf works just as well, and we have to cut it out of the land we will plow," Raaskan corrected him.

"If we carve the ends out a little, we can get them to fit more snuggly, minimize the need for caulking." Konner slapped him on the back. Surely he could fashion some kind of ax out of the collars.

"A log cabin," Kim said, holding up his reader. "Standard construction for European pioneers on the North American continent."

"Roofing material?" Konner asked.

Raaskan pointed to the plains behind them. He bit his lip to hide a smile.

"Hey, we are only human. We can make mistakes." Loki dumped his armload of rocks beside Raaskan.

The former slave nodded his gratitude and continued working. "A god can still be a man. Just better, bigger, more powerful," he said.

"This is way beyond me," Konner replied slowly. "I'm not a philosopher. I'm an engineer." He looked blankly at Kim, the only one of them who might understand the implications.

"Maybe we are gods. Maybe that's what our gods were originally. Men from other places, with other skills, and different philosophies. Philosophies that made more sense than the one before." Kim looked as bewildered as Konner felt. Scared, too.

Mum wouldn't like this conversation. Her faith was firm and tolerated no defiance or probing questions from her sons. She accepted their observance of the forms of her religion, not realizing that when she was absent they never attended services or prayed regularly. Konner wondered if either of his brothers truly believed in Mum's god. He didn't. He believed in his crystals and the science that moved his ship between the stars.

"Who cares what makes a god." Loki shrugged again. "We've got houses to build, and dinner to catch. You guys can sit there staring into space. I'm going fishing."

"I'm going with the women to start collecting edible plants and entering them into the database. And to think about gods and men while I'm at it." Kim punched keys on his reader.

"Then I'd best do what I do best. Build something." Konner moved off toward the line of trees, fitting a new charge clip into his laser cutter and searching his own reader for reference to hardwood trees. Omniscium for the crystal baths and building his forge would have to wait a day or two.

He pounded his fist into the palm of his opposite hand. Two days. He'd wait two days to start the crystal baths. No more. He would not miss his court date with Martin. His son.

"Raaskan, how do I find a blacksmith and a forge?" Konner asked three days later. He stood back to admire their handiwork. Nearly two completed dwellings in only three days of very hard work.

Three days during which his crystals had not had a chance to regrow. If he waited much longer, they might not recover. A blacksmith would know where to find iron ore, and crystal-bearing rock for the omniscium.

"Not many blacksmiths left," Raaskan replied. He stood upon a ladder made of sticks and poles lashed together with vines. The entire contraption looked too rickety to support the man's weight. From atop his perch, the ex-slave and ex-warrior nestled a bundle of grass into position on the roof of the men's cabin. Across the way, his wife Poolie directed a similar operation on the women's cabin. Tomorrow the happy couple would begin building their own smaller cabin.

"What happened to the smiths? How does Yaaccob keep his weapons sharp and strong without a blacksmith?" Konner thought he knew, but he needed the words said.

"Hanassa said the blacksmiths must fight in battle like any other man with strength enough to wield a weapon." Raaskan kept his gaze firmly on his task. "I think the smiths frightened Hanassa. People revered them as magicians because of the wonders they worked with metal."

"And the smiths all died in battle," Konner finished the thought. "Hanassa did not have rivals for his powers."

"Not all of them died."

"A few still live. Where?"

"Two days' march from here. In my . . . in the village where Poolie and I were captured."

"I bet you hid him well just before the attack."

Raaskan replied with a wide grin.

"Delegate this roofing to someone else," Konner ordered. "You and I are going to go find a blacksmith. Then we'll build a forge right here." Strange how "right here" had come to feel like home in only a few short days. He did not want to feel at home. He needed to finish his repairs and be gone.

He'd have to drag Loki away, though. Konner's older brother had become obsessed with the wealth this planet represented. All he talked about was money and buying back his citizenship, no matter how long it took.

Konner would leave him behind before he'd miss his court date with Martin and Melinda.

Kim would come along meekly. He believed in his responsibility to Mum and Mum's plans.

"We can use that boulder over there as an anvil," Raaskan pointed to the west of the village, a short distance from the designated crop area. Kim and his team were cutting the grass down to stubble. The stalks became the thatch for the roofs—not as good as a certain kind of reed growing upriver about ten kilometers, the villagers informed them. Kim painstakingly separated the seeds from the stalks each night and sorted them by size and shape. Only the biggest that were free of rot would be used to plant the fields. Smaller seeds, and ones Kim could not identify became flour or cereal for the village.

"We'll need a plow within a day or two," Konner mused. "Do you think your blacksmith might be able to fashion one by then?"

"Why not use the shoulder blade of a cow or another large grass eater? Sharpen it with grinding stones. It won't bend as much as bronze. But it does need to be sharpened quite often. Since Hanassa decreed that all bronze must be made into weapons, we have used only bones for tools."

"And cows have two shoulder blades!" Konner slapped his companion on the back. Progress. Any step forward in this enterprise put hm closer to meeting his son in court. "We can scout for a cow skeleton on the way. Good thing we cut so much turf to chink the cabins. I don't think bones would plow through it very well."

"We have learned to do quite well without metal, Lord Konner. Why are you so insistent that we build a forge and find a blacksmith?"

"Because I have a few miracles in mind." If he didn't have to make metal tools, he'd have exclusive use of the forge for repairs.

"A forge requires much charcoal. We will have to cut many trees."

"I've located a seam of coal in the southern hills. There is also a stretch of beach north of the river mouth where sea coal washes up. Coal burns much hotter and longer than charcoal." At least that was what the texts on metalworking told him.

"Have you ever tried to draw fire out of coal?"

"Uh . . . no." Konner didn't like Raaskan's tone. He sensed a big disappointment looming.

"Perhaps your magic tools can coax the coal to flames," Raaskan said quietly.

"At least coal will burn wet. Charcoal won't. Does it ever stop raining around here?"

"Eventually. I have not seen the rains last this long since I reached manhood."

"I'll be glad to be rid of these frogs." Konner let out a string of curses aimed at the critter he nearly stepped on. "They get into everything. Found one in my blankets this morning. We'll take the *Rover* to your village."

Raaskan gulped and crossed his wrists, flapping his hands.

"It won't hurt you," Konner stopped and stared at the man in amazement. "Think of this as a tale to tell your children and grandchildren."

Raaskan looked away. Intense grief crossed his face.

Konner could only guess at the fate met by any children he and Poolie might have had. They were of an age to have wed about five years ago. A happy couple in this culture would want children right away. No mention had been made of retrieving children from any village. They could have been killed in battle, enslaved and sent to other villages, or . . . or . . . He would not dwell on Hanassa's thirst for blood. Not children. St. Bridget! Not the children.

What had Hestiia said that first day? Now that Hanassa no longer commanded sacrifices, the women would want to have children again. Right away.

Jaysus, Mary, and Joseph! No wonder he'd seen precious few children and no babes at the village.

Anger boiled deep within him. "If I had not already killed Hanassa, I would kill him again."

He beat one hand into the other, again, and yet again. Sparks flew from his palms into the sopping grass.

"You made fire, Lord Konner. Fire without flint and firerock," Raaskan said. Amazement replaced his old grief. "You will be able to light the coal fire without aid."

"Maybe. If I can figure out how I just did that." Konner stared at the tiny green glow on the tip of his finger. It did not burn him. What would happen if he flung it into dry tinder?

He looked around, burning with possibilities, but not from the flamelet that rose higher with his excitement.

CHAPTER 20

◆ —— · —— ◆ —— · —— ◆

HANASSA CROUCHED BEHIND a clump of sharp saber ferns. Less than ten paces away, three Rover men rubbed sweat and travel dust off the hides of their ponies with tufts of dry grass. Bold bastards to camp so close to the Coron processional way. He admired the cunning fire their women built. Half buried and shielded with a copper tent, the flames remained hidden from view.

The smell of their cooking dinner made Hanassa's mouth water and his stomach growl. The sound alerted the Rovers to his presence. He froze in place, keeping well behind the thick ferns. Not a breath stirred in his lungs for many long moments. At last the Rovers turned back to grooming their sturdy steeds.

Hanassa smiled to himself. Little did the men know that they carried out their chores for his benefit, not their own. He needed a mount to complete his quest. If he had to walk any farther on his path, the wound in his back would rupture again and he might die. The Stargods did not deserve the satisfaction of having killed him.

Those ponies are groomed enough, he thought. If only he could catch the eye of one or all of these three men in their brightly colored shirts, then he could manipulate their thoughts and deeds.

The men kept their attention firmly on their tasks.

Hanassa's legs cramped. He almost groaned out loud. Finger-length by finger-length he eased his legs backward until he lay prone. Gratefully he stretched his back and neck. He was so tired. So hungry and thirsty.

He dozed. And awoke with a jerk. How much time had passed?

Anxiously he scanned the stars and cursed the trees that stood between him and the open sky. The night had grown darker. The Rover fire burned brighter. The three men and their women, plus two old crones and six children laughed and talked quietly around the fire. Their heathenish language grated harshly on Hanassa's ears.

Did not these people ever sleep? And of course they had eaten every scrap of their inadequate dinner. They did not leave so much as a mouthful for Hanassa.

By Simurgh and the dragon nimbus, he needed that food. How could he heal without proper food and drink?

Anger burned within him, warming his back as no fire could. These Rovers would pay and pay dearly for cheating him of his due.

At last the Rovers exchanged friendly, familial kisses and retired to their bedrolls. Within moments, Hanassa heard light snores and steady breathing.

He eased himself away from the sharp fronds of the ferns. His back muscles screamed in protest at the movement. He stopped moving in an awkward crouch.

A string of curses nearly escaped his mouth. Instead, he clenched his teeth and massaged the cramps out of his calves and thighs. Many more long moments passed before he could stand.

Then he had to step carefully. He could not see in the dark and had to feel the ground before him with his toes before taking a step. Twice he stubbed his toe and choked back his cries of startlement. Three times he lost his sense of direction and bumped into trees.

Finally, he found the ponies by scent and by stumbling into one. The beast snorted and stamped. Hanassa stilled his body and his mind. Someone in the camp stirred and settled.

Breathing easier, Hanassa fumbled for the pony's bridle rope. He grabbed a fistful of mane, then followed the thick hair to its source and discovered a smelly rump. In disgust he flicked the tail aside. Feeling his way back along the spine, he eventually found the true mane and the head harness. And a hand.

Hanassa squealed. The Rover guarding the steeds grunted. The pony stomped.

With his heart in his mouth, Hanassa leaped astride the steed. He kicked it sharply with his heels. The beast reared and shied. The Rover guard stumbled backward, shouting curses and alarm in his weird language.

Other men roused.

Hanassa knew they reached for weapons and that they prepared to pursue him. He clung to the pony with every bit of his waning strength as it galloped along the road south. South to his destiny. In the South he would heal quickly and then return to destroy his enemies.

· —◆— ·

Green flames danced within the central fire pit. Shadows leaped and played with Kim's senses. For a moment, he almost believed that a dragon stared at him through the flames and the shadows. Raaskan roared at the top of his lungs and flapped his arms in a parody of flight. The fire highlighted his masked face, shredding holes in reality.

In reality the thick husk of a papacan fruit shaped the mask's muzzle. Flusterhen tail feathers spiked upward in imitation of horns—or antennae. Stain from the papacan fruit twisted around a meter-long horn, broken from a wild cow, mimicking the spiral twist that adorned a dragon's forehead.

"And then, the benevolent white-and-silver dragon deposited Lord Konner and my humble person gently onto the abandoned fields of Faarsee. The remaining villagers, old men and women, beardless boys and girls not yet come to womanhood, cowered in fright. They bowed in awe to see me returned from the enslavement of Simurgh's evil minion Hanassa. But no, I could not allow them to give me the honor. I bowed to Lord Konner, the Stargod, and led him to the fire pit so that the people could acknowledge him as Stargod and worship him.

Kim noted that his older brother blushed as the story of his afternoon adventures unfolded.

"Are you sure it was a good idea to use the shuttle?" Kim leaned over to whisper into Konner's ear.

"We got the blacksmith, his anvil, and his tools here without a hassle. And several baskets of coal from the beach. I'm glad I didn't have to tote that anvil here on my back," Konner replied with a grin. "Found a lode of iron ore in the hills around Faarsee while I was there. We're going back tomorrow to mine it. We'll have to smelt it first in the old forge until we get the new one built."

"That still doesn't get me a plow," Kim grumbled.

"Wait, he's coming to that part." Konner nodded his head toward Raaskan and his rapt audience.

Raaskan continued his story—much embellished, Kim was sure—of how the villagers insisted upon slaughtering a precious bull to feast the new god who had rescued their former chieftain and promised to pass on many magical secrets to the blacksmith. Instead of the bull, Lord Konner in his wisdom chose an aging cow, nearly past the age when she could safely give birth and nurse a calf. As much as he appreciated the honor of a sacrificial bull, the cow would feed them all well and preserve the bull for breeding later.

"What's all this bloody business of the cow about?" Loki grumbled. "I'd have appreciated a little of the meat if you'd deigned to bring some home, Lord Konner." He bowed sarcastically to his younger brother.

"Those villagers were on the brink of starvation. Hanassa had bled them dry with tribute. They needed the meat more than we do. We've been dining high on fish and venison," Konner explained. "Besides, I needed the bones."

"Bones?" Kim asked. He couldn't imagine what Konner wanted with bones when he had the beginnings of a forge to play with.

Then Raaskan produced the shoulder blade lashed to a forked handle.

"A plow!" Kim stood up in his excitement. "Will it work? Will it last?"

"Long enough, little brother," Konner chortled. "Long enough to plow your field tomorrow. By the time we harvest, I'll make you a real plow and scythes and whatever else you need to produce food surpluses."

"A plow. A real plow. We're on the way to turning this planet into our own storehouse of fresh food. The most valuable commodity in known space." Kim basked a moment in his daydreams. One of the brothers needed to stay here, supervise the continued production of food, and enforce the tentative peace among the villages. Why not him. Why shouldn't he marry Hestiia and beget new generations to continue the work of the "Stargods."

"Known space." His last words echoed in his mind. "What happens when all these people start demanding a ride in the 'white and silver dragon'? Your escapade just entered into local folklore. Racial memory of mechanical flight will push someone, someday into re-creating it. We won't be able to keep them out of industralization and pollution and demands to rejoin the GTE. Our storehouse will vanish." And he'd lose his snug cottage and Hestiia and the babies dangling on her knee.

That thought jolted him. What about Mum? Well, he'd just have to come back here after he'd helped Mum find Katie. After all, Mum had promised him a farm. She hadn't said he could choose his own location. That didn't mean he couldn't choose here.

He just had to replace Raaskan's story with something more exciting, more enticing, more *interesting* in order to keep this place free of GTE influence. But what? What miracles could he produce?

· —◆— ·

"Well, Kim," Loki addressed his youngest brother, "you've managed to get the fields scythed, bundled the grasses for thatch, and winnowed out the seeds for replanting, even managed to save some as grain for eating until we can harvest. Now we have to plow the damned field. Any ideas?" He felt his eyebrows rise in sarcasm.

New shelters rose up every few days—as often as Konner could recharge the laser cutters to fell the trees. More slaves joined them every day from the outlying villages. Words of gratitude to the Stargods for giving them the courage to change their lot in life spilled from them like a river pouring down a mountain crag. All of the Coros had heard the decree of the Stargods outlawing slavery. But none of their masters had offered them anything but more lashes and hard work. The slaves had to take the initiative and free themselves by escaping.

And with the increased numbers of inhabitants, came an increasing variety of skills. Weavers, potters, carpenters, livestock wranglers, all seemed to shed the warrior persona and subsistence living Hanassa had imposed upon them.

Lacking woolies—the local version of sheep, Kim had found a way to have the women gather the shed wool from a wild herd of very hairy and long-horned cattle—almost like some of Kim's pictures of Earth cattle, something between a longhorn and a Highland beastie. The women had spun the fibers with a drop spindle and erected a crude loom—long strands of fiber suspended from a rod braced on two standing poles. The warp threads were weighted with pebbles to give them tension. Loki hadn't watched long enough to understand the process, just to appreciate the results. All the women now had halter tops and they were working on tanning deer hides to make trousers for the men.

At least they were all clothed now and Loki no longer spent too many hours day and night lusting after every woman he saw with bare breasts. Two of the former slave women had accommodated his lusts, but they expected favors afterward: loyalty, commitment, and *monogamy.*

Women back home weren't nearly as demanding. But then, women back home exhibited a much higher degree of independence, supporting themselves with careers and living alone quite happily. These women depended upon their men for their very existence. He wasn't certain whether or not he liked that idea.

Cyndi was dependent upon her father for the wealth that provided her a luxurious lifestyle. True, she worked for her allowance, playing hostess when her mother was too drunk to stand up straight, placating rebellious citizens before her father the governor granted them interviews, ferreting out information from rich merchants with black-market contacts. She might choose to marry her father's candidate instead of waiting for Loki. Waiting for an uncertain future with an outlaw.

"We can always harness the plow to a brace of men." Kim stared at the mowed field. Large patches of missing turf made a chessboard of the acreage. He bit his lip.

"Inefficient," Konner added. "Lacking mechanized tractors, we need draft animals."

"The Coros have the finest steeds in all the world. We need only liberate a few," Yaakke, Hestiia's brother, offered with an excited grin. He alone of all those who had followed the three brothers had the strength and stamina of a warrior—Fullmaan, their new blacksmith, was strong, but white streaked his temples and wrinkles lined his face. All of the former slaves had been malnourished to the point of ill health. Raaskan and two others were recovering. But none of them would be able to haul a plow ten feet, let alone around several acres. The patches of intact turf would prove difficult to break with only a bone plow.

"A steed raid! Sounds like fun," Loki answered with a bigger smile. He needed some excitement to offset the incredibly boring tasks of farming. He'd never dreamed making money could be so . . . so *tedious*. His muscles and his brain twitched from lack of use.

"We are not going to steal!" Kim nearly shouted. He looked as if he were ready to tear his hair out by the roots. They'd had this conversation before.

"Liberating steeds from one's neighbors is a time-honored passage into manhood," Yaakke reiterated.

"By St. Marlboro of the Western Range, I like you!" Loki slapped the younger man heartily on the back. He had visions of riding horses across the wide plains of his own personal planet. Well, on this planet they weren't exactly horses, having shorter legs, longer backs, and thicker feet than any of the pleasure mounts he'd ridden on bush planets.

"What about those wild herds of hairy red cows?" Konner asked. "They look fairly placid. We could round up six or eight and have plenty to haul plows or even bring timber in from the woods. We've nearly exhausted the suitable trees nearby, and I'm going to need charcoal to temper the pig iron I bring down from Faarsee. Later we can use the cows in the mines to bring out slag as well as transport ore to refineries." His eyes took on the gleam of fascination, almost as satisfied as he was each time he redesigned the *Sirius*. "I need to get the forge going to repair the thrusters. I need to find some omniscium and get the crystal baths started."

Loki could almost hear the gears clicking in his brother's brain.

Damn, he could hear scattered phrases about angles and torque ratios.

Loki shook his head clear of his imagined eavesdropping.

"Cattle are not honorable beasts!" Yaakke humpfed and folded his arms against his chest.

Loki noted that his friend didn't mention the nearly two-meter spread of the very sharp horns on those beasts.

"I agree, let's go for horses—er—steeds," Loki announced.

"No. I will not be a party to theft. In our own not too distant history, horse theft was a capital crime," Kim said in his sternest lecture mode.

"I have to agree with Kim." Konner pulled on his beard in serious thought.

They all had beards now. Electric razors only worked a few times before requiring a trek back to the shuttle for recharging. Loki and Konner had agreed the shuttle must remain camouflaged and powered down rather than leave it in the open by the village where nosy locals might see and understand too much.

"Theft will merely provoke retaliation," Konner continued his musing. "We will spend all of our time and resources in battle and nothing on production of food or finding raw materials to repair the *Sirius*."

"Hanassa made that mistake," Kim began his next lecture. "The Coros are on the verge of losing all their artisans because the High Priest decreed all men must become warriors or be sacrificed. They are forgetting how to make fine pottery and carpentry as well as smithcraft. The women don't have time to be artistic. They just cobble together what they need, when they need it. The warriors are reduced to making their own weapons—and getting inferior results. Perpetual war can only be supported by a balanced economy with full complements of support populations in ratios of one warrior for every six backups."

"Two men can steal a dozen steeds at the dark of the moon," Yaakke insisted.

"I know a few things about keeping steeds quiet," Loki added. He draped an arm around Yaakke's shoulders and led him away from his brothers. "A matter of letting them catch your scent and becoming familiar with it." And murmuring soothing phrases while holding an image of sweet hay and buckets of grain firmly in mind. Horses seemed more suggestive to mental images than people.

Although lately . . . He wondered if he should try to plant a notion of compliance into his brothers' heads. He'd really enjoy a nice little raid.

"Your plan might work if we were not three days shy of a full moon," Kim called after them.

That stopped Loki short. "Does that mean we have to wait another two weeks for the dark of the moon to go raid the Coros?" He didn't think his restlessness would abide two more weeks of *farming*.

"We can plan a roundup of wild cattle tonight. I've been experimenting with ropes," Konner said. He kept swallowing his grin as if he really enjoyed thwarting all of Loki's plans.

"We'll have enough moonlight, so we won't have to frighten them with torches," Kim added. "Maybe Hestiia could convince Gentian to help us herd the animals."

"They . . . they will stampede," Yaakke said quietly. "The flywacket frightens them beyond reason. They will trample us, trample our village. Their horns . . ." He broke off, swallowing his words and his fears.

"Sounds like fun." Loki dropped his arm from around Yaakke's shoulders. "Let's put together a plan." He rubbed his hands together in glee.

Maybe the brothers had planted compliance into *his* mind. He didn't care. As long as he had *something* to do tonight.

"We should try to separate the mothers with new calves," Kim said eagerly. "That way we can have some milk products and train the youngsters to domesticity. The full-grown males might be too aggressive to train to harness."

"Didn't I read something about castrating the young males to make them docile?" Konner asked.

"Castrate?" Loki couldn't swallow his disgust and his own sense of self-protection. Just the thought of doing *that* to a male, a male of any species, turned his stomach and made his mid-region ache.

"We can try separating out a few young males. Wouldn't want to take on a full-sized bull with those horns," Kim continued nonchalantly.

"Does castrate mean what I think it means?" Yaakke whispered to Loki. He stood with his knees clamped together, just like Loki.

"Yeah, it does." They both shuddered.

"Records indicate prairie oysters make a tasty treat," Kim continued.

Loki almost gagged until he realized his brother was jamming his sensors. Damn, he could hear Kim and Konner laugh deep inside themselves though no sound erupted from their mouths.

Double damn.

Or maybe he could use this newfound talent to his advantage. He needed to push Konner into making more farm tools to improve production and not his precious repairs. Repairs could wait. And he needed Kim to concentrate on organizing work crews rather than wasting time collecting data. This entire enterprise was useless unless they produced a full cargo of fresh food. Time to push them toward his agenda rather than their own.

"Let's have a barbeque out on the range when we finish the dirty work." Loki stared levelly at his brothers, daring them to continue their jamming. He forced an image of a small fire with a spit turning fist-sized lumps of . . . *gag* . . . meat.

Kim gulped with difficulty. Konner squinted his eyes in puzzlement.

CHAPTER 21

✦ ━ · ━ ✦ ━ · ━ ✦

SOFT MOONLIGHT turned the grazing lumps of wild red cattle into troll-like shadows. The great horns pierced the uncertain light in silent warning of the power in the neck and shoulders of the ruminating beasts.

Loki crept forward, keeping below the waving stalks of waist-high wild grasses. Carefully, he skirted a broad expanse of wetland, making certain he placed each step onto firm land and not into the muck. He carried a six-meter length of rope over one shoulder, the end knotted into what Kim assured him was an authentic lasso. Behind him, scattered in a broad semicircle, his brothers, Yaakke, Raaskan, and three supposed animal experts who looked too frail to stand on their own, moved inward with a slow and stealthy gait.

They'd all painted their faces and hands and chests in camouflage patterns with mud. No glimmer of moonlight against pale skin would betray them. Not that Loki believed for one moment that the cattle were smart enough to see a threat coming straight at them.

The huge bull lifted his muzzle, sniffing the air. Everyone froze. The red beast snorted and kept chewing. The females with their calves shifted and found new patches of grass to graze behind the bull. The animals knew something out of the ordinary was about to happen, but they were too stupid or too lazy to recognize the difference between unusual and dangerous.

Loki's heart beat double-time in his ears. He hadn't wanted this crazy hunt, but now that they were in the thick of it, he ached to get on with it. He could feel the adrenaline pump through him in wild pulses, making him feel alive.

The smell of damp, rotting vegetation filled his head. He closed his eyes and blocked it out, thinking instead of the sweet smell of new-mowed hay.

He'd helped with the harvest as a teenager. Mum had insisted. They were living on a bush world three light-jumps from Rigella III at the time. The organic odor had remained with him as something elemental and necessary to life.

"Easy, boy, easy," Loki subvocalized, keeping in his mind images of broad fields of sweet grass, lots of cows and calves, warm sunshine, utter peace. Or was that *udder* peace. He almost lost his concentration with a laugh. At the last moment he swallowed it and focused on the scent of hay.

For a moment his inner vision reflected that image back to him in fuzzy black and white, colored by scent rather than sight. Double images in two different realities sent his balance reeling. He placed both hands flat on the ground, oblivious to the nearby ooze of mud and the frog he disturbed. When he opened his eyes again, the dizziness had passed and his vision righted to a normal single set of images.

What was going on? Had he caught some strange fever?

The bull continued chewing. His eyes drifted closed. The cows wandered back toward the circling men. A dozen of them.

Four cows, two with calves, drifted farthest from the bull. That was all they needed. Surely the bull would not miss four of his ladies when he had so many. He pressed the images of the remaining six cows as the normal size of the bull's harem into the tiny mind.

The bull kept chewing.

Loki unslung his rope. The other men did too, all at the same time, as if they read each others' minds. Whatever. On this crazy planet perhaps he had issued orders with mind-to-mind contact.

The slight breeze shifted direction. The bull worked his nose and stirred uneasily. All the men froze. Once more, Loki projected the peaceful images. All of the cattle settled closer to the wetland, including the four he wanted.

Wily critters. They must know danger was less likely to approach from there.

Raaskan slowly rose from his crouch. He swung his rope easily as he approached a cow on the edge of the herd. A calf at her side munched hesitantly on a tuft of grass. Its rusty red coat shimmered with silver in the weird light. A few paces away, Kim slid into place upwind of another beast. This one looked smaller boned, younger perhaps, with no baby by her side and no droop to her udder.

Then the herdsmen pointed to specific cows. Konner and Yaakke each selected one of them to lasso. Kim selected his own cow to harness. As planned, the animal experts directed Raaskan to the dominant matriarch of the herd. He placed his noose gently around the horns and over the muzzle of his beast. Loki moved into place with his own rope ready to help the former slave. With the "big mama" firmly lassoed, the others would follow.

An image of a semi-sentient thorned vine creeping through the grass looking for victims flashed before Loki's inner vision. "Watch your step!" he whispered sharply.

Almost before the words left his lips, he heard a squish as someone slipped. Probably on one of the ever-present frogs. Then a dull thud sounded as the body hit the moist ground. A suppressed screech came out as a hiss.

A sharp bellow from the bull sounded like a gong in the still night air. He heaved himself onto his feet and nudged his ladies toward the safety of a nearby copse.

Loki flung his lasso toward Raaskan's cow and missed. The former slave leaped astride her back, clinging to her shaggy coat.

Yaakke and Konner pulled tight on their ropes and dug in their heels. The cows sped away, dragging their reluctant passengers. Kim fell face first into the mud. The lunging cow yanked the rope from his hands.

Raaskan galloped past in the moonlight, laughing insanely.

Loki's vision split again. He felt the rage of the bull, saw it charging him from the bull's perspective.

He jumped out of the way, uncaring of direction. He had to avoid the bull's horns and his massive feet. His shoulder hit something soft and fluid, then his hip and head landed. Mud, water, and decaying vegetation rose up around him, choking off his air and his senses.

"Where is Loki?" Kim asked as Konner dropped the last pile of brush to close their crude corral. They only had two cows. Enough to pull one plow. That had to be enough. But Kim's stomach sank with disappointment. He wanted four. A relief team. Or, better yet, a second team to speed up the hard work ahead of them. With the influx of new villagers they'd need at least one more field plowed and planted to feed them all come winter. Should he increase each field from three to five acres? The farming texts were too vague. He needed facts to make a judgment.

"Haven't seen Loki since . . . since the bull charged and the cows scattered," Konner replied. "Raaskan hasn't come in yet either." He mopped sweat from his brow with his bare arm. His mud camouflage smeared. Only the whites of his eyes and his teeth showed palely in the uncertain moonlight.

One of their two captured cows bellowed mournfully.

Kim shivered, not liking the prescient sense of grief in the sound.

"We have to go back for them," he insisted.

"Why?" Yaakke shrugged his shoulders. He looked inordinately pleased with himself. The evening had only been a partial success, yet Yaakke strutted about as if they'd just conquered the world and garnered all its wealth.

The young man had no idea how much wealth these two cows and one calf—which didn't seem to belong to either cow—represented in a galactic empire where everyone ate tanked food. Even the emperor had decreed that the search for bush planets with agricultural surplus must be the top priority of the entire space fleet. He'd also decreed an end to the ages-old policy of stripping planets of all natural resources and moving on.

But the senate would never agree to the corollary proposal granting full citizenship and voting rights to bush dwellers who provided the food necessary to keep the GTE fed and healthy.

The meat and milk from these few precious animals could buy a lifetime of luxury in the empire.

Loki seemed to want more than a quick fortune. He wanted a regular income from the fresh food available here.

Briefly, Kim wondered why Loki of all people needed so much wealth. What had Mum promised him?

What did Kim truly want? Mum's promised family reunion and a farm on a recognized planet? Or did he truly want to stay here, forsake Mum and her schemes and the uncertainty, and . . . everything that was familiar and dear to him, including the goodwill of his brothers?

If Hestiia truly loved him, and wasn't just enamored with the honor of being the wife of a god, he might stay. Forever.

Mum wasn't going to like this.

"Yaakke, patrol along the river for signs of Raaskan. We're going back to the herd," Konner said over his shoulder as he strode away from the corral.

"Again I ask why?" Yaakke sneered. "The slave is of little value. Your brother, Lord Kameron, is a warrior, he will not welcome the smudge on his honor if he has to be rescued. Better to die a hero than live as a weakling."

A resounding crack followed his words. Hestiia appeared out of the darkness and slapped her brother's face. "How dare you place more value on another man's honor than on his life! Every life is precious to us. So say the Stargods," she shouted at him. "Go now. Do the bidding of our new gods and pray that they forgive you when you return with a *man,* from our village, and the cow he rides. We no longer stoop to keeping slaves!"

The fading moonlight cast her shadow long and ominous.

Yaakke scuttled away.

Kim's heart warmed at her strength and her passion. Here was a woman who could stand up to Mum. Here was a woman worth giving up everything familiar for.

"How did you know that Raaskan mounted his cow?" Kim asked. He followed Konner, expecting Hestiia to follow.

"I watched from the shadows," she replied, keeping up with him. "I could not allow my husbands to complete such a wondrous deed without a witness to retell the story." The villagers told stories around the central campfire every night, reliving their history, their laws, and their moral lessons in allegory and song. Rhyme and music made them easier to remember and repeat verbatim generation after generation. Almost more fun than reading the history and lore.

The great cow roundup was exciting, but not enough to supplant Raaskan's account of riding inside a white-and-silver dragon.

Kim had learned more about the local culture from those stories than from any amount of recording data. The lore told him that Hanassa had suppressed references to earlier times. He refused to hear about the civil war that destroyed the society built by the original colonists. He refused to admit any history before his own assumption of power. But the people had kept those stories alive in secret. Pryth's stories and songs made Kim suspect that the mysterious Rovers—Pryth's people—had emigrated here on their own several generations before the official colonists. They had fled centuries of persecution in the GTE. But it had followed them and remained. The original band of refugees trusted her because they knew her. Newcomers avoided her and made the ward against the evil behind her back.

So much to learn. Would he have enough time to absorb it all?

First he had to find his brother.

"Did you see what happened to Loki?" Kim asked Hestiia. The hair on his arms and the back of his neck itched with unspoken alarm.

"Alas, no. He failed to capture one of the wild beasts, so I followed you and Konner to make sure the telling of the end of the story would be accurate."

"I'm afraid the story isn't over yet."

The fading moonlight abruptly disappeared. "Moonset," Konner reminded them.

"I will fetch torches and the others. We must move quickly." Hestiia ran off. Her voice had quavered with apprehension.

"Torches. We need light, Kim. Portable torches from the *Rover*." Konner hadn't slackened his pace at all.

"No time." Waves of fear grew stronger as Kim trotted ahead, leaving Konner in his wake.

Then he heard, felt, saw, smelled a whispering vibration within the ground, a vibration that might have been a whimper from a dying man, a man praying for help.

"Gotta get these boots off." He gave in to the sudden need to touch the ground with his bare feet. Only through his skin could he decipher that odd sound.

The moment the cool ground touched his feet the strange vibration increased. He picked up his pace, treading lightly and surely.

"Wait up, Kim, we can't see a bloody thing until sunrise."

"Follow me. I don't need to see." And he didn't. His feet knew the way back to the meadow and the swamp without the aid of his eyes.

Underneath the sureness of his steps lay a susurration; the land communicating with the trees, with the wind, with the sun an hour from rising, with *him*.

Kim dared not question this strange sense of openness. He had to run. He had to get to Loki before . . .

Then he sensed more than saw the faint flutter of movement within the soft mud and rippling pools of water.

Konner waded into the wetlands. "By St. Norbert of the fens wheezing lungs! This stuff sucks me down as fast as quicksand on Botswana III," he cursed.

Kim jumped from tussock to tussock, keeping as dry as possible. His bare feet found drier patches that would support his weight. Konner's boots must be dragging him down, robbing him of important sensory input.

Blindly, Kim rammed his hand deep. Muck, a branch, something more slimy. He felt around, knowing he was close, knowing he had to persevere no matter how his instincts made him want to recoil from the filth.

Kim grasped something and yanked upward. He couldn't be sure what it was, but it was the most solid thing in this swamp. He came up with a cow's horn.

Konner felt around, too, cautiously, uncertainly. "Sometimes I think life would be easier if we just let our brother drown," he cursed.

"I heard that!" Loki spluttered from his crouch behind a rotting log. His fist followed his words into Kim's jaw.

Kim floundered backward. The swamp rose up to catch him.

CHAPTER 22

◆——·——◆——·——◆

"YOU IDIOT!" Konner exploded with rage. His fist connected with Loki's jaw even as he bent to pull Kim free of the swamp.

But his youngest brother was up already, spitting mad and spitting mud.

And then Loki was up too, fists flying in all directions. Konner ducked one brother only to walk into a left jab delivered by the other.

Kim dove under Loki's next blow and tackled him about the waist. Fortunately, they landed upon dry land. Konner piled on top of the others. He tried to insert an arm between the two. They weren't interested in his halfhearted attempts to separate them.

Hestiia squealed. A cow bellowed. Gentian squawked and took flight. Another body landed in the midst of the pile. The newcomer's knee found Konner's kidney. Konner reared back his head and connected with something solid.

Another body joined the fray. Feet, elbows, and fists tangled.

Konner gave himself up to the glory of expelling all of his pent-up frustrations and energies into remaining in one piece while inflicting as much damage as possible. Relationships, purposes, all the finer points of life ceased to exist.

And suddenly it was over. One by one, the five men rolled out of the conflict.

"How'd I end up on the bottom?" Konner asked. He cradled his jaw in one palm, rocking it back and forth. Deciding he'd lost no teeth and nothing was broken, he gathered himself to rise. A hand reached down from one of the muddy combatants. Impossible to tell who in the flickering torchlight.

"You started it," Kim said. He stood off to Konner's left, teeth gleaming in the uncertain light.

From the clothing, Konner guessed it had to be Yaakke or Raaskan on the other end of the helping hand. He peered closer. Yaakke. Raaskan was broader across the shoulders.

"Loki threw the first punch," Konner defended himself. "And he was hiding, not drowning. One of his practical jokes gone awry. Of course he started it. He always starts it."

"Only after you said life would be easier if you let me drown," Loki retaliated. His fists balled for another blow, then relaxed. He chuckled lightly. "I could say the same for both of you. But easier doesn't make life better." He slapped the nearest man on the back. Raaskan replied by draping a companionable arm around his shoulder.

"Nice to see you consider yourself on equal terms at last." Konner added his own backslapping embrace to the former slave.

"One thing about a fistfight," Kim said around a laugh. "It quickly sorts out all our minor differences." He draped his arm around Yaakke.

"Children, playing in the mud," Pryth snorted. She handed her torch to one of the other women and moved forward. Quickly, she ran knowing hands along arms and legs, jaws, and around eyes. "I cannot tell who is who and which part belongs to which man. But you all seem reasonably intact. You will have aches and bruises tomorrow."

The sharp moo of the cow punctuated the healer's comments.

"Where'd that beauty come from?" Konner asked, surveying the shaggy beast and the calf that nudged her belly looking for milk.

"I have captured and tamed the matriarch cow," Raaskan boasted. His chest swelled and he stood taller.

"The calls of the lone calf have brought its mother to the corral as well. We have them penned back at the village," Hestiia announced.

"Then this evening was a success," Konner said. He took a few steps back toward the village and his bed. Just as Pryth had predicted, the aches began to set in. He could use a hot soak in a big tub. "I guess we can all settle for a dip in the cold river," he muttered. Neither the *Rover* nor even the *Sirius* boasted a true bathtub. Sonic showers just wouldn't do the trick tonight.

This morning. The eastern horizon glowed as a prelude to sunrise. He stopped a moment to watch the dawn creep across the land. "I could get used to this."

But he didn't dare. He had an appointment with his son.

"We ought to name this place." Konner whirled to face his brothers. He wanted to leave his son the legacy, bring him here and let him enjoy the fruits of an unspoiled land.

"Do your people have a name for this world?" Kim asked the men and women holding torches.

"This land is Coronnan, the land of the Coros, descendants of Coron," Raaskan announced. His chest remained puffed out. "Many villages of the Coros make up the people of this land."

"What about the lands across the seas?" Kim asked.

Everyone looked back at him with blank expressions.

"You do know that there are lands beyond the bay?" Konner asked.

"My mother's people tell tales of such lands," Pryth said quietly. "No one living has ever been there and returned."

"The lands beyond the bay are myths. They do not exist," Raaskan asserted. The rest of the villagers nodded in agreement.

"We'll name the planet later, Konner." Loki slapped his back. "After we've explored it all."

"I hope we have time to explore it all," Konner said, looking up to the fading stars. Which one was Aurora where his son waited for him?

"Of course we have time. We'll make the time. This trip or the next," Kim insisted. The light of fascination reflected the sunrise in his eyes.

"Uh," both Loki and Konner said. They looked at each other in embarrassment.

"We have to get home to Mum. She'll worry," Konner finally said, afraid to tell his brothers the truth about his son. The entire experience with Melinda had been just too *humiliating*. The wonderful closeness he'd shared with his brothers at the end of the fight dribbled away.

"You didn't tell us about the boulders, Kim!" Konner shouted at his brother. He eyed the massive glacial reject skeptically. "We've spent three days in hell trying to plow this cursed field and done little more than clear rocks. No plow made of wood, iron, titanium, or even a cerama/metal could break up this ground, let alone the bone one we have."

And all this time hauling rocks kept him away from the forge, kept him from searching out deposits of omniscium.

The three youngsters, who would never have become warriors in their old society, had proven excellent animal handlers under the guidance of the frail experts. Together, they had almost tamed the four captured cows after only three days. In a few more days they'd be ready to harness. And soon they'd be ready to plow—if the rest of the village could clear the rocks out of the fields.

"Yes, we have rocks, but look at the progress we've made in using them as house foundations and retaining walls between fields," Kim replied mildly. "And we've got stacks and stacks of drying turf to insulate gaps between logs."

"That doesn't tell me how we're going to get that damn rock out of the field. It's as big as a house." Well, maybe only as large as a cow, but still too massive to just shove out of the way.

"We could plow around it," Hestiia offered meekly. She was never far from the center of village activity, lately. Konner briefly wondered if she stayed so close because she was always anxious to help or because she was unwilling to get very far away from Kim.

The youngest brother disdained what seemed to be standard male activities—mainly fishing and hunting with Loki and Yaakke. Because of a need to remain close to Hestiia?

"Plowing around it would certainly be the easier solution," Kim mused, running his hands through his hair and beard. "But all of the texts I've found in the library say we need large expanses of uninterrupted rows of grain for efficient pollination. All obstacles *must* be removed. The first year of any farming enterprise is marginal at best. We have to be as efficient as possible."

"Stop sounding like a lecture in a book and help me figure out what to do. Do we plow around it and clear more land to compensate for the loss of planting ground or do we move it. And, if the latter, how?" Konner looked longingly over his shoulder toward the forge.

"You are the engineer," Kim countered.

"Yeah . . . well . . . I guess I am." Konner considered his options. Tools had to be the most basic. Nothing like a challenge to brighten the mind and the mood. "Let's start with a few small explosives from the shuttle. I might be able to reproduce something like cold dynamite with what we've got in the *Rover*. At least we can reduce the mass of the thing." And that would give him an excuse to run more assay tests in search of what he needed for the crystal baths.

First, Konner and most of the villagers dug around the base of the rock. Their primitive picks made from deer antlers broke up the soil enough so that Konner could then move in with a spade he'd fashioned from the small shoulder blade of a calf skeleton found near the swamp.

"This thing is going to be three times as big below the ground," he muttered as he threw off the umpteenth hundred shovelful of dirt. It was fascinating how the women captured the dirt into baskets and carefully dumped it in one place so they could at least partially refill the hole left by moving the rock. These people instinctively conserved and reused everything, including the dirt. A lesson the GTE had discarded and forgotten aeons ago; about the time they rose above subsistence farming and began an industrial age.

Something to think about.

He certainly had time to think about a lot of things as he cleared the reluctant dirt around the immovable rock.

But he'd rather think about his son, Martin, and the wonders he would show the boy as they explored the edges of known space in the *Sirius*.

Long after midday, Konner finally saw the bottom of rock. "Only half again as big below as above," he announced almost triumphantly. "I can get a lever under it. Simple. Give me something to stand on and I can move the world!"

"Do you still need the cold dynamite?" Kim worried his hair and beard, newly habitual gestures of unease.

"Yeah, a few explosives will help," Konner called up from the bottom of the pit around the rock. The rim was nearly shoulder level. "We haven't a lever long enough to move this thing. I need to take off some mass. Get these people out of here. Have them cut and strip some trees. Stout, thick enough to support some weight but not so thick we can't get them beneath."

Three doses of cold dynamite took the rock down to the size of a calf. Still too big to move. "Wish we had some hammers and chisels." They didn't. Bronze tools weren't hard enough to work rock. They needed steel. Next project. Always one more project before he got to repairing his ship. Right now, he needed to move this damn rock.

"And, Kim?"

"Yeah, Konner, you want me to bring Loki and the others in to help."

"That will help. But, Kim, this is going to work. You needn't look so apprehensive."

"If you say so. I just have a bad feeling about this."

"The engineering is sound. It's textbook basic. This is going to work."

Halfway to a late sunset, Konner was beginning to doubt that this would work. The rock did not want to move. They'd broken three lever poles, and the thing hadn't budged a centimeter.

"If I can remove a little more dirt from beneath it, we can push the poles deeper, create greater—leverage," Raaskan offered. He was unfamiliar with the vocabulary, but learning fast.

"It's not safe under there," Kim protested.

Loki and Yaakke had taken off again, claiming they needed to catch more fish for supper. The entire village would be very hungry after all this hard work. Konner was pretty sure they were merely bored—or lazy.

"Maybe we should give up and just plow around it," Kim said with more conviction than he'd said much of anything in the last three hours.

"We've put too much work into this project to abandon it now," Konner replied. "Go ahead, Raaskan, do what you can."

The limber man took Konner's spade, removed the handle, and wiggled under the lower edge of their rock. With broad swipes of his arms he scraped more dirt into Hestiia's basket. Gentian perched on the very top of the rock, peering over as if supervising the operation.

"You are right, Stargod Kim," Pryth whispered. "The rock does not wish to be moved. The land does not want this egg of its bones ripped from its side."

Konner heard the comment. The acoustics of the pit and the woman's voice made her words as loud as if she stood right beside him, pushing the thought into his mind.

"The land and the rock are not sentient. They are not living beings," Konner asserted, as much to himself as to the old woman and his unnaturally skittish brother.

No more than crystals are alive and sentient.

"Who said that?" Konner looked around for the speaker with the almost familiar deep voice.

"It moves," Raaskan said quietly. He reached his arm and half his back under the rock again.

Gentian squeaked and skittered back to the other side of the stone. His movement sent the thing rocking a millimeter. Forward and back. Then two millimeters in each direction.

"Get out of there, Raaskan," Konner called as he leaned against the stone, pushing it away from the man's vulnerable back.

"Just a little more," Raaskan protested. His back muscles worked as he continued to scrape.

"Now!" Konner shouted. He put all of his weight against the stone. Not enough. "Get those poles back under here now!"

The villagers scrambled in a dozen directions. None of them jumped into the pit to help.

The stone rocked.

Raaskan screamed. The sound was muffled by the dirt and rock trapping him.

Konner leaned harder against the stone. "Stay put," he whispered to it. "Please stay put just long enough to get that man out."

The stone levered back as if on command.

Pryth slid into the pit. She murmured soothing phrases all around.

A warm calm spread over Konner. He kissed the rock, feeling the cool surface. His molecules seemed to sink into it, adding his essence to its immovability. As he did with the *Sirius* when he needed to understand what ailed her. "Up just a little, my lovely. Move for your Uncle Konn. Up and back just a little more." Sweat streamed down his chest and his brow. His back and shoulder muscles nearly ripped.

Petram, the stone seemed to whisper its name. Then it complied and shifted up and back.

Konner couldn't tell how far.

"Quickly, Pryth. Get him out of there. I can't hold it much longer." He kept his eyes closed, pouring all of his concentration into holding back the natural movement of the stone.

Some scraping sounds. An agonizing moan. The scramble of many feet.

"You can drop it now," Kim said quietly. He must be standing directly behind Konner, in the pit. Awe tinged his voice.

"I'm not sure I can," Konner replied. His muscles and mind seemed frozen in space and time.

"Just drop your hands and jump back at the same time. I'll help you." Gentle hands touched Konner's shoulders. "Make sure you move your feet, too. You're mighty close to the rock."

Konner nodded, incapable of speaking at that moment.

The villagers seemed very quiet. Too quiet. No whispers or murmurs of a new story formed on the lips of any of them.

"Now!" Kim commanded.

Konner leaped backward, pulling his feet and hands away from the ground monster he'd come to know on intimate terms. He liked the brightness of his crystals better than the dark and brooding rock.

A crash and a deep thud. The ground shook beneath him.

Finally, he opened his eyes.

Petram settled back into the cradle of dirt, right where it belonged. Konner patted it gently. "Okay, buddy, you can stay put. We'll plow around you."

Together, he and Kim scrambled up the side of the pit.

"How's Raaskan?" Kim asked.

"He will live, thanks to the Stargods," Hestiia said quietly. But her face looked grim. "Pryth escorts him to her hut for what healing she can give him."

"Is he hurt badly?" Konner demanded.

"Some." Hestiia lowered her eyes.

Konner's gaze seemed glued to where Pryth directed the others to fashion a litter for the moaning man. His skin looked gray beneath the grime of the day's work.

"How'd you do that?" Kim asked when the villagers had moved away.

"Do what?" Konner splashed water over his head, then mopped off some of the dirt and sweat and fear.

"You levitated that monster a good meter off the ground."

CHAPTER 23

"WE HAVE TO TALK about this," Kim insisted.

"No, we don't," Loki replied. "I didn't see it happen. I don't believe it happened." Chills ran up and down his spine. This couldn't be true. As much as he daydreamed about reading minds, the implications of paranormal talents scared him spitless.

Loki stood firmly in the doorway to their private cabin—the big one built originally for the men. But the others had cleared out, choosing to double and quadruple up in the smaller huts rather than share space with the Stargods. Since the "miracle" this afternoon, everyone had tiptoed around the brothers, speaking in awed whispers and darting furtive glances at them.

Except Hestiia. She had moved herself into the far corner of the cabin and slung a hide curtain between her bed and theirs.

"Believe it," Kim argued. "Konner held that multiton monster a full meter off the ground with only his mind."

"Optical illusion."

"Haven't you noticed anything weird happening, Loki?" Konner asked. He lay back on his bed, fully clothed, face pale with exhaustion. "Like the time I diverted the rock shards from the exploding altar."

"That was the dragon," Loki scoffed. "It fanned its wings and created an updraft. Nothing more." But dragons didn't exist.

"Or the time he scooted the dragon along the nose of the shuttle," Kim picked up the litany.

"I . . . ah." Actually Loki had noticed a lot of strange things happening on this planet. Right now, his brothers truly believed what they told him. He could see it in their eyes and their posture. He heard stray thoughts and caught wispy images of their memories of the incident.

Loki knew he'd eavesdropped on thoughts before, rarely, in times of stress. There were too many times when he finished sentences for people, when he knew Mum was coming to investigate their exploits before he heard her, when he guessed the tactics of the IMPs before they implemented them.

"We need to check on Raaskan. He's too good a fellow to let die if we can help him." Loki stomped out of the cabin and headed across the compound to the circular shack Pryth had put together for herself out of stacked turf and stout reeds.

The entire village hovered around her door, faces grim with grief.

"We aren't going to let him die," Loki reassured them. "He's too valuable to all of us." He patted Poolie's shoulder and gave her a quick hug for reassurance.

But when he saw Raaskan's gray face contorted in pain, his breath coming in short, wheezing gasps, Loki doubted the ability of their technology. Raaskan needed a hospital with a full operating theater and the best medical knowledge available to civilization.

Loki and his brothers carried a lot of medical equipment with them, but not enough for this.

"I brought the ultrasound scanner," Kim said quietly. He pushed past Loki, the palm-sized unit in his hand. The US waves would tell them a lot. Maybe enough. They could set bones, cauterize wounds, treat with antibiotics. But what could they do for massive soft tissue damage and crushed bones and organs?

Kim knelt beside the injured man. Pryth had placed Raaskan on his left side, relieving as much pressure as possible from his inured right side. The US whirred slightly. The minute images on the screen did not look good, even to Loki's uneducated eye.

"If I could just get these ribs back in place, it would take some of the pressure off the lungs," Kim grunted.

"Maybe I can help. If I really did lift a megaton rock with my mind, maybe I can push some ribs back in place," Konner said. He didn't look as confident as his words.

"You have exhausted yourself saving this man's life," Pryth drew Konner away from Raaskan. "You must not try."

"Kim has always been the healer in the family." Why did Loki say that? Just because Kim had read a few medical texts and had a delicate touch with bandages and such didn't make him a healer.

Or did it.

Loki gulped. If he was going to be truly honest with himself, all three of them had special talents. And something about this planet made them obvious. They couldn't dismiss and rationalize anymore.

"You know how to do it, Stargod Kim. All three of you know how, but only he can reach deep enough inside himself right now," Pryth said in her lilting accent. Her olive complexion took on a darker hue in the shadowed hut. Her eyes grew large and moist. Loki felt compelled to look only into those deep wells that opened to another reality. Someone—or something—else seemed to look through her eyes, grab his soul, and yank it out of his body.

Apparently Kim experienced the same compulsion. His eyes remained glued to the old woman while his hands rested flat on Raaskan's side, atop the largest and ugliest bruise.

"Concentrate on where the ribs should be," Pryth whispered.

Loki took the US from Kim and held it over the place Pryth indicated.

Kim looked back and forth between the man and the scanner, seeking the center of the injury.

"Do not look at him!" Pryth commanded. "Look inside yourself. Find the core of energy. Watch it flow from your inner essence down your arm, through your hands. Match the rhythm of your heart to his. Feel the harmony of your bodies melding . . ." Her voice drifted off from its hypnotic chant.

Silence hung around the tiny hut like a smothering wool blanket.

Except for a delicate hum in the back of Loki's throat that matched the US. Loki felt the vibrations move from his heart to his shoulders and along his arms. Without thinking, he placed his free hand on Kim's shoulder. A matching hum rose from his youngest brother. Then Konner joined them, placing his hands on Kim's thighs.

The hum grew louder, amplified by orders of magnitude from the three separate throats that had become one voice, one thought, one will.

Wisps of blue mist enveloped them, isolating them from the villagers. Heat rose with the mist. Sparks of a darker blue appeared in the mist.

Nothing existed but the hum and the blue mist.

The color intensified, condensed into a tight ball, and settled between Kim's hands and the injured man. Then it grew again, spreading out along the damaged torso and across the back.

The hum grew louder to match the pulse and the deepening glow. Loki shifted the pitch upward to ease his throat. His brothers followed and matched him with seamless harmony.

Konner slid from the higher pitch to a lower one. Loki kept the tenor line open. Kim took the middle note of the swelling chord.

As the tuneless music filled them, filled the hut, spread, and enveloped the entire village, Loki thought his heart, his ears, and his mind would shatter with the beauty of it all.

The chord died a sudden death. All three brothers slumped, as if the vibrations of the music that linked them, was all that held them up.

"You have succeeded," Pryth whispered. "Raaskan is healed."

"Impossible," Loki said so quietly he wasn't certain the others could hear him. "Mind magic—faith healing—whatever, can't cure."

"But it did," Pryth confirmed.

Raaskan breathed deeply and evenly. Color returned to his skin. His moans of pain gave way to quiet, healing sleep.

"Now we can talk about this," Loki conceded when they returned to their hut. All three brothers collapsed upon their mattresses, too exhausted to remove clothing or wash or even eat.

Loki wished he'd taken time to eat. His stomach growled ominously. He was so hungry he was almost sick.

Kim rolled over and fumbled with the pack he kept beside him. He tossed a protein bar to each of them. Emergency rations from the ship when local food ran out or proved toxic. "This is supposed to help." He gulped his own bar, barely bothering to chew.

So did Konner.

Loki forced himself to chew the last half of the bar.

"What happened back there?" he asked when his brothers relaxed a little and started in on some local dried fruit from Konner's pack and the nuts, also local, that Loki kept in his own.

"Something more bizarre than anything I've experienced so far," Kim admitted. "It was something out of a fantasy novel. Unbelievable."

Gentian stalked into the room. He looked briefly to Hestiia's half of the room, then back to the brothers. After a moment he hopped onto Kim's mattress, curled up, and began purring. Loki could hear the gentle rumble all the way across the room. His muscles relaxed and his borderline headache vanished before he could fully acknowledge it.

"And yet it happened," Loki confirmed. "You guys have made a believer out of me. Dragons and flying kitties," he pointed to Gentian, "levitation, telepathy, psychic healing, call it magic if you have to. We could sort of do those things before we came here. But now . . . St. Bridget guide us. We've landed on one unusual planet."

Their silence confirmed his opinion. "The question is, what do we do about it?"

"Do we have to do anything?" Konner asked. "Maybe it's just a temporary phenomenon."

"I think it's an augmentation of what we have been doing instinctively before we came here," Kim mused.

Silence again as they all thought about it.

Somewhat restored by the food and a long drink of water, Loki closed his eyes and willed his body to relax. "Okay, you guys, think about something other than what just happened."

"Like what?" Konner asked a little defensively.

"Think about repairing the ship, or about the girl you left behind, or— or—I don't know, just think of something I'm not likely to pick up on."

Rough images flitted across Loki's inner vision, sort of like a dream, half a thought, not exactly words, but concepts.

"Why didn't you tell us you have a son, Konner?" He sat up abruptly, partially outraged. Mostly pleased beyond measure.

"Mum's going to strangle you when she finds out you have deprived her of the joy of a grandchlid," Kim chortled.

"Mum knows. She's going to help me get custody of Martin when we return," Konner defended himself. He rubbed his face with his hands, looking incredibly weary. As they all did.

"You'll tell us the rest of the story in your own good time, Konner," Loki said soothingly. "I presume you were going to tell us?"

"Yeah. When Martin turns fourteen, he can choose his custodial parent. I've spent three months each year for the past seven years as a counselor at his camp. He knows me, but doesn't know I'm his dad. He trusts me, talks to me. He's told me things about his mother . . . things that make the wicked stepmother in fairy tales look like an angel. I *will* be in the courtroom that day and I'll use every persuasion I can think of to get him away from Melinda."

"When is that?" Kim asked.

"In Terran terms, ten months and eighteen days. We can't dawdle here too long. If you two think you need to stay here longer, fine. I'll take off on my own. This is one date I will not miss."

"We'll see to it that you don't," Loki reassured them both. "That gives us a full growing season to get these people started on raising a surplus. The point is, I pulled your deepest, darkest secret out of your mind. I couldn't do that before we came here."

But he'd got nothing from Kim except a few vague flashes of color and the scent of roses.

Strange how Loki always thought of Cyndi when he smelled roses. Their last night together in her father's rose garden . . .

"Loki is a telepath," Kim confirmed. "I'd wondered sometimes the way you seemed to anticipate the IMPs before they acted."

"Except that last time. The captain of the ship seemed to be reading my mind before I thought out what to do. I picked a jump at random and still he was there ahead of us."

"And I'm telekinetic," Konner said around a huge yawn. "Explains why I can get ships to do the impossible; I move parts and energies with my mind instead of tools that are too clumsy for the job."

"And Kim is a psychic healer," Loki finished. "Three talents that could change the course of the GTE if we turned our minds to it."

"I also have precognitive visions," Kim said quietly. Sadly.

"You know something, Kim."

The youngest brother remained silent.

"Spit it out, Kimmer."

"Let's get some sleep." He turned over and closed his eyes.

CHAPTER 24

H ANASSA FELL CLUMSILY from his stolen pony. No saddle or stir-rups for him to hang onto. Only the creature's mane and the rope bridle kept him from landing heavily and painfully. Every muscle in his body ached. His back burned and bled with the unhealed wound. The moon had risen. He should continue his journey by its light. But if he moved one more step, his back would rip into pieces.

The bandages and poultice that Taneeo had dressed his wound with seemed all that held him together.

For nearly two weeks he had fled the retribution of the Rovers. Who would have thought the shiftless wanderers could be so . . . so persistent. His admiration for the entire group rose slightly.

He trembled all over. The tremors racked his body with pains worse than those caused by the jolting gait of the pony as they had climbed this mountain pass.

As soon as his feet steadied, he scanned the skies. Looking up for so long threatened his balance. But still he searched for any sign of the dragon that had circled above him lazily on a thermal current for many hours today.

Iianthe, the purple-tip, the only purple-tip in the nimbus, had refused to leave him alone these thirty years. The flywacket had deserted him years ago. But not the dragon. Not even now when the Coros believed him dead.

But he must keep secret from Iianthe and the rest of the nimbus the destiny that called to him. He was close now. He could feel it. And once he found it . . . whatever "it" was . . . he would be invincible. All the humans and the dragons must bow before him and die. He could feel it. He knew it in his bones.

For the moment, the sky appeared empty of clouds and dragons. At least the rains had ceased. The hot sun had baked much of the infection out of his wound. One more chill in the incessant wet might have killed him.

The wet had not kept the Rovers from tracking him.

With a flick of the bridle rope he released the pony to browse and drink from the nearby spring—a sulfurous, reeking seep. But the pony was smarter than most of its breed and knew when water was safe and when it was not. The Rovers tolerated only the most intelligent creatures.

Because of those Rovers, he dared not light a fire, though its warmth would be welcome on this clear desert night. Rumors of Rover tortures had never bothered Hanassa before. Contemplating them now sent tremors through his body. Rovers did not stoop to inflicting physical pain. They preferred to insert false memories and illusions into their prisoners' minds. And when their victims had screamed themselves into mute terror they removed all memories. A total cleansing of mind and personality. Hanassa was not about to relinquish himself to such abuse. He valued his knowledge, his memories, and his need for revenge too much.

He would give much to learn their mind magic. But Rovers kept their secrets too well. He had learned that much about their race from Pryth. That old crone revealed nothing, and she could not be intimidated. For some strange reason she had no fear of death.

But he knew a few tricks even the Rovers did not know. He had learned the art of invisibility from the dragons. Taneeo had not found him in the altar clearing for six days though he had remained in plain sight, sitting against the bloodwood tree. The loathsome creatures had given him precious little else during his early years with them. When he was through, he would take more, much more from them including their lives.

Long before the so-called Stargods had come to the land of the Coros, Hanassa had vowed to end the tyranny of the dragon nimbus.

Stumbling heavily, Hanassa found a sheltered niche beneath a rocky overhang. The evening wind could not find him here. Not even a dragon could find him here. He slept heavily, huddled beneath a shabby steed blanket.

When he woke, dawn blazed on the desert horizon. He probed his gritty, sour mouth with his tongue and barely raised enough moisture to spit. Desperate for moisture, he crawled to the seep. The pony still stood close by, unaffected by the noisome chemicals. Hanassa plunged his head into the little pool, gulping as much water as he could. When he came up for air, he spat out the water. It left a taste in his mouth worse than the dryness had.

Thirst won out. Breathing shallowly, he scooped water into his mouth and swallowed it quickly. By the time the water had begun to revive him, he had grown used to the taste and drank more. He downed the last of his journey rations and threw himself onto the pony's back.

As long as the beast continued uphill, toward Hanassa's destiny and away from the Rovers, he did not bother guiding it.

Noon came and went. He and the pony drank from several pools, some better tasting than others. They climbed onto a narrow plateau where wild grasses waved merrily in the sunshine. Along the base of the next hill, more seeps made for swampy ground. Hanassa dug out a number of tasty bulbs while the pony grazed hungrily on the grass. Some of it had started to go to seed. Hanassa gathered as many of the grain pods as he could. Tonight he would find a place to risk a fire and roast them.

Then he plaited several strands of grass together to make a primitive snare. Where there was water, animals came to drink. He was so hungry he would welcome even the tiny body of a mouse for his dinner.

When the pony had eaten its fill and ambled toward the little bit of shade along the cliff base, Hanassa mounted it again. This plateau had possibilities. Hidden from below by the mountain at his right, he could see the entire pass.

A swirl of dust told him that someone approached, many someones by the size of the cloud. He refocused his eyes, peering into the distance and beyond—another dragon trick. The Rovers pushed toward him with their packs and ponies, their wives and children and elders. More than the little family band he had stolen from; the entire clan pursued one man who had stolen a pony.

Hanassa admired their pride and determination.

Confident the land would hide him from casual view—but who knew what kind of magic the Rovers possessed for seeing the trail ahead—he aimed the pony around the mountain, seeking another route through the pass.

The sun sank toward its rendezvous with the horizon. The pony plodded on. The Rovers climbed faster than Hanassa had, and by a more direct route.

Perhaps he should go back to the narrow meadow. He sat for many long wasted moments thinking, while the Rovers came ever closer.

A chill wind, born on snow-topped peaks, stiffened. It circled him, seeking exposed bits of skin to torture.

At last, when his body trembled with cold and fatigue, Hanassa kicked the pony forward. The meadow was too far behind him. He needed shelter and water. Soon.

The plateau remained level and consistently two dragon lengths in width. The mountain to his right rose up and up without a break. Only an occasional ravine split its sides. He could tell at a glance that all of them led nowhere. Traps for the unwary.

A tune followed the cold wind. Rover harmonies played with his mind. His pursuers had sent the frigid air to seek him out, follow him, report back to them. They neared the last steep slope to the plateau.

"I have not the strength to send you elsewhere," he whispered to the wind. "I have barely enough strength left to live."

Desperate for a place to hide, Hanassa crowded against the mountainside in what looked like a patch of shade. Perhaps the shadows would hide him from Rovers, magic winds, and dragons.

The shade proved deeper than he thought. He dismounted. With the bridle in one hand and his other feeling along the wall he stepped forward. Less than an overhang. More like a cave or covered ravine. Hanassa probed the passage ahead of him with limited vision and hands nearly numb with cold, privation, and ill health.

On and on the darkness led him. One hundred paces. And then the wall curved slightly to the right. Light appeared at the other end.

The sounds of many feet scrambling over the lip of the plateau sent him scurrying forward.

Hanassa walked into a wide bowl surrounded on all sides by the steep walls of an ancient volcano that had blown itself out aeons ago.

Behind him, several male voices cursed in the abrasive Rover tongue. Neither men nor dragons had heard any other language like it on this world.

Would his enemies venture into the tunnel?

A number of caves opened into the bowl, some at ground level, others far above. He headed for the nearest one on his left. Barely big enough to secrete himself and the pony. He moved on to a larger opening, one with a tiny stream trickling out of it. This cave proved larger with three side "rooms" opening off it. It, too, went no farther.

One by one he investigated the openings, all the while listening with his extra senses for sounds of his pursuers. At last he came to the largest opening, almost directly opposite the tunnel. A good sized creek emptied out of this cave. He ducked into it just as he caught the first glint of the Rovers' torches reflecting off the tunnel walls.

The moment Hanassa stepped within the shadows of the large cave, an overwhelming sense of welcome and security flooded through him. He allowed his body to relax and he opened his mind.

The cave beckoned him to explore.

He crept deeper into the first room, half keeping his eyes on the flicker of light at the opening.

But sunset was coming rapidly in this high desert. He would not have the daylight as a reference point much longer.

The Rovers called to each other across the bowl within the mountain. They sounded happy.

Hanassa picked out the words for water, fire, and camp.

Dragon dung! They were setting up camp for the night.

What to do?

The pony began nuzzling along the edge of the stream looking for whatever plants might grow there. Hanassa gave it a few handfuls of grass he had collected in the meadow, then sat down on a rock and munched his careful hoard of seeds and bulbs. He had to think. Had to plan.

As the moon rose, Hanassa's inner senses awoke. He knew the time of day and the cardinal directions. South tugged at his back like a deep itch.

The pony dozed beside the stream. Hanassa set a little more grass beside the beast. It would not stray far from the water tonight. Come morning, it would wander back toward the plateau and food. The Rovers would recapture the pony and perhaps go away. They could have the creature. Hanassa had no more need of it. Hanassa had come home.

Slowly Hanassa turned in a circle, arms outstretched, palms up and receiving. He did not need light to find his way. Tiny glowing bugs and fungus on the walls and within the stream showed him the path. The cave hummed a welcome to him.

He set off to explore. In some places, he had to squeeze through narrow rifts in the rock. In others, he stumbled over stone obstacles and bashed his knee. But always the cave called to him. He moved deeper and deeper beneath the mountain. And then a long, nearly straight tunnel led him downward at a steady slope. He resisted the urge to crawl. The cave would not trip him here. The cave was alive, and it wanted to share its mysteries with Hanassa, only Hanassa.

The hum in the back of his head became audible. He began to sing along, not needing words to strengthen his communion with the cave.

The path led ever downward.

Sweat poured from Hanassa's brow. It rolled down his back, stinging the still raw knife wound. Only then did he realize how hot the cave was. Like descending into the womb of the Earth ready to give birth.

Give birth to what?

Hanassa had no doubt that he was the intended father of whatever miracle the cave brought to life.

The downward slope leveled off. The heat increased. Still he trod onward, led by the cave's inner music. He splashed through a stream, then tripped through a maze of connected rooms and tunnels until the tune that led him grew almost painfully loud.

The walls began to glow. His body became listless with the heat. Still he plodded onward.

And then the light changed. He was in a large cavern, the ceiling so high he could not sense its presence. A number of small tunnels led off of the room. Garish red light pulsed at the end of three of those short tunnels.

Huge monsters filled the rooms. The light glinted off their metallic hides. He had little space to maneuver around them. He moved cautiously, trying to find the monsters' heads, their teeth and eyes, so that he could anticipate their attack.

Nothing. Just the vibrations of their breathing. They must be asleep.

How could they sleep with the hum beating at them from a dozen directions, bouncing off the walls and the roof at random.

He had to choose a direction now.

Cautiously he stepped into the largest room, the most likely to contain the miracle the cave wished to share. It also contained the largest monster. It sat unmoving, seemingly entranced by the hum that drew Hanassa forward.

He threw an arm across his eyes, protecting them from the bright light issuing from the nearest tunnel. Salty sweat streamed down his face, blurring his vision.

Abruptly, the light softened. Hanassa dared a quick peek to see what transpired. The archway at the end of the passage opened onto a quiet land of harsh grasses and low shrubs. Impossibly large deerlike creatures with massive horns grazed on whatever green they could scrounge. A light snow fell, clinging to everything.

The temperature dropped abruptly just the other side of that archway.

Hanassa hesitated.

The colors of the scene swirled, faded, turned red again.

The only thing beyond the edge of this tunnel was the boiling core of lava at the center of the volcano.

And then the scene shifted again. Red, black, and brown spiraled into green, blue, and brown. The straight trunks of a myriad of old trees formed before his eyes. The light showed pale yellow at a low angle. Birds chirped brightly. Dawn in the forests of home!

He stepped into the new world and smiled.

The cave had shown him a miracle after all.

CHAPTER 25

THE DREAM CREPT INTO Kim's consciousness like fog slithering over the surface of the bay. A wall of confusing images and distorted sounds that enveloped his entire being.

"I'm just dreaming," he reassured himself. "I've dreamed this before."

But the images came clear and fully detailed, much more precise than any previous time.

He thrashed, sweeping away swaths of mist that were immediately replaced by thicker layers—layers that smothered like wool blankets. Somewhere out there was reality beyond this dreamworld.

The dreamworld became more real than reality.

His hands turned slick with sweat. The sweat turned red.

A thick coppery taste coated his tongue. He shied away from it, knowing it portended death.

He'd known death before, shared it with the man he had killed. Pain stabbed his heart and soul at the memory. He dropped a thick veil of forgetfulness between himself and the image of the man's face contorted in agony.

Immediately he found himself back at a local produce fair at the first home of his memory on Aurora. His parents owned and operated a small shipping company. Da was gone a lot, transporting fresh produce to civilized planets for distribution to the wealthy.

This fair was a celebration of a successful harvest. Da had just left that morning. Kim never saw him again. Mum never knew his fate. She hid her grief from her children with stoic pride. Da's name never crossed her lips again.

But this memory was from before they knew that Da was gone forever. Happy times. Togetherness. Family.

Thick smells of fried foods and sugar mingled with the scents of livestock gathered in pens for show and sale. His mouth watered. He swallowed around the almost-tastes that gathered on his tongue.

He remembered the shouts of his older brothers as they ran off to explore the carnival rides, the games, and the treats. His sister—almost forgotten since she'd been separated from the family so long—whined to follow Loki and Konner. Mum clutched both Katie's and Kim's hands tighter, promising a special treat.

Thin plastic cones appeared in their hands topped by clouds of pink spun sugar. He bit into the hot sweet tangles of candy cotton. It clung to his cheeks, hair, and hands like . . . like the fog gathering around his dream. Moist, dark pink, clinging relentlessly.

The fog invaded his lungs, filled his mouth, became solid. Choked him. He gasped for air only to inhale more of the stuff.

His vision reverted to the carnival. The sounds became deafening. Bright lights strobed, blinding him. The fat from a deep fried dinner and the sugar from the later treat roiled in his gut. Strangers crowded closer and closer, pushing him away from the safety of his mother's hand.

"Mum!" he called, hearing it with his real ears but not within his dream. "Mum, I'm lost."

Strangers reached for him. The strobing light shadowed their faces into mockeries of humanity. Bulging eyes, elongated teeth, deeply hollowed cheeks. Ears extended into extra folds, resembling bats. The fingers on each grasping hand became claws, more bone than flesh, impossibly long. At least one extra joint to each digit.

They opened their mouths in parodies of smiles. Gums receded, turned bright red, covered in blood. Eyeteeth grew long and hollow, became drinking tubes.

Kim threw his hands over his vulnerable neck and screamed. His hands stuck to his skin, held there by the melted sugar strands. He pried his hands away, bringing patches of skin with them. Blood flowed from the wounds and from his hands.

The strangers closed in on him, making greedy sucking noises. They flared their nostrils with excitement at the smell of blood.

"Mum!"

His screams woke him.

He lay on his cot in a Tartarean dark hut on a primitive world where dragons were real and magic worked. How could he know for certain that vampires and ghouls did not also exist here?

What strange disease could turn people into such monsters?

He sat up, drenched with sweat and panting for breath. His hands were slick. With blood?

A ghostly white form glided to the foot of his bed. The ghost of the sister taken from the bosom of the family twenty years ago when he was seven and she was nine.

A scream tried to erupt from his throat. Fear paralyzed every muscle in his body. For a moment he thought his heart stopped beating and his lungs failed.

"Lord Kim, are you well?" Hestiia asked softly.

The ghostly white was merely her pale skin reflecting the bits of starlight creeping through the window opening.

"I . . . I don't know. The dream. More real than you." He reached out his arms to her, desperately needing contact with another human to reassure him that what he saw was merely a dream and not another vision. A terrible vision of death and blood ripped from some terrible undead presence.

"Stay with me, please," he pleaded. He clutched her tightly to his chest, kissing her neck and hair, needing her strength and warmth to banish the dream.

Hestiia snuggled into Kim. His warmth cradled her while his heavy arm pinned her back close against his chest. Well-being made her close her eyes and dream of the days to come.

At last she was truly wife to this man. She did not care if Loki and Konner consummated their marriage. Kim listened to her, made her feel safe, respected, special. The other two ignored her more than they paid heed to her presence.

She yawned and felt her legs twitch with the need to be up and about. Today they would plow. An exciting day for the entire village.

Kim's arm clamped tighter about her midriff. "Don't go," he whispered into her hair.

"The birds are singing hymns to the dawn, my husband."

"Another moment, please. You help me forget my dreams." He sounded sad.

She shifted around within the embrace of his possessive arm to face him. Gently she touched his cheek. "'Twas but a dream." She kissed him. He had not told her what transpired within his dream, but she knew it must be terrible to disturb a god. Trouble to come.

But that was the future. This was today.

"We plow today. Your people will need to break their fast with a hearty meal." She kissed his nose playfully. "I will bring you some."

"Best I get back to my own bed before my brothers awake and find me here. We agreed . . ." He did not finish the thought.

Hestiia did not think she was supposed to hear the last of it. But she had suspected for a long time that the brothers had stayed away from her bed by common agreement. They did not believe in the marriage. Perhaps gods did not need marriage. Loki certainly spread his seed far and wide without a word about tomorrow. No promises. No ties to the land or the people.

"You will all leave me one day," she whispered. A hole as big as the pit around the unmovable rock seemed to open around her heart. "But I will cherish every day I have with you until then."

—◆—

Kim watched Hestiia dress and slip around the hide curtain that separated her corner of the hut from the brothers'. Her slim form delighted his senses even in the semidarkness of false dawn.

He smiled from the center of his being outward. Today they would work hard and celebrate what they accomplished. His snug cottage and dream of children suddenly seemed much closer than he'd dared believe. Wholesome food, fresh air, a community working together for the benefit of all, a wife to work beside him, to warm his bed, and give him children. Life didn't get much better than this.

"I don't think I can leave this planet, dear brothers," he whispered more to himself than to the men in the other room. "I know Mum will be disappointed, I know I'll disrupt the family, but this is something I have to do. My dreams are here."

Sadness washed over him. If he stayed, he might never see Mum again. That grief was less than the thought of leaving Hestiia.

He had responsibilities here.

He had responsibilities to Mum. How could he reconcile both?

Kim crept back to his own bed, drawing up his woven metal blanket to cover his nakedness. Where had he left his underwear? The heat of a blush rose from his toes to his eyebrows. Along with his embarrassment came some very pleasant memories. He smiled.

On the other side of the room, Konner snorted and groaned. He opened one eye and rolled over with his back facing the window and the growing light.

Loki lay flat on his back snoring, oblivious to the new day and the emotions bathing Kim.

Best they not know about him and Hestiia. Best he not repeat the exercise. But he'd been so very lonely and frightened after the dream that he thought his soul would shatter if he did not reach out and make contact with the only human being to offer comfort.

"Come on, guys, time to wake up," Kim said loudly. "We've got at least five acres to plow before the next storm comes in." He knew in his bones that thunder and lightning and torrents of rain would come in two and a half days. Drizzle broken by a few brief glimpses of the sun before then. The constant rains had to end soon. By high summer they'd have grains growing tall and ripening.

Once they got the plowing and planting done he'd see about transplanting wild vegetable plants to a portion of the field. Where was that text on sympathetic planting? He was certain he'd read something about mixing squashes with corn. The low growing vines kept the weeds down. Beans interspersed with both replenished nutrients that the other two leeched out of the soil.

What about wheat, barley, and soy? He needed to know what complemented their cereal crops.

Without bothering with clothes, he rummaged through his pack of readers. Five of them, all loaded to maximum capacity gave him access to most of the ship's library. He just had to find the right text. One of these days he'd organize them by subject rather than alphabetized by author.

"I smell sausage," Konner sat up, eyes still closed, sniffing loudly. "Wish we had some pancakes and syrup to go with it."

"And coffee," Loki mumbled. "By St. Starbuck I'd give my eyeteeth for a single cup of coffee." He tried sitting up but flopped back down and groaned, arms outflung.

Hestiia returned with bark trenchers filled with deer sausage fragrant with wild sage and thyme. Gentian followed hard upon her heels. The women had fashioned a flatbread out of ground-up bulbs of the yammat. The swamps yielded a generous crop of the stuff; the only reason Kim could think of to not drain them for more farmland. Yammat flowers came with frogs. Too many damn frogs this year. Gentian pounced on one that dared invade the cabin, catching it in mid-jump. The cat stalked proudly out, prize in his mouth.

Kim took a bite of bread. Maybe later they would drain the swamps. Later. Bread like this was worth a few frogs. In years to come, they would have a surplus of grains and vegetables, domesticated livestock, and good crop rotation. Then they wouldn't need the yammat and could eliminate its habitat.

Wait a femto. He was thinking like a Civil of the GTE. No more elimination of habitat of any kind. He had to think in terms of an interdependent ecology. They must keep industrialization to an absolute minimum. He vowed to avoid any enterprise that could endanger wildlife and pollute the pristine air, land, and water. The land of the Coros would never see their natural resources stripped and their habitat domed.

Before he could pursue a plan to keep this land balanced, Hestiia threw him his underwear. She couldn't hide her grin. Neither could he. He snatched a quick kiss as he stood to slide into the garment.

Seconds later Konner and Loki finally made the effort to get up. They rubbed their faces wearily, scratched, and reached simultaneously for the food placed between their pallets. They both still wore their underwear.

Gentian trotted back in and planted himself in front of Kim's trencher. The frog had fed the fire not the cat. Kim knew that for certain. But how? Gentian looked at him as if he were the stupidest being alive. Then he tucked his tail around himself and sat up straight. He expected a share of the breakfast.

Kim sank back onto the floor, searching his readers, food forgotten.

Gentian edged closer to the food without seeming to move a muscle.

"Pryth says you must eat." Hestiia snatched the reader from his hands. "You must replenish your strength after the magic you worked yesterday." She held the trencher directly under Kim's nose. "And you must hurry. Others have heard of your miracles and wish to join our village. Only you three can accept or reject them."

"Others?" all three brothers asked at once.

"Slaves who have escaped their masters, and two warriors and their families." She named the last ones quite proudly, as if they mattered more than the slaves. In her world they did. But in the new order all people must have equal value, so long as they contributed to the welfare of the community. At this juncture, former slaves contributed more than warriors.

"New recruits," Loki said around a mouthful of sausage and a broad grin.

Gentian butted Loki's hand where it hovered over the sausage. He broke off a bit and offered it. The cat nibbled it daintily, then stalked out of the hut, appeased by the offering to his majestic self.

"The five acres were carefully planned for the eighteen people we originally brought here plus the first round of refugees," Konner cautioned. "More people, more land to plow, more seeds we'll need to plant."

"More boulders we have to work around," Loki groaned, falling back onto his bed. "This would be a lot easier with a couple of steel plows and a tractor."

"Uh, before we do anything, we need to talk," Kim said.

Hestiia scuttled out on cue. She always seemed to understand when the brothers needed privacy.

"Just how much technology do we want to introduce to these people?"

"As much as we need," Konner answered. Having finished his breakfast, he began sorting through his pack for clean clothes. The women seemed to wash, dry, mend, and fold their garments and return them in some clandestine way that the men never noticed.

Except their boots. Konner held up one, inspecting the sole for holes. He punched a finger through two, shrugged, and threw them into a corner, content to go barefoot for a time, like all of the natives.

"But how much before they begin to abandon agriculture for industry and sue for membership in the GTE. Then we will have lost our private reserve of fresh food and a large fortune," Kim reminded them.

"The kid has a point," Loki said. He, too, began to dress.

"Well, at what point in our history did society consistently produce a surplus before the industrial age?" Konner stretched his shoulders, found his shirt tight (they'd all developed more muscle mass with the hard work of starting a farm) and discarded it along with the boots in favor of a leather vest.

Kim fumbled through the readers again. "I'm guessing fourteenth and fifteenth centuries pre-space dating." When artificial geographic and cultural boundaries began to dissolve on Earth, a new calendar had emerged, placing year zero with the year humans had first walked on the Moon—the true beginning of the space age.

"Then that's where we stop the introduction of technology," Loki said. "I think our 'miracles' yesterday ousted the tale of flight in the silver-and-white dragon from popularity. We don't need to worry about racial memory of space flight." He pulled on his worn boots and retained his shirt despite its ill fit.

"But what's to keep people from building on previous tech to develop more? Just like on Earth, once we start the ball rolling, there's no stopping it. These people may be primitive, but they aren't stupid," Kim argued.

"Wasn't the printing press in the fifteenth century the single most important factor in industrialization?" Konner asked, looking pointedly at Kim's pile of readers.

"Dissemination of knowledge, exchange of ideas, preservation of the knowledge of ages past," Kim recited a lesson from a cultural anthropology text.

"So we forbid the art of reading," Loki shrugged again and nearly ripped a shoulder seam.

"And the wheel," Konner added.

"I suppose we have to condemn our friends to ignorance and cultural isolation for our own profit." Kim heaved a sigh. But he wouldn't keep all of them ignorant. He'd find a way to educate a few, teach them to read and write, and preserve their knowledge for future generations. Somehow.

CHAPTER 26

KIM SURVEYED THE ROWS and rows of neat furrows across the first field of five acres. The setting sun cast a rosy glow upon the freshly turned ground. A rich scent of fertile life rose pungently around him. Pride swelled within his chest.

"We did this," he whispered in awe.

"I like that word." Hestiia slipped beneath his arm and snuggled into his side.

"Which word?" He tucked her close against him and rested his cheek upon her hair. She felt so natural there at his side, he couldn't bring himself to push her away, even though his brothers were likely to see them together.

" 'We' is a splendid word," she replied. "We, us, family, together. I like all of those words."

"Family," Kim mused. "We've created that here. A sense of family throughout the entire village. We are building something wonderful here."

What about his obligations to his other family—Mum and the missing Katie?

Mum would never truly have a family again because she would always see it as incomplete. The years without Katie and without her long-lost husband could never be made whole. Kim feared Mum would therefore also be incomplete.

She needed to know where her boys were at all times. They had not yet sent her a message about this current adventure.

A layer of guilt settled atop Kim's happiness.

"We are erecting a festival pylon," Hestiia said quietly, almost shyly.

"A what?" Kim looked down at her. But she would not meet his gaze.

"Do you not celebrate the fertility of the land at your home?" Now she looked up. And he gloried in the love he saw reflected in her eyes.

"Uh . . . not exactly." That would be the last thing citizens of the GTE would consider celebrating.

"This is the way we do it here." She whirled him around to face the center of their village. Raaskan supervised the raising of a silvery log stripped of bark and lower branches. A few heart-shaped red leaves crowned the top, augmented with feathers and flowers. At the edge of the fire pit, several other villagers blew notes into reed flutes or pounded rhythms on skin drums.

A sense of well-being grew from Kim's belly, and a smile creased his face. "A May Pole! We have a variation of this, but only children participate. It's quite fun if I remember correctly." Mum had danced with him when he was five—before the disruption of the family and their troubles with the law.

"Not exactly the way we celebrate." Hestiia giggled.

"We need a bit of a party. Shall we join them?"

"Only if you intend to claim me as wife again." Hestiia blushed prettily from the tips of her ears all the way down the deep cleavage of her halter top.

"Um . . ."

"We must ensure the fertility of the land." She continued to blush.

"Sympathetic magic!" The ritual dawned on him. He'd read about it many times and wondered just how far bronze age cultures took the ritual. Certainly it had deeper meaning than schoolchildren dancing with flower garlands.

"Our fertility must match the land's."

"Of course it must." He squeezed her around the waist. Seed the fields, pollinate the flowers, beget new children. A logical progression. He couldn't stop smiling.

Over by the pylon, Poolie grabbed Raaskan by the hand and began an impromptu dance. Hop, hop, skip, turn, the two pranced in a large circle. Another couple joined them, holding hands and glancing at each other fondly.

"'Twould be better with garlands of flowers strung from the top of the pole," Hestiia said wistfully. "But they take many days of preparation."

"Shall we join them, Hes?" Kim tugged her toward the center of activity.

"If you truly want to." She held back, dropping her gaze.

"Don't tell me you are shy, my Hestiia?" He really liked the sound of that, "*My* Hestiia."

"Your brothers . . ."

"Look at them, Hes." Both Loki and Konner had joined the dance. Beaming women held their hands tightly—two women apiece. "Somehow, I don't think either of them is thinking of you right now." His grin grew wider yet.

"By morning your brothers will wed elsewhere. You and I will be free to be together." Hestiia breathed a deep and satisfied sigh.

"I wonder if they realize what they are getting into." Kim laughed.

"I know who *you* will get into tonight."

·———◆——·

"You realize we still have two more fields to plow," Loki said. He leaned back against his customary log after a soothing breakfast of boiled grains and deer sausage. His head continued to pound from overindulgence in the local brew last night. When had the women had time to brew beer? His muscles seemed reluctant to obey his commands. He didn't care. Last night's party was well worth this morning's discomforts.

"Can we give it a day of rest?" Konner stretched his arms over his head until his back audibly crackled and settled. Then he released a jaw-popping yawn. His fingers trailed along the arm of a young woman who had joined the village only three days before.

Medium brown hair, deeply tanned skin, light brown eyes; she was distinguishable from all the other women only by a small scar splitting her left eyebrow.

Loki hid his grin. He was sure Konner had welcomed the girl most royally. As Loki himself had welcomed the twin blondes who winked at him from across the fire.

Where was Konner's second woman? A petite girl with coal-black hair and almond-shaped eyes. Ah, she helped Pryth stir the morning cereal. From her coloring she could be the old woman's granddaughter. Loki wondered if Pryth knew how the girl had spent the evening, how all the women in the village had spent the evening.

"Why wait another day to plow?" Kim asked. He bounced—positively bounced—out of the cabin. Hestiia followed close upon his heels. Their hands brushed against each other and then they jumped apart. Guilt flashed across both their faces.

Loki didn't need to read their minds to know how they had celebrated the fertility of the fields.

"Some of us are tired, Kim," Loki explained to his younger brother.

"Some of us got some sleep last night," Kim thumped Loki on the shoulder.

"Some of us didn't monopolize the cabin, forcing Loki and me to sleep in the woods just to respect another's privacy," Konner retorted good-naturedly.

"Since we have a second team of cattle and extra people to guide the plow, you poor exhausted men can go fishing. I'll stay and help." Kim wandered off to consult with Raaskan and the others.

Loki looked longingly at the cabin. Perhaps a nap. Then he caught a glimpse of the twin blondes. Their grins and lifted eyebrows clearly asked if they should join him. "Sorry, ladies, I'm not recovered yet from last night," he muttered to himself. If he went fishing, he could doze on the riverbank.

"I'll join you, Loki," Konner said, disengaging his hand from the clasp of the brunette.

Gentian swooped down from the skies, breaking the gentle mood of the morning. He chittered and fluttered his wings even after he landed.

"Someone comes," Hestiia said warily. She stooped beside the flywacket and scratched his ears. Gentian kept up his agitated chatter and vigilant stance.

All of the men reached for tools or weapons, never far from their hands. They turned to face the woodlot as one.

Loki shot to his feet, suddenly alert and ready to confront whatever menace approached. Konner and Kim moved up beside him. Together they marched to the edge of the village, standing stalwartly between their people and danger.

Two men and one woman walked slowly out of the woods. The woman, not much older than Hestiia, trailed behind the men.

Yaakke darted forward. Loki grabbed his tunic to hold him back.

"But that is . . ."

"Not yet, man. We need to see what they want. Don't give up the negotiation edge by showing eagerness."

"They aren't carrying any weapons," Kim said.

"But a horde of armed warriors might be hiding just beyond the first row of trees," Loki warned.

"Hestiia, will Gentian search out the woods and report back?" Kim asked.

Gentian hid his head in Hestiia's arms.

"I guess not," Loki mused. "You say you know these people, Yaakke?"

"Maigrait. We were betrothed until . . . until I left the village."

"And the men?"

"Her father and brother."

"Do they hold positions of power within your father's village?"

"Some. Her father is an honored warrior. He has received many wounds in battle and recovered."

"And the brother?"

"Strong in war but not in opinion. He sided with Hanassa in all things without question. He sought my sister's hand in marriage. Yaaccob denied his suit."

Hestiia seemed strangely absent. She usually stayed in the heart of all village matters or close to Kim's side.

"Would Yaaccob trust them with a message of import?"

"Aye. He knows I will welcome Maigrait."

"Then let's talk to them rather than about them." Konner stepped forward two paces and held his right hand up in the local formal greeting.

The newcomers stopped ten paces from Loki and his brothers. The girl fastened her longing gaze on Yaakke and never looked away. Yaakke stared at her, mouth slightly agape, licking his lips frequently. Last night he'd been one of the few men to abstain from the revelries. Maigrait's father—the older of the two men—looked distinctly embarrassed by the strong emotions displayed between the two young lovers. He cleared his throat twice before uttering a greeting.

"Ahem, well met, my lords." He bowed slightly from the waist, keeping his eyes cast down.

"Well come, honored warrior. Will you join us for refreshment?" Loki asked before Kim could jump into the conversation. One thing Loki had learned was that these people respected their elders. Loki, as the oldest, needed to speak for all of them. Thankfully, he could occasionally tap into Kim's stray thoughts for a glimpse into polite ritual.

"No," the younger man said curtly. His father glared at him. But the son crossed his arms over his chest and stood firm. His face twisted into a disapproving frown.

"We have come to beg a favor," Maigrait said softly. "Please help us, Yaakke." She held up her clasped hands in entreaty.

"Anything . . ."

"If the favor is within our power and will not harm either of our villages," Konner cut off Yaakke's spontaneous reply.

"We have heard that a magician smith has come to dwell with the Stargods," the father said.

"We would know your name before we grant or deny your request," Kim jumped in.

"Niveean." The father bowed again in greeting. "And my son is Nimmrodd." He slapped the younger man on the shoulder. Reluctantly, Nimmrodd sketched a shift in posture that might be called a bow.

Kim shot the young warrior a scathing glance as Nimmrodd's fists clenched in anger. Loki caught a brief glimpse of Nimmrodd raising his fist to Hestiia when she denied his suit for her hand.

"And your request?" Loki prompted. The dynamics of these relationships suddenly bored him. He was too tried to speculate and plot. Hestiia was safe from the brute. Yaakke and Maigrait could work out their own settlement. Loki need deal only with Niveean.

"Our plow and tools are worn and near useless. The rains have rotted our first planting. We need to plow and reseed our fields. But first we need new tools."

"And you seek to borrow our blacksmith," Loki finished for him.

"Yes, Lords."

"And in return for this favor?" Loki asked. He didn't like this. Something sounded fishy.

"We have nothing to offer but our goodwill. We do have a boy willing to apprentice to your blacksmith. He is free to return here with him or stay with us, whatever you choose."

"Whatever the boy chooses," Kim insisted.

"I don't know. . . ."

"Loki, we have to do this," Kim insisted. "They come in peace. We need to build a network of amicable trade and goodwill. If we help them now, they will be obliged to help us later when we need it."

"I don't know. Something doesn't feel right."

"I agree with Kim," Konner said. "No sense building new wars on old arguments. We don't need Fullmaan today. Let him go and sharpen a few tools. Since when are you the cautious one, Loki?"

"Since I started reading minds and motives and I can't read theirs. Maybe if they brought their tools to us . . ."

"Let him go, Loki. You can't control and possess everything. Just let him go. He'll be back by sunset and we'll have another field plowed by then." Kim turned and walked away.

"It all just feels wrong," Loki tried again. But the others walked away, ignoring him and his protests.

CHAPTER 27

◆———·———◆———·———◆

HANASSA STOOD ON THE precipice to the lava pit. But the churning mass of molten rock remained hidden beneath another landscape. A bleak desert scene invited him onward. Stark sand and rock littered the ground as far as the horizon without so much as a single blade of grass. Then the vision swirled before him and dissolved into a myriad of colors. Within another seven heartbeats he saw only the lava pit. He counted ten heartbeats, ten times, marking each group on the wall with a rock that left a chalky residue. On the tenth ten set of ten, the hum began in the back of his head. Excitement leaped to his throat. He lost track of the count. About the time he remembered to breathe, the colors changed once more. Deep green. A wet forest unfolded before his eyes.

Day after day he had watched the changing portals. Once the Rovers moved on with their recovered pony, he had crept back out to the meadow to catch small game and harvest a few plants to sustain him. Always he returned to this special place to watch and study the miracle.

Holding his breath, he took one step forward. The cave would not yank this miracle out from beneath his feet. He had to trust this miracle. He had to trust himself.

A cool misty breeze caressed his face. He smelled the river, he smelled green grass and trees. He sensed the absence of his magical cave, his sanctuary. A circular clearing west of the river delta with its myriad islands looked much the same as the last time he had been here; before the coming of the Stargods and the disruption of his life.

And yet everything looked different. The gate had changed him. His studies of the portal told him he needed an arch shape to create a path home. He observed the shape of the trees carefully, looked critically at places where they formed arches.

The large dark shadow between two of the Tambootie trees looked most promising. He turned and stared at the darkness, waiting.

If only he could control when and where the gate would open for him and him alone.

He needed to learn much more about the phenomenon before he could control it. Now that he knew he could trust the gate, he knew how best to use it. This wonderful gift would help him regain control of the Coros.

Rain dripped from his nose and across his lips. His tongue darted out to catch the precious moisture. He had not realized how dry his mouth and throat had become in the desert air of his blown-out volcano.

The gate would not open again right away. It rarely returned to the same scene in the same day, sometimes waiting three or four days to cycle through all of the locations it visited.

Ten times ten steps took him to the river. Keeping close to the shadow of an overhanging willow, he slaked his thirst and washed dust from his body.

The sun had bleached his leather garments to near white. Examining his reflection in a still pool, a ghostly being peered back at him intently. He realized that his pale blond hair had taken on a silver cast. He had lost weight, too. The bones of his skull and his fingers stood out. His skin crackled like brittle leather. He looked a sight to frighten small children and cast doubt in the minds of their parents.

Good.

Nothing like a little honest fear to bring his people to heel.

(You must not do this!) Iianthe's panicked voice stopped him, still clinging precariously to the riverbank.

"You cannot stop me from returning to my people," Hanassa returned matter-of-factly. He had to look carefully to see his littermate. Each hair on his hide was a natural crystal. Light flowed around the beast, pulling frail human eyes away from the bulk of the body. But Hanassa knew how dragons remained invisible. He forced his gaze to remain directly ahead of him.

The purple-tipped dragon perched in the center of the path leading back to the clearing and the gate. He fluttered his wings slightly and partially reared back on his hind legs in an intimidating display.

"I taught you how to do that when we were but yearlings, brother." Hanassa climbed back to solid ground. He didn't feel any anxiety though perhaps he should. Iianthe could still flame him.

Could. But would not.

(The nimbus has decreed that none of us may interfere with the humans,) Iianthe stated. He dropped his shortened forelegs back on the ground and swung his massive head down to pierce Hanassa with his gaze. His spiral forehead horn came dangerously close to Hanassa's chest.

"I am not a dragon. Not anymore. And if I were, I would not listen to the nimbus."

(Simurgh did not listen to us. He developed a taste for human flesh when we had decreed them poisonous.)

"Why, because humans taste too much like flusterhens?" Hanassa laughed at the old joke. Everything exotic eventually tasted like flusterhens.

(We drove Simurgh into the Great Bay. He was so bloated with human blood and flesh he could not swim. He drowned.)

"I do not eat humans," Hanassa snorted. But that was an interesting idea.

(But you kill them. Blatantly. You have no respect for life.)

"Why should I? The dragons cast me out. Why? Because there were too many purple-tips. Three. They knew how to deal with two. Collapse one into a flywacket or drop it into the bay to drown. None of them remembers why there should only be one purple-tip. They allow any number of reds, blues, greens, yellows, and various shades of each of those colors."

Hanassa drew a deep breath and continued to vent his hatred. "Gentian chose to be the inoffensive and timid flywacket. You and I fought to retain dragon form. But you cheated. Our mother cheated. The entire nimbus conspired for me to lose that battle because they knew I was strong enough and determined enough to dominate them all. So I lost the battle and had to become human. Well, now that my spirit has taken over a human body and molded it to my will, I do what all dragons should have done ages ago. I rule the humans, and I work to eliminate them and their influence from this place."

(We will stop you!) Iianthe charged forward, wings extended, elbow talons exposed. *(Humans are too like us. We must learn to share this world.)*

A shift of light made the crystalline fur of the dragon invisible. Though his eyes could not see his brother, Hanassa felt the warmth of his breath coming closer. He dove back down the bank and into the river. As the cold water cradled his body, he felt the rush of air above him as Iianthe launched into flight. His long claws brushed Hanassa's hair. He yelped and reached up to his sore scalp. A hank of silver-blond hair dangled from the dragon's feet as he flew off into the distance.

"I curse you, Iianthe. I curse the entire nimbus of dragons." Hanassa shook his fist at the departing dragon. "If any human survives my reign, they will hunt all of you down and murder you. As you tried to murder me in forcing me to be human."

Dragon voices deserted his head. None listened to him. None believed him. But they would.

Slowly, Hanassa cleaned the mud from his clothing and began the trek to his village. When he understood more of the magic portal, he would force it to open a gate closer to the center of his power.

But even if he could force the portal to his will, he would never reveal its secrets. Perhaps the portal would show him how to destroy the dragons as well as the humans!

Why is my brother so bitter? Becoming human is an honor among us. Becoming human is a tremendous opportunity to learn and carry that knowledge into the next existence.

I would gladly have taken the body of the dying human child and made it my own, strengthened it with my dragon spirit, and worked with the dragons as well as humans in understanding the joined fate thrust upon us by the gods.

Since taking on the full responsibility of being the only purple-tip dragon, I have learned many things. Only one of us may remain with the nimbus at a time. Only one. We possess special talents that must be learned anew by each generation. We have special responsibilities to use those talents only for cooperation and the gaining of wisdom. With a great deal of observation and study, I will one day advise the entire nimbus. Only a purple-tip can command their loyalty and keep them from tearing apart the nimbus with territorial and mating disputes.

Were there two of us, loyalty would divide. The nimbus would divide. Humans would gain too much power because of the division. The storm that would follow would demolish us all.

Hanassa cannot maintain a balance, cannot avoid pitting one against another for his own amusement. He did it as an infant dragon. He does it as an adult human. Therefore we took from him the name Porffor, which means Purple in an ancient language, and gave him the name Hanassa, which means violent rogue.

Where the river met the Great Bay, Hanassa kept to the shadows until he spotted three fishermen. They sat on the sandy bank facing the bay. A fire crackled happily at their feet, roasting six good-sized fish. The men had turned their boat upside down on the beach. Three sleek, long-legged water dogs dozed in its shelter. Every once in a while, one of the dogs would lift an eyelid just enough to check on the progress of their next meal.

Hanassa took a moment to straighten his garments and his back, brush off a few flecks of dirt, and settle his headdress more firmly on his brow. Then he strode into the midst of the little camp, shaking his staff.

The fishermen, always a surly and independent bunch, looked up, reared back their heads, and scuttled backward three paces on their hands and butts.

One of them crossed his wrists and flapped them in the age-old ward against demons. Another touched his brow, his heart, and both shoulders in a new gesture that puzzled Hanassa. He did not let it trouble him. He had business to attend to.

"I have need of you and your boat," he stated flatly, pointing at the miserable vessel with his staff.

"Dead . . . you . . . you are dead!" gasped the man who had made the new gesture. "I watched you die!"

"You saw what the Stargods wanted you to see. They could not kill me, so they planted ideas in your head. False ideas to steal your faith and your loyalty to Simurgh, the only god in all this world." He raised his staff and shook it again as if summoning a dragon—the last thing he truly wanted.

The dogs growled. The fishermen scuttled farther away.

Hanassa stared at each of them, keeping his eyes fixed upon theirs. One by one they returned his gaze, unblinking, unthinking, unable to resist his commands. "You will take me across the river to the village of the Coros. We will arrived unheralded. As soon as I have stepped ashore, you will return here to your meal and your dogs and forget that you saw me. You will obey me."

"We will obey," the men chorused.

The dogs continued to growl.

"*And* you will forget everything the Stargods have told you. Simurgh rules the skies. Alone and unchallenged," he added.

"We will forget the Stargods," the men repeated.

Hanassa smiled to himself. So easy. For now. All of his previous attempts to control the fisherfolk had been short-lived. They seemed impervious to his control through eye contact.

No matter. As long as they got him across the river dry and unscathed, he did not care about them. Warriors mattered; warriors who gave Hanassa power with each life they took. Only death mattered. Fishermen were cowardly folk who refused to test their mettle in battle. They could die in the Great Bay, unnoticed and unmourned.

At the edge of the village, Hanassa sniffed the air. Acrid smoke teased at his senses. Not the normal wood fires required for cooking, heat, and light. This smoke belonged to something alien.

He moved closer, still keeping to the shadows. Men fed newly turned pots and jugs into the pottery kiln. Their women sat nearby, happily painting finished pieces. The smell came from the coals beneath the clay oven.

A waste of time and a waste of life. The men should be training for war and the women . . . doing whatever women did so long as they cowered in Hanassa's presence.

"How dare you defile yourselves with this mundane chore! Only slaves and women may taint their hands with this work. Men should be warriors and only warriors," Hanassa roared as he stepped into clear view. Three women prostrated themselves before him. He might let them live.

Then a persistent clang bruised his ears. A blacksmith banged away at some project in the ruins of the old forge. The smell of his fire, burning hotter and brighter each time he worked the bellows to feed it air, nearly gagged Hanassa.

A poor imitation of the volcano beneath his mountain. Mere humans could never hope to attain the majesty of lava. Why did they even try?

He thrust aside the men who stood between him and the forge. Anger boiled in his stomach.

How dare these people defy his laws! If they thought him dead, they should revere him more, not defile his memory with . . . with work! He could not tolerate them making tools and vessels that would ease their lot in life. They had no life except what he allowed them.

The potters stumbled and dropped their clay jugs. They shattered with a most satisfying crash.

A string of curses followed the priest's progress through the village.

"Cease!" he ordered the young man banging away at a piece of bronze. The apprentice jumped away from the foot-operated bellows with a guilty look on his face.

"Cannot leave this," another boy spat out the words without looking up. All his attention remained on shaping the bronze on his anvil. A hoe! A stupid, useless hoe. Not even a sword or dagger.

Where was the smith? Both these boys were only old enough to be apprentices. But they stood strong and tall for their ages with bulging muscles gleaming with sweat from both their efforts and the heat of the forge.

"You are not fit to be warriors. Only warriors live among my people," Hanassa hissed. "You shall be my first sacrifices to Simurgh." He shook both his headdress and his staff in warning.

"We no longer have an altar to sanctify your sacrifices," Taneeo said quietly from directly behind Hanassa. "We have decided to change our ways to what they were before you became priest."

Out of the corner of his eye, Hanassa glimpsed the two smith apprentices sneaking away through the back of the forge. He needed to stop their flight. But he needed to deal with Taneeo and his rebellion first.

"How dare you!" Hanassa backhanded the boy.

He fell heavily on his ample bottom. With a couple of quick prods to his jaw, Taneeo gathered his feet beneath him to rise. Hanassa captured his gaze with his own and stared him down.

Taneeo remained on the ground. His eyes fixed upon Hanassa without blinking.

"You are now *my* personal slave, Taneeo. You obey me and only me. Without question. Without thought. All independence and defiance have left you. Forever," Hanassa chanted.

Taneeo said nothing. But he did not shift his gaze away from Hanassa or try to rise again.

"You did not die," Yaaccob said quietly from directly behind Hanassa. The war chief stood in front of the temple, arms crossed, legs braced slightly apart. He looked ready to withstand a physical blow from his High Priest.

Hanassa knew he could not fell this man with a single blow as he could Taneeo and a host of others. Nor could he control the war chieftain with mere eye contact.

"The Stargods have stolen much from you. Only I can show you how to regain all that you have lost and more." Hanassa stepped up to the only man who stood between him and control.

"Once conquered, the secrets and wealth of the Stargods will be yours, Yaaccob," Hanassa continued his persuasion. "Your son will return to you and your daughter will become my wife. Your grandsons will rule the Coros as both warriors and priests." Hanassa applied his cunning and guile to Yaaccob's greed. "You will follow me because my way is the only way to power!"

His control held.

CHAPTER 28

HESTIIA TAPPED DORAAN on the shoulder. "I will sit and spin for a while. You should rest and eat." She motioned the newest woman of the village away from the circle of women who were spinning and weaving. They had gathered near the central fire pit to enjoy a day without rain while they worked. The growing village needed many skeins of wool to weave protective clothing for the coming winter and the cool rainy days that still came between short dry spells.

Doraan nodded mutely and sidled away. She never raised her eyes, never spoke, never lifted her head or straightened her back.

Hestiia rested a friendly hand upon the woman's shoulder. Doraan cringed away from the touch. Any other day, Hestiia would have followed her, tried to talk to her, reassure her. No one would beat her here. Or starve her. Or rape her. She was no longer a slave. But not today. Hestiia had too much to think about. She reached for Doraan's dropped spindle. Her shaking hands missed the spindle by half a hand's width. She took a deep breath, squeezed her eyes shut, and tried again. This time her vision cleared enough to coordinate with her hand.

So many layers of color surrounded everything, she had trouble finding the core. Yellows, blues, greens, red, and every shade between piled one atop the other, in a different order for each object. The colors blazed brighter than any hue she had ever seen before. The yammat in full bloom paled in comparison. The leaves and sap of the silver bloodwood tree looked like two drops of blood diluted in a bowl of water next to the colors she saw.

The familiar activity of dropping and retracting the spindle gave her time to think. Cautiously, she raised her eyes to watch the women in the circle. At first, the blinding colors confused her and made her eyes ache. Their gossip and laughter washed over her, as garbled and confused as her vision. A few words filtered through to her mind. They talked of the planting, of the plowing festival, of the Stargods and their miracles, of the blessing of the weather finally clearing.

Hestiia remained silent through it all. She watched and she studied, as Lord Kim watched and studied everything, trying to make sense of the unfamiliar. Gradually, she began to understand that when a woman talked about the virility of the Stargods (Lord Loki and Lord Konner had blessed many women since their arrival) the red in the layers of color around her head thickened. When Pryth talked of the spices in tonight's stew, green dominated.

Hestiia smiled to herself. The colors represented emotions. She took a deep breath and relaxed a little. Her spindle spun more easily.

Pryth looked at her sharply. Her brows came together in a deep puzzled frown. The old Rover woman set aside her own spinning. She made a show of admiring each woman's efforts as she worked her way around the circle to Hestiia's place. With a jerk of her head, she sent the two spinners on either side of Hestiia away. Then she sat, wiggled her ample bottom into a comfortable position, and stared at Hestiia.

"What ails you, child?" Pryth asked.

Under the weight of her stare, words spilled out of Hestiia's mouth.

"You never saw auras before this?" Pryth nodded her head, keeping her face neutral.

"Never."

"What is different, Hestiia? What has changed in your life recently."

"Nothing." Hestiia could not help blushing.

"Ah!" Pryth nodded. She picked up someone's discarded spindle and began to spin. The red cow wool shimmered with silver as it twisted and coiled. Blue and purple glowed along the edges.

"What do you see in the wool, Hestiia?" Pryth asked. Her voice never rose or changed. The wool continued to spin.

"The thread looks like . . . it looks like a baby's umbilical cord. And more."

"Your baby's umbilical. It carries the blue of the Stargods, your deep ocher, and the silver of the dragons."

"But . . ."

"You only slept with the man a few days ago. You should not be able to tell that you carry new life yet. But your mate is one of the Stargods. The magic shimmers in him, as brightly as it does in your baby's umbilical. The baby has magic. His magic flows within you now. Learn from it while you can. Learn so that you may teach your baby." Pryth stood up.

"How do you know this, Pryth?" Hestiia asked. She did not quite believe Pryth. But how else was she to explain the colors.

"I am a Rover by birth and by rearing. Rovers know many things. For many centuries, Rovers were the only people with true magic. Now the Stargods come with a different kind of magic. It may be stronger than all the Rovers put together. I cannot tell yet. You, Hestiia, are the mother of a new race of magicians. When you hear your baby's thoughts, come to me. You will need help understanding them." She walked away, humming a bright tune.

Hestiia continued to spin and think. The sun seemed to shine a little brighter. She smiled, quite happy with her life and her love. "You will stay with me now, Lord Kim. When I tell you this news, you will stay forever. Even your brothers will not be able to take you away from me."

Loki walked warily along the edge of the river. He whistled nonchalantly, as if he had nothing better to do than spend a lazy morning fishing. As he spent most mornings now that three fields had been plowed and seeded.

The rains only came every other day now rather than constantly.

Lately, Kim and Konner seemed to feel the weather in their bones long before it happened. Just like old men who had lived all their lives on bush planets, in tune with the seasons and the phases of the moon.

Loki shook his head in bewilderment. His brothers were as much creatures of space as they were any number of both bush and Civil planets. He thanked his own personal god that he had not been cursed with an affinity to any one place. Cyndi wanted a life on the busiest and most exciting Civil world they could find. He'd gladly spend a lifetime with her looking for that place. Mum had promised him the freedom and the money to do that once they completed this last run and they found Katie.

While Kim mucked around with dirt and seeds, Konner had taken the two adolescent apprentices and the blacksmith Fullmaan into the hills near the old sacrificial altar to dig out more iron and coal. The first efforts at making an iron hammer had failed miserably. The hammer had shattered with the first blow.

The boys had not explained why they had suddenly deserted the old village two nights ago.

No amount of persuasion or eavesdropping on their thoughts had made them talk about why they had left in such a hurry, or why they were so eager to go in search of new mineral deposits. Their silence was one of the reasons Loki prowled the riverbank today.

Konner would find the deposits with a scanner. He was still looking for a source of omniscium for the crystals as well. He planned to learn the visible signs of ore deposits. Then he'd teach his men to find them on their own.

Soon, Loki hoped and prayed, the new village would move from a bronze culture to an iron one. And none too soon. This first planting looked to be a poor crop, just enough to feed the village but not enough to produce a surplus.

Loki also wanted iron swords and pikes at hand for defense. He didn't trust the Coros and their offers of cooperation. The precipitate return of the smith's apprentices had only deepened Loki's suspicions. The Coros were warriors born and bred. They'd not remain peaceful for long. Their honor was at stake.

Loki knew it in his bones. Just as he knew the IMPs lay in wait back at the last jump point. No matter how long he and his brothers stayed here, the IMPs would wait. Their honor was at stake.

Besides, he'd seen the troubling signs of watchers. When he'd cut his fishing pole this morning, he'd made certain it was stout enough to serve as a quarterstaff. He also carried his fully charged stunner just in case he ran into someone bent on malicious mischief. Loki's normal path ended near his favorite fishing hole, east of the village. Still whistling, he pretended to scan the river, the tree that shaded him, and the sky. The skin on his back and the nape of his neck crawled as if hundreds of bugs had lighted on him. Someone watched.

He sensed a seething hatred. Thoughts and images remained a kaleidoscope of color without form or texture. Sooner or later the watcher would let something slip. Everyone did. Loki had learned that much in practiced eavesdropping before and after he had learned the extent of his talent.

With a casual shrug of his shoulders that repositioned his pole in his hands, he continued along the edge of the river. Periodically he cursed as he stubbed his toe or stepped on something hard or barbed. Everything seemed to penetrate his boots these past few days. But he would not stoop to the barbaric custom of going barefoot. Just because his brothers were in danger of going bush didn't mean he had to.

Loki strayed from the river's edge. But he kept the image of the river flowing a few meters to his left firmly in his mind. He made a show of walking around obstacles that weren't really there. But each time he allowed his footsteps to aim a little closer to the line of trees one hundred meters to his right. Still he projected the image of the river close to his feet to mask his true destination.

There! Something moved. Not much. Just enough to show him that one shadow had detached itself from a tree and shifted to another. Still whistling and maintaining his casual posture, he picked up his pace.

The shadow shifted again. Loki stopped and stared. He focused his eyes more keenly on the man-shape that stood just inside the tree line. At times like this he wished he could tap into the flywacket's senses as Hestiia claimed to. The way things worked on this planet, he wouldn't be surprised if the girl and the flying cat were mentally linked.

An image of a corpse, blood flowing from a gaping wound to the neck, flashed across Loki's mind. The coppery smell of hot blood collecting in a bronze basin assaulted his nose. Loki recoiled instantly. He stepped back, away from the shadow and the source of the mental image.

Shock robbed him of breath and made his heart stutter. The corpse was himself!

The shadowy image disappeared into the trees. Loki pressed his hands to his temples, trying to force the image from his mind. He dropped the fishing pole and forgot it.

Then an onslaught of other thoughts, other images, from two dozen minds sent him running back to the village.

Could it be? Finally! Konner checked the graph on his scanner a second time. The peaks looked right. If he read this correctly, he was looking at an entire boulder of omniscium, enough of the mineral to grow a whole family of crystals. A chunk this large was worth the entire planet's wheat crop for five years.

Relief swept away weeks of tension in his neck and shoulders. He was going home. In three months he'd be on his way back to Aurora. By the end of the year, he'd have custody of Martin.

He had to sit down a moment. The block of omniscium cradled his bum quite nicely.

Below him, Fullmaan and the boys chipped away at an iron-bearing rock, a task that would take forever with their stone and bronze tools. "Mining will be easier with steel tools," he promised them. They did not hear his quiet words. Just as well.

Before he went down there and extracted a load with his sonic cutter, he needed a chore up here for them. He, Kim, and Loki had agreed to keep technology secret from the locals. At times Konner cursed the decision. Like now, when he needed help with the heavy work. But when he remembered the filthy air of industrialized planets, the perpetual staleness of recycled air that never got totally clean, and the taste of tanked food, he applauded the decision.

Quickly, he examined his hunk of omniscium. It seemed to be a free-standing rock. He pushed at it with his foot. It shifted a little. Too heavy to pick up and carry down this mountain.

Konner whipped out his sonic cutter and sliced the rock into four neat quarters. The work of perhaps five minutes. Then he opened his pack and retrieved a meter-square tarp. He spread the whisper-thin and pliable plastic beside the closest hunk of rock.

He tried to lift the rock onto the tarp. No luck. Too heavy. So he rocked it, twisting it a little with each shove. At last the thing dropped on its outer shell and rolled halfway onto the tarp. The newly cut faces lay exposed to view.

It should show a multitude of crystals embedded in a composite of six other inert types of rock. Not that any rock on this planet was totally inert. His experience with Petram in the middle of the wheat field had taught him that.

Konner saw only raw granite with a few streaks of marble running through it. No crystals. No omniscium. Frantic, he whipped out his scanner. The screen showed a resonance graph of granite. At the surface of the rock he saw strong traces of omniscium; traces only. He slammed his fist into the scanner. The graph jumped again, showing uranium.

"The batteries! Stupid. I haven't charged the solar batteries. No wonder I'm getting anomalous readings." He sank down hard onto a companion rock. Sharp jabs to his backside, back, and thighs jolted him upright again. None of the nearby boulders was shaped to accommodate the human anatomy. Nothing on this friggin' planet accommodated him.

And he was stuck here. Forever.

Worse, his son was stuck with Melinda.

CHAPTER 29

"**T**HEY'RE COMING TO KILL US!" Loki shouted as he pelted into the village center.

Kim looked up from a complex discussion with the ancient herdsmen and Raaskan about breeding possibilities of their livestock.

"Who?" Kim steadied Loki before he collapsed in a heap by the central fire pit. His brother panted heavily and looked ghostly pale.

"Yaaccob and his men. They are led by the ghost of Hanassa."

Raaskan immediately jumped up and began shouting orders to everyone within hearing distance. The women gathered the few children and scuttled toward the shelter of the river.

"Only two of you take the children! Cut loose the fishing raft and take shelter among the islands downriver," Raaskan yelled at them. "The rest come back here. We need every hand to repel our enemies."

The women stopped and looked at him in confusion and horror.

"Simurgh may forbid women to defend themselves, but the Stargods do not," Kim informed them all. "Take the shovels, boil water to throw in your enemies' faces. Digging sticks, fishing poles. Anything can be used as a weapon."

A big grin lit Hestiia's face. She dashed inside their hut and returned a heartbeat later carrying a primitive bow and a quiver full of arrows.

Her glowing strength and beauty filled Kim with a swelling pride. He loved her so much in that moment that he hated the thought of leaving her—even for Mum. He was willing to die to protect her.

"We will fight side by side," he told her around a quick kiss to her cheek.

A wall of sound roared toward them like waves racing before a storm. Two dozen men, screaming their bloodlust, burst from the tree line. They stopped about fifty meters from the villagers while they shouted insults and challenges. They rattled their weapons and made a fierce display of intimidation. Masses of uncombed hair about their heads and faces turned them into the howling demons of childhood nightmares.

Behind them, young men beat a thunderous tattoo on their drums. The vibrations coursed through Kim's bare feet. His heart hammered a discordant counter beat that set his teeth on edge. He needed to run away.

He had to make a stand for his people.

Kim swallowed deeply, caught up the pointed stick he'd used to draw in the dirt, and took his place between the invaders and his village.

Hestiia stood at his left, bowstring pulled back to her ear, a large flint arrowhead aimed at the attackers. Yaakke took his position to Kim's right, short sword at the ready. The two new warriors arranged themselves among the former slaves. Loki stood at the far end. He held his stunner in his right hand. But in his dominant left hand he carried a long pole with a huge flint point lashed to the end.

Kim didn't bother to ask where his eldest brother found the spear. As long as it came in useful. As for the stunner? One or two long blasts would drain the charge. Then it would be more useful thrown at the heads of the enemy.

Most of the women in the defensive line piled up rocks beside themselves. One of the men on the far left, beyond Hestiia, produced a sling as he limbered up his throwing arm.

Kim's mouth went dry, and his palms turned sweaty. He'd fought in brawls before without guilt. But this? The invaders had murder in their hearts. It was kill or be killed.

"I don't think I can do this," he muttered. "I can't kill another man. Not again. Even the IMPs don't try to kill in battle. They aim for engines and weapons arrays."

Then a spear hurtled toward him. He had no more time to think.

Hestiia loosed an arrow. Men charged at full speed. Rocks flew from the sling in rapid succession.

Kim's stick splintered under the first blow of a bronze sword. He ducked under the warrior's arm and head-butted him in the abdomen. His opponent staggered back with a grunt. His bronze helmet—little more than a bowl—went flying. Before he could get up again, Yaakke was upon him with sword and dagger.

Shock paralyzed Kim. Darkness closed in upon his senses. An *other* stood beside him, waiting. Waiting to be led to the other side. The other side of what?

He felt his knees crumple. The darkness faded. The *other* drifted away, content to find his own path.

"Not again. I don't know if I can do this again." Kim dropped his forehead to the ground, seeking an anchor for his reeling senses.

An arrow sped past his ear, digging into the dirt centimeters from his hand.

Kim dove for the rock pile. Rocks wounded. They hurt like hell when they hit your head or your gut. But they rarely killed with just one blow.

"I can do this," he told himself over and over. "I have to defend myself and my people."

Hestiia's next arrow embedded itself in the leather armor of an advancing warrior. The man grinned with malice as he raised his sword to take off her head.

The rock flew from Kim's hand before he had time to think or aim. It struck the grinning man in the temple, knocking his helmet askew. He staggered. Kim sent another rock flying toward his nose.

Blood spurted in all directions as the missile crushed bone and cartilage.

Hestiia had already aimed another arrow, this time for a vulnerable throat.

Kim grabbed rocks in each hand, closing all of his senses away from death. He had to concentrate on keeping his people alive. He looked around for a target. Everyone seemed engaged. No leftovers. Fair fight.

And then the ground tilted. The sky disappeared. The air became a wild clash of colors. Red in a myriad of hues. Brown, black, yellow swirled in a perverted imitation of the funnel of a tornado. Hot winds born in the furnaces of hell blasted him with dust. He stumbled backward, throwing up his arm to protect his eyes. His villagers huddled together.

The warriors pressed forward unhindered. The wind was at their backs.

And out of the color storm strode the wraithlike form of Hanassa. His skin, hair, clothing, even his staff were bleached translucent white in that eerie light.

The villagers screamed and ran. Kim grabbed Hestiia and followed them all toward the river.

Loki stood his ground. The hot wind washed waves and waves of fear over him. Fear stored in his soul from a lifetime of tales of hell and Satan.

But he did not believe in this Satan. He had read his mind. A human mind with emotions: greed, lust, power, jealousy, and anger. Above all else, anger. But also a keen intelligence that learned quickly and remembered fine details with amazing precision.

While Hanassa was still within the tunnel mouth of this bizarre vortex, Loki aimed his stunner and fired one long continual blast. He blocked out the screams of his people. He resisted the urge to flee from the warriors charging forward. All of his concentration focused on keeping that beam of energy aimed at Hanassa's heart.

All the while a voice taunted him. *Your mortal weapons cannot kill a ghost!*

But his mother's training was older, more firmly implanted in his mind. "In the name of St. Bridget, I reject this shade from the otherworld," he shouted over the din of battle and retreat.

Hanassa tumbled backward under the continuous stream of energy from the stunner. He grabbed hold of the collar of his apprentice who stood in the back ranks of warriors and drummers. The boy fought his master with flailing arms and thrashing legs.

The swirling mass of colors narrowed, then reversed.

Hanassa kept a tight grip on the boy. The vortex dragged them both backward.

The stunner fizzled. The tunnel mouth closed upon the two struggling figures, and the wind died. Only a lingering waft of sulfur remained as evidence of the apparition.

Loki sank to his knees in exhaustion.

The villagers halted their retreat.

Without the hot wind propelling them, or Hanassa leading them, the warriors looked about in confusion.

Yaakke raised his sword once more and engaged the nearest invader. The other villagers followed suit.

Loki could only watch. A small circle of reality seemed to surround him. All else was just an ugly dream, surreal. It did not and could not touch him.

Warriors retreated.

The battle wound down.

"But we'll never know if Hanassa truly lives or not," Loki muttered to himself. "I don't think I killed him. Next time. I swear, next time I will kill him."

"Don't say that, Loki. Don't even think it. You won't want to live with yourself if you ever kill a man," Kim admonished him with Mum's inflection and authority.

"Where'd it go?" Konner ran the last kilometer to the battle site. He and his apprentice smiths had watched it from afar, hurrying as fast as they could, hoping they'd arrive in time to help. Fullmaan limped along in their wake, falling farther behind with every step.

"Where did what go?" Kim asked. He and Hestiia bent over the moaning figure of one of their warriors. Pryth tended to two other injured men.

Loki seemed too far out of it to talk. Was he hurt? Konner touched his older brother's neck to check for a pulse. Too fast, but strong and regular. No overt signs of blood. He decided Loki could wait.

"The wormhole. What happened to the wormhole?" Konner asked again. "Do you know how long scientists throughout the galaxy have tried to find a natural one? No one has even come close to creating one. Theories only. Speculation on what it would look like. And that thing looked like the theories!" He walked toward the line of trees, determined to find evidence that the vortex in space and time truly existed. If only he could resurrect it, solve it, re-create it, he could eliminate the problems of jumping vast distances in space with delicately balanced crystals forming a barely safe envelope.

With a wormhole he could be back on Aurora within days instead of months. He could stay here a little longer and still claim his son in time.

"Heat, cyclonic winds. What else went into creating this thing?" He sniffed and grimaced. "Sulfur. Lots and lots of sulfur."

"We just fought a battle here and nearly lost, Konner," Kim reminded him.

Konner pretended not to hear him. He had to find out more about that wormhole. Something about the shadows between those two trees formed an arch . . .

"We have wounded who will need all three of us to perform a healing," Kim continued. "Not to mention a brother trying to imitate catatonia."

The shadow shifted. Konner lost the scent of sulfur. All trace of the wormhole vanished with it. He shrugged, trying to let his brother know he didn't really care. But he knew he'd be back tomorrow. He'd search every inch of those woods for the wormhole.

"So, you find the dragongate fascinating," Pryth said quietly behind him.

"Dragongate? You know of this phenomenon?" Konner turned to face her. Out of the corner of his eye he noticed the villagers organizing first aid and comfort for each other. He wasn't needed until Kim decided to do something interesting with the more severely wounded.

Pryth shrugged noncommittally.

"Tell me about it, Pryth. You have to tell me everything you know." He shook her shoulders. "This is important."

"More important than finding yourself?" She seemed unmoved by his desperation.

Konner released her and took a step back. "I know who and what I am. I've always known."

"Then why did holding rock Petram aloft with your mind come as a surprise?"

"Because . . . because there is something about this planet that augments psi talents. I did not expect it."

"Did you know of your . . . your psi talent, your magic before you came here?"

"I . . . I . . . We have no dragons where I come from." He didn't know why he associated the dragons with his newly realized telekinetic abilities. But then, dragons and flywackets were the most obvious difference between this world and the familiar planets of home.

Why was he arguing with Pryth about it anyway?

Kim waved for him to join the villagers.

"Then look to the dragons for answers." Pryth turned abruptly and retraced her steps to the site of the battle. "When you understand the dragons, you will understand yourselves. Tell that to your brothers."

CHAPTER 30

◆—▬—·—◆—·—▬—◆

"MY LORD KONNER!" Fullmaan ran up to Konner, panting. He grinned from ear to ear as he brandished a small adze still warm from the forge. "We have done it! We have solved the problem."

"Which problem?" Konner asked, refusing to allow his blacksmith's enthusiasm to raise his own hopes. They'd had too many disappointments. He'd missed something important in his reading about smithcraft. Something that left all their attempts at ironwork brittle and near useless.

He was stuck here on this lost planet too many light-jumps from his son. Days passed and nothing happened but futile battles and worthless experiments.

"It is the coal!" Fullmaan continued. "The coal is impure when we bring it from the sea and from the land."

"Let me see that!" Konner grabbed the adze away from Fullmaan. He grasped the haft where a wooden handle should slide through to give him better leverage. With little pressure the tool dug into a nearby stack of firewood. A neat slice of wood peeled away from the downward curve of his swing. The point remained sharp and intact. He swung again and again. Each time, a long curl of wood separated from the log. Konner worked the tool as long as his shoulders could maintain a strong swing. He'd been working the forge for nearly a month. He had built a good deal of muscle as a result.

When the first log was reduced to a pile of shavings, he began on the next and the next. The adze held.

At last he looked up at Fullmaan with a wide grin. "How?" he asked, unable to voice the emotions coagulating in his throat. If the answer was impurities in the coal, he could only blame his own stupidity. Modern texts *presumed* that mining practices would purify the minerals. They never said how. Machines handled that dirty little task.

"When we arrived at the end of the battle, I started a fire in the forge—in case we needed to heat knives for amputation." Both men shuddered at the primitive surgery that was often the only way to save a life. "But Pryth called me away for other chores. So I threw a handful of sand upon the burning coal to put out the fire. I did not want to burn down the fine forge you built for me. Then, between helping with the wounded and celebrating our victory and a few dances with Doraan . . ." The big blacksmith blushed at the budding relationship he had formed with the timid woman who had escaped from a distant village and crawled toward the hope of a new life with the Stargods. "I did not get back to the forge for two days. I presume the sand I threw on the fire was not enough to put it out. Nor was the light rain that dampened the coal. The coal smoldered and smoldered. The smoke it gave off was—dirty. Lady Hestiia called it to my attention, but I had no time to get back to it. Then this morning I worked the bellows a little to clear off the smoke. The flames climbed high, the smoke turned white and the tool I made is strong and clean." Fullmaan ran out of breath.

Konner couldn't find any air to make a reply. He just grinned.

Finally he broke through the lump in his throat. "Let's go make something else."

"A sword for you, Lord Konner?"

"No, a plow for my brother, Lord Kim. And a hook and swinging arm to hang the stewpot over the fire. Pryth will like that. We aren't in the business of killing." A chill ran up his spine. Five dead bodies—three of the attackers, two of their own—along with ten wounded had brought home to him just how painful, messy, and *final* a fight could be. He didn't ever want to be a part of one again.

Something else to teach his son. When he got off this planet once and for all.

The simple tools he made for the village would give him practice before tackling the more intricate work of casings for the thrusters.

"But surely you will need knives? Knives are tools," Fullmaan insisted.

"Yes, we can make knives, long and short. We can make scythes and rakes and anything else we can dream up."

"The Stargods make dreams come true."

"No, each person must make his own dreams come true." He dreamed often of his son. He'd seen Martin just before Mum had called him away from the junior camp where Konner worked as a counselor and Marty attended during the long break between school terms. The boy had his mother's medium brown hair, but the O'Hara midnight-blue eyes had bred true. At thirteen he looked as if he'd inherited the O'Hara height and strong chin as well.

Each year, Konner spent weeks undoing the corruption Melinda instilled in her son—the love of money over honor, ethics, and justice. Any action was justifiable so long as it netted Melinda more money.

Martin belonged with his father.

"Come, we have a lot of work to do. I've a ship to repair." Konner practically dragged Fullmaan back to the forge.

Twice now the forces of darkness have eaten the moon since the humans fought a battle. Always the moon recovers. Not so the humans. The ones who call themselves the Coros sulk and complain and do no work. Hanassa seems to have abandoned them.

But I know my littermate. He leaves nothing unfinished. He plots and plans in his lair. I would know what. He no longer shares his thoughts with me, and I cannot penetrate the depth of the mountain that shields him. The web of life that channels our thoughts has a gaping hole in it around that cursed mountain. Without the web of blue light that holds the universe together, Hanassa and his evil can grow in power.

The dragon nimbus must stop him. The others prefer to watch and wait. They will never DO anything to interfere. I must. But I do not know how.

Hanassa marched along the strand toward Yaaccob's village, leaving behind the fishing fleet and the surly boatmen who respected nothing but the sea and their dogs.

He had strengthened the false memories he gave them this time so they would not remember ferrying him and Taneeo across the river on this trip or any other.

After eavesdropping on the Stargods, Hanassa knew that the strongest and most feared tribe of all the Coros were as nothing. Thousands upon thousands of humans would follow the Stargods here.

Unless Hanassa eliminated the three Stargods here and now.

Twice, they had wounded him gravely. An ordinary man would have died from either of those injuries.

But Hanassa was not an ordinary man.

At the battle, Yaaccob and his warriors had rushed into the attack too soon, too filled with righteous fervor. They had depleted their energy before Hanassa appeared as a ghost to strike terror into the hearts of the escaped slaves so that they would flee.

Now Yaaccob's mighty warriors sulked at their first defeat. Mighty warriors? Bah! Spoiled children needing discipline. A new round of sacrifices would put the fear of Simurgh into their hearts and make them obey.

This time their blood would sanctify the dim recesses within the temple made of bloodwood. This time his victims would see only shadow and flame as the light of life went out of their eyes. No more the reassuring sun or moon to light them on their way to the void between the planes of existence.

Hanassa did not care for their comfort or their next existence. Death gave him power. Death made him invincible. Death gave him control over the people.

Hanassa had had to retreat to his caves within the volcano to retrieve his ritual knife. The one the Stargods had plunged into his back. The one that must be the weapon of death for his sacrifices.

The strange light from the magic rock wielded by the Stargods had disrupted Hanassa's portal to the land of the Coros. It was a rare portal that only appeared at noon on the day of the dark of the moon. He had timed the battle for that portal. Now it was gone. The closest access to the Coros was the clearing north of the river and west of the village. He could travel anywhere else in the world in an instant. But to Coronnan he had to walk and he had to deal with ungrateful fishermen to get across the river.

Taneeo trailed listlessly behind him, carrying a heavy pack of supplies. Bruises marred his face and covered his ribs. He had lost the ugly flab around his middle and his face had taken on a gaunt look that made him almost handsome. His resilience saved his life. If the boy failed in any of his duties to Hanassa, he would be the next sacrifice.

Hanassa must walk warily now, make certain Yaaccob and his villagers did not see his approach. He must appear among them suddenly without explanation. They must continue to believe him a ghost, an immortal who could not be harmed.

Soon the land would rebel against the new iron tools of the Stargods. The omens ordained this year as a year of the curse of the broga. Many years had passed without a single victim falling to the diseases their ancestors had soaked into the soil. A decade ago the curse of the broga had taken every fifth person in all the villages of the Coros and those they had conquered. This year the curse would rise again. The frogs sang of it.

And when it did, Hanassa planned to be ready to fell the newcomers and reclaim his slaves for the sacrificial altar.

Hanassa grew warm with pleasure at that thought. He paused a moment to glory in his vision of the future.

Sounds of fishermen making their way across the stony strand toward the village and their supper made Hanassa step into the shadows and watch. The villagers must not see him until he was ready.

Taneeo, the coward, scurried as far away along the embankment as he could. Away from Hanassa, but not far enough to escape. The worthless slave did not have the ambition or the courage to escape.

Hanassa found invisibility in stillness and shadow. He watched many long moments while the men laughed and told tall tales of the fish that got away.

So far they did not seem to remember having brought Hanassa across the river on this or any other day when he had spied upon the Coros and the newcomers. The dogs sniffed warily in his direction.

They passed on, into the village. Hanassa smelled their suppers cooking.

"At sunset when the light is uncertain, I will enter the village," he told Taneeo. "I must ease my back, slave. I have walked long and far." He did not like the weakness the Stargods had inflicted upon him. If the wound in his back would ever heal properly he would no longer require his slave to tend to his needs and his aching body.

Hanassa's spirit longed for the peace and quiet of his cave; for the rich smell of sulfur. There, the noise of the web of life the dragons prized so highly could not reach him. In the quiet dark he could think and plan in solitude. Soon . . .

He paid no attention to Taneeo's fatigue and weakness from hauling the pack for many a mile.

Hanassa smiled. He would force Taneeo to slit the throat of the next public sacrifice. The boy must overcome his weakness of mind and spirit or he would never survive.

The first sacrifice must be made by Hanassa in the dark and within the privacy of the temple, without an altar or his apprentice. He needed the blood for power to heal himself.

Soon he would no longer be forced to lean heavily upon his staff when he walked any distance. By this time tomorrow the Coros would cease to cower in fright. Tomorrow at noon he would gather them all in the center of the temple to watch while Taneeo sacrificed the rebellious potters. He wished he had captured the blacksmiths as examples. Big strong men with plenty of blood to wet the altar. He must teach the Coros to obey him and only him.

CHAPTER 31

HESTIIA MOPPED HER BROW in the morning sunshine. The day seemed unusually warm for this early in the season. The Solstice approached and the rains finally eased.

Despite the rain, the Stargods organized the work so skillfully, brooking no argument or slackers, that every chore seemed finished almost as soon as it was begun. The entire village rejoiced daily that the Stargods had come to rescue them from Hanassa and Simurgh. They made a point of placing offerings of thanksgiving upon the rock Petram in the center of the fields; flowers, a bit of the first fish caught, or sometimes a precious bone bead or other ornament.

Fertility blessed the village and the soil. Nearly every woman showed signs of quickening after the dances around the festival pylon.

She listened to the frogs sing from the marsh. A welcome sound that had been missing for too many long dry summers. The frogs sang in celebration of the rain and the fertility it brought. Frogs were sacred and could not be eaten even in the leanest of years.

Since the village had defeated the Coros, more and more people had joined the village of the Stargods. They now had three fields plowed and planted. They had pushed the cultivation right up to the edge of the marsh. The huge rock that had nearly killed Raaskan sat proudly undisturbed in the center of their bounty.

Pride filled Hestiia. Though Kim had not returned to her bed, she knew he held a fierce affection for her. And even now her belly had begun to swell with new life. The other women looked at her with knowing smiles and winks as they, too, swelled. Three swore that Lord Loki had planted his seed within them. Two more named Lord Konner as the father of their children. Only Hestiia could claim Lord Kim as mate.

Only Hestiia knew for certain that her child carried the magic of the Stargods in his blood. Pryth asked her daily if the child spoke to her. So far Hestiia heard nothing unusual. The bright halos of colors around every object she saw made more sense to her now. People and animals had very bright colors and deeper layers. Grass, trees, flowers, and the sprouting crops had smaller, paler auras. Rocks and dirt reflected only a single layer of yellow or white light. The huge rock Petram, though, shone white, yellow, and pale, pale blue.

The rock was alive in a dim sort of way.

Hestiia threw her handful of weeds into the basket. One of the disadvantages to the wet year was the number of weeds that sprang up each morning after the night's rainfall. These noxious leaves were not fit to eat. She would add them to the compost heap at the edge of the field.

She sneezed repeatedly, then coughed. A nagging problem she had taken pains to hide from her all too observant husband. He and his brothers had too many worries already. They should not fuss over a minor illness that would pass in a few days. Surely by the Solstice she would feel like dancing again with Lord Kim.

Only two handfuls of days until the Summer Solstice and already thick green shoots of wheat poked through the rich soil. Never had she seen a field respond to plow and seed with such bounty.

As she scanned the field with joy, her gaze fell upon Petram. The thin blue layer of light at the edge of its halo shimmered in the sunshine and seemed to spread. It flowed out in a network of lines, like a spiderweb at dawn with the dew still upon it.

She placed one foot on a thin tendril. Perhaps it tickled her sole, perhaps she merely imagined it.

"Are you talking to me?" she asked the baby within her.

Nothing changed.

Hestiia shrugged. "Not yet, little one. You are just showing me new things."

A long-haired brown hopper nosed out of the wild plains grasses at the edge of the field.

"Hoo! Away there," she shouted at the creature as it nibbled the succulent new growth.

The audacious hopper wiggled its nose and twitched its long ears as it stared at her a moment before continuing to eat the fresh stalk of grain down to the roots.

"Dragons take you and your entire burrow for dinner," she screamed. She waved her arms wildly and ran after it.

Her feet moved sluggishly and the heat weighed her down. Her vision narrowed, black night seeming to come at her from the sides, leaving only a thin blue line directly in front of her eyes. All the while the hopper ate daintily amidst a too bright light.

She held back the cough that threatened to tear her chest apart.

At last, she came within two very long paces of the hopper. The creature wiggled its nose one last time and returned to the tall grasses.

"You will not disappear on me quite so easily," Hestiia murmured as she launched herself after it. Her mouth nearly watered at the thought of fresh hopper for dinner. She was getting tired of fish and venison.

And then she nearly gagged at the thought of hot blood spurting from the hopper's death wound. Her jaw ached with clenching it so tightly.

The land seemed to rush up to greet her as her hands closed around the throat of the hopper. It squirmed and squealed in distress. She squeezed her hands tighter. Her prey kicked back with strong legs and sharp claws.

Blood oozed from the scratches it left on her arms. She wrenched her hands, breaking the neck of her dinner.

And promptly vomited her breakfast.

Just the baby upsetting her system. This happened to many women in the early days of pregnancy.

Strange that it should not hit her until nearly three moons after the conception.

Triumphant glee erupted from her throat. But the only sound that emerged was a painful croak. Her throat hurt as if she had strangled herself. And her teeth remained firmly clamped shut.

Gentian swooped down and landed beside her. He licked the blood from her arm, emitting a soothing purr.

"And where were you when I needed you to keep the wild things out of the crops?" She wanted to say it. Tried hard to say it, but her jaw would not open.

Her face grew hotter. Her arms weaker. Maybe she just needed food. What was left of the boiled grains and fresh brambleberries from her breakfast spilled over the wild grasses. She had no appetite. Only weakness.

Still holding the hopper, she gathered her knees beneath her. Her back seemed heavy. Had Gentian climbed atop her? No, the flywacket mewed beside her. Concern radiated from him. Her vision split, making two, no, four, possibly five of him. She shook her head, blinked, and looked again. Gentian resolved into a single creature. The layers of bright light that surrounded him flashed and turned white. Too bright. She closed her eyes against the glare.

After a moment, she tried to rise again. This time she dropped the hopper before pulling her elbows back to brace herself. The effort sent her head reeling. The spinning ground rose up to greet her face again.

Kim kept a wary eye on the wild bull. The ruddy long-horned beast rested in the shade of a lone tree, chewing his cud. But he had grown cautious of the villagers. His gaze fixed each of them with wary concern.

"I know I stole some of your ladies," Kim murmured to Big Red. Its shaggy coat was darker and thicker than any in the O'Hara clan. The reddish sunlight reflected off it—something crystalline in the soil that permeated the grass and therefore the grazing animals? In certain lights the herd looked like a sunset moving across the plains.

"How would you like to have one of those ladies back again, for a while, Big Red?" Kim continued to coax. He had no hope that the bull understood a word he said, but the soothing tones felt good.

The bull flicked his gaze and his tail to the right where Raaskan approached. Then he flicked left, observing two other men. He shifted his weight, preparing to rise.

"We could probably catch one of the lesser bachelors wandering around the fringes of your herd of ladies, Big Red," Kim continued. "But I want only the strongest and most enduring bull to service *my* ladies."

Big Red swallowed and heaved himself upright. He looked around once more and lowered his head, aiming those massive horns directly at Kim. He must sense that the center of the closing circle represented a threat to his freedom.

In the distance a cow bellowed.

Big Red reared his head up again and worked his nostrils.

"You see, one of my ladies has come into heat. She wants you and only you, Big Red." Kim chanced a glance behind him to where Pryth and Doraan kept firm grips on the halter of the young cow who had come into her first season—probably out of season.

Hestiia had wanted to come today, but she hadn't looked well for days. She'd tried to hide her sneezing and coughing, but Kim had heard her and grown concerned. Doraan didn't look so good either, pale and listless, lacking appetite and saying little. But then she rarely spoke and hadn't recovered from the abuse of her enslavement. Her grim expression relaxed only under the gentle gaze of Fullmaan the blacksmith.

She'd sneezed and coughed several times today, too. Not good.

Doraan had no skills. She was too thin, bruised, and scarred from her hard life as a slave. Pryth feared leaving her alone, lest her guilt and fear overwhelm her will to survive. How she ever had the courage to run away, no one had been able to pry from her trembling lips.

Kim would have chosen any other person to help them get the bull and their cow together. But everyone else was busy. The forge, fishing, hunting, gathering, weaving, pottery, fashioning clothing, and refreshing mattresses with dry grass, cooking, and caring for the children took up all the villagers' time. Everyone had a task assigned to his or her strongest skills.

As the unofficial doctor in the village—paired with Pryth as a midwife/nurse—Kim had checked both Hestiia and Doraan for specific symptoms of malaria. The nearby wetlands were probably breeding mosquitoes and other nasty bugs by the millions. He didn't know enough about local diseases to guess what else could ail them.

Pryth looked worried, too. But she said nothing.

Back home, infant inoculations protected everyone from all but the worst ailments bred by recycled air and tanked food.

"He has noticed the cow," Raaskan said softly to his compatriots.

"I'm going to ease out of his way," Kim said. "As he starts moving toward his lady love, let's come up behind him and slip the harness over his neck. He should have only one thing on his mind." They were being very audacious, trying to capture the bull for breeding. What corral would hold him?

Raaskan snorted. "That is all this fellow ever has on his mind." He nodded toward Big Red with good humor.

Indeed, the big bull already showed signs of excitement.

His first three steps were slow and steady. Eyes and tail still flicked back and forth with continued wariness.

Pryth and Doraan backed off, leaving the lowing cow tethered by two stout ropes to a good-sized sapling.

The bull picked up speed. His biological imperative overrode his learned caution.

Kim and Raaskan ran after Red with ropes at the ready.

Big Red skidded to a halt beside his lady, leaving long gouges in the turf from his hooves. They engaged in a brief mating ritual—more an acknowledgment of each other than a real courtship. Then the bull mounted her with a delicacy surprising in such a huge beast.

Doraan put her hand to her mouth in horror, backing away from the lustful bull. Her eyes grew wide, the dilated irises crowded out most of the white, filling with tears. She grew even paler as she coughed uncontrollably.

Kim and Raaskan both made sure they fastened their ropes firmly around the bull before turning their attention to the woman. They expected her to crumple in a faint. Instead she turned and ran. At the edge of the swamp she stopped. Still without uttering a sound she threw herself into the murky water.

"Shite!" Kim cursed. He handed off his rope to Raaskan and dashed after the girl. What now?

He could only guess that her slavery had been a long endurance of rape, beatings, and starvation. In his heart he cursed the unfeeling brutes who had used her so. Even Big Red was more considerate of his mate than Doraan's captors had been.

Rotting vegetation clung to Kim's ankles as he waded after Dorann's alarmingly limp body.

He almost yanked his hand away from her wrist when he felt the fever that burned her.

"Pryth!" He called for help. Grimly, he overcame his instinctive fear and repulsion as he hauled the girl free of the muck. "Pryth, we've got a problem."

"Silly child. She has not had time yet to learn she is safe here. No man will touch her without her permission." The aging Rover woman met him at the edge of firm land. She waddled as if her ankles ached. Her arms hung limply at her sides, and her eyes looked overly bright. She sneezed abruptly.

"St. Bridget! Have you got the fever, too?" Kim waded out of the swamp with an unconscious Doraan in his arms.

"I believe I do," Pryth said weakly. She sat abruptly. "If I had been thinking clearly, I would have noticed. But the fever . . . Oh, dear. This will not do. This will not do at all." The last came out in a hoarse whisper as her jaw clamped shut.

CHAPTER 32

✦ —— · —— ✦ —— · —— ✦

HOURS LATER, Kim stumbled into his cabin. His brothers awaited him. "I don't like this," he said as he threw himself onto his pallet. "People have been getting sick all day. I've never seen anything like it." He wiped sweat from his brow with the edge of his shirt—he'd ripped the ragged sleeves off days ago. Konner had confiscated the rags for some arcane use in his precious forge.

"How many?" Loki asked. He looked up from mending the soles of his boots with a strip of hide and strands of sinew for thread.

Kim wondered why he didn't just give up on the flimsy things and go barefoot like the rest of them. He could at least resort to moccasins if his feet were too tender.

"Five down so far. Three more don't look so good."

"All with the same symptoms?" Konner came alert. He'd been reading something with great concentration. Until now. "Raaskan reported that we lost the bull. No one could hold him once he'd finished with the cow."

Kim ignored the last statement. He'd suspected they'd never hold Big Red for long. "Symptoms: coughing and sneezing followed by fever, muscle aches, the usual kind of flu symptoms, but their jaws are locking. We can't even force water into them."

"What does Pryth say about it?" Loki set aside his half-mended boot. Deep furrows creased his brow.

"Not much. She's sick, too. But her last words called it the curse of the broga."

"What the hell is a broga?" Konner asked

Kim could only shrug his shoulders. Pryth couldn't talk right now to answer that question. "This curse apparently reoccurs frequently but without pattern. Casualties can be anywhere from two individuals to twenty percent of the population."

"This planet is underpopulated as it is!" Loki protested. "We've got to do something."

"What?" Both Kim and Konner nearly shouted at him.

"Maybe we can heal them like we did Raaskan after the rock fell on him. And the wounded after the battle."

"I don't know." Kim shook his head. "With the others, I had specific injuries that needed correcting, bones to shove into place, blood vessels to mend. This is different. How do I root out all of the bacteria or viruses or whatever that cause this thing?"

"Could we manufacture an antibiotic?" Konner asked.

"Using what as a base?"

"Chemicals?"

"Like what? We have precious little available to us from ship's stores. We're smugglers—not doctors."

"If only we had access to the original colonists' records. If they encountered this thing, maybe they knew how to fix it." Konner began to pace, running his hands through his hair and beard.

"Or maybe this is the disease that reduced their numbers to a bare minimum and threw them back into the bronze age."

"You'd think, if that were the case, that some trace of technology or records would have been secreted away, revered and protected as holy artifacts." Loki sat next to Kim. Excitement warred with worry on his expression. "So far, we've found no references to the original settlers in their folklore, or their customs. St. Winship of the Minstrels knows we've heard enough of their folklore around the campfire every night. But we know this planet was partially terraformed by humans. They had to have had heavy machinery, fuel cells, computers, and botany labs. They left nothing aboard the colony ship. Where is all that tech now?"

"Dragons only know." Konner threw up his hands, adopting an expression and a gesture from the locals.

"Dragons only know," Kim repeated softly. "Maybe the dragons do know. We've got to talk to a dragon."

"How?" Loki asked. "And where? They aren't exactly as common as mosquitoes and flies. And we don't know if they are sentient. Not for sure anyway."

"I'll ask Hestiia. I haven't seen her all day." His heart warmed with the thought of a few private moments with her. "Maybe Gentian can fly around and spot a dragon for us."

"She hasn't been looking well lately," Loki remarked. "Maybe I should try communicating with Gentian and let her rest. Don't know how this village would function without her."

"Even Loki noticed that she's not well," Kim said quietly. The brief observation scared him. Scared him from the roots of his hair down to his bare toes. Loki usually noticed only the most obvious about other people. Nothing about them was as important as himself.

But Hestiia was sick.

Kim ran through the village, looking briefly in each little cabin for Hestiia. No one had seen her since early morning.

All work seemed to have ground to a halt as the villagers stood in tight groups carrying on hushed conversations. Those conversations ceased abruptly as Kim passed. And then the villagers turned their backs on him.

What?

He wanted to scream at them that the disease was not his fault.

Before he could vent his frustration, Gentian landed at his feet with a great deal of flapping wings and squawking noise.

The villagers backed farther away from Kim, crossing and flapping their wrists in a ward against evil.

"Where is she?" Kim asked the flying cat. He looked directly into the animal's eyes, hoping he was telepathic enough to communicate with Gentian.

Gentian continued squawking and fluttering his wings in agitation.

"Show me," Kim demanded. He stooped down closer to get to eye level with Gentian.

"Merawk!" the animal protested.

But Kim had a flash of the edge of a field where it met tall grasses. And Hestiia lying facedown in the dirt, a dead, rabbitlike creature beside her.

He took off running. Gentian flew overhead, squeaking for him to hurry.

"Why did you wait so long?" Kim asked the flying cat. "You could have come for me when she first fell."

Gentian flashed him an image of laving Hestiia's face and arms with his tongue; of sheltering her from the hot sun with his wing; of being so frightened he did not know what to do.

"I'm scared, too, Gentian."

"Not so fast. Did you bring anything to help her?" Loki asked, running right beside him.

"Like what?" Kim hated wasting breath on talking when he could put it into running. He increased his speed.

"We've got basic analgesics in the first aid kit," Konner added. He kept pace with Kim while Loki lagged behind slightly. "Alcohol baths to bring down the fever and broad spectrum antibiotics."

"Only a few. Not enough for everybody," Kim countered. He had to slow down as he leaped off the beaten path to the verge of tall grasses. Near the edge. Gentian had been certain she was near the edge. But which edge, which field?

Gentian circled once and then flew beyond the huge rock in the center of the first field. Kim tried to keep his foot placement between the rows. The young wheat shoots were so delicate, he was afraid to trample them. His brothers followed his example.

The flywacket kept circling. He seemed to center his flight on the third field, the one planted in a soy-gone-wild.

Over the rock wall, across the infant barley field, slightly downhill all the while, then over another wall and into the just planted soy field—and hadn't he had a grand time separating out the seeds and beans from the mix in the wild field.

Nothing. Kim couldn't see anything out of the ordinary in the evenly tilled soil. Just beyond lay the marshes and beyond that Big Red's pastures. If Hestiia had come to the soy field, he'd have seen her, maybe even heard her earlier when they mated the cow and Big Red.

"Where, Gentian? Where is she?" He looked up to see the flywacket. He had to shade his eyes against the glare of the sun reflecting off a new bank of clouds rolling in from the east. "We've got to find her before the rain hits. She'll chill worse if she has a fever. I won't lose her."

"We won't lose her," Loki said calmly. "Gentian's in panic mode. He's useless. I'll walk the circumference of this field. Konner, check every inch of the barley. Kim, go back to the wheat. Quarter the field. Check every inch. She may have crawled off into the grass looking for shade from the sun."

Kim nodded mutely. Between the long run and his rampant emotions he couldn't speak. Firmly, he prayed to his mother's god and every other one he could name that he'd find Hestiia in time, that he'd find a cure for her and for the others.

Gentian swooped down and grabbed a beakful of Kim's hair. He screeched as loud as the flywacket. "Get out of my way. You aren't any help at all!" he called as Gentian returned once more to the verge of the marsh.

Keeping his wings spread and his talons extended, Gentian perched on a deadfall log that hung over the shallow water. Seconds later he thrust down with beak and claws. He came up with a wriggling frog. With a jerk of his head that looked like disgust, Gentian threw the frog back onto solid ground where it landed with a squishy thud against a rock. It could not have survived.

"Is he trying to tell us something?" Kim asked his brothers.

They, too, had observed the murder of the frog in fascinated horror.

Gentian repeated the process. Another frog bit the dust. Literally.

"Whatever he's saying is too obscure for me." Konner shook his head and began his search of the terraced barley field.

"My telepathy sees only the frogs lying dead next to Hestiia," Loki said. He shook his head, too, more vigorously, as if to rid it of the images, or a headache. "I wish I'd practiced more on him and less on eavesdropping on Yaakke and his girlfriend."

Kim chose not to comment on Loki's conviction that Maigrait was a spy for Yaaccob or Hanassa. He needed to concentrate on Hestiia. At the edge of a field. With a dead rabbit.

The image flashed across his mind again. Green shoots, about fifteen centimeters high (the locals called it a hand). That would be the wheat. He headed back to the first field, pumping his legs against the slight uphill slope.

At the rock he tripped over one of the offerings left there. Briefly he touched the cool granite for balance. A jolt of awareness sent him careening to the far corner of the field. Somehow the rock had known that something was not right and directed him.

Gentian dove down upon the same corner. Apparently convinced that either his message with the frogs had been conveyed or was useless, now he tugged at something half hidden by the waist-high grass verge.

Kim nearly flew across the last piece of field, heedless of the precious plants, or the numerous frogs that had come out to greet the evening drizzle. He found Hestiia slumped against the verge, her bare legs had been tanned to match the soil by a lifetime of living in concert with the land and the elements. She looked as if she needed to merge with the wild that surrounded her; gave her sustenance and soul.

"I can't lose you yet, Hes," Kim cried as he gathered her against his heart. "Leaving you behind when I go home will be hard enough. I can't bear to watch you die!"

Her unconscious body lay limply in his arms. Fat tears rolled down his cheeks, mingling with the rain.

CHAPTER 33

"SHE'S STILL BREATHING, Kim," Konner said gently. He pressed his fingers to the girl's jugular. Thready, rapid, not at all good. "We can still save her. But we have to get her under shelter. Quickly."

"How? How can we save her?" Kim looked up at him with haunted eyes.

St. Bridget, the boy must truly love her, with the same depth that Konner loved Martin. In that moment, Konner regretted all the time he had not spent with his son. Three months a year, for a few short years working as a camp counselor to the boy weren't enough. Not once in all that time had he acknowledged his relationship with Martin. Not once when his son cried himself to sleep from loneliness or with a problem that really needed a dad's advice had Konner come through with the one bit of information that would help his son.

He took a deep breath. One problem at a time. But he would *not* be late to the final custody hearing on Martin's fourteenth birthday.

"We can find a cure, Kim. We have the knowledge, we just have to figure out the details."

"But we need microscopes, gene splitters, test rats, an entire laboratory. All we have is a few emergency supplies onboard—badly depleted, I might add—and one bronze age village on the verge of accepting iron." Kim's tears increased.

Loki bent over to relieve him of Hestiia and carry her back to the village. Kim held her tight, rising to his knees and then to his feet, all the while retaining his precious burden.

"We have the *Sirius* and the computer," Konner reassured his younger brother.

"And Gentian showed me flashes of machinery and equipment," Loki added with more excitement than reassurance. "There is a stash of the original technology in the southern mountains. There's a lush plateau and a mountain rising sharply above it. He'll show us where. I'm getting through to him with stronger and clearer images all the time."

"But we need the girl conscious to call a dragon for us. We can't land the shuttle in the mountains to the south," Konner added. "I'm going ahead to pull an emergency IV drip and antibiotics from the shuttle. We have to keep her hydrated, Kim. Loki will help you with the antibiotics in the first aid kit." By using his brother's name frequently he hoped to break through the mental barrier of his grief, make him think, make him act rather than merely react.

"IV. Yes, we have to rehydrate her, break the fever. Get her conscious." Kim just kept walking blindly, squishing frogs and delicate wheat sprouts with every step.

"What about the others?" Loki asked.

An entire village on the verge of dying. A pit gaped in the center of Konner's soul.

"I guess we have to spread out the supplies. Give the IV to one, the antibiotics to another. What else can we do?"

Konner settled into a kilometer-eating jog along the river until he came to the camouflaged *Rover*. Rain drenched and chilled him. He ignored it, letting the exercise warm his blood. But nothing could warm the chill of fear in his heart. They had to find a cure for this strange disease—and soon. He sincerely doubted childhood inoculations would immunize himself and his brothers for long.

The bulk of the shuttle loomed out of the evening mist like some haunted castle in a Gothic holovid. Superstitiously, Konner crossed himself, as his mother had taught him. He prayed for guidance and luck and whatever else he might need in this quest—if God could find him in this forgotten corner of the galaxy.

Gentian flew above him, following while he chirped concern. Konner's talents didn't lend themselves to interpreting the flywacket's messages. And he didn't feel like talking.

The shuttle was locked tight, just as he'd left it. But the ground around it had been disturbed. The current rain had not washed away the footprints of many men. They'd dug at the landing gear and scratched the ceramic/titanium alloy of the hull around the hatch.

The thrum of the compressors distilling nitrogen out of the atmosphere had betrayed the shuttle's presence despite the cloaking.

He counted five drowned fires near the nose of the craft. Yaaccob and his men, probably egged on by Hanassa, had tried everything they knew to break open the white dragon of their nightmares. None of their skill could match the technology of a race that had wandered the stars for nearly five hundred years.

Many times humans had chosen to lose themselves out in the wilderness. Space was just one more wilderness.

For good or for ill? Konner didn't know anymore. As much as the need to go to his son burned within him, he also longed to remain, teaching, experimenting, working hard, sleeping soundly, and eating well. The simple life free of outside interference had its advantages. He and Kim seemed to thrive on it.

Loki was taking a lot longer to accept it.

But then, the eldest brother had ambitions Konner could only guess at. Not for the first time, he wished he could read Loki's mind and understand what drove him.

And Kim still seemed committed to returning to Mum. When would he learn that Mum's machinations had little to do with her sons' well-being and were mostly about giving Mum control over them.

Konner opened the hatch, careful to shield the keypad with his body. He couldn't sense any watchers, but no sense in taking any chances. Stale air whooshed out of the shuttle. No one had infiltrated. Otherwise, the air would be fresher.

The emergency kit yielded all he'd come for. But, while he had the computer, he decided to review the initial surveys. He called up the coordinates for the southern mountains, looking for a narrow but lush plateau with a barren mountainside soaring above it.

Strangely located magnetic forces had disrupted the focus on the survey sensors. Konner peered closer to the frozen image on the screen. He enhanced and extrapolated as finely as he could. The picture he called up was still out of focus but revealed a few more details. He didn't like what he saw.

The plateau was watered by underground streams. But that was the only water he could find in the vast and barren landscape. The blurred hole in the picture at the mountain peak could be the mouth of a volcano. No way to be sure without on-site visuals. If the volcano was dormant, then lava tube caves within it would provide an excellent hiding place for a cache of technology. No rain, no humidity to speak of, would eliminate rust and corrosion. If protected by a force field, or even a thin wrap of plastic, everything left there should be intact.

"Well, Gentian. If you can call up a dragon for me, I'm going tomorrow."

"I'm the telepath, I need to go. You can't communicate with the dragon," Loki said from the doorway to the cockpit. How had he gotten here so quickly?

"But I'm the engineer. I need to assess the condition of anything left behind," Konner replied.

"One of us needs to stay and keep Kim on an even keel. He's on the brink of an emotional breakdown."

"Then you stay." Konner wasn't about to give up on the project just because Loki ordered differently. "How is Hestiia?"

"Still feverish. But we got her jaw unlocked enough to get some water down her throat. I made sure everyone boils the water from now on. Just in case there are nasty microbes hiding in it."

"We tested it before we set up camp."

Loki shrugged. "We tested for bugs GTE equipment could detect. Who knows what strange nasties this planet breeds along with dragons." He froze, staring out the viewscreen of the cockpit.

Konner followed his gaze. In the drizzle and low light he couldn't be sure, but he thought he saw the outline of a dragon reflecting the interior lights of the shuttle.

"I guess Gentian called in transport to the cache of technology for us."

"No, I want the throne there," Hanassa ordered.

Taneeo glared at him for a brief moment of defiance.

Hanassa maintained his stony expression until his slave dropped his gaze and shifted the heavy chair made of silver bloodwood two handspans to the left. With the seat in the precise center of the raised portion of the floor, Hanassa sat and surveyed his throne room.

Neither elegant nor filled with awestruck worshipers yet. But soon. Soon Hanassa would have throngs of faithful followers bowing to him in this very cave. Those followers would bring him long lines of sacrifices until he had eliminated the infestation of human vermin from his home.

"We will put an altar there," Hanassa waved vaguely to the open area in front of his throne.

Taneeo blanched but said nothing.

"I *like* caves." Hanassa settled into his throne, appreciating the security of the thick walls and ceiling. He felt the mountain fold around him, protecting him from the vast openness of the skies.

Taneeo edged toward the labyrinth of tunnels and caverns that led to the open air and sunlight. The boy had rebelled against being confined inside the mountain from the first moment Hanassa had brought him here through the portal. More reason to keep him close at hand. Hanassa kept him uneasy and obedient during the day; then let him sleep in one of the small outer caves at night—enough relief to give him the courage to survive one more day underground.

"I have need of a bed," Hanassa announced. He rose from his throne, keeping his chin lifted and his gaze level upon his slave. "We shall remove one from . . ."

"Master, the Rovers come," Taneeo interrupted. He cocked his head toward the entrance, listening intently. Hope blazed in his eyes.

"The Rovers, yes. A profound nuisance. They will not rest in their pursuit of me even though I returned their pitiful pony to them." Hanassa heaved a tremendous sigh.

He did not know for certain that the dark-eyed wanderers sought him. Quite possibly they used this mountain as a way station and shelter in their continuous trek from one end of the world and back again.

"Should you not confront them, and evict them from your domain, Master?" Taneeo persisted.

"Not yet. Come. I have need of you in the lower caverns." Hanassa strode evenly toward the passage deeper into the mountain.

"Wh . . . where will you take me this time?" Taneeo asked. He had balked every time Hanassa pushed him through the magic portal. His fear of the unknown made the caverns look comfortable by comparison.

"Some place new, I think. I have not yet explored most of the regions open to me."

"You retreat," Taneeo accused. His voice rose in pitch and volume. If he was not careful, the Rovers would hear him. "You run away from the Rovers rather than face them. You are afraid of them!"

Where had the boy found the courage to voice those thoughts?

Hanassa slammed his fist into Taneeo's nose. The boy dropped heavily to the ground. "How dare you speak so to your master?" Hanassa kicked him soundly in the ribs. Taneeo rolled over, moaning and clutching his middle. Even the sound of his moans echoed down the corridors of the labyrinth.

"Your punishment for blasphemy, slave, will be to step first into an unknown land, to explore it and return to me with your report," Hanassa hissed into Taneeo's ear as he hauled him to his feet.

"No, Mashter," Taneeo moaned through his bloody nose. "Please, no. Let me go with the Rovers. Let me be their slave, and they will cease to persecute you."

"Not bloody likely. I am not giving up so valuable a possession as your strong back for the illusion of safety. Everyone knows that Rovers promise whatever you want to hear and then break those promises before they finish speaking. Rovers are also tenacious beyond reason. They will never forgive me for stealing one of their wretched ponies. Never. And their tortures are horrible. You will take five days and more in the dying. They will make the sacrificial altar of Simurgh look merciful before they are done." Hanassa warmed to his topic, making up "facts" as they occurred to him.

As he spoke, he shoved Taneeo toward the long downward passage. His slave stumbled several times, sobbing and bleeding all the way to the lower caverns.

Hanassa paused only long enough to grab a torch from a niche in the wall. Despite his affinity for the caves, he could not see in the dark.

"I will not go alone," Taneeo said. He regained his footing and attempted to right himself on the level floor of the creek room.

"Yes, you will, slave. Why should I risk myself in a foreign land when you are so much better able to prove to me the safety or danger of the place?" Hanassa chuckled at the boy's fear. Warmth and energy poured through his body, drinking in the pain and terror as if sampling the richest milk.

"Then I will not go." Taneeo ran deeper into the cavern. He tripped over his own feet, flailed for balance a moment, and kept going.

"Come back here, slave!" Hanassa roared. "You may not disobey me."

Taneeo kept running, careening off columns and protrusions from the cavern walls.

Hanassa hurried after him. With the aid of the torch to avoid obstacles, he gained on his slave's erratic progress.

A narrow slit appeared off to their right. Taneeo headed for it. He managed to slip his now gaunt body through the tight opening just as Hanassa grabbed the collar of his tunic.

The slit did not want to accommodate Hanassa's stockier body. He persisted, tightening his chest and stomach muscles and never letting go of the struggling slave's clothing.

At last he squeezed into the new room with a popping sound. With room to maneuver, he slammed Taneeo against the wall with yet another blow to his face.

Light flooded the room.

Strange shapes, all the same shade of gray, sat atop three long tables made of metal.

The slave moaned and slumped to the ground. He pressed his hands against his nose and eyes, trying unsuccessfully to staunch the flow of blood.

Hanassa circled slowly, drinking in the strange sights. He blinked in the too bright and uniform light.

"What miracles are these?" he breathed. "For revealing these wonders to me, I will not kill you today, slave."

CHAPTER 34

◆— · —◆— · —◆

LOKI APPROACHED THE DRAGON with caution. It perched sedately on the nose of the shuttle, preening its chest. When Loki came within twenty-five meters, the dragon ceased its grooming. With each of Loki's steps, the creature lowered its head to look more closely at him.

Loki gulped back his apprehensions. "This will be a grand adventure, Konner. We'll see things no one else on this planet can dream of."

"Easy, brother, you don't want to rush into this like you do everything else. Luck and latent telepathy might not pull you through this time." Konner hung back, close to the hatch. "We need to get back to the village with the emergency supplies."

"In this case we have to take the initiative. The battle goes to the bold." Loki took three more steps forward, then halted. "Our emergency supplies won't help much. We need to find a cure, and this dragon is the key!"

A dragon eye came level with his own. The immense creature twisted its back to an impossible angle while maintaining its grip on the shuttle's nose and peering intently at Loki. Great swirls of color invited him to delve deeply into the dragon's soul and discover . . .

Loki shook himself free of the compulsion to lose himself in the dragon. He kept his eyes closed or gazed elsewhere.

"Why is the dragon shaking himself as if trying to rid himself of a nightmare?" Konner asked. He'd apparently gained enough courage to step out of the shuttle.

"Maybe he looked too deeply into my soul and got scared," Loki laughed. He smiled, showing his teeth, hoping his expression wasn't the true grimace of fear he felt in his gut.

"So what do we do now?" Konner asked. "If we're taking off with the dragon, shouldn't we wait until we tell Kim what we're up to? He's expecting us with the med kit and an IV."

"Kim is so bound up in his own personal grief and misery I don't think he's going to notice we haven't come back."

(Come.) The voice sounded as if it rumbled up from the bowels of the planet.

"Did you say something?" Loki looked back at the dragon, keeping his gaze away from the creature's dangerous eyes.

"I didn't say anything," Konner replied.

"Did you hear anything?"

"Just a sense of urgency and a high-pitched gibber. I thought Gentian was ranting about something again."

(Come.) The deep voice reverberated through Loki's head like the biggest bass bell ever cast. A single controlled strike of the clapper, bronze against bronze.

Every nerve ending in Loki's body vibrated in sympathy with that voice.

"Do we climb up on your back?" Loki asked the dragon, not at all sure he wanted to do that. He preferred flying while fully enclosed by a cockpit, strapped in by a harness and in control of the joystick. In control.

(Yes.) Another single gong sent vibrations through the soles of Loki's boots and up into his belly.

"Um—could you come down from there so we can reach you?"

The dragon partially unfurled his wings and hopped down beside Loki. His muzzle with the twenty-centimeter fangs came much too close to Loki's head.

"Maybe we should ask it if it has a name," Konner said. He'd come closer but was still hanging back.

"Why would it have a name?"

"Well, you are talking to it like it is a member of a sentient species. It must have a name and a gender. Do you realize that we've discovered a sentient alien race that doesn't want to kill us?"

(Iianthe.)

"He said . . ."

"I heard it, Loki. Iianthe. What is that?"

(Purple.)

"Purple?" Loki asked, making sure he understood it correctly. "Purple as in the color of your wing tips and veins and horns?"

(Yes.)

Could this guy only speak in single word sentences? Maybe if he said/ thought two words in a row, the vibrations from the bronze-bell vocal cords would shatter him.

"Isn't Gentian a shade of purple?" Konner asked.

"Hush," Loki demanded. His brother was demanding far too much information. Couldn't they just get on with this?

(Yes.)

"Is Gentian related to you in some way?" Konner continued.

"Don't be ridiculous. Gentian is a black, flying cat, with the barest hint of a purple sheen, and less than one-tenth the size of this guy," Loki splurted.

(Yes.)

"Yes to what? That Gentian is related or that he's merely a flying cat one-tenth your size?"

(Both.)

"That doesn't make sense." Konner ran his hands through his hair and beard in consternation.

"So what. We can figure it out later. Right now we need to get to the cache of tech so we can take care of this disease that's felling our people." Loki almost danced from foot to foot in his excitement.

"I wish I could talk to Iianthe directly. I have a lot of questions," Konner moaned, backing up three steps from the dragon.

(Ask as we fly.)

St. Bridget! Four words, and the bell didn't shatter.

Iianthe hunkered down on his forelegs, giving them access to his shoulder and back.

Loki hopped aboard with his heart in his throat beating in double time. This could be so wonderful, or so *bad*. But wasn't that what adventure was all about?

"Hey, this guy's got fur. I always thought dragons were supposed to be reptiles," Loki chortled. "And each hair is like a crystal filament. It bends light around the dragon so it appears nearly invisible." Maybe if he could engage Konner's scientific curiosity, he'd lose his fear.

Konner didn't comment. He mounted behind Loki, hesitating at each move. He wrapped his arms around Loki's waist and clamped his knees tight against the dragon's sides.

(Ready?)

"As ready as I'll ever be," Konner said through clenched teeth. "But I'm keeping my eyes closed."

(Hold tight.) Iianthe took six long hopping steps.

Loki's stomach bounced the way it did during a chancy landing.

The dragon covered the length of the clearing, mighty wings flapping. The wind of their passage threw Loki back against Konner, his hair and beard instantly tangling.

"Yahoo!" Loki shouted.

And then they were airborne. Treetops fluttered below them. The river became a thin red line in the last of the sunset.

Mist closed around them. Loki was chilled to the bone in the dampness. Konner shivered, his teeth chattering.

Then they were above the thin, rain-soaked clouds. A nearly full moon made a silver path along the insubstantial blanket below them.

Loki's stomach lurched as he realized that nothing stood between him and the ground—so very, very far away—but the strength of a mythical creature and a destination he knew nothing about.

"I used to dream this when we were kids," Konner whispered into his brother's ear. "I dreamed this and then I began redesigning atmosphere craft so I could live this adventure."

"I used to dream of falling off a platform above the clouds. The flight was glorious. Fortunately, I always woke up before I landed." Loki squeezed his eyes shut, but he couldn't block out the memory of those nightmares. This grand adventure had turned scarier than he'd imagined.

Adrenaline pumped fiercely through his veins. And still he could not open his eyes without fear.

"Would you look at the structure of this wing, Loki!" Konner said on a breathy exhale. "A model of efficiency. I wouldn't believe that something so fragile looking could support this much weight."

Loki opened his eyes. Now that he had grown used to the wind in his face, he could look around with less fear of falling off. Both he and Konner gripped the long spinal horns fiercely, though.

(Ask your questions.)

"Oh . . . um . . . yeah. How are you and Gentian related?" Loki stammered.

(There can only be one purple-tipped dragon at a time.)

"No. You don't mean that Gentian was a purple dragon," Konner replied in disbelief. "He's too small."

Yet he was the largest cat of the domestic variety Loki had ever seen and weighed much more than he should.

(Purple dragons are always born multiples. The redundant—one—must become something else by the turning of the second year.)

"On this planet I'll believe anything. So, Gentian was born your twin." Loki mulled that over in his mind. That would explain the near telepathic communication between the flywacket and humans.

(No.)

"What?"

(The one you know as Gentian is one of three.)

"Triplets? So where is the third?"

(I do not know. He has traveled far. I cannot always find his mind amongst the muddle of all the illogical humans.)

"Are you saying that the third purple-tip dragon became human?" Loki gulped again. This was getting too weird even for this planet.

(My littermate chose to assume the body of a human child that ailed and was near death rather than restrict himself to collapsing his own body into that of a flywacket. He

enjoys the power he thinks humans wield, one over another. Something he could never do within the dragon nimbus.)

"Why not?"

(Dragons are solitary creatures. We listen to no one and obey only ourselves.)

"Are there more of you?" Konner asked. He leaned over a bit too far for Loki's taste, merely to get a closer look at the musculature of the dragon wing.

(No.)

"But how do you mate, get born, pass on your lore?" Now Loki was interested in this bizarre story.

(I am the only purple-tip.)

"But are there other dragons? Other colors?"

(Yes.)

"What other colors?" Konner almost shouted. "I thought your color came from blood veins showing through translucent skin."

(The males can be any color-tipped, red, yellow, blue, green. Females are all colors and yet no color at all.

"Iridescent," Loki supplied the word.

"Purple-tips must be special if there is only one," Konner coaxed.

(I am the only dragon who will watch out for the humans.)

"Is that because your littermate is human now?" Loki wondered if he had met the dragon-become-man who liked to wield power.

(If my twin still walks the land, I cannot find him.)

"Did he die?"

(Doubtful.)

"What name does he use?" Loki had a sudden suspicion he knew the answer, and he didn't like it at all.

(My twin sees you as a threat to his power, and he will try to kill you. And he lives still. You did not succeed in killing him. I doubt any human can. He answers to the name Hanassa.)

Kim wandered to the doorway of the hut he shared with his brothers and Hestiia. Where were Konner and Loki? They should have been back an hour ago. Hestiia's fever was rising again, and she desperately needed moisture. The few drops he coaxed down her throat weren't enough.

The villagers stood around the central cook fire in tight knots that admitted no others to their conversations. From their hushed whispers, he gathered they were frightened out of their wits. They'd seen this curse of broga before, knew it for a killer, and wondered who would be felled next.

Every once in a while, someone would look over a shoulder at him, catch his eye, and then turn away furtively. As if they blamed him for this disaster.

He didn't want to think about the others who had fallen already. He just didn't have enough antibiotics with him to treat them. Basic remedies for fever were his only tools.

Did these people have a penicillin-producing mold? He had no idea what kind of conditions that mold required for propagation. Or what was needed to distill it down into an antibiotic.

If he could just keep Hestiia's fever down while he hunted for a solution. Where did salicylic acid come from? Something about willows. The leaves, the roots? The bark! That's what he had read. Willow bark tea.

Hope welled up in him and died just as quickly.

He couldn't call upon Pryth for information. She needed his help more than either Doraan or Hestiia did.

The fever racked her aging body and locked most of her joints, not just the jaw. Already, after only a few hours, her gums had begun to bleed and pull away from her teeth. Her eyeteeth looked more like fangs than human denta-lia. Whenever he'd checked on her, super-dilated eyes implored him to end her pain one way or another.

He wasn't desperate enough to practice euthanasia. He'd never be that desperate. Not after . . .

CHAPTER 35

✦ —— · —— ✦ · —— · —— ✦

TWO YEARS AGO. The O'Hara family had taken the *Sirius* into New Nashville. The cargo had been legit, music recordings for delivery to three bush worlds. Bigger shipping companies couldn't be bothered with such a trivial cargo to marginal markets. But the bush worlds had paid well for the luxury items that bordered on necessities. They'd even given the *Sirius* papers that looked almost authentic.

But Loki had gone off on an errand of his own.

Mum sent Kim in search of his errant brother.

Twinkling lights, soft music from a real string quartet, laughter. Kim smelled the roasting vegetables and the perfume from banks of flowering plants. Nothing computer generated about this party. And all of it added up to a great deal of money. Loki certainly knew how to pick out the wealthiest girl on the planet.

But this time Mum had ordered Kim to cut Loki's affair short. Loki had turned off his comlink. The one unbreakable rule in the family enterprise: never, ever, while dirtside sever communications with the shuttle and/or the mother ship.

They had to get off planet quickly, tonight. Mum and Konner had been recognized in town. Even now, port authorities closed in on them. But they couldn't leave Loki behind. Especially if the governor, the host of this party and father of Loki's latest inamorata, should look too closely and find an O'Hara in his inner sanctum.

And they could not raise Loki on the comlink.

Kim slunk close to the garden wall that separated the governor's residence from the rest of the domed city. No one bothered to patrol the wall. The cit-

izens all respected the privacy of their elected ruler. (The emperor had recommended one candidate. No one dared oppose him in an open election.)
Obeying the law had become the planetary religion among the civilized
worlds.

A few couples strolled among the blossoming fruit trees, clumps of roses,
and grassy paths. The ladies wore sparkling jewels and floaty gowns. The
gentlemen sported bright particolored suits; all the latest rage in fashion. But
Loki was not among them.

Kim eased away from the sheltering shadows of the wall. Keeping to the
periphery, he scanned each of the paths. Where could his brother be? Surely
Loki was not fool enough to venture *inside* the governor's mansion!

"One last kiss, my own true love," a high-pitched feminine voice implored.

Kim almost turned away, not willing to eavesdrop on the mating rituals of
the rich and powerful.

"I have to go, Cyndi," Loki said. Reluctance made his voice heavy and
scratchy.

Right on that one, big brother.

Slow footsteps passed beside Kim's hiding place. He decided to be diplomatic for once and not corner Loki over his tardiness and having turned off
his comlink. His oldest brother would be hurting that he had to leave Cyndi
behind.

Oddly, Loki seemed to think his affair a secret.

Kim shook his head sadly. This relationship could lead only to heartache
for Loki, for Cyndi, and for both families.

A number of long moments passed in silence before Kim heard his brother's soft movement through the garden toward the wall.

He turned to follow.

Heavier footsteps moving rapidly. Two men.

Kim listened more closely. He had to be sure Loki's escape from the
grounds had not alerted the guards. Loki wasn't being too careful at the moment, or very alert. Two men dressed all in black hurried past him. Kim
didn't like their furtive glances or their beady eyes. Trouble.

The footsteps, at first so firm and sure, became scuffles. A muffled scream
cut off, replaced by moans.

Images flashed across Kim's mind. A hypo spray of narcotics pressed into a
soft feminine arm. A lithe blonde collapsing against one of the roughly clad
men.

Without thinking, Kim drew his stunner and stepped out of hiding. He'd
already seen the placement of the bodies, the motive of kidnapping for ransom or revenge. He already knew what he had to do.

The man holding Cyndi's limp body shouted something. His partner
whirled.

Kim's thumb pressed the red button firmly. The full beam of blue light streamed from the stunner directly into the mouth of the man holding Cyndi. He went rigid with pain. Kim continued to fire. The man's face turned red, redder, pulsed. His mouth turned black, split, charred. The tongue lolled as his body jerked. He collapsed.

The partner ran.

And still Kim kept the pressure on the stunner. His hand seemed to have a mind of its own. His mind closed down, he saw only the clean beam of blue light.

Then darkness enfolded his sight. One heartbeat later blinding light flashed across his inner vision. Pain invaded every joint and muscle. Burning. His head was on fire. Nothing existed but the pain and the too-white light. And then nothing. No pain. No body. Just the light and a compulsion to move forward.

Fear paralyzed his movements. If he'd still had a body, he would be trembling and sweating. If he'd still had a mind, he would retreat. But he couldn't. He *had* to follow the light. An *other* depended upon him. The *other* fled before him into the light.

He had no choice but to follow. He should have led the *other* through this void into death.

And then the light swirled, turned into a multicolored vortex. Each layer of green, red, blue, purple, and every shade in between was too vivid. Surreal.

The other was caught up in the violently rotating lights. Vertigo shimmered around Kim. A little more. He needed to go forward only a little more and he would be safe. Safe was forward into death. Safe was away from all that he knew.

Blackness. Nothing.

He awoke with a jerk. Cyndi wept grateful tears onto his face. Her father commanded medics to care for Kim.

He could only tremble with a terrible chill and vomit.

Kim jerked away from the awful memory once again. Each time it possessed him it was worse than the last time. But he could not dwell upon it. He had obligations to the living.

Did he dare leave Hestiia long enough to search out some willow bark? He had no choice. All of these people needed help. Helping them eased his guilt over causing a death a little. But only a little.

He retreated into the dark hut interior to read up on willows and their bark, praying that the original colonists had included the vital tree in their terraform package.

A thump behind him alerted him to Gentian's presence. The flywacket stalked into the hut before completely furling his wings. Except for the agitation radiating from him in psychic waves, he behaved just like a normal cat that owned the place and graciously allowed a few humans to share it with him.

But the agitation wasn't all coming from Gentian. The hushed whispers of the villagers became louder, angrier. Kim paused to look at them more closely.

The green firelight cast bright afterimages around every face turned to him in anger. Red arrows shot through the layers of yellow and black.

He recoiled from the anger in those red arrows sparking away from their heads. Their entire culture had been built around appeasing unexplainable natural forces with blood sacrifice. An animal for minor issues. One of their own in case of disaster.

The reoccurrence of the curse of the broga marked a major disaster for them. Who would they take to their new altar in the center of the field? The altar where they placed their offerings and votives in honor of the Stargods.

Gone from their faces was the respect they had held for the Stargods this morning. Their murmurs of discontent and fear rose around him like a malevolent wall.

·———◆———·

"Look down, Loki," Konner gasped.

"I'd rather not. Reminds me of just how high we are flying," Loki replied through clenched teeth.

"This is important."

"Uh, what is it?" Loki's head swivelled back and forth, scanning the landscape below them in all directions.

The cloud cover had dissipated. Moonlight shone across rolling hills, some forested, some bare. Off to their left, the waters of the Great Bay glinted with phosphorescent life on the crest of the waves and below.

Across it all, Konner saw a faint web of delicate blue lines.

"Can't be stunner fire," Loki said, peering more intently.

"Energy. Like the web of transactional gravitons that holds the universe together."

"Impossible. No one has ever seen a graviton." Loki didn't sound as certain as his words indicated.

"No. But we can measure them. We know they exist because of the energy they manifest. We can push against them and block them to allow space travel. The king stones use the web of energy for sub-light communications. Every theory I've ever read or heard postulated suggests they look just like that, only smaller and farther apart. All we need is the proper device."

Konner gestured broadly with one hand to encompass the entire landscape.

"Hold tight!" Loki ordered.

Konner clamped his free hand back onto the dragon's horn.

(You have discovered the web of life,) Iianthe stated.

"Web of life." Konner mulled over that phrase a moment. "Good description. It's like everything is connected throughout the universe."

(Yes.)

"Cosmic strings?" Loki asked. "That's the only useful phrase I've ever pulled out of quantum physics."

"In a way."

(Strings. Webs. Umbilicals. All the same.)

"But why are they visible here and now, yet the best physicists and engineers in the galaxy can't find a way to make them visible?" Konner mused out loud.

(This is the beginning.)

"Huh?"

(When you understand, you will be ready to understand.)

"That sounds like a Rover conundrum," Loki snorted.

(Rovers understand.)

"Understand what?" Konner demanded.

Silence.

"Can you at least set us down to explore this?"

(Later.)

"Can we find this web of life again, on the ground?" Loki asked.

(If you search. But first you must learn how to look.)

"That makes as much sense as the conundrum." This time Loki sounded disgusted.

And then the lines disappeared, as if a vast hole had been cut in the web and it had not repaired itself.

(We are here.)

"I have a funny feeling about this, Konner."

"So do I."

(Trust your feelings. You will survive longer.)

CHAPTER 36

◆ — · — ◆ · — ◆

IANTHE LANDED IN THE middle of the lush plateau beside the mountain. Konner dismounted first, taking several moments to run his hands along the crystalline/silver fur of the dragon. It felt softer than he expected. It looked like it should resonate like the crystal drive of the *Sirius*, and have the same hard texture. Instead, it tickled his palms like Melinda's hair on their ill-fated and short-lived honeymoon. Gentian's fur was softer than the dragon's but not by much.

"I didn't know that dragons could be mammals, or so beautiful," he said quietly.

(In another few decades I will mature, and my fur will be as transparent as the crystals you treasure. Then I will be beautiful,) the dragon chuckled in the back of Konner's mind. *(In your terms, I am only a teenager.)*

"And yet your twin is a fully grown man, in his prime," Konner replied. Hanassa had to be in his early thirties at least. An elder by the standards of the locals because so many died young, but younger than Konner and Loki.

(Dragons live long. Our memories live longer. Hanassa's evil will be remembered and guarded against in future generations.)

"Why didn't the dragons stop him before now?"

(Most dragons do not care for the fate of humans. They see you as an infestation. The sooner you kill each other to the point of extinction, the better they will like it.)

"Then why should they care now?"

(I have persuaded them that Hanassa presents a danger to the dragon nimbus; that he will drive his human followers into a fervor to sacrifice us to the false god, Simurgh. Then they will care.)

"Thank heaven for small miracles." Konner rested his forehead wearily against the dragon's muzzle. It had been a long day already and likely to get longer. "Who is—or was—Simurgh anyway?"

(One of us.)

"And?" Loki jumped into the half silent conversation. "Why does Hanassa worship him?

(He took a liking to the taste of human blood.)

Konner gulped. This conversation bordered on many uncomfortable thoughts about how and why humankind found it necessary to make gods out of *something*, good or evil. The only qualification for godhood seemed to be incomprehensibility. Or fear. His own beliefs came into question. He didn't want to think about it. He just wanted to believe in the benevolent creator that Mum worshiped so wholeheartedly and that he paid lip service to.

Loki looked almost green with similar uncomfortable thoughts. He broke the cycle of questions that had no answers by sliding off Iianthe's back—awkwardly.

Konner stepped away to survey the landscape.

They were far enough south that twilight still lingered and would for perhaps another hour. They neared the Summer Solstice when this area would see little true darkness on the longest day of the year.

The ground beneath his feet felt springy—as if it enjoyed moisture frequently but had gone from muddy to squishy to this bouncy texture fairly recently. Already the little creek that crept out from beneath the soaring mountainside flowed sluggishly. In a few weeks it would dry completely and the greenery crowded along its bank would die of dehydration, much as Hestiia, Pryth, Doraan, and the others would die if they did not find a cure soon.

Within hours.

"Is there a reason you dumped us here rather than inside the mountain?" Loki asked with his usual lack of tact.

As Iianthe had circled the mountain, they had seen the blown-out interior of an ancient volcano. A number of irregular dark shadows suggested caves. Dry caves in a dry climate to store delicate technology.

(I need to drink. The water here tastes better than that within the mountain. The minerals leech into the plants, leaving the water sweeter.)

The mental message carried the distinct taste of sulfur.

"Will you wait for us?" Konner asked.

(If I can.)

"What would take you away before we finish?" Loki looked belligerent.

The dragon did not dignify the question with a reply. He merely waddled over to the creek and lowered his muzzle. He looked as ungainly on land as Konner felt after spending hours with his hips nearly dislocated while clinging to Iianthe's sides with his knees.

"How do we get into the mountain?" Konner asked, trying to keep this conversation reasonably polite and professional. No sense in allowing Loki's usual lack of caution and tact to get them into more trouble than they needed.

Iianthe directed them around the plateau, through a tunnel entrance and across the bowl of the volcano to a very large cave almost directly opposite the entry. As they began the long walk around the mountain—five or six kilometers to their destination—Iianthe curled into a tight ball and closed his eyes. Before they were out of sight of the dragon, they could hear his light snores.

"Do dragons dream of magical sheep?" Loki quipped.

Konner replied with a grin.

By the time they reached the tunnel, they had to use portable torches to keep from stumbling over the rough terrain.

"Someone has been here," Loki said, sidestepping a too-regular pile of rocks. "Steed dung. Really dry. Probably only a week or two ago in this climate."

"I guess all the time you've wasted reading those biographies of explorers is paying off a little."

"Yeah. Never knew adventure would be this scary."

They crept on, hesitating often to search the immediate area with their pocket lights—brighter than any artificial light on his planet, but still inadequate to see more than thirty meters or so ahead.

"This is an old volcano. Fifteen, maybe twenty, kilometers across the bowl. Do you suppose it's blown itself out or is just dormant?" Konner asked. All of his studies of geology for mining helped a lot in understanding the landscape.

"That all-pervasive reek of sulfur has to be coming from somewhere hot. My guess is sleeping lightly rather than dormant or extinct." Loki wrinkled his nose.

"There's the cave." Konner pointed his torch around the edge of a hut-sized boulder. The light did not penetrate far. "Bet the passage bends just beyond the opening."

The entire passage was a maze of twist and turns. Chills ran up and down Konner's spine as they plodded on. "Is it me or is it cold in here?"

"I'm sweating."

Konner turned his torch onto his brother, checking for signs of fever. His skin was no paler than usual, and his eyes contracted normally under the increased light.

"Your jaw feeling tight or sore?"

"No, I'm not sick." Loki batted the torch away. "I'm concerned. That's the remains of a campfire over there." He pointed his torch into a large room off to their left. "More steed dung and lots of scuffed footprints."

"Who would want to camp here?" Konner bent to examine the desiccated remains of the camp. "From what our surveys revealed, I don't think this place is on the way to or from anywhere."

"I don't know who was here or why, just that part of me really wants us to be alone and another part of me prefers chatter and music and company in this forbidding landscape." Loki ran his torchlight along the ceiling. "See those cracks? They look fresh. I bet there's been an earthquake here. Recently." He hunched his shoulders as if he expected rocks to start crashing down around them.

"Not a big quake, or we'd have seen fresh rockfall. This place is stable for now." Konner needed to move, to get away from the ghostly camp. In the back of his mind he could almost hear people talking and laughing as they munched a light meal and chased away the shadows with the inevitable stories and history ballads. But the echoes didn't sound like the strangely accented dialect of his own mother tongue that he'd grown used to among the Coros.

They continued on, keeping to the largest passage as much as possible, backtracking and examining room after room. Their path led downward. The air temperature grew warmer. But Konner did not.

"We're following one person now, maybe two. One set of firm prints and a bunch of shuffles and scuffs slightly to the right," Loki announced. "Can't tell if anyone came back up. Someone is waiting for us down there."

And then the floor became solid rock, sloping downward with little or no dirt to betray the passage of others. Konner instinctively moved closer to the rock wall and pointed his torch down rather than ahead. Loki followed suit. They stayed close together, shoulders touching frequently.

"Lava tube tunnel," Konner whispered. "It's nearly as straight as if man-made."

"No place to hide," Loki added in hushed tones.

Their whispers echoed slightly.

By mutual agreement, they said no more.

And then they burst into a large cavern. A sulfurous creek ran through it. Tall columns of rock supported the soaring ceiling. A maze of outcroppings and cave growth hinted at a tangled labyrinth of caves large and small.

They stopped to drink. Konner ran his scanner over the surface. The bouncing graph showed a veritable soup of nearly every known mineral. Excitement ran through him. Could this creek possibly carry omniscium as well as all the other stuff?

He needed a micro molecular detector that read an actual sample to tell for sure. Or, better yet, a gas chromatograph.

After a moment's indecision, he nodded that the water would not kill them.

Next time they visited a civilized world, he'd buy a palm unit that contained both devices, and maybe a nuclear magnetic resonance sampler.

Loki gagged and spat out the foul-tasting liquid. Konner forced himself to drink, knowing he needed water.

"Drink," he ordered.

"We'll find the storehouse somewhere around here, I guess," Konner said, finally feeling the heat. He mopped his brow with his forearm. "Drink some more. We'll need it in this heat."

"Our other visitor was here," Loki pointed to more footprints and the remnants of fire. "Let's follow him before we begin a systematic search. This place hasn't been disturbed in aeons. I'm suspicious that someone else found this place just when we need it."

"Agreed."

All of the side rooms seemed to lead off the main cavern where the creek ran, rather than interconnect. Outcroppings and rockfall obscured the fact that they always returned to the same cavern before exploring a smaller cave.

The very next room set them back on their heels. "Is that what I think it is?" Loki asked. He made the strange flapping gesture to ward off evil used by the locals.

Konner resisted the temptation to mimic him, or to cross himself. "A steam generator. Old," he breathed.

"And big."

"Pipes go through this wall." Konner jumped up to see where they led. Then he backtracked to another room. "Transformer here. Someone used this place as an electrical power plant."

"Why not just use fuel cells?" Loki scratched his head. Sweat dripped from his face.

"Fuel cells need major industrial complexes to replace and recharge. In comparison, steam-generated electricity is cheap and easy. But it can be dirty and takes massive machinery."

"Where's the heat source?"

That stopped Konner. "We're inside the heart of a volcano," he finally whispered, almost afraid to voice this newest revelation.

As if to emphasize his words, the cave rumbled and rolled beneath their feet for a few heartbeats.

"Just a little quake," Konner reassured his brother. "No more than a two point five." But they had to be right on top of the epicenter to feel a quake that small.

"So where would the original colonists have stashed their tech when the rest of their world fell apart?" Loki looked around apprehensively. "Let's find it and get out of here. I'm getting claustrophobia. That ceiling wants to come down on top of my head.

Konner tracked wires from the transformer. "They'd need a power supply when they came back after the devastation had run its course."

"Only by the time it was safe to come back for it, too many generations had passed, and the descendants had forgotten that it existed let alone how to use it." Loki shook his head. "I'd almost be willing to bet that civil war followed the curse of the broga. Generations of warfare that continues today."

"Could be that the civil war triggered the curse." He stopped short in his exploration of the next room. "No, it couldn't be. They wouldn't."

"Wouldn't what?"

"Biological warfare."

"St. Bridget! That explains it. A germ engineered to mutate every few bug generations so no one develops full immunity—even those who catch it and survive." Loki turned pale. "But it goes dormant. What revives it?"

"Water. Remember Pryth saying she hadn't seen a spring so wet in about ten years? And then Raaskan tells us in a separate conversation that the curse hit his village hard about seven years ago."

"Frogs. We're plagued with frogs this year. Pryth remembered the wet year was the last time she heard the frogs sing so loud and so long. They hibernate in dry years, don't they?"

"Frogs. That's why Gentian was killing frogs. He was trying to tell us that they had caused the problem. They carry the disease but are not affected by it. First thing we do when we get this disease cured is drain that bloody swamp." Konner's brain finally cleared of questions, and he began to think straight.

"Bloody in more ways than one."

"Ah. Here's the lab." He squeezed through a narrow crack in the cave wall into a good-sized room. He reached to his left for a switch. The moment his palm found the panel, blue-white light flooded the room.

Workbenches lined the walls, and two more ran nearly the length of the room down the center. Each was topped with its own variety of equipment. The computer terminals seemed to be independent rather than networked. Full-sized nuclear magnetic resonance (NMR) samplers, gas chromatographs and stills to break down the organic matter for the GC to read, gene splitters, racks of beakers and test tubes, and, miracle of miracles, a micro molecular detector (MMD), palm-sized, with a digital readout even he could read. Everything had been neatly covered with dust protectors.

"What do we take and what do we leave?" Loki fingered a terminal lovingly.

"We haven't any power back at the village. We'll have to do the work here or aboard the shuttle." Konner shook his head sadly. He ran his fingers lightly over the MMD. So much of his work would be eased by this little piece. He pocketed it, praying its batteries recharged with solar energy.

"Running back and forth from here to the village is going to be a lot of work for our dragon. Let's hope he's willing."

"Let's hope he stayed on the plateau. We'd best get back to him and get home. We'll need blood samples. And a frog to dissect. And I want to test the creek water. I think it might contain omniscium."

"Before we go anywhere, shouldn't we look for journals and reports on the terminals to see if there's a formula for a counteragent?"

"Next trip. I've got to test the creek water." Konner hit the light panel as he exited. Loki was forced to follow or stay in the dark.

"No, wait a minute. You've got a reader with you. You downloaded a bunch of stuff on it just before we left. Only take a few moments." Loki slapped the light panel again and aimed for the nearest terminal.

He had it uncovered and booting up before Konner could think through his objections. He just had a nagging feeling that they needed to be gone from here.

The two of them searched all four terminals, text only mode, before finding the references they wanted. The voice commands had either broken down or did not recognize their accents after three hundred years of language evolution—the equipment couldn't have been newer than that.

A civil war three hundred years ago on Earth had disrupted communication with all of the colonies. Not all of them had been found again. Since then, the more stable replacement government, the Galactic Terran Empire, kept better records. "No cure, just how they made the bug," Konner reported.

"I found a personal journal about the breakdown among five differing factions," Loki reported.

"Let's download both and read them later." Konner's anxiety rose with each passing hour.

But the archaic terminals did not want to interface with the modern reader. Konner eventually made the two machines talk to each other, reluctantly and hesitantly. Then they seemed to take forever in transferring the data from one to the other with numerous pauses for passwords and other security precautions. Fortunately, Loki excelled in breaking through those barriers. At last, they exited the lab with the information they hoped would save their village and their plans for the future.

In the femto before Konner turned his torch on, while his senses were tuned beyond his visual perceptions, a sound disturbed his balance.

"What?" Loki bumped into him.

"Did you hear that?" Konner replied, keeping his voice as quiet as possible.

"My ears are ringing from the silence and the heat."

"More than that. Stop and listen." A soft humming seemed to tug at his soul, drawing him toward his right, back toward the transformer and generator and beyond. Down into the core of the mountain itself.

"Yeah. Someone singing," Loki breathed in Konner's ear. "Who?"

"Or what?" Konner took two steps to the right, toward the alluring voice. He ran into a wall.

"Can't travel in a straight line down here." Loki steadied his balance.

Konner reluctantly turned on his torch. The humming increased in volume and intensity. He *had* to find it, follow it, meet his destiny.

The trip to the cavern with the huge generator took less time than going in the opposite direction. Konner knew where he had to go. He started jogging, barely noticing the rubble he tripped over.

"This isn't like you, Konner," Loki called after him. "I'm the one who rushes headlong into new situations."

"You don't understand. I've heard this before. I know what I have to do."

"So have I. But where?"

"It's the wormhole. Pryth called it a dragongate. It can take us home in about ten femtos rather than two hours of dragon flight or a week of walking."

"I don't trust this."

"I do." Konner skidded into the large cavern. He swung his head back and forth several times, zeroing in on the source of the hum. It continued growing louder. It drowned out the echoes of their footsteps, their thoughts, everything but their racing heartbeats. Konner heard it all.

And then he saw the wild swirl of color at the end of one of the short passages near the generator.

"I see it," Loki whispered.

The colors mutated from the wild red, black, and yellow of the cavern into the softer greens and browns of a forest. Everything was bathed in the ruddy light of dawn.

"I recognize that place," Loki nearly jumped through the passage. "It's just upriver from us. A near perfect circular clearing in the woods."

In that instant a figure walked through the arched opening of the tunnel from the forest. With supreme confidence Hanassa strode directly toward them.

CHAPTER 37

◆ —— · —— ◆ —— · —— ◆

KIM BACKED INTO THE CABIN, away from the irate villagers, uncertain and afraid. His people had murder on their minds. The hut offered little protection other than out-of-sight-out-of-mind.

"I thought I had convinced them that sacrifice isn't necessary. I saved most of them from the altar!"

Someone rattled the bone beads on the outside of the hide curtain. The closest thing to a doorbell. At least they retained a semblance of manners.

Kim pushed the curtain aside to confront whoever had come for him.

"We want the flywacket," Yaakke said. His voice betrayed no trace of hesitation or misgiving.

"Gentian?"

"The flywacket. It brought the curse of the broga to us." He fingered the hilt of his bronze sword where it still rested in the scabbard.

"I doubt that Gentian is responsible."

"We know he is. We who have lived here all our lives. Our people, who have lived here for all time, know that flywackets bring evil. The curse of the broga is evil." He drew the bronze sword, keeping it at his side. A menace but not yet a threat.

"Just yesterday you praised Gentian because he showed you a nest of fresh duck eggs. Yesterday he was not evil." Kim resisted the urge to back away. He needed to block the doorway and keep these people out. At least until Gentian found a place to hide or slipped out the little window Loki had insisted upon cutting into the eastern wall. He said he liked to watch the sunrise, but he was never awake that early.

"The creature lulled our senses. Today we know the flywacket is evil. The evil spawn of Simurgh come to exact vengeance for its God."

"Bul . . . nonsense. The flywacket is gentle. He helps us because of his love for Hestiia. Your sister will never forgive you if you take Gentian from her. They share firm bonds. I will never forgive you if you hurt Hestiia in any way."

"My sister will die anyway. There is no cure for the curse of the broga. But we must make sure the flywacket bestows it on no one else." Yaakke clenched his jaw and narrowed his eyes as he peered over Kim's shoulder in search of Gentian.

"I can't allow you to sacrifice an innocent animal. To sacrifice anything or anyone for your perverted beliefs. My brothers will be back any time now. They promised to find a cure."

"We have no faith in your promises." The sword came up level with Kim's belt.

"You had faith in my brothers and me this morning. You placed an offering of flowers on the rock in my name!"

"But we know . . ."

"How do you know that the Coros did not come down with this disease first? How do you know that Maigrait, your lover, did not bring it with her when she visited your hut last night, or the night before that?"

Silence.

"We will find a cure," Kim pressed his slight advantage. "We can work some miracles. But we need a little time to study the . . . the essence of the curse, to understand it and then destroy it at its root."

"Who is to say your brothers did not fly away in their great white dragon, never to return. They have left you here to die, just like the rest of us." Yaakke lunged, bringing the sword up to Kim's throat. His other fist balled, ready to pound out his frustrations.

Kim felt cool metal pressing against his voice box. A trickle of warm blood snaked down his throat. He heard his heart thunder in his ears. Black spots popped before his eyes. Desperate for control, he grabbed Yaakke's sword hand, pressing his thumb against the pressure point on the inside of the wrist. With his other hand, he groped for a weapon. Something. Anything to distract or disrupt the attack.

A frightened squeak in the back of his mind alerted him to Gentian's presence.

No! he commanded the flywacket with all of his willpower. *Hide yourself.* An attack by the flying cat would only confirm Yaakee's conviction that Gentian embodied evil.

Gentian seemed most willing to remain out of the conflict. Kim almost felt him burrowing deeper into a pile of dirty laundry.

"Leave him," Hestiia croaked. She had crawled from her bed and half-lay, half-crouched by the curtain to her room.

"Hes?" Yaakke dropped his sword and pushed past Kim to kneel at her side. "Hes?" He cradled her weak body against his chest, kissing her hair. "Hestiia, you live!"

Mutely, she raised one weak hand to Kim.

"Beloved." He took her from her brother and rose to his feet. "You should not have left your bed."

She favored him with a weak smile. Her hand lingered on his bearded cheek as she caressed him.

"Never before has one stricken risen from their bed, even briefly, nor do they speak again," Yaakke gasped in awe. He flapped his crossed wrists, looked at his hands. A blush crept up his cheeks to his ears. Then he crossed himself in the gesture Kim and his brothers habitually used.

"You have indeed worked a miracle," Yaakke gasped. He stayed kneeling and bent his back so that his forehead touched the ground.

"She's not cured yet. But once my brothers return, we will find a way to make everyone in the village better, and keep the others from falling victim to this hideous disease," Kim promised. He prayed fervently that this was a promise he would not have to break.

"And the Coros?" Yaakke could not look him in the eye.

"And the Coros, too, if they will allow it."

"My Maigrait . . ."

"Why don't you just marry the girl and bring her into our village?" Kim eased Hestiia back onto her bed. He straightened her covers and bathed her brow gently with cool water. Anything to keep from looking at the embarrassing sight of Yaakke bowing to him.

From a separate pitcher he took a clean cloth and squeezed it so that a few drops trickled into Hestiia's mouth. She worked hard to swallow. Half of the water spilled from her mouth.

"Marriages are not so easily arranged," Yaakke explained, coming to his feet. "She must have her father's permission. He must offer a dowry. I must give an equal bride-price. Honor demands it."

"And if you throw your honor to the wind because you love her?"

"Then there will be war between us. Not just one attack easily repulsed. Full war to the death of everyone in both villages."

Kim shook his head in bewilderment. What had brought these people so low that they sought any excuse at all to go to war? "We'll worry about that later. For now, help me get some more liquid down Hestiia's throat. Then we must watch her carefully. Make sure she gets as much water as we can force her to swallow."

"And we must watch for your brothers, make sure the Coros do not fell them before they can return."

Loki pulled Konner behind the monstrous generator. With a wave of his hand he signaled silence and dark. For once Konner complied without protest.

Hanassa struck a spark from flint and iron onto a torch he must have stashed beside the cave entrance. He looked ghostly. But runnels of sweat marred the white paste he'd smeared over his body and clothing.

He's a fraud and a charlatan! Loki thought.

The flaming torch would deepen the shadows beyond the meager circle of light. Loki and Konner should be safe from him as long as they remained silent.

"Ah, my beauty." Hanassa caressed the metal plating on the outside of the boiler. "I do not know your purpose. But I shall delve into your secrets soon. Your magic will not elude me long." He circled the huge machine.

Loki and Konner kept stealthily to the opposite side. When they reached the section of cavern where the little tunnels branched off, Konner grabbed his sleeve and dragged him into one of them. Not the one with the dragongate at the end, Loki noticed.

Hanassa never looked beyond his own chosen path, confident that he was alone and unobserved. When he had finished his circuit of the generator, he yawned hugely and ambled off toward the lab.

Konner started after him.

"What are you doing? That man is dangerous!" Loki hissed.

"We have to find out how much he knows. And keep him from figuring out more," Konner replied.

"We have to get back to the village. Lives are at stake."

"And how do we do that? We have to go past Hanassa to find our way out of this complex and back to the dragon."

"There is always the dragongate."

"Untested," Konner replied. But his eyes shone with excitement in the meager light of his shielded battery operated torch. "If I can harness a wormhole . . ."

"Hanassa used it. Apparently he uses it all the time. Why can't we?"

"It isn't humming. Who knows what triggers it."

"Magic?"

Konner shrugged. "More likely a natural occurrence, born of the heat, pressure, and some natural phenomenon within the volcano. These people don't have real magic. We've got psi powers, and that's the extent of the supernatural here."

"Are you forgetting the dragons?" Loki arched one eyebrow.

"Seen one breathe fire yet?" Konner grinned. "But Iianthe showed me transactional gravitons." Confidence dissolved from his face.

"Let's observe the gate and see if it opens on its own. We'll give it long enough for Hanassa to settle in for a nice long nap. If nothing happens, we go back to the plateau and our dragon," Loki suggested.

When the echo of Hanassa's footsteps and the glimmer from his green fire torch faded to nothing, Loki and his brother slipped into the adjacent tunnel.

"Um . . . Konner, turn off your torch." Loki had a funny feeling about this. More than just the jumping beans in his stomach from excitement and pumping adrenaline. The heat increased to barely tolerable levels. It was worse than standing next to a roaring bonfire.

Konner touched the off button. The cheery yellow light vanished, but after a few femtos Loki's eyes adjusted to the change.

"There is still light!" Konner said in surprise. "Red light glowing at the end of the tunnel. Unknown source."

"Too much light," Loki muttered.

"Almost like we are walking directly into the sun."

"Not that bright. Even if it is too hot for comfort."

They crept forward, examining the details of the tunnel at every step. The closer they got to the end, the more intense the heat and the brighter the glow. Three paces from the edge they halted abruptly, afraid to take one step closer.

One thousand meters below them, the molten core of lava churned and heaved. At irregular intervals, spurts of liquid rock burst upward, covering at least half the distance to their precarious perch.

Loki threw his arm across his eyes, shielding them from the sudden flare.

"Now what?" Konner asked.

They both retreated several steps.

Then the humming began again. They watched in awe as the red glow swirled and faded to shades of blue and fierce white. The temperature dropped suddenly. The sweat on their bodies chilled.

A snowscape appeared before them. Falling snow drove through the portal into their eyes. They both began to shiver.

"I'm convinced. This portal leads to other places," Loki said, hugging himself against the sudden chill.

The humming intensified. A drift of snow piled up on the edge of the tunnel.

As suddenly as it had come, the snowscape disappeared. The light fell back to its normal red glow. Heat returned, more fierce than before in contrast to the cold snow.

Only a small puddle remained on the lip of the chasm to remind them of what had been.

"St. Bridget!" Konner crossed himself.

They waited a while longer. The next scene to appear was a barren desert. Not a single cactus or other moisture-conserving plant peppered the land. Just coarsely eroded rocks and near endless sand. In the distance, perhaps one hundred meters away, a jumble of outcroppings looked suspiciously like the broken hulk of the interstellar colony ship. Scattered around it was the debris of the burned-out communications satellites.

"I'm hoping that thing came down after being hit by a comet. I shudder to think that the colonists sabotaged it during their civil war." Loki stared at the wreckage. They hadn't learned much from it on their first visit.

"Can't tell without closer study. I didn't detect pre-landing collision damage," Konner mused. "Glad we scrubbed the *Rover* in the bay after we saw it, though. Hate to think what the plant growth in the upper atmosphere might have done to it."

"Something tells me that I don't want to know what on this planet had the power to bring down the mother ship. It should have remained in orbit a thousand years, even derelict and untended. Automated systems would have kept the orbit from deteriorating." Loki shivered again, but not from the temperature.

Right on the heels of the barren desert came an underwater view. A school of nearly man-sized fish streamed past them, obviously in a hurry. A fish the size of the legendary Earth whales chased them. As they watched, the behemoth opened its mouth, baring fangs as long as the dragon's. It caught a fully grown fish, cutting it in two with one bite.

The surviving members of the school scattered. They splashed Loki and Konner, drenching them in salt water.

When the heat of the volcano returned, the water evaporated quickly.

"I could spend a lifetime studying this." Konner sighed heavily. He sounded a lot like Mum when she was proud of her boys.

"The question is, how often does it return to the location we want?" Loki reminded him.

"Often enough," Hanassa said right behind them. "I use this magic portal whenever I need to appear among my people." He lifted his staff and aimed it at them as he would cast a spear.

For the first time, Loki saw that the bones and bronze ornaments were actually blades and arrowheads, designed to penetrate and kill mere mortals.

"Can we talk about this?" Loki asked, looking hastily over his shoulder. He didn't have a lot of room to dodge the staff. The volcano remained stubbornly flaming behind him. The former High Priest nearly filled the tunnel entrance with his broad shoulders and sturdy legs. He reeked of the sulfurous water he'd used to wash off his ghost makeup.

"You destroyed my altar. You denied me access to Simurgh's power. Now I will destroy you." Hanassa advanced.

Loki stubbornly stood his ground. He might survive an attack by Hanassa. He would not survive a fall into the lava core.

"Die, you foreign dogs, false gods!" Hanassa threw the spear directly at Loki's heart.

"Come on!" Konner yelled, dragging Loki back.

Loki flattened himself against the nearest wall.

The spear bounced off the swirling red/black/orange at the end of the tunnel.

Hanassa dove for his weapon, raised it ready to stab with all of his muscled weight behind it.

"Where?" Loki kept his eyes on Hanassa as he dug in his heels. He really did not want to fry in the lava.

"The portal opened again," Konner said. He shifted his grip from Loki's collar to a surer one on his belt.

"But where are we going?"

"It's green and away from here."

Sense-numbing blackness enveloped Loki.

CHAPTER 38

KIM STOOD IN THE DOORWAY of his hut watching the dawn creep
through the forest. A thin cloud cover turned the sky a dozen shades of
red. Many years ago Mum had made him recite an old adage:

> Red sky at night,
> Sailors delight.
> Red sky in the morning,
> Sailors take warning.

He could guess the weather without technological advances or cute say-
ings from the past. Rain. More rain. And when he grew tired of rain, there
would be humidity so intense the air felt as heavy as a blanket and appeared
so thick one could barely see through it.

For a few moments anyway, the air was cool enough to be comfortable.
Later, it would oppress the spirit as well as the body.

St. Bridget, he was tired. Tired of this planet, of the superstitions of the
villagers, of his brothers leaving him to cope on his own. He wanted to go
home.

But where was home?

Neither he nor Yaakke had slept much. They'd taken turns bathing Hestiia
in an alcohol/water mixture, dribbling water between her teeth. Between
vigils by her bed, they watched the village warily.

So far no one had attacked them or repeated the demands to give up the
flywacket. But if anyone else succumbed to the curse of the broga or, worse
yet, died of it, he didn't trust the villagers to stay away. Someone would be

sacrificed at the new altar. They knew of no other way to try to affect natural forces that were beyond anyone's control.

Gentian had slipped away in the middle of the night without so much as a farewell to Hestiia. Kim had seen him go only because he had been standing in the doorway hoping for a breath of fresh air when the creature's silhouette flew across the crescent moon.

"By St. Camillus of Lellis, I pray that Hestiia and the others recover." He bowed his head a moment in honest supplication. "And by St. John Muir of the itchy feet, I need my brothers to come home with some answers."

"She is not any better," Yaakke said wearily. He stretched and yawned as he, too, watched the light gradually increase and banish the shadows of night. But not the fears.

"Is she any worse?"

"I do not think so. The fever is still high, but her jaw has not locked again."

"Swallowing still difficult?"

"Yes, but she does swallow."

"We can ask for nothing more until my brothers return. I truly hope they found some answers."

Both men were silent for a long time.

No one stirred in the village. Someone should be up stoking the fire, fetching water and more firewood, making preparations for breakfast.

Fearfully, Kim moved to the next hut. He rattled the beads over the hide curtain. Silence. He rattled again, harder, more urgently. Just when he was about to enter uninvited—a terrible breach of etiquette in this society despite their communal lifestyle—a hesitant voice growled something from within.

"Are you well?" Kim asked, afraid of the answer.

"We live," came the curt reply.

"Do you need anything?"

"No. Go away."

Kim moved on. At each door he asked the same questions. At each hut he was sent away without any new information. They lived. He did not know if they ailed or not.

Not knowing what else to do, he grabbed a yoke of buckets and headed for the river. They'd all need more water, no matter what their condition.

"See there, that's the unstable gene that causes the mutation." Konner's voice carried across the river.

Kim looked up, startled out of his depressing musing.

"And where have you two been all night?" he asked angrily. Suddenly all of his fatigue and anxiety boiled up. The most convenient target was the sight of his two brothers lolling about on the opposite bank with their feet dangling in the cool water.

"Kim!" Konner jumped to his feet. He was altogether too happy and energetic. "We've found some answers."

"Thank God for small miracles. Do you have a cure?"

"Not yet," Loki jumped up to join his brother. He, too, looked very pleased with himself. "Konner's going back to the shuttle to run some things through the computer. I'll be over in a minute to tell you about it." With that, Loki dove into the river and began swimming its width.

"I just hope I don't have to jump in and rescue you, too," Kim muttered. "I'm getting tired of saving everyone."

While he waited for Loki to make his way to him, Kim filled the buckets and set them on the embankments.

As usual, Loki had some trouble with the current in the center of the river. He drifted downstream as he struggled. But he managed to push through it.

Kim rolled his eyes and shrugged. His brother would make his way back to the village in his own good time. At least Loki and Konner were safe. One less worry to drag Kim down.

If only he could be certain the rest of the village was safe from the disease.

Loki caught up with Kim at the back side of the first cabin. "You won't believe the adventure we've had!" he enthused.

"Would you believe the villagers are ready to turn on us? They wanted to sacrifice the flywacket last night. Yaakke was ready to throw both Hestiia and me on the fire with the blasted cat," Kim replied sourly. "I talked him out of it—or rather Hes did. She's in better shape than Pryth or Doraan. I guess that means something. No one has ever recovered from this thing before."

"That's because it's an engineered bug, bacterial—so the antibiotics helped—designed to mutate every few bug generations so that no one develops full immunity to it." Loki slapped Kim's back in high good spirits.

"What's so good about that? And where did you find that important little factoid?"

"The dragon showed us how to find the cache of tech from the original colonists!" Loki proceeded to relate the events of the previous night, with all of his usual sidetracks and embellishments of his own part in their eventual escape.

Kim proceeded to dispense water to those willing to thrust a bowl or pottery beaker out their door. No one presented himself to Kim's view. He could just imagine the crossed and flapping wrists behind those doors after he left.

He had to go back to the river twice for more water before Loki wound down his narrative. He was so caught up in his excitement he even carried extra buckets and filled them.

"Bottom line, how long before we have a cure?" Kim finally asked as he lowered the last bucket of water inside his own hut. A glimmer of hope smoldered somewhere behind his heart. He wouldn't allow it to fan into full flame until Hestiia was up and walking, free of fever and locked joints.

He didn't dare think about her bone loss in the jaw and receding gums.

Her eyeteeth protruded strangely, looking far too much like those of the vampires of old Earth legend.

"I don't know how long it will take Konner to isolate whatever will complete that unstable gene. He'll also have to synthesize a bonding agent."

"Does he have the equipment?"

"Back in the caves he does. But we have to come and go when Hanassa is elsewhere. Either that or risk confronting and eliminating him again. Sometimes I think we should just kill him." Loki slammed his right fist into the palm of his left hand.

"We tried that already. He didn't die. Maybe we should take that as a lesson that all life is sacred. We have no right to take a life, for any reason." He shied away from the memories that had plagued him all night.

"Why not!" Loki looked ready to push his balled fist into Kim's face instead of his own palm. "The GTE claims to revere all life, but that doesn't stop them from blasting away at 'suspect' ships, destroying engines and sensors, and then leaving them to drift alone in space until they starve to death or run out of air or kill themselves from space sickness."

"We are not the GTE. Nor are we Hanassa. If we kill him, we reduce ourselves to his level. We cannot kill him." Kim began to sweat with just the thought of taking a life. Not even the citizenship granted him by Cyndi's father—a planetary governor—was worth the pain of sharing the experience of another life passing and fighting that passing from this existence into . . . into whatever lay beyond.

"Then we have to be circumspect and avoid Hanassa." Loki shrugged off Kim's emotions. "Otherwise he might destroy the machines when we aren't there to guard them."

"We've got the stunners. Surely they will subdue him for a time. If we can remove all that stuff to the shuttle, we wouldn't have to worry about him."

"Good idea. But that volcano is a long way away. Until we've figured out how and when the wormhole works—Pryth called it a dragongate—we'll have to either hitch a ride with a dragon or risk landing the shuttle on that plateau."

"Is the caldera bowl big enough to land?"

"Caldera?"

"A volcano that's blown out its insides and collapsed back in on itself."

Loki shook his head. "You come up with the dangedest factoids and vocabulary. But maybe I can land inside the bowl if I use the VTOL jets and hover. Real tricky."

"Think about it. We need to find a cure fast. If we don't, we could find ourselves fighting our own people for our lives. Konner hasn't regrown the crystals or fixed the thrusters on the *Sirius*. We can't leave here yet, with or without a load of food to sell back home."

"This bug can be beaten, Kim. Anything engineered by humans can be broken down by humans. Sometimes we just have to be tricky about it. I have faith in you and Konner being cunning enough to dismantle something cobbled together by bushy colonists three hundred years ago."

Hope burned a little brighter in Kim. Deep down, he did trust his villagers. He and his brothers had shown them a better way than appeasing a bloodthirsty god with endless and useless sacrifices. They were frightened now and wanted a return to the familiar even though the familiar was not safe. Once that fear was appeased, the villagers would calm down and proceed on a peaceful course.

"Doraan! Sweet Doraan is dead," Fullmaan screamed. He ran into the brothers' cabin, eyes blazing with fear and anger. "She did not deserve to die. Why did you take her? Who will you take next? 'Twas better to die swiftly on the altar." He looked about wildly, not fixing his gaze on either brother or the room.

My brother will never be satisfied with life. As an infant he resented Gentian's and my presence as well as that of our littermates. Then he resented my absence when the fates determined one of us must leave the dragon nimbus. Now he resents the changes that have come to his life. He will never acknowledge that change is as much a part of life as breathing. To remain static is to die.

That is the curse of the entire nimbus. None of the others wants to believe anything is different since the humans came among us; the humans who are nearly like us in intellect and cunning.

I have always loved my brother. But I cannot allow him to live if he persists in his current course of action. He plans the complete extermination of the humans.

For the first time in his life he has the power to do that. The ancients left him the means. He does not know how to use it for the preservation of all. He no longer has a sense of good and bad, right and wrong. I fear that nothing will stop him.

"The Stargods have invaded my privacy," Hanassa said quietly. Bad enough they had found the mountain with its wondrous cave system, and they had looked into every room.

He knew who had found his treasure cave. They had escaped through the portal. He had not been able to follow them before it closed. Now he must discover why they had invaded his sanctuary.

He explored the side cavern with the light and his very sensitive fingers. Thanks to his heritage, all of his senses were more adept than those of mere humans who relied too heavily on sight and not enough on what scent, taste, sound, and skin told them. Now that he had extra light, marvelous light that banished all of the shadows in the room, he intended to discover its source and duplicate it.

Taneeo must not watch him and learn. For now the boy gathered water and greens on the plateau outside the mountain. Left on his own, he would not stray far. The trail carved by the Rovers frightened him almost as much as being trapped underground.

Hanassa planned to learn the secrets of this place before Taneeo returned with their dinner.

The boxes and beakers and other strange objects in this hidden cavern meant nothing to him. Yet. He would discover the purpose of each before he returned to the Coros and prodded them into another war. After the curse of the broga had run its course.

Patience was something these Stargods did not understand. The disease could not be cured. The lives of the Coros meant nothing. So why hurry about accomplishing nothing. All that mattered in the end was power. And whatever fueled the light was power he intended to tame.

Carefully, he pushed aside a number of things arranged on one of the center tables. He did not want to damage anything, lest it prove valuable when he had completed his investigations. Then he climbed upon the table and reached up to touch the light.

His fingers met a smooth flat object. Hard like rock and yet not rock, nearly clear but not quite. The warmth emanating from the panel was not enough to harm him. He pushed against it. It shifted upward with slight pressure. A harder push revealed a cavity above the piece of false rock. This time he slid the flat piece to the right. The left-hand corner dipped downward.

Chortling with glee he rearranged the object until it came free. He set it aside for study later. The first thing he had to do was to find the source of this strange blue-flavored light. No natural light would burn anything but green.

Two long tubes seemed to contain the light. Warm and getting warmer. He wiped his sweaty palm on his vest before reverently touching one of them. It sizzled and crackled like a fine drizzle hitting a fire. The light flickered like a newly lit torch, popped, and died.

Hanassa jerked his hand away. A strange tingle arced from the now dead light to his hand. He knew how to kill this magic. But how to create it?

He jumped down from the table, puzzled. From this angle he could see thick hairs growing from the remaining tube into the rock beside it. Once more he climbed onto the table and inspected the hairs—more like tiny ropes or the yarn spun from the lotten plant. Did they grow from the light into the rock, or from the rock into the light. A closer look showed him that the strings were tight against the holder for the tube but loose in the rock. He jiggled one of the strings on the now dead tube. They were hard but flexible. The bundle of them moved in and out of the rock a little but remained fixed to the end of the tube. When he bent one, it retained the curve. True string would be limp.

Where did it go once it left this cavity? And what in the rock attracted it?

A memory image flashed across his mind. One of the large machines had bigger strings made of a similar hard substance growing out of it and passing through the walls. Maybe that machine could tell him more.

A quick look at the oddly shaped boxes on the tables around the perimeter of the room showed that they, too, had hard strings passing into the rock. Perhaps all of the machines, big and small, were connected by these strange strings, imitations of the web of life.

He ran out into the main cavern. In a patch of sand beside the creek, he began drawing crude outlines of all that he had found so far. His keen memory, trained to repeat verbatim all of the lore of the Coros without faltering, as well as report accurately the events and transactions of the people, reproduced more detail than he was conscious of. He must be careful not to disturb this reference. He would add to it as he discovered the wonders of this cave. His wonders. His treasure.

In a little while he would set traps so that the Stargods could not return and steal the magic from him.

CHAPTER 39

✦ —— · —— ✦ —— · —— ✦

"SELENIUM," Konner breathed. He looked up from his reading of the genetic engineering that went into creating biological warfare among the early colonists. He had skipped the personal journals retelling what had prompted such devastating civil war that required chemical warfare at its most vicious. Only hard science would keep him from vomiting at the thought of what these people had done to each other.

"The blood needs selenium to block the bacterial invasion. But where in hell do I find selenium on this godforsaken planet?"

A quick reference into the *Encyclopedia Galaxia* confirmed that the chemical conducted electricity in photoelectric cells. It was frequently found in combination with sulfur—either bonded to it or to separate molecules in the surrounding environment.

"Sulfur. I know where I can get that in abundance." He ran a scenario through the computer.

"You really should find a computer programmed with medical software for this," Mum's voice grumbled and complained at the unfamiliar task assigned to the machine.

"Just complete the assigned task using engineering programs. I look for metal viruses all the time and ways to defeat them in alien star systems," he ordered. St. Bridget, it felt good to give Mum an order for a change.

"This may take a while," Mum retorted.

Sometimes Konner almost believed his mother inhabited the cranky computer. With all of the modifications he and his brothers had added to it as well as to the ship, it could have developed a degree of artificial intelligence.

Nah! That had been proved impossible time and again. Every time scientists came close to creating a computer capable of thinking for itself, it went insane and suicided. A couple of colony worlds had been rendered uninhabitable by berserk AIs.

"Sulfur will stop the virus from spreading further once introduced to the body," Mum sighed. "But selenium will render it inert. The body will pass it off and recover."

"What about inoculation?"

"What am I? A medical genius? Go find a better computer." Mum shut herself off and refused to acknowledge his commands.

"I programmed you with Mum's voice just so I could order you around! Now get back here so I can shut you off," Konner muttered on a laugh.

So he had to go back to the volcano for sulfur. But he wouldn't go alone. Hanassa was probably still lurking about. Konner wanted at least one brother with a fully charged stunner on the lookout while he collected a minimum of five liters of water from the underground stream. It was heavily laden with sulfur. Maybe selenium as well. No, make it ten liters if it contained omniscium like he thought it did.

While he was in the caverns, he'd run a few tests with the medical equipment. "No, I'll bring back as much of the equipment as possible and network with you. Will that make you happy, Mum?"

He received a disgruntled "humpf" in reply.

Spurred on by the excitement of discovery and a lightening of the humidity, Konner arrived back at the village faster than usual. He found chaos.

Fullmaan had Kim pinned against the wall of a hut. Raaskan was trying to pry them apart. Loki waved a blazing stick of firewood at the other enraged villagers. One of the former slaves made a feint to Loki's right. A warrior type rushed his left.

And ran into Konner's fist.

The warrior reared back and reached for a piece of firewood. Loki swiped his burning brand across the man's wrist. A woman leaped upon Loki's back. She pulled at his hair and scratched at his eyes.

Konner yanked her off his brother's back and dumped her into the chest of the hovering warrior. They tumbled. The villagers stumbled out of their way.

For half a moment the group's attention was on the two fallen fighters.

Konner snatched up his own torch and flashed it back and forth in warning.

Then Yaakke marched into the center of the fray carrying his sister. The villagers fell back, crossing themselves and flapping the ward against evil.

Hestiia opened her mouth. Her voice came out a croak. She swallowed and tried again. "Trust the Stargods," she whispered. "Only they can help us." She fell limp again, exhausted by the brief effort.

"She lives," Poolie gasped in awe. "A miracle she speaks. Stargods tell us that she will recover, that we are free of the curse of the broga!" She crossed herself and fell to her knees.

"Simurgh may have brought this curse of broga to us because we dared defy him and his High Priest!" Yaakke finished for his sister. "But the Stargods are stronger. They will help us! They will defeat Simurgh once and for all." Then he turned abruptly and carried Hestiia back into the hut.

Fullmaan released Kim slowly, almost reluctantly. Tears streamed down his face. "Doraan did not deserve to die."

"I did not know you cared for Doraan so deeply," Kim said. His voice sounded harsh after the blacksmith's strong hands had been about his throat.

"She was helpless. And frightened of everything. 'Twas my duty as a warrior to protect her, and I failed." Fullmaan hung his head in shame.

"Doraan was weak of body. She had no resistance to the disease," Loki said. He kept his flaming brand while he paced a circle around the central fire pit, keeping the villagers at bay.

"She had just found freedom with no chance to enjoy it," Fullmaan continued his litany of grief.

Poolie rose up from her attitude of prayer and wrapped her arms around the man's shoulders. "She is at peace now. Perhaps in her next existence she will find happiness and an easier life."

"Could she have enjoyed freedom?" Konner asked. He hadn't known the woman well, no one had. All he remembered about her was big eyes and a cowed posture. She expected to be beaten and raped for doing anything, even completing her assigned chores efficiently and on time.

"I vow by the altar of the Stargods, that I will search out the men who enslaved her and kill them all, most hideously," Fullmaan swore. He stood straighter, squaring his shoulders. A determined glint sparked in his eyes.

"And I will seek out and destroy every priest and altar dedicated to Simurgh," Yaakke added, emerging from the cabin.

"Violence is not . . ."

"Violence is all that Simurgh and his priests understand!" Fullmaan insisted.

Including Hanassa, the High Priest, who still roamed Coronnan at will with the aid of the dragongate.

Kim stared at the reader. He could not believe what he read. "Deliberate genocide."

Bile burned the back of his throat.

"Did you say something?" Yaakke looked up from dribbling a few drops of moisture into Hestiia's mouth.

"Nothing." Kim dismissed him. He could not repeat what he had just read, not to Yaakke, not to Hestiia, not to any of the locals.

But Loki and Konner needed to know this. At least the outline. The grim details would have to wait for long lonely nights beside a campfire with a lot of whiskey.

Three hundred twenty-two years ago, in the dead of winter on this planet, the original colonists had faced devastating storms. Snow piled high, drifted higher. Temperatures plummeted. The old, the young, and the weak died of privation. The remaining two thousand colonists, out of an original five thousand men, women, and children, retreated to the volcanic caldera for warmth.

They broadcast a distress signal back to Earth for help, for rescue, for life. But the old Earth Republic was already dead, collapsed under the weight of its own bureaucracy. The new constitutional monarchy that solidified the government into the Galactic Terran Empire had not yet arisen.

Fighting broke out among the colonists. They fought over food. They fought for medicine. They fought for power.

Spring came, the land thawed, food became plentiful again. And still they fought. Factions moved to various parts of the planet, often with ethnic or language groups sticking together. And still they fought each other.

Fighting and killing became an addiction.

But one faction remained in the caves of the old volcano. The scientists.

In their supposed godlike wisdom they decreed that the lesser mortals did not deserve to live. So they released their engineered microbes to take out their enemies. When a year had passed, the scientists crept out of the safety of their volcano fastness and ventured into the world.

The journal writer figured they could now plan their own community based upon the "higher" principles of science and logic prevailing over the emotionality of politics. Scientists would rule in a well-planned and orderly oligarchy. The unnamed scientist had left his/her journal with the other equipment when he/she left the mountain.

The plan worked too well. The scientists, too, must have fallen victim to their own disease, or the perpetual warfare. Some of the colonists had survived. So had their dedication to war.

"I say we take the shuttle," Kim said to his brothers. They sat beside the central fire while the women attempted to put together some kind of breakfast. "The shuttle is the fastest and most efficient way to solve many problems."

For once, the morning rains held off. The frogs seemed quieter, too. As if they'd croaked themselves out for a time.

With luck they'd take this abominable disease back into the mud with them.

"But travel by wormhole is so much faster, and more discreet," Loki insisted. He put on his I-am-the-captain-and-you-will-obey-me face.

"We're running low on fuel," Konner warned. "I'll need time to synthesize more."

"We'll have a lot of equipment to bring back as well as sulfur-laden water. I'm hoping the gas chromatograph and the spectrometer are still working. They will tell us if there is selenium and omniscium in the water, too," Kim countered. His brothers might trust the wormhole, but he sure didn't.

"Didn't Iianthe say something about the water *outside* the caldera being sweeter?" Konner asked half to himself.

"I wasn't paying that much attention. I was too entranced by the web of life. Maybe it's just magnetic fields of some kind," Loki changed the subject.

"Plants leech minerals out of the water and the ground. That's why you have to rotate crops and fertilize, to replace the minerals," Kim said, ignoring Loki's change of subject. He'd read a lot about crop rotation in the past few months.

"So if there was selenium in the water, then the plants along the edge of the creek would have selenium in their leaves and roots. Once we determine the levels of the mineral in the plants we could make a more controlled— dosage in a decoction—or infusion! I could—distill a counteragent." As usual, Konner's mind raced ahead of his words. He had to hesitate while he backtracked.

"Distillation takes time. Too much time. Getting an infusion or decoction into the mouths of the patients is the problem. Their jaws are locked." Kim started pacing. Life looked promising once more. They just had to keep Yaakke and his fellow warriors from launching a war against the Coros as soon as the sick rose from their beds.

"We'll work out a way to insert a wad of leaves into their mouths and have them suck for a while," Konner dismissed the problem. "That should unlock their jaws. Come on, let's fire up the shuttle and get moving. From the looks of those women, we don't have time to waste."

Kim eyed the pale skin and bulging eyes of his people. "Yeah. We need that cure by nightfall, or we're likely to lose them all."

"If they don't kill us first." Loki shook his head. "Who stays with them?"

"I trust Yaakke and Raaskan to look after things for a few hours," Kim said, hoping he wouldn't regret it.

"Good, I need to get out of here." Loki shook his head. Strain showed in the creases around his eyes. "I can't seem to block out all these fevered minds. All their distorted dreams are circling in my mind." He tried putting his fingers in his ears, shook his head again, and wandered away, his breakfast untouched.

After a hasty meal, Kim and his brothers trotted to the shuttle's landing strip.

Though they'd each returned to the shuttle several times since their abrupt landing, on this trip Kim felt uncomfortable—alien amongst the artificial alloys, synthetic materials, and electrical power. He'd grown used to simple, handmade tools. His fingers wandered over his console, seeking familiar patterns. The stretch from one interface to the next was wrong, as if he was trying to grasp a rock that was too big for one hand. He'd done that a lot while clearing a field. The shuttle smelled funny, though it should have no smell at all, being inert and lifeless without humans to activate it.

Maybe he was inert and lifeless without Hestiia and the other villagers to activate him.

Oh, Mum, forgive me for that thought, but it's the truth.

During the flight, Loki paid more attention to the ground than to their flight path. "Scan for electromagnetic fluxes," he ordered Kim. "Or any other kind of energy field, natural or man-made. I want to know what those blue lines are."

"I told you, they are a manifestation of transactional gravitons," Konner said blandly. "Nothing magical about them. Just energy strands."

Kim scanned the full spectrum of light and energy through his console and detected nothing out of the ordinary. This was just another bush planet as far the electronics were concerned. But he knew it was so much more. He looked out the real-time viewscreen. At first, he saw nothing. Gradually, afterimages and sparkling shadows danced across his vision. He allowed his eyes to lose focus.

Then he saw them. Straight lines here and there in varying shades of blue. Some thin, others fat. And where they crossed, a kind of fire flared out from the intersection.

"I don't get it. You should be able to detect something," Loki muttered. "Maybe it had something to do with the pattern of storms and moonlight."

"Maybe those dancing blue lines were figments of our imaginations," Konner scoffed. "We shouldn't be able to *see* gravitons, just push them aside to counteract the inertia they impose."

"On this planet, the imagination pales in comparison to reality," Kim muttered as he stared at the lines. "Psi powers can't be measured either. Maybe Loki's blue lines are akin to our talents that blossomed on this planet and nowhere else."

Too soon, the dry mountains came into view. The volcanic caldera seemed short and squat in comparison to the towering peaks around it. "That must have been one monster of a mountain before it blew its top!" Kim breathed. His sensors measured the distance between the rim and the bowl as being close to five hundred meters of near vertical cliff.

"When the volcano blew, it must have torn a huge hole in the graviton web. Maybe that's what caused the wormhole. There is absolutely no inertia there!"

"Strap in tight, boys. This is going to be a less than smooth landing," Loki called as he began a slow vertical descent.

Giant boulders littered the bowl, leaving little clear ground for the shuttle. But Loki made room by setting a jet at an angle to roll smaller rock debris out of the way. They tilted back and forth, nose down, and then sharply up several times.

Kim had to close his eyes. He'd spent too much time dirtside to feel comfortable with these abrupt changes. He needed a steady horizon and his feet firmly planted on solid ground. Could risking the trip on dragonback or through the dragongate be any worse?

Giddy rhymes and riddles played games with his thoughts. Heat waves and halos of light shimmered around the protrusions from the uneven ground. He blinked to rid himself of the images. They intensified.

"Am I feverish?" he asked his brothers, suddenly sober.

Konner touched his wrist to Kim's forehead. "A little warm. Not bad. But I think we'd best get on with this chore and get back home."

"Home," Kim said wistfully. "I've never had a home before."

He noticed his brothers exchanging concerned glances, but didn't care.

"I'll round up the equipment I need and take it out to the plants. You two load up the shuttle with as much of the cache as you can," Konner said.

"Who put you in charge?" Kim asked, only mildly resentful.

"That's supposed to be my line," Loki interrupted. "But I agree with Konner. You don't look so good, Kim. We don't want to leave you alone or let you stray too far from the shuttle in case you have to take it easy. Konner's the logical one to inspect plants. You and I can handle equipment. Grab a torch and a head mount for it. You'll want both hands free."

CHAPTER 40

D ISASTER! Hanassa braced himself against the roaring and shaking out-side the cavern where he slept. Taneeo visibly shook with fear. The whites of his eyes shone all too clearly. The boy would have bolted if Hanassa had not bound his ankles.

The High Priest crawled to the entrance and watched the noisy white dragon descend ungracefully into the bowl of his hideaway.

The Stargods had returned to rob him of his treasures, just as they had robbed him of Hestiia. He had not had time to set more than two traps and they were both deep inside the cave system, near the magic portal; where he had expected them to return. He had forgotten that they had other access to the caverns than the wondrous gate.

But he did have a few surprises for his uninvited guests. He knew these caverns well, all their tricks and turnarounds. He had also learned a few things about the machines and the weird yellow lights. The ancients had left behind more than just their toys. They also left diagrams and pictures painted most cunningly on thin slices of some substance akin to tree bark or leaves, all of a uniform shape with unnatural sharp corners. Arcane symbols filled most of the leaves. He could not yet decipher them. But he would.

In the meantime, he had taken samples of several pieces of equipment and hidden them well. The Stargods would not find everything.

And when he had made these caverns into a palace with a village to sup-port it, he would bring Hestiia here to reign over it as his queen.

"Get up, boy." He kicked Taneeo to get him moving. His apprentice struggled to sit upright. A difficult task with his bound hands and ankles and gagged mouth. Bruises covered his face and bare torso. But Hanassa had been careful to leave the boy's arms and legs undamaged. He needed his strength and youth.

Taneeo's eyes grew even wider and more fearful.

"Do not worry, I will not beat you for the insult of your life today. As long as you obey me. We have work to do."

Loki stepped warily into the large cavern. His brothers were eager to get the lab equipment back to the shuttle and leave this eerie place. He was, too. But he sensed something was wrong. The hair on the nape of his neck stood up, and his finger itched on the stunner.

Echoes of a voice lingered. Not a voice, a mind. An active one, very close.

He forced himself to listen to the echoes of this mind. A few hours ago he had run from the village because he could not separate himself from the disjointed ranting of fevered brains. The noise had nearly driven him insane. Especially Hestiia. She was worried about her baby. Her baby.

A half smile tugged at his mouth. Kim had found solace in her arms at the plowing festival. Hopefully the relationship had progressed beyond mere sex. The boy needed a friend and confidante as well as a lover.

Just once, Loki wished he knew Kim's secret and what Mum had promised him to get him to come on this run.

Loki hushed his brothers with a finger to his lips while he listened with all of his senses. They complied immediately. Loki guessed they, too, had sensed the presence.

The mind was behind them, chortling with glee. Hanassa! Another, quieter thought process lay beneath the laughter. The second person whispered one word of warning. *Trap.*

Loki searched every visible crack and crevice of the large cavern. His portable torch brought details into sharp focus. He couldn't tell if anything looked out of the ordinary.

Konner and Kim mimicked his actions. All their lives, he and his brothers had read each other's actions and attitudes without words. Perhaps the telepathy that had blossomed in Loki since coming to this place had been within them all from the beginning.

Konner's light lingered on a particularly large and nasty rock perched precariously on top of a pile of rubble. Only on second examination did Loki realize that the rubble nearly reached the ceiling, right beside the narrow entrance to the lab. If disturbed, the big rock would crush anyone beneath it. The rubble would slide in front of the doorway and seal it.

Loki jerked his head behind him to indicate that whoever had set this trap would willingly collapse the rocks on top of them.

The three brothers drifted slightly apart. Konner and Kim extinguished their lights. No sound followed their circling movement. Loki clamped down on his thoughts lest he inadvertently broadcast them to the lurker behind them. He focused on the lab as his eyes picked out the rocks he must avoid touching as he squeezed into the smaller room.

"Loki, freeze!" Konner called out.

The word reverberated around the cavern.

Loki stooped moving in mid-step. He teetered on his left foot. Cautiously he set his right foot back down precisely in his previous footprint. When he felt anchored, he looked around for the source of Konner's warning.

A tiny shift in the patterns of light and dark at his feet leaped out at him as unnatural. He shone the light where he would have set his foot. A slender thread stretched across his path at mid-shin. The coarse maroon wool from the wild cows was nearly lost in the darkness. One end of it seemed to be fixed to the center of the rubble pile by the lab.

"Breathe, Loki," Kim said quietly.

Loki did so. He hadn't realize he'd held his breath so long that his lungs ached.

"Now what?" Konner mouthed.

Loki looked around for inspiration. He bent down and hefted a good-sized rock, added a smaller one to it, then he grasped two more with the other hand. Easy to see where Hanassa got the raw material for his tilting rock sculpture.

Konner grinned as he picked up his own ammunition. Kim was a little slower to catch on; the fever must have been interfering with his thought processes. They had to finish this quickly. For Kim's sake. For Hestiia and the baby. And all of the others.

Silently Loki counted to three, mouthing the words clearly for his brothers to coordinate. On the last count they each launched all of their collected rocks at the same upright column of stone, well away from the rock sculpture and the trip thread.

Deafening crashes burst from the collisions. The sound amplified and compounded as it bounced around the cavern. Konner added an appropriate scream. Loki wanted to cover his ears. But he had to keep his stunner aimed and ready.

Hanassa bounded out of the passage into the cavern before the dust had cleared. Loki fired. Konner fired. Kim fired.

Three blinding pulses of energy pinned Hanassa upright. He jerked and convulsed and screamed. The smell of burning hair and flesh nauseated Loki. Kim doubled over in a coughing spasm (or was he gagging?) before his stunner drained of energy.

When Loki was certain that no mortal could survive the blasts, he released his iron grip on the trigger. Konner did the same.

They tiptoed over to the still jerking form that had collapsed onto the rough ground.

Loki knelt beside Hanassa, feeling clumsily for a pulse. Residual energy tingled through his hand and forearm where he touched the man's skin. That shouldn't happen. The body shouldn't store the stunner blast.

Hesitantly he opened his mind. He heard Konner's internal mutters about delay and equipment and plants. He heard a gibbering edge of panic from Kim, but nothing coherent.

And a third mind from behind him. But nothing from the inert body of their enemy.

"Is . . . is he dead?" came a tentative voice from the passage.

Loki looked up into a battered face bruised beyond recognition. "Who are you?" He already knew he didn't have to aim his stunner at the newcomer.

"T . . . Tan . . . Taneeo."

"The apprentice priest," Kim supplied the information.

"What in martyred St. Stephen's name did he do to you?" Loki asked. He rose from his crouch to catch the young man before he collapsed.

"H . . . he m . . . made me his slave. He pu . . . pu . . . punished me for everything you did to wrong him."

"I don't know if he's dead or not," Konner said. "I can't find a pulse. But we couldn't find a pulse last time we thought we'd killed him either."

"Throw the garbage into the corner," Loki ordered. "And pile a bunch of rock on him to keep him there. Maybe this time he'll stay dead and buried." Anger at the way Hanassa had so blithely mistreated Taneeo and all of the Coros burned within him.

"L . . . let me m . . . make certain he d . . . died." Taneeo pulled a knife from Hanassa's belt and began to plunge it into his heart.

"No," Kim said quietly. His voice carried a note of authority even Loki did not want to defy. But it also sounded hoarse. "If any man survived a triple blast of stunners, then we are not destined to kill him. Bind his hands and ankles, then place his body out of the way. Self-defense is one thing, murdering a downed man another. We have to have options other than murder."

"You don't sound very good, Kim." Loki eyed his youngest brother skeptically. "Your voice is getting weaker."

"I can do what we have to do to dismantle the lab." Kim squared his shoulders and marched determinedly toward the lab.

"Just be careful you don't trip that booby trap," Loki called after him.

"I will help," Taneeo offered, his voice gaining in strength and confidence. "I am yours to command now."

"We don't keep slaves," Loki growled. "But your help is most welcome. You may return with us and join our village."

"I would feel s . . . s . . . safer if you all . . . all . . . allowed me to drive a kn . . . kn . . . knife through his heart."

Loki shuddered. "He's gone. At least his mind has fled the body." Some of

Kim's trepidation leaked through to him. Maybe killing another being was as bad as he'd been told.

"If you do not kill him now, then you will die by his hand," Taneeo warned.

Kim slumped onto the padded bench in the lounge of the shuttle. Taneeo lifted his feet for him and swung them onto the far end of the bench.

"Tancs," Kim slurred. *St. Bridget,* his jaw ached. Just opening it far enough to utter the single word sent sharp pains up to his temples and down into his shoulders.

"What may I fetch you, Lord?" Taneeo kept his head bowed and his shoulders slumped as if he expected Kim to throw a blow at him as well as instructions.

Shaking his head in the negative hurt less than trying to tell the apprentice priest that all he wanted was sleep. He closed his eyes and prayed that all of his childhood inoculations would protect him from the worst ravages of the curse of the broga. But he knew they hadn't. Only his healthy, well-hydrated body had delayed the onset of the disease.

Several moments passed while Kim kept his eyes closed. Even the filtered light through the various ports made him wince in pain. Snatches of conversation and the sounds of movement drifted around him.

Dimly, he was aware that Loki and Taneeo stowed the equipment they had liberated from the lab of the original colonists. All of the extra water tanks were full of the foul-smelling creek water. Konner had gone off to the plateau.

"I could have sworn there were three terminals in the lab," Loki said at one point. "But we only found two today."

Something about the comment raised a tingle of alarm in Kim. He couldn't rouse far enough to say anything.

Kim drifted in and out of consciousness.

"What I want to know is what drove those people to such bitter hatred that they resorted to germ warfare," Loki said in disgust.

Kim tried to tell him he didn't really want to know, but he should read the journals downloaded into Konner's reader. His jaw ached too much to move it. He tried to massage the joints. His oh-so-terribly-heavy hand refused to lift.

More time elapsed. The sunlight seemed dimmer. Had the sun fallen behind the rim of the crater? Or had the disease affected his vision? Strangely, Kim did not care. He could die peacefully here and now with few regrets. All he really wanted was to hold Hestiia in his arms once more. He really should tell Loki where to find Kim's citizenship records. Cyndi's father had given him the precious status in thanks for saving the young woman. Kim wouldn't take the man's money. He refused to profit from the death of another—especially a death he had caused.

Maybe Loki and Konner could manipulate the papers to cover their own names. Their description was already close enough to Kim's. That was the least he should do for his brothers. With citizenship—even a faked one—they could realize their dreams much more easily. They could help Mum find Katie.

He would like to see Hestiia one more time. Just once hold her hand and tell her he loved her, without fear or guilt.

"Here, suck on this," Konner said, stuffing something between Kim's gum and cheek.

The wad was soft and cool. But it started to tingle and then burn. The taste made him gag. He couldn't control his muscles enough to swallow or spit. Maybe he'd die soon. He hoped he wouldn't take this bitter taste to heaven with him. It was a horrible thing to have to endure for all eternity.

"Eeouw!" Loki made horrible gagging sounds. "Couldn't you sweeten it up a bit?"

"Sorry. More important that we get the goodies into our systems than that we enjoy the taste," Konner replied sarcastically.

"This is an herb we use in soup," Taneeo offered tentatively. "A most interesting flavor in this batch."

Kim risked opening his eyes. The artificial lights had come on. His eyes focused easily, though he still needed to squint a little against the brightness.

"Think you might live, little brother?" Konner asked, holding his wrist against Kim's forehead.

"Do I want to?" His jaw still hurt, but it worked better than it had before Konner gave him the wad of plants.

"I think you might. Hestiia will be waiting for you."

"Hes." Kim swallowed. The ugly wad of plants remained stuck in his cheek. "Can I spit this out yet?"

"Better wait a while. Or better yet, swallow it when you can. That should mean the selenium is in your system and neutralizing the bacteria."

The plants helped him in the early stages of the disease. What about those who had succumbed earlier? How much internal damage had the fever and dehydration caused?

"Hes. We have to get back," Kim whispered, praying his brothers heard and understood the painful words. "She's dying. We have to help her." Healing sleep enfolded him before he could press his brothers further.

CHAPTER 41

H ANASSA SHOVED A PILE OF ROCKS off himself. He lay quiet a
moment, testing each part of his body. Scrapes and bruises from the
rocks, though no broken bones or internal injuries. But his neck jerked and
his abdomen spasmed. He breathed deeply, fighting to master the uncon-
trolled movements.

Eventually, he crept from the dark corner where the Stargods had tossed
his body—quite ungently. The ground beneath his feet trembled slightly. He
heard a distant roar. They had left him alone in the dark without his slave. His
body still trembled. A blue spark shot from his open palm. He stumbled to
the entrance to the room his enemies had called a "lab." A flexible strip, like
partially hardened tree sap, defined one side of the doorway. He leaned
against it for several long moments, seeking control of his body. Gradually,
the tingling and the jerking slowed.

"I am whole. I am alive," he said. Then he repeated it loudly. The sound of
his own words echoing around the cave confirmed his statement.

A lesser man would have given up hope and died. Only a man descended
from dragons could have survived the blasts of lightning from the Stargods.

The Stargods might think they had defeated him. They had lessons to
learn about him and his power. They had spoken openly while they thought
Hanassa dead or unconscious. They had used many of the machines before
stealing them, making certain they "worked." Though what work they performed Hanassa could not imagine.

He must find out. He possessed one of the terminals.

Hanassa had watched them and learned how to bring the thing to life. He
had recognized the arcane symbols as similar to the ones on the picture leaves.

He studied the terminal closely. He had seen images of it and how it connected to the "wires" growing out of the rock wall. He had also watched one of the Stargods, the healthy one, as he traced the wires to the "transformer" and the "generator." The generator had balked at his commands. He had removed a patch of its skin and manipulated several nodes. Then he kicked the thing and said: "Just like Great Aunt Bertha. Too bulky to move and too thick-skinned to listen to anyone else. Well, Big Bertha, you are going to listen to me." He had kicked the thing again, and it roared to life, clanking and puffing.

Then the transformer had whirred, and all of the machines came to life at once.

"I know your secrets now, false Stargods. I will learn everything these machines can teach me, and then I will bring you down. For you are no gods at all. A true god would not succumb to the curse of the broga. A disease for which there is no cure. The lore of the ancients made certain there is no cure, only remission."

Kim knelt beside Hestiia's pallet. She lay there, limp and pale. Her skin looked sallow and drawn.

"I haven't been able to get her to swallow any water for several hours," Yaakke confessed. His head slumped upon weary shoulders.

"The antibiotics I gave her weren't enough." Defeat weighed as heavily on Kim's shoulders as on the warrior's. An emotion alien to both of them. "I hope we are in time."

Still weak and shaking from his own fever, he pressed some crumbled and bruised leaves into her mouth. Her gums were blood red and had pulled away from her teeth. She did not even have enough strength to resist the bitter taste.

"You take some, too," Kim ordered Hestiia's brother. "It will keep you from getting sick."

Greedily, the young man stuffed a wad of the watercress-like plant into his own mouth. He gagged and tried to spit it out.

Kim held his hand over Yaakke's mouth. "Endure the taste. Keep it in your mouth as long as you can, so your saliva breaks down the chemicals in the leaves and stems."

Yaakke winced and curled his lip but obeyed.

Kim waited breathlessly for some sign of change in Hestiia. His heart seemed to beat overly loudly as he counted the seconds, minutes, hours.

"Nothing happens," Yaakke said. Defeat seemed to drag him down once more.

"It takes time. She's been very ill for two full days." Kim tried to make his voice as hopeful as his words. He did not think he succeeded. "I was beginning to be ill. The plants helped me within hours. We may not see a change in Hestiia until morning." He dribbled some more water into her mouth.

Her throat worked as if trying to swallow. Not much of the moisture disappeared from her mouth. Still she should absorb some of it through her sensitive gums. As long as he didn't drown her with too much at a time.

"May I take some of this cure to Maigrait?" Yaakke asked. "The Coros will have been struck down. The curse of the broga always fells an entire region at the same time."

"Yes, whatever. Go." Kim dismissed him, not truly certain he heard or understood his request. Not that he cared. He only wanted to see Hestiia get better.

"Don't leave me, Hes," he whispered. "I don't want to live without you, beloved. I want to marry you. Settle here on this planet with you. Help you raise our children as we guide these people toward peace and prosperity." A fat tear streaked down his cheek. It landed on Hestiia's hand.

Not even her skin twitched in reaction.

"Um, Loki, I, ah, something is bothering me." Konner detained his older brother from leaving the shuttle with a hand on his sleeve.

"Don't tell me we can't cure this cursed disease after all!" Loki's eyes grew wide. His nostrils pinched and his lips thinned.

"No, the selenium in the plants should render the bacteria inert. The problem is . . . well did you notice anything strange back in the cave?"

"The entire cave system is strange." Loki tried to move away. Konner kept him anchored with a firm hand on his shoulder.

"But in the lab. The light panels in the ceiling."

Loki stilled. His eyes glazed as he searched his memory. "Now that you mention it, one of the lights was out. The panel was off. I presumed you opened it to check it. Maybe to see if there were any spare tubes."

"I didn't touch it."

"Kim was too weak to do more than plod from the lab to the shuttle and back twice. Taneeo and I carried most of the equipment."

"Then who opened the panel?"

"Hanassa." Loki mouthed the word, almost as if he were afraid saying the name would bring their nemesis back to life.

"You don't suppose he survived," Konner said, hoping that the man was out of their hair forever, but also afraid that he had been responsible for another man's death.

"I don't think we have that kind of luck."

"So what do we do now?"

"I don't know. But we only have two terminals here. I know there were three the first time we were there."

"We cleaned the lab," Loki insisted. He did not like the trend this conversation was taking. "I double-checked. All we left were the tables."

"Then where is the third terminal?"

Loki gulped back his fears. "You don't suppose Hanassa hid one before we got there?"

"Just pray that he isn't smart enough to activate the voice control and have the computer teach him everything it knows."

"Have you slept at all?" Pryth asked. She hobbled into the big cabin supported by two women. One of them carried an IV bag still attached to the old woman's arm. The last IV bag Kim had stashed in the shuttle.

Dawn crept over the horizon, promising a clear day. The pattern of rain and high humidity seemed to have broken, at least temporarily.

The frogs were quiet for the first time in three moons. Hopefully they had gone underground again and taken the curse of the broga with them.

"I nodded off a few times," Kim admitted. He didn't tell the Rover woman that those few times had been when he was in the grips of the fever.

"Then go back to your own bed. Now." Pryth and her assistants crowded him away from where he crouched beside Hestiia's pallet.

"I don't want to leave her. If she dies, I must be beside her. I can't let her go alone."

"She will not be alone."

"But . . ."

"Go! This is women's work."

"Nursing is an honorable profession held by men as well as women."

"Nursing. Yes. But what ails her now is best left to women."

"What do you mean, what ails her now?"

"Have you not noticed?"

"What?" Anxiously Kim scanned Hestiia's slight form. Her face looked less pale beneath the dark circles around her eyes. He touched her arm. The skin blanched a little beneath his touch. It felt springy rather than so dry it might crumble to dust. The fever had broken during the night, and he'd coaxed her to drink a few milliliters almost every hour.

"If you do not know, then best you do not know. Go. Sleep. We will tend her."

"I need to know, Pryth." Kim stood up to his full height and caught her gaze with his own.

"You can intimidate warriors with those bluer-than-blue eyes, but not me. I have survived worse."

Pryth's assistants pushed him to the other side of the hide curtain that separated his quarters from hers.

"But, Pryth . . ."

"We will call you when she awakens and is fit to see men again."

"See men again?" Kim drifted out of the dim cabin that had begun to smell of fever and fear. His own sour smell was enough to drive him toward the river.

Waves of fresh air helped clear his head. His stomach grumbled and nibbled at his backbone. How long since he'd eaten? He couldn't remember. He should eat. Soon. Bath first.

Loki and Konner seemed to be on the same errand, headed for the deep pool downriver from the village. They carried roughly woven squares for towels and a small pot of a boiled root that sudsed up into a wonderful cleansing lather.

"Why is Pryth up and moving while Hestiia remains barely conscious?" he asked his brothers as soon as he caught up with them.

"We gave Pryth the only remaining IV. She was the worst off. Hestiia had some antibiotics," Konner said. He kept his eyes averted.

"But Hestiia was drinking. She took the cress plant readily. Her fever broke. She should be better."

"Complications," Loki said. He, too, kept his glance averted.

"What complications?"

Silence.

"What complications?"

"He has a right to know," Konner mumbled.

"Know what?" Anger added its own foul scent to Kim's body odor. It grew stronger the longer his brothers remained silent.

Loki stared at Konner. Konner returned the gaze. They looked as if they carried on a long conversation without words. With Loki, that was possible.

"Answer my question," Kim ordered. His fists balled. The cords of his neck knotted.

"Hestiia is pregnant. She'll probably miscarry as a result of the fever and the bacterial damage." Konner spoke in a monotone, as if reading from a medical text written by someone else.

Kim's knees collapsed. His butt met the ground before he realized he wasn't standing anymore.

"How—how do you know?"

"Before we left for the mountain, I overheard her dreams. Dreams full of fear," Loki admitted. "I couldn't block her out. She was broadcasting on a wide band. I'm surprised you two couldn't hear her."

"Oh."

"I already asked Konner. Neither he nor I has . . . ah . . . violated . . . no not violated . . . broken . . . is that the right word?"

"I had a nightmare. I didn't know then that it was a vision of the curse of the broga. I saw how the disease eats away at the jaws and gums, making the teeth look elongated, like a vampire's. Hestiia brought me out of it. Held me until the shakes passed." Kim confessed. "But it only happened once. Unless you count the plowing festival when everyone found partners for the night. I wanted to be with her. But I knew it was wrong, knew you two would . . . but I never thought it would lead to this."

"We know, Kim. We know. We understand. We've all thought about it. And we don't condemn you. St. Fidelio knows, I've visited enough of our women."

"I've . . . ah . . . consoled a few of the women myself," Konner admitted on a cough. "But not Hestiia. Neither of us . . . Well, we wanted to leave the field clear for you. You and she are obviously in love."

"Love. Yeah. I guess so. But pregnant?" His thoughts whirled. He couldn't think straight. Didn't know what to think, what to feel. "A baby."

There was something else, but his mind wouldn't settle on anything but the miracle of new life growing in Hestiia. His baby. *Their* baby.

Now he knew he couldn't go home, no matter how much Mum needed him.

"Can you imagine Mum's reaction? She's finally going to be a grandmum. She's wanted grandchildren for ages," Loki babbled.

"She already is," Konner reminded them. "And I intend to bring Martin back to the compound to meet Mum as soon as I gain custody. I will gain custody."

"I'm going to be a father!" The smile started somewhere around Kim's heart and spread outward.

"Congratulations!" Loki slapped his back. "Never thought the baby of the family would beat me to the punch. Cyndi and I . . ."

"Before you two start knitting little things, remember, Hestiia's not well. Pryth was pretty sure she'll miscarry. This could be dangerous for Hestiia. We don't exactly have advanced medicine and knowledgeable doctors here," Konner reminded them. "I don't think we have enough data to help with the damage a miscarriage could cause her."

Kim's vision dimmed. The elation drained out of him, leaving him deflated. Empty. Scared.

What good was all the progress they'd made in curing the curse of the broga, planting fields, teaching nonviolence if Hestiia wasn't there to share it with him?

CHAPTER 42

HESTIIA DRIFTED THROUGH NOTHING. If she moved nothing, thought nothing, then nothing hurt. Holding perfectly still, she could ignore the raging thirst and aching joints of the curse of the broga.

"Is this death?" she wondered. The words echoed in her mind but not her ears.

(Almost.)

Hestiia risked moving her head in search of the speaker. The pain did not return. "I must be dead if I do not hurt."

(Almost.)

The speaker sounded as if he had more to say. It must be a "he" to have such a deep and resonant voice.

(Open your eyes.)

Hestiia resisted. If she opened her eyes, the light of a thousand suns would burn up her soul as well as her body.

(Open your eyes, Hestiia, daughter of Yaaccob, wife to Stargod Kim.) The deep voice carried the weight of many voices, many ages of experience and wisdom.

She complied. Absolute darkness greeted her.

"I have lost my eyes!"

(Then open your mind.)

"How do I do that?"

(You know how to do it. You have always known.)

Had she?

(Your baby opened your eyes to new colors, a new way of looking at the world, a different way of watching others.)

Yes. Hestiia called into her memory images of colored halos around every living thing.

Some of those colors remained with her. She allowed her memory to peer deeper into those lines of bright red, green, yellow, blue, and purple that twisted around her.

(Now that your eyes are truly seeing, open your mind in the same manner.)

The colors pulsed with life. A vivid blue coil reminded her of Kim's eyes when they darkened with passion. She reached for it, needed to hold it close. It came to her readily.

An ache surrounded her heart.

"My Lord Kim grieves," she said sadly.

(And the green one?)

"Green for the fire of enthusiasm in Lord Loki." She grabbed hold of that one and felt the anger that always simmered just beneath the surface of his emotions. She dropped that coil rather quickly, frightened by the intensity.

On her own she drew the bright yellow light within her grasp. Strange numbers and precise shapes flooded her mind, sometimes chaotic, sometimes ordered. "This one must be Lord Konner. Always thinking, always looking for answers."

(And this one?) The voice pushed a deep ocher coil toward her. Purple twisted with it, the two colors separated by a constant clear space—not clear, white shimmering elusively with all of the colors.

"I think this is me, me and Gentian bound together."

(Not Gentian. You and the dragons. From you comes a solid link between humans and dragons that will last for many generations.)

"Gentian is gone from my life." Sadness weighed heavily against her.

(Yes.) The voice sounded as sad as she felt.

She fought to master her grief for many moments. At last it lifted from her soul. A little.

"Gentian was never truly mine. He sheltered with me because Hanassa frightened him and he knew that Hanassa would never truly hurt me."

(Gentian protected you from other humans when he could. Courage was not his strongest quality. We must find another quest for him. There is still another coil of life you have not touched.)

"I see no others."

(You do not look. This one frightens you more than you know.)

"Hanassa." Black and purple and red, all twisted together in tight knots. She shied away from it, looking elsewhere. Anywhere but at Hanassa.

(Take it.)

Hestiia stared at the ugly coil a long time.

(Take it. Now, before he hides again.)

Reluctantly, Hestiia stretched toward one of the dark knots. It untwisted at her briefest touch.

"He loves me as fiercely and possessively as he hates everything else about his life. He blames the dragons, he blames people, he blames everything but himself for his unhappiness."

(Yes.)

"He thinks I will fill the emptiness inside him. But only after he has murdered every human that walks the land of the Coros. But he is wrong!" She thrust the coil away from her. Immediately it twisted up again, tighter than before.

(Hanassa will not be complete until he dies. No mortal can kill him. Only the dragons can do that. But they will not kill one of their own. Killing one of their own will trap the entire nimbus in the void between the planes of existence forever.)

"Is that where I am?"

(Yes.)

"Then I am dead."

(Almost.)

"Can I live?"

(You have one more life you must touch.)

Bodily pain invaded her. She closed her eyes/mind, seeking the blissful nothing from before this alien voice had invaded her.

(You must touch. You must know.)

"I cannot."

(Why?)

"The life is not fully formed."

(Yes it is. The life is only a part of the body. 'Tis the body that is not fully formed.)

"If I touch it, it will die," she wailed.

(If you do not touch it, then it will cease to exist. Touching it now will give it life in your memory. Touching it now will give it a chance to find its way across the void to its next existence.)

Hesitantly, she opened herself a little. Just a little. All of the colors of life washed over her in a single wave. She could not experience it all at once.

She opened her heart a little more. Exuberant joy cascaded through her.

"Hello, little one."

The colorful joy danced and bounced in greeting.

"Child of my heart."

The colors embraced her fiercely. Then they slackened and retreated.

"Do not leave me." If she had a body, tears would streak down her face.

(We must.)

"I love you."

(We know. We love you, too.)

"Will you come again?"

(If we can.)

"Thank you for . . ." Sobs choked off her thought.

(Listen to your heart. Look with your soul. Love with your entire being. Farewell.)

"Farewell," she whispered as the life drifted away.

Pain ripped through her middle.

She opened her eyes to see Pryth's stern frown. The world beyond the wisewoman looked pale, faded. The colored halos had gone back into the void along with her baby's life. An emptiness vaster than the void she had traversed gnawed at her. But a little bit of joy remained near her heart.

"My baby talked to me, Pryth. Just as you said it would."

"Where is Yaakke?" Loki asked the villagers as they assembled for breakfast. A strange nervousness twitched between his shoulder blades. He needed to be up and moving. A nice long hunt would help. Hunts always went better with a partner. Like Yaakke.

"Haven't seen him since we got back from the mountain," Konner said around a mouthful of cereal.

"He took some of the cress plants to the Coros. He was worried about his girlfriend," Kim added. He played with his bowl of mixed, boiled grains. Loki couldn't tell if he actually ate anything or not.

"That was yesterday," Loki reminded them all.

"Maybe he stayed overnight to nurse the girl." Konner shrugged. "I have to go back to the *Sirius*. I need parts to cobble together a still to take the omniscium out of the mountain water. Then I have to start the crystal bath. Anything you want me to hunt for on the scanners?"

"Wetlands," Kim said. A spark of animation finally moved his face out of his depression. "We should start draining them if they harbor the frogs that carry the curse of the broga."

"Think a bit before you jump to that conclusion," Loki warned. If he'd learned nothing else on this adventure, he now knew the advantage of leaving the planet's ecology alone. People had survived here for three hundred years without interference from the outside, or improvements. They had to move cautiously.

St. Bridget! Was that thought his own? He'd never been cautious before. Never needed to be. And here was Kim on the verge of drastic action based on an emotional response. He was the one who always urged caution and planning.

What was happening to him? To them?

"I have thought it out. If we are ever to bring these people into prosperity—actually producing a surplus that we can sell elsewhere, we need to eliminate this artificial disease once and for all." Kim stood up, letting his breakfast bowl fall to the ground.

For the first time in a long time, he hadn't said anything about how much Mum needed the money from that surplus.

"There are ways to do that without altering the landscape beyond repair. Remember your history. What was the key trigger to dome the major cities on Earth and start breathing canned air?" Konner remained calm. But it took an effort. Loki read his apprehension as if it were his own.

Kim's face looked blank. Did he honestly not remember the lesson Mum had pounded into their heads from earliest childhood? Or did he choose to forget?

"The frogs all died. When the last of them were gone, the ecology that had been breaking down for a long time took a drastic plunge. The declining numbers of frogs were an indicator of an underlying problem, but they also served a valuable niche," Loki recited Mum's words. "The wetlands are the homes of the frogs."

"We need to look at long-term weather patterns instead," Konner mused. "From all that I've heard, winters here are wet and cold. The cold sends the frogs into hibernation. Spring is short—just long enough for the frogs to mate. Then a long dry summer when the frogs burrow deep into the mud and stay out of the way of people. But in very wet years, they stick around long enough to infect the populace. I think I'll start a weather database while I'm scouting iron deposits."

"This has been an unusually wet year. The first one in a decade," Loki hammered the final point of his arguments.

Kim sat back down, deflated. But his mind was working. Loki could hear scattered half thoughts as he sorted and organized them, devoid of the strong emotions that drove him earlier.

"Wet spring, move inland, away from the swamps. And plant late, after the rains stop. We're going to lose part of our crop this year due to rot from all the rain." Loki shrugged his shoulders. He felt lighter, as if he'd just solved a major problem all by himself.

"Or, by the time the next one comes around, we'll be able to sow the wetlands with selenium and neutralize the disease," Loki finished the argument.

His usual good spirits returned. "I'm going to look for Yaakke and take him hunting. We need some protein to restore weakened bodies after the fever laid so many of us low." He stood up and stretched.

"I'm staying here. Hestiia might need me." Kim looked longingly at the cabin. Pryth and her acolytes had not emerged since they went in over an hour earlier.

"I'll be gone most of the day," Konner said, also rising and stretching. He left the campfire circle, heading for the open grassland upriver where they'd left the shuttle last night.

Loki surveyed the village a moment. A dirty place by civilized standards back home, but neat. No garbage lying about, a few fusterhens—a cross between a local fowl and the chickens brought from Earth—and dogs—another crossbreed—strutted around, nosing out any dropped food. Mud splashed the stone foundations of the huts, but otherwise the locals kept the place clean. Even the latrines remained unobtrusive and rarely stank, thanks to a liberal application of lime.

Satisfaction replaced Loki's earlier unease. He and his brothers had built something here, something worthwhile, something that would earn them citizenship and financial independence back home. Then he and Cyndi could be together.

His contentment shattered. A psychic scream lanced across his mind. Darkness crowded his vision and made his knees tremble.

He knew with absolute certainty that Hanassa had returned from the dead and taken a sacrificial victim.

"Yaakke," he said on a long exhale that ripped through his lungs. "He's killing Yaakke!"

CHAPTER 43

HANASSA SENT A SHORT BURST of energy from the stunner toward Yaaccob, the warrior chieftain of the Coros. He had found three of the little weapons hidden in a cache within "Big Bertha," the largest of the generators. The computer had taught him how to use them, how to charge them with energy, and how long a blast a man could withstand before passing out or suffering permanent damage.

Neither the computer, nor any of the texts in the hidden library told him how to kill a man with the stunner.

Yaaccob crumpled at the end of the second short blast.

"You have killed my father! Now I will kill you," Yaakke screamed. The young warrior rushed from one of the houses with his blade upraised and murder in his eyes.

Hanassa noted that the young man carried one of the new iron knives fashioned by the Stargods. That metal was more dangerous to Hanassa than the bronze carried by the other warriors. But Hanassa doubted that Yaakke could break through his thick and unusual bone structure to find the few vulnerable places that might kill him.

Casually, the High Priest turned the stunner on the man charging toward him. Yaakke screeched like a gray hopper at the moment a hawk crushed its neck. Like his father, Yaakke continued forward, ignoring the pain. A second blast brought a louder scream from him. The third felled him.

"You have all wavered from your faith in Simurgh, and from *me!*" Hanassa informed the rest of the village. They backed away from him. A few fell to their knees in fear and awe. As they should.

"Choose your sacrifice so that I might choose to release you from the ravages of this curse of the broga!" Hanassa shook his staff; the bones and beads rattled ominously.

Everyone still standing backed farther away. They did not try to rouse the fallen men.

Hanassa smiled. "You have chosen your two finest warriors. Their blood will cleanse you all of the taint of disbelief. Carry them to the altar."

"But . . . but we no longer have an altar. The Stargods destroyed it," a timid voice said from the back of the crowd.

"Then find a new one. Preferably where the Stargods can observe and know their downfall, know that they will be next to die on the altar if they continue to defy me." He cast off the last pretense that these people served any god but himself.

Hanassa had few doubts that the Stargods would continue to defy him, possibly make war on his people. But he knew how to kill them. They were mortal and not gods at all. Unlike himself. Unlike the dragons he was descended from.

When he had killed the Stargods, Hestiia would have to return to him. No man must have her but Hanassa.

A slim, dark-haired girl crawled out of the hut where Yaakke had been hiding. Her skin was pale beneath her normal dark coloring and her eyes bulged like those of a curse victim. But her teeth and gums looked healthy. She wailed her grief, so her jaw could not be locked. She smoothed Yaakke's hair from his brow, murmuring words of comfort.

The villagers moved closer, gaping in amazement.

"She lives."

"She speaks."

"The curse of the broga wanes."

"The Stargods sent a miracle."

"The Stargods sent nothing! Simurgh roused the girl." Hanassa had to think fast to counter the actions of his enemies. "Yaakke knew the truth and returned to us from the village of unbelievers. His return was rewarded with the life of his beloved. Fall down and worship Simurgh the all-powerful."

"But Yaakke brought me some plants from the Stargods," the girl said quietly.

Hanassa felled her with a single shot from the second stunner he had hidden in his left hand.

"Loki!" Kim grabbed his brother beneath the arms and held him upright by sheer force of will. "What's wrong?"

Konner bounded back to them. He cradled half Loki's weight. Together, they managed to set him back down on the rock where he had eaten his breakfast.

In short broken phrases, Loki told them of the telepathic vision.

"Are you certain?" Kim asked, checking Loki's pulse and temperature.

"More certain than you are when you have one of your freaking visions. This was real. I saw it. I heard it. I friggin' smelled it. We've got to save Yaakke."

"He's one of ours," Konner agreed. "O'Haras don't abandon their family."

Kim did not remind his brothers that they'd left their sister Katie to the not-so-tender mercies of the planetary governor who illegally stole their home, their business, and their citizenship. None of them had heard from Mari Kathleen O'Hara since.

But Kim agreed with Konner. They could not abandon Yaakke.

"Once Hanassa eliminates Yaakke and his father, he'll come for us. He'll regain his power over the people through a reign of blood and terror."

"Where are they taking Yaakke and his father?" Kim asked.

"I don't know. They had not decided when the vision cut out."

"Where would they take him? We destroyed their altar." Konner paced around them, running his hands through his hair and beard. "They don't like to use the temple. The walls and ceiling hide the view of the sacrifice from Simurgh."

"Hanassa told them to find a new altar," Loki choked.

All three of them whipped around to stare at the massive rock in the center of their wheat field.

"Petram," Konner breathed. "He won't let them use our Petram for sacrifice."

"The rock isn't sentient, Konner," Kim reminded him. "At least, I don't think it is. Who knows on this crazy planet. We need Gentian to spy on them."

"Or the dragon. Iianthe is more—literal—no telepathic. He speaks in words. The flywacket communicates in images," Konner said.

"Images are enough. Has anyone seen the flying cat since Hestiia convinced you he didn't bring the curse of the broga and shouldn't be killed?" Loki asked the villagers lingering around the campfire.

Kim looked into the eyes of each one seeking the truth. They all shook their heads. Strangely, most of them had gone about their daily chores and returned to a normal routine despite the disease that had almost felled them all.

"I think Gentian flew into the woods," Raaskan said for them all. As he usually did.

"Hes is the only one who can call him," Kim said quietly. He turned his attention back to their cabin. A tremendous weight pressed upon him, dragging his face into a frown. "If she dies, we are leaving. With or without repairs. With or without a profitable cargo."

"There might be another way to find Yaakke," Loki said. His voice was confident, but his eyes looked clouded with doubt.

"I could take the *Rover* up and scout activity." Konner said. "Tricky flying low enough and slow enough to look that close."

"I was thinking in terms of engaging my telepathy again," Loki said. "This time deliberately. If only there was a way to concentrate my powers."

"There is a way. If you are serious. If you are willing to risk it," Pryth said, emerging from the big cabin.

But Kim barely heard her. He rushed past her to Hestiia. Nothing else mattered.

• ——◆—— •

"Is Hestiia all right?" Loki asked. He felt he should inquire for Kim's sake before he got to the more interesting and exciting prospect of expanding his telepathic talents.

"She will live." Pryth's face carried no expression.

"Will she bear more children?" Konner asked. At least he had the courage to catch the old woman's eyes with his gaze.

She returned his look with a penetrating stare. "Perhaps. Perhaps not."

"What, by St. Nicholas, patron of children, does that mean?" Loki asked. Impatience to get started made his feet itch. But he had to know about Hestiia for Kim's sake. His brother would not remain sane if she died.

Loki crouched down and removed his boots, something he'd not been willing to do before. But he needed the feel of the beaten soil on his soles. Almost immediately, the itch ceased to bother him. Then he tossed off his shirt. The cool morning air, warming up by the femto as the sun rose higher, eased the crawling sensation on his back and chest.

"Hestiia is young. Her body heals. How it heals is always a question." Pryth shrugged in that annoying way of hers. "If you wish to save the warriors from Hanassa's knife, you must go to the island where you first appeared in the white dragon-that-does-not-smell-like-a-dragon. Gather the leaves of the Tambootie tree. Bring them back to me."

"Tambootie? What kind of tree is that?" Loki asked.

"According to Kim's botany text, there was a tree in South Africa on Old Earth by that name. Supposed to be extinct," Konner replied, scanning the reader rapidly.

"The Tambootie is what makes a dragon . . . a dragon." Pryth shrugged again. "Eating of the leaves will bring out the dragon in you. But you must return here before eating of them. They will kill you if you make a single mistake in their preparation."

"Okay, what does it look like?" Loki wasn't sure he liked this.

"Thick leaves. Oily leaves. Mottled pink and green. Young leaves from the top of the tree are best. But any leaf will assist you in your task."

"Do the leaves have to be from that island? It's a long way from here, and we don't have much time." There. He'd acknowledged the urgency of the mission. Some of his anxiety lessened. He knew the cause of it. But knowing the deadline added more unease.

"Across the river. A clearing in a perfect circle. Near the opening of the dragongate."

Loki and Konner exchanged a look. They knew the place. They'd returned from the mountain crater to that spot. How did Pryth know that? How did she know anything?

"She is a Rover," Raaskan said, almost as if he'd read their thoughts. Maybe he had. "I will go with you. You will need a guard. That clearing is one of the places Hanassa may choose for his altar."

"He respects circles, then."

"We all do."

"Then I will give him circles next time we meet."

"How, Lord Loki?"

"I don't know yet. Let's go find some of the Tambootie."

"You are up to something, Loki," Konner accused.

"Of course I am."

"Then, I'm coming, too. I want to see if this tree of magic will enhance my power as well."

"Remember, do not eat of the dragon tree. You have not undergone the trial by Tambootie smoke. Eating the leaves without preparation will kill you," Pryth reminded them.

CHAPTER 44

HESTIIA ENDURED Pryth's ministrations. She drank the foul-tasting brew forced upon her. She answered questions. She cooperated with the elaborate cleansing process. Echoes of old pain tried to reach her through the knot of her cold grief.

She retreated to memories of the void, seeking once more the vivid colors of life. She sought out again the bright joy within one splash of life. Her child had not yet had the chance to resolve into a defined coil. It had washed through her rather than taking on a form she could touch. Neither male nor female. The child had been simple joy, unscarred by life.

Her memory lingered on a deep blue cord, the same color as the Great Bay in the sunshine. She drifted with the memory for a long moment.

Sleep claimed her.

In her dreams the blue coil tugged at her. She wanted to follow, knew it would help fill the empty void left by the loss of her child. But she had to go through the pain and scarring to get to the other side.

She retreated. Hid deep within the colors, letting them mask the deep ocher of her own identity.

The blue followed her, relentless in its pursuit. Wherever she hid, it found her. No matter how fast she ran, it caught her.

The chase became a game. Her own cord vibrated with growing brilliance. The blue throbbed with a responding laughter. Deep, melodious, compelling.

Like Lord Kim's laugh when she coaxed him to smile. He was too serious, too much in need of her lightness to counter his dark moods.

At last the blue cord caught her, wound around her, tangled, melded, and helped heal the aching emptiness within her.

She sighed and opened her eyes.

The first sight to greet her was Kim's smile. He held up their entwined hands and kissed her fingers.

"I thank all the saints that you have returned to me, beloved," he whispered.

"I thank you for giving me a reason to live."

Then memory caught up with her. She wanted to retreat again into sleep. But she could not. A knife-sharp pain in her belly reasserted itself.

"I have failed you, my Lord." She wept.

"Never, Hestiia. You live. That is enough."

"But I lost your baby. I have betrayed you."

"Never. I promise you there will be other children. We will be together for a long, long time. Together, we will raise a dozen children."

"But your brothers will take you away. You must return to your mother."

"Mum will get by on her own. I am yours body and soul. That part of my family no longer has a hold on me."

"Those must be the trees," Konner pointed to the tall deciduous tree with the thick succulent leaves. The aromatic bark filled the clearing with a clean scent, almost like the incense Mum's priest burned. The heady fragrance threatened to unbalance his senses.

He'd felt just like that when Yaaccob and Hanassa had tried to burn the *Rover*. Something in the smoke . . .

He gritted his teeth and curled his toes into the mat of decaying leaves. Over the generations the shed leaves had composted down into a rich soil. His entire body felt nourished, anchored, by the contact.

"A good mixture of hardwoods." Loki walked the perimeter of the clearing, kicking at the layers of dead leaves on the ground. He picked up a long branch and began stripping off the smaller branches with his good alloy knife.

"First we need to send Hanassa a signal," Loki said grimly.

"I don't like the look in your eye, brother." But a chill of excitement shivered from his shoulders to his fingers, to his gut.

"You sound like Mum. She never liked any of my plans." Loki pouted. The gleam in his eyes belied his expression.

"Someone has to keep you from getting us all killed." Konner couldn't help watching his brother's meticulous stripping of the long stick.

"What kind of signal do you wish to send, Lord Loki?" Raaskan asked.

"I intend to let the vicious little prick know that we will not be intimidated and we will not allow any of our people to become his victims." Loki began gathering deadfall branches.

Raaskan followed suit.

Konner rolled his eyes and shook his head. But he, too, began gathering firewood.

Loki arranged their offerings in a tall pyramid.

"You building a bonfire?" Konner asked. "I think I like this plan, but it scares me a little. You scare me sometimes, big brother."

"Sort of a bonfire." Loki scooped piles of desiccated leaves around the base.

"A fine bonfire," Raaskan said. He puffed out his chest with pride. "This one will burn long and bright for an entire night of dancing and storytelling."

"You forgot one." Konner proffered the two-meter-long branch Loki had meticulously stripped when they first arrived.

"No, I didn't. I saved it for something special." Loki fished in his pockets with studied determination. He came up with a fistful of small bones, fish and rabbit probably. Each bit had already been strung on a separate strand of yarn in the ubiquitous maroon from the wild cows.

"By the Holy Sisters of the Stars, what are you doing?" Alarm warred with laughter deep inside Konner.

"I'm making a staff. Haven't you always wanted a finely decorated staff? We deserve staffs as symbols of our godhood."

"I'd think we'd want something a little different, a little more elaborate than Hanassa's staff." Konner fingered the dangling bones.

"Your staff does not have an animal skull on top." Raasakan looked around the clearing as if expecting to find one lying about.

"Correct. That's the signal. We are depriving Hanassa of his sacrifices, animal and human." Loki jammed the improvised staff into the center of the carefully arranged firewood. "And this bonfire will burn more than just wood." Then he pushed into the base of the fire, right next to the butt of the staff, a small black plastic box.

"That's a bomb, Loki. A vibration sensitive concussion bomb you liberated from Kim's private stash aboard the shuttle. It won't kill, but it will knock a person out and give him a monstrous migraine for a few days."

"Shush, Konner. We don't want to give away the party surprise."

"Yeah. Right." Just what Hanassa deserved. Konner just hoped no one else was hurt by the device.

"Now it's time to gather some leaves of the Tambootie. Who's going to climb a tree?"

"I will, Lord Loki." Raaskan bowed low, then bounded forward. He leaped and caught the lowest branch of a huge tree some three meters above the ground. Clinging with hands and feet, he scrambled upward. Soon he was lost to view in the thick foliage.

Konner marked the man's passage by the rustling of the branches.

A few moments later Raaskan shouted in triumph. The sound of breaking branches and crashing limbs followed. Then a branch covered in small tender leaves thumped to the ground.

Loki rushed forward and grabbed the branch. Another nearly landed on his head. He caught it before it hit the ground.

Loki's screech of pain and the thump of the branch hitting the ground reached Konner's ears at the same time.

"Loki, what is it?" Konner caught his brother before he fell to his knees.

"St. Bridget!" he whispered as he staggered back. He held up his hands. A thin oily residue dripped from his palm.

Konner tried to wipe his brother's hand clean with the leather of his vest. The oil jolted and burned his fingers where he touched the plant goo. Not unpleasant. With a gesture, the oil flew from Loki's hand, landing harmlessly among the leaf litter.

"Just touching the leaves, I know where Hanassa is going," Loki whispered.

"Just touching the oil, I feel like I can move the world." Konner circled his hand. A cyclone of dead leaves rose up. He gestured to it to scatter a meter away. It complied.

"Hanassa didn't even think of this clearing," Loki continued. He stared into the distance, focusing on something only he could see or hear. "He's going to defile the place where we first landed the shuttle. He wants the place to be sacred to him rather than to us."

"Can we get there in time?" Konner asked. The heady influx of power dissipated as quickly as it had come.

"He's waiting for the full moon to rise tonight."

"Then we have time to gather weapons and raise an army."

"An army of forty former slaves and half-trained warriors."

"This time, you and I will wed in a proper ceremony. Just the two of us. A normal marriage. I will not share you with my brothers," Kim insisted. He held onto Hestiia's hand fiercely. Once they were together, in a true marriage, he would protect her from danger and illness with every bit of knowledge and technology he could lay his hands on. Even if he had to kill every frog in the land.

"But we are already married," Hestiia replied. She lowered her eyes briefly, shyly, then raised them to capture his.

Kim willed her to read all of his love for her in his direct gaze.

"What must we do?" Hestiia asked.

"What do your people do?"

"The man must ask the woman's father permission to court her. The father will demand a fat bride-price, fatter than the dowry he offers. There is much negotiation carried out over many days of feasting and drinking and dancing. When the two men have negotiated a settlement—the bride-price always equals the dowry—then the woman moves from her place behind her mother to sit beside the man. He covers her breasts with a garment signaling that no other man may have her body and they retire to his hut. They are married."

"Not unlike our own preliminaries. But we believe marriage is a partnership. The man and the woman must exchange vows before a priest. They vow to love, honor, and respect each other through good times and bad. The negotiations of bride-price and dowry are called a 'prenuptial agreement' or a 'prenup.' They are very important and usually handled by lawyers—people who are very learned in the law and the art of manipulation."

He could no longer meet her gaze. "I cannot go to your father to request permission to marry you, Hestiia. His village and ours are not yet on cordial terms."

"Could you please ask my brother? He is one of us. We should forge a new ceremony that is the best of both our worlds."

"I . . . um . . ." How could he tell her that both her father and brother had been captured by Hanassa and marked for ritual sacrifice? In her weakened state, the shock could make her condition worse.

"Please, my Lord Kim. Please hold to at least this little part of our customs. So much has changed since your coming, we have lost touch with customs that anchored our sense of self and connected us to the roots of our past." Hestiia grabbed his arm in a strong grip that belied the weakness of her condition.

"But . . ." In order for Kim to ask Yaakke anything, he would have to free him and his father from Hanassa's grip. The High Priest kept the Coros chained to him by terror and some kind of hypnotic enthrallment.

If Kim chose to honor Hestiia's demand, he put himself in grave danger. If he and his brothers sought to impose their laws and beliefs on this society, they faced equal danger.

The time had come to rid these people of the evil influence of the demon Simurgh and his High Priest.

Just then Loki and Konner burst into the hut. "We need weapons and a battle plan," they said together.

"Then we have to rally every able body to join us in a crusade against Hanassa," Loki finished. "I won't allow my friend Yaakke to die, nor his girlfriend, nor his father. This time Hanassa will die if I have to behead him myself."

Hestiia gasped and fell back against her pillow of soft bird feathers. "My brother? Hanassa has my brother and my father?"

"Yes, my dear." Kim cradled her shoulders and pulled her tight against his chest. "I wanted to shield you from this horrid news." He glared at Loki, wishing he could silence his unthinking, incautious brother with just a look.

"Sorry." Loki shrugged as he began rummaging through his scattered possessions. "You two are so big on honesty, I presumed you would have told her."

"You must not leave me alone, Lords." Hestiia clutched Kim's head, forcing him to look directly into her eyes. "Hanassa uses my father and brother to draw all three of you into a trap. And when he has murdered all three of you, he will come to claim me by right of conquest. He will force me to be his wife. I will kill myself before he has the chance to touch me."

CHAPTER 45

◆ —— · —— ◆ · ◆

KIM TOUCHED THE OILY LEAVES that Loki held before his eyes. His mind flashed with images in alien colors. Horror and revulsion pulsed through him. Heat pounded at his temples and left his cheeks and his hands icy cold.

He breathed deeply and evenly, counting each inhalation and matching it to the exhalation. Desperately he pressed his fingers against his temples.

The vision waned. He took another deep breath.

The colors swirled around him, more vivid than color had a right to be.

Hanassa neatly severing Loki's head with his bronze sword. Konner already lay dead beside him. Hanassa's staff impaled him through the heart.

"This is only a vision," he told himself. "This isn't happening. I won't let it happen." The sound of his own voice beat against his ears and shattered the images before his eyes.

"I have to stop this! Why would God give me visions if not to warn me, help me prevent it from happening." Who could he call for help?

"I told you, you must wait for my instruction and guidance!" Pryth burst into the cabin. Her face darkened with her ire. Her black eyes blazed.

All three brothers recoiled from her instinctively.

"How can you interpret these visions? How can you understand what knowledge the gods send you? You have not undergone a trial by Tambootie smoke to settle your talents, bring them to your instant command. And now you touch the leaves and think you know everything!" She spat into the corner.

"We don't have time for trials and training, Pryth." Loki returned her stare with one of equal intensity. "We have to act tonight, before the full moon rises. We have to save the innocents and destroy Hanassa once and for all. I will kill him myself this time."

Don't say that, Loki. You don't know what you mean, Kim pleaded with his brother silently.

"Then you and you alone are responsible for the disaster you bring upon yourselves. What is the cost of three lives compared to the safety of an entire world?" Pryth stomped out of the cabin.

"What did she mean by that?" Loki and Konner asked in unison.

"Pryth speaks in riddles. She knows what she knows. She is a Rover," Hestiia replied softly.

"What makes you think you can stop Hanassa this time?" Kim asked his brothers. Or did he truly ask only himself? "Twice before we have dealt him lethal blows. He has survived both times. Indeed, he seems to thrive on our efforts." His mind worked furiously. He had to protect Hestiia. He also had to keep his brothers from plunging into a situation they only half understood.

Not that Kim understood it any better. Whose eyes had provided him with the terrible precognitive vision? If the colors had not been too bright and oddly placed—beige skin, pink leather clothing, blue grass, green sky— he might have believed himself the originator of the vision.

He'd worry about what this all meant to Mum later.

A sharp taste on the back of his tongue jerked him out of his self-defeating thoughts. The vision had tasted sharp, like incense. Like the aromatic tree sap that lingered on his brothers and their clothing.

"The Tambootie!" He stared at the branch with the weird leaves. "Hanassa added some of that tree to the fire beneath the *Rover*. We've already undergone the trial by Tambootie smoke. We can handle the stuff and survive."

"This time we will fight Hanassa with weapons he understands, bronze and iron blades, fire, and magic." Loki grinned. He was too smug, too pleased with himself.

"What do you mean, with magic?" Kim did not like the colored vibrations radiating from Loki. The aftermath of the vision had left him overly sensitive to every nuance of Loki's body language as well as his thoughts.

"Like you said, we've undergone the trial. Our talents are settled. These leaves fuel my telepathy." Loki held up a broken branch filled with vibrant leaves. Hours after plucking, they were still thick like a succulent, deep green, veined in pink, and dripping with oil. The greenery gave off the odor of incense.

"They also increase my telekinesis," Konner added.

"I'm going to try planting ideas in Hanassa's head."

"I'm going to throw everything I can at him. Rocks, knives, fire, water, whatever is close at hand."

"We'd have better luck sending the dragon after him," Kim countered. He ushered them into the other room of the hut and closed the curtain behind him. He had to keep this discussion from Hestiia. "If Hanassa was born a dragon, and the dragon spirit has altered his human psyche—and, I think, his skeletal structure from the time I examined his knife wound—the dragons may be the only things that can stop him."

"Yeah, but how do we find a dragon? And, once found, how do we persuade it to help us. The dragons haven't done anything to interfere up to now other than giving us a ride," Loki argued. His fists balled and his shoulders tensed. He was ready to fight anyone who stood in his way, even his brother.

"We cannot kill. What are we if we stoop to Hanassa's level?" Kim insisted.

"This has gone beyond that, little brother." Loki's fists tightened even more. The waves of energy radiating from him became redder and more intense. "One of our people is in mortal danger, so are his father and his girlfriend. We stand to lose a lot more than our self-esteem if we don't rescue them."

"Honor in battle is the only thing the Coros understand," Konner added on a gentler note. "Our honor has been compromised. We have to do everything in our power to save Yaakke and the others. We'll gain a lot more than we lose."

"Please stop and think about this. You are talking about killing another human being," Kim pleaded. He grabbed Loki's shoulders and shook him. Other images flashed through him. He did not think he could survive another trip to the "other side" with a dead soul. Could Loki withstand even one trip?

Loki broke Kim's grasp. His hands remained up and ready to exchange blows at the least provocation.

"We have thought about it. Hanassa is no longer human," Konner pronounced. "We leave within the hour. Will you join us, Kim?"

"I cannot condone murder."

"Then we have to make sure you don't stop us," Loki's fist connected with Kim's jaw. Bright spots blossomed before his eyes as he reeled backward.

"You need more than one poke in the jaw to stop me, Loki. I can't let you do this." Kim surged up. He launched his full weight into Loki's chest. They sprawled across Konner's pallet. Loki gasped for breath. Kim kneed him in the groin.

They wrestled. Loki came up on top.

Kim choked as Loki's fingers tightened on his throat.

Konner shouted something.

Loki yelled back.

Kim fought for air. In a mighty effort he inserted one finger between Loki's hands and his throat. Then he heaved. They rolled to the ground. Kim reversed his position. He forced Loki's shoulders to the ground, trapping his hands with his knees.

"Sorry, Kim," Konner said.

A searing pain crashed across the back of Kim's neck. Darkness swamped his senses. The last thing he saw was Loki's satisfied smile.

"We've got to hurry. With Kim's hard head, he won't be out for long," Loki said. He rubbed feeling back into his hands and arms. The continual ache in his groin would have to wait. He could walk. He could breathe. That would have to suffice.

"I haven't had time to forge much in the way of weapons," Konner said. He produced a long belt knife from his pack. "A few axes and spades, skinning knives, blades for gutting fish. That sort of thing. I've been working on spare parts for the *Sirius*."

"They will have to do. Anything iron is superior to the bronze Hanassa's people can produce."

"But they outnumber us more than three to one. And all of them are trained warriors. We have more women and children who can't or won't wield a weapon."

Loki swallowed hard at that thought. "Then we will have to be trickier. We have right on our side."

"We've got the shuttle. The noise alone should scatter some of them."

"Let's hope."

Outside, Raaskan and ten other men awaited them. They had already found the best axes, scythes, and blades at the smithy. Five women joined their ranks, each carrying a club and a skinning knife. Not enough. Not nearly enough people to confront the more than one hundred trained warriors Hanassa had at his command.

Loki grinned. He licked one of the Tambootie leaves he'd brought back with him.

Knowledge burst upon his tongue in a flurry of colored images. He knew precisely how many men Hanassa had and the strength of their weapons and their strategy.

He also knew that most of the men from outlying villages quaked in their moccasins at the thought that they might become Hanassa's next victims if they displeased him. Or if they pleased him too much. He selected sacrifices capriciously.

"Hanassa is insane and getting worse," Loki whispered to Konner. "That's our advantage."

"It's also our disadvantage. No way to predict what he'll do next," Konner countered. He loped toward the shuttle parked upriver from the village. Their tiny army followed him, two paces behind.

"With these magic leaves I can read Hanassa's thoughts."

"Until he figures out what you are doing and blocks you out. He's smart, it won't take him long. Just like Kim blocks you out at every turn. Neither of us have ferreted out his deep, dark secret yet."

Their army crowded into the lounge area. Taneeo slammed the hatch shut.

"You do your part. Keep throwing rocks and fire at Hanassa. Once he is felled or retreats, the rest of the army will collapse," Loki ordered. "Then we can move in for the kill. Maybe his own warriors will help."

"Let's hope." Konner slipped easily into the cockpit of the shuttle. He fired up the engines.

Loki plunked down in the pilot's station. Familiar routines settled the jumpiness in his stomach.

No more delay. They were ready.

Loki closed his eyes and launched. "I'd rather face a whole fleet of IMPs than this crazed priest. *St. Bridget,* I never thought I'd have to enter into hand-to-hand combat for my life and the lives of all those I care about," he said quietly. "And I do care about these people. I don't want any of them hurt."

"The chances of coming out of this unscathed are few and none," Konner warned.

"I know. And I don't like it. I don't like the odds."

"Do we have a choice?"

"No choice at all."

I am forbidden to interfere. I may not help the helpless. Only a flywacket may do that. Gentian is too frightened of the humans to act. He hides beneath my wing, trembling and ashamed.

But I cannot remain aloof and aloft. If the flywacket will not act, perhaps . . . Perhaps there is a way.

Kim moaned. He knew he did. He heard the sound. The noise hurt his aching head. Moving made him hurt more. Best if he lay still a while longer.

But he couldn't. He had to stop this battle before it escalated.

Just as with the original colonists, civil war could erupt from this one battle. Power was a heady drug. So was Hanassa's bloodlust.

He slumped over.

He almost wept. Once men tasted the power of life and death in battle they became addicted. Hence the warrior society of the Coros. All honor, all sense of achievement, all self-worth stemmed from prowess in battle, to the detriment of society as a whole.

Humans on this planet had become so enamored of shedding blood, they had begun worshiping a demon who demanded blood. They had forsaken peace and prosperity for the "glory" of war. "Glory" that led only to death and more death.

The wars and the resulting diseases had reduced the numbers of the local population to subsistence levels. And still they warred.

Kim had to stop it all. Now. Before it got any worse. His mission in life—his God-given destiny was to stop this war.

He thought he had some leverage over Hanassa this time. His obsession with Hestiia. Kim might be able to placate him. Draw off the energy of battle.

He knew how to do it. Mum and her religion had taught him how from earliest childhood.

Loki and Konner had the shuttle. Kim heard the roar of its takeoff even as he contemplated chasing after them. They would arrive at the island in moments.

Kim would need several hours to walk there over rough terrain.

He could not call the dragon for a quick ride. He did not know how to communicate with one. How else could he reach the islands in time? The dragongate? No natural portal would bring him closer to the site of sacrifice than the one across the river from the village.

He had only the river. With luck, the raft rested at the nearest inlet. If not, he'd swim with the help of a floating log to the delta.

Groaning with each movement, he rose to his knees, then to his feet. Cautiously he waited for the dizziness to assail him. The cabin did not spin around him. Good. He had no concussion. One foot in front of the other.

"Forgive me, Hestiia. Forgive me for leaving you alone. Eventually, you will see the wisdom in this and thank me. I hope."

CHAPTER 46

◆ —— • —— ◆ —— • —— ◆

"KIM!" Hestiia sat up suddenly. "Kim, where are you going?" she called through the closed curtain. She had heard some of the conversation among the brothers. The fight between Kim and Loki had frightened her. She had wanted to go to them then, but knew they would not listen to her. Nor would they appreciate her interference.

Now, when she finally had the courage to confront them, make them stop and think, Kim spoke as if he knew he could not return from the coming battle.

"Kim, do not dare leave me. Not now," she pleaded as she rushed to the door of the hut. She had to grab onto the wall for support. Her head spun. After a few moments of deep breathing the world righted and she had the balance to step through the break in the curtain. The medicines Kim had given her made her stronger than she thought she should be. She had drunk a lot of water to replenish her system upon his orders. The cure seemed to be working.

Kim had already run halfway to the river. Her words fell to the dust without a listener.

"I cannot allow him to do this." Her mind whirled with fear and half-finished plots.

"Gentian!" she called to the sky. "Gentian, please come to me. I need your help." Maybe the flywacket could stop Kim from foolishly stepping between Hanassa and his need for blood and death.

She listened hard for a hint that Gentian returned to her. She had not seen him for two or more days. Where could he be hiding?

"Gentian!" she ordered as if her familiar were a small child in need of a reprimand. "Gentian, I need you."

At last she heard the faint cry of a hawk in the distance. It pierced her ears but not her mind.

Puzzled, she stepped out into the center of the nearly deserted village for a better view of the sky. There, she spotted the small dark shape flying toward her. As it neared it grew in size, took on shape, became the familiar outline of the flywacket.

Hestiia sighed. Her friend had not deserted her.

In a flurry of squawks and ruffled feathers the flying cat landed at her feet. He continued to shake and preen, pecking at dust or mites hidden at the base of his wings. Strangely, he did not retract his predatory talons.

"Gentian, where have you been?" Hestiia stooped to scratch his ears.

He lifted his muzzle to stare at her. Strange, incomplete images passed to her.

"You are not Gentian," she accused. Anger kept her upright when shock wanted to buckle her knees. "Where is Gentian?"

(Help you.) The flywacket continued to stare at her.

"How can you help? Can you attack Hanassa and make him cease his bloody sacrifices?" Her tone remained accusatory, as if this strange creature had stolen her most valued friend.

(Come.) Tucking his wings partially into the extra fold of skin on each side, the flywacket marched in his most haughty manner toward the grasslands where the Stargods had rested their white dragon.

"What do you want with me?" Compulsion pulled Hestiia in the fly-wacket's wake even though suspicion made her want to remain within the protection of the village. She grabbed a skin filled with fresh water on the way and took a long drink.

(Come.)

"Why should I trust you? You are not my Gentian."

The cat stalked on.

Hestiia almost lost sight of the creature in the tall grass. Wild stalks and seedpods scraped her skin and tugged at her woven clothing. She should have worn leather for an extended trek across country. She should have eaten more.

"I have to sit," she told the flywacket. She plopped down and took another long drink.

The strange cat paused impatiently in its journey and came back to butt his head into her arm, just as Gentian did when he prodded her into action.

"In a moment. I am still weak from loss of blood and the fever."

With a huge sigh her companion sat and waited. His stare made her uncomfortable, edgy, needing action. She needed more rest. But how to deny a cat full of superiority?

Before she was truly rested, Hestiia rocked to her feet and once more followed the cat. This time he moved more slowly and looked over his shoulder frequently to make sure she did not stray or lag behind.

Soon enough they reached the area of flattened and scorched grass where the white dragon had crouched, hidden like a true dragon. The flywacket stopped in the middle of the clearing and spread his wings.

"Now what?" Hestiia asked.

(Wait. Do not be frightened.)

A blue-white halo shimmered around the cat.

Hestiia shielded her eyes from the glare with her hand.

The light increased. Through her clenched eyelids, Hestiia saw rays of purple. She risked opening her eyes once more and closed them again, abruptly. The light was too much. She could not see. Could not think.

Off-balance, she staggered back and turned away. She dropped to her knees trying to make herself as small and as invisible as possible.

(You may look now,) a deep voice, deeper than the far reaches of the Great Bay, rumbling and vibrating to the core of her belly, told her.

Cautiously she peeked over her shoulder. The silver-and-purple dragon stood where the flywacket had been a moment before.

"Dragon Lord." Hestiia scuttled around and prostrated herself before the dragon.

(Get up, child. We must hurry.)

"Yes, master. Er . . . What do I call you?"

(Iianthe.)

"Iianthe." She tasted the word on her tongue. "What does this mean."

(Purple.) A hint of a chuckle followed that word.

"As does Gentian. Where is Gentian? I miss him."

(The flywacket will take a different assignment. He is no longer needed here.)

"But I miss him. He was my . . . my friend."

Silence.

Hestiia sighed. The dragon would say no more. "What must I do now?"

(Swallow your fears and climb upon my back. I will take you to the Stargods. You and you alone can stop this madness.)

Hestiia swallowed heavily and climbed to her feet. "Climb?" She surveyed the dragon's form, seeking footholds. Spines and scales seemed to glow in the sunshine. She saw the pathway to his back, a gap between two of his spinal horns where she could perch. "Not so different from riding an overlarge steed," she muttered as she placed one bare foot on Iianthe's foreleg.

(Quite a bit different, the brothers tell me. You must cling tightly with hands and knees as we fly. If you fall, I cannot rescue you. You are too important to this mission to risk.)

Hestiia wiggled into the place on Iianthe's back that seemed made for her body. The dragon's muscles bunched beneath her. He spread his wings and took three long steps forward. She gulped and clung and closed her eyes. Wind rushed against her face and hair. It pressed her backward. Tall spinal horns held her in place.

She sensed upward movement and did not dare open her eyes. This must be what Kim and his brothers felt when they flew inside their white dragon. Or did they? Would the dragon's metal hide protect them from this chill air rushing past her?

Then the wind eased and Iianthe flew straight. Curiosity forced one of her eyes open a crack. The land rushed past beneath them. She saw the river, brown and green from the heavy rains. "Did you give the Stargods your memories of flight so they could choose the village site?" she asked. The wind snatched her words away.

(*The men you call Stargods had their own memories of flight.*)

"The white dragon took them on a flight, then."

(*Yes.*) Another deep-bellied chuckle.

By the time Hestiia could think up another question, the islands came into view. Iianthe tilted sideways and descended. Hestiia's stomach lurched. She closed her eyes again.

(*You must look. You must see what is happening so that you know what to do.*)

"I am afraid." She risked opening her eyes a crack. The land rushed up to meet them. Too fast. The wind threatened to blow her off the dragon's back once more. She found comfort in the darkness of not seeing.

(*Will you allow your fears to dictate your actions? Actions that will bring your beloved's life into grave danger. Gentian is just such a coward, and he will hide forever now.*)

"But what can I do? I am just a woman."

(*The woman who defied Hanassa and risked death to take up weapons to feed those she loves. The woman who married the Stargods against the wishes of Hanassa and brought others to follow their teachings of peace. The woman who will end this adventure as she started it with her eyes wide open and her fears consigned to unimportance. Only you can bring Hanassa to his knees.*)

"But I do not know how."

"Careful with the fire you throw," Loki said quietly to Konner. "He's got fresh tinder waiting to explode at the feet of his victims."

In the center of the clearing, three stakes had been pounded into the ground. Yaakke was firmly tied to one. His father to another. The third stake, in the center stood empty. Both captives seemed barely conscious. Around their feet, two dozen Coros, men, women, and children, piled branches. The mounds of firewood reached to the captives' waists.

Nearly one hundred locals stood between the brothers and their quarry. All of the men were heavily armed with bronze axes and swords. The women and children hefted rocks, ready to throw at Loki's army of a meager dozen.

"Wet wood. Hasn't had time to dry out. It won't burn easily," Konner replied. He shifted his gaze constantly, assessing the situation.

"But wet wood will smoke. They'll die quicker from the smoke than the fire."

"True. Suggestions?"

"We take out Hanassa. Without him, the others will lose their motivation."

"How do we get to the bastard."

The High Priest of Simurgh stood behind two ranks of seasoned and scarred warriors.

As if sensing their thoughts, Hanassa raised his staff and shook it. His headdress towered above his protectors, but nothing of his face or form showed through the tight ranks of men.

"Is he even there? That could be anyone wearing his headdress and carrying his staff." Taneeo whispered to Loki. His eyes scanned the entire are. But then he looked up and beyond the clearing.

Loki shifted his attention to the trees. An odd movement among the branches seemed wrong.

"Twenty degrees right of center. Third tier of branches," he whispered.

"I see him," Konner replied. He held out his hand, palm up. "I've never tried this before. But if I can call fire into kindling and coal, I should be able to gather it into my hand." He stared long and hard at his palm. The light around it began to glow, coalesce and then brighten.

Konner's whole arm trembled with the effort. He threatened to drop the ball of cold light before he could do anything with it.

Gasps of awe came from the army they faced. They looked to each other in confusion. Many looked into the trees where Hanassa perched rather than to the imposter behind them.

"Gotcha, Hanassa. Your own troops betrayed your whereabouts," Loki chortled.

Konner tossed the ball of fire. All eyes followed its arc across the clearing into the trees. It landed square in the center of the figure. Sparks erupted. Flames and smoke rose.

Loki and his army surged forward, weapons drawn. He held an image in his mind of Hanassa slapping uselessly at the fire that ate at his clothes, his hair, his skin. With every bit of energy he could muster, he sent that image into the ranks of the enemy.

Three soldiers in the first row hesitated. Three more advanced five paces, swords at the ready to engage the screaming dozen.

Metal clashed against metal. People screamed. Blood spurted.

A scarecrow stuffed with straw fell from the branches of the tree, burning gaily.

Loki lost his projection of images. Konner faltered while trying to gather more fire.

Hanassa jumped forward from behind the ranks of his soldiers, rattling his staff and shaking his headdress. The warriors surged forward, swords at the ready.

"He tricked us," Loki stammered. His mind closed down. He couldn't tell anymore what Hanassa planned. His head remained empty. He drew his stunner and dagger, not knowing quite how to use them.

Two of the enemy fell beneath stunner blasts. The rest kept coming, trampling their fallen comrades in their rush to eliminate Loki and his few followers.

His army fell back. Raaskan nursed a long cut across his ribs that spurted blood. One of the woman lay upon the ground, staring blankly at the sky. Blood poured from a gaping wound across her throat.

Konner and Raaskan rallied the small band. They stood firm, meeting the heavy wave of advancing troops. Weapons clanged. Men screamed. Others shouted.

Someone knocked the stunner and dagger from his hands.

"Fall back," Konner shouted. "Fall back to the *Rover*. Defend the *Rover*!"

A rock flew from the back rank of warriors. It struck Konner in the temple. He staggered and went down.

"What have I done?" Loki whispered. He stumbled over a dead body. The dying thoughts of the man beneath him stabbed him behind the eyes. He experienced pain, terror, blackness, peace, nothing. "What have I done?"

The enemy rushed forward.

"I want the false gods alive," Hanassa ordered.

Harsh hands grabbed Loki and forced him to his feet. The warrior who grabbed him smiled around black and broken teeth as he yanked Loki's arms behind him and bound them with wet rawhide. Hanassa slammed the butt of his staff into Loki's jaw.

Black stars danced in front of his eyes. His knees turned to jelly. He crumbled.

"Now you shall burn for your crimes against me," Hanassa announced. He held a flaming torch up, ready to ignite the brush at the base of the stakes.

CHAPTER 47

K IM HALTED HIS SOGGY DASH toward the clearing at the edge of the tree shadow. He was dealing with fanatics. He had to act with calm dignity. He had to make himself appear superior to Hanassa.

He had to become a god.

"St. Bridget, forgive me," he whispered as he crossed himself. "With my mind, my heart, and the strength of my shoulders, help me end this. Amen."

The High Priest looked up from his gleeful arrangement of firewood at Loki's feet. He stood up slowly, assessing Kim as if he were prey.

To Kim's sensitized vision, a silvery dragon head with a long spiral horn coming out of his forehead seemed superimposed upon Hanassa. He still had many of his original defenses and instincts. Could anything but another dragon kill him?

At least the High Priest had freed Yaakke and Yaaccob to make room for the three brothers at the three stakes. He must have planned to trap them all along.

"I won't underestimate you again, Hanassa," Kim said. His words carried across the clearing.

Konner roused a bit. Red marks on his jaw and temple were bruising fast. Even tied to the stake he slumped awkwardly to his left. The warriors must have beaten him senseless and then beaten him some more.

Loki continued to stare off into space, lips moving in a silent conversation with some unseen entity. Was Loki actually praying?

"Seize him," Hanassa ordered.

"I deny your right to speak for Simurgh, Hanassa. You are no true priest of any god. You are not worthy of your office." Kim kept his voice low and calm, despite the cold sweat on his back and the trembling of his knees.

"Seize him, I said."

No one moved.

"You have perverted the rituals of Simurgh from a voluntary offering to a needless bloodbath. You have kept tribute designated for Simurgh for your own personal use. You have denied these people the *right* to fulfill their god-given talents and channeled all of their energy into war, solely to glorify yourself. You assign vital tasks to slaves and women to free all of the men for war. And if they are not suited for war, then you murder them in the name of sacrifice, all to feed your pride and make you feel more important than you are."

Murmurs and questions broke out in the crowd.

"I guide these people with the true wishes of Simurgh. Do not listen to him," Hanassa said loud enough for everyone to hear. "Only the strong survive war. Simurgh deserves only the strong."

"Think, people." Kim continued to face Hanassa, but made sure his words carried to one and all. "Did Simurgh demand such high tribute or so many sacrifices before Hanassa came among you? Did your women and children go hungry because they were not worthy of Simurgh's notice *before* Hanassa told you so? Check the fine dwelling he forced you to erect for him."

Questioning murmurs rose around Kim like a flood tide. Still he kept his eyes on Hanassa. "You will find all of the foodstuffs, furs, and artworks you gave to Simurgh hidden for his own use. But he does not use it. He sits atop it and gloats, just like the dragons of legend he belittles."

"'Tis the tribute offered to Simurgh. Kept for Simurgh." Hanassa narrowed his eyes and stepped forward three paces.

Kim matched him step for step. When they stood nose-to-nose, Kim spoke again.

"Admit it to yourself, Hanassa, if not to these others, 'tis me that you want. I stand between you and Hestiia, the only woman who ever refused you. You lust after her. You pant for her and dream of her. But she loves me. Until I am dead, you will never possess Hestiia's body or her soul. She would kill herself first."

Hanassa snarled rather than reply.

Then Kim lifted his voice again so that all could hear. "Release my brothers. They are unwilling sacrifices and therefore unworthy. I offer myself, one god sacrificed to another. That should satisfy Simurgh for all time. Let this be my gift to all the Coros and all the people of this land. Let me die so that no other must ever sacrifice himself to a god."

Kim's skin turned cold as he contemplated what he had just offered. Was there anything else that would save any of these people from Hanassa's greed for blood and yet more blood?

"Witness my death, people of Coronnan, and know that I am the last to die for Simurgh. There. Will. Be. No. More. Sacrifice!"

"And if Hanassa tries to sacrifice anyone else, ever again, we will know that he lies and has no real connection to the gods!" Taneeo shouted. "If Hanassa violates this covenant, then he must be the one to die. We honor you, Stargod Kim." He bowed deeply.

"Do it!" Hanassa drooled in anticipation. "Release the others and place this man at the center stake. Take the firewood from the others and place it all at his feet."

"Are you crazy, Kim?" Konner shouted. "I can't let you do it."

"You can and you will. Take care of Loki. Take care of Mum. And take Hestiia offworld. I want her safe, with Mum." Kim did not resist as two warriors bound his hands and led him to the empty stake in the center.

"No, Kim. No," Konner continued to protest as other men dragged him and Loki away from their execution. "What will we tell Mum? Think of Mum. Think of Hestiia, for God's sake."

"I am thinking of them."

Hanassa raised his torch.

———◆———

Hestiia ran as she had never run before. She pushed her aching body to the limits of her strength and still she ran. Tall trees flashed past her. Leaf litter gave way to underbrush, and then she was free of the forest and into the clearing. She did not slow her pelting pace. Two dozen long strides and she leaped the pile of firewood and kindling. She landed in a heap at Kim's side. She flung her arms around his neck.

"If you kill him, you must kill me, too!" She drank in the warmth of his body, his unique scent. As she pressed her body closer to his, she surreptitiously slit his bonds with her knife.

"Oh, Hes, what have you done?" Kim buried his face in her hair. "Go with my brothers. Please. This is for the best."

"If you die, I die," she insisted.

"Arrgh!" Hanassa growled. And he flung his torch away.

Hestiia dared relax a little. Kim was safe, for a time. "This is very scary," she whispered to her love.

"Very scary indeed. But you are brave enough to come between me and death. Only you are brave enough." He kissed her hair.

Then rough hands grabbed her shoulders. "I will not let him have you!" Hanassa said. He spun her around and pressed his open mouth to hers. His tongue forced her lips apart, ran along her teeth. His saliva mingled with hers.

She gagged.

"Never." She wrenched away from him.

Kim pressed her little knife into her hand. Without thinking she shifted her grip and plunged the blade into Hanassa's chest.

He screamed. Blood spurted from his wound.

Chaos erupted among the warriors. Iron weapons rang against bronze. Hestiia heard the distinctive chirp of the blue light weapons of the brothers.

A warrior with broken teeth raised his sword to slash at Yaakke's back. Gentian—or was it Iianthe in flywacket form?— swooped down and grabbed the warrior's hair with his talons. He squawked noisily, flapping his wings in his victim's face. The warrior dropped his weapon, batting ineffectually at his attacker.

Yaakke picked up the fallen sword. He swung it wildly at his enemy. His opponent gasped once, clutched his belly, and collapsed. Blood dribbled from his mouth and from between his fingers.

Kim sagged slightly beside Hestiia.

"No more death," he whispered. "Please, no one else should die."

Yaakke and Iianthe moved on to new combats. There were many. At least half of Hanassa's warriors battled alongside Loki and Konner.

"My people turn against me," Hanassa said flatly. He did not even acknowledge the little knife embedded between his ribs.

A rain of arrows flew from the edge of the woods toward Hanassa and his army.

Kim grabbed Hestiia's waist and pulled her back. "We can get out of here now," he shouted over the din of battle.

"A very good idea," Hanassa agreed. He pulled a black rock from his belt. Bigger than the weapons, it had two small circles, one on each narrow side. One red and the other green.

"What is that?" Kim asked. He stared at it as he tried to back away from Hanassa. He tugged at Hestiia's hand to separate her from their enemy. But the piles of firewood and the stake kept them confined.

Hestiia felt Kim go hunted-still.

"Something the ancients called a remote," Hanassa replied. He slammed a fist into Kim's gut. He doubled over, loosening his hold on Hestiia's hand.

Hanassa grabbed her upper arm and forced her to follow him through the mound of firewood. The more she resisted the tighter his grip. Her fingers began to grow numb.

Kim clasped her other hand and stumbled after them, still clutching his middle. Together they ran for the shelter of the forest.

"You don't need this, Hanassa. We can live in peace if you just stop murdering people." Kim's voice came out strangled. He continued to clutch his belly with one hand and cling fiercely to Hestiia with the other.

"Peace is for cowards," Hanassa sneered. He continued his relentless course toward the first line of trees. The branches of one tree met another in a tall arch. Like the imposing entry to Hanassa's temple to Simurgh. Bright light from the remote struck the center of the shadow. It expanded, intensified, swirled, erupted into a thousand colors spiraling inward.

"My magic portal," Hanassa said. "Magic more powerful than anything the Stargods will offer you, Hestiia. My Hestiia." He seemed oblivious to Kim's presence.

"You're figured out how to harness the dragongate." Kim stopped short. His tug against her left hand became as fierce as Hanassa's grip of her right arm.

Hestiia couldn't tell if his gasp was from pain or awe.

"Another trick of the ancients." Hanassa pulled harder on Hestiia's arm.

Her shoulders ached. Great weights seemed attached to her legs. Her strength drained out of her.

With one last desperate surge of energy, Hestiia yanked her arm away from Hanassa. She had to escape the High Priest's crushing grip. "I am not going into that," she screamed. This was more frightening than flying on dragon-back.

"You have no choice." Hanassa shifted his hold on her and hauled her in his wake.

Hestiia clung all the harder to Kim's hand, pulling him behind her.

The colors swirled around her. She fell, tumbled rolled. Up and down, right and left, her contact with Kim, her sense of self, all dissolved along with the rest of her senses.

CHAPTER 48

HANASSA HAS STOLEN the lady. How could this have happened? From the moment I became a flywacket her thoughts filled the back of my mind. I was free to aid the Stargods in their battle because she was safely in the arms of her lover. And then a cloud fell over her thoughts.

My brother has learned extraordinary powers if he can control the minds of others. He must be stopped. Now.

What can I do? As a flywacket I am allowed to aid the humans. But the tiny body of a flying cat is useless against the powers of a former dragon. No wonder Gentian still cowers in fright.

If I am to save our lady and the revolution against Hanassa and their worship of Simurgh, I must break all the rules of the dragon nimbus. I am frightened that they will exile me as they have exiled Hanassa. What is a dragon without a nimbus?

Still a dragon, but one with a purpose and a mission.

"The dragongate. He triggered the dragongate," Konner said in awe. He dropped his guard to stare at the swirling phenomenon. "I've got to follow them. I've got to see how he did that."

Out of the corner of his eye he caught a glint of sunlight on bronze. Some instinct for self-preservation made him duck and roll away from the killing blow.

"Hanassa has deserted you!" he yelled as he came up aiming the blunt edge of his iron ax at his attacker's temple.

A few stout warriors paused in their berserker rage to stare at the fading colors at the edge of the forest.

Konner stepped in and disarmed them before one of his own people could fell them with a killing blow.

As quickly as it had opened, the dragongate closed. More quickly than when it followed its own natural pattern of random connections.

"Loki, to the shuttle. We have to follow them. Hanassa has Kim and Hestiia. He's taken them back to the mountain."

A few isolated duels continued around him, most of them blocking his path to the shuttle.

(Too noisy.) The deep-bellied voice of the dragon reverberated around Konner's skull.

He looked around for sight of the enigmatic creature.

All he saw was Gentian crouched in the middle of the field, radiating light. Or was it Gentian? This beast seemed larger, heavier, more purple than black along the tips of his feathered wings.

The halo around the flywacket expanded and intensified. All of the light that the black fur and feathers had absorbed, pulsed outward. Konner had to shield his eyes against the blinding glare.

Battle sounds ceased. Hardened warriors dropped to their knees and cast down their weapons.

And still the light grew. As did the black form at its center. And as the light intensified the black core faded, turned silvery with purple edges.

Only Taneeo faced the wondrous transformation with courage. The apprentice priest stood taller, straighter, more self-confident than ever before. With great dignity he crossed himself in the manner that Konner and his brothers did under extreme duress. But Taneeo made the gesture with respect and awe.

"A miracle. The dragon nimbus has granted us a miraculous sign. Simurgh is defeated. We must follow the light of the Stargods!" Taneeo proclaimed. "I claim the right to dismantle all evidence of Simurgh and his priest."

"And I claim the right to dispose of that meddlesome priest myself," Loki said.

"But not until I find out how to harness that wormhole and replicate it," Konner added.

"Priorities, little brother," Loki warned. He placed a heavy hand upon Konner's shoulder. "First things first. We have to rescue Kim and Hestiia. If that means killing the bastard before you interrogate him, so much the better."

(Correct.) Iianthe added the weight of his opinion. *(Your white dragon cannot fly or land quietly. I can. We will need stealth to remove the captives from Hanassa's control.)*

"You and Taneeo fly with the dragon," Loki instructed his brother. "I'll recharge all the stunners and follow in the shuttle." He looked as if he swallowed other words that wanted to burst forth.

"The stunners don't have a lot of effect upon Hanassa," Konner reminded him.

Loki set his jaw and narrowed his eyes. Konner couldn't read his intentions. But he could guess. That scared him more than if he could actually hear Loki's thoughts.

"No, Loki. You aren't going to break out the needle rifle." Konner swallowed heavily. His Adam's apple bobbed several times as he fought for words. "Look around you, Loki. In all this horrible battle, only a few have died. Some of ours. Some of theirs." He gulped back sorrow at the bodies that littered the ground. Most writhed in pain. He'd feel the same agony if he allowed himself to. No time. He had to rescue Kim and Hestiia.

"Most of these people—*on both sides*—have stopped short of killing. As we do. Poolie is badly wounded, but she will live. If I've learned anything in this mess, it is that life is sacred. We have no right to take the life of another, even in battle or self-defense."

"Hanassa has our brother and the woman he loves. Hestiia is now as much family as you or Mum. I will stop at *nothing* to save them. If that means firing the needle rifle directly into Hanassa's black heart, I will. You can study the same remotes he did to learn to control the dragongate." Loki stalked off, ever the pilot in control.

"You never believe anyone can finish a job as well as you can, Loki. But sometimes you believe wrong."

Kim stumbled in Hestiia's wake, unable to rescue her from Hanassa's grip, but unwilling to let her go. He reared back on his heels, trying desperately to keep from falling into the sense-robbing darkness of the dragongate.

If I had a stomach, I'd vomit, he thought. But all he had was his mental essence. No body, no mind, nothing but pure thought.

Then awareness of dim light and hard ground penetrated slowly to his reeling consciousness. At last an end to that endless and instantaneous journey . . .

Kim caught his balance, realized he still clung to Hestiia. And then Hanassa swung his staff at Kim's head. Kim flung himself to the side, bouncing against the basalt wall of the narrow access tunnel. Hanassa's blow glanced off the side of his head and shoulder. Kim reeled across the tunnel into the opposite wall. He couldn't risk falling back into the lava crater.

Those narrow walls saved his life. Hanassa swung again. Blindly. Desperately.

Kim ducked and rammed his head into Hanassa's gut. They tumbled the length of the tunnel into the cavern. Hanassa kneed him. Hot waves of pain filled Kim's being, stole his breath and the dim light around him. One more blow to the back of his head and even the pain deserted him.

Awareness crept back into Kim slowly. Warmth at his back. Cold on his side. Every joint and muscle ached. He lay on the ground. Probably inside one of the caverns near the bowl of the caldera.

He wiggled around. His left arm was numb and sore. Neither of his arms wanted to move with the rest of him. A body blocked his movement backward. A warm and soft body.

"Hes?" he asked. The word came out a croak through his dry throat and split lip. "Hestiia?"

"My Lord Kim?" She rolled over and placed her hands upon the sore spot on his temple. "You are awake. Your eyes are clear. The bleeding has stopped."

He winced away from her touch. But she persisted. When she kissed the sorest spot, the pain receded to a manageable level.

Kim sighed in relief, but only for a moment.

"We have to get out of here, Hes. You know Hanassa won't let me live long."

"I know. But . . ." She bit her lip and looked pointedly at Kim's hands, still pinned behind him.

He tried to move again. Sharp burns wrapped around his wrists and shot up to his shoulders with every twist.

"Force bracelets. A favorite of IMPs and pirates alike. Prisoners can't wander more than a kilometer from the jailer before the electrical current kills them. Wonder why the original colonists had them?" He gritted his teeth against the pain. Then he rolled to his knees and scrunched his body up. With a great deal of twisting and rolling he managed to wiggle his hands beneath his feet and around to his front. The bracelets burned. His hips and shoulders resisted the awkward movement.

He persisted. With each movement, the bracelets sent shock waves through his body until the cave spun around him. Black spots appeared before his eyes.

Then his shoulders rotated and his hands cleared his feet. The world righted itself, and some of the pains faded. He clenched his eyes shut, fighting the persistent dizziness from the electrical jolts.

Then he could finally examine the plastic wires encircling his wrists with thirty millimeters of coiled plastic connecting them. A tiny transmitter was embedded in the plastic in the center of the coil. His eyes still wouldn't focus properly on the seamless bracelets. He had to breathe deeply for several long moments.

"Modern technology has made only a few improvements on these." He peered closely at the bonds. "St. Bridget, I need more light." He rolled to his knees again, then staggered upright. He followed the light to a crack in the cavern wall. Noonday heat penetrated even that tiny opening.

By comparison the dim interior was cool and moist.

The light offered no more inspiration on the force bracelets. He needed an electronic key to open them. Cutting the wires with a sharp tool would electrocute him before he was free. But if Hestiia smashed the transmitter with a rock? A big and heavy rock.

No such luck. The finest judicial minds in known space had developed force bracelets to control hardened criminals, smugglers, and political malcontents alike. Twice Kim had endured time in IMP holding cells, controlled by bracelets. Both times his brothers (once with Mum in the lead) had rescued him. Even Konner's ingenuity with anything mechanical had not broken the locks. Only a key would open them. Thankfully, Loki was adept at picking pockets and had found one.

"I wonder why Hanassa has left me alive this long?"

"Humiliation," Hestiia replied softly. She stood at his shoulder, examining the bracelets intently. "Hanassa claims he needs you as his slave. Just before he felled me with his black rock weapons, he said that when you are reduced to a beast in man's rags, when you beg him to kill you to put you out of your misery, then I would cease to love you."

"And will you cease to love me?"

"Never. He will only make me love you more and hate him with all the fierceness of my heart."

"Good." He bent to kiss her lightly. "I know where Hanassa is likely to hide. We have to find him and the key to these things." He held up his bound wrists. "We also have to destroy the remote that allows him to control the dragongate."

"He keeps all of his remotes in his belt. He will not be parted from them easily. He is very strong. I stabbed him in the chest and he barely bled, barely knew that he was wounded."

"Then we have to be smarter than he is."

"You have changed." She traced his cheek from temple to jaw with a delicate fingertip.

"How?" He kissed her fingertip when it lingered beside his mouth.

"More confident. Convinced that your path is right."

"I guess when one walks through the valley of the shadow of death, he comes out the other side a little different."

"Stronger."

"Hopefully strong enough in purpose to eliminate Hanassa's influence over any of the Coros." He took a deep breath. "Which way to the big cave?"

Hestiia led him through a series of connected caves. The first room revealed a large opening, fifty feet above the caldera bowl. Heat rose in waves around the opening. Sunlight reflecting off pale rocks nearly blinded him. The heat made him dizzy. The bracelets sapped his strength as much as the heat. Sweat poured down his face and back. The appetite that had been growing in him died abruptly. Hestiia drooped in the heat as she trudged beside him.

They descended several levels. The interior offered relief from the sun glare and the heat. But they had no light. They had to stay close to openings.

Then they found a large cavern with a throne set upon a natural dais, and a path lighted by torches.

"Hanassa is leading us to his lair," Kim muttered. "He knows I have to remove the bracelets before I can escape."

The dim interior offered a little relief from the heat, but not much. Kim imagined that the lava core joined the sun in heating these tunnels.

They descended to the columned cave with the sulfurous creek running through it.

Dim light flickered from panels in the ceiling. Not every room had light.

"You should stay here. Rest," he told Hestiia. "You haven't had time to recover."

"Where you go, I go. I will not be separated from you again." She thrust out her chin in defiance.

Kim had a feeling he would grow to dread that determined look. That thought warmed his heart. He wanted the time to learn everything he could about her.

"Come, then. But when you need to rest, let me know. We will both stop."

"I could use a drink of water."

"So could I. The stream is the only water around. Foul-tasting stuff, but it won't hurt you."

Kim drank deeply of the sulfur-laden water. Hestiia did, too. She grimaced at the taste. Kim motioned for silence. She swallowed any sounds she wanted to make.

He tried to use telepathy to tell her that sound carried through the caverns in odd patterns. He had no way of knowing if his thoughts carried to her truly or if she understood.

One more gesture for her to stay by the water. Turning away from her was the hardest thing he'd done since walking up to Hanassa and surrendering.

On tiptoe, Kim made his way to the lab.

"You awoke earlier than I expected," Hanassa said from his post at the terminal in the room. The oldest machine with the smallest memory, suitable only for recording data, not for processing problems. Had Loki overlooked the machine, or had Hanassa hidden it before they came? Kim couldn't remember seeing it in the lab. But then the fever had kept him from thinking clearly.

With 20/20 hindsight, he knew they should have made the effort to retrieve the terminal as soon as his brothers realized they missed this third one. Hanassa had learned too much from it.

"I came for the remote, Hanassa." Kim edged closer to the man.

"I imagine the force bracelets are making your arms weaker and weaker."

"An antique design flaw. Modern restraints leave the prisoner capable of hard labor," Kim commented. He had to keep Hanassa off-balance, make him doubt his judgment.

"A flaw I will have to correct," Hanassa said. "With your help, of course. I shall master engineering in time. However, I do not wish you to become useless or damaged beyond repair in the meantime."

"I'm a scholar and historian, not an engineer. I can't help you."

"But you will." Hanassa aimed a remote and pushed the button.

Pain ripped up and down Kim's arms, all the way into his chest. He gasped. The world turned white. He couldn't breathe. Unholy red light snaked from the bracelet transmitter in long, continuous coils.

But he'd be damned if he would collapse and whimper in Hanassa's presence.

"Stubborn," Hanassa said with a note of approval. "I shall have to beat that out of you."

An image of Hes creeping up behind him revived Kim a little.

"Not bloody likely." With the bracelets still radiating energy, Kim snagged Hanassa around the neck. The transmitter pressed against the priest's jugular. His entire body jerked.

"Kim, what must I do?" Hestiia said. She had crept up on them.

He'd always know where she was.

"Get the remote," Kim gasped through gritted teeth. He couldn't hold Hanassa for long. His arms felt as if they were dislocating at every joint.

"Which one?" Hestiia asked. She gathered two of the black boxes from Hanassa's belt.

"All of them!" Kim lost his hold on Hanassa's throat.

The priest thrashed. He managed to get his hand between the choking plastic and his vulnerable neck vein.

Kim twisted his hands. Shock after shock raced up his arms. His prisoner jerked, and his eyes bulged. The punishing current in the bracelets must be affecting him as well.

Hestiia juggled at least four of the black boxes. At last, she pried the last remote from Hanassa's fingers.

The burning energy ceased flowing. Kim slumped against his enemy. His arms slid down around Hanassa's chest, imprisoning his enemy's arms.

"Put the narrow end of the remote against the bubble in the center of the bracelets," Kim instructed Hestiia. "Then press the blue button."

"Button? What is a button? I see no blue."

"The round spots slightly lower than the main surface. The paint is worn off. Should be the center of three circles."

Recognition brightened Hestiia's face. She pressed the button.

Instantly the force bracelets opened. Kim sighed in relief.
Hanassa burst free of his grip. The priest ran.
Kim followed. He tripped over the rough floor.
Hanassa laughed at his clumsiness. The lights went out. Kim fell.
Hestiia screamed in fright.
The dragongate hummed.

CHAPTER 49

◆——·——◆——·——◆

"COMPUTER, LIGHTS," Kim ordered as loudly as he could. The lab came to life behind him. None of the other panels responded.

"Computer, all lights."

"Command denied," came the tinny, artificial voice of an unknown man through the computer.

"Command denied," Hanassa giggled in front of them.

"Hes, give me the remote," Kim said.

"Which one? Where are you?"

He saw her outline in the light from the lab. Twelve long paces separated them.

"All of them. Push every button you can. Damn, I wish I could call fire like Konner does."

"Done, little brother," Konner tossed a ball of cold light toward him. It hit the ceiling and stayed there. Details of the obstacles littering the cave floor sprang into focus.

"St. Bridget, you brought the rifle!" Kim stared at a solemn Loki standing with feet braced, holding the needle rifle cocked and ready.

"Thought you might need some help." Loki patted the gun affectionately.

Taneeo lurked behind Loki, eyes darting about the cavern seeking trouble. They'd find it soon enough.

"Command denied!" Hanassa shouted. He appeared briefly in the passage to the transformers and the big generator. He aimed a remote at the light.

The lights flickered but held.

Kim dove after his quarry.

Hanassa turned and ran. The dragongate hummed louder.

"You won't get away this time," Kim yelled as he closed in on the priest.

Hanassa kept stopping and aiming his remote at various things. Nothing happened to the mechanicals. But the tone of the dragongate opening and closing altered with almost every action of the remote.

"The remote he's holding only works on the gate," Kim mused. He paused in his headlong dash to take a closer look at the tunnels. A thick tube filled with fiber optics traversed the ceiling above Big Bertha. It ran into a hole cut precisely to the tube's diameter beside the little tunnel that led to the dragongate.

Making a snap decision, Kim veered away from Hanassa within tackling distance. He leaped and grabbed the tube. It sagged.

The dragongate changed tone again.

"I can't escape to the desert!" Hanassa roared his frustration.

"Halt, priest!" Loki ordered. "One more step and I nail you to the wall." He shouldered the needle rifle.

The tube of fiber optics sagged more. A groan oozed out of the tunnel. Hanassa or the dragongate?

The priest retreated from the edge of the lava pit three steps toward the mouth of the tunnel. He held his hands out to his side. But he still had the remote. His thumb still tapped buttons.

A black shape swooped through the caverns.

Kim ducked instinctively.

"Merawk!" the flywacket screeched.

Hestiia followed the creature into the generator cavern.

"Gentian?" Kim craned his neck for a better view of the action.

"Iianthe," Hestiia told him.

"Iianthe? The dragon?" This was all too strange. "Where's Gentian?" His feet touched ground now while his hands clung to the tube. He swung around without releasing the guidance system for the dragongate.

Before anyone could answer his question, Iianthe swept past Hanassa, wings partially furled for a dive. He extended his raptor talons. Hanassa held up his hands, protecting his face and throat. The flywacket screeched in delight, flapped his wings once and continued into the tunnel, a remote clutched firmly in his talons.

"NOOoooooooo!" Hanassa's wail echoed and built into a wall of despair.

Iianthe continued through the tunnel with only a single flap of his wings.

The lava core glowed menacingly red. Up and up Iianthe flew, beyond sight of the humans. They all rushed into different tunnels to the edge of the lava pit.

Hanassa stopped abruptly, his preternaturally long toes clinging to the rocks. Taneeo ran into him. They rocked. Four arms spread wide for balance. They teetered.

They righted.

Kim's heart leaped to his throat. He dashed back into the dragongate tunnel. With a desperate grab he clutched the back of Taneeo's shirt and hauled him away from the edge. Hanassa continued to cling to Taneeo.

Heat blasted them all as the lava flared.

High above, almost out of sight, Iianthe dropped the remote into the boiling rock a thousand meters below.

Then the flying cat plummeted to their level. At the last moment he snapped his wings wide and glided into a tunnel opening off the pit on the opposite side from the dragongate.

Kim sensed Hestiia sagging in relief. She latched onto Taneeo.

Kim helped her drag Taneeo back into the big cavern. Hanassa continued to cling to his former apprentice. Before they had traversed half the narrow tunnel, Kim abandoned his hold on Taneeo to assist Hestiia. He could almost feel the strength draining out of her.

Loki and Konner met them in the larger room dominated by the big generator. They needed maneuvering room.

The fiber optic tube still sagged. Its connection to the gate was interrupted but not broken.

"Out of the way, Taneeo," Loki ordered. He shouldered the rifle once more and stepped to the mouth of the portal tunnel.

Hanassa whirled around, grabbing his former apprentice by the throat. "To kill me, you must kill him as well." He grinned. "I no longer control the dragongate. But it still lives. In a few moments it will open again. I will escape you once more."

Taneeo slammed his elbow into Hanassa's gut. The priest's grip loosened. Taneeo wrenched free. He pelted back down the narrow tunnel.

Hanassa flung out his staff, tripping him.

Teetering for balance, Taneeo slashed backward with flailing arms. He stumbled and fell to the ground, facedown.

Hanassa tumbled atop him.

Loki fired the rifle.

Hanassa's spirit slipped away from his body. A hundred and more tiny barbs pierced him; each tipped with a poison that froze his muscles. He let go of the temporary mortal shell.

Beneath him, Taneeo's body stirred. He collapsed again. Ten of the barbs had gone through Hanassa to the boy. The poison froze his will as well as his body.

Gently, Hanassa eased into Taneeo's body. He pushed aside the weak flailing of the resident spirit. It would soon learn that resistance was futile. It would soon fade to nothing, leaving Hanassa with a younger body, taller and more slender than the one he left behind.

Best of all, no one would recognize him in this new body. He would begin again. Somehow, someday he would remove the entire infestation of humans from this land. All of them except Hestiia. And then she would worship him in awe and terror.

— ◆ —

"They . . . they're both dead," Loki whispered. He knelt beside the bodies. Every part of his being trembled.

He couldn't think, couldn't focus beyond the lives he had snuffed out with the needle rifle.

"Oh, God, I didn't mean to." Loki cast aside the rifle and buried his face in both his hands. "Hanassa has such thick skin and strange bones, I didn't think the needles would go all the way through him. Oh, God, I felt him die. I shared that last moment of pain and reluctant release." He looked up, eyes closed, hands clasped in an attitude of prayer.

"Self-defense," he tried to console himself. It didn't work.

Kim sought a pulse. His hands trembled and his face looked pale and clammy. "Wait, there's a pulse, weak and fluttery. Taneeo is alive for the moment."

Relief almost knocked Loki flat on the ground. He kept his head up by sheer force of will.

"Ten needles shouldn't have done more than stun the boy," Konner said. "Why's he so weak?" He helped Loki carry Taneeo into the main cavern. They left Hanassa where he had fallen.

"He's not like us," Kim replied bitterly. "His system hasn't been bombarded with pollution and antibiotics, tanked food and canned air, so that he'd build up resistance to the toxins in the needles. He's in shock. We've got to revive him before he gives up."

Hestiia rushed up with a beaker full of water. She began dabbing it on Taneeo's wrists and brow.

Iianthe leaped into the tunnel with Hanassa. A second flywacket flew into the cavern and landed at the mouth of the tunnel.

"Gentian?" Hestiia exclaimed. Tears formed in her eyes. She crawled the few feet toward her pet.

But Gentian had eyes only for the inert body.

Iianthe grabbed the neck of Hanassa's shirt in his mouth, unfurled his wings and tried to lift the body.

Reluctantly Gentian joined him,. He grasped one of Hanassa's ankles in his teeth and began tugging it toward the lava pit.

"What?" Kim asked.

(Dragon ritual,) replied Iianthe in his deep, sonorous voice. They must have all heard, as each nodded in acceptance.

"I have to help." Loki choked out the words. He scrambled to his feet. His hands trembled and he walked unsteadily. A headache stabbed at the back of his eyes.

"Stay with Taneeo," Konner touched Kim on the shoulder as he joined Loki and the flywackets in the tunnel.

"No, Konner, I have to do this myself," Loki sobbed. "I killed him. I have to bury him." He gathered the body in his arms and lifted with a mighty heave. He staggered under the weight.

Konner rushed to help.

Loki shrugged him off.

An overwhelming sense of gratitude flooded him from the flywackets.

The black cats stalked beside him, wings partially unfurled, as he traversed the twenty paces to the edge of the crater.

"Jaysus, Mary, Joseph, and St. Bridget, guide his soul to the other side," he whispered as he released the body. The two flywackets launched above him, flying solemn circles. The body dropped, a dark speck amid the roiling red lava. It grew smaller and smaller. Flame ignited the pale hair, the leather clothing. Then it was gone.

The flywackets flew one last circle and exited through a tunnel opposite the point where Loki kept vigil.

"We must take him home and help him get well," Hestiia said quietly.

Kim couldn't tell if she meant Taneeo or Loki. Loki had to heal himself. No one could do it for him.

Kim took a deep breath and released it. Life had to go on. He'd learned that much from death.

He wished Mum had learned that when she lost Katie and their father.

"The day after Taneeo can stand on his own, Hes and I will marry, properly, formally, with all of the villagers as witness, and this young man as the priest," Kim insisted. He pulled Hestiia to his side and faced his brothers in defiance.

"Fine with us. Just don't forget our primary mission," Konner reminded him. "I have an appointment in less than a year."

"Keep your appointment, Konner. My life is here now."

"And what about our responsibility to Mum?" Konner asked. "Seems to me you are the one who always threw that in my face when I wanted to go off on my own." Konner persisted.

"Mum can take care of herself. She has for twenty years now. She'll keep her own agenda, no matter what we do."

"'Bout time you realized that," Loki growled from his vigil by the pit.

"I'm not leaving either of you behind," Konner insisted. "The only reason we survived this is because we stuck together."

"Perhaps. Perhaps not," Kim replied.

Kim and Konner stared at each other through long moments of stubbornness.

Konner looked away first. "Let's load up the last computer and get out of here. No sense leaving it for someone else to discover." He shuffled toward the lab. "I want more of that mineral water, too. For crystal baths."

"Come along, Loki. I'll buy you the first drink back at the village." Kim offered his hand to Loki.

Loki looked over his shoulder from the edge of the crater. His eyes were ringed in dark shadows. "I almost killed a man. I did kill that monster. But he was just another man. Another soul . . ." He broke off on a sob, still shaking.

"You'll have to learn to forgive yourself, Mathew Kameron O'Hara. *Loki*. But it's going to take time," Kim consoled. "For now, getting drunk and recording a confession to Mum are the only things that will help."

"How do you know?" Loki snarled.

"Because I killed a man once. Two years ago." Easier to admit it to the world now. Perhaps because he knew that at last Loki would understand.

"How? When?" Loki stared at him mouth agape.

"The last night you said good-bye to Cyndi."

"Cyndi. My love. She'll never forgive me now." Loki buried his face in his hands.

"Just after you left her, before she had time to return to the party," Kim continued, ignoring his brother's wails. "Mum had sent me to drag you back to the ship. Apparently some dissidents had been waiting a long time for the opportunity to kidnap Cyndi and demand release of political prisoners as her ransom. They grabbed her. I intervened. I fought dirty, like we have to on bush planets sometimes just to survive. One man ran away. The other pulled a knife on Cyndi. I was meaner and more ruthless. I poured a stunner at full strength into his open mouth." He gulped, trying hard to flatten the memory into something less than a realistic nightmare. "Cyndi made me look like a hero. Her father pardoned me and returned my rights as a full citizen in the GTE. A gift from a grateful father and planetary governor." Kim paused and swallowed deeply.

"None of that helped. I had *killed* a man, a sentient being. Part of me died, too. I confessed to Mum. I confessed to a priest. And now I confess to you. In time, it hurt a little less. I still haven't been able to eat meat. My vow to never, ever take another sentient life helped the most."

"Promise?"

"Promise. Let's go get drunk."

"The local beer won't be enough."

"I know. I've a fine bottle of twelve-year-old Scotch stashed in the shuttle for just such an occasion. You and I will drink it dry."

"I will still remember and regret."

"Always remember and always regret. That way you won't ever do it again. Come on. I need a drink as badly as you. But let's celebrate life as well. I'm getting married. We have liberated a lot of people from Hanassa."

"I think I know what to name this planet," Loki said meekly.

Kim raised an eyebrow in query.

"Kardia Hodos."

"Greek for the path of the heart," Kim mused. "I think I have found that. When will you?"

EPILOGUE

HANASSA KEPT HIS EYES CLOSED. Bit by bit his new body responded. The paralysis drained away, beginning with his lungs.

He allowed Hestiia to fuss over him, relishing her touch and compassionate words, almost believing she meant them for him, Hanassa, and not for Taneeo, whose body he had stolen.

His enemies did not take long in removing the terminal and several remotes from the lab. They cast the rifle into the pit along with his old body. But they left behind six stunners, and five remotes he had hidden in various places around the cavern.

Then they returned for him. He lay limply between the two older brothers as they hoisted his body up through the tunnels.

Through slitted eyes he watched Kim tuck Hestiia neatly beneath his arm. The bastard kissed her deeply. She snuggled tight against his chest.

Hanassa burned with hatred. He consoled himself that when the time came, she would welcome a resurrected Taneeo into her arms where she would never consider Hanassa. The time would come when all three brothers must leave this land forever.

So be it. He would be waiting for the woman who truly belonged only to him. She would learn to enjoy his punishment for her lack of loyalty to him.

For now, he had the magic portal—no, they called it a dragongate, so he must, too. He had books left by the ancients. They had brought them from their original home as great treasures and antiquities to be honored and worshiped. The terminal had taught him to read. The books would teach him to reconstruct the magic of technology.

Once the dragongate stabilized, he would travel throughout the world, gathering his followers, offering them sanctuary and purpose.

With that magic he could rule an army of men as merciless and bloodthirsty as himself.

With an army at his back he could finally rid this world of the infestation of humans. Then he would rid himself of the army as well.

All except Hestiia. She was the only worshiper he needed.

The Coros had not heard the last of Hanassa. And neither had the Stargods.

THE
DRAGON
CIRCLE

This book is dedicated to all my
Circle of writer friends
Who have kept me going
Through thick and thin.
Thank you one and all.
Karen, Lea, Lace, Mike, & Bob

PROLOGUE

*T*HE DRAGONS *of the nimbus hear a new voice. Or is it an old voice become new. It speaks to the stars. We do not know this thing.*

Stargod Konner, tell us who converses with the places beyond our ken. Tell us, so that we may be wary and know who listens to this voice and why.

CHAPTER 1

MARTIN KONNER O'HARA stared at the tiny device. Hardly as big as his palm and yet so dangerous. A red LED blinked at him in an ominously slow pattern.

He could almost hear it shout across the light-years "Here I am. Come get me."

It had to have been here for months, possibly a full year . . . since the last time he and his brothers had space-docked.

His ship *Sirius* was currently in silent orbit around an uncharted planet. While he made vital repairs, he had shut down all but the most essential systems, including spin. The star drive was quiescent, awaiting regrowth of a number of the directional crystals.

Konner and his brothers had just run out of time for repairs.

He pried the foreign device out from where it hid under the red directional crystal. It came away from the cerama/metal hull reluctantly. After a few curses, two broken fingernails, and a new set of bruises on his knuckles, he grasped the device in his palm, still blinking, still alerting authorities to his location.

How could she have done this to him?

Only his ex-wife Melinda could have taken one of his patented locator beacons and perverted it so. Many had a motive to track the O'Hara brothers and their . . . independent cargo shipments. The Galactic Terran Empire called Konner and his brothers smugglers.

The people who received highly taxed and increasingly hard to get essential goods, like food, from the black market, called them saviors.

Melinda had more personal reasons. She had probably sold the frequency of this beacon to the highest bidder. Or bidders.

She could afford to spend a great deal of money to retrieve the damning evidence Konner had secreted aboard *Sirius* and a number of other key locations.

Konner wondered if Melinda would brag about her betrayal to their son Martin. Did she know how her need to banish Konner from Martin's life would destroy more than just her ex-husband?

When the Imperial Military Police found the beacon, they would also find a pristine world ready for exploitation. Konner shuddered at the thought of thundering tractors, a myriad of people, mechanical threshers, and machine after machine throwing out air and noise pollution. Chemical fertilizers would seep into the groundwater and run off into the rivers, making them unsafe to swim in, drink from, or fish out of.

Nine tenths of what the farmers produced would be shipped off planet to feed a hungry empire. The Coros would lose not only their way of life, but would have to learn to do with less than they had now.

The Galactic Terran Empire would not stop there. They would strip this place of every valuable resource, beginning with the timber and ending with the minerals, until there was nothing left. Then the inhabitants would dome their cities, breathe artificial air, eat tanked food, and sue for full citizenship.

And another bush planet would have to be found to feed the growing empire.

He had to destroy the beacon. Now. Before the IMPs found the right jump point to bring them here.

Konner bent his knees and pushed against the climbing rungs of the rabbit hole that afforded access to the outer array of crystals. As his body sprang back from his push through null g, he launched himself forward. Every ten meters he touched one of the climbing rungs on the inside of the conduit to adjust his angle of glide to match the curve of the saucer-shaped spaceship. At his back, the red directional crystals hummed a muted chatter only he could hear. As he sped along, the crystals became less harmonious.

One hundred forty-four directional crystals lined the outer rim of *Sirius*. They linked to twelve green driver crystals by kilometers of fiber optic cable. At the center of the ship, the drivers were linked to a single blue king stone. The two-meter-high monster kept the crystal drive harmonious and connected. In gravity, the king stone would weigh nearly one hundred fifteen kilos. But an active king stone never entered gravity. It had to grow in concert with its family of crystals in null g and lived at the center of the vessel where gravity from spin never reached.

He came abreast of the source of the strident note. A tiny crystal bud kept the port open while a new crystal grew at the center of *Sirius*. Five other reds had to be replaced as well. The disharmony among the array gave him a headache.

"Soon, friends. Soon you'll be whole again," he murmured soothingly. "And we can get out of here."

All the while his guts churned. Melinda had betrayed him to the Imperial Military Police.

If the IMPs showed up in this forgotten star system, they would take him and his brothers prisoner. Konner would never make it back to Aurora in time for his son's final custody hearing.

No wonder the IMPs had been able to follow Konner and his brothers across the galaxy. Their frantic flight from the law had kept Konner from meeting his son Martin at summer camp this year.

His fist clenched around the beacon. Would the boy be disappointed? Or would he even notice that his usual counselor had gone missing.

Five months ago, with the crystals damaged and the IMPs closing in, Konner and his two brothers had jumped blind into this uncharted star system three sectors off the maps. They had plunged into the adventure of a lifetime and found a place they could call home. A place where Konner could bring Martin to experience his true family away from Melinda's self-centered greed, amoral manipulations, and emotional abuse. As well as her lies.

And away from Mum.

Useless making plans now. As long as the beacon sent its signal, the IMPs could find the O'Hara brothers and terminate their dreams. All that had kept the law away from here till now was finding the weird jump point.

"We have to leave," he muttered.

He stared at the device again.

"We can't leave until the crystals regrow." Konner launched again along the narrow access shaft at the extremity of *Sirius'* rim. At the next hatch he grabbed a handle and changed direction. One deft somersault put him into the largest cargo hold.

Strangely, the load of black market pearls remained undamaged, despite the wild maneuvers through which Loki had put the ship in escaping IMP patrols. Konner had added to the hold the antique computers and lab equipment that had been left behind by the original colonists of the planet. A wealth of information about the first colony and the civil war that destroyed them lay encrypted on the hard drives.

From the hold, he dove into the crystal room. A vacuum-inducing force field encased each of the monopole drivers. Nitrogen flooded the field, causing the green crystals to spit out electrons along the fiber optics to the red directionals. Six new directional crystals stood in sealed baths shaped to the exact dimensions of the finished crystal. The original seeds stood at the peak of the bath cage and grew down and out. Limited by the cage and the precisely measured minerals in the baths, the red crystals would stop growing

when they reached the shape and size needed. Each would need a little pol-
ishing and tuning to finish them, but they could be used the moment they
completed growing.

Each bath was connected by fiber optics to the king stone and thus to
every crystal on the ship. The ship's power, navigational, and communication
systems had to grow as a family in order to synchronize and propel the ship
across the vast distances between stars. More than that, the king stone had to
be connected to a mother stone at its place of origin in order to find its way
around the galaxy.

Konner had disconnected the crystal drive from its mother stone upon
entering this star system. Just as Konner and his brothers were out of contact
with Mum.

They weren't going anywhere until he reconnected that dangling orange
fiber optic lying just outside the crystal circle. But if the ship could not find
its way home with the connection severed, the IMPs could not find them
through the connection.

Except for the damned locator beacon he still held in his palm.

"Another week to finish growing," Konner grumbled. "Another week for
the IMPs to search for the jump point that should not exist but did."

Another twist and rebound took Konner up the gangway to the bridge.
He slapped the comm port even before he anchored himself in his chair.

The lights blinked furiously red for an interminable ninety seconds. Then
they dropped back to normal black.

"Damn!" Neither of his brothers had an active communicator close at hand.
"We haven't got time for this!"

A quick sensor sweep showed the inner planetary orbits free of man-made
objects other than *Sirius*. He hadn't time to search the vast distances of the
outer planets for a tiny moving vessel.

He pounded his fist against the edge of his interface. The locator beacon
dug into his palm.

He had designed the thing to survive the fire and ice and massive radiation
of space travel. He needed more weight than he had access to to crush the
thing.

Only the sustained heat of molten lava at the heart of the planet would fry
the femto-bots inside the beacon beyond their self-repair capabilities.

A half smile crept across Konner's face. He had access to that molten core.
If he dared.

Could he face the ghost of Hanassa on his own?

·——◆——·

"Captain Leonard, sir." Kat Talbot nearly squirmed with delight in her chair
at the helm of Imperial Military Police Cruiser *Jupiter.*

Commander Amanda Leonard, captain of the *Jupiter*, glanced up from the screen full of reports she studied. She looked bored.

"Captain, I think I found it."

"Found what?" Commander Leonard lost the bland vacancy in her eyes. She touched the screen in front of her own chair so that it corresponded with Kat's.

"The jump point, Captain." Now Kat could not contain her excitement. "And the beacon."

"Show me," Leonard demanded. At the tone of her voice, the rest of the bridge crew keyed their own screens to share in Kat's discovery.

Lieutenant Josh Kohler, Chief Navigator and Kat's best friend aboard ship, flashed her a begrudging grin. They had a bet on this jump point. If she found it first, he would do her laundry for a week. If he beat her to the discovery, then she would sleep with him. Kat had no intention of allowing him to win the bet.

"Summon Lieutenant Commander M'Berra to the bridge, Englebert," Leonard said to the communications officer. Kat figured she would want the second-in-command in on this discovery.

Lucinda Baines, the diplomatic attaché who had hitched a ride aboard the IMP cruiser, hastened to Kat's side. She bent her petite body over Kat's shoulder, resting her hands on the back of the helmsman's chair. Her perfume suddenly overwhelmed all other scents. The usual citrus smell of the recirculated air took on rotten overtones, as if it had spent too much time in waste recycling and not enough in the scrubbers.

Kat shifted as far away from the woman as her station chair allowed. Then she highlighted the anomaly her sensors had discovered with her electronic pencil.

"I don't see it," Commander Leonard hesitated.

Kat brought up some new data. Commander Leonard's thick eyebrows raised as she digested a string of numbers and symbols that showed a femto's difference from normal space energy fluxes. In the past week of parking in deep space Kat, with M'Berra's help, had adjusted and fine-tuned the ship's sensors to detect smaller differences than any other IMP vessel could find.

And there was the beacon blaring through the tiny hole in space. If you only knew where to look and what to look for.

Lieutenant Commander M'Berra ducked his curly black head as he stepped onto the bridge. He suppressed a yawn. Other than that single sign that he'd just gone off a twelve-hour shift, he looked as refreshed and crisply fresh as he had half a day ago. He immediately went to his station beside the captain. Leonard briefed him on the latest development in hushed tones.

"Are you certain that is a jump point and not just a reflection of the normal radiation currents?" Commander Leonard was known as a cautious leader. Bets aboard *Jupiter* favored that she'd easily make full captain, and get a bigger vessel at the next review board.

"Captain, sir, the outlaws jumped from these exact coordinates to somewhere. That anomaly is the only indication of something *different* about this area. And I am getting a hint of the beacon frequency that was highlighted on the memo from Command Base."

"Ms. Baines, do you have any objections to a further delay in delivering you to Annubis IV for your annual leave?" Commander Leonard asked.

"If the notorious O'Hara brothers disappeared from here, I have no objections to chasing them," the diplomatic attaché replied. Her eyes narrowed and the planes of her perfect face became sharper. "Commander Leonard, do you have to be reminded that capturing those three is highest priority for all Imperial Military Police."

Kat wanted to rear away from the menace in her tone.

Lucinda Baines, daughter of a planetary governor, granddaughter of an Imperial Senator, and great-niece of the previous emperor had a grudge against the O'Haras.

So did Kat.

"Inform Judge Balinakas that his services will soon be required," M'Berra ordered.

Ensign James Englebert busied himself at the comm board.

"Prepare for jump," Commander Leonard ordered.

"Aye, Aye, sir," Kat replied with enthusiasm.

CHAPTER 2

KIM O'HARA stared at the pristine piece of dried pulp in front of him. He'd spent hours peeling layers of stringy wood fibers, soaking them, and finally pounding them into an approximation of paper. Each day he made a few new pieces. Each day he scribbled notes recording the day's events.

Nearly five months had passed since Kim and his brothers had landed—almost on their butts—on a planet where dragons were real and magic worked. He had filled nearly three pages of his primitive paper with a description of Iianthe, the nearly invisible purple-tipped dragon. He'd given up trying to bind his scribblings. He now had five neat stacks of the papers, each confined within a separate box made of the same fibrous wood. One for each month of their time shared with the Coros—the name the local inhabitants gave themselves.

He could have cleared some space on a reader and used it as a daily log. He wanted more. He needed a journal he could leave behind, as well as an alphabet and basic grammar. Reading was a precious gift. He did not agree with his brothers that they should forbid the skill to the Coros. *His* people. He had to create something for them to read and learn from.

Enforced ignorance might keep the local tribes from developing industrialization, but it would also stunt the growth of the civilization, stunt the minds and souls of people who deserved better.

Where to begin today? His mind spun with the facts of the harvest. Five acres of barley to cut tomorrow. Five acres of wheat threshed yesterday. Three acres of soybeans gathered and drying. The yield was bigger than he expected in all three fields.

Still, the harvest should stretch to feed them all if no more outcasts joined the village.

Two more refugees from outlying villages had made their way here today, swelling their numbers to seventy-five. Many of those who sought out the Stargods—Kim and his two brothers—had disabilities, missing limbs, or chronic ailments. Some of them had simple minds and damaged emotions. No one else wanted them.

How did he *know* to plant the extra acres to feed seventy-five rather than the thirty-two who began the village? How did he *know* events to come? How did he lay his hands upon an injury and make it right?

Time to think seriously about it. He gritted his teeth and grabbed a reader with a few gigs of free space. When he had a coherent text, he'd transfer his musings to his journal. Paper was too precious to waste.

Begin at the beginning, his mother's voice whispered in the back of his mind. Not quite Mum, though. The voice took on the sonorous overtones of Iianthe, the purple-tipped dragon.

Kim thought back to the beginning of the current adventure; to the day when he and his brothers had run so desperately from an IMP cruiser. The captain had seemed to anticipate every evasive maneuver, every jump through space, and every weapon blast the O'Hara brothers could imagine. It was almost as if the IMPs read his and his two brothers' minds. Since then, Loki, the eldest brother, had developed and learned to control his telepathy. Quite possibly, in the stress of the escape from IMP patrols, he had broadcast his thoughts on a wide band.

Konner had begun to hone his ability to move objects with his mind. Mostly, he did it unconsciously in moments of stress.

Kim's precognitive talent kicked in when he least expected it. Aboard *Sirius* he'd had a vision of a safe haven inhabited by dragons. The vision had given him the symbolic coordinates of the jump point that had brought them here.

How to describe it?

He took a deep breath, felt refreshed, and filled his lungs once more. Ideas and flickers of memory crowded the edges of his vision. One more deep breath and . . .

He relived the numbness that shot through his body, the disembodied sensation of floating in a null g sensory deprivation chamber. Then the bright tangle of lights streaked across his vision. More than lights. Chains of light, each a different hue pulsing with life. Then blackness again.

He looked into the reader screen. Words scrolled rapidly across the screen as he dictated. The mini computer inside the reader prompted the word "void?" As good as any to describe the place in the mind between here and there.

His memory, triggered by the vivid description, pulled forth more images and sensations. Tumbling through darkness into atmosphere. The shuttle *Rover* tumbling toward a planetary surface and a . . . a dragon. A huge dragon with all the colors of the rainbow on its wing veins, horns, and claws, irides-cent and awesome in its beauty, appeared out of nowhere. The wondrous creature shot forth a river of flame. Its dagger-length teeth and claws reached forward to rip . . .

Kim woke with a start and a whimper. He'd come out of the true vision with the same startling abruptness. Were the images more vivid in his mem-ory than they had been originally? Or had the symbols become clearer with time and recall?

Only one way to tell. Deep breathing seemed to help the process. He'd read somewhere about mystic adepts who spent years learning how to breathe. Must have something to do with the infusion of oxygen into the red blood cells.

"I don't have years." He keyed a few notes about breathing into the reader.

Then he exhaled as much air as he could through his mouth, clearing his lungs of any leftover toxins and chemicals. When he felt as if his chest and backbone had nothing between them, he drew in a long healing breath through his nose.

Immediately, his vision intensified. Each basket and article of clothing strewn about the cabin he shared with his wife Hestiia came into sharper focus. This breath he exhaled as deeply as the previous one. A second con-scious inhalation brought the now familiar dazzle around the edges of his vision. Rather than banish it, he nurtured it, giving the sparkles and half images a little time to develop. This time the aura remained as he got rid of that breath and took the third.

The void opened clearly before him. Pulsing chains of light and life in-vited him to explore. He reached for one that scintillated with every color and yet seemed to have no true color at all. . . .

The void snapped closed.

Kim landed on the packed-dirt floor with a thud. Rubbing his butt, he righted his stool and climbed back up on it.

His head ached and his stomach growled. He thought he heard a chuckle in the back of his mind. A chuckle with the deep bronze bell tones of Iianthe. Or did all of the dragons have the same bass voice?

Amazingly, all of his impressions and sensations revealed themselves in precise wording on the reader.

But what did it mean?

"Am I working magic?"

(*Magic is in the perceiving*,) the dragon voice said. It continued to chuckle.

Konner gulped. Before he could change his mind, he locked down commu-nications and secured the hatch to the bridge. Then he jumped into a long dive for the launch bay where he'd parked *Rover*.

Before launching the shuttle, Konner tried to call his brothers again from the cockpit. The comm port remained silent. He set the device to repeat the call.

"Come on, Loki. Answer the damn phone." The light continued to blink red.

Konner vented the bay atmosphere as he opened the bay doors. He used the explosive release of the remaining air to push his shuttle out into the darkness of high orbit. He oriented to the planet beneath him. *Sirius* held position on the night side, over the horizon from the southern continent where he and his brothers had made homes among the Coros.

He passed his hand over the computer screen once more, in a pattern only he knew. *Sirius* disappeared from his sensors. His confusion field continued to work.

"What's so damn important you dragged me away from my work?" Kim O'Hara growled through the comm port.

Kim, the least likely to respond. The youngest brother had embraced the primitive life of the Coros. He'd taken a native wife. He'd announced his plans to remain dirtside when Konner and Loki returned to civilized space.

"Trouble coming. I need you and Loki to meet me at the landing site. Be there in one and twenty." Konner discomed before Kim could argue with him. Before Konner's own fears could choke him into immobility.

Ninety digital minutes later, they waited for him in the open meadow west of the village and tilled fields. The shuttle's landing draft blew their red hair and beards into their faces. Loki's blue eyes flashed with anger and he braced his long legs for confrontation. Kim leaned his lanky body against a boulder.

All three brothers had the same overt characteristics. But studious Kim was taller and more slender, audacious Loki broader, the shortest of the three with more brute strength. Konner was very much the middle brother in build and temperament, the placater, the one who tried to hold them together as a family when troubles threatened to split them.

"What?" Loki asked the moment the hatch irised open.

"Trouble. Get in." Konner pushed the shuttle toward a rolling launch before Kim had time to slap the portal controls closed. Both Kim and Loki stumbled as they fought for balance in the rapidly moving vehicle.

"What?" Loki asked again when they had all strapped in.

Konner tossed him the beacon.

Strained silence stretched. Konner realized he was holding his breath only when the pain in his chest became unbearable.

"Who?" Kim asked.

"Melinda. Who else."

"Aurora markings on the casing. Definitely manufactured in one of her factories," Loki mused turning the thing over and over. "But then she manufactures all of these things."

"Who else could modify it so that *I* would not find it until I reset one particular crystal. None of my sensors noticed it. None of my routine inspections noticed it. The bit of recessed LED that shows was shadowed by an equally red directional crystal. The casing is painted the same gray-green as the rabbit hole. We got that color by mixing a bunch of leftovers from other ships. Only Melinda would have the audacity to try to match that paint or bribe the few people outside the family who had access to it."

Another long silence.

"So what do we do with it?" Loki asked.

"The lava core of the volcano."

All three brothers shuddered.

"I thought we decided never to go back there," Kim said.

"We have no choice."

"Are the IMPs within the star system yet?" Loki asked.

"Didn't take the time to do a full search."

"Mum will never forgive us if we get caught," Kim reminded them.

"Mum isn't going to like anything about this run." Konner checked the computer setting. Still on mute. None of them needed Mum's voice droning in their ears right now, even if it was just a mechanical device reporting the information of their interface displays.

"Can't we just dump this at the bottom of the deepest ocean?" Kim asked. His fingers ran over the sensor array with precision.

"Not deep enough," Konner replied. He kept his attention on the engineering rather than the mountain range looming ahead of them.

"What if we shot it into the sun?" Loki prompted. He piloted the craft with ease, posture relaxed, dominant left hand resting upon the joystick. He liked to interface with the ship directly rather than rely on computer readouts.

"Take too long to reach the sun's corona if we launch it from orbit. Besides, the window is wrong. *Rover* doesn't have enough power to get us away from the sun's gravitational pull once we get close enough, and we can't move *Sirius* until the crystals finish growing."

"How much longer on that?" Loki asked.

Kim frowned and turned his head away rather than face the issue of leaving the planet.

"A week at least. Maybe a day less," Konner replied. Even then he'd be cutting it close to make it back to Aurora in time for Martin's court date. He only had one chance to gain custody of the boy and he would not miss it.

They reached the yawning mouth of the mountain caldera all too soon.

They sat for a long time after Loki set *Rover* down inside the bowl of the volcano. The dust settled. The shuttle ceased to click as it cooled. Still they sat in silence. Waiting.

For what?

"We have to do this," Konner said finally.

"I'll stay and guard *Rover*," Loki said flatly.

"None of us should have to face this place alone. We all go, or we all stay." Kim swallowed deeply.

"We killed a man in there," Loki reminded them all.

"We killed a monster who tried to kill us and our villagers any number of times." Konner gathered a portable illuminator and a canteen. He tossed other survival gear to his brothers.

"We all go and face our personal demons together." Konner decided for them. "Come on. Let's get this over with before the IMPs have any more time to find us."

CHAPTER 3

L OKI STOPPED in the shadow of the ragged cave entrance. The sun beat
down in a blinding glare upon the dry bowl of the caldera. High, steep
walls of the blown-out mountain rose nearly one point five kilometers above
him, trapping the heat and the dust, keeping out the wind. Nothing disturbed this lonely and hidden outpost in the Southern Mountains.

Even in the shade, sweat poured from his brow and back. He smelled himself and did not like the acrid taint of fear.

Deliberately, Loki scuffed the dust with his foot. Anything to delay entrance into the cave. He spotted traces of footprints, remnants of his retreat
from this place a few weeks ago. He discerned the shape of his boots, Konner's lighter steps, Kim's bare feet, the tiny prints made by Hestiia, Kim's
wife. In the middle, he barely made out the shuffling smudge made by
Taneeo, the village priest. He'd been weak, ill, and sorely abused when they
rescued him from violent Hanassa's clutches.

Then he saw something else. Someone with firm steps and a confident
stride had been here. The most recent visitor had worn soft boots—unusual
among the local population. Male by the length, breadth, and depth. Those
prints were fresh.

"Wait!" Loki called to his brothers. They had already entered the relative
coolness of the first chamber.

"What now?" Konner asked impatiently. He swept his illuminator along
the walls, creating more shadows than it banished.

"Someone has been here. Recently," Loki said. He clamped his teeth shut
to keep them from chattering.

"Rovers camp here when they travel the pass," Kim explained.

"Yeah. Rovers." Loki gulped. He took a swig from his canteen.

His family had given him the nickname of the Norse god known for his adventurous spirit and lack of caution. He was always the first one to wade into a brawl and usually the last man standing. Why did he fear this place so?

Because you took a life within these caverns, his conscience reminded him. That inner voice always sounded just like Mum. Anger began to replace his hesitation. Anger at Mum for her martyr complex and her manipulation of all three of her sons. Anger at himself for listening to her for so many years. Anger at Hanassa for being the bloodthirsty priest of the false god Simurgh. Anger at the dragons who had originally spawned Hanassa and then kicked him out of the nimbus for his lack of honor and his taste for human flesh.

He let the anger propel him forward. He caught up with his brothers and took the lead.

He could not help watching the ground closely for that alien footprint. It danced off to the side, then rejoined the direct route to the lower levels. A few paces farther on it disappeared again. Loki breathed a little easier.

The three brothers wound their way silently through the maze of caverns into the large room with a natural dais. At the entrance they all paused and held their breath.

Someone had placed a large, high-backed chair made of silver bloodwood in the exact center of the platform. Before it, a massive boulder had been carved and shaped into an altar. Outlines of a dragon dismembering naked humans, male and female, young and old, helpless and in their prime, appeared half finished on all four sides of the stone.

"The chair . . . it looks like a throne," Loki gulped. He could not stand to look at the grisly altar. He drank deeply from the canteen to keep his stomach under control.

His lover, Cyndi, would love that throne. She looked good in red with her blonde hair and fair skin.

"Who can tolerate sitting on that wood? The sap toxins would burn right through clothing." Konner squirmed uneasily.

"Hanassa would sit there. I don't think he'd notice a little thing like discomfort," Loki said quietly. Cyndi would also find a way to discount or avoid skin rashes and welts. Enhancing her looks was her primary occupation. That and defying her father.

"The dragons dumped Hanassa's body into the lava core," Kim reminded them. "He could not have survived. I know it, you know it. The dragons know it." He slapped his illuminator on his thigh with each statement.

"Maybe the Rovers?" Loki offered. Anything to banish the thought that Hanassa might still live to plague them.

Or his ghost might haunt them. Who else would *want* to erect and carve that altar? The rock looked untainted. At least it had not yet been consecrated with human blood.

"Maybe Rovers." Konner sounded as if he did not really buy that explanation. The Coros blamed all misdeeds and bad luck upon the homeless tribes. "We need to get moving and destroy the beacon," he said. Now he took the lead and marched across the cavern toward the lava tube tunnel that would take them downward, into the bowels of the mountain.

"It's so beautiful." Kim drawled his words, his accent declining into the slow and drawn-out enunciation of the locals. He ran his hand above the intricate carving of the throne. He seemed to caress it without actually touching it. Horned dragon heads looked over the shoulder of anyone who sat there. Dragon wings formed the arms and sides. Dragon legs and large dragon feet with extended talons supported the piece. The openwork back looked like more dragon horns interlaced.

"They've left bits of the silver bark on the wings to represent the shimmering translucence of the membrane." Kim looked as if he was about to sit.

"Poison permeating the wood makes it red," Konner reminded the youngest brother. "Polish and time will reduce the toxins, but never eliminate them."

Kim sighed heavily as if breaking a trance. Then he rejoined his older siblings. "I wonder who carved it," he mused.

"I don't think I want to know," Loki said, careful to keep his speech crisp like any properly educated civil back home. "The artist's hands would be ruined forever from working with the raw wood."

"The artist who carved the altar would also have a ruined psyche after working those images," Kim said with a shudder.

They began the trek downward. The smooth lava tube tunnel offered an easy path. They made good time. The temperature rose dramatically with each half kilometer. By the time the path leveled off into another cavern, all three were drenched with sweat. They exhausted their canteens about halfway down.

"I'm so thirsty even that creek water will taste good," Loki admitted. He rushed to the streamside and splashed some of the sulfur-laden liquid on his face. He dipped his cupped hands once more for a drink.

"Hold on, Loki," Konner grabbed his shirt collar and pulled him away from the creek bed. "Let me test it first."

"What could change the content since the last time we were here? It's potable even if it does taste like morning breath with a hangover," Loki argued.

"This is an active volcano. The mineral content of this stream changes frequently." Konner knelt with one of his gadgets extended over the water. He dipped a sensor in and waited.

They all waited. Probably only a few femtos, but it seemed like an hour. The gadget beeped. Konner nodded.

Loki slurped up a double handful of water and spat it out. He screwed up his face at the foul taste. His brothers laughed.

"At least I wet the inside of my mouth," Loki excused himself. The sourness at the back of his throat overcame the strong aftertaste of sulfur. He sipped a few drops from his hands. It didn't taste quite so bad this time. A few more sips and he could tolerate enough to slake his thirst.

He noticed his brothers taking a few cautious sips as well. Eventually, they all drank their fill.

"The beacon," Konner reminded them.

As one, they rose to their feet and headed deeper into the maze of caverns. Half walls, boulders, stalactites, stalagmites, and columns forced them to take a twisted path that doubled back and wandered far from a straight line. Small dead-end rooms branched off the convoluted cavern. They paused at a metal door blocking a large room. They'd removed the computers and technical gadgets left there by the original colonists and stored them aboard *Sirius*. None of the locals could stumble upon the equipment and use it destructively without understanding it.

As Hanassa had.

Their steps took them past the site of their last confrontation with Hanassa, the place where Loki had pulled the trigger of a lethal needle rifle and killed the man. Each brother murmured a quick prayer and moved on.

Loki resisted the urge to make the sign of the cross. That was Mum's religion, not his. Still the old habit died hard.

Suddenly, the darkness and the weight of the mountain above pressed heavily against Loki. His breathing grew difficult.

He relived the moment he had last faced Hanassa. He raised his arms, as if still holding the needle rifle, took aim, and pulled the trigger. Cold sweat broke out on his face and hands. His knees trembled.

He saw again the hundreds of poisoned slivers of steel pierce Hanassa's back. Felt with him the agony as the deadly missiles passed through his body into the chest of Taneeo, his apprentice priest and hostage.

The world went white. Too bright.

As life escaped Hanassa, Loki knew several moments of deep agony of body and soul. And then nothing.

He shivered, remembering the cold numbness that had frozen his mind and his will to go on living.

He still dreamed that he died with Hanassa.

A hum began in the back of Loki's head. It sang in his back teeth and quivered along the fine hairs on his spine.

"Konner, is this what you hear when you work with the crystals?" Loki whispered.

"Similar. Nothing is as beautiful as the siren song of a crystal array in harmony," Konner replied.

"I have never heard a crystal array, Konner. This is irresistible." Kim smartened his steps and walked forward eagerly, the way he went to greet Hestiia.

A flicker of movement in Loki's peripheral vision diverted his attention from the allure of the hum. He turned quickly and swept his illuminator over the walls. The light glinted off dripping limestone. Ominous shadows played with his depth perception. Was that the shape of a man hiding behind a column? Or was it merely another stalagmite in the distance?

He shook himself free of the creepy imaginings.

Then he heard it. A low chuckle rummaging around his mind.

"Someone is here," he hissed to his brothers."

They halted in their tracks, not moving a muscle.

"Are you certain?" Kim asked. He stared around him, keeping the illuminator low.

"Yes," Loki breathed. "I can feel him."

"Him? Who?" Konner also searched the immediate environs.

"Not sure who. Only sure that a mind brushed against mine. It was . . . was totally alien."

Five months ago either of his brothers would have questioned Loki's statement. Since coming to this planet they had learned a new respect for psychic powers. Each possessed a different one. Loki was telepathic if he tried hard enough. Kim had visions of the future and the healer's talent. Konner could move things with his mind.

Each talent seemed to grow stronger the longer they stayed on this world of dragons and magic.

"We'll deal with the intruder after we dump the beacon." Konner moved forward.

Kim followed him, letting his illuminator wander from the direct path seeking anything that did not look right.

Loki took up the rear. He turned in frequent circles, checking behind him and off to the sides. Nothing showed in the feeble light. But the presence of "another" still weighed heavily on his mind.

They passed into the next cavern. The light was better here. Openings to the churning lava pool allowed the red glow from planetary fire to penetrate a few of the shadows.

The rusting hulk of an ancient steam generator, left over from the original colonists, loomed over them. The brothers had nicknamed the machine Big Bertha after a very cranky and very lazy aunt. Out of some superstition, Loki touched the boiler.

And jerked his hand away. He sucked on his palm, drawing out some of the burn.

"Why is this thing hot?" he asked around the fleshy part of his hand.

Panic lighted Konner's eyes. "It should be cool, unless . . . unless someone connected the pipes." He moved around the machine and shone his illuminator on the line of pipes that channeled creek water over the heat of the lava pool and into the boiler. Indeed, the broken and rusting pieces had been patched together with bands of bright bronze.

"Those welds won't hold." Konner shook his head.

"The question is who did it?" Loki persisted. He fought to control his own panic. "The only person on this planet with the technical knowledge to repair this thing, other than us, is dead." He gulped. "He *is* dead, isn't he?"

Silence.

"Isn't he!"

"He has to be. We watched Iianthe and Gentian dump his body into the lava pit," Kim insisted.

Loki replayed the scene from his memory, checking for errors. The two purple-tipped dragons had shrunk to the size of house cats. Eerily black and winged, they had grabbed the limp body of Hanassa in beak and claw, flown it through this side tunnel, and dropped it. Loki had not watched the corpse burn. He didn't need to in order to know it could not survive in any form.

"This beacon follows Hanassa into the pit before anything else diverts my attention." Konner ran into the nearest tunnel giving access to the open cauldron of churning lava.

At that moment the alluring hum increased to raucous song.

"The dragongate," Loki breathed.

The light changed from eerie red to a green-blue. The natural wormhole, born of the tremendous heat and pressure of the volcano, bridged the distance between the volcano and the depths of an ocean. And out of those watery depths loomed the biggest fish Loki had seen or read about on any of the worlds they had visited. The infamous behemoth. A voracious feeder, known to charge large boats and take bites out of the hulls.

"Shite, I need burning rock to destroy this thing, not water!" Konner shouted.

A mottled blue-and-gray hide made the behemoth nearly invisible until it was upon them. Its gaping maw showed row upon row of dagger-sharp teeth. Seven beady eyes probed the watery depths for prey.

Loki barely had time to breathe before the fish spotted Konner, turned, and lunged through the water into the mountain cavern. Konner reared back, stumbled, fell. The beacon rolled away from him.

A shadowy figure, clothed in concealing dark robes leaped out of the darkness, pounced upon the gadget, and raced off with it. He chortled and giggled as he pranced away.

"St. Bridget and the angels, he sounds just like Hanassa," Loki choked as he scrambled after the retreating shadow.

CHAPTER 4

decorative divider

MARTIN FORTESQUE checked the corridor outside his suite. He'd already misdirected the normal surveillance equipment. This wing of the residence was empty of his many tutors, bodyguards, accountants, spiritual advisers, and athletic young sports companions, who were well paid by Melinda to see to Martin's well-being, and to keep him out of her hair. For once Melinda Fortesque had relaxed her vigilance over her son's safety—and his privacy.

Melinda carefully scheduled ten Earth Standard Minutes into her day to be a mother. The rest of her time was dedicated to making Aurora the wealthiest planet in the Galactic Terran Empire and the much larger Galactic Free Market.

"No one around to interfere," Martin chortled. He'd just spent two hours hacking into his mother's day-planner to make certain every one of his prison wardens believed that someone else occupied Martin's time.

He leaned back in his Lazy-former®. The inflatable cushions filled the contours of his posture and supported him while he concentrated on the blank white wall in front of him.

Where to begin?

"Scaramouch," he commanded his computer unit. "Bank balance upper right-hand corner."

A figure representing the total liquidity available to him appeared in both GTE credits and Adols, the Aurorian monetary unit. Not enough. For all of her wealth, Melinda kept her son on a strict and limited budget. Largesse came sporadically for reasons only Melinda understood.

"Scaramouch, holoimage of the HD™ 37000 jet pedcycle with optional foul weather bubble in lower left-hand corner. Full size." A three-dimensional two-wheeled vehicle with foot pedals for cycling, jet ports for minor elevation over obstacles, and collapsible wings for higher gliding materialized in the room. Only a slight distortion of sunlight coming in from a bank of tinted bioglass windows hinted that the coveted cycle was made only of colored light.

"Price of the HD 37000 above it, please." An astronomical figure appeared above the image in both credits and Adols. "Difference between bank balance and price of HD 37000 in the center."

The new figures represented an additional year of savings from his allowance.

"Well, Melinda told me to do my own birthday shopping. She's always saying I don't get enough exercise, so she can't object to the cycle in principle. Let's see what we can do. Scaramouch, show me Melinda Fortesque's day-planner for my birthday."

The computer already had the day memorized since Martin had accessed it several times in the last three AMs—Aurorian months. He skimmed the usual round of conferences, lists of judges and legislators to be bribed, and deadlines that littered his mother's life. Fifteen minutes allocated to an appearance before a judge. Not an unusual occurrence. Probably some paperwork designed to keep planetary laws within GTE guidelines while concentrating a maximum amount of power and money in Melinda's hands. After the court date, she'd budgeted an entire hour for his birthday celebration. The fact that it coincided with the evening meal surprised him. Mealtimes were prime opportunities to access business associates and rivals in supposedly casual settings. An Adol figure beside the mealtime must represent the amount of money Melinda was willing to part with for Martin's birthday present.

He raised his eyebrows, surprised at the amount. Quite a bit more than he expected.

"Wonder what she wants to bribe me for this time?" He mused. "Add this figure to my bank balance." He touched the day-planner image and dragged it up to the right-hand corner. The numbers ran upward.

Still not enough.

"Scaramouch, delete foul weather bubble from HD 37000."

The holoimage wavered and distorted, then reassembled itself without the protective force field that would keep rain, wind, and unpleasant temperatures from disturbing the rider. The price numbers flickered and changed. The difference between the price and the amount of money he might expect to tap decreased but remained far too high.

"Scaramouch, replace bubble. Since I've got to get creative, let's go for the whole thing." Martin memorized the number in the center of his field and blanked the screen. "Scaramouch, boot up BigMoney program."

Martin spent the next hour moving figures around the program. He bought some high risk stock with his available allowance and sold it almost immediately at a slight profit. He bought a confiscated cargo sitting in the police warehouse and sold it through the port authorities. That brought him closer to his goal.

Then something in the port records caught his eye. The entry was listed in bright red and displayed in letters three times the normal size.

"M. Konner O'Hara, ship *Sirius*. No entry under any circumstances on or before above date."

Martin looked closer. The "above date" was his birthday. Why had the port—and therefore his mother—banned Martin's summer camp counselor from the planet on his birthday?

Melinda sent Martin away for three AMs every year for "education and socialization opportunities." In other words, she wanted her son out of sight and out of mind. Konner O'Hara had been his counselor for four years. Except this year. Melinda had kept Martin home with no explanation other than a new tutor with loads of homework assignments.

Martin skipped back to his mother's day-planner. The judge to be bribed that day also included a court time handwritten in tiny letters rather than computer generated. An unusual entry. Electronic pencil markings could not be changed easily and Martin had yet to discover a program to hack them. The computer had difficulty reading the print and kept blanking it out.

Martin enhanced that portion of the schedule and set it on decode mode in case Melinda had gotten creative with her private entries. She did that every once in a while, as if she feared industrial espionage. She should.

"Final custody hearing. Make certain Martin has a new suit."

"I don't believe it. Melinda is actually going to go through the motions of obeying a law that is good for the masses but not necessarily good for her. She's going to let me choose my custodial parent. That myth she's been telling me, and everyone else, that she chose artificial insemination to gain an heir is a big fat lie! But why outlaw Konner. Maybe he knows my father. He could get my dad here in time for me to legally choose him instead of Melinda."

In order to maintain good standing with the GTE, Melinda Fortesque had to make a show of a republican government for the people who lived on Aurora—all of them her employees. Anything that she disliked or found inconvenient was taken care of with a bribe of money or influence. At some time in the past, she had allowed a law to pass that in cases of contested custody, the child had the right to choose his/her final custodial parent at the age of fourteen.

The fact that a hearing had been scheduled meant that Martin's father—whoever he might be—had challenged Melinda. He hadn't totally abandoned Martin.

"I wonder who my dad is?"

He zoomed back to the port authority and moved the order banning Konner O'Hara from Aurora to the previous year. No mention of banning him on or after the birthday and crucial court date. "Konner went out of his way to become a counselor at my summer camp. Maybe he's my dad."

Martin hoped so. The three Aurora months each summer that he spent with Konner represented more time than the accumulated amount Melinda allotted him on a daily basis.

"If he is my dad, then his name is on the custody suit." Martin hesitated. Did he dare hack into the official court records? The GTE maintained those records, not the local judicial system. If he got caught, even Melinda would have a hard time bailing him out.

He called up the message center of his computer. Sure enough, Bruce Geralds, his cabin mate at summer camp had left three messages. Martin opened them. All three were innocuous greetings and gossip about other friends.

Martin opened a mailbox and dashed off a hurried message for a conference. He needed the help of all of his friends to hack into the court records—especially Bruce whose father was a freelance bounty agent.

"Martin!" Melinda appeared in the center of his screen, life-sized and in three dimensions, as if she actually stood there. Her lustrous brown hair was sculpted into the latest fashion of the sleek professional woman. Her suit had cost the annual income of several small worlds. And anger blazed from her amber-brown eyes.

"What do you think you are doing with this money program?" she demanded.

"Just shopping for my birthday present, like you asked me to," he answered innocently. Hopefully she wouldn't find out until too late exactly what he planned to get for his birthday.

·——◆——·

"Konner, grab the beacon with your mind," Kim called out to his brother even as he ran after the thief. They had to destroy the device before the IMPs found the jump point. Before Kim was forced to leave Coronnan and Hestiia.

Hestiia. A gaping hole opened in his gut at the thought of leaving her. Of never coming back.

Because once the GTE found this planet, nothing would be the same. The life they had built here would vanish as ashes from an evening campfire scattered, trampled, and drowned by invaders.

He and his brothers would not be allowed to return.

The black-clad figure darted through the maze of caverns. He stopped and looked at Kim from the depths of his hood.

"Show yourself, bastard!" Loki called from right behind Kim. "Are you afraid to show your face?"

The intruder giggled, high-pitched, hysterical. Insane. And took off again in a new direction. He danced and leaped and cavorted as if leading a festival celebration, all the while making certain Kim and Loki followed.

"He's toying with us," Kim panted. He put on a burst of speed.

"St. Bridget, and Mary, and all of God's little angels help me!" Loki cried as he took a flying leap.

Loki landed hard, fingers entwined in their quarry's cloak.

"Eeeeppp!" the man squealed. He flailed.

Loki tugged on the sturdy cloth. Not black. The ubiquitous rust color of the local shaggy cattle.

Kim grabbed the man's shoulders. Must be male by the breadth and musculature. He wore soft boots made of deer hide, the same as the footprint Loki had seen earlier.

And then the thief wiggled once and slid out of their grasp.

The intruder left Kim holding the cloak as he disappeared into the shadows.

Loki pounded the ground with his fist. He remained prone, shoulders slack in disappointment.

"I can't . . . get . . . it," Konner panted coming up behind them. "I can't find the beacon with my mind. And I don't have any Tambootie to augment my powers."

A hum began in the back of Kim's neck. His teeth itched and his feet did not want to remain still.

"The dragongate," he breathed. "It's opening."

"By St. Bridget, does this ghost know how to use the gate?" Loki looked up. Horror dawned in his eyes.

"If anyone but us knows . . ." Kim did not dare finish that thought. Instant transportation to almost anywhere on the planet offered near-limitless power. Another unscrupulous megalomaniac like Hanassa. . . .

"Hestiia knows," Konner reminded him.

"So does Taneeo," Loki added. "Hanassa sent him through the gate dozens of times while he was enslaved."

"We can trust them. Hestiia is my wife. Taneeo is a friend. He presided at my wedding. They understand why this must be kept secret," Kim insisted.

"Then who?" Loki asked. "Sure, we all want to trust everyone. But who else did Hanassa show this to?"

"There he is." Konner dashed after the flicker of movement at the edge of the light.

Kim and Loki stayed at his heels. They had to catch the man now. Before the IMPs locked onto the beacon and everything he held dear crashed around him. They ran full out. Kim's lungs began to strain in the heat. His thighs ached and his heart thundered in his ears.

The hum in the back of his neck set his teeth on edge. "He's headed for the dragongate!" he called out.

Big Bertha loomed ahead of them. The eerie red light from the lava grew brighter; took on tones of gray and pale green.

"Stop him before . . ."

Their quarry darted into the tunnel, little more than a silhouette. Did he have only two dimensions?

Kim blinked his eyes several times, trying to focus on the figure, find some point of familiarity, or substance in him.

"Good-bye, my friends. Even the dragons can't catch me." The stranger's voice deepened and rang through the tunnels. The soaring caverns took up the cry, twisted it, amplified the reverberating tones, and sent it back to them.

The hair on Kim's nape stood on end. Chill touched his heart.

Loki made the sign of the cross without breaking stride.

The light shifted again, going red and dark.

Konner came to a skidding halt at the lip of the volcanic crater.

A stream of lava flared upward coming within a thousand feet of the precipice where they stood. The heat threatened to scorch exposed skin.

"He's gone," Konner whispered.

"Where?" Kim asked. "Did you see where the dragongate took him."

"No place I recognized. Gray-green soil, rocks jutting through like broken bones in a compound fracture, scant plant life. Deep ravines revealing black rock beneath the soil."

"We have to find him."

"How?"

CHAPTER 5

◆—·—◆—·—◆

KAT TALBOT yanked her safety harness across her shoulders and fastened it between her legs. All around her, the bridge crew copied her movements. All except Lucinda Baines, the diplomatic attaché. That august personage, not much older than herself, continued to brace herself behind Kat's chair, staring eagerly at the sensor readings.

"Are we truly on the trail of the infamous O'Hara brothers," Ms. Baines breathed.

"You won't be unless you find a place to strap in," Kat warned her. The woman's beauty and pedigree did not grant her special dispensation from the laws of physics. Scientists had yet to figure out how jump points worked. They only knew that they opened holes in space to distant places and that they were dangerous.

"Strap in, Ms. Baines, or get off my bridge," Commander Leonard ordered.

Ms. Baines flashed the ship's captain a resentful glare. Then she flounced over to a jump seat with a harness.

Kat slapped the jump alarm. A loud klaxon resounded throughout the ship three times, followed by the captain's prerecorded voice. "Prepare for jump. All personnel, prepare for jump." Thirty long seconds later, each section of the ship reported in; med bay, judiciary, anthropology, Marines, engineering, and all the other smaller departments that kept the judiciary cruiser running. If anyone aboard was out of position and injured in the coming minutes, they had only themselves to blame.

"I certainly hope this means we have finished this wild-goose chase and can proceed toward civilization," Judge Balinakas intoned from the hatchway. His stout body filled the portal, his black judicial robes draped about him with majesty, reflecting the glossy black of his hair. His swarthy skin had higher color on cheekbones and nose than usual.

"Strap in, Judge," Leonard ordered. She gripped the arms of her chair until her knuckles turned white. "I am taking this ship in pursuit of criminals wherever I must follow them. That is, of course, our mission."

"We are well overdue for our rendezvous, Commander Leonard. Not even the infamous O'Hara brothers are worth yet another fruitless side trip." The judge looked down his beakish nose at the captain of the ship.

"Take a seat, Judge, or suffer the consequences of jump." She turned her head back to the screens, clearly dismissing the man who represented a rival authority aboard ship.

"I shall report you, Commander, for this deviation." The judge did not seek the jump seat on the opposite side of the hatch from Ms. Baines.

"Your conduct goes into my official report. Need I remind you *again* that I am in command of this vessel? You command only the judiciary process for any criminals we apprehend." Leonard's voice gained intensity and volume.

"Need I remind you that I have absolute authority over this mission?" The judge remained calm.

"Bridge personnel secure, Lieutenant Talbot," Commander Leonard reported. "Take us into jump."

Kat slapped the final alarm.

Judge Balinakas remained standing.

Kat took a deep breath and began the sequence of commands transferring control to the central computer. No human could react fast enough during the sensory overloads of jump to navigate. Three hundred lives depended upon the computer's judgment.

"Someday, I'm going to prove that I can fly a jump by myself," Kat muttered to herself.

The klaxon sounded again. Three loud and annoying blasts that no one could ignore, including Judge Balinakas. He threw himself into the jump seat and secured his safety harness, every millimeter of his posture shouting resentment. He'd called the captain's bluff and lost the bet.

Lights flashed red and dimmed with each blast.

Kat's own jaw began to ache from clamping her teeth together to avoid biting her tongue.

The ship surged forward. Two gs, three gs. Acceleration pushed Kat hard against her chair. The high back kept her neck from whiplashing. Pressure built. She fought for every gulp of air.

Black stars crowded her vision. She forced her eyes open. She had to watch. Just once she had to see what jump was truly like.

Dry grit weighed heavily against her eyelids. She had to blink. Just once.

Before she could open her eyes again the pressure ceased. Gravity dissolved. Light vanished.

Kat lost contact with her body. She was only a soul drifting in a vast noth-ingness. Her mind tricked her into believing she witnessed bright coils of light pulsing with life. Each coil was a different color and brightness. They chained and twined together, braided and looped back upon themselves in an intricate mesh.

She could almost reach out and touch them. If the harness did not restrain her. If she had a body to be restrained.

Time passed. Aeons of memories flitted past her mind's eye. She tried to sort them, catch hold of one for longer than a single heartbeat. Each evapo-rated. Space ghosts without form or substance or purpose.

(*Why do you come?*) a deep sonorous voice that was many voices and minds combined echoed around her skull.

"Who are you?" She could not hear her words. A space ghost? Who else inhabited the empty places between the stars?

(*We are who we are. Who are you and why do you come?*)

"I come to find . . . myself."

(*Welcome.*)

The ship burst free of jump. Sensations slammed back into Kat's body, all at once, too quickly to absorb. She welcomed the headache as proof that she lived. The moment she had something to see, and eyes to see with, she scanned her instruments. Nothing looked familiar. The computer looped through incoming data from the ship's sensors. It found nothing familiar and repeated measuring the scan.

"That was definitely a jump point," Commander Leonard said. Her voice shook. The unflappable captain looked disoriented and uncertain.

"That was one hell of a jump," Chief Navigator Kohler said. He rubbed his eyes with trembling hands. His normally dusky skin looked gray.

"Longest jump I've ever endured." Ensign James Englebert, the communi-cations officer on duty, said on a choking laugh, as if he had more than two or three jumps notched on his belt.

But he was right. The jump had lasted longer than usual. Although the ship's chronometer showed the passage of only a few seconds, Kat knew her body had passed through perhaps as much as an hour.

Jumps played hell with linear space and time.

"So where in Murphy's continuum are we?" Commander Leonard asked.

"I wish I knew, Captain," Kat whispered. "I think we are lost."

"I track the Stargods," Dalleena Farseer stated simply to the village headman. She had observed the protocols and sought him out first. But the tug on her senses drove her onward. Those she must find did not dwell here.

"Many seek the brothers from the sky. Why do you *track* our lords?" The middle-aged man with the heavy muscles of a warrior looked her up and down with care. The interest in his eyes had little to do with her femininity and a lot to do with her choice of words.

Not much of her body showed beneath her leather breeches, boots, vest, and linen shirt. Unlike most women of her acquaintance, she did not need to highlight the swell of her breast or the nip in her waist to earn her keep. She had other talents.

"'Tis something I need to do," she replied.

"Why?"

"I need not explain anything to you without the courtesy of a name or hospitality." She stood firm, not wavering under his fierce gaze.

"Forgive my lack of manners, Tracker." The headman bowed his head slightly. But he never took his gaze from her eyes. "We have learned caution. Many seek the Stargods and their chosen people, the Coros. Some do not wish our saviors well."

"I have heard that the three brothers descended from the stars to save your people from a deadly plague. They also ended slavery among you." She scanned the array of houses behind the headman. The town was nestled between the bay and the river, a half hour's walk above the flood line of either. Nearly one hundred sturdily built homes and a temple. No mistaking the huge building with the silver bloodwood columns topped by carvings of dragons. These people had worshiped the bloodthirsty Simurgh before the coming of the Stargods.

"My father still resents the loss of his slaves." A younger man with a hooked nose to match the headman's and a similar cast to the brown eyes, sauntered over from the largest of the homes, at the opposite end of the town from the temple. "I am Yaakke. My ill-mannered father is called Yaaccob the Usurper. You will not find the Stargods here."

"But they have been here. Recently."

"Your tracking senses are correct," Yaakke replied. "They came to bless the pregnancy of my wife. My sister is mate to the youngest of the Stargod brothers."

"Ah," Dalleena said. She turned in a slow circle, right arm extended, palm raised. West of this riverside town. Not far. Too far after a long journey afoot before sunset.

"I go to visit my sister," Yaakke said. "Would you care to join me in the boat journey? Company relieves the tedium of the travel."

"Boat? Yes, I will join you," Dalleena said with a sigh of relief. She could rest her aching feet. Gratefully, she followed the man to the riverbank.

After weeks on the road, he had offered the first evidence of actually having seen the Stargods. But everyone who lived south of the big river and north of the fiery mountains had heard of the three brothers who descended from the stars on a cloud of silver fire. Their great deeds done liberating the tribe of the Coros had become the subject of song and ritual.

Dalleena settled into the hollowed-out log of a boat. "How did you smooth the inside so evenly?" She ran a hand along the inner sides, amazed that no splinters pierced her skin. Even the outside remained free of bark or ragged patches.

"A miracle of the Stargods." Yaakke grinned hugely. "There are advantages to allowing Stargod Kim to marry my sister." Then he handed Dalleena a paddle.

She looked at it skeptically. Tracking sometimes required her to travel long distances over a variety of terrain. The people who required a Tracker to find lost livestock, errant children, or missing lovers usually did all the work.

This time the quest was her own. Therefore she must work for herself. She dug the paddle into the water with strength equal to Yaakke's stroke.

Before long, her back and shoulders began to ache. Her palms blistered. The sight of the setting sun sparkling red upon the waters of the river numbed her mind and her talent. She knew nothing, felt nothing but the pressure upon her body each time she pushed the boat a little farther upstream.

"Nearly there," Yaakke told her. He pointed to a muddy embankment. Many feet and more than a few boats had slid up and down it. Two rafts and another log boat were tied to large stakes driven into the dirt on either side of the slippery access.

To Dalleena's surprise, Yaakke continued paddling beyond the point. Her shoulders ached even more. They had passed their objective and her guide expected more work from her. This was more tiring than if she'd walked!

"Ease up on the paddle," Yaakke called.

Finally. She obeyed him, resting the paddle across the boat sides. Her back slumped and her head felt a little too heavy. She should not be this tired. She worked hard every day on the family farm when she was not tracking. She could match muscle and stamina with any warrior.

Why?

Yaakke let the boat drift back toward the landing area, using his paddle to steer them closer and closer to the bank.

At last the boat grounded. Yaakke jumped out, calf-deep in the water. He grabbed the bow of the craft and waited.

"Are you getting out or not?" he asked testily.

"Oh," she replied dumbly. Heavily, she dragged herself out of the bottom of the little boat and into the water. The current tugged at her. She grabbed the boat for balance.

"Push," Yaakke ordered.

She did so. He hauled. Together they brought the craft up onto the bank. A crowd of people gathered above them, watching. When Yaakke had tied his craft to one of the stakes protruding out of the mud, a young woman jumped down and grabbed him in an embrace. She had the same set to her eyes as both Yaakke and his father, but a more delicate nose structure. Her thick brown hair cascaded down her back, covering most of her body. At first Dalleena thought she and the other women adhered to the old custom of not covering their breasts until a man had claimed them. Slave women were never allowed to cover themselves except out of doors in deep winter. A shift in Hestiia's posture, a ripple in her hair, revealed a halter woven of red cow wool above her leather sarong. All the women seemed to wear the same clothing with little variation.

Dalleena suddenly felt too tall, too awkward and out of place.

"My sister, Hestiia," Yaakke introduced them.

Dalleena gave her own name and talent, nodding her head.

"Welcome, Tracker." Hestiia marched over and stuck out her right hand to her.

Dalleena stared at the hand wondering if she was supposed to touch it.

Hestiia took the decision away from her, grabbing her by the elbow and shaking her arm. Dalleena returned the gesture as well as the woman's smile.

"Come, the hospitality of this village is open to you. We have hot food ready. My husband and his brothers should return any time now." The little woman led them up the bank and toward the cluster of cabins as if she held the honored place of headman.

Dalleena followed, curious about a village that allowed a woman to speak for them. At the top of the track, an ancient woman of impressive girth and swarthy coloring waited. She stood with hands on hips, legs spread sturdily, and a fierce scowl upon her face.

A Rover. What was she doing here? Rovers never settled in a village. Villagers never allowed them to linger near. Suspicion and distrust kept them always apart.

"I be Pryth," the Rover woman announced. "You be Tracker. Why do you feel needed here?"

"I do not know, only that something, someone needs tracking." Her senses awoke under the intense gaze of the old woman. Her hand burned and itched as it never had before. She raised her right arm and supported it with her left. Palm out she turned in a slow, methodical circle, pausing at every quarter of a quarter turn. Her head spun with the need to find the nameless thing before it destroyed itself. Or destroyed them.

But she could not find a direction to look.

CHAPTER 6

◆ — · — ◆ — · — ◆

KONNER STARED into the campfire.

Villagers bustled around him. Women carried trenchers piled with roasted venison, chunks of wild yampion, a sweet tuber served raw or roasted or mashed with fresh milk, and globs of boiled greens dressed in fat and fruit vinegar.

The Tracker sat among the men across the fire from Konner. She did not participate in any of the usual female pursuits. Her eyes wandered restlessly around the village, across the sky, and toward the deep shadows beyond the fire.

Konner did not have the thoughts to spare this night to wonder why. All he could think about was the missing beacon and the audacious thief. Which led him back to Melinda and her betrayal of him.

Hestiia offered Konner a platter without meat. He waved it away.

She pursed her lips in disapproval and offered it instead to her husband, Kim.

He took it from her with a smile that lighted his face all the way to his eyes. Their gazes locked on each other, grew intense. His hand covered hers, lingered, and caressed before she relinquished the bark platter.

Konner turned his head away, embarrassed by their intimacy, jealous and lonely in his own isolation.

Fifteen years ago he had believed he and Melinda could learn to love each other like that. She'd offered him one million Adols, the most stable currency in the galaxy, in exchange for a legal marriage ceremony. She wanted control of her inheritance, the corporation that owned the entire planet of Aurora. But her parents' will had specified she could not sit on the board of directors or have access to capital funds until she married or turned thirty years of age.

At twenty-two she decided to take control of her fate and made her proposal to Konner. He'd been only twenty and on his first solo reconnoiter for the family business. Aurora produced a number of high-tech items needed on bush worlds that could not afford to buy them legally. Mum had sent him to Aurora see if they could empty a warehouse without paying for the merchandise.

Then Konner met Melinda. They had spent a giddy week together on a newly opened bush colony world. No one had asked questions or required much in the way of paperwork before the wedding ceremony. Seven days of sex and wine and laughter and more sex had not been enough for Konner.

Within hours of returning to Aurora, Melinda had seized control of her corporation, had Konner arrested, and permanently exiled without a single fraction of a coin in payment of the prenuptial agreement.

Notice of annulment of the marriage appeared on the bush world within hours.

The humiliation and the loneliness burned so deep in Konner that he had not told his brothers about his marriage.

Loki planned and executed the theft from Melinda's warehouse based upon Konner's information. Konner had participated in the plan without a single guilty thought to slow him down. Only Mum knew of his failed marriage, and she used the knowledge ruthlessly, to keep Konner in the family business when all he wanted was to go off exploring on his own. Mum promised him the time and money to fight Melinda for the prenuptial sums and custody of his son Martin when she completed a project of her own. The time never came when Mum had enough money to bribe the right officials to regain family citizenship. Without those essential papers, Konner had not a prayer of winning anything from Melinda in a legal court.

But he had kept a copy of the prenuptial agreement and stashed extra copies in key places.

Shame for his youthful misalliance still ate at him. His only consolation was a chance meeting with a mechanic who had worked a short time at the Aurora Space Docks and gave him the news that Melinda had a son.

As soon as Martin was old enough to go to summer camp, Konner made a point of working at that camp as a counselor. He'd forged citizenship papers to pass their security screen. He and his son had bonded over many an evening campfire.

Those flames had burned normal red and gold with a blue heart.

In front of him, on this early autumn evening on a forgotten planet beyond explored space, pale green flames around a deep yellow layer licked branches greedily. Copper sulfate, he told himself, made the fire burn green. Copper sulfate impregnated every living thing on this planet. He'd never get used to the colors. Wondered if his blood would turn green if he lived here long enough.

"I have to leave in five days," he said aloud. "I have to leave by then or miss my . . . appointment."

Loki nodded his acknowledgment. Kim frowned as he jerked his head down and up a single time.

Konner's brothers now knew of his court date on Martin's fourteenth birthday. He'd confessed everything to them after Loki had learned how to read minds with some regularity and consistency.

Pryth, the ancient matriarch of the village, stood up and began reciting a long saga of the first coming of the Stargods to rescue the slaves of Hanassa. She directed the story to the new woman, but included the entire village in her audience.

Konner winced. He'd heard this story every fourth or fifth evening sitting around the campfire during and after the communal meal. That he and his brothers were the heroes of the story embarrassed him.

One of the younger men picked up a skin drum and began beating the rhythm of the old woman's recitation. A middle-aged woman added deft tones on a reed flute to punctuate the story.

"You and Loki can't leave until we find the beacon," Kim insisted in hushed tones. "I won't have this planet at the mercy of the GTE, even if you two do leave."

"I told you that you should have dumped the beacon out *Rover*'s loo and let it burn up in reentry," Loki grumbled.

"No, you didn't. You weren't even there," Konner replied.

"Well, you should have thought of that solution."

"They are designed to withstand reentry and crash." Konner returned to his contemplation of the fire.

"So where did the thief go?" Loki leaned forward, shoulders and spine rigid.

"Raaskan," Kim hailed the village chieftain.

The man Konner and his brothers had rescued from a life of slavery and death as a sacrifice to Hanassa's god, ambled toward them. His soft leather knee breeches and vest molded to his muscular frame. The buttery color made a nice contrast to his permanently sun-bronzed skin. Konner guessed him to be in his early thirties, about his own age. But in this primitive society, just growing out of bronze and into iron technology, Raaskan commanded the same kind of respect as a senior CEO of a galactic corporation.

"Pryth always tells stories better than anyone else. She has an energy and sense of timing possessed by few," Raaskan said as he lowered himself to sit cross-legged beside Kim in one smooth motion.

Konner never had been comfortable out of doors before coming here. He preferred ships and big buildings filled with mechanicals. He could bond with machines more easily than people.

But something about these people and their simple values tugged at his heart with an emotion akin to his love for machines.

"Must be Pryth's Rover heritage. Her people are renowned for their ability to take ordinary events and make them into life-changing sagas," Konner replied.

"Pryth has been with us for more than three generations. We forget that she is not originally one of the Coros," Raaskan said.

"She has seen many places in Coronnan." Kim followed the casual conversational rules of this society. Pleasantries must continue for some time before coming to the meat of a subject.

Loki fidgeted beside Konner. The oldest brother did not like waiting. Any second now he would plunge in and demand information.

"Rovers wander far," Raaskan said. He nibbled a bite of venison from his trencher.

Kim turned his head away. Loki looked longingly at the meat before yanking his gaze away to watch the women.

Hestiia and Raaskan's wife led a dozen villagers in a dance around the fire, acting out the story Pryth told. They recounted how Konner and his brothers had unleashed their magic—fully charged stunner guns—and blasted the sacrificial altar rock to pieces. No more would the stone taste human blood in homage to the winged god Simurgh.

"How far have you wandered?" Konner pressed Raaskan. "What have you seen beyond the meadows and rivers of Coronnan."

Raaskan clamped his jaw shut. He looked directly into Konner's eyes for long moments.

Konner did not look away. "You may speak of this among us."

"I flew with you, Stargod Konner, inside the belly of your white dragon that is no dragon."

"And when you traveled with my brother to the hills south of here," Kim said, "to the huge outcropping that juts out into the Great Bay so that you could bring a blacksmith to this village, did you see a land with tufts of grass more gray than green, with scrubby shrubs and long fissures cutting deeply to reveal black rocks, like the bones of the land scorched by the sun?" Kim easily fell into the convoluted formal language of the bard. He excelled in calling up language that spoke in metaphors as easily as fact.

The scientist in Konner rebelled at the imprecision these people loved. They liked many layers of meaning that they could peel away bit by bit to reveal truths of human nature that could not be quantified by science.

He ached to be gone from here, back on the space lanes where he knew the risks and the dangers and how to overcome them.

At the same time he knew he would miss the evenings spent in the community of friends sharing a meal, entertaining each other with stories and songs, and keeping the nightmares away with a cheering fire.

"I have never seen such a land," Raaskan admitted. "You must ask Pryth if her people know of it."

"Are there more Rovers we could ask? Clans who have traveled more recently than Pryth?" Loki asked. He twitched with the need to move.

"There are always Rovers. Finding them is not easy unless they wish to be found."

"Great!" Konner exploded, letting his words propel him upward. The momentum of anger fueled his muscles so that he did not need to brace or balance himself. "What good are these people? What good are any of you?" He stalked off into the night, tromping heavily through the underbrush.

He did not care how much noise he made. He did not care if he got lost. He just had to move; to do; to think.

His feet automatically steered toward the meadow west of the village where he had parked *Rover*. The cloaking field gave off a slight hum, more muted than the dragongate, a different frequency. This tone lulled the senses into believing it did not exist and neither did the object it hid.

Konner half smiled at his foresight in designing the system. After spending five months on this planet with its unique ability to augment psychic powers, he understood that the cloaking field worked with brain synapses to fool the mind.

A sliver of a moon showed just above the horizon. He slowed his pace.

He had to destroy the beacon. To do that, he had to find the thief. Should he go back to the volcano and wait for the dragongate to open to the same location as where the thief escaped?

That could take days, even weeks. The gate was unreliable and random in choosing its destinations. He did not have that kind of time to waste.

"I'll take *Rover* up at first light. I'll find that semiarid land on my own."

(*Will you?*) a voice came to him out of the night.

"What? Who?" Konner turned in a full circle seeking the source.

Moonlight glinted off the nose of the shuttle. The cloaking field should mask even the reflection of light off the cerama/metal hull. He peered closer. His steps became more cautious.

(*Will you find the land that you seek on your own?*) the voice repeated.

The moon rose above the tree line at the edge of the meadow. To Konner's trained eye the outline of the shuttle became clearer, still insubstantial because of the cloak, but he knew where to look and what to look for.

Something marred the sleek silhouette of the vessel. A big lumpy something sat on the nose. A lumpy something with spikes. It looked a little like one of Mum's pincushions.

"Not again."

CHAPTER 7

K ONNER SANK to the ground just outside the cloaking field. Evening dew moistened his knees. A chill breeze reminded him that summer had come to an end and he needed a shirt beneath his leather vest. Like the fine white one worn by the new woman, the one who dressed as a man and sat with the men rather than working with the women.

Still he sat there, staring at the nose of the shuttle.

"Iianthe?" he asked the living pincushion.

(*I have not the honor of purple tips to my wings.*)

Typical enigmatic dragon thoughts. If Konner did not know that Iianthe was another word for purple and that Iianthe's horns, wing veins, and wing tips were a shade of purple he would not have understood the statement.

"I am Martin Konner O'Hara," he said politely.

(*Irythros,*) the dragon replied.

"Irythros? Does that mean anything?"

(*I am Irythros. What should it mean?*)

"Does the word name a color in some other language?"

(*Ah,*) the dragon sighed in understanding. It remained silent so long Konner wondered if it would say anything more.

(*Some might believe my name means Red.*)

"Red. You have red horns and spines and your wing tips and veins are red."

(*Yes.*)

"Just like Simurgh."

(*Never!*) The dragon rose up on its hind legs, flapping its wings and roaring its displeasure. A single long flame shot forth from its open mouth.

"Touchy subject?" Konner asked. But then he knew it would be. "Dragons don't like to admit that one of their own became thirsty for human blood. You don't like to remember that you had to destroy one of your own."

The dragon's silence seemed to take on weight. Konner felt a heaviness in his mind that wanted to push his knowledge of Simurgh's true nature deep into the forgotten recesses of his lizard hind brain. A place that knew instinctive fear and had no sense or reason.

He fought the compulsion to forget.

"So, Red, are you waiting for me?" Konner crept a little closer.

(*Irythros,*) the dragon insisted.

"Whatever. Why are you here? Dragons don't show themselves to mere humans without reason." Konner dared rise to his feet. This brought his eyes level with the dragon's claws where they gripped the sleek nose of the shuttle. Each of those talons was as long as his forearm. He winced at the thought of punctures in the cerama/metal hull.

No mere dragon could pierce the hull of a shuttle designed to withstand the heat, radiation, and pressure of reentry, he reminded himself. Again and again.

"You are bigger than Iianthe," he commented, tentatively checking to see if any cerama/metal hull scales had broken off beneath the talons. He needed every one of those scales intact to protect the ship—from space travel as well as corrosion of the interior.

They all seemed intact. But he would not know for certain until the dragon moved.

"Would you mind coming down from there?" He looked up to where the dragon's eyes should be. Hard to tell in this light. Hard to tell in *any* light. His eyes wanted to slide around the dragon rather than look directly at it.

(*Is there a reason?*) Irythros asked. Suddenly, he snaked his head down to Konner's level.

Hot breath bathed his face. A spiraled two-meter-long horn of red and crystal teased his hair.

Konner resisted the temptation to jump back. He'd learned over the months of dealing with Iianthe, the purple-tip who was very fond of Kim and Hestiia, never to show fear. One had to earn a dragon's respect. They had no use for cowardice. They considered Simurgh a coward for hunting weak humans rather than more honorable prey, like the huge predatory fish in the Great Bay. Like the one that had startled Konner in the dragongate and caused him to lose the beacon.

Konner took three deep breaths to keep his feet from shuffling backward. The dragon exhaled.

Konner winced at the thought of the fire the dragon could produce. (They liked their meals cooked.) The wind that passed his ears was cool.

"I would like you to get off my ship because your claws are ripping holes in its hide," Konner said mildly.

(*Oh.*) The dragon leaped free of the shuttle. Its talons screeched against the cerama/metal.

The sound became needle darts in Konner's ears. Again he cringed but did not back away or cover the offended organs.

(*Forgive my trespass,*) Irythros said as he settled to the ground beside Konner.

The beast towered above him, as big as the shuttle. It spread its wings before furling them. The moonlight turned them into shimmering translucent veils. For a moment, Konner thought he could see star maps in the vein network. Or maybe transactional gravitons, the theoretical energy force that held the universe together and at the same time conspired to keep everything in place.

Overcoming the inertia of the gravitons posed the single largest obstacle to space travel. Or atmosphere flight, or rolling a cart.

Konner shook his head free of his fanciful thoughts. Dragons were planet bound. They might speak enigmatically with a great deal of wisdom, but they did not carry star charts etched into their wing membranes.

"Now why did you seek me out?" Konner asked again.

(*Hanassa speaks to the stars. We need to know why.*)

"But Hanassa is dead." Konner began to shiver with a new chill. Twice he and his brothers had thought they had killed the man. Twice he had recovered and come back to threaten their friends as well as themselves. The third time they had made certain he stayed dead. Two flywackets, purple-tip dragons shrunk to the size and shape of winged house cats, had dumped Hanassa's body into the lava pit. The same pit where Konner wanted to dump the beacon.

(*The body of Hanassa died. Yet still he speaks to the stars. We need you to tell us why.*)

"Speaks to the stars," Konner mused. "The beacon! You know where the locator beacon is. Can you take me to it so that we can destroy it?"

(*No.*)

Konner stared at the dragon, expecting the beast to fly away.

Instead Irythros parked his haunches on the ground and returned Konner's level gaze.

"You may be able to see in the dark, but I need more light to see you properly," Konner said at last.

(*Fetch it.*)

"You will wait?"

(*Yes.*)

For the first time in this bizarre conversation, Konner realized the difference between this dragon and Iianthe, the purple-tip who had helped him and his brothers through the last crisis. Iianthe spoke in bass tones very like a large bronze bell tolling across the landscape of his mind. Irythros was more of a tenor, sounded more like an Ubberlund doodlehorn chattering away with the crisp notes of a military march.

Konner wasted no more time. He touched the keypad in his pocket to banish the cloaking field and open the hatch. He'd stashed the portable illuminator just inside. A simple matter to grab it and exit without taking his eyes off the dragon for more than three heartbeats.

He blinked rapidly. Where had the beast gone? And why had Irythros contacted a human with such a very frightening and bone-chillingly cryptic remark?

Kim kissed Hestiia lightly on the cheek. "I have some work to do," he whispered.

She looked at him sharply. "Will you use the weed?"

"I don't know. Depends on what I find." He could not hold her gaze.

"You know it is dangerous."

"I know that Pryth thinks it is dangerous." He walked back toward their cabin, the one he and Hestiia had built for themselves the day they married. Well, actually, the village had built it for them as part of the wedding ceremony. They were still chinking the logs with moss and turf to insulate it against the winter cold. The moss they used was as ubiquitous as the red cow wool. It absorbed moisture in babies' diapers, became good tinder when dried, and insulated against cold and noise quite effectively.

Once inside the cabin, Kim pulled out his reader. It came to life precisely where he had finished his notes this morning. Before the hasty visit to the volcano, before the news of the beacon had upset the tidy life he had made for himself here.

He took a deep breath and concentrated upon the reader. He needed to record today's events.

The woman, Dalleena, and her supposed talent drew his thoughts away from the implications of the lost beacon. The locals respected her claim to track anyone. How did she do it?

For that matter, how did he achieve his own miracles of healing? Raaskan was alive because Kim, with the help of his brothers, had rebuilt the man's crushed rib cage and pelvis, using only the power of his mind. He had cauterized internal bleeding. And he had pushed a dislocated shoulder back into place. All without invasive surgery or the technology of modern medicine.

"Something born in me and my brothers lets us do this. So how do we access it on a regular basis?"

This morning, Kim had been on the verge of doing that with controlled breathing. But once he'd fallen out of the trance he'd been exhausted, ravenous, and nearly incoherent. "My body lacked the fuel to perform the magic."

His eyes sought the basket in the corner. Inside lay the wilting leaves of the Tambootie tree. Once before, he had ingested the essential oils that seeped out of the leaves. They had opened his mind and his talent, allowing him to perform one last miracle to rescue the Coros from Hanassa's control. He had read Hanassa's mind from a distance of nearly ten kilometers.

"Just a little. I need just a little of the leaves to experiment." Without thinking about it, he had walked across the room and shoved his hand deep into the mass of leaves. His skin burned slightly from contact with the essential oils permeating the leaves. He withdrew his hand, grasping a particularly fat leaf dripping with oil. He licked it.

Colors burst upon his tongue. Outside, he heard every word whispered by his people. He shared Hestiia's concern for him as if experiencing his own emotion.

His vision sharpened on the periphery at the same time that he lost focus on things directly in front of him; as if he needed to look at life sideways, around the barrier of his own emotions and prejudices to get a clear view.

Halos enveloped every object in varying colors and brightness. He reached out slowly for the basket of Tambootie. His fingers had to stretch a long way into the corona, or aura, or whatever, before he touched the woven grasses of the basket. Further experiments showed the aura less deep on his bed and the stool in front of his working table. A quick peek out the door showed flashes of living fire surrounding the heads of all the people still gathered around the fire. He found Hestiia rapidly by the brown, rust, and orange flares growing out of her hair. Others he had to think about until he noticed distinctive colors and combinations for each person.

Darkness yawned before him. A bright tangle of colored chains similar in color and combination of colors to the auras beckoned him to grab hold and explore. . . .

(*Be careful when you delve into the realm of dragons.*)

Kim thudded to the packed dirt floor and promptly vomited.

CHAPTER 8

◆—·—◆—·—◆

DALLEENA EXCUSED HERSELF from the rapt company of the village men. Raaskan, the headman, and Yaakke from the other village, both had questioned her intently about her talent. Trackers were not born into every generation. Her family had produced one in each of three successive generations. Both men wanted her as an asset to the village.

Something bigger and more important drew her here. She had listened to reports of the Stargods for moons now. They offered a new view of life and spirituality. They offered freedom from the old ways.

And the Stargods had lost something important. She had to find it for them. Whatever it was, no matter what dangers lay in finding it. Her talent would not allow her to rest until the lost was found and the Stargods were safe once more.

Stargod Konner was not hard to follow. He had left a trail a child could see. She did not even have to engage her talent.

She followed him across two fields separated by a narrow creek. She jumped the creek without even thinking about it. Then over a small hill, with just enough elevation to obscure from the village what lay beyond.

Dim moonlight and a soft glow from the other side of the hill lit her way. She used her eyes rather than her talent to pick her footsteps.

At the top of the rise she halted. Her throat froze. She forgot to breathe.

Shimmering in the moonlight a long white dragon rested easily on its haunches. That sight alone was worth a second glance. But the other dragon, the one that was hard to see, the one that demanded that she look anywhere but at it was even more beautiful. Illuminated by the Stargod's magical torch, she saw that dark red, the color of blood, outlined its horns, wing tips and veins.

She swallowed and stuffed her hands into her pockets. She must not cross her wrists, right over left, and flap them in ward against Simurgh, the winged god that had demanded blood sacrifice at every turn. Touching her head, heart, and each shoulder in turn, the ward of the Stargods, did not seem protection enough.

Beside the dragon stood a lone man. Stargod Konner. The dragon was a worthy companion of a god.

She swallowed her superstitious fears and walked down the hill toward the man and his dragon. A red-tip.

Simurgh had been a red-tip.

As she approached, the dragon took wing and disappeared into the night. Shielding her face from a blast of wind and dust raised by flapping dragon wings, Dalleena followed his flight path with her eyes. For half a moment she thought she saw a nearly transparent wing cross the moon. Then it was gone.

"Irythros!" Stargod Konner called. "Irythros, come back here. I'm not finished with you."

The dragon ignored him, of course.

"Dragons obey only themselves," she said as she came closer.

"Who are you?" Stargod Konner whirled to face her.

"Dalleena Farseer. I sensed that you had lost something."

"Sensed?"

She shrugged. "I am a Tracker. I find lost things."

"Why should I believe you?"

"You have my word."

He looked at her closely then. He focused on her eyes.

"I believe you. I shouldn't. But I believe you."

"What have you lost?" She could not break eye contact. The depth of his blue eyes promised her much. Promises she knew he would keep or die.

"Um . . ." he licked his lips.

She mimicked his action. Her throat still felt dry. She had to remember to breathe.

"We call it a beacon."

"A bee-kan."

"Close enough. About this big." He held up his hand and traced his palm. "It is made out of the same material as the shuttle." He gestured toward the huge white dragon beside them.

The beast emitted a low hum, but otherwise seemed strangely quiescent.

"I do not know this bee-kan." She placed her right hand flat upon the cool skin of the white dragon.

Her hand grew hot. Tingles shot up her arm to her brain. A numbness grew from a knot into a broad band at the base of her neck.

"Far away. I hear the bee-kan calling to its home. It calls to . . . a . . . king stone. It begs the king stone to come rescue it," she whispered.

She shook her head to free herself of the tracking trance. A little of the numbness eased. It would not leave her completely until she removed her hand from contact with the white dragon.

She lifted her hand. It felt too heavy. She braced her arm with the other hand and pulled back. Her hand was heavier still. Then she wrenched her arm.

Her hand remained glued to the shuttle.

Kim wrapped his arms around Hestiia, tucking her beneath his chin. She just fit there. Together they stood for long moments watching the last of the daylight fade beyond the western horizon.

"What troubles you, husband?" she asked.

His senses still reeled from the Tambootie. He dared not mention his reaction to the weed. He'd cleaned up after himself as best he could. But he had to lock his quaking knees and pretend nothing had happened.

"Kim?" Hestiia prompted him.

"Trouble comes," he replied.

"What form does this trouble take?"

Kim sighed. She'd not allow the subject to drop until he told her all. He did not like secrets. His family had too many. But some things were best kept private among his brothers.

"Tell me." She tried to step away from him.

He pulled her back against his body, savoring her warmth and her love.

"More people from my homeland approach. They will bring many miracles. But each miracle comes with a price. They will poison the air and water. Our ears will be assaulted with noise day and night until we can no longer hear birds sing or crickets chirp." How else could he explain the cost of industrialization?

Magic would do nothing to stop these people.

"Many, many more people will come to live here. At first the land will produce enough for all, but eventually the fields will grow tired and give forth smaller and smaller crops. My people will poison the soil to force it to grow more and more crops. And still more people will come, blind to the pollution, blind to the conflicts that arise when too many people fight for the same small piece of land. They will destroy everything we hold dear."

"Then we must stop them."

"Not so easy."

"But you and your brothers are the Stargods. Surely you and your white dragon *Rover* can defeat them, send them back where they came from."

"There are too many of them. They have bigger ships and more powerful weapons than we do."

"There must be a way . . ."

"We have one small chance. We have to find and destroy a small device before they find us."

"I saw the Tracker follow your brother Konner. She can help."

"I pray that she can." But Kim doubted it.

"Your silence tells me there is more trouble than a device that calls these Others."

"Are you sure you do not read my mind?" He kissed the top of her head.

"I know you well, husband. What else troubles you?"

"The beacon we seek was stolen."

"Who would dare!"

"Who, indeed?"

They both stared in silence at the silhouettes of trees against the last glow of light.

"Hanassa died. Your brother killed him. Gentian and Iianthe dropped his body into the fiery heart of the mountain," Hestiia said.

"Indeed. But Hanassa began life as a purple dragon, triplet to Gentian and Iianthe. But only one purple-tip may exist at any time. Gentian shrank to become a flywacket, Iianthe remained a dragon. Hanassa sent his spirit into a human body. Are we certain Hanassa's spirit died with his body?"

"Yes!"

"Then he must have had more disciples than Taneeo. We know how much our new priest hated Hanassa. We know we can trust Taneeo. Another must be haunting the caverns and making mischief for us."

"We must ask Taneeo. He would know if Hanassa trained any followers."

"I hate to bother him. He has not yet recovered from . . . from his ordeal." Ten drugged needles from Loki's rifle had run all the way through Hanassa's body into Taneeo's. One hundred or more of the needles had lodged in Hanassa's vital organs and muscles. The priest of Simurgh had died instantly. Taneeo had been knocked unconscious. Already weakened by months of privation while Hanassa's slave, the apprentice priest had taken a long time to recover from the wounds and the drugs. Even now, after more than a month, he failed to gain weight or rebuild muscle.

"We must still ask. Now better than later." Hestiia insisted. Decisively, she grabbed Kim's hand and led him back to the campfire.

A quick look at the assembly showed Konner and the new woman still missing. Taneeo had not made an appearance.

"I took food to his hut," Pryth, the old wisewoman said. "He often eats alone and sleeps early." She dismissed his behavior as normal.

But it was not normal. The Coros lived communally. The evening gathering was important to them. They sang, told stories, and shared their lives as no one on the civilized planets of the Galactic Terran Empire would. Survival on this primitive planet depended upon mutual cooperation and sharing of burdens.

"Perhaps I should examine Taneeo again. See if he needs healing," Kim mused as he and Hestiia trudged over to the circular hut set a little apart from the larger, square cabins of the rest of the village. With a bit more of the Tambootie, perhaps he could leech some residual poisons from Taneeo's body with his magic.

Hestiia politely rattled the strands of beads hanging outside the doorway. Kim counted one hundred heartbeats. Then he gave the beads a more vigorous shake.

No one answered.

"I'm coming in, Taneeo," Kim called as he ducked beneath the low doorway.

Inside, the single room was dark and deserted.

"*St. Bridget!*" Konner cursed. The Tracker woman had merged with *his* shuttle in a way he never could. If the ship wanted a human partner permanently attached, it should be him. Not . . . not this female from an alien culture. A *primitive* alien culture that knew nothing of machines or electronics or space travel or . . . or . . .

Damn.

"Um . . . has this ever happened to you before?" Konner stared at Dalleena's hand. He could not see where her flesh separated from the cerama/metal hull of *Rover*. He ran a blunt fingernail around the edges of the merge. One seamless bond.

Puzzled, he scratched his head.

"I . . . I do not usually have to touch the sheep and children who wander off to find them," she said. A tiny note of apprehension crept into her voice. Not panic. Not hysteria. Neither emotion would help and so she kept them at bay.

An eminently practical woman, to go with the sturdy broad palm, nails cut nearly to the quick, and shortish fingers. A sturdy hand used to hard work.

"This certainly complicates life," Konner grunted as he walked around Dalleena to study the problem from another angle. He also studied her figure. Nice curves were outlined beneath her masculine clothing. She stood quite tall for a woman, as tall as many of the men on this planet. The top of her head reached the bridge of his nose. All of those curves would fit very nicely snugged against him. "Perhaps I should call my brothers."

"No!" Now she sounded closer to panic.

Konner cocked an eyebrow at her.

Immediately, she seemed to realize how her hasty reply had sounded. She squared her shoulders and returned his stare, measure for measure.

"Then what do you propose to do?"

She swallowed deeply and held out her other hand. He clasped it in his own. A tingle shot up his arm.

Who is this stranger, Konner? Mum's voice demanded in the back of his mind. Not Mum. The computer voice he had programmed to sound like Mum. He and his brothers had agreed that at times they needed her voice of authority to calm them when the IMPs were hard on their heels and all seemed lost. At other times they took immense satisfaction in telling the voice to "Shut up" and slapping the mute with enthusiastic vigor. Something they would never do in Mum's presence.

Dalleena's eyes opened wide and she bit her lower lip.

"You heard that?" he asked.

She nodded, eyes still wide.

He knew she was frightened, but she kept it under control. He liked that.

"Don't worry. Mum won't hurt you. At least not as long as you stay on this world," Konner chuckled.

"Your . . . your m–mother? This dragon is your mother?" Her knees knocked together and her face grew pale.

"Nothing quite so simple." Although to describe Mum as a dragon . . . Well, she did pretend to the wisdom of the ages and keep her own counsel. Margaret Kristine O'Hara could be as enigmatic as a dragon. She also defended her offspring with a ferocity reminiscent of a battle between a dragon and a behemoth.

Somehow Konner's fingers became entwined with Dalleena's.

Her other hand began to glow. And so did the hull beneath it.

Konner slapped his own hand atop hers, careful not to touch the cerama/metal scales. New warmth permeated his being from his points of contact with the strange woman.

"I expected the glow to be hot," he muttered. Just flesh. All he felt was soft, warm, feminine flesh beneath his hand.

He suddenly found Dalleena's lips very close to his own. She licked her lips. Their gazes met. The world seemed to stand still.

"Konner!" Loki called from the edge of the meadow. "Konner, we need you. Taneeo is missing."

"St. Bridget, his timing is perfect as usual." Konner broke free of the thrall of Dalleena's luscious mouth.

"Go," Dalleena whispered. She sounded more than a little breathless . . . and perhaps reluctant. "I will free myself. Somehow. They need you more than I do."

With the last statement she stood taller, straighter, and thrust out her chin in stubborn resistance to his charm.

"Fine." Inexplicable anger shot through him. Konner jerked both of his hands away from hers. The moment he was free of her, he regretted the distance between them.

Without thinking he clamped both hands around her right wrist, braced his feet, and pulled on her arm.

"If I can levitate a three-ton boulder, I can separate you from my ship and my life." He shuddered in memory of the disaster that had forced him to use the latent psychic talent in order to rescue Raaskan.

He should concentrate on separating Dalleena's flesh from the hull.

"Not so easy a task," Dalleena chuckled. She remained firmly attached to the shuttle.

Had she referred to the now famous levitation or to freeing her?

"Not easy, but possible." Konner shifted his weight and balance a little. With a firmer grip, he concentrated on the line of skin that met cerama/metal.

A ripping sound alerted him. He caught her as they tumbled away from the shuttle. She landed atop him on the ground. Again her mouth was a bare breath away from his.

"Free of the dragon, but not free from me," she said softly. Her gaze seemed concentrated on his own mouth.

Before he could reply, she brushed his lips with her own. Then she scrambled away from him.

He rose quickly, brushing grass and debris from his trousers and vest.

Now what? Clearly the woman wanted him. He could not deny the evidence that he found her very attractive. "St. Bridget and all the angels, I don't have time for a relationship," he muttered, hoping she would not hear him. "I have to get off this planet and claim my son. I have to find the beacon and keep the IMPs from finding us. I have to finish too many things before I get serious about a woman."

"I will meet you here at dawn. We will hunt your lost bee-kan together," she announced and stalked back toward the village campfire. Not once did she look back over her shoulder.

Konner pounded his fist into the hull of the *Rover*. Pain immediately cooled his ardor . . . but not his frustration.

CHAPTER 9

"I AM WAITING for an answer, Lieutenant." Commander Leonard drummed her fingers against her screen.

"For the life of me, Captain, I can find no record, ever, of this space configuration," First Lieutenant Kohler said, shaking his head. His fingers never stopped moving across his screen.

"Sir," Kat interrupted. Never good to jump into a conversation with senior officers too quickly.

Commander Leonard nodded for Kat to proceed.

"Sir, there is a habitable planet. Fourth from the sun. We are too far away to read signs of life. It looks green. No man-made satellites. One moon. And I'm getting a faint echo of the beacon."

"Communications, you picking up any traffic?" Commander Leonard swung her chair around to face Ensign James Englebert and his array of screens.

"Nothing coming from any of the planets, sir," he replied. "Except that beacon. But *my* instruments cannot pinpoint a location. It seems like it's coming from everywhere and nowhere."

"Any other habitable planets?" Commander Leonard asked.

"Not without artificial habitat," Kat replied.

"I would guess that if people lived on the inhospitable planets, they'd have radio traffic," Englebert said.

"If our quarry did indeed come to this system through that wild jump point, then my guess is they would head for the one place they could breathe. Helm, take us in. Slowly, with due caution."

Kat smiled to herself. She set course for the little green planet. "Now we'll see what kind of audacity and courage the O'Hara brothers truly have. I'm sick of following legends and rumors. Time to bring them to justice."

"We'll find you, Taneeo," Loki said. "One skinny, young priest couldn't run too far away. There aren't that many places you could go."

He jammed a long branch into the green fire at the center of the village. The fat-soaked moss bound to the tip flared immediately. He pulled it free and held it up. The eerie light illuminated a small section of the compound beyond the evening gathering space.

Just on the edge of the light was the doorway to the large square cabin he shared with Konner. Kim and Hestiia had built their own home adjacent to this one.

Primitive. Logs crossed and stacked, chinked with moss and mud. Lots of the moss. For many months the thatched building had been home. A place to call their own. A home Mum had not invaded and stamped with her personality. He liked that. When he returned to civilization, he would insist upon a home of his own, a place where he could take Cyndi. A place where Mum had to knock on the front door to gain entrance.

Suddenly he wanted nothing more than to get away from the people of his village and their demands upon his time, his energy, and his integrity.

But first he had to find Taneeo. He was eldest. It was his responsibility. "It's not like Taneeo to be gone for more than an hour or so," he said.

"He's not well," Hestiia added. "Where would he go?"

Kim raised his own torch and illuminated another sector of the village.

"*St. Bridget,* I hope Taneeo hasn't been kidnapped by the ghost we encountered in the caves," Loki muttered. Surreptitiously, he made the sign of the cross. He found no comfort in his mother's ward against evil. What he truly wanted to do was cross his wrists and flap his hands in the gesture used by the locals to ward off the winged demon Simurgh.

"We could rescue him from kidnappers. Let's just hope he doesn't run into that big red bull who hangs out in the far meadow beyond the wetlands." Konner added his own torch to the pool of light.

"The priest is that way." The new woman, the Tracker, pointed in the direction of the wetlands and the bull. She started walking. Each stride was strong and confident, like a man's. She did not look back, as if she expected them to follow her without question.

"How can she be sure?" Loki asked. The hair on his spine bristled. Who was this woman to come into the village alone and start giving orders.

"She knows what she knows," Konner said. He followed the woman with the same long, determined stride.

"Konner?" Loki scrambled to follow, more worried about his middle brother than the little bit of dignity he forfeited with his hasty, ungraceful steps. "Konner never follows anyone. Not even me—or Mum."

"Looks like he found Mum's equal," Kim said with a chuckle. He and Hestiia paced alongside Loki, Hestiia taking two steps to every one of Kim's.

"I like Dalleena," Hestiia commented, a little breathlessly. "She will be a good addition to the village. To all of the Coros."

"Hmf," Loki grunted.

He caught up with Konner just as they all came alongside the woman. She kept her right arm outstretched, palm facing forward. Kim and Hestiia stayed a few steps behind, holding hands.

St. Bridget! They'd been married two months and they still held hands, and smooched at any excuse. Sooner or later Kim would come to his senses and realize he had to leave the girl. Better sooner than later. If they did not find the beacon soon, they'd have to leave. Crystals or no crystals.

Loki did not want to be around to deal with the copious tears that would fall upon the departure of the Stargods.

Dalleena stopped short at the stone wall that divided the wheat field from the wetlands. The wheat had been reduced to stubble over the last week. She stepped forward, barked her shins upon the piled rocks, then backed off one pace. Then she repeated the process, seemingly blind to the obstacle.

"Doesn't she see the damn wall?" Loki growled.

"Apparently not. I guess that she has fallen into a tracking trance," Konner mused.

"Trance?" Loki asked. "Like when Kim does his healing magic?"

"Or like you when you eavesdrop, or like I do when I 'commune' with the ship's crystals." Konner sounded so calm, so trusting of this strange woman.

"This way," Konner said gently, taking Dalleena's arm. He led her to a crude stile over the wall. She followed docilely. But her right arm shifted to maintain her bead on whatever she sought.

Loki hung back. He did not want to leave the perceived safety of the cultivated fields. Primitive as they were, these fields represented civilization. Beyond was wilderness, the unknown. Disaster.

He knew it. He knew it as clearly as he knew his own name, and Cyndi's name, and how anxious he was to return to her and claim her hand in marriage.

Once clear of the retaining wall, Dalleena moved her arm back and forth, scanning, as if her hand were a sensor. Then she started off, faster than before. Her pace increased until she ran. She stumbled often, heedless of the rough ground and soggy patches. Konner was always there, steadying her, guiding her to an easier path.

Kim and Hestiia hastened after them.

Loki had no choice but to do the same. They had to find Taneeo. Had to protect their friend.

One thing Loki had learned over the past few months was that the Star-gods did not let their people down. He'd be glad to get rid of that responsibility when he returned to civilization.

They circled the wettest of the wetlands. Not as soggy or dangerous now as when the brothers first landed on this remote little planet.

Konner's torch burned low. Loki's and Kim's didn't fare much better. The moss had its limits after all.

Dalleena kept moving. Could the woman see in the dark? Off to their left a series of barely perceived lumps shifted. One snorted and stood. The shaggy red bull warned them away from his harem.

Their path took them past the cattle and back around toward the cultivation.

"We could have gone straight through the barley to get here faster and safer," Loki complained.

"She follows the path that Taneeo took," Hestiia explained.

"Does she detect his scent?" Loki asked, intrigued despite his reservations.

Hestiia shrugged, as much as she could while keeping up the pace.

And then they were back in the middle of the barley. Loki dug in his heels. He nearly catapulted onto his face. The lump in the center of the field loomed menacingly. But this was no cow. This was a rock. A rock that might be sentient. *The* rock that Konner had lifted with his mind to free Raaskan and save his life.

Taneeo sat at the base of the rock. He rested his back and head against the solid granite. His face was streaked with dirt, his trousers and vest ripped. His leg stuck out in front of him, twisted at an odd angle.

"We didn't kill him. We can't kill him," Taneeo whispered.

"Kill who?" Kim knelt before the village priest. He ran his hands over him assessing his injuries.

"Hanassa. Only the dragons can kill Hanassa."

The blood drained from Loki's face. The ghost of their greatest enemy was real.

Kim concentrated hard. His hands burned every time he came close to an injury on Taneeo's battered body. Two cracked ribs that would heal with time and tight bandaging. One eye swollen shut. The Bruise Leech® would take care of that. But that leg.

"We've set broken bones before, Kim," Konner reassured him with a firm clasp on his shoulder.

"Yeah. But I need the portable ultrasound unit. And some splints, and a stretcher and a bunch of stout men to carry him on the stretcher back home." A quick look around told him that Loki, as usual, was edging away from them—useless in a crisis. The oldest brother tended to charge into situations and then leave Kim and Konner to clean up the aftermath.

"Loki, he needs the US unit and the Leech. Can you get it for us?"

Loki bristled and clenched his fists.

"That is, unless you'd rather set some bones and . . ."

"Never mind. I'll get what you need," Loki grumbled. He turned sharply and set off across the acres of barley at a brisk trot.

"I'll go, too," Hestiia said quietly. "Pryth and Raaskan can help."

Kim's heart swelled. He knew she'd do her best to calm and soothe Loki. She was good at that. But would even Hestiia be able to ease Loki's mind tonight?

Firing the lethal needle rifle at Hanassa had cost Loki a great deal of emotional stability. Taking a life . . .

Kim shook his head to clear it of his own memories of the one time he had caused another man to die. Years later he still had nightmares about it.

Now to find out that perhaps Hanassa had not died must upset Loki's equilibrium.

Dalleena produced a skin of clean water. Kim accepted it gratefully. He took a long drink, offered some to Taneeo, and used the remainder to cleanse the priest's face.

"I tried to keep him out," Taneeo whispered. Suddenly he grabbed the fronts of Kim's vest with a strength that belied his injuries. "I fought him as hard as I could, Stargod Kim. I promise you I tried. But he is strong. Much stronger than I thought."

Taneeo swallowed with difficulty. Kim brought the guttering torch closer. What he had thought were streaks of dirt on the young man's face and throat turned out to be bruises. In the shape of fingerprints.

Kim's vision fractured and he suddenly saw ghostly hands clasping his friend's throat. He shook himself free of the frightening sight. He needed some Tambootie to make the vision clearer.

"Drink, Taneeo." Kim offered the skin of water once more.

"He punishes me. Even now he punishes me," Taneeo whispered. He clawed at his throat. Somehow his hands precisely fit the bruises.

Again Kim had to separate himself from the sight of a second hand atop Taneeo's guiding it, clenching it.

"Who? Who punishes you?" Kim pressed. He felt cold with the certainty he knew what was coming. If only he had some Tambootie, he could sort this out.

"Hanassa."

"We killed Hanassa. The flywackets dumped his body into the lava pit. No one, not even a dragon could survive the heart of the volcano," Kim insisted.

"Dragons are not limited to the life of the body," Taneeo squeaked.

"Dragons can't shapechange into humans," Konner insisted. "They can shrink to the shape of a flywacket, a flying house cat. If they choose human form, they have to—borrow a body. I wonder if they can later move from one body into another." He hunkered down beside Kim. The little lines around his eyes deepened and his shoulders arched toward his ears, sure signs of inner stress he did not allow to reach his voice.

"I have an awful feeling they can." Kim swallowed deeply, then turned back to Taneeo with resolution. "Whose body did Hanassa take?"

He had a sudden sinking feeling in his gut. How long could the ghost of Hanassa linger in the caverns before it forced its way into a human body? Which human?

Taneeo's eyes opened wide, staring into the distance. He gurgled and choked. "I fought him. I continue to fight. He will not have me!" Then his eyes rolled up and he slumped into unconsciousness.

A second aura appeared around his head, separated, and drifted free.

CHAPTER 10

◆——·——◆——·——◆

DALLEENA STUDIED the white dragon. The rising sun cast interesting shadows upon the gleaming scales. Was that a slight indentation in the shape of a palm and fingers? She wanted to trace the outline with her finger, test the perceptions of her eyes with touch.

Resolutely, she crossed her arms under her breasts and buried her hands in her armpits. No sense tempting fate and permanently bonding with the dragon that was not truly a dragon.

An inner voice told her to leave. Leave the village. Leave the influence of the Stargods. Leave the all-too-handsome Stargod Konner. She had to forget his gentle touch, the way their bodies seemed to fit together when she landed atop him. No good would come from continuing.

But she had promised to track a lost one.

That nagging inner voice insisted that she had found the lost priest Taneeo. Did that fulfill her promise to Stargod Konner?

No, it did not. She still needed to find the bee-kan for Konner. Only she could do that. Her word of honor as a Tracker was at stake. She had to find the bee-kan. Then she would leave. As fast as she could. She would go as far away as she could and never, ever see Konner again.

No good could come from a relationship with a god. Even a temporary relationship. Hanassa, the priest of the god Simurgh, had spread his seed far and wide. No good had come to any of the women he seduced or raped. Unfortunately, or fortunately, most of the children of these liaisons had died young.

Dalleena had decided years ago that she would stay away from gods and their priests.

Resolved, she turned away from her scrutiny of her handprint on the white scales to watch the sunrise.

Konner stood right in front of her.

S'murghit, she had been so absorbed in thought she had not heard him approach. Unforgivable in a Tracker.

He stepped closer. Barely the width of her hand separated them. He bent his head just a little, bringing his mouth level with hers.

She moistened her lips.

"Are you planning on usurping control over my *Rover* again?" he snarled.

Dalleena reared away from contemplation of his delicious mouth. Her head banged against the solid surface of the dragon.

"Never. The thing is alien and dangerous. I do not know why you put up with the beast," she returned. Her head hurt. Her scalp tingled. And she'd caught another whisper of the strange feminine voice he'd called "Mum." What had it said?

Nothing complimentary, she was certain. Mothers never liked other women entering their sons' lives. Her own grandmother had complained constantly about Dalleena's mother for as long as she could remember. Right up until they both died in a slave raid led by Hanassa.

"Is the beacon still to the east?" Konner asked. He stepped aside and tapped the white scales in an interesting pattern right beside her handprint. Only after he dropped his hand did she notice a series of bumps and indentations.

The dragon hissed in response to the tattoo he'd beat on its side.

Dalleena jumped back.

The belly opened, like the pupil of a cornered animal's eye.

But no eye peered out at her from that opening. Just . . . just the inside of a cabin. A richly furnished cabin with soft cushions dyed a blue too vibrant to have come from any plant or mineral she knew, and strange storage chests made of a metal shinier than the new iron, and . . . all manner of things she could not identify.

Her head reeled trying to make sense of it all.

"Well, are you coming with me to find the beacon?" Konner asked. He marched up the two steps to stand in the doorway.

His angry tone shook Dalleena out of her befuddlement.

"The beacon is due east. At the other side of the sea beyond the Great Bay." She dug in her heels and braced herself, lest he force her into the dragon's belly.

"I need more information than that, Dalleena." He stood with hands on hips and a tense posture. "I have never explored the continent across the sea. You have to come with me."

"Not inside that dragon. I will not be its next meal."

"*Rover* doesn't eat people." Konner's entire countenance brightened. His eyes twinkled with mischief and his shoulders relaxed. The laughter in his voice sounded so inviting.

"Come along now. We can't waste any more time." Konner held out his hand.

She could not help putting her own hand in his and letting him draw her up the two steps. Her hand lingered in his as she surveyed the inside of the dragon's belly. Most of what she saw still did not make sense. But she noticed that the too-blue cushions showed fading and wear patterns. The square edges looked frayed. Indentations marked the places where male bottoms had sat too often and too long.

A morsel of pride crept into her posture. She would never allow such wonderful possessions to be treated so carelessly.

"This way." He tugged on her hand, leading her to the right and the head of the dragon.

Dalleena promised herself she would explore the well-used cabin later. More curiosities awaited. Whatever magic this dragon possessed, it seemed designed to help Konner and his brothers, not devour them.

The Stargod held aside a shiny curtain. It had the same reflective surface as the storage chests. She had presumed it was just another wall. Curious. She fingered it, finding it slick, as if Konner had spread grease upon thin wood shavings. But her fingers came away clean.

What other marvels could Konner show her?

Eyes wide, absorbing as many details as she could, she entered what could only be a sacred temple. Soft flames from hidden candles glowed and blinked at her. Colored flames! Red and blue and yellow as well as the normal green. But not a normal green. Deeper and more intense than a saber fern just washed with spring dew.

Dalleena resisted the need to drop to her knees in adoration of whatever god Konner had dedicated this temple to.

But why would he worship another god? He was one of the three Stargods. He deserved adoration. He did not need to give it.

"Sit," he ordered her, pointing to a seat formed of metal and covered with the same worn blue cushions as the cabin.

Dalleena plunked herself down on the floor of the temple. She wrapped her arms around her knees and remained motionless. She just could not bring herself to sit where a Stargod had been enthroned within his own temple.

Stargod Konner frowned at her. "Don't be stubborn and ridiculous. I said sit and I mean there." He glared. His intensely blue eyes—the same color as the cushions before they had faded?—glinted with emotions Dalleena could not read.

She swallowed protestations of unworthiness. Somehow she sensed he would not respect groveling.

Hesitantly, she rolled upward without touching anything. Two short sidesteps took her to the throne. It swung beneath her, rotating in a full circle. She popped back onto her feet. "Is it alive?"

Konner chuckled briefly. Then he fiddled with something at the base of the chair. "Try it again. The chair won't bite." He gestured grandly for her to obey.

Dalleena bit her lip and lowered herself into the chair. She kept her weight balanced on her toes, ready to flee if anything moved.

The chair accepted her weight. Indeed, it welcomed her, snuggling to fit her frame.

"Now buckle up. I don't want you flying about the cockpit." Konner pulled long thongs about as wide as his palm over her shoulders and then fastened them to the chair between her legs. Then he sat and produced two more of the broad, flat thongs from the back of his own chair and "buckled up" himself.

He turned his attention to the altar of colored flames. As he touched first one and then another, the sounds within the dragon changed. It rumbled. It vibrated. The sunlight coming in through its eyes dimmed. If the thongs had not held her in place, she would have bolted. She could not. So she gripped the edges of her chair with her hands. Her knuckles turned white. Her fingers grew numb. And still she clung to the chair.

Then a tremendous weight pressed against her chest. She could not breathe. The meadow outside the dragon's eyes rushed past, faster than any person could run. Faster than a bird could fly. Faster than . . . than she could pray to whatever god might listen, even the hated and feared Simurgh.

"Easy, Dalleena. The worst will be over in a minute."

But it wasn't. On and on they sped. Faster and faster. The pressure increased. The landscape flitting past and . . . gulp . . . below them made her dizzy.

Desperate to maintain some sort of equilibrium she fastened her gaze on Konner. He remained solid, in place, and seemingly untouched by the terrible forces assailing them.

And then, with a jolting suddenness, they broke free of the pressure. And floated above the land.

"Is that the river?" Amazement overcame her fears. Birds flew. Dragons flew. Why not this bizarre dragon that was not a dragon. She had to trust that the beast would not spit her out to fall back to the land. She had to trust Stargod Konner to keep her safe.

"Yes, that is the river that gives the Coros life. And up ahead, that broad expanse of blue, that is the Great Bay." Konner pointed with his left hand, keeping his right on the array of winking lights.

"Will we see a behemoth?" She had only heard tales of the monster fish that had been known to take bites out of frail fishing boats, but when captured, could feed a large village for a week. And its thick hide could be tanned like leather to make warm winter clothing for most of a village as well.

"I doubt we'll see one, unless it comes to the surface." Konner frowned. His eyes clouded. "Can you point toward the beacon?"

Dalleena stretched out her hand, palm forward. She concentrated for a long moment on the small thing made of the same material as the hide of the white dragon. At first nothing. Then the tingling began in the center of her palm. Faint at first, then stronger.

"That way." She pointed straight across the endless blue of the bay that continued on into the distance until it met the sky. She shook her head with the enormity of their search. No one she had ever heard of had sailed beyond the reaches of the Great Bay.

Konner made a few adjustments to the lights beneath the flat surface in front of him. The nose of their dragon shifted slightly until it aimed precisely where her finger pointed.

"Will we fly to the edge and fall off?"

"No." Konner flashed her a grin. "The world is like a ball. There is no edge. A special energy called gravity keeps us anchored to the land so we do not fall off."

"But we are not on the land. We fly above it."

"I could fly up above the gravity." He pointed up through the top of the dragon. "I have a bigger ship up there that travels the stars. *Rover* isn't big enough or powerful enough to go beyond this planet."

"Oh." She did not know if she understood all that. The knowledge that Stargod Konner and his brothers could leave this place so easily only confirmed her hesitation to accept friendship or anything else from them. She must fulfill her duty. Nothing more.

She looked through the dragon eyes below them. The land gave way to the bay. She could see the muddy bottom beneath the surf. Must be high tide. Then she discerned the deeper channels through the mudflats. A miniature boat floated on the water, following one of those channels. Was that one of the waterdogs in the bow? The waterdogs had talents akin to Trackers. They directed the fishermen through deep water so that they did not run aground on the mud.

"They look so small. And growing smaller."

"Distance. A tree at the edge of the meadow looks no bigger than your hand. As you walk closer, it gets bigger and bigger. We are very far away."

"How far?"

"Higher than ten of the tallest trees you have ever seen."

She gulped. But her curiosity overcame her misgivings. A wispy cloud passed beneath them. More clouds appeared on the left, near the horizon. Dark clouds. "It will rain tomorrow."

"Probably," he grunted. "I hope Kim gets the last of the harvest in today."

They traveled on in silence for a long time. Dalleena had dozens of questions. He answered them politely. But she sensed he never gave her all of the information she needed to fully understand.

After a time she held up her arm again and scanned for the beacon. They came closer. But it was still very far away. She directed him to aim a little to the south. He did so.

Another space of time passed. They still traversed the ocean. She scanned again. Instead of the tingle in her palm, her entire body began to shake. Her muscles jerked. Forward and back, side to side. She swayed as far as the thongs allowed her.

"What?" Konner asked. He released his own restraints and jumped to hold her in place. "Dalleena! What's wrong."

Her teeth chattered. She clamped her mouth shut, lest she bite her tongue. Her throat swelled with the need to speak. To warn Konner of the strange apparition that pulled at her senses, demanding she find it.

"Up there," she finally managed. "In the sky. Beyond the sun. Something is lost. Something bigger than a behemoth. Much bigger than this dragon."

Then she forced her arm down and gripped the edges of the chair.

Konner looked up to the sky, then back to the flashing lights. Many more lights than before.

And then the strange voice of his mother spoke. "Warning. Open jump point detected. Unfriendly vessel approaches."

"You spotted the IMPs before my sensors did!"

CHAPTER 11

◆ — · — ◆ — · — ◆

KONNER TOUCHED TWO interfaces and set the shuttle on autopilot. Then he returned his attention to Dalleena.

"How did you do that?" He ran his fingers over her damp brow and along the stress creases above her nose. Worry made him clench his jaw. He had to show a calm face. He had to keep her from going into hysterics.

"I do not know." She stared at her palm. The skin looked red, not quite raw, but definitely painful. "It burns," she whispered.

He should have known Dalleena would not panic.

"I have some salve for that." Konner released the first aid kit from its place beneath the console. His hands felt empty and cold when he released her, but the kit was awkward to haul into position with only one free.

A quick swipe of Electro-Steri® killed off any stray bacteria. St. Bridget only knew how much bizarre bacteria lurked on the planet. Then a squirt of cooling gel sealed the burn.

"What miracle is this?" She held up the hand. Already the redness faded as the medicines leeched the heat out of her skin before it could blister.

"Just keep your hand up, above your heart, for a few seconds until the gel dries." He held her hand in position. The softness of her skin despite the calluses sent micro amps of electricity up his arm and into his heart.

He jerked his gaze away from contact with her big brown eyes before he lost himself entirely.

"Is this strange ship in the skies friend or foe?" Dalleena asked. Ever practical. Ever logical. She returned to the cause of her hurt rather than dwelling on the injury itself.

Melinda, Konner's ex, had taken to her bed for three days when a splinter lodged in her finger on their honeymoon.

"Most likely a foe." Konner let go of his memories of Melinda gratefully. As soon as he retrieved his son from her ungentle custody, he need never think of her again.

He could concentrate on Dalleena.

No. His place was not on this benighted planet. He belonged to the stars. He would not enter into a relationship knowing he had to leave very soon.

"What must we do to evade this enemy? Or defeat it?" Dalleena asked.

"Our first step is to find that beacon and destroy it." Konner returned to his seat and put the shuttle back on manual control. Without hesitation, he boosted the speed. "The heck with fuel conservation." He pushed the speed up another notch. "If we don't kill the beacon fast, we won't need the shuttle. We'll need holes in the ground to hide in."

"I know of a number of caves on the headlands at the south end of the bay. Children often get lost exploring them. 'Tis up to me to find them when they go too deep," Dalleena offered.

"I'll keep that in mind."

The coastline came into view. Konner called up the maps from Kim's initial survey of the planet. The central continent dominated the scans. It spread across nearly an entire hemisphere north and east of here. Only a few large islands and semicontinents, like the land of the Coros, dotted the ocean that covered the rest of the planet.

Konner and his brothers had dismissed the continent because the clusters of human habitation hugged the coasts with little or nothing in between. The climate of the interior appeared barely hospitable to human life.

He shed altitude. Somehow the initial survey had not picked up on the lively boat traffic that now came into view.

"Now where?" Konner asked. He might be close enough to pick up the beacon on one of his scanners. But he had to stay high enough not to disturb any locals.

"North. At the head of that bay." Dalleena pointed and he changed course.

The scanners spit images and a data stream into the interface. Then the beacon blipped. An obscure frequency well below normal scan ranges. If the IMPs did not know where to look, they would never find it. Another strike against Melinda. She had to have sold the frequency to his enemies.

Konner suppressed the boiling in his blood. Giving in to his anger with Melinda would not help him this minute. He needed to save his emotions and be in control for the court date.

And use his copy of the prenuptial agreement she had not honored.

He locked in the frequency and pinpointed it on the map the computer formed, layer by layer as he circled the port.

"Just wonderful." He nearly slammed his fist into the console. "An entire city full of people." Several thousand crammed into a tiny space. Any one of them could have the beacon.

Frantically, he sought a landing place beyond the hordes of people, but close enough to walk into the city.

For some reason, the city seemed to be confined within a stout wall. It formed a large half circle around the harbor. Warrens of alleyways filled the enclosure. Buildings piled one atop another, threatening to tumble in a stiff breeze. The scanners picked up a large concentration of pollution in the water of the harbor. Mostly human and animal waste.

Konner wrinkled his nose at the thought of the stench of the city. Most civilized worlds were as crowded as this place. But air scrubbers built into the protective atmosphere domes replaced unpleasant odors with a citrus scent. Sewage disposal remained unseen and unsmelled, returning sanitized minerals and liquids to the environment and food tanks.

"Why do they not move beyond the wall?" Dalleena asked. She shifted her gaze from the growing map to the knot of dark brown below them.

Smart girl to have figured out the relationship between the map and the real view.

"I'm guessing the wall is protection. Marauders, dust storms, large predators. Something mean and dangerous lives in the steppes beyond that wall."

The land stretched out in near endless waves of undulating hills dotted with low shrubs, covered with tall grasses, golden in the autumnal sunshine, and creased by ravines. A few lakes glinted in the distance.

Konner decided to hide *Rover* behind a long hill that rose slightly higher than its fellows a few hundred meters beyond the city wall and away from the small flocks of sheep and goats that dotted the hillsides. Did the shepherds bring all of the livestock within the protection of the wall each night?

He circled around, banked, and cut the engines as he glided to his selected landing. He smiled as he rolled to a silent stop, completely hidden from the city. Loki could not have executed the maneuver any smoother or quieter.

Locking down the shuttle was an easy and familiar procedure. Collecting supplies required some thought.

"Water," Dalleena said. She looked around the cabin.

Konner touched the pressure panel on one of the cupboards. An array of native waterskins, cloaks, knives, and other survival gear tumbled out.

She sighed and rolled her eyes at Konner. Immediately she began to sort, stack, and organize the jumble.

"Water is in here." He stepped into the head and turned on the tap. Dalleena watched every move he made.

She quickly made sense of the sink and tap, filling the skins efficiently, with minimal waste. Then she inspected the shower with minute care. Very quickly she nodded in understanding. But the toilet seemed to mystify her.

"For waste," Konner informed her succinctly. A quick flush and the light of understanding dawned on her expressive face.

He felt inordinate pride in teaching her this simple thing. This one part of civilization that seemed so elemental.

"Hats," Dalleena said as she emerged from her inspection of the marvels of modern plumbing.

"Hats?" Konner looked up from his array of portable sensors and other gadgets. Almost as an afterthought he thrust six small diamonds into his pocket. The jewels were accepted as currency throughout the GTE when cash and credit limits did not cross borders into the Galactic Free Market—or black market.

"Hats?" he asked again as Dalleena peered into the corners of the supply closet.

"Desert sun. All of the locals will wear them as protection."

He nodded compliance. He added brimmed straw hats to the collection of gear.

And then there was no more reason to stall and every reason to find that bloody beacon and destroy it. He estimated they had approximately seven hours before the IMP vessel descended upon the planet.

After that, the history of the place, the very nature of society here would change irrevocably. For members of the Galactic Terran Empire could not leave a planet pristine. They always had to "improve." Improve, as in industrialize, exploit, overpopulate, pollute.

Destroy.

"Come on, we're running out of time." Konner flung the loosely woven cape of ubiquitous red cow's wool over his shoulders and began marching up the hill. He barely remembered to touch the remote to cloak the shuttle behind its light-bending force field.

Dalleena trotted behind him, uncomplaining, matching him long stride for long stride.

They crested the hill quickly. Looking downslope, the city lay before them, crammed into barely ten square kilometers. Every building was made of the same reddish mud bricks. At one time, the place had begun on a square grid with a well at every major intersection. But those spacious blocks had been divided and subdivided time and again. Alleys ran between buildings at odd angles. People crowded around the wells, now too few to accommodate them all. Dust covered everything, giving it a uniform reddish-brown pallor. No trees. No flowers. Nothing living except too many people and a few stray pigs and goats.

"Now where?" Konner asked.

"There." Dalleena held up her hand, palm out. She indicated an area near the port, north of center where a larger than usual congregation of people shoved and pushed their way through the narrow streets.

Konner took a bead on her direction with his portable scanner. Dead on. He could not have pinpointed the beacon any closer with electronics.

He hurried down the hill and through the open gate in the wall. Five gates. All open. No visible guards. Whatever the wall protected the locals from, must not come out during daylight, or this phase of the moon, or until it rained. Just not right now.

Unchallenged, they made their way into the heart of the city. Roughly clad people with swarthy complexions and blond hair bumped against them, shoving to get past, too eager to go about their own business to pay attention to two strangers.

But then maybe strangers were not all that unusual here. This was a port, after all.

The pervasive odors of rotting fish, salt water, and seaweed lay atop the more subtle scents of humanity pressed into too tight quarters, dust, and a hint of exotic spices.

"Where did all these people come from?" Dalleena asked in hushed tones. She clung to a bit of his cloak, as if she feared becoming separated from him. "Did they sail here from Coronnan?"

"Possibly. A long time ago." Konner did not want to give her a history lesson about the original human colonists who had fallen into civil war and genocide with a bioengineered plague. That plague still cropped up occasionally. He just hoped he'd managed to neutralize it last spring.

The babble of voices refused to settle into a recognizable pattern. The Coros spoke a dialect of Standard GTE, slowed to a creeping drawl and mutated over the last three hundred years. The denizens of this city spoke a rapid dialect that was similar. He almost caught a word here and there. And yet . . .

"Possibly they have been here as long as the Coros have held their lands. My brother Kim will be very interested to study the history of these people." Perhaps the original colonists split, some coming here, others staying in Coronnan, before the devastating winter and crop failure drove Dalleena's ancestors to fight among themselves for generations until they fell back to bronze age technology and a tribal culture.

Perhaps there were many remnant cultures throughout this world. His feet itched to explore more. But he had to get the beacon. Now. Before the IMPs had a chance to pinpoint its location.

But once the IMPs landed, and they certainly would, now that they were in system, how could Konner and his brothers prevent them from informing the authorities back home about this pristine little planet ready for exploitation?

"The bee-kan is in there," Dalleena said. She nodded discreetly toward a jumble of people and makeshift structures.

Voices rose higher and higher as people shouted at each other, waving their arms in wild gesticulations. Konner was about to jump in and separate two men seemingly bent upon throttling each other. Then a few coins changed hands and one of the men scooped up the pile of goods between them.

"It's a *souk!*" Konner smiled with understanding.

"A 'sug?'" Dalleena asked, never taking her eyes off the arguments and exchanges.

"A market."

"Ah! We have these two times each year, at end of planting and end of harvest."

"That is a market fair. This bazaar is open every day. All year." They stepped beyond an invisible line that separated the normal crush of people going about their business from the frantic crush of people dealing with their business.

"Those metal disks they exchange. Are they markers against goods and services?"

"In a way. We call them coins where I come from. They are made of valuable metals."

"But what good are they?"

How to explain the concept of money to a woman who had only known the concrete evidence of barter?

Before he could think of a coherent sentence, she darted ahead of him. He had to hurry to keep track of her in the shouting and milling crowd. They wended their way around rickety stalls, fragrant cooking pits with roasting beasts, and cauldrons of aromatic stews. Everywhere people pushed and shoved and raised their voices, doing their best to separate Konner from the Tracker.

Then he caught a brief glimpse of her cloak. Good thing she stood nearly as tall as he, half a head taller than most of the shoppers and merchants. He elbowed aside an insistent purveyor of a frothy beverage that smelled strongly alcoholic, and stepped over a tumble of fabric rolls to keep her in view. Halfway around a cart piled with leather goods he saw where she had stopped.

Crystals and rough-cut gemstones dangled from the crossbeams of the stall. Agates and polished metal pendants were strewn about the counter. A beady-eyed merchant kept one hand on a dull green object the size of his palm while fixing his gaze upon Dalleena's face.

Konner's sensor went berserk, flashing lights and beeping in chords of tones.

A second dull green object nestled into a pile of gems in the back of the stall. Two of them? Where had the second beacon come from?

"How much?" Konner asked the merchant. His jaw trembled and his hands wanted to shake. He put Dalleena behind him, away from the lustful eyes of the thin man wearing a robe of garish-colored stripes and a matching turban. Unlike most of the people he had encountered in the *souk*, this man had pale eyes and sun-burned pale skin. He looked very much out of place in this land of dark-eyed and swarthy-skinned natives. Even his blond hair was too fair, almost artificial.

"The girl. I trade you the artifact for the girl." He grinned, revealing too-white, too-perfect teeth.

CHAPTER 12

LOKI THRUST ASIDE the leather curtain from the doorway of Taneeo's hut. He did not bother rattling the strands of wooden and clay beads hanging outside, nor did he ask permission to enter.

"Taneeo?" Loki called as he ducked beneath the low lintel of the circular reed hut. For some reason these people seemed to think that priests needed a dwelling without corners. Or amenities, by the look of the spartan interior. A reed mat on the floor. A single blanket of cowhide. A fired clay beaker of water on the dirt floor, and nothing else.

Nothing.

Not so much as a window to let in the glorious sunshine and fresh air.

The place smelled of sweat and vomit and sickness.

Loki did not believe Kim's tale of Taneeo possessing a second aura that separated from his body. Not one little bit. The boy had hit the Tambootie a little too hard in his magical experiments.

Taneeo hated Hanassa. He'd never allow his old master's spirit to possess his body. *Never!*

Loki refused to believe Taneeo capable of harboring the enemy in any form. If he did, then that would mean . . . that would mean that Taneeo had beaten himself in order to get rid of the offending spirit.

Impossible. No one could inflict that degree of injury to themselves.

Loki squinted and blinked, trying to force his eyes to adjust to the dimness. His mind knew Taneeo was here. He could "feel" the man's fearful shrinking against the wall.

Where else could the young man be but here where Kim had left him last night. He could not walk. Not with a broken leg and various other injuries.

"Taneeo," Loki said again, more gently.

A startled gasp came from the farthest curve of the hut.

"Didn't mean to scare you, Taneeo." Heat flushed Loki's ears. He squatted down, closer to eye level with the man.

Taneeo struggled to sit, dragging his splinted leg. He nearly collapsed twice as his arms and shoulders weakened with the effort. The pain in his cracked ribs must be excruciating.

Loki rubbed his side in memory of a vicious brawl on a bush planet notable only for its horse-piss beer and ugly women. He'd fought with a man twice his size, over the "honor" of a barmaid who did not want either man's attentions. Loki was lucky to walk away with only a cracked rib and a few bruises. The pain had taken his breath away and made his knees wobble until Konner got him to an ER. The medicos had bombarded his body with micro amps of electricity and ultrasound tuned to healing frequencies. Loki had whistled as he left the hospital mere hours after entering.

Taneeo did not have the luxury of modern medicine. Only Kim's limited magical talent that sped healing but did not cure. The portable ultrasound unit in *Sirius'* medi kit did not have enough power or life in its batteries to do more than indicate if Kim had set the bones properly.

Loki moved to help Taneeo to a sitting position.

The priest's instinctive jerk away from him kept him in place. "What do you want?" Taneeo's voice cracked with dryness. "To accuse me of treachery, as your brother did?" He glared at Loki with resentment.

Loki pushed the water beaker closer to him. The priest lifted it and drank long and deep. When he put the vessel down, he looked at a point above Loki's head and to the left.

"What do you want?" His voice was stronger, and clearer. "I am clean of the tainted spirit. I have fought him off and suffered the consequences."

"I need to know what happened to you," Loki said, careful to keep his voice even. "Who beat you?"

"I do not remember."

"You have to know something. Our enemy fought with you, broke your leg, cracked two of your ribs, and left you with a black eye that might permanently impair your vision. How could you forget that experience."

"I . . . I fainted. He came from behind."

A growl tried to climb from Loki's gut to his throat. He swallowed heavily to suppress it. "Did you see the man who attacked you?"

"Dark. Too dark." Taneeo turned his head away. He started to slip back down to his previous reclining position.

"Was the man dark?" Loki seized upon the adjective. "Dark hair, dark eyes, swarthy skin, like a Rover?"

Rovers, the local version of Terran Gypsies, used the blown-out volcano and the cave system as a way station in their endless wandering. They would have been the first humans to enter the scene of Loki's last battle with Hanassa. The spirit of Hanassa might have taken over one of their bodies.

Hanassa would then use that body to move closer to his enemies. What better way to strike at the heart of the Stargods and their followers than to possess the body of their priest and friend?

Loki liked that explanation. It put a lot of his fears to rest and gave him a concrete enemy to hunt down and neutralize.

You mean murder, a little voice in the back of his head sneered at him. It sounded a lot like Mum.

No. He'd never take a life again. Even a miserable sadist like Hanassa had a sacred life force Loki must respect. His sanity would not withstand another episode like . . . like that time in the caves two months ago.

"Rover?" Taneeo's eyes brightened and cleared a little. He rested a little easier on his mat. "Yes! Yes, I do believe 'twas a Rover who attacked me. A very tall Rover. Nearly as tall as you and your brothers, Stargod Loki. But dark in every way. Dark of complexion and of spirit. His clothing . . . black tunic and trews. Black shirt. How do you suppose the Rovers mix a black dye for cloth and leather that does not fade?"

"They probably use the squid ink."

Just last week Kim had found a multilimbed blob of flesh on the beach that had produced a body fluid he could use for indelible ink in his endless scratchings and recordings of events and thoughts and who knew what else. He'd named the creature a squid after some long extinct denizen of Earth's oceans before pollution killed them all.

Loki frowned. He did not like the idea of Kim leaving behind so much information that could be deciphered by the locals. All three of the brothers had agreed that in order to keep this planet agrarian, prevent them from developing industry that would eventually cause pollution and drive them to quest for the stars, they had to forbid reading and the wheel from their culture. Otherwise, they'd become just another colony of the GTE.

Kim seemed bent upon violating the agreement. Loki made a mental note to gather up *all* of Kim's records and journals and take them with them when they left.

Otherwise, everything that was good and honest about this place would disappear. And so would the supply of fresh food Loki intended to sell on the black market back home. One cargo hold full of fresh vegetables would make his fortune for life. He'd finally have enough money to buy back his citizenship and marry Cyndi.

Loki could not allow this place to be despoiled. He had to stop Hanassa. All he had to do was find him.

"I will bring Pryth to you. She was born a Rover. She may be able to give us more information about your attacker." Loki rose from his crouch. He could not stand upright, even in the center of the conical hut.

"The old woman speaks not the truth. Born of Rovers, bred as Rovers. Truth eludes their kind as mist in sunshine. We . . . I will not speak to the woman!" With great effort, Taneeo turned his face to the wall.

"Pryth used to be your friend, Taneeo. She has helped us all with her wisdom and her knowledge."

"No more. She speaks for the tribe that shelters our enemy. She has *become* our enemy."

"How can you know that?"

"Even now she corrupts your brother. Together, they will bring change that destroys you."

"Kim," Loki whispered. "He's teaching some of you how to read." The truth washed over him like a cold dip in the river. He knew that Taneeo spoke true. He "felt" it in his mind as clearly as if he had read the priest's thoughts.

"Have you found anything interesting, Bruce?" Martin dictated a brief message to his friend.

Within femtos of sending his reply a message appeared in his mailbox.

"Couldn't wait to hear from you, Marty. My dad just accepted a contract with your mom. Usually he tells me where he's going and something about who or what he is supposed to find. This time he left abruptly without telling me anything. He didn't even come home between jobs. I thought maybe you could give me a head's up on what is so important that your mom hired a 'Sam Eyeam,'" Bruce's voice and image came through the computer screen.

"Now that is a good question," Martin muttered.

"This news comes right on top of finding a delete in the marriage records of Meditcue II. That delete has my dad's computer telltales all over it. I'm digging further. Too bad neither of us has a Klip. We could track Dad's activities a lot easier then. But, of course, they are illegal."

Martin gulped. A marriage record deleted by Melinda's private Sam Eyeam. Melinda was up to something. The timing was too coincidental. She didn't want key information to come up at the custody hearing.

If Melinda and Bruce's father had negotiated a sensitive contract, perhaps the man had come to Aurora for a private meeting. Data waves could be intercepted no matter how much security Melinda paid to put on them. Financial transactions tended to be more secure than private correspondence, but even then the data had to cross open space at many times the speed of light. Dedicated hackers could find even those messages.

He accessed his mother's appointment book for the previous month. Many meetings. Many contracts. Nothing resembling Bruce Geralds, Sr.

What about the AM before that?

Martin had to go through three more AMs and nearly a thousand entries to find what he was looking for. A cryptic remark, "Freelance. Midnight. Altered beacon," followed by an estimated expense account that allowed considerable travel was his only clue.

"Travel. He had to enter and leave Aurora space." Martin sent his snoopers over to the port authority. Sure enough, at 0600 hours the next morning, a private, one-man transport left the port. It carried Melinda's personal ID on the logbook.

"But Melinda was home that day. I remember because she introduced the new math tutor to me personally."

"Master Martin, I believe you are supposed to be working on wave differential equations at this moment, not playing with your friends." The image of the hated math tutor appeared in the upper right-hand corner of the screen. A twenty-something man with a sallow complexion and thin hair, who tried to look older by adopting a stern frown and an artificial touch of white at his temples, Adam Wun never approved of anything Martin accomplished.

"I finished the homework an hour ago," Martin replied. He pulled up his calculations and transmitted them to the tutor.

"If you completed all this so easily, either you were careless and made many mistakes, or you need more advanced work. I will have a new assignment for you as soon as I correct these equations."

"I'm due for physical training in ten minutes. You, Mr. Wun, will have to wait."

Fencing was one activity he enjoyed in the structured time Melinda arranged for him. Easy to imagine his opponents in the salle as his mother. He worked hard at aiming each lunge and thrust for her heart.

"Who are you and where did you come from?" Konner spat at the gaudy merchant with teeth so clean and firm they could blind a deer in the moonlight.

"I know not what you mean." The merchant backed up one step, holding his hands at chest level, palms outward. The gesture spoke of innocence.

Then his right hand snaked behind him to capture the second beacon.

He had used the same crisp dialect of Terran Standard that Konner used, not the languid prose of the Coros or the mutated dialect spoken elsewhere in the souk.

Konner raised one eyebrow in question and waited.

"I am but a seller of pretty trinkets," the merchant continued. Speaking too rapidly, as if to convince himself as well as Konner of the truth of his words.

"Then sell me the artifacts for a fair price. Both of them," Dalleena jumped into the conversation. "You paid nothing for them. They serve you no purpose."

"Ah, but they must serve you a purpose," the merchant crowed and smoothed his mustache and beard with one finger. "Else you would not be so anxious to purchase these pretty toys."

"The 'toys' serve only a captain of an IMP vessel," Konner said quietly. "I would make certain this . . . ah . . . sailor never finds them or the man who possesses them."

The merchant's eyes opened wide.

"Take the cursed thing, now. Before it is too late." The merchant pushed the beacon on the counter at Konner. The second one had disappeared into his clothing. Then he jerked his hand away from it as if burned. And soiled.

"Not until you tell me who you are and why you are on *my* planet." Konner folded his arms across his chest. He leaned slightly away from the proffered device, all the while seeking a telltale irregularity in the man's clothing for the second beacon. Where had it come from? More importantly, why did this black market denizen have it?

"I'm just trying to make an Adol." The merchant began folding his trinkets into brightly colored cloths. Still no sign of the second beacon.

"Here? This planet has little of value to the outside world. Few precious metals or raw resources."

Dalleena peered curiously first at Konner, then the merchant, seeking answers to the puzzling words they spoke.

Konner hated to do this to her. But they had to keep the conversation cryptic lest the locals hear and jump to wrong conclusions, and possibly drastic action to rid themselves of things they did not understand.

Konner and his brothers had survived one attack by locals only by cunning and a hasty retreat inside their shuttle. The shuttle was a long way away from this souk.

"If you cannot see the bounty of this place, then leave it to me and take this cursed beacon with you." The merchant strapped all of his wares, except the first beacon, into a crude satchel with straps that tied rather than buckled. He left the beacon on the counter.

"What I see is a man in a place he does not belong. Now who are you?" Konner reached across the plank counter and grabbed the merchant's robes at the throat.

"Sam," the merchant choked out, eyes wide and frightened.

"Sam Who?"

"Sam Eyeam."

Konner snorted at the old joke stolen from a children's text. Freelance agents, black market merchants, and bounty hunters all used the ubiquitous pseudonym. "You'll have to do better than that, Sam. What's your real name?"

"Yours first."

"Fair's fair. Konner."

"Not Konner O'Hara. Please tell me you aren't Konner O'Hara, the smuggler with two brothers." The Sam Eyeam closed his eyes as if in prayer.

"And if I am Konner O'Hara?" Konner did not release the man's robes. Off to the side, Dalleena began looking around hastily, as if she sensed danger coming closer.

Damn.

"If you are Konner O'Hara, then I will run away from this place as fast as I can, by as stealthy a route I can find, and never mention to anyone being here, or seeing you."

"You fear me that much?" Konner eased his grip a little. "Then give me the second beacon as well."

"I know nothing of a second beacon. Only this one given to me by . . . one I did not know. I will return the bribe that came with it."

Dalleena tugged on Konner's arm. "Men with clubs and whips approach. A large number of angry men follow them."

"Ah, the hue and cry has been raised. The locals do not like brawls of any kind in the souk." Sam ducked out of Konner's grasp, grabbed his satchel and . . .

And Konner stepped in front of him before he bolted out of the back of the stall. "Tell me why you fear the name Konner O'Hara so much. And where you came by the beacons."

Sam's gaze darted to the shouts rising from the dock side of the souk.

"Tell me, or I turn you over to them as a thief."

"I don't fear you. I fear the GTE. Anyone important enough to have a reward of 100,000 Adols has to be the most dangerous man in the galaxy."

"Melinda fears me that much?"

"Melinda Fortesque, the owner of Aurora?"

"My ex-wife."

"The father of her son!" Understanding seemed to dawn in his eyes. "Heaven help us all." Sam darted away.

"The second beacon . . ."

Dalleena grabbed Konner's hand and dragged him deep into the market at a breathless pace. She clutched one beacon against her chest.

"Wait! I have to know why he didn't detect my ship when he landed. Why I never saw his."

"Later. I will find him later. He is a Tracker. He will be easy for me to find. My talent will find his."

She was right. They had to take this beacon to the volcano and destroy it before the IMPs landed. Five and one half hours from now. Max.

"Let's go."

CHAPTER 13

✦ —— · —— ✦ —— · —— ✦

THE AIR AT THE HEAD of *Rover* shimmered. Dalleena gulped. She dug in her heels. The caked dirt of the hillside crumbled under her feet. She continued her downward slide toward the dragons—the white one she could see and the red-tipped one that was almost visible in the harsh noon-time glare.

"Now what?" Konner grunted and moved forward at a faster pace. He barely left a footprint in the ground at the speed of his passing.

"The Stargod does not fear the dragons. They are his messengers and allies," she whispered to herself. "If he has no fear, then neither should I." The thought did not reassure her. If the dragon wished, it could blast her with fire and eat her in one gulp.

Last night it had ignored her. Today it might be hungry.

The beast bent its head toward Konner. Steam or smoke rose in small puffs from its nostrils. Dalleena guessed it spoke to Stargod Konner in some mysterious way.

She struggled to remain upright, wrapping the shreds of her courage around her.

If she had nothing else, she had her dignity. If she died in the next moment, she would not quail before the Stargod. She was Tracker and had fulfilled her duty.

"I know," Konner said to the dragon. "Dalleena spotted them before I did."

So they discussed the invaders. Dalleena took her next step with a little more firmness than the last. *She* had served the god better than his dragon messenger did.

Then the beast turned one of its multicolored eyes upon her. Red glinted on the eyelid, echoing the color outlining its horns and wing veins.

Her stomach tied itself into a knot.

The red spiraled inward, drawing her attention, her consciousness, her soul. . . .

"Irythros, release her!" Stargod Konner shouted and slapped the muzzle of the creature.

The sound of his voice seemed to sever a physical tie between Dalleena and the dragon. She shook her head to clear it.

(*Apologies. I do not wish to offend.*) The dragon's eyes dimmed and it ducked its muzzle.

Dalleena shook her head again. "Did I truly hear him speak?" For half a heartbeat she shared a sense of deep shame with the beast. How could that be?

"Probably," Konner replied. He rubbed the knuckles of his left hand with his right palm.

"Apology accepted." She resisted a near compulsion to move closer and touch the place where Konner's fist had connected with its muzzle, just below the right eye. Hard to tell if the skin beneath the crystal fur bruised or not.

"Dalleena is under my protection, Irythros," Konner said. "Keep your hypnotic powers to yourself."

Dalleena tasted the strange new word. Hypnotic. It meant nothing to her.

(*Dragon dreams reveal a true nature,*) the dragon replied in a defensive tone.

"Unnecessary." Konner continued to stare at the huge creature with authority. "If you want to delve into the secrets of a human, go find the merchant who calls himself Sam Eyeam. He carries a second beacon that must be destroyed."

A niggle of pride ran down Dalleena's spine. This handsome man, this *god,* defended her before the most awesome being in her world.

"The news of the intruders is momentous, Irythros. I appreciate you bringing the news yourself. I have need of a favor, if you are willing." Finally Konner stroked the place on the dragon's muzzle that had begun to darken. The dragon leaned into the touch as it would a healer's caress.

(*Name your favor,*) the dragon nearly cooed.

Dalleena had to stifle a grin. This monster behaved as any steed, or dog, or cat, given adoring attention by its master.

"I have to drop this beacon into the volcano to destroy it. I would like to leave the shuttle hidden in the crater. The magnetic forces of the mountain will mask its presence from the intruders. Will you carry Dalleena and me back to the village from there?"

(*We cannot. The transition place of Hanassa is sacred. We may not go there.*)

The mighty wings of the dragon unfurled. He raised and dropped them once. Dust swirled into Dalleena's face. She threw up her arm to protect her eyes. With her other hand she groped for Konner. His hand entwined with hers.

The dust increased. The roar of the wind from pulsing dragon wings drowned out all other sound. All other thought.

Wind buffeted her, forcing her back and back again. She clung to Konner. She bumped against the solid hide of the white dragon *Rover.* And still the wind pressed against her, stole the breath from her, tried to crush her chest.

And then Konner was between her and the wind, sheltering her with his body. She risked looking up at him. His eyes darkened. Barely a breath separated their lips. A strange stillness washed through her, replacing the terrible pressure of the wind.

Then the wind died. The agitated dirt settled on her clothing, in her hair, and on her face.

"He left," she said.

"In a huff," Konner replied, averting his gaze from her mouth. He heaved himself back, away from the shuttle and close proximity to her.

"Now what do we do?"

"We destroy the beacon."

"How? Do we return to the village of the Stargods?"

"I will leave you there before I go to the volcano."

"How will you return?"

"I must walk for many days, or trust my luck to the dragongate."

Dalleena crossed herself, swallowed her fears, and looked him straight in the eye. "So be it. I go with you."

"Captain?" Ensign Englebert sounded hesitant.

Kat stole a moment of attention from the helm to watch the communications officer's face. He looked puzzled.

"Watch it!" Kohler warned her quietly.

Kat jerked her attention back to her own screens and interfaces. She barely veered to port fast enough to avoid scraping *Jupiter* on a mid-sized boulder in a crowded asteroid belt.

At least Ms. Baines had retreated to the comfort of her cabin. Kat didn't have to worry about the woman watching and criticizing every move she made. Nor did she have to smell the cloying perfume.

"This space junk looks tricky," Kohler continued. "Computer can't find a pattern to the movement. We're going to have to wing it."

"Captain, can we get weapons on some of these rocks?" Kat asked.

Commander Leonard gestured to a pair of SBs to handle the chore. In three quick blasts, Kat had a clear path before her.

"Captain?" Englebert said again.

"Yes, Ensign." Commander Leonard did not look up from her screens as she answered.

"Sir, I'm getting an echo from the beacon. It's moving away from the primary."

"What?" Kat and Commander Leonard exclaimed at the same time. Kat dared not swing her chair around. A rock the size of a moonlet loomed before her. It tumbled fast enough to generate a gravity field.

"It's almost as if there are two beacons, sir," Englebert said.

"Impossible. Fortesque Industries swore they only built one at that frequency," Commander Leonard protested.

"I read the memo, sir. You can look for yourself. Something strange is going on down on that planet."

"If I may, Captain," Kat said, never taking her eyes or her hands off her screens. "The second beacon could be why we could not lock onto the signal earlier. We were getting echoes of both off the atmosphere."

"True, Lieutenant. Investigate further, Ensign Englebert. I want to know more about this.

"Uh, Captain . . ."

Leonard shot Englebert an impatient glance.

"Captain, sensors detecting a fireball on the big continent. It's burning hot enough to fry cerama/metal."

Kat gulped. What were the O'Haras up to?

"Status of the beacons, Ensign?" the ship's captain demanded.

"Both still beeping."

"Estimated time to orbit, Lieutenant?"

Kohler answered for Kat. "Five hours, twenty-seven minutes, sir."

"Providing someone doesn't start throwing these rocks directly at us," Kat muttered. Another blast from the pulse cannons sent a big one lurking behind the moonlet spinning out of their path. Chips from it splattered a sensor on the rim directly in front of Kat. She cursed.

A tech scrambled to get her a clear view again.

Kat veered sharply to starboard. Everyone on the bridge reached for safety harnesses. "If only I had a joystick," Kat breathed, "I could jockey around this planetary debris with no problems at all."

"Joysticks are not standard military equipment," Commander Leonard reminded her. "This is a Military Police Cruiser, not a cybernetic fighter."

"I know, Captain. Just wishing out loud."

"Are you sure you can get us through this safely, Lieutenant?" Leonard asked.

"Yes, sir. I'm rated ace on everything in the fleet. Just keep those cannons working on the little stuff and I'll get us around the big ones."

Kat let her eyes lose focus a moment while she listened to the crystal drive. She "felt" nearly every electron pulse shooting from the drivers to the directionals. Three arrays, all working off one king stone. She isolated the forward array in her consciousness. Suddenly the scene outside jumped into her awareness clearer than any computer display. She saw in her mind the position of every asteroid, moonlet, and chip. She understood the gravitational pulls from sun and planets upon each. She became a part of the web of transactional gravitons.

Her fingers flew over the computer interfaces on her screen guiding the ship through the obstacle course.

"You're smiling?" Josh Kohler broke into her trance.

"Just meditating on what I'll do with my part of the reward from capturing the O'Hara brothers."

"Just keep your mind on steering this boat," Josh grunted.

Kat's smile grew broader. "I am, Josh. I am."

"The O'Haras may be the most wanted men in the Empire, but they aren't worth the lives of three hundred people and the loss of my ship, Lieutenant," Commander Leonard said. "Slow and easy. If you don't feel we can get through here safely . . ."

"I've waited too long for this moment to give up now, sir." Kat firmed her chin and narrowed her eyes. Nothing would keep her from finally confronting the O'Haras and bringing them to justice. Nothing.

I watch as Sam Eyeam meets another; one I should trust, but he smells wrong. They fight. The device that Stargod Konner seeks drops to the ground. It speaks to the stars in a voice we believed to come from Hanassa. Now we know that the man Hanassa has become wishes to misuse it.

The fight between Sam Eyeam and the one I cannot trust grows desperate. One man rises, grabs the device, and disappears into the dragongate. Who is left? I cannot tell from my watching distance. Dust obscures color. Injury disguises posture.

Ah, I see now that Sam Eyeam rushes to take refuge in a creature similar to Stargod Konner's Rover. This creature is bigger than Rover. I loose a little flame to encourage Sam Eyeam to emerge and speak to me.

He remains secreted. A little more flame. Too much? The creature catches fire.

The man jumps free and flees.

The heat from the fire singes my wing tip. I retreat to the clouds. Sam Eyeam and his device disappear from my senses.

Kim checked the village center. Two older women he knew only a little stoked the fire and hefted the stewpot onto the iron crane Konner had forged. Both women looked too frail for the heavy work. One had lost an eye, the other the use of her left arm. Both were past childbearing. No other village wanted them.

"Stargod Kim," the one-eyed beldame hailed him.

He smiled at them and took a moment from his mission to lift the heavy bronze cauldron onto the hook and swing it over the low fire. Enough distance separated the bottom of the pot from the flames to keep the metal from melting. An iron cauldron was near the top of the list of improvements for the village, as soon as Konner and his team of blacksmiths found time to forge one.

The old women returned his smiles with profuse thanks and bows and vows of eternal gratitude.

He scuttled into his cabin before they could enlist his help with something else. Everyone else who could work even a little was in the fields finishing off the harvest. A third grandmother watched the bevy of children too young to help. Five year olds helped gather the sheaves into stooks.

The perfect time for him to work in privacy without Hestiia hovering over him or Pryth clucking at him.

He did not wait for his eyes to adjust to the dim light inside. He found the basket of Tambootie by smell. As his pupils opened and he detected outlines and shapes within the shadows, he thought that particular basket glowed with an unusual aura. A corona of green mottled with pink, just like the new leaves, shone around the entire basket. He picked out two leaves, both mature, having lost all traces of pink. Oil still gleamed slickly on the fat foliage, though he'd picked these leaves nearly a week ago.

Checking once more that no one observed him, Kim licked the oils. The now-familiar taste sparkled inside his mouth. He felt lighter, freer, stronger, and more alert. The dimness of the cabin receded. Every object stood out in clear detail, as if he stood in bright sunshine. Now he could truly work magic on Taneeo's injuries, maybe speed the bone healing and swelling. Perhaps even restore the man's full eyesight.

And delve into his mind deeply enough to see if Hanassa was still there or had left booby traps for the Stargods.

He stuffed the leaves into his pocket and ducked out of the cabin. The old ladies smiled and waved at him once more. He ignored their invitation to talk to them and perhaps get snared into helping with more heavy chores. He had to act before the Tambootie wore off.

At the entrance to Taneeo's hut, Kim barely took time to rattle the strings of beads before entering. He heard the rustle of someone moving quickly. To his Tambootie-enhanced ears it sounded like a wind racing across the tops of the trees.

"S'murghit!" Taneeo cursed.

At least Kim thought it was Taneeo who invoked the deposed winged demon. Who else would inhabit this crude circular hut?

But the voice was deeper, raspier, harsher than the young priest's.

Then Kim's eyes registered the shape of Taneeo's sparse belongings and the man himself by the light of the auras.

Taneeo seemed to be two men, one lying atop the other, each with his own separate aura, touching but not blending.

Kim blinked. The outermost halo of red and black faded to Taneeo's more usual green and blue spiked with orange pain.

What had he seen?

For a moment Hanassa's coarse features had masked Taneeo's.

Kim reached for the Tambootie in his pocket. Taneeo reached a hand to stay his movement. "Nay, friend. You need no more of the weed. I have rejected my former master once and for all."

"I wished to try more healing on your leg," Kim said. His mouth went dry. A dozen questions choked him.

"Do not bother, my friend and Stargod. Your magic cannot touch my wounds."

"How do you know that?" Kim knelt beside the pallet. The hut smelled of sweat and fear and fever. He held his breath.

Taneeo's aura spiked again with red and black, then calmed to its normal colors.

"Because Pryth has filled your head with false tales of your powers. You can do nothing for me. You only think you can because you listen to the ancient harridan. Go. Leave me in peace to meditate. I will heal in my own good time." Laboriously, he rolled to his side with his back to Kim. As clear a dismissal as possible.

Kim rose to his feet, swayed a moment. The Tambootie seemed to burn its way through his pocket, begging him to chew just a little. Already his vision dimmed back to normal limits and his ears felt blocked with the lessening of sounds reaching him.

"I have to try, Taneeo."

"No."

"We will never know if my magic is valid or not until I try. _I_ have to know."

Had he seen Hanassa trying to invade Taneeo's body again? Or had it been a hallucination born of the Tambootie?

"Kim?" Loki's voice summoned him from outside. "Konner just commed. We've got trouble."

Kim closed his eyes and regrouped his senses. Already he longed for the clarity Tambootie gave his mind.

Clarity or hallucinations? He swallowed deeply and kept his hands out of the pocket that held the Tambootie.

Without another word he ducked out of the hut to join his brother.

Taneeo's grunt of satisfaction bothered him more than all of his other questions.

CHAPTER 14

◆——·——◆——·——◆

"WHERE ARE THE IMPs now?" Konner asked, closing down his comm unit.

"The Others come closer," Dalleena whispered. A glaze covered her eyes and she kept one hand extended toward the windscreen, palm questing outward.

"How much closer?" Konner spared her an extra few moments from his instruments.

The shuttle flew clear of the continent. The sea sparkled in the autumnal sunshine. He picked out the frolicking forms of dolphinlike creatures. The locals called them "mandelphs" and considered them warriors of old who had angered the gods. Their souls had been condemned to wander the seas for eternity. Their hunger for their lost humanity made them follow ships and rescue drowning sailors.

"Less than one third of daylight."

"Then they will have to orbit to pick their parking spot and deploy a lander. Six hours until they home in on the beacon's last location." He prayed to his mother's god and St. Bridget and whomever else might be listening that he destroyed the thing in time to confuse the enemy.

"Is it enough time?" she asked. At last she turned and looked at him full on. Other than wide eyes, she showed no trace of fear.

"Since I do not have to return you to the village first, we have enough time. Thank you."

She cracked half a smile.

"You realize that once we destroy the beacon, we will have a long and hard trip back to the village. Many days, with minimal provisions."

She nodded.

"Good girl." He patted her hand.

"I must see the task through to completion. 'Tis part of the code." She did not withdraw her hand from his touch.

This could get interesting.

"Whose code?" he asked, leaving his hand atop hers. "I wasn't aware there were any laws at all except for the ones Hanassa made up in the name of Simurgh to suit his own desires."

"The code of my father and his father and grandfather before him. 'Tis part of being a Tracker, seeing the lost thing returned to where it needs to be. Your bee-kan needs to be destroyed in the fiery mouth of the volcano. I will see it through." She looked off to their left, staring at the empty sea.

"I do not think that Sam Eyeam has the same Tracker code that I do."

"Why do you believe that?" Konner wished he understood why she considered the freelance agent a Tracker. Now if the man was a bounty hunter, a Tracking talent might come in handy.

"He did not acknowledge the secret sign I gave him."

"I did not see you . . ."

"I told you it is secret, passed from one Tracker to the other. Only we may know it. He does not know it. He does not follow the code."

"In other words, don't trust him."

They flew on in silence. Dalleena raised her free hand occasionally to sense the approach of the IMPs. As much as possible, Konner slipped his fingers around hers. Sometimes she seemed hesitant to continue touching him, then she'd sigh heavily and relax into the gentle bonding.

"My villagers welcomed you without question. They honored you. I do not understand," he said after a while.

"Trackers are rare. We provide a service no other can. We earn our keep." Sam Eyeam could make more than his keep if he had a true tracking talent. A lot more.

"But my people did not question your word that you are a Tracker."

"I showed them this." Dalleena swept her mass of dark hair off to her back, then slipped vest and shirt free of her left shoulder.

Konner's gaze rested upon a small blue tattoo of a right hand, palm out. Meticulously drawn, he could almost pick out her fingerprints on it.

He dared look no further than the emblem. Her breasts swelled nicely above their confining band. He traced the tattoo with a delicate finger, wishing he dared drop his hand lower.

"Only Trackers are honored with this symbol. I had to successfully find three lost ones and return them home alive before I could call myself a Tracker."

She replaced her shirt and vest and raised her hand in questing pose once more. "They come. More quickly," she said quietly. Her grip on his hand tightened.

The shoreline of the Great Bay smudged the horizon.

A quick glance at his instruments confirmed the presence of a ship near parking orbit. Had they found and boarded *Sirius*? Had they left his ship intact? Or did they simply follow the beacon?

"They didn't stop to take in the sights, that's for certain," Konner quipped. But then, they'd had the beacon to follow and didn't need to do full surveys before making decisions about landing. How did they make it through the blasted asteroid belt so quickly? "We'll beat them to the volcano. Just." He boosted speed, heedless of the sonic boom he created and the vast amount of fuel he consumed.

Within a few moments, *Rover*'s instruments lost track of the IMP cruiser. "Damn. No satellites to bounce signals!" He slammed his fist into the console. He couldn't even tap into the more extensive sensors aboard *Sirius*. He'd parked her over the horizon to keep the locals from noticing a new "star" in the firmament.

The IMPs would not be so careful. They had no vested interest in keeping the locals ignorant of the outside and tied to a self-sufficient agrarian economy.

"Where are they?"

"They have not yet launched a . . . 'lander?' " Dalleena made the last word a question.

He jerked an abrupt nod that she had remembered the word correctly. Then he eased his speed up a notch. Inwardly he cringed at the thought of the noise his passage must create for the inhabitants below.

The Southern Mountains loomed ahead. Konner shed altitude and speed. The butterflies in his stomach grew to the size of bats.

Dalleena's knuckles turned white where she gripped her seat. Her sensing hand came up once more. She'd checked on the IMPs a lot since they had left the sea behind. And removed her hand from his, leaving him isolated and alone. "The . . . ship splits. Two pieces. One very large. One smaller. Moving fast. The lander?"

Konner gulped. Moving fast could mean any speed to Dalleena who had grown up expecting paces no faster than the hybrid horses domesticated by the tribes.

"Faster than us?" he asked, not expecting an answer.

"Much faster. Spiraling through the air. Aiming for us."

"Damn." After a few seconds' thought he half smiled. "I'm not the pilot Loki is, but I still have a few tricks up my sleeve."

Dalleena cocked her head in question but said nothing. If she did not understand the phrase, she'd figure it out soon enough.

He liked that.

Abruptly he changed course and dropped altitude. Mountain peaks now rose above him. His magnetic readings began to spin. He let his mind go blank a moment before looking out the window. Spidery blue lines flickered in and out of sight. Lines of unexplained energy akin to transactional gravitons. Pryth and the dragons called them ley lines. They dribbled away to nothing in the foothills of the blown-out volcano. The eruption must have exploded with massive power to disrupt magnetic forces and the ley lines.

Konner could use the disruption to lead the IMPs a merry chase.

He popped up above the mountain peaks and the electronic magnetic fluctuations or EMF disruption long enough to give the IMP sensors a glimpse of him, way west of his target. Then he dropped down again and wove a serpentine course back north. When he judged himself far enough away from the volcano, he rose up again, briefly. Only long enough for the sensors to blip before he dove back down again.

If this IMP captain was even a degree less perceptive than the last one who had chased the O'Hara brothers, he should plot a trajectory based upon the last two sightings and look for the shuttle along the line of mountains running north and south to divide the continent nearly into two equal parts.

Konner circled around and took the fastest course toward the volcano, as high as he could, giving himself sufficient distance from the ground, but not to be out of the mask of EMF.

Dalleena bared her teeth at him in a half grimace half smile. "Is this what living in your world is like?"

"Pretty much." Konner suppressed a laugh of exhilaration as the broken mouth of the volcano crater came into view. He did not bother with finesse. He did not bother with comfort. He needed to set the shuttle down within the confines of the crater as quickly as possible.

Rocked and jolted by rapid changes from the VTOL jets he barely secured the vehicle before grabbing the beacon out of Dalleena's lap and diving out the hatch. She came right on his heels, not even wrinkling her nose at the hot dry air stench.

"What about the lander?" she gasped, trying to keep up with him.

"We'll worry about that later."

They maintained silence on the trek down into the heart of the mountain. Konner could tell that Dalleena was fairly bursting with questions. Still, she saved them. She even took his lead in sipping from the sulfurous stream, rolling the precious moisture around in her mouth before swallowing. The grimace on her face gave him a brief chuckle.

"You like this stuff no better than I," she retorted, then took a second, longer drink. This time she raised her eyebrows in puzzlement. A third mouthful and she quirked her mouth up on one side. A delightful dimple made the expression into a silent exclamation point. "I could get used to this."

"You may have to. The lava pit is over here." With careful, almost reverential steps he wound his way around the obstacles in the big cavern, through several smaller ones, each housing a generator or transformer, into the room where Big Bertha, the monster steam generator, dwelled.

Thankfully the dragongate remained silent, between cycles. He did not know if he would be able to think straight with the hum in the back of his head.

Dalleena stopped short at sight of the machine that filled nearly an acre of cavern. Her questing hand came up. She shook her head and thrust the hand forward with determination.

"Big Bertha is not lost," Konner chuckled.

"Perhaps not. But I think I may be." Tentatively, she used her questing hand to touch the metal surface of the generator. The first contact led to a more thorough tactile exploration.

"Come, we still have a chore to perform." Konner stepped into a side tunnel well away from the dragongate. No sense in taking a chance on the wormhole opening and taking the beacon to yet another destination. Though, if he could send it to the south pole, it might divert the IMPs long enough to finish repairs on the *Sirius* so that the O'Hara brothers could get the hell out of Dodge.

But that would not protect Dalleena and her people from the ravages of civilization that must follow on the heels of the IMP invasion.

He balanced on the edge of the lava pit.

The beacon weighed heavily in his hands. A stream of molten rock shot upward. Heat blasted him. Sweat broke out on his brow and back.

He had to destroy it. He and his brothers would deal with the IMPs somehow. He could not take a chance on another ship following the beacon here.

Without further thought, he hurled the beacon far out over the pit. A pitiful distance compared to the wide stretch of the opening. He watched it arc gracefully, a diminishing speck that dropped and dropped, a thousand feet or more into the roiling mass of the pit.

"Good-bye, Melinda. So much for your treachery," he sighed. He prayed that Sam Eyeam had taken the second beacon out of the system.

But it was already too late. The IMPs had found the O'Hara brothers and a pristine planet ready for exploitation.

The dragongate hummed loudly. Dalleena jerked her attention away from the tiny burst of flame that was the beacon. She cocked her head, listening acutely. Her right hand came up. Konner steadied her balance.

The gate silenced abruptly. Too quickly. Normally, it took a full minute to open completely and then another to close. This opening had lasted only a few heartbeats. Or had he been distracted with thoughts of the beacon and not heard the beginning of the cycle?

Too soon the thing began to hum again. He headed back to Big Bertha's cavern. Before he could gain a sighting on the dragongate tunnel, the thing reached a climactic pitch and grew silent.

"What the . . . ?" Konner nearly ran to the edge of the portal, Dalleena close upon his heels.

All he saw was the roiling mass of molten lava shooting flaming rock high enough to force him back from the lip as he flung his arm over his eyes to protect them.

· ——◆—— ·

The enemy is come. They cannot be allowed to destroy us or our home. We are responsible for the safety of this world. We will guard it at whatever cost. Even the death of the Stargods.

What is this? Sam Eyeam returns to my senses. He is stranded. He has no device that is the voice of Hanassa and speaks to the stars. He has no shelter, no food, no transportation. I must return him to the land of the Coros. But not too close. A band of Rovers will protect him as they wander westward. They will also keep Sam Eyeam from returning to the land of the Coros until his time is proper. Stargod Konner will find him later.

CHAPTER 15

$\blacklozenge$ —— $\cdot$ —— $\blacklozenge$ —— $\cdot$ —— $\blacklozenge$

KONNER STOOD IN THE dragongate tunnel for many long moments. He wished for a wrist chrono to time the portal. He'd left his on *Sirius*. What need of digital time in a society that measured its passage in seasons and generations.

He sighed heavily. What two places had it opened to in rapid succession before he watched it so diligently?

As best he could guess, the portal had not opened in half an hour. He could not wait any longer hoping that in the next few heartbeats he would see the green clearing across the river from his village.

In the last battle with Hanassa, he had destroyed the only remote that controlled the gate. The dragongate reverted to its own unmappable schedule.

"Dalleena, we'll have to take our chances with the desert."

"Shall we fill the waterskins at this creek?" She looked reluctantly at Big Bertha. He could not read her thoughts or emotions.

"There is a plateau nearby where the water is sweeter. We can harvest a few fresh greens there to supplement our rations." Time was he'd have been perfectly happy with reconstituted vegetable protein. Now he knew the true joy of flavor and texture, spices that burst upon the tongue, crisp vegetables, and juicy fruits. He had learned to appreciate sharing his meals. True food nurtured the palate and the soul as well as the body. After five months of eating food cooked over an open fire, he'd never settle for ship's rations in their Insta-hot® packets again. No wonder fresh food was the most valuable commodity in the Galactic Terran Empire.

On the trek back to the surface, Konner paused in the throne room. He scanned with his senses as well as his portable instruments for signs of recent habitation. The throne carved of silver bloodwood remained where he'd last seen it. The dust around the throne and the half finished altar remained free of new scuff marks since he and his brothers had been here . . . was it only yesterday?

The remnants of an old fire in one of the outer caverns looked cold and undisturbed. Whatever body Hanassa might inhabit, he had not come back since stealing the beacon and selling it to Sam Eyeam.

"Konner, wait," Dalleena whispered. She clutched at his sleeve.

Instantly, he froze in place. "What?" he mouthed.

She cocked her head toward the narrow opening with harsh sunlight streaming through it.

Then he heard what she had sensed. Voices. Footsteps. The hatch of a shuttle opening. The IMPs had penetrated *Rover.*

"Hide!" Konner shoved her behind him. Together they crouched behind an outcropping. He wrapped his arms around her, making them one object. With luck, and if God and all the saints looked upon them with favor, the desert heat concentrated into the bowl of the crater and the screwed magnetics would scramble their sensors.

"Lieutenant, I'm picking up a reading," an anonymous female voice announced in excited tones. No doubt she already had designs on the reward for the capture of any O'Hara. Doubled by Melinda if Konner were the one captured.

What could he do?

"We have to run back to the pit," Konner whispered to Dalleena. "The heat will confuse their instruments, and maybe the dragongate will open for us."

She nodded mutely.

With one ear tuned to the proceedings outside, he whispered, "Ready, set, go."

They pelted back the way they had come as fast as they could.

"Two of 'em. Running," the same female voice cried.

Dozens of feet pounded the baked dirt. Then came the distinctive thud and "Oof," of someone measuring their length against the ground, or one of the columns.

"Lights! Someone get some lights," an authoritative male voice called.

Konner ducked into the throne room. He risked his own light to orient his sense of direction to the exit. Together, he and Dalleena skidded around the corner and into the long tunnel that led downward. Ever downward.

Sweat dripped into his eyes and drenched his shirt. His mouth dried and his heart pounded too fast. The full length of his thighs ached and the soles of his feet burned.

At the creek, both he and Dalleena paused long enough to scoop up a few mouthfuls of water. If they were hurting from the mad dash through rough terrain with the intense heat, the IMPs must be in a sorry state. They had a few moments to breathe. And think.

"How do we get out of this?" he asked the air, not expecting an answer.

The dragongate hummed in the back of his mind.

Footsteps pounded on the long downgrade of the tunnel.

"Come." He grabbed Dalleena's hand and dragged her back through the maze of caverns.

Shouts sounded behind them as the IMPs emerged into the large room near the creek.

"Ewww! It smells like something died and rotted," a nasal tenor voice protested. It had the singsong pattern of one of the Hindu cultures.

"Sensor's scrambled," a female voice reported. Cool and precise. "Magnetics disrupted. This chamber is hotter than body heat. Can't get a definitive read."

More mumbles and grunts.

"Footprints, this way," yet a third voice cried excitedly.

The dragongate hummed louder.

"St. Bridget and all the angels, please let it be the portal I need," Konner prayed as he entered the short tunnel. He kept a wary eye on any signs of activity behind him.

Close. They came ever closer.

He couldn't let them find out about the wormhole.

The harsh yellow-and-orange glow from the lava below cooled to a soothing green. Bright sunshine on a circular clearing, ringed by Tambootie trees.

Konner grabbed Dalleena's face with both hands. Without thinking, he kissed her hard. He didn't want to let her go.

"That place is across the river from the village. Go!" Konner pushed her. "I'll find you. No matter what, I'll find you."

Dalleena stumbled over the ledge of the pit and into . . . the greens and browns swirled and shifted back to the normal colors of a volcano thinking about exploding. The insistent hum in the back of his mind died.

He dove back out the tunnel, running fast. He shoved uniformed men and women aside, heedless of where they landed. All he wanted was up and out of this cave system; away from the dragongate.

"I must advise you that resisting arrest will not endear you to the judge." That had to be one of the lawyers. A judicial cruiser had followed them—a ship full of judges, lawyers, investigators, and police enforcement. That meant a minimum ship's personnel of three hundred.

Shite. They'd carry word of this planet back to civilization. The stories of its fertility would exaggerate into legend. Civilization would ruin and pollute the land as it had every planet the GTE had settled.

"Are we certain this man is our quarry?" asked the singsong voice. "Are we certain he understands our language?"

"I'll lead you all a merry chase right back to the beginning," Konner muttered to himself as he scooped up one more handful of water and braced himself for the uphill trek.

This time he set a moderate pace, needing the IMPs to follow him. Anything to keep them away from the dragongate. Halfway to the throne room he had to slow even more, dragging in deep gulps of air. His hands shook when he dashed sweat out of his eyes. The back of his throat tasted sour and gritty. He couldn't keep going.

He had no choice.

From the sounds behind him, the IMPs fared no better. Konner at least had spent the past five months working hard outdoors, plowing, planting, building a smithy and forging parts for *Sirius* as well as tools for the locals. Single-handedly he had dragged the Coros up from dependence upon bronze to a full embrace of iron. And in the course of that achievement, he had built muscle and stamina. The IMPs had been in space for months with no physical activity outside a gym in the heaviest gravity portion of their ship.

If he stayed this far ahead of the main party, he just might be able to gain access to *Rover* and take off.

They'd leave a few guards at his shuttle.

They'd shoot first and ask questions later.

He had to come up with a better plan.

Hard to think in this heat; working this hard. If only he had a drink of cool water. A swallow would help. He trudged on.

Visions of the cold waters of the Great Bay wavered before his eyes. A mirage. Surely a hallucination born of heat and dehydration.

Or a plan.

All he needed was a distraction.

"St. Bridget, send me an idea."

He burst into bright daylight, blinking and cursing. Two uniformed men lounged at the hatch of *Rover*. They'd slung their stun rifles loosely on their backs. A third figure showed in the cockpit window. She worked furiously and with frustrated gestures trying to start the shuttle. She would not succeed. Ignition, communication, and navigation were keyed to O'Hara DNA.

Where the hell had they parked their lander? Surely not in the crater.

Clearly the IMPS had not expected their quarry to come running out of the caves alone.

Konner dove behind the nearest boulder. It was as big as a hut and shielded him admirably. Finally he had the time to breathe and think.

Not for long. IMPs had their limitations on bush planets. But they were not stupid. He heard two sets of footsteps approaching from two directions. Where was the third?

He darted to the next outcropping, a nest of smaller rocks.

Two weapons burped stunning bolts of energy. Both missed.

Konner ducked and rolled into his new position. The IMPs kept coming.

A quick glance between the rocks of his new shelter showed him three of his pursuers. They came at him cautiously, with silent but firm steps. Slowly. Each was balanced and held a stun rifle easily, comfortable with the weight.

If he crawled, he might make the next obstacle before they spotted him. Another quick look canceled that idea.

Then he heard the bulk of the party emerging from the caves. A full squad of Marines plus the lawyer, an anthropologist, and assorted forensic technicians.

"S'murghit," he cursed. Three he might have handled. Twenty steepened the odds far above his budget of options.

He looked up at the sheer walls of the caldera. Aeons ago, the volcano had blown out its interior. The walls had been left so thin they collapsed back into the heart to form the crater. How stable were they?

He had one chance and one only. "Let's just hope this works." He'd worked a couple of miracles with his mind when he did not know what he was doing. Could he perform similar feats consciously?

He took a deep breath.

"I surrender!" Slowly he rose to his feet with both hands above his head.

The three IMPs closest to him looked skeptical. They swung back and forth, making certain the muzzles of their weapons covered a wide area.

"Where're your brothers?" the lieutenant called from the mouth of the cave.

A tech corporal beside him looked anxiously from Konner to her instruments. "I read only one civilian," she said. No emotion colored her voice.

"Where are your brothers, O'Hara?" The lieutenant approached with a confident swagger. Mid-thirties, unremarkable brown hair and eyes, politically correct stature. The top of his head might reach Konner's chin. And he had the muscle bulk of an efficient metabolism.

Kind of old to still be only a lieutenant.

"I'm alone," Konner called.

"Not likely. You three never go anywhere without at least one sibling. Where are they?"

Konner shrugged, keeping his hands up and nonthreatening. But he fixed his gaze high, about the middle of the slope above one of the smaller cave entrances. While the IMPs muttered among themselves, he concentrated on a rock teetering precariously on nothing but packed dirt. In his mind he pictured the rock rolling, gaining speed, collecting more rocks and debris in its path. Over and over, he willed the rock loose from its perch.

He breathed deeply. The picture of the rockfall became clearer in his mind.

And then he heard it happen.

Twenty IMPs looked up. Fifteen weapons swung up in the same direction.

Konner wasted no time. He dove for the next outcropping. Three meters closer to the exit. All the while he kept picturing the rock rolling down the steep cliff.

He heard the soft *chunk* of one stone bouncing off another. Then a sharper sound as the first hunk of rock slammed into a larger one. He spared a glance at the slope. Sure enough, a minor landslide had begun. The first rock had a long way to go and a lot of hillside to collect from before it reached ground. It gained momentum as it tumbled and gathered more of its kind in its wake. If the IMPs did not move soon, they'd be caught in a major cliff slippage.

All twenty of the GTE's finest law enforcement personnel stared at the cliff, dumbstruck.

"How did O'Hara know it was going to fall," one noncom whispered. Her words sounded loud in the hush that had fallen among them.

"Take cover!" The lieutenant recovered from astonishment first.

Konner launched himself toward the exit tunnel before anyone had a chance to think about him.

A mighty roar punctuated the sound of a rockfall. Konner risked a glance at the source of the sound. The vague form of a dragon outlined in red swooped into the crater belching flame.

"Thank you, Irythros."

(*They would hurt you,*) the dragon replied indignantly.

Then the dragon flew upward, the squirming, screaming body of the lieutenant clutched in one set of talons.

"They only wished to capture me and my brothers, not kill me! Put him down, Irythros."

(*Would capture not hurt you?*) The word "capture" appeared in Konner's head as himself imprisoned in a small room behind a glowing force field. Electronic force bracelets confining both hands and feet.

"Very much so."

(*Is that why you created the landslide?*)

"Yes, but you must not hurt the lieutenant. Isn't that part of dragon honor? You value life in the same way I and my people do. Put him down. Gently."

(*Very well,*) the dragon sighed. He almost sounded disappointed.

At the top edge of the crater walls, the dragon hovered and set his quarry down.

The lieutenant yelped. "Razor wire! What the frig . . ."

The dragon flew off.

Konner chuckled. Irythros had set the IMP lieutenant atop the rusting fence line erected by the original colonists.

Nineteen IMPs scrambled to find a path up the steep slope.

"That should keep them occupied while I get out of here." Konner took off again, forgotten by the law enforcement officials.

(*You may ride on my back.*) Irythros flew past the outside of the exit tunnel.

"I thought you could not come to this place."

(*You needed my help. Sometimes aiding brethren is more important than rules.*)

"Thank you." Konner allowed a moment of silence to emphasize his appreciation. "I do not wish you to get into more trouble with the nimbus. I have a better idea for getting out of here."

(*Be careful.*)

"Aren't I always?"

(*No.*)

CHAPTER 16

◆ —— · —— ◆ · —— ◆

DALLEENA TUMBLED into nothing. Thoughts of a horrible death in the heat of the lava struck her dumb. She could not even scream.

Cool air drifted past her face. Cool?

She opened her eyes. Time and space twisted and distorted around her. She had no sense of up or down, right or left. Her head spun and her joints ached. Her stomach threatened to turn inside out.

A groan erupted from her throat. But she could not hear it. She decided to keep her mouth and her eyes clamped closed.

Contained within herself once more, her senses found orientation. She shifted to face up.

One heartbeat later, a firm surface pressed against her butt. With her fingers she explored the surface. Grass. Bracken. Stone.

Her eyes flew open. A near perfect ring of trees surrounded a grassy glade. She caught a whiff of the pungent Tambootie tree. Off to her right she heard the rippling of the river. Farther in the distance she picked out rhythmic voices chanting a harvest song.

Dalleena rolled quickly to her knees and then to her feet. She sought the protective shadows of the trees, all the while holding out her questing hand.

"Konner?" she whispered. The memory of his kiss lingered on her mouth.

The breeze in the treetops seemed to pick up her words and whisper them into the far distance.

Dalleena circled with her hand out. She had no sense of Konner, near or far. "Konner!" she called louder.

Her hand remained empty of directional tingles.

"That place is across the river from the village." She remembered his words. Did he mean here? "I'll find you. No matter what, I'll find you."

"I'm supposed to do the finding, Stargod Konner. So where are you?" Until she figured that out, she needed to find the village. He'd come looking for her there first.

She set her mind to picturing the village. Her questing hand came up and pointed directly in front of her. She followed her hand and the sound of the river. One pace for each of her heartbeats. Very shortly the expanse of the river came into view, shallow and narrow this late in the year. Once the winter rains began, it would swell. For now, she could probably swim to the other side with ease.

Before she plunged down the bank and into the water, she shaded her eyes and scanned the opposite bank. Two adolescent boys approached with fishing poles. She recognized the youths from the village.

"Wonder what tale they spun to avoid helping with the harvest," she muttered to herself.

One of the boys looked up at her words, as if he had heard her. He shouted and waved in greeting.

Konner was correct. She was just across the river from the village.

She pulled off her boots and tested the water with her toes. Cool. Refreshing after the intense heat of the volcano crater and caves. With a lace from the front of her shirt, she bound her soft leather boots together and slung them around her neck. Six steps brought the water up to mid-calf. Another five steps and it was deep enough to strike out with long strokes. Barely a dozen body lengths and the gravelly riverbed scraped against her toes.

One of the boys scrambled down the embankment. He offered her a hand out of the water. She accepted it, though she did not need assistance.

"You the Tracker?" he asked.

Dalleena nodded, wringing water out of her hair and shirttail.

"Stargod Loki has been looking for you and Stargod Konner." He looked beyond her shoulder as if expecting the errant brother to appear. Something in the urgency behind his words sent a frisson of warning up Dalleena's spine.

"He's not there," she said, trying to keep the worry out of her voice.

"Dalleena, where is *he!*" Stargod Loki called from the top of the embankment. His usually neat hair looked as if he'd combed it with repeated hand gestures, and bits of chaff clung to his beard.

"I do not know," she replied, more irritated than she intended. A knot of worry grew in her belly. She looked at the boys, all eyes and eager grins. And ears atuned to the slightest nuance of her voice.

She climbed the bank rather than voice her concerns in front of them.

Loki extended his hand to help her up the last steep incline.

She took it gratefully, hoping his strength would calm the shaking she could feel beginning in her hand and extending up her arm and shoulder and into her jaw. If she weren't careful, her teeth would chatter in a moment.

She should not care this deeply about someone she needed to find; only about the finding.

"Where did you last see my brother?" Loki pressed her in a quieter voice.

She drew him away from the edge of the bank and the listening adolescents. "We destroyed a bee-kan in the volcano," she said quietly.

"You found it! Where was it? Were you in time?" He grabbed both of her shoulders in a tight grip.

"We found it in a . . . sug." She fought for the word Konner had used.

"Souk. A marketplace," Loki confirmed. "Where?"

The top of a tousled head appeared at the edge of the embankment. Dalleena disengaged herself from Loki's hands and walked another ten paces closer to the village before speaking again.

"Far across the sea. A place where many boats gather and many numbers of people live in a very small space."

"A city on a harbor. Fine. Did you destroy it in time?"

Dalleena shrugged. "Intruders came."

Loki paled. He looked as if his knees would collapse. "No," he mouthed. "No," he said louder. "Not after all we've worked for. They can't come now!"

"They have come. About twenty men in a . . . a lander." She remembered the word Konner had taught her. "They chased us. Stargod Konner pushed me into an opening into the lava pit, but I landed there." She pointed across the river to the clearing.

"What about my brother? Didn't he follow you?" Loki's hands shook. He stared at them for a long moment, then stuffed them into his pockets. The face he turned to her was calm, but his eyes blazed with anger and fear and a number of other emotions she could not read.

"I do not know. He said he would find me."

"If he's still there, then the IMPs have him. He might be dead by now. We have to go into hiding. We have to . . ."

"We have to wait for Konner to return. He promised he would return. I believe him." This time she grabbed his shoulders and shook him.

He gulped and seemed to gather himself. "If you could track the beacon across an ocean, why can't you track my brother in the volcano?"

"I do not know. I have never failed to find someone before. But he does not answer to my call." She held up her hand again and slowly turned in a circle.

Nothing.

"I must also tell you that a second bee-kan exists." She dropped her hand in defeat. That artifact did not tingle on her palm either. Her heart and belly began to feel as empty as her palm.

Loki's blood ran cold. Another beacon to find and destroy. Another trip into the volcanic craters. And IMPs beginning to crawl all over the planet.

He watched Dalleena's face and shoulders sag. She must know how dire their situation was. Moisture gathered in her eyes. He draped an arm about her shoulders ready to comfort her. He spent a lot of time comforting women on this planet. They seemed to enjoy the process of their weakness drawing his affections.

Dalleena surprised him. At his first touch she mastered the defeat in her posture and stepped out from under his embrace.

He raised his eyebrows. Not his kind of woman at all. His Cyndi could exhibit a spine of titanium when crossed, but she at least put on a show of needing a strong man to help her. She was the daughter of a planetary governor and knew when a woman should be soft and when she had to be strong.

The Tracker didn't know how to be soft. The men of the village had welcomed her as an equal. No questions about her masculine garb, her father, brother, or husband. She was a Tracker and that was all that was important.

Well, he could be strong and insistent as well.

"Try again, Tracker," he ordered. "I have to find my brother before the IMPs take him back to their ship."

She held up her right hand, palm out, and once again made a full circle. She paused briefly as she faced south by east, shook her head, and moved on.

"Nothing."

"What about where you paused?" Loki turned to face in that direction. All he could see were undulating hills of forest and meadow. Great swaths of pristine land waiting to be to put to the plow.

If the IMPs were already here, then the process of destruction was about to begin.

Unless . . .

"We can't let any one of those twenty IMPs from the lander, or the rest of the ship's complement leave the planet. We have to find and destroy the second beacon before another ship comes."

"We must kill the Others for what they have done to Stargod Konner," Dalleena said. Her voice sounded neutral, but her clenched teeth and fists told another story.

Loki's face grew cold and his stomach knotted. He'd taken one life. Even in self-defense, the death throes of Hanassa, the agony Loki's soul had shared with the man, haunted him still.

"I will not countenance their deaths. I must find a better way."

"Stand down, Lieutenant Talbot," Commander Leonard ordered.

Kat pursed her lips, biting back the angry words on the tip of her tongue. She wanted to pace the tiny office of the ship's captain. Protocol demanded that she remain at parade rest. She felt hunched and confined beneath the low ceiling. Her bushie height and long legs made all standard military living quarters claustrophobic.

Rigid training kept her posture erect even if her cap did brush the ceiling.

"May I ask for an explanation, Captain, sir?"

"If I give you one, it is not because I cater to your bloated sense of superior knowledge in this issue." Commander Leonard sighed. She fiddled with her electronic pencil and the series of screens built into her desktop.

A long stretch of silence. Kat did not break the tension with further questions.

"I do not want you taking point on the pursuit of the O'Haras because I believe your emotions are overriding your judgment," Leonard said at last. She did not look at Kat. For some reason, her screens seemed more important than her helmsman.

"Accompanying the next contingent of Marines dirtside is hardly taking point, sir." Kat almost snapped a salute to emphasize her words. At the last moment she realized the reflexive gesture was not necessary.

"I know you, Kat. You would not allow any mere Marine to lead." In the ship's convoluted hierarchy, the Marines ranked well below those who actually ran the ship, and below the judiciary arm that directed criminal investigations and capture.

Kat almost smiled.

"I obey *your* orders, sir. I take them very seriously. Leading the Marines is not an option, though most of the time they need to be led."

Commander Leonard swallowed a smile.

"You are too close to the issue, Kat. I will not have you turning a normal police pursuit into a personal vendetta."

"Sir . . ."

"I know your history, Lieutenant Talbot."

Kat clamped her mouth shut on her protest. No one knew her full history. No one. She'd made certain all records of her first seven years of life had been destroyed.

"I know that Governor Talbot adopted you when you were quite young. I also know that the O'Hara clan originated on your home planet. The connection is there. For some reason I will leave unexplored, you have a connection to the men we chase. You will have your opportunity for confrontation after they are captured. Not before."

Kat opened her mouth to say something, anything to get herself on the next lander.

"You will not sneak aboard the landers even if I have to confine you to quarters under armed guard, Lieutenant. Dismissed."

"Yes, sir." Kat saluted crisply, did a precise about-face, and marched out of the captain's office.

She muttered seven oaths in six different languages, none of them Terran Standard. If she disobeyed orders and sneaked aboard a lander, then her career was over. Everything she'd worked for, all of the disadvantages she'd overcome, were for naught.

Was revenge against the O'Haras worth it?

CHAPTER 17

"GET YOUR NOSE out of the book, professor, and come help us."
Kim looked up from his journal, blinking at Loki's silhouette in
the open doorway. Dalleena stood just behind him. "What?" he managed to
stammer, his thoughts still on the sequence of events he was cataloging for
preparing the body to engage psi powers—or magic. He needed help if he
was to understand how and why Taneeo had become Hanassa's victim once
more. Kim was also puzzled about Taneeo's sudden antipathy toward Pryth.
A few days ago they had been great friends, heads together discussing the
value of this herbal infusion over that salve to treat a rash among the children
who played too close to the wetlands.

Did his sudden dislike for the old woman indicate a residual of Hanassa's
hatred for Pryth. If so, could that kernel of distrust leave a pathway for Hanassa's malignant spirit to return to the village priest?

Something about Konner's earlier communication. A warning of some
sort. The locals and the planet were in danger from . . . His mind refused to
focus on anything but the text he input to his reader. He needed to finish
before the Tambootie wore off.

"You know we really should name this planet," he mused. "I think we
should start calling it Kardia Hodos, the name you suggested." Consolidating
his thoughts on developing their psi powers was much more important than
Loki's panics. Perhaps a little more of the Tambootie would inspire him.

"Later, Kim. We have a problem." Loki yanked the reader out of Kim's
hands and tossed it aside. It landed with a thud on the mattress.

Kim winced. Loki's violent treatment of a reader indicated more than just
his usual simmering temper.

"What is so important that you have to interrupt . . ."

"The IMPs have Konner."

The world stilled for a moment. Kim heard his own heartbeat.

"They've landed? Already?"

"Already."

"We have to evacuate. Raaskan mentioned some caves to the southeast. The harvest is almost in and stored. We can take everything. Pack it onto the backs of the cattle and the steeds. The women and children need to go first. The men should stay behind to dismantle the village, obliterate all trace of us . . . Hestiia. Where is Hestiia?"

"We need to rescue Konner."

"We need to rescue Konner," Kim echoed. His brother's words sank in. "We still need to evacuate. Raaskan can handle that while you and I find Konner."

"If we make certain none of the IMPs ever leaves this planet, we don't have to evacuate."

That thought stopped Kim. Could they strand the entire crew on this planet? Tantamount to a prison sentence for life. For future generations. That would be treating the IMPs worse than they had treated Kim and his brothers.

"They are foreign invaders. We are defending the planet and its people by doing this," Loki said with force. Obviously, he had read Kim's mind again. He grabbed the front of Kim's vest and stared directly into his eyes. "We have to do this."

"How?" Kim swallowed his misgivings. For Hestiia and her people, for the future of an entire planet, they had to do it. They had to defend themselves against foreign invaders, just as Earth had defended itself against the Kree.

Kim did not like that analogy. Humans had stolen tech from the winged aliens and used it to expand their own empire beyond their own solar system.

"I shall gather warriors from all of the villages. We shall ambush the Others and kill them all. There are only twenty of them," Dalleena said from behind Loki.

"Oh, there are a lot more than twenty of them," Loki replied almost on a sneer. "Twenty came down in the lander. That was just the first wave. There are probably three hundred more up on the cruiser."

"Three hundred?" Dalleena looked as if she needed to sit down. "An entire city of the Others."

Then she jerked her head up and over to her left. Her nose worked like a cat's did when scenting the air. Then she raised her right arm to shoulder level, palm forward. She waved it back and forth until she settled on a generally easterly direction. "Konner," she breathed. A great deal of relief flooded her face.

Kim felt the same emotion.

"Where?" Loki and Kim asked on the same heartbeat.

"There," she pointed due east, toward the river mouth.

"Near or far?" Kim asked. He'd seen the woman in action last night. This was another talent he needed to record. The basket of Tambootie and his reader called to him, in an almost audible siren song.

NO! he told himself. First they needed to rescue Konner.

"Not across the ocean, but far." She began walking out of the village and along the riverbank toward the bay.

"I did not hear the shuttle go overhead," Kim said.

"You wouldn't with your nose in a book," Loki replied.

Dalleena just kept walking.

"Is he safe?" Kim asked her.

"Cannot tell." She stepped over a moss-covered log.

Last night she'd been oblivious to obstacles. Did distance from her target weaken her trance?

"We may need help," Loki said practically. "Raaskan, Yaakke, a few of the men with warrior experience. Weapons."

"Hestiia. I can't leave without telling her." Kim turned back. His wife would be in the fields with all the others, bringing in the last of the harvest. The wheat he had helped plant. The people he had helped rescue from a bloodthirsty priest. The village he had helped build. "I have to stay and defend this place." If he left now, he might never return.

Dalleena just kept walking.

"What about Konner?" Loki stopped long enough to stare at Kim. "What about rescuing our brother?"

"I don't know. I can't just . . . I . . ." For the first time in his life Kim knew the terrible indecision of choosing between protecting the people he loved as family and his brothers who had shared most of his life's adventures.

Dalleena just kept walking.

"I'll catch up. I'll bring men and weapons." Light dazzled around the edges of his vision. His gut churned with premonition. "I have to hold Hestiia in my arms one more time."

Kat prowled *Jupiter*. Each long stride only fueled her frustration. The ship's passageways were too small for her. The half-mile circumference and the one-mile length of the torpedo-shaped vessel were too short. There was not enough space to burn off the energy that pulsed through her system. She headed for the outer areas of heavier gravity. The constant hum of the king stone at the exact center of the ship quieted just a little. She breathed easier.

Good thing *Jupiter* possessed only one king stone. If each of the three arrays of twelve drivers and one hundred forty-four directionals—equally spaced along the length of the ship—fed into a separate king stone, she'd probably go crazy.

Or was that crazier?

Despite Commander Leonard's orders, she still sought a way to get aboard the next lander to the surface. She needed to confront the O'Hara brothers face-to-face. *She* needed to be the one to bring them to justice.

Her path led past the Marine ready room. Twenty men and women strapped on spider silk armor, cleaned and charged weapons, checked EVA suits, and excitedly traded insults. Kat itched to share in the precombat cama-raderie. She'd done her share of combat training. But since going into space, all of her preparations had been with ship's weapons and shielding, space tac-tics, and flight plans. Her dirtside skills must be getting as stale as unscrubbed air.

Could she use that as an excuse to get a Marine officer to request her pres-ence in the landing crew?

"Balinakis is going soft. He's afraid of a tough criminal recovery," a female corporal muttered. Her short, squarish figure suggested civil lineage. But her speech patterns and diction had a lisping whistle that came from a bush planet on the outskirts of GTE space.

Kat paused outside the ready room's open hatch to listen.

"I heard that the judge actually ordered Capt'n Leonard not to follow the marking beacon attached to *Sirius*," a tall, blond sergeant, decisively bushie in his size and speech, replied. "Clear violation of judicial protocol, if you ask me."

Kat knew that gossip and rumor flew through the ship at faster-than-light speed. Eavesdropping on enlisted personnel often provided her with more accurate information than official notifications. She pressed herself against the bulkhead, willing herself to remain unnoticed by the Marines.

"I'd like to see us strand the judge on a Bush planet and let Captain Leon-ard take his place. She's fairer and just as knowledgeable about the law," Ser-geant Kent Brewster grumbled. That tall, dark-haired noncom had beaten her three times in poker, the only person aboard who could.

"We're Marines, not SBs," a young private protested. "We owe our loyalty to the judiciary, not the ship's crew."

"We owe our loyalty to justice," the female corporal sneered. "Fat lot of justice anywhere in the GTE." Her last statement was so quiet Kat had to strain to hear it.

A rumble of agreement rippled around the ready room followed by silence.

If she were leading this squad, she'd be hesitant to have so many bushies in the group. They sounded angry enough to find excuses to strand themselves dirtside. If this lot of combat veterans sided with the natives and mounted a defense against the rest of the crew, they'd have a full-blown mutiny aboard.

It had happened before. Three times in the last decade. Bushie crews had deserted ship en masse and sided with Free Market merchants. One crew surrendered to the Kree rather than serve under a particularly harsh civil captain.

Kat hastened back toward Captain Leonard's office. Now she had a reason to join the landing crew. Someone had to keep the Marines in line and fighting for the right side.

She ran right into Lieutenant Commander M'Berra.

"Excuse me, sir. I wasn't looking where I was going."

"Stand down, Lieutenant," M'Berra smiled. His large white teeth bit at his lip.

"I have serious breaches of loyalty to report, sir. I need to get to Captain Leonard." Kat tried edging around the big black man.

"I heard the talk as well, Kat." He looked back toward the Marine ready room. Still he did not budge from the narrow passageway.

"Then you know, sir, that I must report . . ."

"Consider your report given, Lieutenant." He stared at her with a stern expression Kat could not read. She was too far away from a crystal array for her senses to open and look beyond the surface of the man.

"Sir, in *Jupiter*'s best interest I believe I should accompany the next landing mission." Kat squared her shoulders and stared the man in the eye. They were nearly of a height. She could match him stubborn for stubborn.

"In *Jupiter*'s best interest, I am leading the next landing mission. You stay here and keep an eye on the rest of the Marines."

"But . . . sir."

"Stand down, Lieutenant. You have your orders. And not a word of this to anyone else."

"Yes, sir." Her words lacked her usual enthusiasm.

Konner ran his hands lovingly over the control interface of the IMP lander that had carried him far away from his enemies. Such an efficient machine, well maintained, responsive, and fast. It leaped to obey his slightest touch on the control screens. He didn't even need an electronic pencil to trigger the ignition.

But it had no personality. The ship's voice had no expression, no quirks, just the bland computer-generated tones, neither male nor female. Obedient and unthinking.

"Sorry to do this to you," he said to the colorless voice embedded in the computer.

No response. He hadn't asked for one. That blind obedience of a machine made his task so much easier. He'd never be able to consign *Rover* to the same fate. *Rover*, like *Sirius*, was nearly a member of the family.

"Autopilot on," Konner said firmly.

"Autopilot on," the computer confirmed. The sound irritated Konner with its artificiality.

He punched in the coordinates he wanted.

At the last moment he remembered to program in a thirty-second delay. Then he dove for the exit hatch, quite convenient to the pilot's seat rather than halfway back in the vessel as on *Rover*. The hatch closed automatically as soon as he cleared it.

With a roar that set Konner's teeth on edge and sent a flock of birds into squawking flight, the lander lifted straight up. Beach sand, small rocks, and bits of shell blasted his face. He had to turn and cover his eyes until the debris settled. He risked a look at the vessel as it reached an elevation of thirty meters. At that moment it shot forward. A nice arcing flight up to thirty-five hundred meters, then a straight plunge down into the watery depths at about the center of the ocean.

He watched it fall. "It's just a machine," he reminded himself. "The thing needed a bath anyway, to get rid of that green plant stuff in the outer atmosphere that eats metal." He needed to wash *Rover*. His mission to destroy the beacon had consumed his thoughts for the last full day to the point where he'd forgotten that little idiosyncrasy of this planet. If he left that chore another full day, the plant would begin to compromise the outer hull of his shuttle.

From orbit this world looked green because of a layer of diatomaceous plant life in the upper atmosphere. Passage through the layer left a coating of the metal-eating substance on the vessel. A quick dunk in the bay seemed to take care of it.

"I've got to go back to the volcano," he muttered. Exhaustion suddenly weighed him down. He had to sit a moment. The thought of a return journey to the crater, with twenty IMPs waiting for him with charged weapons did not entice him in the least.

Letting his mind go blank, Konner wrapped his arms around his knees and contemplated the waves lapping at the shore. Low tide. He guessed the sun was well past the zenith by now. He'd been moving every minute since he arose before dawn from a restless night. He'd been running nearly all of his life. Running from the law, running from Melinda, from Mum.

Running from himself.

Who was *he* when not running? A man more comfortable with machines than with people. And he'd just destroyed a magnificent machine.

The hairs on his right arm and at his nape tingled with another presence. He looked, expecting Dalleena. He'd only met the woman yesterday. But after today's adventures, he had grown used to having her at his side.

Disappointment sat heavily in his belly.

"Hello, Irythros."

The dragon sighed as it settled its haunches into the sand beside him. No words. He just sat beside Konner in companionable silence.

Konner felt like he should say something more, but the words lumped in his throat, along with his fatigue and his questions about himself and his life and what he needed to do next.

After many long moments, when the lander was out of sight and its distant roar but a memory, Irythros spoke. (*Your sense of duty is strong. Almost as strong as among dragons.*)

"Is that a compliment?"

(*If you wish.*)

"Right now duty and responsibility are not very attractive to me."

(*They seldom are.*)

Another long silence.

"I'm just so tired, Irythros. I want to stop running. I want . . . I don't know what I want."

The dragon let him think in silence.

(*I do not understand. You are an honorable man. Yet you flee the enforcers of the law. How can you violate law and remain honorable?*)

"Not all law is honorable."

(*Law is law.*)

"Not among humans. You saw how Hanassa perverted law when he was priest to the Coros. He created laws at his own whim and called it religion."

(*Hanassa did not create law. He dictated rules for his own convenience.*)

"Among my people that happens as well. They call it law. They have lawyers, people who do nothing but debate the law and make it more contradictory." Konner let that thought stand between them for a while.

The sun crawled toward the west, changing the angle of light. Shadows grew.

"When I was about ten years old, my father flew away on business. He promised to come back. We never saw him again. The planetary governor, a man appointed by our previous emperor, decided Mum made too much money from a small shipping business. He wanted that money. So he made up a lie and called it law. He sent armed men to arrest Mum. But a friend warned her. She managed to gather her children and flee. The governor's men arrived sooner than we expected. They set fire to the house. In the confusion, my sister Katie got separated and lost.

"Because we fled rather than allow ourselves be arrested, the governor convicted Mum of imaginary crimes *in absentia*. We lost citizenship. We lost our home. We lost our family. We lost everything."

(*And what of your lost sister?*)

"Mum is obsessed with finding her. Without citizenship, we don't have access to resources that will pinpoint her. Without citizenship, we can do nothing legally. So we operate outside the law, always in the hope of one day regaining what was stolen from us."

(*Your lawmakers act much as Hanassa acted.*)

"And so honorable men like me and my brothers must run from the law. And now the law has found us. I am tired of running."

(*Then you must stay.*)

"I have duties and obligations." To his son. To his mother. To the Coros. "And a finite amount of time before I must leave."

(*Then you must allow your enemies to find what you hold dear and make it dear to them.*)

"What is that supposed to mean?"

Irythros did not answer. He rocked to his feet and spread his wings. A few heavy steps with wings flapping and he took flight.

Konner watched him work his way to a respectable altitude before diving into the bay. He entered the water with wings tucked tightly to his sides, horns folded back. A small amount of splash accompanied him. Three heart-beats later, the dragon shot back to the surface with a huge fish wriggling in his maw. Irythros' wings snapped out and he took flight once more.

"I'll never understand how he maneuvers so much bulk so gracefully."

(*You must learn to make air and sea a part of your soul,*) the dragon chuckled as he flew away.

Before Konner could think of a retort, a shout from the embankment behind him drew his attention.

"Dalleena!" he cried as she trudged through the sand toward him.

His body and mind felt lighter. She was safe. He did not fully trust the dragongate he'd thrust her into because he did not understand it. He had not built it, did not know its specifications and vagaries.

He should have known she would be safe. This woman could survive many tribulations and learn from them.

"Dalleena," he said again and gathered her close to his chest. Where she belonged. He kissed her hungrily, as if he had the right. As if her familiar response to him had been a part of their lives forever.

Suddenly he knew what he had to do.

"Let's go surrender to the Imperial Military Police," he said.

CHAPTER 18

✦━·━✦·━✦

THE AIR LIGHTENED within the shadowed arch of a branch of a Tambootie tree in the clearing across the river from the village. Konner took a deep breath of lava-heated air through the opening wormhole. He waited on a count of one hundred. The greens and browns of the forest shifted, brightened, took on reddish tones. Luck smiled upon him. The dragongate opened.

"This won't be easy, but it's our only choice," he reminded his brothers.

"Let's go." Loki bent his knees, ready to launch into the dragongate the femto it fully opened.

"I still don't like this idea," Kim said sotto voce. "Someone could get hurt. Even killed. I don't like leaving Hestiia alone."

Konner grabbed his arm and dragged him through the swirling colors of the portal. He would not think about taking a life. Any life. All life was sacred. Even the IMPs believed that.

Kim grabbed at a low-hanging branch to keep from stumbling. Konner pulled harder to get him through the portal.

He lost contact with all of his senses. He thrust out his arms for balance. But his body was not there to respond. *I will not panic, he told himself.* He tried breathing deeply and regularly. Even though he could not feel his body responding, his mind calmed. The pattern and rotation of the wormhole began to make sense. If he followed this particular eddy of red . . .

He fell out of the portal into the narrow tunnel next to the lava pit.

Sweat streamed down his face and chest. His stomach turned sour in the heat. The smells of hot dust and sulfur could not mask the scent of his own fear. Fuzziness surrounded his vision. His knees wanted to give way. But this was his plan; he had to appear strong and determined for his brothers.

Kim still held the broken branch of Tambootie. A rash began to form where the essential oils in the bark and leaves had penetrated his hand. That should not have happened so quickly. Unless the dragongate intensified the reaction. Or Kim's system was saturated with Tambootie and only needed a little bit more to turn toxic.

Konner took the branch away from Kim. He considered dropping it back into the pit. But the leaves tugged at his senses. He concentrated on breathing, deeply, regularly. His mind cleared. Objects near at hand jumped into focus so clearly and precisely, they appeared to be almost enhanced digital images. He lost the limitation of periphery.

"Let me scout ahead," Loki whispered at the head of the tunnel. He peered out of the opening, took one step, and then two toward the rusting hulk of the generator.

Konner dropped Kim's arm. His left hand began to burn and itch where he held the Tambootie. He transferred the branch to his right hand. Instinctively, he sucked on the worst of the developing rash. Was this the irritant that had caused a similar breakout among the children? If so they had not been playing by the wetlands as they claimed, but had crossed the river and played in the forest against orders from every adult in the village.

Tambootie oils burst upon his tongue. His ears popped and cleared, his eyes honed in on the details of the cave. The solidified lava that encircled him paled and lost density. He peered right through the barrier to the larger cave system. Shadows of men and women wandered past. He saw insignia on collar and sleeve of each uniform, knew the ranks, specialty and . . . and name of each of the techs who prowled the lower caves for hints at the origins of the machinery left by the original colonists.

"Five down below. Confused and uncomfortable. Resentful of that discomfort," Konner said quietly. "They're worried about the water in the creek. The lieutenant issued orders not to drink it."

"How did you know that?" Loki whirled to face him. "Reading minds is my talent." He sounded almost accusatory. Jealous.

Konner thrust the Tambootie branch at him. Kim intercepted it. He looked at the bright green leaves, thick with oil. They'd lost the pink mottling of new leaves.

"We tried this once before, just before Hanassa tried to burn Kim as a sacrifice," Konner reminded them. "It enhances psi talents."

"The drug helped me listen to Hanassa's thoughts and comprehend his motives and his plot," Kim said. He looked back at the silent dragongate. "I knew then how to counter his megalomania. Perhaps, if I listen hard enough, I can find his ghost and the second beacon."

"Later. We need to concentrate on the IMPs. Give me a leaf. We need all the help we can get for this lumbird-brained plan." Loki grabbed the branch and began chewing on a leaf without bothering to strip it from the stem.

"Let's get on with this. I promised Hestiia we'd be home in time for supper. A promise I intend to keep," Kim said.

"And I promised Dalleena," Konner whispered, almost hoping his brothers did not hear him. At the same time he wanted them to know of his growing attachment to the Tracker.

"I vote we surrender to the most junior and gullible of the forensic techs. They have no authority." Loki marched forward.

"Inflate his ego with our surrender and he'll protect us with his own life," Kim chuckled.

Loki walked right up to a smooth-faced recruit—young enough to be on his first assignment—with a receding chin and dark blond hair plastered to his skull with sweat. More sweat stained his uniform shirt.

Loki tapped the boy on the shoulder.

The tech jumped and nearly dropped the instrument he pointed at a column made from cave drip.

"Easy there, son." Konner caught the instrument. He stared at the screen, saw a decimal point out of place and adjusted it. "It will read easier now." He handed the palm-sized gadget back to the boy.

They all stared at each other, shuffling their feet. The tech's mouth hung open in surprise.

"We surrender," Konner said. The corner of his mouth twitched.

"Su . . . surrender?" the boy gulped.

Konner did not need to read his name tag. "Yes, Mr. Saunders. Surrender. We are tired of hiding out in these caves and decided to let the Imperial Military Police feed us. Mighty hot down here." He wiped sweat from his brow.

The boy mimicked him.

"Mind if we get a drink?" Loki asked, taking his cue from Konner.

"I . . . I . . . my canteen is empty," Saunders apologized. He swallowed heavily, as if he had little spit to lubricate his throat.

"That's okay, we'll just get a sip from the creek." Konner began moving toward the stream. They had a lot of cave to traverse before they reached it. But the tunnel upward was right beside it. The Tambootie made him feel as if he could float there, or maybe fly.

"What does the kid want most?" Kim asked Loki on a whisper.

"What all nineteen-year-old men want." Loki shrugged. He looked at the boy long and hard. "Only he's twenty-one. Just inexperienced and socially immature. But good at what he does with forensics."

Saunders stumbled behind the three brothers. He touched his left hip as if expecting a weapon to be holstered there. He was a tech, armed only with instruments. He jerked his hand back and blushed.

"Inefficient of the lieutenant not to issue weapons to all personnel on a dirtside mission," Loki muttered. "Or at least provide more Marines to protect these kids."

"You never know when three desperate outlaws will surrender to you." Konner grinned back at his older brother.

At last they approached the creek. Beside it stood the muscle of the patrol. A squarely built woman surveyed the lower caves. She had a corporal's two chevrons on her sleeve and a stun rifle in her hands. Her dark hair was pulled back into a tight, no-nonsense bun. As Konner and his brothers approached, with Saunders in tow, she watched them warily, bringing her weapon to bear and pointing it squarely at Loki's chest.

He raised his hands in mute surrender. Kim and Konner mimicked him.

"Corporal Sanchez, mind if we get a drink?" Konner asked. The woman's name had jumped into his head at first sight of her. Strange that she thought of herself in terms of her surname rather her given name. He had to search a moment to come up with Paola.

The Tambootie still sang in his blood.

But what did she want most in life?

"Promotion," Kim whispered to him. "She wants control over those who don't measure up to her standards."

"Queen bee with a whole bunch of drones at her beck and call," Loki finished. He scowled. Konner knew Loki had never liked strong women with opinions of their own.

You don't know what you are missing, Konner sighed to himself with thoughts of Dalleena leading the others over the dunes with her hand extended until she spotted the one she tracked. Konner. She had not given up on him when he pushed her through the dragongate. He loved that she took action when she saw the need and never looked back with regret.

Kim looked at the cave ceiling and rocked back on his heels. A light whistle escaped his lips. His wife Hestiia also knew when and how to make decisions, take action, and defy the world when it needed changing.

From what Konner had heard of Loki's lost love, Cyndi, the planetary governor's daughter, she never decided anything—even the selection of a day's wardrobe—without long and deliberate consideration of all the options and the ramifications of each. Then she'd ask for a dozen opinions before selecting and changing her mind three times.

Loki stooped to take a drink, Sanchez followed his movements closely, keeping the rifle pointed directly at his back.

"Report," she barked.

"Th . . . they surrendered," Saunders stammered.

"Surrendered? Unlikely," Sanchez growled.

"True. We surrender," Konner said. He took one step closer to the creek. As foul as the water tasted, he really could use a drink. The heat from the lava core made him long for the hot days of summer in the desert as a relief. He noted the sweat stains on Sanchez's uniform, smelled the rawness of her discomfort as well as her frustration at being stuck down here when the action was supposed to be taking place above this cave.

"We need water. We're tired of hiding out and spending our lives on the run." Konner said. Both true statements.

"This water isn't safe," Sanchez spat.

"Sure it is. We've been living off it for weeks," Loki said. "We cured a plague with this water."

"If you've been here so long, then you must know where this machinery came from." Sanchez gestured with her rifle toward the various generators and transformers.

"Left behind by the original colonists," Konner said. He, too, stooped beside the creek. He took several long slurping drinks, then splashed more water over his face and hair, letting it drip down onto his vest and naked chest. The slight cooling helped banish his doubts about this plan.

Sanchez and Saunders licked their lips and swallowed. Konner deliberately took another long and noisy slurp of water from his hand.

"The remnants of the first colony are scattered all over the planet in small tribal groups," Konner continued. He splashed some more, making sure that some of the drops reached Saunders' pant leg. They evaporated quickly, but not before the kid felt a tiny dot of relief at those spots.

The young tech succumbed to the temptation of the water. He pocketed his sensor and crouched between Loki and Kim. He spat out the first mouthful and screwed up his face in disgust. But then thirst and dehydration overcame the taste of sulfur.

"Very few of the tribal groups are united. The people seem *thirsty* for leadership," Kim said, looking pointedly toward Sanchez.

"Saunders, hold this," Sanchez ordered. She handed the tech her rifle. Dutifully, the boy stood and aimed the weapon in the general direction of the three brothers while the corporal drank. She was made of sterner stuff and swallowed her first taste of the nasty brew. She looked as if she might gag on it, but she kept the liquid down and took more. She, too, doused her face and head, then sighed in momentary relief.

Loki leaned back and looked directly at Saunders. "You know, I'm mighty grateful for the relief you are going to get me. Nothing like a nice long space voyage back to civilization to recover from this planet."

"Re . . . recover from what?" Saunders gulped.

"Being treated like a god by superstitious natives. I don't know about you, but after the first two dozen virgins, the routine gets a little boring. I'm ready for a woman of *experience*. But the locals don't think such a woman is worthy of one of the Stargods." He almost could not keep his chuckles under control.

Certainly Loki had shared his bed with more than a few women in the last five months. Konner, too, had sampled several. Kim had been satisfied only with Hestiia. But none of the village women had to be forced and few had been virgin. Vastly underpopulated before Hanassa's sacrifices depleted their numbers, the Coros had learned to value the birth of children and expanding the gene pool more than worrying about the identity of the father. In a communal village, no child was ever orphaned or disparaged for not knowing his father.

Then, too, the men of this planet took parental responsibilities seriously. Few children were born out of wedlock, but the first one often came three or four moons early.

"Now that tale is just a mite too tall to believe," Sanchez snorted. "Who would think you three thieves are gods?"

"The locals don't know our history," Kim said. He heaved himself to his feet.

"Time to report to the lieutenant. Saunders, bring in the others," Sanchez said. "I imagine Pettigrew will relish locking the infamous O'Hara brothers into the deepest hole, in a heavy gravity hold aboard *Jupiter* and throwing away the key. We'll have you tried, convicted, and into psychological rehab before the next landfall." She grabbed her rifle away from Saunders and gestured with it for them all to stand and march up the tunnel. "Which one of you stole our lander?"

All three brothers stared at her blankly. Konner willed his mind away from all thoughts of a transport vehicle. Any vehicle. He thought of Dalleena's big brown eyes and long dark hair. He thought of her quick intelligence and her courage in the face of the unknown.

"Without the lander, how are you going to get back to the *Jupiter*?" Konner asked mildly.

"We'll find a way to hot-wire your shuttle, if they don't send down a second boat to retrieve us," Saunders said confidently.

"Don't be so sure of that," Konner muttered. He glared at the kid from beneath lowered eyelids.

On the trek back to the upper levels Loki kept up a friendly banter with the kid Saunders, lauding the charms of the local women. The three additional techs who joined them kept rapt attention on Loki's tales.

When they arrived at the hatch of the shuttle, a frantic quality permeated the men and women who bustled about, taking readings with sensors, jumping in and out of *Rover* and reporting back to the lieutenant who lay on a stretcher in the shade of one of the house-sized boulders. Long shadows nearly filled the bowl now that the sun came close to setting behind the western ridge.

Lieutenant Pettigrew struggled to sit up as Sanchez spat her report to him.

Instead of uniform trousers, his legs were now encased in a series of bandages. Konner looked up to the ridge where the dragon had deposited the man this morning. Sure enough the setting sun glinted off the rusting razor wire the original colonists had strung during the civil war that nearly destroyed the entire population.

He hoped the man's tetanus boosters were up to date. They were a long way from a new supply of any but the most basic of natural medicines.

"Which one of you stole my lander?" the lieutenant screamed at the three O'Hara brothers.

Konner and his brothers strove to return his glare with blankness.

"Don't answer that," the lawyer, Sasha Demochitsky called from a knot of IMPs on Pettigrew's other side. In a flash of images, Konner knew everything about her, including her passion for defending the downtrodden, convinced that the GTE accused bushies of invented crimes just to persecute them.

"You mean you didn't parachute down from your cruiser?" Loki asked. His eyes were wide and he sucked on his cheeks to avoid outright laughter. The way his eyes twinkled, he must be having a gay old time.

"You know damn well we didn't," the lieutenant began to froth at the mouth. He spat out the precious moisture.

Sanchez looked as if she wanted to spit, too, but conserved her bodily fluids for more important things.

The techs just found the sky fascinating.

"What do you know of the local cultures?" the anthropologist with the singsong voice rushed up to the brothers and shoved a recorder into their faces. "Are they ready to join the GTE or will they need persuasion?"

Arthur Singh, Ph.D. The title was as much a part of the man's identity as his name. Konner did not need to read this man's mind to know his prejudices against all bushies.

"Had any luck starting up *Rover*?" Konner looked over his shoulder at his shuttle, ignoring the anthropologist.

He saw three figures in the cockpit shaking their heads. "Didn't think so. *We* can fly all of you out of here. Our village women are preparing a hot dinner with lots of fresh water and ale. The river valley offers a much more pleasant climate, too. You and your men can refresh yourselves while you wait for someone to come get you."

A number of the people now milling about licked their lips.

These twenty IMPs had no true shelter and no conditioning to endure the extremes of the desert climate. In about twenty minutes the air would begin to chill as the sun set.

"What's our guarantee that you three won't attempt to escape again?" a sergeant asked. He stepped between Konner and the still spluttering lieutenant.

Konner had no trouble reading his name tag, Duggan. The Tambootie must be wearing off if he couldn't pluck the name from his mind.

"I must advise you . . ." Both men cut off the lawyer with a glare.

Corporal Sanchez relaxed a little. She clearly felt comfortable with Duggan's leadership. But not Pettigrew's.

Konner wondered which family had purchased Pettigrew's commission in the Imperial Military Police. How many promotions would their largesse buy? Mid-thirties and still a lieutenant. He'd not go much farther without a lot more money. And how could Konner and his brothers use that information to implement their plot?

"I'll see you all in hell before I, or my men, fly anywhere with you, O'Hara, unless you are in chains in the brig!" Pettigrew snarled. He lunged to his knees, grabbing at Konner's wrist. His fingers clamped tight, like force bracelet restraints.

His touch sent sharp pains through Konner's arm to his brain. The horizon tipped and twisted. Colors reversed. Pettigrew's head blanched to a grimacing skull.

Konner's head buzzed. His stomach roiled. And his heart felt crushed within his chest.

In that moment, with a trace of the Tambootie still augmenting his senses, he knew without a shadow of a doubt that Pettigrew would die and Konner would be responsible.

CHAPTER 19

◆ — · — ◆ — · — ◆

KIM FOUGHT THE URGE to kneel beside the lieutenant and draw some of the poison out of his wounds from the razor wire. No sense in broadcasting his healing talent to skeptical IMPs.

"Lieutenant Pettigrew has become feverish from his wounds," Sergeant Duggan announced. Then he faced all three brothers equally. "Mr. O'Hara . . . um . . . et al . . . I will gladly delay your arrest for smuggling dangerous and outlawed substances, for resisting arrest, for unauthorized exploration of a lost colony, and for . . . whatever else is on the books against you and your brothers if you will fly us to a more hospitable place where we can get help for Lieutenant Pettigrew."

"And get communications working," a tech advised him. "This place is just plain weird. I can't get a signal in or out."

Kim found it interesting that the man had not asked them to use the shuttle to take them all immediately back to the cruiser in orbit. Why?

"We have enough fuel and lift to get us all back to our village," Loki said. "I'm the pilot in the family." He immediately marched toward *Rover* and entered the shuttle. Half a dozen troops followed him, holstering their weapons.

"We will, of course, need to use your communications equipment to signal *Jupiter* once we are clear of the magnetic disturbances here in the crater," Duggan continued.

"We expected as much," Kim replied. But they'd not get much use out of the system. Kim would make certain of that.

"Ah, Mr. O'Hara," Sanchez insinuated herself between Konner and the sergeant. "What was that creature that nearly killed Lieutenant Pettigrew, and how did you control the beast?" She cleared her throat. "An interesting potential weapon."

Konner smiled. "Irythros is very protective of me. He acts on his own initiative. Dragons don't take kindly to control."

"Just be glad Iianthe was not here," Kim added. "The purple-tip dragon dislikes strangers even more. Especially strangers who brandish weapons indiscriminately."

Lieutenant Pettigrew screamed something incoherent.

Sergeant Duggan gestured to another IMP with a medical caduceus on her collar. The blonde woman sprayed something directly into the lieutenant's face. He fell back against his makeshift litter with a thud and a grin on his face. The medic looked around as if daring anyone to question her cavalier application of strong sedatives.

"Drag . . . dragon!" Saunders and three other recruits within earshot crossed themselves. Paused. Repeated the gesture and began murmuring prayers.

Kim smiled.

This plan might work after all.

The sun was well down below the rim of the crater before all twenty of the IMPs were crammed into the shuttle. Sergeant Duggan and Corporal Sanchez elected to stand behind Loki and Kim, peering over their shoulders and marking every touch they made on the interfaces. Saunders took up a post in the cramped corner of the cockpit. He maintained a proprietary air about the O'Haras, as if they were his personal prisoners.

The engines fired to life at Loki's first command. The sensors and communications responded easily to Kim's touch.

"How'd you get a commercial shuttle to give readouts like that?" Sanchez gasped. "You've got every one of *Jupiter*'s comm satellites on line and we aren't even out of the bowl yet?"

"Who says we have to leave original equipment intact?" Kim smiled at her.

"But the manual . . . ?"

"Got lost on the first shakedown run," Kim muttered.

"Bet Commander Leonard would give her eyeteeth for an array this accurate aboard *Jupiter*," Saunders said.

"Engineer Jorges would go flapdoodle and faint at the violations to the manual," Duggan chuckled.

The flight back to the village seemed to take forever. With the heavy load and limited fuel, Loki kept the speed and altitude low. The grumbles and mutters of discomfort from the main cabin grew louder with each kilometer. Then a few of the IMPs standing near portholes gasped. They were flying over the Great Bay. Phosphorescent life-forms crested the waves. In the diminishing daylight, the ocean sparkled and danced. A behemoth breached and splashed back into the depths right below them.

"Quite a place," Duggan said, his voice tinged with awe.

"We've kept the local culture primitive," Kim said. He wanted to say "unpoisoned" but bit his tongue.

"Makes them more malleable," Loki chimed in.

"They think these clowns are gods," Saunders added, as if he knew everything about the situation—or at least more than the sergeant.

"So we are landing half a klick away from the village and cloaking the shuttle," Kim explained. "And we would appreciate all of your people keeping their instruments and weapons holstered when in contact with *our* people. Your anthropologist should back us up on that."

"From what I hear, there's another instrument we don't have to keep holstered," Saunders said on a deep blush.

"Keep it to yourself," Sanchez barked before Kim could.

Suddenly, this part of the plan did not seem so good. Kim knew what they had to do, but to expose Hestiia and the rest of the Coros to these crude . . . barbarians . . . Marines!

Loki killed the internal and external lights.

"Brace yourselves. This isn't going to be pretty or comfortable," Loki called out. The shuttle bumped the ground, bounced, tilted, and thudded into place. All of the IMPs teetered and crashed into each other. The three O'Hara brothers shared a mischievous glance. They were strapped in and weathered the rough landing with ease.

"We're gonna crash!" A voice screamed in the back.

Surreptitiously, Loki moved his hand to another control while Duggan and Sanchez were righting themselves.

"Hey! The hatch won't open," a voice called from the cabin.

"Get us out of here. Life support is going down."

"I can't breathe."

"Lights! I can't see."

Duggan shoved aside the metallic cloth curtain that separated the cockpit from the cabin. "Quiet down!" he ordered the troops. "We'll get you out in due order." Then he turned a malevolent visage upon all three brothers. "Open the damn hatch before I forget that all life is sacred and throttle the three of you with my bare hands."

"Certainly, Sergeant," Loki replied as if nothing were wrong at all. He touched a different control. All of the lights came on in a blinding glare.

Kim edged his hand toward the red triangle in the corner of his interface. Once the men were outside, he could render them all unconscious with a quick blast of the sonics.

Konner shook his head at him. "Not yet, little brother. Don't reveal your cards until the last chip is played."

"You've been quiet since we took off," Kim said.

Duggan bellowed orders for the orderly dispersal of his troops. Kim did not think anyone heard his own comment over the noise.

Suddenly the cockpit emptied of excess people and noise. Even Loki had disembarked. The silence seemed alien.

"How did you live with yourself when you killed that man?" Konner asked suddenly.

Kim searched his brother's face for signs of distress that triggered his question. The incident had happened years ago, but he'd never told his brothers until after Loki had been forced to kill Hanassa. Like Kim, Loki had shared the moment of death with his victim, nearly willing himself to die in the process.

"I had to go through the motions of living. For Mum. For you and Loki. I had to keep putting one foot in front of the other, day after day. Why? Did you kill someone on your adventures today?"

"No. I have not killed a man yet. But I had a precognitive experience. Must have been induced by the Tambootie. I haven't done the deed and I already feel as if my guts have been ripped out." Konner slumped.

Kim had never seen him so upset. So . . . reduced.

"Then maybe you don't have to kill anyone. The one thing I have learned from experimenting with psi powers and Tambootie: the future is fluid. The few glimpses we get are warnings of one possibility. Each choice we make opens dozens of new possibilities. Maybe you were granted the premonition so you *won't* kill another human being."

"I certainly hope you are right." Konner looked a little brighter, a little less fatigued.

"Come on, big brother. Let's go get some supper." Kim slapped Konner on the back and urged him out of the shuttle.

Outside, they found the IMPs grumbling about the hike across open country to their destination. Duggan commandeered Kim and his brothers to handle the lieutenant's litter along with the medic. They led the way toward home.

Home. Kim savored the word. This forgotten planet three sectors off charted space had become home. The villagers and Hestiia were his family now. He never wanted to leave, even to see Mum one more time and explain to her why he had to stay.

Mum would get over his absence. He didn't want Hestiia to try to get over it if he left.

The savory smell of roasting meat and vegetables reached the troop before they sighted the cooking fires. All around Kim, men and women started licking their lips and hastening their steps.

"I thought you told the girls no meat," Konner whispered to Kim across the litter from him, and heedless of the medic in front of Kim.

"I did."

"Meat won't stop this greedy bunch of hypocrites," the medic snorted. "Every bush planet we encounter, that's the first thing they head for. I can't convince them they don't need meat to satisfy their nutritional needs. I can't tell them anything. They are too busy bickering among themselves to listen to anyone. You think the class system at the Emperor's court is strict? Try getting workshirts to sit down at the same table in the officers' mess with cleanshirts. Try getting the defense team to talk to the prosecution. Try getting forensics to talk to the Marines. Or one anthropologist to agree with the other on the time of day or day of the week. Then there's Captain Leonard and Judge Balinakas." She looked as if she wanted to pound her fist into someone's jaw—anyone who got in her way.

"In that case, half the plan is already implemented." Konner quirked up half his mouth.

But his smile did not convince Kim. "Must have been one nasty precog episode," Kim muttered.

"It was."

"Getting a headache yet?" he asked. His own head had begun to throb. Withdrawal from the Tambootie. He'd only ingested a small amount of the oils. His mouth salivated at the thought of tasting the oils again, of feeling the flavors burst upon his tongue and open his senses. His hands began to shake.

Just how addictive was the drug?

"Sometimes it takes a month to get the stink of meat out of the ship," the medic continued her litany of grief. "Even with the best air scrubbers available."

Kim looked closer at her uniform. In the gloom he thought he saw a name tag that said "Lotski." Did she have any gamma blockers in her kit to break addictions? Maybe all he needed were a few judiciously placed micro amps to the affected brain synapses. Then he could use the Tambootie with impunity.

The troop crested the last low hill before the village. The glow from the central fire lit the ridgeline.

"Duggan," Loki called the sergeant. "Best my brothers and I lead the group. Don't want you punctured by a spear or brained by a club. The blacksmith totes a really mean hammer."

The IMPs halted their plunge down the hill to wait for Kim and his brothers. The weight of the litter had slowed them down considerably. Or was it reluctance to let these invaders into their home?

Several figures stood between the troop and the fire. Backlit, Kim could not distinguish features. But he picked out Hestiia at the front of the welcoming committee. He'd know her anywhere. His heart speeded up in anticipation of holding her close once more.

He hastened his steps, forcing the other three with the litter to match his pace.

The rest of the waiting figures became clearer. All women. They moved forward bearing armloads of flowers, greens, and gourds. Just as they began bestowing their fragrant gifts upon the IMPs, Kim realized each and every one of them was naked to the waist.

Including his wife.

CHAPTER 20

◆—— · ——◆—— · ——◆

DALLEENA SWALLOWED her embarrassment at having twelve strange men stare at her naked breasts. In her home village, and all the villages that had employed her as Tracker, she had been separate from womenfolk and their customs. She was Tracker, different, independent. She had worn men's clothing as a sign of her equality with them. Women had worn a simple sarong in spring and summer and little else until a man claimed them. Then and only then could they expect to cover their breasts in any but the coldest seasons.

Now Dalleena and all the other women exposed themselves to trap the invaders in their own lust. She swallowed her self-consciousness for the sake of the plan.

Then she caught sight of Konner staring at her. A deep frown creased his face. She straightened her shoulders with pride and met the next foreigner with a proffered blossom and a smile. Konner's scowl deepened.

Her assurance firmed.

The few women in the group of foreigners mimicked Konner's expression.

Then Raaskan, headman for the village, and three other men, wearing only their short buckskin trews and vests moved up and bestowed flowers upon the females. Bright smiles spread all around.

"Remember what happened to the *HMS Bounty* when they received a similar greeting from primitives," a man shouted even as he accepted two flowers from Poolie, Raaskan's wife.

"The mutineers from the *Bounty* succumbed to the allure of the native women and embraced a primitive way of life," Konner whispered in Dalleena's ear. "They went bush."

Dalleena just twitched her hips and moved on. She had one more flower to give. She stared at it a moment. Then she stepped daintily back to Konner and gave it to him. He dropped his corner of the litter abruptly. The injured man moaned and thrashed. The others set down the rest of the litter with a little more care. Not much though.

Kim rushed to Hestiia's side and draped his arm possessively about her shoulders.

Loki ambled toward the center of the group. He accepted a cup of ale and began a jolly round of swapping tall tales with the visitors.

Konner grabbed Dalleena about the waist with both hands. He looked at her long and hard from beneath heavy eyelids. Then he kissed her. Hot. Possessive. Insistent.

"You know what you have to do?" he whispered into her ear.

"But what do you *want* me to do?" Languor made her limbs heavy and her mind slow. The heat throbbing from his hands where he grasped her tightly sapped her strength and her will. She could no more separate from him now than she could cease to obey the tracking instinct.

"Later." Konner kissed her quickly and thrust her aside.

She almost stumbled. Strange, rough hands steadied her from behind. Those same strange hands began wandering all over her chest.

Dalleena gritted her teeth and turned to her would-be rescuer with a smile.

"You giving her up for the night?" a voice as rough as the hands asked Konner. The man had slowed his speech to a recognizable dialect. Probably the effect of hastily quaffed ale.

"Her choice," Konner replied. He turned his attention back to the now thrashing figure on the litter. "Always the woman's choice here. Not the man's." His voice grew heavy with warning.

Did she detect reluctance to leave her in his posture?

Pryth waddled over with her pouches of herbs and salves. She, too, had left her breasts uncovered. The pendulous sacs swung as she moved.

She and the blonde woman who had helped with the litter entered into a detailed discussion of infection that led to locking jaws.

Dalleena detected a sneer on the face of the man who tried to hold her. Then he turned his disproving gaze back to her and smiled.

"I don't like a lot of fat on my women," he muttered.

Dalleena decided not to take offense at his comment. Today. Tomorrow might be different. Deftly, she inserted her arm in his and led him to the cask of ale. His hand grabbed her bottom as she walked. She let her own hand drift about his hips until she found the square outlines of a comm unit in his pocket. She slid it free and tucked it into the waist of her sarong.

All around her the Coros, male and female, relieved their guests of every trace of contact with the mother ship. As they passed a one-eyed old woman, seated just outside the circle of light from the fire, they dropped the instruments into her lap. She then secreted them about her person with a near toothless grin.

Taneeo sat in the place of honor beside the fire with his splinted leg stretched out before him. He scowled into his cup of ale, never meeting the gaze of any who greeted him.

A shiver ran down Dalleena's spine that had nothing to do with the evening breeze on her bare skin.

Loki grabbed a handful of fresh vegetables from the heaping bowls scattered around the village common. The sweet yampion root crunched under his teeth. He let the tastes and textures linger in his mouth a moment before launching into his next recounting of his adventures. He carefully avoided mentioning that he had pulled the trigger on the needle rifle that finally felled his nemesis. This bunch of IMPs might be a bloodthirsty lot in comparison to most civils—those raised on civilized planets as opposed to those raised in the bush. Still, IMPs had taken oaths to uphold the sanctity of all life, even the lives of outlaws such as himself.

"So this guy actually slit the throats of his victims?" Sergeant Ross Duggan grimaced. Then he quaffed a cup of ale.

"And he enjoyed it," Loki said. "Three times we thought him dead. Twice he came back to life." And maybe a third time.

Loki looked around hastily. The hairs on his nape prickled as if someone watched him. Pryth, the ancient wisewoman and local healer seemed to follow his every move with her eyes. Had she been corrupted by the spirit of Hanassa as Taneeo suggested?

Pryth was strong of will as well as body. She had never succumbed to Hanassa during his lifetime. Yet Loki could not trust her. She never accepted help if she had any other option. And she made her own decisions.

She was too much like Mum.

Loki could not trust her.

"We had no choice but to take him out the only way we could," he finished the story. He repeated to himself that he had had no other choice. He had to pull the trigger of the needle rifle and end Hanassa's tyranny over all of the Coros. He had to end the wholesale slavery. He had to destroy the bloody worship of the false god Simurgh.

No one else could have done it. No one else would have done it.

"Yeah, this place would never grow with a meat eater like that keeping the population down and instilling superstition and actually fostering slavery." Sanchez munched on a handful of crisp wild onions. She moaned in ecstasy as she savored each bite. "This place is some kind of Utopia. Can't see why you guys want to leave."

Loki grinned and handed the corporal a bowl of stewed sweet yampion. She had the compact stature of a civil, but something about her accent and the fierceness in her eyes suggested a different ancestry.

Duggan reached over her shoulder and snitched a chunk of roasted lily. He nodded his head in eager agreement with Loki's words.

A drum and flute began a lively tune.

"Who said we intend to leave?" Loki raised his eyebrows.

"But . . . but you surrendered?"

"Did we? Or did we kidnap you into the local version of Nirvana?"

A busty brunette, dressed only in a short sarong, grabbed Duggan's hand and dragged him toward the festival pylon standing tall at the center of the village. Long streamers of red-leafed vines trailed from the top. Flowers, grains, and tiny squash decorated the pylon as well as the vines. The brunette skipped and hopped in the opening steps of a celebratory dance. Grinning, Duggan copied her movements.

Loki allowed himself to be dragged into the dance with Sanchez.

Other couples joined them. Newcomers, men and women alike, had streamers thrust into their hands. The locals pushed and maneuvered them around and around the pylon until they were all quite dizzy.

All the while, the drum and flute kept up a throbbing and sensual rhythm. More ale flowed.

Locals changed partners and places. Corporal Sanchez's sturdy hand caressed Loki's as she passed him. A thrill of excitement coursed through his body. Or was it revulsion. She was another strong woman who made her own decisions.

But, unlike Mum, her expressions remained open and honest.

Couples wandered off into the darkness, limbs entwined, mouths locked together.

Loki accepted the invitation in Paola Sanchez's eyes.

The drum pounded in time with the hot blood pulsing in his veins.

CHAPTER 21

◆——·——◆——·——◆

MARTIN STARED BLANKLY at the holoimage of the HD™ 37000 in the center of his screen. He'd left the image there to distract Melinda when she hacked into his system. No matter how many fire walls he erected, she always had better software. So he left decoys to send her off in wrong directions.

"Marty!" Bruce's image jumped to the top layer of programs running on Martin's screen.

"What? Did you find something?" Martin sent a series of algorithms and wave differential equations to sleep, boosting Bruce's image.

"I think I hit the jackpot," Bruce almost whispered. He looked over his shoulder as if he suspected adult eavesdroppers. "I found a minority report on the accident that killed your grandparents."

"A minority report?" Martin had never heard of such a thing connected to anything but judicial opinions.

"Yeah, an IMP detective wasn't convinced it was an accident. He filed a report differing from official record. The guy must have had enough rank and prestige the courts couldn't ignore it, but they didn't agree with his assessment. So they buried the report, pretended it didn't exist without actually destroying it."

"Does Melinda, my mother, know about this report?"

"Probably not. She didn't have my dad destroy it." Bruce grinned.

"What does it say?" Martin suddenly felt cold to the core of his being.

"Major Van der Hooten said, and I quote, 'Weapons residue on the hull surface indicates the vessel exploded from an external blast rather than an internal malfunction. Such residue is consistent with weaponry carried by independent merchants for defense against pirates.'"

"An independent merchant? Anything else?"

"Nothing useful. I've got Jane Q backtracking flight plans for the dates one month either side of the accident. That would be a lot easier with a Klip, though."

"Good work, Bruce. And forget the Klip. We don't want to get caught tapping private data and draining power from bigger systems." Martin began to shiver. He did not like the implications of the minority report. His mother's corporation owned most of the vessels piloted by "independent merchants" who flew in and out of Aurora. Her parents had been barely out of the Aurora system on their way to the first jump point when the "accident" occurred. A small independent vessel attacking them would have to come from Aurora.

"Any luck on finding your birth certificate?" Bruce asked.

"No. No adoption papers either in any of Aurora's courts. Of course, Melinda could have gone offworld for my birth. Still, you'd think she'd want to stay here with her own doctor and nurses in a private clinic."

"That's what I think, too. Kurt has a new program for tracking deleted files. He's working on that marriage license. I'll have him download a copy of the software to you so you can check more deeply."

"Thanks, Bruce. I did find out that Melinda had Konner O'Hara arrested and exiled about a month after the date of the deleted record. Eight Terran months before I was born."

"Just long enough for her to confirm her pregnancy and be pretty sure she wouldn't miscarry." Bruce whistled through clenched teeth.

"Evidence is mounting that Mom married Konner, got pregnant, and then got rid of him," Martin muttered. "But why would she arrange her parents' death and not Konner's?"

"Look at the money trail, Marty. It's always about money."

"Something about the inheritance, I bet. I should be able to flush out a copy of my grandparents' will."

"If you can't get it locally, I might be able to find something at Earth Central. An inheritance as big as an entire planet would have to be registered there."

"Keep in touch, Bruce. This is getting interesting."

"Sure 'nough. Konner's a good guy. Best counselor at camp. We missed him this summer. Missed you, too." He signed off.

"Konner—Dad?" Martin tried out the sound of the word on his tongue. It sounded fine, slipped out of his mouth much easier than "Mom" or "Mother" when he thought about Melinda.

"Scaramouch, call up Super Snooper™," he ordered his computer.

The icon of two fencers clashing blades progressed back and forth across the screen indicating the machine needed time to process the request. Martin watched the chronometer tick off the seconds while he waited. When the fencers stabbed each other and their blood burst forth in a kaleidoscope of unrelated dots and lines, Martin donned his VR gear.

The dots and lines resolved into the three-dimensional image of a slender man with sharp features wearing a tweed Inverness cape and deerstalker cap who strode purposefully into the screen area. He carried a large meerschaum pipe and an old-fashioned magnifying glass.

"The game is afoot, Master Martin," he said in clipped tones. An edge of excitement tinged his voice.

"I need to know if anyone over at the port has noticed that I moved the 'no access' order for Martin Konner O'Hara, ship *Sirius*," Martin said.

"A disguise is in order, Master Martin." The detective shed his cape and cap to reveal the rough coveralls of a dock worker. He shifted his posture to suggest broader shoulders. His aquiline features spread and flattened.

These changes merely symbolized the signature masking taking place deep within the computer. Every computer on Aurora—except possibly Melinda's—had a registered signature that could be traced by the authorities back to the user. Alteration of that signature carried heavy monetary and criminal penalties. If he got caught.

Martin had no intention of getting caught. All he needed was one quick look at the harbormaster's calendar.

"You will need more memory available to complete this task, Master Martin," the detective said in a monotone—a clear indication that the huge Super Snooper™ program struggled to work within the constraints of Martin's computer. Melinda's would have been able to handle both the program and the holoimage.

"Scaramouch, cancel HD™ 37000." He waved his hand across the holo screen. In the wake of his gesture, a telltale afterimage of green fire followed his hand movement. Someone monitored his activity.

Guess who? Melinda. She was the only one in the entire corporate headquarters/mansion who had the hardware and software to beat him at his own game.

"Super Snooper, remove observer."

"Are you certain, Master Martin, that you wish to alert the observer by forcing them out of the program?" The detective had resumed his costume of Inverness cape and deerstalker cap.

"Alternatives?" Martin asked.

"Diversion." The detective smiled. Mischief glinted in his holoimage eyes.

"Do it!" Martin agreed. The detective pulled a leathersynth strap about one meter in length from the capacious pocket of his cape. A canine—the likes of which had never been seen on Aurora except in holoimage—sprang from the white background and loped over to the detective. It sat on the man's foot and looked up at him imploringly.

Martin wanted to reach out and pet the creature. He'd always wanted a pet, but Melinda had frowned on the practice of domesticating alien species. Besides, she did not want to live with the dirt she supposed such creatures carried around in their fur. The air filters in the mansion design could easily compensate for any foreign particles, but Melinda still refused Martin permission. She probably did not want to deal with any being she could not control through money or coercion. The emotions of love and loyalty were too foreign to her.

On the holo screen, the detective snapped the end of the strap onto the dog's collar, then he pointed at the remnants of the telltale around the still intact pedcycle. The dog sniffed around the image and then took off howling in a new direction.

The detective let the long strap slide through his fingers and turned back to Martin. "Toby will lead the observer into the marketplace where you presumably are shopping for your birthday present," he said as he resumed his dock worker disguise. "Now, Master Martin, we shall proceed on our current mission."

The white screen dissolved to be replaced with the cubicle in the port authority offices where the harbormaster presided. The office was small but just as pretentious in furnishing as Melinda's. A large woodsynth desk filled nearly every square centimeter of open space. One blank wall was dedicated to holo equipment. Another wall looked out on the spaceport through a bioglass panel nearly as large and expensive as the one in Martin's suite. The other two walls were covered in holos of antique vessels designed for atmosphere flight only. Nothing lay upon the shiny surface of the desk; no notes, writing implements, day-planners, calendars, or maps. Since the demise of paper as a communication medium—even before faster-than-light travel—desks had become obsolete. Melinda Fortesque had one in her office that she used as a symbolic barrier between herself and whoever dared approach her. The harbormaster must have adopted the tactic in imitation of his boss.

The harbormaster himself leaned back in his Lazy-former® while he shifted icons around on his holo screen. Vessels and cargoes moved from box to box, indicating times and docks at the orbiting space station above Aurora. Shuttles indicated the ferrying of goods and personnel between the station and the big FTL vessels in orbit and the surface. Dock crews and equipment moved from the shuttles to assigned warehouses. Customs officials scuttled behind the operations every step of the way.

Martin's detective wiggled his way around the desk and stared at the screen from behind the harbormaster's shoulder, examining every aspect of the operation. Martin watched from the viewpoint of the doorway—without ever leaving his Lazy-forme® in his own suite.

A communication icon popped into the habormaster's screen. The port official froze his manipulations to touch the icon with a single fingertip.

Before the caller could appear on the screen, the detective used the interruption to step into the screen behind a warehouse.

Martin sensed his man working his way from one place of concealment to the next while the harbormaster yelled at one of his underlings for having lost a box of freeze-dried artichoke hearts intended for Melinda Fortesque. The Terran delicacy would not grow on Aurora. Melinda loved them and imported them regularly. Only she, on all of Aurora could afford the exotic food.

The calendar in the corner of the harbormaster's screen blinked twice and faded. A replica appeared in the center of Martin's screen, the harbormaster's office disappeared. The entry barring Konner O'Hara and his ship *Sirius* from landing on Aurora or docking at the space station for anything other than emergency repairs and medical service was still circled in red and remained on today's date. No one had moved it back to two weeks from Tuesday.

Martin breathed a sigh of relief. Deftly, he moved the item again to *three* weeks ago and recalled his detective.

He expected the man to walk out of the screen. Instead, a glowing green blob of light appeared at the bottom of the screen. It grew rapidly, expanding with many flashes of red, yellow, and purple flames bursting from its edges. Three seconds later, Melinda Fortesque exploded onto the screen. A lock of her sleek brown hair strayed from her coif and drooped over her brow. Her green suit jacket rode her shoulders slightly askew and a scuff marred her green shoes.

Whatever she had been doing had demanded all of her attention and energy.

"Yes, Melinda?" Martin ripped off his VR gear and faced his mother, trying desperately to school his face into impassivity.

"Martin, you have no business snooping around the docks." She didn't say he had no business using the Super Snooper™ software.

"But, Melinda, I wanted to know if my birthday present has arrived yet." Not a total lie.

"Konner O'Hara will not be bringing you anything. That man will never pollute our planet again." She nearly hissed in her anger. With a snap of her fingers, her red-circled entry moved to today's date with a permanent ban icon beside it.

"But, Melinda, he's my friend. Last summer he promised to come to my birthday party!"

"Last summer?"

"He's a counselor at my camp."

"Not anymore! He will be fired and blackballed as of today. And you are grounded. No more networking. I'm putting a lock on your screen. The only work you are authorized to do from now on is schoolwork. And don't try to get past me with your snooper software. It's outdated. I have the only copy of the upgrade. That's how I traced your activity. Now get back to your assignments. I believe you have wave differential homework. I shall also replace your tutor for allowing you too much free time for this—this disgusting activity."

Melinda dissolved from the screen, leaving Martin with a pile of graphs and equations. All traces of the pedcycle and his detective vanished along with Martin's hopes for escaping Aurora and his mother.

The one I should trust but cannot because he smells wrong seeks to deceive Stargod Konner. He plots in secret with the Invaders. What can I do? I dare not kill this man. Dragons have made a pact not to kill these lesser beings. The rogue dragon, Simurgh, hunted them for many decades with malice rather than hunger. We will not follow his behavior. What to do? What to do?

Loki woke with a smile on his face. Until Sanchez spoke.

"I hope you realize that last night does not mean I want any kind of commitment from you," she said.

Loki looked up through heavy eyelids. She stood over him, literally, feet braced on either side of his knees, hands on hips, and her lustrous dark hair cascading down her back.

She had donned her uniform shirt and underwear, scanty undergarments at that, but left off the trousers and boots. A magnificent Amazon.

Part of Loki thrilled at her stark beauty. The rest of him recoiled from her strength and decisiveness. In a brawl or wrestling match she might come out on top. He'd never lost either.

Sanchez reminded him of Pryth. He could not trust Pryth. Taneeo had warned him against the woman.

"Who said anything about a commitment?" Loki shrugged. "We were just celebrating the harvest. These people make any excuse they can to celebrate."

"If this place is as underpopulated as initial scans indicate, the influx of twenty newcomers to swell the gene pool is also cause for major celebration."

Loki stared at her without comment, wondering what leap of logic she would take next. Would she land on his side of the struggle for control of the planet? Or would she be like Pryth and betray him?

He'd trust Mum before he trusted Pryth or Sanchez.

"Though I did notice at the end of the evening all of the couples were strictly local," Sanchez continued. "Most of my people are passed out around the remnants of the bonfire. I seem to be the only one who got lucky. Strange behavior for people more interested in genes than parenthood."

Loki nearly choked. "You noticed."

"Yeah, I noticed a lot of things. Like your people stole all of our comm units. I figure Captain Leonard will send down a rescue boat as soon as dawn reaches that volcano, our last known location. When they don't find twenty IMPs and three prisoners, and a lander, they'll come looking for the rest of us and spot your shuttle. What level of tech are you planning to bring these people up to? I presume you'll find a way to stall it just short of industrialization."

"What?" Loki sat up, scooting backward and drawing up his knees so that she no longer trapped him. "The . . . uh shuttle is cloaked. They'll never find it."

Sanchez shrugged, dismissing his comment. "You and your brothers aren't as dumb as Lieutenant Horatio Pettigrew. But your plan to entice the entire crew dirtside and then keep them here so your precious little Utopia remains a secret is obvious."

"Only if you say so." Loki stood up, ready to bolt around her and out the door. He should be whispering enticements to this woman to induce her to stay. Instead she laid out *her* plans as if organizing a battle.

"Why would you want to stay here, if, that is, I was planning such a thing?" he asked. He really did want to know, besides distracting her.

"Because back home my family is poor, and bushie. I enlisted ten years ago. Graduated first in my class at Basic and every bit of training since. If I'm lucky, I might make sergeant in another ten years. Meanwhile, dome-breathing rich boys like Horatio Pettigrew buy into a commission and get promoted every time the family comes up with more money. I figure I can sign on with some petty king here and command an entire army." She shrugged as if her explanation were obvious.

The movement drew Loki's attention to her well proportioned attractions. He had a sudden image of her striding into battle, wearing only a sarong and carrying a sword and ax, yelling obscenities at her enemies. His body grew tight with longing.

"How many IMPs will follow you?" Loki stepped closer, ready to kiss Sanchez with all the passion he'd reserved for Cyndi if she gave the right response.

"I can count on fifteen. Five already dirtside, ten more on board. Duggan is the one we have to convince. Give him a job he can sink his teeth into and he'll bring at least one hundred troops to our side. Marines, communications, and forensic. Our other anthropologist will go bush at the least provocation. Don't count on Singh for anything."

"And I have just the job for Duggan," Konner said. He poked his head around the curtain that divided the cabin. Dalleena's head appeared just below his. Neither of them had on much in the way of clothing.

Instead of surprise, Loki registered satisfaction at the evidence of a growing relationship between the two. Konner needed human companionship. He spent too much time talking to his crystals and machines.

"What job?" Loki and Sanchez asked in unison.

"Something big and dangerous that is keeping the biggest port city on this planet from growing outside some very stout walls." Konner stepped into Loki's half of the cabin, pulling on his trousers as he talked. "And your rescue boat will not find the shuttle. I've got it cloaked."

"Like your mother ship. Best sensors in the galaxy and we couldn't locate it. Not even by looking where there appeared to be nothing." Sanchez grunted with something akin to admiration.

"Did you find another ship in orbit, possibly a small one-man merchant vessel?" Dalleena asked.

Where had she come up with the vocabulary?

"No, but I did hear reports of a fireball hot enough to burn cerama/metal. Hate to think what could trigger a fire that hot on this primitive place."

"Sam Eyeam," Konner breathed. "Did he and the second beacon survive?"

"Second beacon still beeping, last I heard," Sanchez replied.

"What?" Loki took a step closer to his brother.

"Tell you later." Konner grabbed his shirt and finished dressing.

"Could Irythros set fire to Sam Eyeam's ship?" Dalleena asked. She moved closer to Konner as if seeking shelter.

"Unknown."

"Irythros, the dragon?" Sanchez looked as if she needed to grab a weapon.

"Yeah, a dragon," Loki replied. He began to make connections. Sam Eyeam, the name most black-market merchants took to hide their true identity. A dirtside ship on fire. A dragon in the vicinity.

And a second beacon.

He shuddered and resisted crossing his wrists and flapping his hands. He did not want to think about the possibility of a human being caught in that blaze.

"If we open up that port to more than a small portion of the coast," Konner continued, "we'll have the beginnings of a major trade network. We need trade to grow to a high medieval level of society and technology."

"You'll also need sailing ships and some primitive navigation," Loki mused. Better to concentrate on future plans than dwell on yesterday's horrors.

"I've got just the people you need for that." Excitement glowed in Sanchez's eyes. "You two just signed on your first ally." Suddenly she looked quite beautiful.

Loki wanted to trust her. He really did.

CHAPTER 22

✦━━━•━━━✦━━━•━━━✦

"THERE'S A ROGUE DRAGON preying on trading caravans," Konner told Sergeant Duggan. He made up a reason for the port city to remain huddled behind stout walls.

He sat beside the blond sergeant on matching rocks near the communal fire. Konner absently stirred his morning porridge with a wooden spoon. The grain mixture was sweetened with berries and fresh milk. Normally, he gulped his breakfast, too concerned with what he had to do that day to think about the fuel he put into his stomach.

Now he contemplated how well the cereal "stuck to his ribs." He often went five or six hours after breakfast without even thinking about food.

If he thought about what he needed to do today, he'd feel guilty about the lies and deceptions he spread among the IMPs.

"What concern of mine is a rogue dragon?" Duggan asked. He, too, stared at his bowl. "This is really good. I could make a fortune packaging and selling this back home."

"The GTE won't let anyone make a fortune on food." That at least was the truth. He had to give each and every member of the *Jupiter*'s crew a vested interest in preserving this planet. "The powers that be will move in their corporate employees to run the farms. All surplus goes into Imperial warehouses for distribution."

"Smugglers could make a great deal of money . . ."

Konner turned a blazing smile on the man.

"But we'd have to keep this planet's existence a secret from the rest of the galaxy," Duggan finished for him.

"How big a cut do you want?" This was the hard part. Talking money when all Konner wanted was to grab Dalleena and run for Aurora. Martin's fourteenth birthday approached. Two weeks from today. Would the crystals aboard *Sirius* be ready?

Rover ran low on fuel. He needed to steal the next lander from *Jupiter* and drain its fuel cells.

"Not certain you can give me what I truly want," Duggan said quietly.

"This planet is under populated. You could claim a big hunk of it and crown yourself king."

"Can you get my parents and my wife and kids out of debt indenture?"

"Shit! Which planet?" Only fringe worlds of the Galactic Free Market (translate that as pirates) still practiced debt indenture. Konner and his brothers had taken refuge on most of them at one time or another.

"Mehican V."

"Shit." The worst pirate world in the known galaxy. No laws. No rulers. Just bullies lording it over weaker folk. Weaker translated as poorer, less cruel, or less self-serving. Debt indentures might as well be slaves working mines and factories in bleak conditions.

"Yeah. Shit. Only reason I signed on with the IMPs was to earn some cash to pay off the debt. Trouble is the interest grows faster than my annual salary."

"You help us and the first profit goes to paying off those debts."

"What about your own profit? Heard you three are trying to bribe your way back to citizenship. You need to clear your names. Going to take a heap of A dols to do that."

"Auroran currency is the most stable in the Empire. Melinda Fortesque owns all of Aurora and therefore all of the A dols. She has a big grudge against me. Getting my hands on any of her money is next to impossible." Going to be hard enough to liberate his son from the woman's greedy claws, even if he won legal custody.

"Do we need to take care of this rogue dragon in order to open up more farmland?"

Konner took a deep breath before spitting out his next lie.

He couldn't do it. Duggan was being honest and helpful.

"Truth is, I don't know what is preying on the largest port city we've found. I do know that we need those trade caravans to bring produce to a central market."

"Let's go scout the territory." Duggan stretched up and stood. He looked at his bowl quizzically. "We supposed to wash these or something?"

"Big cauldron beside the fire. Filled with warm water and a root that makes good suds. Also a fine antibacterial." Konner stood and added his own empty bowl and spoon to the mix. "Uh, rinse your spoon and keep it. Along with your utility knife. We all carry our own utensils. That way we don't deprive someone else of theirs if we happen to be away from home."

"We've got mess kits aboard the lander . . ."

"Ditched it."

"In the ocean?" Duggan looked pained. "We could have cannibalized it for tools, bedding, canteens, rations . . . survival."

"I know. Hurt like hell to kill a machine, but it had to be done. I couldn't let *Jupiter* find us too quickly by locking sensors onto the lander. But now I can't even steal fuel from it."

"Shit! Now what do we do?"

"Set a trap for the next lander?" Konner grinned at his new friend.

"Guess we better find something to do away from camp before Pettigrew starts bellowing orders." Duggan rotated his shoulders and surveyed the perimeter of the tidy village.

"And Arthur Singh, Ph.D, tries to convert us to the joys of rejoining civilization."

They both grinned at the man who stretched groggily on the other side of the fire. His turban tilted over one eye and his uniform looked as if a dragon had stepped upon it. He held his head in his hands and moaned.

"Hangover," Duggan said and pointed the anthropologist toward the bright-eyed medic who was dispensing analgesic sprays to all comers. "His first, I think. Guess he didn't recognize your local brew as alcoholic since it didn't come with a label. He's big on putting labels on everything, including people."

"Pryth has taken Lieutenant Pettigrew to . . . ah . . . her bosom so to speak. We won't worry about him for a while."

"Pryth?"

"Local wisewoman and healer."

"Big—?" Duggan held his hands in front of his chest, cupped.

"That's our Pryth. Earth Mother personified. She won't take any nonsense from him and she'll probably keep him restrained to let his wounds heal."

"Can't exactly call her an 'Earth Mother' since we aren't on Earth."

"We've been thinking about that. Haven't agreed on a good name for this planet yet. We certainly need something better than MKO-IV."

"Something close to the heart." Duggan grew silent for a moment while he stared at the flames beneath the cereal cauldron. "*Jupiter* is very close to Captain Leonard's heart. As long as there is a ship in orbit and a chance to fly it home, Amanda Leonard will not leave *Jupiter*."

Was he envisioning his ship going down in flames?

"All we have to do is get the orbit to decay. Once it passes through the outer layer of atmosphere, the green diatomaceous plants will eat the hull beyond repair. We have to bathe *Rover* every time we return from visiting *Sirius*."

"Not enough." Duggan shook his head. "She's smart. She knows that ship inside and out. You don't have enough firepower to take it away from her. You have to destroy the king stone before Leonard communicates with civilization. As long as the king stone is intact, this enterprise is in danger."

"I have to destroy a king stone," Konner muttered. The giant blue crystals that communicated along transactional gravitons to mother stones and kept the rest of the crystal array working as a unit lived. All life was sacred. He'd already had a premonition about killing a human being. Killing a king stone . . . "I'd rather rip out my own heart."

"Maybe we should uncloak again," Loki suggested, nervously tapping his fingers against his thigh. The three brothers and Dalleena lay prone beneath *Rover*, waiting, watching the sky.

"Patience," Kim counseled him. He, too, felt the urge to move. He settled for running his hands through his unruly red hair. He tugged at the leather thong that tied the mane at his nape.

"How long has it been?" Loki asked.

"Less than ten minutes," Kim replied. He looked up at the sun's position and checked it against the length of the shadows. The Tambootie in his system told him more precisely the time, their location, the nearest magnetic pole, and that he needed another dose to keep those senses enhanced. But he could not determine the location of the lander *Jupiter* had launched just after dawn local time.

"If we uncloak again, they'll know the blip on their sensors isn't a fluke," Loki said.

"It takes more than ten minutes for a lander to fly from the volcano to here," Konner spoke up at last.

He'd seemed very moody this morning for a man who had found his soul mate. At least Kim presumed Konner and Dalleena had found each other last night. The way their shimmering auras merged when they leaned their heads together told him more than the whispered confidences they shared. Dalleena had no business on this adventure. But Konner had insisted.

Kim should have brought Hestiia with him. His wife had more right to accompany them than the Tracker.

Right had nothing to do with it. Skill and talent decided the duty roster, he reminded himself. He winced at how his vocabulary returned to the jargon of space farers and how his speech seemed more clipped and rapid after only a few hours in the company of the newcomers. The lazy dialect of the locals lingered on his tongue and he savored the poetry of the idea behind the words. Efficiency lost importance among people who measured time in moons, seasons, and generations rather than digital femtos and metric minutes.

"They come," Dalleena said. She held her right hand up, palm outward, facing south."

"How far?" Konner asked.

Dalleena raised her left shoulder in a half shrug. "Far. They come closer."

"They must have emerged from the shadow of the volcano," Kim mused. Communications, sensors, magic went haywire within the confines of the crater. The meadow outside, where the water was sweeter than in the cave offered marginally better electronic performance. "So what do we do when they get here?"

"You, Kim, surrender to them. Offer to lead them to where the others are hiding. Loki and I will take the lander back to *Jupiter*." Konner did not look happy about that.

"The rest of the crew will have to evacuate once we break the king stone." Loki looked positively gleeful. "Once we do that, the crystal circles will lose connections and stop working, their orbit will decay, and the ship will crash. The crew will have ample time to evacuate with adequate supplies."

"You should take Ross Duggan and Paola Sanchez with you. We should cannibalize as much as possible from the ship. Like fuel for *Rover*," Kim suggested

"No." Konner put on his stubborn face, jaw thrust out, eyes narrowed, and shoulders reaching toward his earlobes. "If something goes wrong, they'll be tried for mutiny. Maybe treason. I won't let them take that risk."

"Not your choice," Sergeant Duggan said. He walked boldly up to their hiding place beneath the cloaked shuttle. Corporal Sanchez stood right behind his left shoulder where she was in a good position to protect his back.

"You can't see us," Loki choked.

"I can if I know what to look for and where. Besides, you three are making so much noise even Pettigrew could find you."

"The Others wander," Dalleena said. She held her hand out, more to the north.

"They are probably following the signature of the lander. Salt water will confuse the signal. What part of the ocean did you ditch it in?" Ross Duggan asked.

"Deepest trench I could find," Konner grunted.

He and Kim got to their feet at the same time. Both reached to open the hatch.

"Time to uncloak again," Kim said.

"I can do this, little brother," Konner muttered.

"But you don't want to. Let me help, Konner." Kim tried to place two fingers from his dominant left hand upon his brother's temple. Experimenting with Hestiia had helped him find this the best way to enter a person's mind and soothe disturbing dreams and thoughts.

Konner ducked away from his touch.

"I know what I have to do, Kim. You can't ease that burden."

"It should not be a burden."

"But . . . a king stone?" Konner shivered.

"Maybe Loki or I should dismantle the king stone. Neither of us is atuned to the crystals as you are."

"That is just it. One cannot remove a crystal from the array unless one is atuned to them. Especially the king stone. It has its own defenses."

Kim gulped. "You should not do this alone. I'm coming with you and Loki." And he'd take a stash of Tambootie with him, in case he had to intervene with more than his wits and his strength. He fingered the dry leaves in his pockets. Was it enough?

A roar approached from south by southeast.

No more time to think. The IMPs had found them without uncloaking again.

"We have to do this. To preserve our home. To save Hestiia and all the rest," Kim muttered to himself.

"Amen," echoed his brothers and their two new allies.

"Something is wrong." Dalleena looked at her tracking hand. "There are two landers." She shifted her palm to face due east as well as south.

"We need two distractions now." Kim pounded his fist into his other palm.

The first vessel approached slowly from the south. It circled three times and hovered before settling to the ground thirty meters from the cloaked shuttle. The long tubular vessel, painted black with white IMP insignia looked alien and menacing in the waving grassland. Five heavily armed Marines poured out of two hatches. They surveyed the area with weapons at the ready. Three techs holding sensors emerged more slowly. They sported holstered pistols, and rifles slung across their backs.

"That's Lieutenant Commander M'Berra. Executive officer of the *Jupiter*." Sanchez pointed to the ebony-skinned man with tight black curls clinging to his scalp who jumped down and surged forward, pistol cocked and trigger finger itchy. He had the tall stature of a man raised on a bush planet. Unusual for a bushie to rise so high in the ranks. His family must be very important back home.

Another ten Marines followed him out of the lander. Immediately, the vessel lifted and hovered.

The second lander touched down, deployed another twenty Marines, and took off. The two craft circled the area, one clockwise, close in. The other circled higher, in the opposite direction two kilometers out. Both ships opened ports for pulse cannons.

"Now what?" Kim slumped down and stared at the grass. "They are smarter than we expected."

CHAPTER 23

◆───·───◆───·───◆

ERYTHROS, I need your help, Konner called with his mind. If only he had a bit of the Tambootie that Kim touted so highly.

"Loki, your telepathy is better than mine. Call a dragon," he whispered.

One of the techs jerked his head and his instrument in their direction.

Konner held his breath. No one moved. The tech shook his head and moved his instrument around. Lieutenant Commander M'Berra waved his troop forward in the direction of the shuttle. They, too, remained silent.

Only a matter of a few steps before they ran into *Rover*, even if they could not see it. Upon contact, their instruments would penetrate the cloak, understand it, and never again be fooled by it. With that information, *Jupiter*'s crew would be able to find *Sirius*.

He needed to act. Fast.

"Just be ready to disappear." Sanchez scooted out from under the shuttle. Before Konner, or anyone else could stop her, she ran around the vehicle and approached the IMP squad from an angle at a fast trot.

"Hurry," she said, breathless. More breathless than she should be after such a short sprint. "They're after me. They . . . they have a dragon!" She pointed to the east and north, across the river.

Instantly, all the techs shifted their instruments away from the shuttle to the direction in which the corporal pointed.

"Calm down, Sanchez," Lieutenant Commander M'Berra said. He placed a comforting hand on Sanchez's shoulder. "You must be hysterical, Corporal. There are no such things as dragons. Now report. Slowly. Calmly. And rationally."

"Yes, sir. Thank you, sir." Sanchez took two long slow breaths. The techs and their protective phalanx of Marines edged a little to the north and away from Konner and the others.

"The locals welcomed us with open arms and a feast last night," Sanchez said. She shifted her weight and shuffled. Her movement forced M'Berra to make nearly a quarter turn.

"When we woke this morning, all our comms and equipment had been stolen, the locals had disappeared, and this immense creature was perched on a boulder the size of a house staring at us. Lieutenant Pettigrew tried to shoot it. It attacked. Then the noise of the landers frightened it off. It . . . it flew, sir. On wings a full five meters wide." She gulped. "I believe Lieutenant Pettigrew is injured, sir. Legs a mess of abrasions. Medic Lotski has nothing but water to wash the wounds. Everything else was stolen, sir."

"Why in Allah's name did Lieutenant Pettigrew trust the natives. And where is the lander?"

"I do not know, sir."

"Where are the rest of your squad, Corporal?" M'Berra sighed heavily and shook his head.

"Back this way, sir." Sanchez pointed upriver, well beyond the village and the shuttle.

Duggan ground his teeth.

Konner touched the sergeant's shoulder, much as M'Berra had calmed Sanchez.

"Sensors indicate a population center of about one hundred bodies due east of here," a tech pointed his instruments directly at the village, half a klick away.

Konner swallowed his frustration.

"Corporal Sanchez?" M'Berra raised an eyebrow in question.

"Could be, sir. I got twisted around running to catch you. Lots of landmarks look alike. The natives took all my equipment. I ran too fast to observe my position as carefully as I should." She wiped sweat off her brow and looked very pale. The medic grabbed her elbow to steady her as she swayed in her tracks.

"One fine actress," Loki mouthed without a sound.

M'Berra activated his comm. "Find a landing place with good cover and wait for us," he barked.

"What about the smugglers?" a sergeant reminded his commander.

"They aren't going anywhere. Our first responsibility is to our own." M'Berra stalked in the wake of the tech toward the village. The entire squad followed without question.

When the last of them disappeared over the rise and the roar of the landers had receded south, Konner crept out from beneath the shuttle and its electronic cloak.

"Now what? Sanchez saved our skins, but we didn't get a lander. Nor did we get fuel for the shuttle." Disappointment rode heavily on his shoulder.

He breathed easier, though. Relief. He would not have to kill a king stone today.

"Magnificent woman," Loki let his gaze linger in the direction Paola Sanchez had disappeared with the landing squad. "Too bad she isn't my type."

His brothers looked at him strangely.

"Open your eyes, Loki. She is precisely your type," Kim chuckled.

"She's too much like Mum," Loki protested.

"Not in the least." Konner smiled and looked lovingly at Dalleena.

Loki's back itched with something more than physical irritation. Could they be right?

He decided to change the subject rather than examine his emotions too closely. "How far away do you suppose the landers went?"

"Couple of klicks from here," Duggan said with a shrug. "The pilots don't want to be too far off, in case the villagers, or the dragon, gives them any trouble. But I wish Paola hadn't gone down a crystal conduit without a sensor like that. She'll be up on charges before the day is over once M'Berra discovers she lied." He rubbed his knuckles against his teeth in a worrisome gesture.

"Don't worry. We'll find a way out of this. Now let's see if we can find the landers." Loki slapped his new friend on the back hard enough to shake him out of his doldrums.

"Minimum flight crews aboard. But every member of *Jupiter's* crew is fully trained and most are combat veterans. Even the judge and lawyers," Duggan said.

"I'll fire up *Rover's* sensors and find the landers," Kim said. He keyed open the hatch. "We've got some stunners and probably the element of surprise."

"We'll have to uncloak to get a reading," Konner warned him, hard on his heels.

"You aren't the only one who manipulates systems beyond factory specs." Kim smiled widely.

"The landers are there." Dalleena held up her hand palm out and faced due west. "A short walk, hardly a full sun mark."

Duggan looked to Loki for an explanation. "Primitive timekeeping. One sun mark or one candle mark is roughly one hour."

"About three klicks." Konner beamed with pride as he pulled Dalleena against his side. "She's almost as good as your sensors, Kim, and untraceable."

"Get the stunners, Kim. We're walking," Loki called to his youngest brother.

"A body could get mighty tired of walking," Duggan grumbled.

"Get used to it. Once we take care of this little problem, walking is about the only form of transport," Loki replied. "Unless you want to round up some wild horse hybrids. Locals call them steeds. That's a good name for them; can't really call them horses anymore."

"Um, Loki," Kim stammered as he handed out stunners, even to Dalleena. "I think I should go back and check on Hestiia, the village . . ."

Loki snorted. Kim wasn't complete anymore without his wife. A total waste of a good man.

But he had to admit that when Hestiia stood at Kim's side, his logic was clear, he acted more decisively, and he led the natives with superb instincts.

"Pryth and Hestiia have taken them all to the next village. Hestiia will be safe with her brother and father," Konner said. "M'Berra will find only his own people trussed up like wild lumbirds ready for the spit."

"You could have told us that!" Loki protested.

"Didn't want to spoil the surprise." Konner and Dalleena grinned at each other like moonstruck Acadian Jolilbirds. They mated for life, and if one lost a partner, never found another mate, and often died of loneliness and a broken heart.

Loki shivered at the thought of tying himself so completely to any woman. Even Cyndi. Certainly he planned to marry the love of his life, but he'd never imagined either of them being completely faithful. Life was too full of adventure for that.

Paola Sanchez would demand monogamy from her mate. And St. Bridget help the man who strayed from her side. Good thing she'd announced that she expected no commitment from Loki. She had a larger agenda than finding a spouse.

"What about Taneeo?" Kim asked. "Is he still free?"

"Hardly, with splints on his leg and his other injuries." Konner shrugged. "Even if he does harbor Hanassa's spirit, he can't move around enough to betray us."

"I don't like that Captain Leonard sent M'Berra down with the second wave," Duggan said, rubbing his knuckles across his teeth. "She usually saves her big guns for more desperate situations."

"She's lost track of twenty of her crew and an expensive lander. I'd be part of the second wave if I were her," Loki replied.

"Not our captain. She stays with the ship unless she has no other options. That's accepted military protocol. And believe me, you don't want to get her into a corner with no options. She's one fierce lady with a mind as sharp as a laser cutter."

"Was, um, er, the *Jupiter* chasing *Sirius* about five months ago?" Loki's stomach felt like it wanted to sink to his toes.

"Yeah, we were. Thought the captain would split a few skulls when Command called her off the chase. She wanted to capture you guys like her life depended on it."

"If *Jupiter* was called off the chase five months ago, why are you all here now?"

"Captain Leonard got hold of the report of how *Sirius* disappeared through an uncharted jump point. She detoured from delivering a diplomatic attaché to chase you down."

"Tenacious, isn't she?"

"Obsessed."

"Just like Mum?" Kim piped in. His voice sounded mischievous. His face looked grim.

"Just like Mum. This mission could be a real pain in the ass," Loki muttered. He shook his head.

An idea slammed into his brain with the force of a pulse cannon.

"Your Captain Leonard wouldn't be tall and red-haired, would she?"

"No. That would be Lieutenant JG Kat Talbot, our helmsman. Captain Leonard has black hair and blue eyes. Pale skin and a figure to make a man look twice. Maybe four times. But she's all business aboard ship. Doesn't tolerate flirting among the crew, especially not with her."

"This Kat Talbot . . ." Loki prompted. "Tall with red hair. Green eyes?"

"Green eyes that spit fire. Another woman you do not want to cross."

Just like Mum. *It can't be. I'd know if it was her. Wouldn't I?* Loki could not dismiss the nagging questions.

(*Would you?*) The voice in his head flitted by so quickly he almost did not hear it.

"Yeah, I'd know," he replied, as much to himself as that obscure mental intruder. "I'd feel her in my thoughts and dreams. *I'd know.* It's my responsibility to know." He kept walking toward the two landers and whatever encounter lay ahead, wishing he'd never discovered this godforsaken planet MKO-IV.

Commander Leonard drummed her fingers on the arm of her chair on the bridge. "What is going on down there?" she asked the air.

Beside Kat, Josh Kohler hunched in on himself as if trying to make himself invisible. He did not want to capture the captain's attention when she was tense, concerned, and thinking out loud. He could end up cleaning bilges for breathing wrong.

Any of the bridge personnel could.

"I told you this detour was unnecessary and dangerous," Judge Balinakas said calmly. He punched notes into his handheld, recording every misdemeanor.

Kat presumed on Leonard's superior rank by answering her question without having been specifically addressed. "If you ask me, sir, the O'Haras have begun a guerrilla warfare campaign." She sat up straight and caught the captain's gaze with her own. She had too much at stake to let a superior officer's bad mood get in the way.

And she did not trust M'Berra or any of the Marines dirtside to complete their mission successfully.

"I did not ask you, Lieutenant. But go ahead, explain your thoughts." The captain leaned forward. She kept her face and expression neutral. Her right fist continued to clench and release her electronic pencil.

"Classic opening sortie, sir. Ambush and retreat. Force the enemy to commit more troops. Those, too, will be sabotaged. Cut communications and supplies. Lure more troops dirtside. My guess is that they will try to eliminate, incarcerate, or seduce most of ship's personnel to the planet, then sneak aboard and steal *Jupiter*."

Leonard's electronic pencil snapped loudly in the silence that followed Kat's words.

Kohler flinched as if his neck had been the intended victim instead of an inanimate tool.

Leonard turned and glared at Balinakas, daring him to add his now familiar diatribe.

"Alert. All ship's personnel. Secure all launch bays. I want armed troops stationed in or near each hatch with full counter-grav gear," Leonard nearly shouted into ship's comms. Without equipment to neutralize the heavy gravity of the outer sections of the ship, troops would have to be rotated every hour to avoid undue fatigue and physical stress. "No ship comes aboard without command codes and passwords. Sight recognition is not enough."

Somewhere deep in the ship an alarm blared in response to the captain's orders. Faint echoes filtered through to the bridge. Leonard did not relax.

Kat grinned to herself. She'd taken steps to prevent a mutiny without violating her orders not to speak of the complaints she'd overheard.

"Captain, if I may suggest . . ." Kat prompted.

Leonard pursed her lips in disapproval, then nodded for Kat to continue.

"I would like to set a trap for my . . . for the outlaws. Let them come aboard. Lull them into believing we are unaware of their presence. Then set an ambush for them in the heavy grav section, where their maneuverability is limited and we have the advantage of counter-grav units."

"I don't know . . ." Leonard looked long and hard into the eyes of every person on the bridge. No one offered her any alternatives.

"Dangerous," Balinakas said. "But I like it. Easy to set up and execute and we get out of here all the faster."

"What makes you think they will come aboard, Lieutenant Talbot?" Leonard ignored the judge.

Kat noted a few drops of blood on the captain's fingers where the broken electronic pencil had cut her. She proffered the first aid kit from beneath her console. Leonard nodded brief acknowledgment of needing it. She sprayed an antibiotic cleansing compound onto her fingers, followed by a touch of sealant. The blood evaporated and only a little telltale swelling lingered from the injury.

"I have studied these men, Captain," Kat said. "None of their operations have been on this scale before. But they've never had an entire bush planet at stake before. They will fall back to patterns that have worked in the past. Just bigger and a little more complex."

"An entire bush planet at stake," Leonard repeated.

"Aye, Captain. What else would make them linger here long enough to risk capture?"

"Do it, Kat. Do what you have to. I want those bastards captured, tried, locked up, and mind-wiped by shift change in the morning."

Kat jumped to her feet, saluted, and jogtrotted to the exit hatch. Her heart nearly skipped a beat with excitement. After twenty years, she'd have vengeance.

CHAPTER 24

✦ ━━ · ━ ◆ ━ · ━━ ✦

"WHO'S ABOARD THE LANDER?" Konner asked. He and his party lay flat in the tall grasses one hundred meters from the first parked lander. The second lander lay two klicks west and out of sight. Dalleena had led them to this spot without hesitation and without error.

"Pilot and copilot, both armed, and a sentry, probably a corporal armed to the teeth and capable of killing you with one hand tied behind his back and both feet in shackles," Duggan replied.

"I thought IMPs weren't allowed to kill anyone," Kim muttered.

"Marines are trained to the extreme. Have to know how to kill in order to disable. At least that's the theory. A lot of bushies go into the Marines. Their viewpoint is slightly askew of standard GTE." Duggan grinned sideways.

The sentry emerged from behind the lander, making a circuit of the craft, rifle at the ready, two pistols holstered at his hips, a knife in his belt and another in his boot. He scanned every sector warily.

Konner kept his head down, hardly daring to breathe. The sentry returned his gaze and his rifle aim to their direction several times before moving on to the front of the lander.

They'd not approach him undetected.

"I haven't done anything like this before unless I was desperate with the adrenaline pumping like mad," Konner whispered to himself. He hefted a palm-sized rock he found conveniently by his hand.

"A simple thrown rock won't divert him for long," Duggan warned.

"I'll just graze his temple a bit. Enough to knock him out without hurting him," Konner replied, weighing the rock and judging its mass.

"At a hundred-meter distance?" Duggan raised his eyebrows skeptically.

"Try some of this. It might improve your aim." Kim handed Konner a Tambootie leaf with a grin. His eyes looked a little bloodshot and unfocused. How much of the weed had Kim taken?

The leaves looked a little dry and wilted. Kim had probably been toting them in his pocket since yesterday. No oils to lick off. Konner nibbled a bit of the leaf tip.

Kim nodded approval.

Loki took a second leaf from Kim and devoured the entire thing in three mouthfuls. He smiled dreamily.

"I am champagne and my body is the bottle that barely contains me," he said wistfully.

Konner took a bigger bite of the leaf. He felt too light to remain lying prone on the ground. He wanted to fly!

Kim offered Tambootie to Dalleena. She shook her head and kept her hands tightly clasped.

Duggan's eyes grew wide, but he did not take any.

Konner hefted the rock in his hand one more time. Then he peered at the sentry. His vision focused in on the precise spot on the man's temple he wanted the rock to hit. High enough to render him unconscious, low enough to avoid permanent injury.

As he narrowed his focus, fuzzy blue lines snaked across the land beneath his feet. The same web of energy he likened to the transactional gravitons that held the universe together. He shifted his balance a little. His left foot touched one of the lines. Energy pulsed up his leg to his arms and his eyes.

The Tambootie hit a high note in his blood, threatening to shatter glass, or the stone in his hand.

And then he tossed the rock. He followed it with sight and mind. The gravity-defying flight made him laugh.

The sound must have alerted the sentry. He turned to face him. The rock thudded against his forehead, right between the eyes. He sagged. His knees collapsed. He fell forward.

"St. Bridget and all the angels, have I killed him?" Konner immediately sobered. His heart beat too fast. Black spots burst before his eyes followed by a too white light.

"Easy," Kim whispered. He clamped a hand on Konner's shoulder. "Not dead. Just unconscious. I felt it, too. He's not dead."

Konner clung to those words as he gasped for breath. If he shared this much with a man he merely injured, what would it feel like when he had to kill someone?

He crossed himself, muttering prayers.

Loki jumped up and ran toward the lander, Duggan right on his heels.

Dalleena helped Konner to his feet. He fought for balance, leaning too heavily on her.

"Go," she said to Kim. "Help your brother Loki. I have Konner. I will protect him."

Kim nodded and followed Loki. He caught up with him and Duggan at the open hatch.

"Do you know how dangerous that Tambootie is?" Dalleena said. Anger deepened her frown.

"Yeah, I am getting that idea." His vision flashed and once more he felt the splitting ache in his head. His knees threatened to give out, just as the sentry's had.

"The more you use, the more you need to use. And more often. The need for the leaf never leaves you."

Konner's view of the dangers were decidedly different from hers. Addiction was moot with gamma blockers, available in any advanced med kit. But this awful sharing of emotions could kill him eventually. Especially if he managed to end someone's life while in a Tambootie thrall.

"My father used the Tambootie to increase his tracking skills. The stuff killed him in the end," Dalleena continued.

"We have to help my brothers," Konner muttered. He took one hesitant step. His knees held. He took another and almost fell. Dalleena kept him upright though he could see the strain in her arms and face.

"I can walk," he insisted. He visualized himself darting the one hundred meters to the lander. Then he was doing it, faster than he should have. His breathing came easy and his heartbeat did not rise.

Dalleena had a hard time keeping up with him.

One of the pilots glanced out the cockpit windscreen at that moment and spotted Konner. A hasty conversation ensued between the two. Konner read their lips and knew they quickly organized their own defense. They drew their weapons.

"Why can't these things ever go easy like we planned?" Konner asked the sky.

(*Because life is never easy.*)

"You got that one right."

Still feeling as if he could fly, Konner launched himself into the open hatch. His head connected with the midriff of one of the pilots. They went down in a tangled heap. While the IMP fought to catch his breath, Konner knocked the stun pistol from the pilot's grip and restrained both wrists in one of his hands.

"Get up very slowly and raise your hands," the other pilot said. His voice was low and menacing.

Konner looked up to find a stun pistol aimed at his eyes.

Very slowly he disengaged from his victim. The man still breathed heavily, but he no longer gasped from the stunning blow to his diaphragm.

"Now who are you and why did you attack this vessel?" the IMP asked.

The pips on his collar made him a first lieutenant. The sprawled man was a junior grade. He'd be the copilot. The senior officer held him captive with that stun gun. Was it larger and more powerful than most?

"Martin Konner O'Hara, at your service." Konner made a slight bow, still keeping his hands up.

Where were his brothers?

In his mind, he saw Loki beckoning him to ease backward.

Konner shuffled his feet and nearly tripped over the copilot. He flailed his arms seeking a balance he did not need. The Tambootie in his blood kept him light and placing his feet without error.

The pilot stepped forward instinctively to keep Konner from falling.

Loki's hand shot out from the cover of the hatchway and grabbed the pilot's ankle. He yanked. The pilot fell. His gun spun away.

Konner caught the weapon neatly and trained it on both men.

"Tie them up and leave them outside," Konner ordered. "Kim, use the comm system to jam all dirtside frequencies. Loki, fire up the engines. Dalleena, you and Ross go back to the village. Keep track of the others."

"Konner . . ."

"I'll be back. I promise."

"Be careful."

"Aren't I always?" He cocked her a wide grin.

"No." She sounded remarkably like the dragon with that comment.

Their tasks accomplished, Loki slammed the hatch shut. "Let's go kill a king stone," he said with glee.

"Kill a king stone. I have to kill a king stone."

In that moment Konner knew he couldn't do it. He had to find another way.

(*There is always another way.*) Was that the dragon or Mum who spoke?

Konner, you travel too far and too fast. Betrayal awaits you where you go and when you return. Look before you leap into the void. Reach for us when you do leap. No one else can catch you. We will aid you the only way we can. The invaders will not survive.

"This is too easy," Kim said quietly.

Loki edged the nose of the bulky lander into its docking clamps. "Just like we planned," he chortled. "They asked for codes. We gave them codes. They opened the bay door and we docked."

"They will wonder why twenty-plus Marines and three prisoners do not pour out of the hatch at touchdown," Kim reminded him.

"Requesting decontamination and temporary quarantine." Konner spoke into the comm.

"State your problem, Lieutenant," a brisk feminine voice filled the cockpit.

Shivers of familiarity ran up and down Kim's spine. Where had he heard that voice before?

"We encountered some bushies, ma'am. The prisoners have been living among them for quite some time. They may be carrying a local plague. We have all been exposed."

Loki grinned from ear to ear. "We did encounter a local plague and were exposed to it."

That was months ago. Kim remembered his own bout with the debilitating fever, locking jaw, and dehydration. He'd almost lost Hestiia to the bioengineered disease left over from the original colonists and their civil war. Hestiia had lost their child before she knew for certain she carried it.

Kim still ached for the loss of the babe. They needed to wait another moon or two for Hestiia to fully recover before they tried again. A secret smile crept across his face.

"Docking bay three cleared of all personnel. Decontamination in progress," the feminine voice came over the comm.

The shiver of familiarity became a frisson of disquiet. Kim knew that voice. Knew that woman from somewhere.

"Now we get out of here, before they realize this ship is empty," Konner whispered."

"The hatches are sealed until the decontamination is finished," Kim replied in an equally hushed tone. He had a feeling that familiar female was listening.

"There is always an emergency exit. Into the rabbit hole with the crystals if nothing else," Konner said. Any ship that used a crystal drive had to have access to the outer circle of red directional crystals. In the torpedo-shaped cruiser, three separate circles, evenly spaced the length of the craft, kept it on course and spinning for gravity.

All three brothers scanned the bay for signs of an access hatch.

"There." They pointed to the imperfection in the hull plating. Just the barest sign of a crack and latch. With the uniform gray-green paint on bulkheads and hatch, only those looking for it would notice it.

They made for the exit. Konner led them along the rabbit hole. They climbed. Gravity pulled at their muscles. In moments Kim was sweating, breathing heavily. He felt as if he crawled two hand-widths above the floor. Every meter presented a new, sharply-pointed red crystal ready to spear him if he lost his grip.

Konner had suffered a similar injury aboard *Sirius*. Kim had healed him with magic, without knowing how or what he did. He had no confidence that his brothers could tend him as well.

He needed more Tambootie to strengthen his body and his will.

Sirius didn't produce this much gravity while spinning. But this was a much bigger ship. It had to spin faster to generate gravity in the interior portions, making the outer rim proportionally heavier.

At last Konner paused. Seemingly, they had traversed half the diameter of the cruiser. But they had passed only one other hatch. If he remembered correctly, they had come only one eighth of the way around.

"Loki, can you sense another mind beyond this door?" Konner whispered.

Loki held his hand flat against the bulkhead beside the hatch. After a moment he shook his head and shrugged.

"There's a long tunnel to the main corridor about as long as the docking bay is wide. It's empty. Can't tell what is beyond."

Without another word, all three pulled stunners and aimed at the hatch. Konner flipped the latch and waited. The hatch opened a crack. No voices. No unseen hand eased the portal farther open. Loki nodded and swung through, pushing the hatch with his feet. Another uphill crawl. Because of the spin, "down" seemed to be the rabbit hole. At the end of the tunnel he shifted his angle of approach. A cautious look around the exterior and he pushed up through a hatch in the deck of the corridor. He rolled onto the deck and came up in a crouch, weapon at the ready.

Kim counted to ten and followed his brother. Eventually he, too, rolled to his feet, alert and ready to fire his weapon, or jump back into the tunnel. The corridor was empty. He scooted to the side to make room for Konner.

Konner heaved himself upward onto the deck. He stayed on his knees, breathing heavily, pale and sweating.

"Maintenance," Loki mouthed. "Mid shift. Bet they are all in the mess hall."

Kim nodded his acknowledgment of the assessment. But something wasn't right. With nearly three hundred people on board, in uncharted territory, with men and a lander missing, surely someone should patrol every corridor at all times.

"Well, if it isn't the infamous O'Hara brothers dumped right into my lap," the familiar female voice from the comm system sneered.

Kim looked in the direction of the voice. A tall woman, as tall as Loki, with a cap of red curls, long legs, and green eyes that spat fire, stood in the shadow of a cross corridor to their left. Her khaki uniform with emerald trim was crisp and clean and shouted authority. She leveled a needle rifle at his heart.

Counter-grav units strapped to the soles of her boots and just above her elbows gave her the advantage of maneuverability.

All three brothers froze.

"Lieutenant JG Kat Talbot?" Kim asked.

"I bet she was christened Mari Kathleen O'Hara." Loki grinned from ear to ear.

"And if I was, why shouldn't I nail all three of you to the wall?"

"Because IMPs don't kill."

"I've cleared this corridor. Captain won't ask questions if I dump your dead bodies out an air lock. No one with a conscience will come looking to save you."

"Then you will not shoot because the blood in your veins speaks to the blood in mine," Kim said calmly. He felt the draw of kinship. Her physical resemblance to himself and his brothers said more than words.

"If blood speaks so strongly, why didn't you come back for me twenty years ago?" She let loose with a single blast from the stun pistol in her right hand. The bolt of energy landed at Loki's feet. The counter-grav equipment made her body jerk with the recoil.

All three brothers jumped away.

Kat lifted the muzzle of the needle rifle. It rested easily in her left hand—a miniature counter-grav unit clamped to the butt negated the weapon's weight for her. Her trigger finger twitched nervously.

"We did not go back for you because we could not go back." Loki took one cautious step forward, hands raised. His stunner dangled uselessly from a wrist cord. "Not then. Not with Imperial troops authorized to kill Mum."

"Imperial troops do not kill. All life is sacred," she snarled and let loose another blast from her pistol. This one sent Konner scrambling to his right, farther away from her. Closer to the next cross corridor.

Kim coughed heavily as he scrambled left. Kat sent him a scathing look. Had she seen how far away Konner had gotten?

"Tell that to Governor Mitchell," Loki growled back. "Dead men—or dead women—tell no tales and carry no lawsuits back to Imperial Justice on Earth. We've been on the run for twenty years because of that man."

"Mitchell is dead," Katie said, quite calm. Her eyes looked dead. She'd lost the fire. "I watched him die."

She did not add that she had shared the moment of death. She did not have to. Her eyes said it all. That fact alone made her one with her brothers. They all had borne the curse of nearly following victims beyond the mortal realm.

"Mitchell's decrees of outlawry remain," Loki said. Bitterness colored his words and his posture.

"Mitchell's falsified evidence against Mum remains." Kim took up the recital. He forced a loving tone into his words. He tried to reach out to her with every scrap of healing empathy he could. If only he had more Tambootie! "We've been running away from a dead man for twenty years, Katie. But not for one moment did we forget that we left a family member behind. We've been trying to find you for twenty years."

"You didn't try hard enough," she spat. "And my name is Kat. Kat Talbot, I took the name of the man who adopted me. The man who loved me as a daughter. The man who was there for me when my *family* deserted me." She aimed the stun pistol and blasted again.

Kim knew she would do it. Knew precisely where she would aim and that she had as good accuracy with her right hand as with the needle rifle in her left. He did not move out of the way.

He had to give Konner a chance to disappear.

Pain lanced through his bare left foot. Flame shot up his leg followed by numbness. His knee was on fire.

And then he fell. He tried to catch himself against the bulkhead. He couldn't find it with dead hands.

"She shot me!" he mumbled through leaden lips. "My own sister shot me."

Konner took off into the blind cross corridor without a backward look, as fast as the heavy gravity would allow him.

CHAPTER 25

K ONNER KNEW what he had to do. He had to abandon his brothers, much as they had all abandoned Katie twenty years ago. He hated himself for leaving Kim wounded.

Kim must know that he had to leave. They had planned for this. At all costs Konner had to dismantle the king stone.

None of the IMPs could be allowed to leave this planet. Ever. All communication with civilization must be severed. The king stone was the key.

(*Do not forget the other beacon,*) a disembodied voice warned him. (*One you should not trust has the beacon.*)

"Later. First things first." He ran. A blast from Katie's stunner nipped at his heels. He ran faster.

She had the advantage of counter-grav. But her quarry had split. Which would she keep under guard?

He heard footsteps behind him.

His heart thudded. The heavy gravity dragged at his muscles. He kept going.

Right ten paces, left two. He grabbed the rungs of an emergency ladder and pushed himself up to the next deck and slightly lighter gravity.

The footsteps behind him fell away. He thought. He couldn't be certain. His heart pounded in his ears so loudly he heard nothing else. Too fast. Gravity was too heavy. He had to slow down and think.

This corridor ended in a blast door. Kat had said that she'd cleared the area before confronting her brothers.

Konner spun the lock. It slid open.

He heard voices off to his left. A cross corridor ahead. People. IMPs.

He ducked into a storage locker. Cables and grapples and magnetic couplers filled every available inch. He pried a space for himself between two neatly stacked coils of cable. One long breath in and out. Then another and a third. His pulse calmed to a more reasonable level. He listened. A coupler pressed painfully into his back. One hundred heartbeats later the voices moved on.

Not bothering to fully close the locker, he crept out. Now where? He had to work his way into the heart of the ship to the king stone.

Konner drew his stunner, a toy compared to the pistol and the needle rifle his sister packed. He checked the charge and the setting. Mid range. A solid hit to the chest would render most adults of civil height and mass semiconscious. No sustainable injuries. But this crew seemed to have as many bushies as civils. Their greater height and weight might take a stronger charge.

The vision of Lieutenant Pettigrew's death's head grinning at him wiggled into his mind once more. He left the setting in the middle. He'd take his chances.

One corridor at a time he worked his way inward, toward ever decreasing gravity. The area grew more and more populous. Everyone carried a sidearm. Many packed larger weapons. He detected no more needle firearms. They were illegal after all. So why did Kat have one?

Knots of people gathered around viewscreens peering at the planet below them. Two fistfights broke out when someone refused to give way.

Konner gulped and pressed himself deeper into the shadows. The fight broke up. Three men drifted away directly past him. They searched the area warily, but their gazes slid right over him without a flicker of acknowledgment.

Maybe the Tambootie continued in his system, allowing him to misdirect their attention.

He passed crew quarters and a mess hall. The scent of textured protein and tanked greens did not entice him at all. Voices raised in disagreement sent him scuttling past the open hatchway.

Just beyond the mess hall, he found a lift, an open affair, merely a series of platforms rising on a continuous belt. Beside that was a closed stairwell. He took that up one level. The corridor there seemed to go only north and south. He couldn't see any cross ramps going east-west or up and away from the concentration of gravity.

Up two more flights. He found it! A ramped passage going east-west. He stepped into it. On the bulkhead a terminal blinked at him. He pressed two buttons and found a map. But he did not truly need it. He could hear the crystals whispering to each other up ahead.

Gravity eased. He moved more quickly. Each step bounced and threatened to send him in oblique directions. He could not afford the time recovering from rebounding off the bulkheads.

Concentrate, he admonished himself. *One step in front of the other. Straight lines. Straight ahead.*

The crystals came alive in his mind. One king stone and twelve drivers. Always a symmetry of twelve. But this ship had three circles of drivers, twelve each, at bow, aft, and midship. Each ring of drivers had one hundred forty-four directionals spread around the circumference of the torpedo-shaped vessel. *Sirius* had a more efficient design—to Konner's mind—with a single ring of drivers around the king stone and a directional circle around a saucer.

He heard/felt the magnetic monopole drivers sharing the nitrogen that bathed them. They spat energy along fiber optics to the twelve directionals assigned to each driver. Each crystal was connected to the others. They needed no opposing pole to complete them. They had a circle of like crystals. An entire family of green drivers, red directionals and a single blue king stone that interpreted computer commands for direction and speed. Every crystal in the three arrays was grown together. The king stone maintained an invisible tether to a mother stone at the place of their birth. As long as the king stone was in communication with its mother stone, it could always find its way home. It could also communicate with every other king stone tethered to the mother faster than the speed of light.

Crystal scientists theorized that the stones used the invisible transactional gravitons to communicate almost instantaneously anywhere in the galaxy.

Konner had seen the local equivalent of transactional gravitons crisscrossing the planet below. He'd used the energy in those blue lines when he needed to move heavy objects with his mind. Could he use them to throw his thoughts across great distances as well?

He sped onward toward the sealed door and the crystal he had to kill. Without the king stone, the crew would have to manually input each tiny correction into each driver and directional. The strain of the constant work allowed shifts of only two hours with the next four hours in heavy, drugged sleep.

Konner had seen men go mad after only two days of maintaining a crystal array. They became so atuned to the crystal matrix that they could no longer communicate with humans.

"St. Bridget and all the angels!" Loki exploded. He dove for Kat Talbot's knees. The heavy gravity made him sluggish. She sidestepped easily, buoyed by her counter-grav units.

Loki snagged her ankle with one fist. His palm covered the power unit of the counter-grav. He switched it off and yanked her foot out from under her. She fell atop him, unbalanced in the heavy gravity. The needle rifle skidded across the deck. She still had the stun pistol. Grasping it, she slammed both fists into his kidneys.

Loki rolled and gasped. Fire raced up his back. *Jaysus!* She was strong.

But the counter-grav units had reduced the force of her blow. He'd be bruised but would recover.

He twisted, pinning her beneath him. She writhed like a Denobian muscle-cat, spitting and hissing curses in at least three languages.

He had the advantage of weight and reach and a hundred barroom brawls where fair had nothing to do with winning. He made certain he switched off both of her arm counter-grav units. Her muscles grew slack beneath him.

Kim groaned. They both stilled. Loki watched as Kim's eyes rolled up and he passed out.

"Jaysus, Mary, and Joseph, what did you do to my baby brother?" Loki stared into Kat's eyes.

"Baby brother? That's Kim?" she breathed.

"And you have no grudge against him. He was but a toddler when we lost you. You were barely two years older. Hate me, and Konner, we were teens and should have gone back for you. Hate Mum for failing to find you later. No way you can blame Kim."

"You all look so much alike . . ." she said quietly. Beneath him, her stomach muscles contracted.

Either she prepared to deliver a massive blow to his head or she was going to vomit. He hoped the later, as he crawled over to where Kim lay.

Kat rolled to her knees and retched. Dry heaves. They had to hurt under these g forces.

Loki busied himself with checking Kim's pulse. Slow and steady. His eyes dilated when Loki rolled back the eyelid. He'd live.

Konner had taken responsibility for the king stone. Loki had to make sure they all escaped. That meant keeping Kat occupied and the corridor clear.

"The docking bay was empty. Should have been three more landers there," he said casually. And another five in a bay on the opposite side of the ship. Plus a number of smaller shuttles and fighters.

"On the surface. Deployed in a broad search," Kat replied. She seemed to have regained control of her stomach, but stayed on her knees, holding her head in both hands. She probably lied about the ships. All O'Haras inherited the ability to spin yarns at will. "I swear I only stunned him. He's not dead, is he?"

"You'd know if he was. You'd share the passing with him, maybe even let yourself pass beyond the barrier with him." Loki grabbed a pair of force bracelets out of Kat's uniform pocket. Before she could recover, he slapped them around her wrists. Two thin strands of plastic, linked by an electrode. Every movement of the wrists and hands sent jolts of electricity through the special conductivity of the bracelets. Loki had endured incarceration with bracelets before. They were no fun.

Kat would have to have more endurance and willpower than he had to do more than sit quietly and answer his questions.

"How long will your captain keep this corridor free?" Loki grabbed her stun pistol and slid it through his belt. It rested neatly, as if it belonged there. The rifle he kicked farther down the corridor, never wanting to touch such a weapon again.

Kat stared mutely at the force bracelets.

"I asked you a question." He grabbed the bracelets by the electrode.

Kat gasped and paled. Her lips remained sealed.

"You're tougher than I thought. But then you are an O'Hara." Loki stepped back and thought a moment.

"Help me get Kim back to the lander."

"No."

"What do you mean, 'no?' "

"I am a prisoner of war. I do not have to aid and abet the enemy."

"We aren't your enemies. We're family."

Again she remained silent. But this time her venomous green eyes were riveted on him.

Loki squirmed. She looked very like Mum in that moment. He'd never been able to withstand Mum's stare. He always succumbed and told her everything when she fixed her gaze upon him like that.

"Very shortly, all hell is going to break loose and you will want to be in the docking bay." Loki looked around for an easy way to get them back into the rabbit hole without impaling Kim on a directional crystal. Or better yet, convince Kat to escort them through the corridors.

The heavy gravity of this deck was wearing on his thought processes. Or maybe the Tambootie he had ingested earlier had worn off.

"What can you three do to bring down an IMP cruiser alone?" she scoffed.

"Never underestimate the ingenuity of your brothers," Loki returned. He knelt and checked Kim again. His eyes opened and closed fitfully as he fought back to consciousness. Having him awake would help, but the numbness in his legs would take too long to wear off for him to handle the rabbit hole by himself let alone be of much use out here.

"Where is Konner?" Kat sat up straighter and looked around. "He disappeared halfway down that corridor." She jerked her head in the direction she had chased the middle brother.

Loki smiled and held her gaze. He could be enigmatic, too, when he wanted to.

"If I remember correctly, and I remember everything in precise detail, Konner is the engineer in the family. He was always dismantling things and rebuilding them better," Kat mused.

She sat in silent thought for a moment. "Oh, my God!" She struggled to stand. She winced several times as the force bracelets shot jolt after jolt of electricity through her.

Loki did not offer to help her.

"He's going to destroy the king stone. Why?"

"If you'd paid attention to the surveys of the planet below, you'd know," Loki replied.

"Every crewman and officer not assigned otherwise has their noses glued to portholes and surveys. This is an uncharted system with a habitable planet. They are all excited."

"And getting greedy. Big bonuses for discovering habitable planets. Bigger bonuses for discovering lost colonies," Loki said.

Kim stirred and moaned. But his eyes opened and stayed that way. He moved his head cautiously, checking his surroundings. Then he opened his eyes wide and moaned.

"She shot me. My own sister shot me."

"Yep. And she'll do it again if we give her half a chance." Loki handed the stun pistol to Kim. "Use it if she tries to escape."

Kat snorted.

Loki helped Kim to sit up, bracing his back against the bulkhead. His long legs straddled the hatch to the rabbit hole.

"You getting any feeling back?" Loki ran his hands down Kim's legs, looking sharply for any muscle reaction at all.

"Flashes and tingles," Kim replied.

Loki could not read his reaction as his youngest brother eyed their sister.

Come to think of it, she was mighty quiet, concentrating on the electrode of the force bracelets.

"Try to move your legs, Kim. You've got to be up and running by the time Konner finishes."

Kim's knee twitched under slight pressure.

"Breathe deep and even. Concentrate."

Kim flashed him a grin as if he knew more than Loki about the subject of breathing.

"He recovers fast," Kat said. She finally looked up from her study of the bracelets.

"We all do. A matter of survival."

"And possibly something else?" She twisted her wrists. The bracelets flashed. She winced.

The bracelets weren't supposed to flash. The current threading through the conductive plastic was designed to be silent and invisible.

Loki shifted his attention to Kat and the bracelets. Did they rest a little looser on her wrists than they had a few moments ago?

"You can't open the bracelets without a key," Loki said, somewhat puzzled. "I'm an expert with those things and I know the locks inside and out. You can't open them." He walked over to her, bent on examining the lock to make certain.

While he crouched beside her, Loki relieved her of the counter-grav units and strapped them to his own arms and feet. All the while he studied his sister and how she held her wrists.

"Wanna make a bet I can't open my own bracelets?" She smiled sweetly even as she lunged to her feet. She kept her hands together as she shoved them into Loki's jaw.

She no longer had the counter-grav holding back her blows.

Black-and-yellow stars burst before his eyes. His balance tilted. He shifted his weight forward. Veteran of too many brawls, he knew how to compensate and stay upright under a sucker punch. Without thinking, he swept one leg behind Kat's feet.

She fell backward. The bracelets dangled from one hand only. Her left swung back, preparing a new blow. If she was like the rest of the family, her dominant left hand was free.

Bad news.

Kat twisted as she went down and caught herself. She drew her feet back under her and jumped upright, only slightly hindered by the heavy gravity.

But she jumped back, toward the cross corridor.

Loki cursed himself. He should have manacled her feet as well. She had two more sets of force bracelets in her uniform hip pocket.

He dove after her, still fighting for clear vision and balance.

He caught up with her easily, propelled by the purloined equipment. She did not go far before he grabbed her right shoulder.

Too late.

Her left hand slapped a comm unit set into the bulkhead just below a ship's diagram.

"Captain Leonard. They're going after the king stone!" Kat yelled.

CHAPTER 26

KONNER FLEW INTO the crystal room at the exact center of the ship. The king stone and the first twelve drivers lived here.

He could not think. He just had to do.

An engineer turned at the sound of the portal irising open. Konner let loose with a blast from his stunner. It caught the man square in the chest before he had time to sound a protest. His body plunged backward, toward the bulkhead. In null g he bounced off the exposed pipes and conduits and spun in a new direction.

The recoil from the gun sent Konner into a roll. He compensated, firing in the opposite direction.

But the crystals' chatter rose to an unharmonic seventh chord.

Konner braced himself low against a driver crystal to prevent recoil from his weapon that would send him flying about the room.

A second and a third man went down as easily as the first. They, too, were propelled from wall to wall.

The crystals shrieked at the disruption of their routine maintenance.

Konner closed his ears and his mind to them. Deftly he caught each of the engineers and tethered them to the leashes attached to the bulkheads. If the ship had to dive into evasive maneuvers, the momentum could severely damage vulnerable humans. They had to have the leashes handy at all times.

Crystals, however seemed to glory in the challenge of rapid changes of direction and speed. As long as they were connected to the king stone. Without it, they grew confused and spurted energy in odd, and often dangerous, directions.

At the consoles around the room he checked each display. One of the drivers was out of alignment. It needed to be rotated a micrometer or two. It happened sometimes after a magnetic storm or when the ship achieved too low an orbit too quickly. The unusual planetary magnetics of MKO-IV could be playing havoc with the crystals.

Every instinct in Konner demanded he perform the adjustment.

Blindly, he slapped every console into sleep mode. Each crystal had to come off-line in order. No time for the long safety protocols. He had to get the king stone disconnected quickly.

First he cut the flow of nitrogen to the stones. The gaseous fuel flooding the crystals caused the monopoles to spit energy along the miles of fiber optics to the directional crystals. He could shut off the fuel source, but the stones still had massive amounts of energy contained within their force field.

Konner braced himself against the console labeled due north of the king stone. He found the fiber-optic cable in the first position. "Let's hope these guys use standard left to right." He closed his eyes, said a brief prayer to whatever God might listen, and pulled.

The cable did not want to let loose its connection. "S'murghin' stubborn dragon!" he yelled and yanked with all his might.

The cable broke loose.

The crystals shrieked loud enough to wake the techs.

Konner flew to the opposite bulkhead. He grabbed a leash with one hand to keep from bouncing around the room. "Hush now. This is for the good of my people," he whispered to the crystals.

Sparking energy spat from the end of the clear tubing. He capped it with a special clamp from the workbench beneath the console.

The south console was now directly beneath his butt. He loosed the first cable and began working on the number one here. It, too, resisted his attempt to disconnect it. But, eventually, it yielded to his pressure.

Too much time. He had to get on with this. On to the west and east consoles. Each disconnect came a little easier than the last. He was down to the last twelve when the clamps ran out.

Curses streamed from his mouth. He had to improvise. How?

Praying the next crystal did not decide to blast him he tied an overhand knot in the cable just before its connection to the console. Then he gritted his teeth and prepared to endure pain.

The cable came free. A dribble of sparks leaked out, not much in comparison to a fully live fiber optic, but enough to light a small city for a day. He kept his hands above the knot, hoping he remained safe. Now to keep the leaking energy from making the cable dance about. He wedged the knot between two exposed pipes along the bulkhead. So far so good.

At last he had all one hundred forty-four red directionals free of the king stone.

The king stone whined and strained loud and long as it sought to compen-

sate for the loss of the center array by tapping into the other two circles of
directionals at the bow and aft.

"I'm sorry." Konner felt as if his heart might break. With a few commands
to the computer, he isolated the other two circles of directionals.

Now he had to tackle the twelve green drivers.

The king stone wailed a mighty protest. The big blue stone was dangerous
when isolated. At any moment it could unleash forces no man had encountered and lived.

Konner could not listen. He could not think. He had to keep going now
before he lost his nerve.

The green drivers were bigger than the reds and channeled proportionally
larger amounts of energy. The cables did not want to knot. The leakage was
more volatile. His hands grew raw from contact with the raw power.

The crystal techs began to stir in their tethers.

Konner looked over his shoulder for any indication that the blue king stone
would protect itself and its family of crystals from disconnection and death.

"I have to do this," Konner apologized to the stone.

A headache slashed Konner like a laser wrench to the base of his skull.
Too-white lightning flashed before his eyes, nearly blinding him.

"I'm sorry. But I have to do this. There is no other way."

(There is always a better way.)

Was that the stone speaking to him?

No, it could not be. The stones might be alive, but they were not sentient.
Were they?

The voice became a chuckle. The headache eased. But it did not go away.

Konner took a deep breath and cut the connections to the other two circles of drivers.

The force field went down.

The king stone was now alone.

He thought he heard a sob.

The ship lurched slightly. He grabbed hold of the console edge to keep the
null g from throwing him into the bulkheads along with the semiconscious
engineers. Without the crystal arrays, the vessel no longer compensated for
collisions with space fragments. Most were too small to notice. Anything
larger than his fist could throw the vessel off alignment.

Surely someone would notice that the arrays were off line and come to
investigate. He had to hurry.

He took a deep breath to steady himself. Then another. The crystal chatter
became less strident. Almost took on meaning. He inhaled again. Held it. Let
it go until he felt as if his belly button met his backbone.

His focus grew more acute in the center. Fuzzy layers of bright yellow and
blue surrounded the crystals. He peered more closely and saw deep into the
core of the king stone. Light and energy blossomed outward, enveloping him.

He had to touch the blue stone.

Slowly he approached the stone and placed his hands on it, near the base.

Awareness of his body drifted from his mind. He knew only the channels to each crystal. A tiny beacon called to him from far, far away.

The mother stone.

If he just reached a little, he could touch her, become a part of the massive family of crystals communicating throughout the known galaxy. Every ship became a part of him. He understood each of their idiosyncrasies. They teased him. Flitting in and out of his perceptions, needing him to adjust this, fix that, align a pathway through the universe to connect them all.

He sighed. A sense of family welcomed him. Stronger, keener than the domineering embrace of his mother, the grudging respect of his brothers. More massive than the love that he shared with Dalleena, but not better.

Dalleena.

He knew what he had to do.

Still dazed from the oneness he shared with the stone, he withdrew his mind.

And then he twisted the king stone free of its base.

The king stone screamed. The sound battered his ears and his mind.

He jerked his hands away from the stone's agony.

"I can end your pain," he whispered. He grasped the stone with both hands. The cool facets blazed hot and angry.

He ignored the pain and yanked the king stone free.

Tears ran down his face. He cradled the stone in both arms, ready to hurl it against the bulkhead. But he couldn't. He was the stone. The stone was he.

He'd rather kill a man.

(*There are always alternatives.*)

Sobbing openly, still holding the king stone as if it were an injured child, he stepped out of the crystal circle.

"Put it back," an angry female demanded. "Put it back or I shoot you with a full load from this needle rifle."

CHAPTER 27

✦ ——— • ——— ✦ ——— • ——— ✦

KONNER STILLED. His emotions evaporated. "If you shoot me, you damage the king stone."

He shrugged, shifting his grip on the king stone. In null g it weighed nothing. But the two-meter length of the thing made it awkward. By the time he reached the docking bay on the outer rim, the crystal would weigh more than he did.

Before that, he had to get past Commander Amanda Leonard, captain of the *Jupiter.* She blocked the only exit to the crystal room.

The engineers thrashed against their tethers. The simple straps would not restrain them long.

If only he had some way of getting Commander Leonard out of the way, for just a few seconds.

Nothing loose floated about the crystal array. Everything was strapped down and out of reach. As was his stunner.

Leonard raised her rifle and took careful aim. "In null g the stone will not drop. I'm a crack shot. I can kill you with a single needle in the eye." The newest upgrade had the option of firing a single needle. The weapon Loki had used to kill Hanassa could only fire a wide spray.

Konner couldn't take the chance she was bluffing with the capabilities of her weapon or her ability.

Well, the magic had been working for him so far. He concentrated on his stunner, holstered on his belt on the right side, for easy draw with his left hand. He shifted the king stone again, bringing the left end up in front of his face.

"Care to take a chance on hitting the stone?" he asked. The words spilled forth, but his mind was on the stunner, willing it into his right hand where he cradled the base of the crystal. "Those things don't shoot on a straight line. They spray the needles across a target area. You'd also hit one or more of your own crew behind me." He pretended ignorance of the new design.

The stunner remained in place, impervious to the prod from his mind.

How comfortable was Amanda Leonard in null g? She seemed to have braced herself against the doorjamb to keep herself in place and prevent recoil.

Konner was in the middle of the room with only some fading directional crystals, barely a meter high, as a brace. Just a little spring upward would propel him as high as he wanted to go. The right amount of pressure against the balls of his feet would keep his movement slow, give him more control over his trajectory.

Without thinking further, he sent himself up. Maybe he could kick the ship's senior officer in the temple and knock her out.

Commander Leonard followed his passage with the muzzle of her needle rifle.

Then the stunner nudged his right fingers. He was so startled at the delayed reaction to his mental command, he almost brushed the weapon aside. Before it floated away, he snagged it with one finger. A little shift of his hand and he had it braced against the crystal and his index finger on the trigger.

No way to aim. No time to regret.

"Sorry about this, Commander." Konner pressed the firing button on the black box of the stunner. A bolt of red energy hit Leonard on the side of her face.

She slapped the place as if she had been bit by an insect. Her fingers caught the tail end of the stunning blast. Her hand fell to her side twitching as her knees collapsed and her eyes rolled up.

"Hey," one of the engineers shouted.

Konner twisted and shot all three of the tethered men. They rocked like pendulums at the end of their leashes. The recoil sent Konner against the bulkhead near the ceiling joint. He banged his head against the cerama/metal plates. Black stars bloomed before his eyes.

And so did the web of blue energy connecting the transactional gravitons and the planet. The crystal in his arms seemed to expand as it drew the energy inside itself, inside Konner.

How could the king stone still be connected to the rest of the universe? Did it communicate with the mother stone even now?

He swallowed, trying to understand.

The crystal array came closer. Konner fought to restrain his drift across the room. He checked the air circulation ducts. He should be moving toward them as unseen compressors moved the air about and scrubbed it of CO_2.

No, he was moving toward the center of the crystal array. The king stone wanted to go home. He could not allow that. He had to get back to the docking bay. Fast. Before either Commander Leonard or the engineers awoke and sounded an alarm.

Cautious about recoil, Konner twisted around. Then he pushed against one of the driver crystals. He aimed for the hatchway and the exit. Years of practice in free fall made his aim true. But he had to shift the king stone to keep from banging it against the doorjamb. A damaged stone would solve many problems. It might also kill him. At least break his heart.

An image of Dalleena rose before his mind's eye. He smiled. If anything could heal him after a catastrophe with the crystal, she could. He did not want to put that kind of burden upon her. He had to protect the stone.

At the next intersection Konner pushed against the first solid object he encountered. He sped down the long ramp to the next level. Near the end of it, gravity began to grab him. He anticipated and landed with both feet on the deck, knees bent. And another long spring until heavier gravity forced him back on the decking. With each pace toward the outer decks and each descent down a ladder, the stone grew heavier in his arms. By the time he reached normal Earth gravity, sweat poured down his face and back. His toes were bruised and his calves ached.

He spotted the passageway he needed into the heaviest gravity and hoped he'd land somewhere near his brothers. He needed help with the stone. His fingers were numb from grasping it so tightly. His shoulders felt as if the stone were wrenching both his arms free of the joints. Air burned all the way down his throat to his lungs.

His heart beat too quickly and irregularly.

And still he felt the giant crystal pushing him backward to its home. It screamed in his mind at the loss of its family.

"I promise, I'll reunite you to at least one array," Konner soothed the crystal.

It did not believe him.

"How about if I find a new task for you?" Though what that would be, he had no idea.

"Intruder Alert! Intruder Alert!" A male voice came over the comm system. He sounded so calm.

"All crystal techs report to manual stations. Repeat, all crystal techs to manual. This is an emergency. All decks, all shifts. Be on the lookout for the O'Hara brothers. They are aboard. Do not shoot. They have the king stone. Repeat. Do not shoot them. Approach and apprehend with caution.

St. Bridget! Konner was willing to bet that all the bay doors had been sealed. No one was leaving the ship with the king stone or without it.

·———◆———·

What are we to do with the intruder in orbit? Stargod Konner tells us we cannot allow it to fly away. This requires much thought and subtle action.

We have powers we have not used in centuries. A little tug here, a push there. The intruder will not stay in orbit long now. Nor will they fly away.

Dalleena lay flat amid the tall grasses on the verge of the plowed fields. From here she could watch the village. Raaskan, the headman, and his wife Poolie lay just beyond her.

Inside the village, dozens of armed men and women from the landers ransacked the huts, pulling out baskets of food, tools, clothing, everything portable. They laughed and hooted over the fine spears and arrows men had labored over for many nights around the fire. They gobbled handfuls of raw grain and spat them out again. One woman tore off a hunk of dried meat with her teeth. She made an ugly face and spat. One of her teeth came out along with the soggy blob of jerky. She howled and rubbed her jaw. The others nearly doubled over in laughter.

"All our stores gone to waste," Raaskan muttered as he pounded the ground with his fist. "They'll squander every morsel of grain, every basket of jerked meat. And we will starve this winter. I have had enough of starving." He began to rise, eyes glinting dangerously.

"No!" Dalleena and Poolie both said through gritted teeth. They hauled him back into the protection of the grasses.

"We saved most of the stores. Stargod Konner told us to leave behind just a little as bait," Dalleena reminded him.

"We did not save enough to feed our village all winter," Raaskan replied, still scowling.

One of the intruders looked their way, narrowing his eyes.

Dalleena held her breath, willing the man to forget he'd detected movement out of his peripheral vision. Apparently, she did not have Stargod Loki's talent for influencing minds. The man turned and fully faced her and the others. He raised his weapon and shouted something at his comrades. She had to concentrate a long time to understand the rapid stream of clipped syllables.

"Jimmie, did you see anything?" The guard took a step forward. "I'm going to investigate. This place is spooky. Cover my back."

A second guard stepped into his place, weapon at the ready, eyes scanning the fields, back and forth. Back and forth. He'd spot anything that moved. "Watch your step, Brewster," he said.

The first guard, Brewster, came closer. His weapon moved with his gaze across the stubble in the fields. For half a heartbeat, his gaze lingered right above where Dalleena crouched. Then he moved on, stepping cautiously, alert to his surroundings.

Silently, Dalleena cursed whatever gods had cursed the people of the Stargods. Then she cursed the intruders from another world.

The guard looked sharply above Dalleena's head, toward the marshlands that separated the fields from the pasture of wild cattle. He raised his weapon and aimed.

"What?" Dalleena mouthed to Raaskan.

He shook his head.

One finger length at a time, Dalleena turned her head in the direction where the guard looked so intently. Raaskan and Poolie edged backward, deeper into the high grass.

"S'murghit!" Another curse escaped her lips, this one not so silently.

"Halt!" Brewster called. He shifted his attention and his aim up, away from Dalleena, toward the tree line.

Dalleena froze. The ground beneath her vibrated slightly. She placed her tracking hand flat upon the dirt. Many feet. Human feet tramped toward her.

She risked turning her head a little farther.

A wild red bull, his long fur ruffling in the breeze, sprang to his feet. No longer warily chewing his cud, he pawed the ground and lowered his head at the line of men approaching.

Taneeo, the priest with the broken leg, led two dozen men. He had discarded his splints. He walked with only a slight limp.

How? After only two days! Stargod Kim must have worked a wondrous miracle for such a cure.

Then she noticed that each man in the line carried one or more of the weapons and communications devices the villagers had liberated from the intruders last night. They carried them across open arms and open palms.

And Taneeo carried a bit of white cloth dangling from a stick.

She recognized the fine weave of the "handkerchief" Konner had used last night to cleanse his face before retiring.

CHAPTER 28

"AT LEAST WE CAN TELL Mum that you are alive," Kim said to his sister. He studied her intently for familial resemblance.

Her sparkling green eyes were truer in color than Mum's paler hazel. All three of the boys had midnight blue eyes. Kat Talbot had the same length of leg, red hair, and fair skin as the rest of the family. Mum was shorter but not by much. Their father must have been quite tall.

Kim had no memories of his father other than a long shadow offering comfort when he awoke with a nightmare.

Hard to tell if Kat had a figure at all beneath the now rumpled uniform. But she gave the impression of lean fitness.

She possessed a dangerous, feral quality, ready to lunge at any moment without warning; even with force bracelets restraining her wrists and ankles above her soft ship boots.

Kim edged a little away from her.

They sat along the interior bulkhead, resting as much as possible in the heavy gravity.

"You expect to get out of this escapade alive? Your Mum will be lucky to ever see you again," Kat said. She'd lost the sarcasm in the last half hour. "Do you have any feeling yet?" She touched his right leg tentatively with both hands. Hard to separate them with the force bracelets.

Kim fought to keep from twitching under her touch. Survival might depend upon the element of surprise. For the first time in months he wished his boots had not worn out. Boots would hide his feet when he flexed them, trying to restore circulation and feeling.

"Barely." Kim sighed deeply. "When you go dirtside, will you tell my wife that I died honorably, from battle wounds?" He tried to make his expression imploring. "I just hope our son will understand why he does not have a father."

Both Loki and Kat raised their eyebrows at him. Kat looked a little wistful. And sad. No one had ever found their father.

"I have a nephew?" she whispered.

"You didn't tell me that Hes is pregnant again," Loki said accusingly.

"Not enough time," Kim shrugged off the half-truth. Last night as he lay beside Hestiia he'd placed his hand upon her belly with affection. She'd been asleep when he finally crawled into bed after hours of experiments with the Tambootie. With the drug still coursing through his veins, he had sensed an extra presence beneath his fingertips. A heartbeat. A stirring of personality. "I only found out last night myself."

"And you can tell so soon that it's a boy? I thought the natives were primitive." Kat sat up a little straighter. Alert curiosity banished her soft expression "Even the most sophisticated medical equipment cannot determine fetal gender until the end of the first trimester."

"We don't need medical equipment. We just need Kim on this planet." Loki looked very smug.

"Explain."

"Psi powers augmented by local conditions." Kim jumped to explain before Loki went off into some wild tale.

Kat's face went blank. She was hiding something.

Kim caught Loki's gaze. He nudged his brother with his mind to read their sister's thoughts.

Loki's eyes crossed. He concentrated for a long moment then shook his head. "She has erected barriers." He sounded exhausted. The Tambootie must be wearing off.

"Psi powers have never been documented," Kat said. She sounded as tired as Loki.

"Just because they have not been documented, does not mean they do not exist. We discounted them, too. Until we went dirtside here." Loki picked up the train of thought.

"This planet is magical. But it won't be for long once your esteemed GTE gets hold of it," Kim continued the persuasion. "The first thing the GTE surveyors will do is kill all of the dragons."

Kat shifted her attention from one brother to the other. "Dragons?" she gulped. "Dragons do not exist."

"They do here," both brothers jumped in.

"I've ridden on the back of one," Loki said. "More magnificent than piloting any craft built by humans."

"You've had psychic experiences, haven't you, Kat," Kim pressed her. "Probably just flashes. Hardly enough to document. But enough to make you wonder."

"What happens to you, Kat?" Loki asked. "Do you sense what others are thinking? Do you know what will happen before it happens? Or do you move things with your mind? Like the force bracelet you opened earlier."

"Perhaps you have touched someone who has received a mortal wound and watched them heal beneath your hands," Kim added. To emphasize his point he raised his right knee, the one that should still be paralyzed, until she touched him.

She gulped and opened her mouth as if to speak.

"Intruder Alert! Intruder Alert!" came over the comm system. The lights turned red and began to flash.

"Captain Leonard must have found Konner." Kat struggled to her feet. The force bracelets must be burning into her flesh. She reached with both restrained hands for the stunner that should have been holstered right at her hip.

Loki held up the weapon with one finger. He grinned sardonically. "Looking for this?"

"You have to get back to your ship immediately. Before she seals all the doors." Kat looked frantically up and down the corridor.

"You come with us, Kat," Loki said with the authority of the senior member of the family.

"You need to find out what your mind is capable of, Kat," Kim added. "We can help you do it. But only if we have some time, free of pressures from your crew."

"Where the hell is Konner?" she asked rather than answering.

"Here," Konner said from the end of the cross corridor. "Loki, I need help." His voice came in gasps and grunts.

Both Loki and Kat took off down the corridor, as fast as they could in the heavy gravity. *St. Bridget,* how much pain could she endure before she collapsed? Kim followed more slowly. Every joint and muscle from his waist down ached from the stunner blast. The gravity did not help much.

Kat seemed to be made of sterner stuff than he.

He found Loki and Kat supporting the magnificent blue king stone. Konner slumped against the bulkhead, half upright. Sweat glistened on his skin and soaked his shirt.

Loki and Kat tugged in opposite directions, neither willing to give up possession of the crystal.

"Can't you three get it through your thick heads? If you won't run far and fast right now, your only hope is to turn yourselves in, without violence. I'll see that you get a fair trial," Kat yelled.

"There is another way," Kim said more calmly than he felt. Alarms blared all around him. He sensed panic heading toward them.

Then he heard a fierce pounding upon the sealed doors on either end of the corridor.

"There is only one way in the GTE. Obedience to the law," Kat argued. "You three may be my long lost family, but my loyalty is to the GTE, this ship, and my captain."

"Our loyalty is to the family and the people dirtside who depend upon us for safety. Neither the family nor our people can have that within the GTE," Loki spat. "You are invading private space."

"You are coming with us, Kat," Kim said. He closed his eyes and prayed for forgiveness. With luck his mental plea would reach her.

Then he slammed his fist into her jaw.

He just barely caught her end of the king stone before she collapsed against the bulkhead.

"Grab her, Konner. We are getting out of here. All of us." Without looking back, Kim led his brothers to the nearest rabbit hole hatch. His back and leg muscles screamed in protest and threatened to buckle with every step.

Loki checked both of his brothers where they slumped in the cockpit of the lander. The king stone rested snugly in crash webbing. Why had Konner insisted on bringing the monster? Escape would be so much easier without the crystal.

Kat fought her force bracelets from the jump seat where Konner had deposited her. Her wrists had already turned raw. At this rate they'd soon bleed.

"Will you please give me the codes to override the captain's seal on the bay doors?" Loki asked Kat with a veneer of politeness.

"Go feed yourself to your dragon," she spat and tried to kick him.

He dodged her blow and caught her knees with one hand. Slowly he lifted, throwing her balance back against the bulkhead.

"This is the last time I ask politely, baby sister. Mum always taught us to be polite. Will you please give me the codes?"

She glared venom at him.

"Okay, we do this the hard way." He dropped her knees abruptly. Her feet landed with a thud. She winced from the pain of the force bracelets.

"I have a little Tambootie left in my pocket," Kim said. His voice sounded strangled. All three of them were exhausted and hurting from too strenuous activity in too heavy gravity.

"What is this Tambootie?" Kat asked.

"Give it to me. We need those codes." Loki put out his hands.

Kim deposited one partial leaf and several fragments into his palm. He kept the largest piece for himself, chewing on it hungrily.

Loki's skin begin to tingle upon contact. One layer of fatigue washed away from him. He popped all of the pieces into his mouth. He sucked on them a moment, moistening the dried leaves and drawing out any lingering oils.

A now familiar rush of sensation sharpened his focus. A layer of energy emerged from atop every object. Mostly he saw a white after shadow. But when he looked at Kat, flares of bright red shot forth from her brow and the top of her head. With her red hair, she looked like a sun's corona.

Or the lava pit boiling beneath the blown-out volcano.

Loki banished thoughts of that place. Too many bad memories crowded out what he had to do.

"What are you hiding, baby sister?" he asked quietly. Immediately her corona of colored light shrank and blanched to a mere glare.

Loki clenched his eyes closed a moment and shook his head.

"Breathe deeply," Kim coaxed him. "Inhale long and hard. Exhale long. Get rid of all the air inside you. Good. Now inhale. Exhale. Again."

Loki obeyed the soothing voice. More layers of fatigue and worry slid off of him. He opened his eyes again.

Kat sat before him. If he looked closely, he could see through her skin to subcutaneous fat, muscle tissue, and bone. Her jaw muscles tightened. She ground her teeth.

Fascinating.

"Deeper," he whispered to himself. "Deeper."

Her skull seemed to dissolve before his gaze. He thought he saw tiny bolts of lightning firing across the surface of her brain.

"Past the brain, into the mind." Deeper he went, following chains of synapses into the center. The chains became tunnels. They took on colors. Yellow for muscle reactions, blue for autonomic functions. Green for memory. Red for knowledge.

And a black wall standing between him and the piece of knowledge he desperately needed.

"Open," he commanded. A few bricks seemed to fall away from the wall.

She threw up new ones as fast as he tore down the old.

"She's blocking me," Loki said. At least he hoped he said it.

"Relax a moment. Gather your resources," Kim instructed. His voice remained quiet, calm, soothing.

Loki withdrew to the outer surface of her mind. Then Kim began talking. He spoke of fathers and sons. He whispered about the sweetness of holding his baby son when the child arrived. He spoke of Konner's loneliness, missing his son, and needing to get back to Aurora in time for the custody hearing. He talked of Mum's obsession with finding her missing daughter.

The black bricks began to crumble and thin. Kat had held firm against frontal assault. She dissolved under the subtle pressure of her own need for family.

How did Kim know what to say to her? He'd taken the Tambootie. It must have opened his telepathy.

Loki turned his attention back to his mission. The moment he sensed Kat relaxing, he dove through the barrier in her mind.

A beautiful black rose opened before him. The lush velvet petals spread. Each one contained a string of numbers. Some made no sense to him. But deep within the rose he found what he needed. Three words followed by six numbers.

"Got it." He pulled out. Dizziness and disorientation. The cockpit looked strange, harsh, unreal. Nothing fit. He put out his hand expecting to brace himself upon the back of the pilot's chair. He missed by three centimeters. The rest of the cabin tilted to the right by the same distance.

Konner slid an arm beneath Loki's shoulder. Kim just sat and grinned.

"Breathe, Loki. You have to breathe. It takes a moment to clear your mind after an intense session," Kim said quietly.

"You've been practicing," Loki said. His words sounded slurred.

"You should, too. And so should Konner. We have to be able to control these powers."

"Let's worry about that after we get out of here."

Loki opened an interface with *Jupiter*'s computer. He scanned the menu presented on the screen.

"Is it voice activated?" he asked, keeping his back to Kat.

Kim watched her. He was better at reading faces. He'd alert them all to minute changes in her expression.

No answer from either of them.

"Konner, hack into the system. I need to override voice and go to manual."

Konner swung around and began working the copilot's screens. Some of the worry lines had eased around the middle brother's eyes. "Good to go. You have a manual connection to the central computer."

Loki typed in the three words and the string of numbers.

Access Denied. The words flashed before him. *Access Denied. Begin countdown to automatic defense system.*

Loki gulped. He swung around to face his sister.

She smiled blandly at him. "I'll die before I give you the correct codes. We'll all die in thirty seconds."

CHAPTER 29

◆——·——◆——·——◆

"WE HAVE TO HIDE!" Dalleena said as she slithered backward on her belly. She'd moved only a few feet when her bare feet touched mud. She shuddered. She hated swamps. The murky water and unknown depths hid bloodsucking creatures, flesh-eating reptiles, and plants with leaves as sharply edged as one of the new iron knives.

Or so she believed.

Taneeo and his followers continued to march toward the intruders, weapons and communications devices still proffered as peace offerings. The men's eyes did not focus. They stared blindly ahead, walking as if bewitched.

Taneeo grinned widely. He almost sauntered in triumph. The limp evaporated with each step.

"I must stop the idiot," Raaskan said. "How did he escape Pryth's vigilance?" He tried to stand. Once more, Poolie held him in place. Nearly as tall as Dalleena, she was strong from long hours of working the fields and spindle.

Raaskan glared at his wife.

She returned his gaze levelly and with meaning.

"Taneeo has to learn that not all problems can be solved with peace and compromise," he hissed.

"Especially when it means he's betraying us," Dalleena muttered. She didn't care if the others heard her or not. She was leaving. One of them had to remain free and safe to tell Konner and his brothers about Taneeo's betrayal and the defection of half the men from the village.

Gritting her teeth, she dared the swamp. At least the mushy edges of it.

When her knees felt soggy, she risked rising to a crouch. From that position Taneeo and his men were clearly visible. The intruders still gathered twenty paces away. They carried their weapons warily and balanced on the balls of their feet, ready to run forward in attack, or flee as events evolved.

Neither group seemed to notice the rustling grasses where Raaskan and Poolie crept toward Dalleena. Beside a rotting tree snag they peered around, seeking the best path. Dalleena motioned retreat.

"Big Red," Raaskan whispered. He jerked his head toward the shaggy wild bull that had risen to its feet.

It plodded toward the marshy verge of the pasture. Morning sunshine showed the sharp tips and smooth curve of his horns. From tip to tip, those horns spread as wide as a man could spread his arms. Big Red's cows shifted their grazing closer to the tree line, away from the village and the armed intruders. Their red fur seemed to fade to gray and shadow as they merged with the protective cover. Movement alone would betray their presence to predators.

Big Red, on the other hand, drew attention away from his cows. He pawed at the ground and bellowed his annoyance at the proximity of so many people.

The bull stood between Dalleena and safety. He made enough noise to attract the attention of the intruders, across three fields and a swamp. Laughter from the intruders at the bull's antics. They did not fear it. They should.

"Stillness," Raaskan said under his breath. "The hunted stands so still he blends into his cover. The hunter cannot see him until he moves."

Dalleena took a deep breath and willed herself to obey. Every instinct in her body told her to flee.

If only Konner were here to protect her.

But he, too, needed to stay free of the invaders.

If only she could hear the words passed between the Others and Taneeo.

The priest made a gesture and each of his followers moved forward in turn and deposited the weapon or communicator he held at the feet of the foremost guard. Other intruders crept out of the village. The ones with the most decorations on their clothing grabbed guns and comms from the growing pile first.

When all of the stolen gear had been returned, the intruders, as one, turned their weapons upon Taneeo and the others.

They crumpled to the ground, startled looks frozen on their faces.

Fine thanks for their act of goodwill.

Dalleena swallowed back the bile that threatened to choke her.

Poolie rested a hand upon her shoulder in mute comfort. "We saw much the same actions from Hanassa before the Stargods liberated us from him. But Hanassa drew blood and gloried in death. The invaders have only stunned the traitors. These weaklings fear death and do not kill lightly. We must use this against them."

"Yes, we must," Dalleena agreed. "I will watch. You two go and gather the others. You are more used to hunting stealthily than I. Go in secret. After sundown, before moonrise, we will liberate our neighbors. Also in secret."

But Konner and his brothers would return before then. She had to warn them. She would not allow them to stumble into a trap as wicked as a patch of devil's vine.

How could she watch the village and wait for Konner at the place he told her he would return?

The betrayal becomes obvious. We must stop this. But we cannot. With our magic and awesome defenses, too many innocents would be caught in the storm. Even a dragon dream will not affect the traitor. For he is one of us.

We will concentrate on the Others. We can accomplish something positive there. We pull upon the ship in orbit with our united minds. We will it to crash and never fly again.

"Read the codes back to me from right to left," Konner demanded. His voice sounded harsh, bruised to his own ears. He didn't have time to worry about it.

Twenty-four, twenty-three. The computer counted down the seconds.

"Um, 763997 Alpha, um," Loki stammered.

Konner watched his brother's eyes swivel right to left, left to right, and back again.

Nineteen, eighteen, seventeen.

"Standard protocol is left to right," Loki protested.

Konner felt like shaking his older brother. "Kat is left-handed. Like the rest of us. Her brain wants to read right to left even though she's been forced to learn to read left to right. Give me the codes backward."

Kat opened her eyes wide. Her nostrils pinched and she clenched her teeth. He had guessed correctly.

Ten, nine, eight, seven.

"Alpha 7997367, beta, omega, pi." Loki looked deflated.

Konner punched in the code. His fingers moved rapidly over the interface. The countdown stalled at *three.* The bay doors creaked open, slowly. Oh, so very slowly.

He breathed in short gasps.

Kat slumped against her jump seat.

"Strap in, everyone. We're blasting out of here. Fast. Before Commander Leonard has a chance to scramble fighters." Before the doors finished opening.

Konner punched in the launch protocol. Engines fired beneath him. Cockpit lights dimmed.

He felt lighter. His lungs drew in air more easily. Gravity lessened its drag on his muscles.

That had to be his imagination. His body reacted to the surge of adrenaline and made him feel lighter. Momentum should keep *Jupiter* spinning and, therefore, the gravity at a normal rate far longer than this. Planetary gravity should only assert a minute influence on the ship at this time.

He prayed. All they needed now was for the ship's orbit to deteriorate too quickly, before Commander Leonard had time to evacuate all personnel and salvage much needed stores.

Would hearing the death screams of hundreds of trapped innocents be worse than his vision of Lieutenant Pettigrew dying?

He had to weigh the loss of innocent lives among the Coros if he failed in his mission to ground the IMPs for all time.

Konner's hands began to shake.

"This is going to need some finesse, Loki. Can you take command?"

"Finesse is my middle name," Loki said on a big grin.

"No, it isn't. You are Mathew Kameron O'Hara," Kat said.

"A lot you know," Loki said back. "Let me show you some real flying. Hang on."

Kat snorted. But she held on to the edge of her seat between her knees as best she could. The simple waist restraint on the jump seat offered only minor protection.

Konner's head snapped back as Loki slammed the lander forward. Gravity increased with acceleration as it compounded the spin on the primary vessel. Pressure built in his chest. He found it difficult to breathe.

He heard metal scrape against metal. His teeth ached and his spine cringed. The lander edged through the partially opened doors with no room to spare.

Then they burst free of the cruiser. Gravity fell back to an acceptable level. Loki flipped the lander around to circle *Jupiter* and aim for the planet.

A squadron of fighters scrambled into position to block them.

"We'll have to shoot our way through," Loki muttered.

The weapons array lay at Konner's fingertips. Everything looked odd, out of reach, misplaced. Kim monitored sensors and engineering. The layout was backward from *Rover*. Konner should have engineering and communications. Kim should have sensors and weapons.

"If I know Captain Leonard, she's ordered her flyboys to take out the cockpit," Kat said. A smug smile crept across her face. "They'll leave the cargo area intact. She wants the king stone back. She won't let your death stand in her way."

"We've a few tricks up our sleeves," Loki muttered.

"Why didn't you just smash the crystal, Konner? Life would be easier," Kim asked.

In the back of Konner's head, he heard the king stone crying out to its family of driver and directional crystals. It had never been alone since before it was a tiny seed in an omniscium bath.

"Look out! Vultures at three o'clock," Kim shouted.

Konner slammed his palm flat on the interface, firing whatever responded. He closed his eyes and prayed that the fighters would veer away and no one would get killed. Least of all the king stone.

Loki closed his eyes and pushed the throttle forward. One nice long smooth motion. Acceleration pushed him back into his chair. He listened to the ship. Listened to the constant hum of active minds. Waiting. Waiting until it felt right.

He jerked the ship right and "down" relative to his internal horizon. Only when the ship began to shudder from the speed and angle of reentry did he ease up. Still without looking he thrust the controls to port, up, down, starboard, down.

To his right he heard Konner mutter a prayer every time he fired weapons. Kim shouted orders to both of them. Kat sneered at every word said, every action taken.

Loki tuned them out. Now he listened for the planet. The obscure, primitive, raw, and unforgiving place that had grabbed his heart and promised him everything he'd dreamed of. The place he had to protect at all costs.

Without the king stone, the IMPs could neither leave, nor communicate with civilization. If every crystal tech aboard took continual shifts of two hours on, four off, *Jupiter* might achieve something close to light speed. Not enough to make it to the jump point in less than a year. Without the king stone, they could not jump. He had to keep them from retrieving the stone. Even if it cost him and his siblings their lives.

Why hadn't Konner smashed the crystal when he had the chance? But he could not read his brother's mind and evade the fighters.

Up, down, port, and starboard, always angling closer to the planet. The green atmospheric layer glowed beneath him. He plunged into it. Leveled out. Shot to port.

His right side tingled where a bolt of energy seared the edge of the cockpit. A strange whistling came to his ears. More than tinnitus ringing against his eardrums from the rapid changes in direction and acceleration.

"Sensors clogged," Konner said on a sigh of relief. He'd not be shooting any weapons for a while.

"Femto point hull breach," Kim reported. As he said the words, he unstrapped and reached for the repair kit.

"What is that stuff?" Kat leaned forward to peer out the windshield.

"Diatomaceous plant life, lives in the uppermost reaches of the atmosphere," Kim replied. His hands were busy with a caulk gun filled with liquid cerama/metal. It would harden quickly and seal most small holes up to the diameter of a man's pinky finger.

"It eats the metal out of the hull alloy unless we bathe the shuttles every trip," Loki added.

"No wonder the planet looks green from space," Kat said. Curiosity seemed to have calmed her antagonism.

Loki felt like he had to say something. Anything. He couldn't think what. The ship and his evasive course demanded all of his attention. If he thought about his maneuvers, he'd overthink and make a mistake.

He kept up a course that made the foothill approach to the volcano look flat and easy. Occasional shots zinged past them. A few came close.

"They are shooting blind," Konner said quietly. He looked pale and shaken. Shooting back at IMPs had never bothered him before. Why now?

Loki was a fine one to ask. He'd killed a man, Hanassa, and nearly followed him into death, linked to his mind by psychic talents.

Another shot pinged the tail of the lander in a glancing shot. Enough to send him careening into a spin.

"Have the fighters got new technology for listening to us?" he asked, not expecting an answer. "Tech we don't know about."

Kat said nothing. She looked pointedly at the ceiling rather than return his gaze.

"Not that I've heard," Konner said. He usually heard about every innovation, public and military. "But we've been gone for months. Between civilized worlds for months before that. I thought I was up to date when we jumped to this planet. Maybe I wasn't."

Kat bit her cheeks and kept her mouth closed.

"Okay, little sister," Loki whispered. "I'm trusting your silence to be a 'yes' answer. Not a word out of anyone. They may be listening to echoes of our voices." Loki abruptly changed course. He nosed upward. A sharp climb almost took him out of the green layer of microscopic plants that should have blinded the IMPs' ship as well as the lander's sensors. He'd never spent so long a time in the green and wondered how much damage the plants would do to the hull before they safely hit dirtside.

The shots continued, barely missing. They must be following engine emissions.

"Going back to surrender?" Kat asked hopefully.

Kim grabbed the ubiquitous duct tape and started strapping it over her mouth.

Loki put the lander into a dive and shook his head at Kim. No sense in maintaining silence.

"Not on your life. I wouldn't give Captain Leonard the satisfaction," Loki whispered.

"You may have severed communications, but we have a diplomatic attaché aboard. Her father will move galactic parliaments to get her back."

A funny feeling began jumping in Loki's sternum.

Kim moved to close Kat's mouth with duct tape anyway. Loki shook his head "no."

"You haven't been in orbit long enough for the GTE to triangulate your position," Konner said, also on a whisper. He didn't sound as happy as he should. "And I'm betting that when you found the jump point you did not have time to transmit the coordinates."

Kat just sat there smiling smugly.

Damn.

"The diplomatic attaché can't be too important if she allowed the captain to divert onto a wild lumbird chase," Kim said. He shrugged.

Loki breathed a little easier. The last time he'd communicated with Cyndi she had said she'd enter the diplomatic corps before she married the sniveling flunky her father had selected for her. But Cyndi would never allow a mere commander captaining an IMP cruiser to divert her for long.

Unless . . .

"Whose idea was it for *Jupiter* to sit long enough to search for the jump point?" he asked Kat, looking directly into her eyes, praying that he'd be able to detect a lie.

"Mine," she replied. "I knew you had disappeared at those coordinates. I've been searching for you guys for a long time. Easy to convince my captain that IMP priorities required us to investigate outlaws and smugglers before shuttling a dippo around the galaxy."

"And you just happened to mention to your blonde dippo why you could not deliver her to her destination on time," Loki said quietly. His gut wanted to sink to his feet.

"Of course." Kat did not contradict the dippo's hair color. "As soon as I mentioned the name O'Hara, she agreed wholeheartedly that we must pursue you. In fact, Lucinda Baines even took a turn at the sensors."

"Shit."

Loki forgot evasive maneuvers. He forgot the king stone. He did remember to polarize the hull as he put the lander into a steep dive into the atmosphere. Like he should have done in the first place. Instead he had needed to show off for his long-lost sister and impress her with his piloting skills.

Nothing would impress Kat. She was an O'Hara.

Dirtside, he and his brothers had allies. The O'Haras were gods on the planet below. A few fighters would not have a chance there.

But he left his heart and his enthusiasm aboard *Jupiter*.

"Cyndi," he muttered over and over. Lucinda Baines. "Cyndi" to friends and her **lover**. How could **he** justify stranding every last person aboard *Jupiter* dirtside when one of them was the love of his life. The reason he had endured Mum's manipulations and obsessions just to get enough money to bribe his way back to citizenship.

He'd never get that precious change in status on the official database.

And he'd never earn Cyndi's forgiveness for hijacking her transport and stranding her in the middle of nowhere.

CHAPTER 30

(WELCOME! WELCOME, WELCOME,) Irythros chortled in Konner's mind. The red-tipped dragon flew loops and twirls around the fighters and the lander.

"You're going to crash into that thing!" Kat choked.

Konner's respect for her courage rose a facet. She didn't scream, though clearly she wanted to. She clenched her eyes closed and began murmuring some personal prayer. He couldn't catch the words.

"Irythros is smarter than we are," Konner replied, almost chuckling at the sight of the red-tipped dragon. "He will avoid us."

(Of course I will. Only a yearling silver dragon just out of the nest has so little control over his wings that he would make contact with Rover,) the dragon crowed.

The others in the lander did not react as if they heard Irythros. He must be transmitting on a tight beam to Konner only.

Hello, my friend, Konner replied, also on a tight beam. This telepathy talent was growing stronger with practice. Or maybe proximity to the dragon helped him. *Any news?*

(Trouble.) The joy vanished from the dragon's voice.

What kind of trouble? Alarm built in Konner. Fear of IMP troops capturing and molesting Dalleena crowded out coherent thought.

(Your mate is safe,) Irythros reassured him. *(Safer than you. I must protect you when, and however, I can.)*

Konner's head emptied of external thoughts. He felt a little light-headed and disoriented.

What in St. Bridget's name did the dragon mean?

(We of the nimbus have exiled the one you call Sam Eyeam, though he gives himself

another name. But the beacon still speaks to the stars. One you should not trust has betrayed you.)

Who, Irythros? Who should I not trust? Konner asked. Worry began to gnaw at his stomach and the back of his neck.

(*We of the nimbus may not speak his name.*)

Hanassa.

Irythros squeaked a loud protest that stabbed at Konner's eardrum as well as his mind.

"What is that thing?" Kat asked. Her voice still sounded strained but she had opened her eyes.

"That, baby sister, is a dragon," Loki said. He beamed with pride.

"St. Bridget, those things really do exist," she breathed. Now she leaned forward for a better look at the creature through the windscreen. Sunlight sparkled along his crystalline fur, reflecting it back to them in a myriad of prisms.

"Is that blood showing through his horns and wing veins?"

"Doubtful," Kim replied. "Each adult male dragon sports a different color. I understand the females are iridescent, all colors blending into no color at all. This one still has hints of silver in his hide—signs of a juvenile. They are born a dark pewter color and get more silvery as they mature until they are as transparent as glass. By my guess and from what Iianthe has told me, I presume the purple-tip and this red-tip are from the same litter. They are less than three decades old." He too leaned forward.

"Litters? Not clutches?"

"Litters. Our dragons are mammalian, bearing live young, suckling them. They have fur instead of hide. Each hair is like an individual crystal that directs the eye around the dragon," Kim continued to lecture all he had learned about the elusive creatures.

"How long is a year on this planet?" Kat cut off his monologue. She sat back, gathering information now as well as satisfying her curiosity.

Konner needed more information, too. What kind of trouble did Irythros warn him of?

"Three hundred fifty-two point six local solar days," Konner replied, forcing his mind back into the conversation. He'd spent time observing the stars and moon, verifying what the computers had told him. He agreed with the calculations, but found satisfaction figuring it out for himself.

"And how long is a day around here?" Kat tried to look casual, but she kept leaning farther forward for a better view. The huge continent below them gave way to the ocean. Soon they would be over the Great Bay and home.

"Twenty-seven Earth standard hours," Konner replied. He suddenly realized he'd had no trouble adapting to the longer day or shorter moon cycles. As if his body knew what his mind only recently began to accept. This planet was home.

His lover lived here. This was home. But, oh, how he missed traveling the stars. There had to be a way he could do both.

Presuming they all survived the coming encounter with the IMPs.

Irythros continued to fly around them, more maneuverable than the man-made craft. He offered no more conversation, even when Konner prodded him mentally.

Loki slowed the vehicle as he descended. The atmosphere glowed around them from the heat of their reentry. Shields automatically slid across the windshield, deflecting light as well as heat. The interior lighting snapped on to compensate. Yellow-red light similar to Earth's sun.

And seemingly alien to Konner after five months of the redder but dimmer light of Star MKO in the local heavens.

"Any sign of pursuit?" Loki asked.

"Can't tell. Sensors still gummy from the green layer. We need a bath before we land." As Konner spoke, Irythros plunged into a steep dive. He entered the choppy waters below without a splash. Seconds later he swooped up. A fish, nearly as large as himself, was clutched in his talons.

"Can your dragon sense intruders?" Kim asked, eyes glued to the dragon.

Konner stilled himself, waiting for the clarity of mind to listen to the dragon. His vision dimmed. Colors lost intensity. Edges lost their definition. And then . . .

(*I caught it!*) Irythros chortled. (*I caught a behemouth. Tonight I feast.*) With his last words the dragon dropped his prey upon an open desert behind them.

Konner cringed, almost hearing the thud of its landing through his contact with Irythros. The fall killed the monstrous fish. Then the dragon landed gracefully beside his dinner and loosed a long spurt of green fire.

Irythros continued to ignore Konner's mental probes.

"Dragons are civilized. They cook their food before dining," Loki informed their sister.

"Nothing about this place is civilized. Yet. Including you three."

"You'd be surprised, little sister," Konner said. His mind remained open to the dragon. He listened to his siblings with half his attention. "Loki, let me take control. I want to try something the dragon taught me."

Maybe Irythros would release more information if he saw the lander and its passengers as kindred spirits.

Reluctantly, Loki shifted piloting interfaces to Konner.

"What are you going to do?" Kat asked skeptically.

"Drown some unwanted passengers." Konner grinned at her. If she was ever to be part of the family, she had to learn to accept their teasing.

She blanched at Konner's words, but held her tongue.

"No. You aren't going to do what I think you are going to do." Loki looked pale as well. His fingers curled and brushed his interface. He wanted control of the lander back.

"Why not?"

"Because this thing was built by the GTE, not to our specs." Loki's voice rose an octave as he braced himself for a steep dive.

"We'll see." Konner let go of his contact with Irythros. He'd learned enough from the dragon. Now he needed to listen to the ship. "Kim, does this thing have atmosphere wings?" he asked. His voice came out hoarse and barely above a whisper.

"Little ones," Kim replied. He moved his hand to a lever above his head. The manual override. If the craft lost power, the wings could catch the winds and glide to a softer landing than a straight plunge. Modern pilots rarely used them for anything but emergencies. There wasn't even a place on the pilot screen for activation.

"Little is all I need." Konner adjusted his angle of entry and slowed.

"One hundred meters to impact," Loki said. He called out the numbers as they descended.

Twenty meters above the water with the engines slowed to a near stall Konner called out, "Wings. Now."

The lander shuddered and creaked and abruptly slowed.

Two heartbeats later they impacted the water. Konner's head whipped back and slammed into the headrest of his chair. His teeth clanged together and he bit the inside of his cheek. He tasted blood.

His spine jolted. An ache spread outward.

Their world became blue. Bubbles streamed past them along with fish and seaweed. Light played games with shifting currents. He wanted to linger and observe. He couldn't.

Fighting gravity and pressure, he reached for the interface. The ship did not respond.

Water trickled in from around the seal of the tiny hole in the hull. Steady drops hit Konner's face. The trickle became a stream.

"Sluggish as a garbage scow!" Loki spat. He wrenched control away from Konner. "Kim, get the sealer out. Now!"

Kim reached for the tube of cerama/metal caulk. He moved gingerly, not jarring his body further.

The lander wallowed in the water and sank deeper.

"I'll have you know, this lander is the latest model. Engineers can't design anything better!" Kat spluttered.

"You could design something better in your sleep," Loki replied. "Not even a joystick to control this heap of junk."

"Imitating dragons diving into the depths of the ocean is not the kind of maneuver any sane pilot would put a ship through," Kat retorted. "If you'd just let me . . ."

"Forget it, Kat. You may be the best pilot the GTE can produce, but I taught you how to fly." Loki's fingers flew over the interface. Hard as he looked, he could not find anything resembling full manual control. The computers kept compensating for every correction he made.

"Our father taught me how to fly before he left. You just followed up on his lessons," Kat retorted.

"You know, if you hadn't put that red-tailed spiny lizard inside her pants when she was five, she might be more cooperative." Konner grinned at Loki.

"That was you!" Loki spluttered. "You put the lizard on her. I was there to protect her."

"But it was your idea," Konner protested.

Loki couldn't even remember what game had inspired the prank.

"Manual is in the kneehole. Far right corner," Kat said. She sounded as if she begrudged the information. At the same time a memory clicked behind her eyes. That look always led to mischief; mischief that got Loki and Konner into trouble with Mum. "I'd have had us out of here by now if you'd just let me . . ."

"Forget it. I'm in charge," Loki spat at her. "You can help Kim seal around the windshield. I'm surprised this barge has held together this long!"

"Manual is a last resort," Kat continued. "You shouldn't reach for it, unless you are desperate."

"We are desperate," Konner whispered.

Loki glanced at Konner. He was pale and sweating.

"I know I copied every last move Irythros made. Including the twist upon entry. It should have worked."

"But we don't have a tail as long as the body for a rudder and you didn't collapse the wings the moment we entered the water," Loki reminded him. He reached left instead of right. If manual control was a last-ditch effort, then it would be opposite the dominant hand of most pilots. But convenient for the left-handed O'Haras.

Kat swallowed hard and scrunched her eyes closed the moment Loki found the toggle. She obviously did not like that he could second-guess her even without using telepathy.

"Wings?" Konner looked a little brighter. "Are they down now?"

"Kim, do it!" Loki called

The ship shuddered slightly as Kim shoved the lever upward. The wings locked into place with a clank that reverberated around the cockpit and inside Loki's skull.

He clenched his jaw against the beginning of a headache as he manipulated for manual control while trying to keep one eye on the windscreen and the other on the interfaces. "Damned inconvenient release when you're desperate," he muttered. At last the computer released control. The interface went blank, a small joystick rose from the panel.

Loki breathed a sigh of relief. The ball fit loosely into his palm. Designed for someone with smaller hands; a smaller *right* hand. A quick rotation of the stubby control and he had the feel of it. The lander's nose edged upward. It nudged something pliable, but heavy.

A startled dolphinlike creature stared at him through the bioglass windscreen. It blinked, then nosed the craft. When it encountered the resistance of the screen, it bounced back, working its fins and tail to maintain position.

"That must be a mandelph!" Kim exclaimed. He brought his nose up to the screen and made faces at the creature. "The original colonists brought dolphin embryos from Earth. They had genetically engineered language into their intelligence, looking for partners in fishing and exploration. But the creatures disappeared. The colonists thought they died out when released in the wild. But they went feral. Maybe interbred with something native. Local fishermen gave them the name because they have been known to help drowning fishermen back to shore and are quite adept at stealing fish from the nets. No one has mentioned anything about them speaking to humans, even telepathically."

"Is he always so . . . ?" Kat asked.

"Kim is our family scholar. He reads everything and remembers every word. He's collecting local lore now," Loki said. A smidgen of pride swelled in him. He'd helped Mum teach Kim how to read and encouraged the boy to study everything that came to hand since he could never go to school while they were on the run. Kim had quickly outstripped the tutorial programs available through local educational systems. Now he qualified for three doctorates. Someday, when he was no longer on the run, he would collect them.

"But how did you find out about the original colonists?" Kat shifted her gaze from the curious sea creature to Kim.

"We found journals. A full record of . . ."

"If this is a lost Earth colony, then why are the locals so primitive? No communications to monitor, no industry, nothing but farms and those are few and far between."

"Their own technology killed them. We don't intend to ever let that happen again," Kim said. Anger made his voice husky.

"This planet remains free of GTE interference," Konner added with equal vehemence.

"That's why you stole the king stone."

"That's why we stole the king stone."

"Make me understand why you think primitive life in the bush is more valuable than all the benefits of the GTE," she pleaded.

"We'll show you as soon as we get this garbage scow out of the water," Loki reassured her. "Observe closely, because if you do not understand, you will never leave this planet again. None of your people will be given a chance to hint to folks back home that this place exists."

Kat snorted as if she did not believe him.

Loki gritted his teeth. She was more stubborn than all three O'Hara brothers combined. Maybe as stubborn as Mum.

With that thought he shuddered.

All he needed was *another* strong-willed woman in his life.

So why did the image of Paola Sanchez rise before his mind's eye rather than Cyndi, the love of his life?

CHAPTER 31

◆ —— · —— ◆ —— · —— ◆

DALLEENA WATCHED the Others in indecision. Her tracking talent sensed that Konner returned. She knew that water surrounded him, but he did not drown. Had he flown another vessel into the Great Bay? He did not need her at the moment. But she needed to tell him that Taneeo had disappeared in the move to the other village, then reappeared with two dozen men in thrall and returned all of the weapons and comms to the Others.

She also needed to warn Konner about the Others. They had broken a flag of truce. They honored nothing.

Even now the guards tramped about the fields and swamps, crushing delicate plants and heedlessly scattering wildlife in all directions. One of them took aim at the red bull with his long weapon.

The bull! The heart of the village livestock.

He could not be allowed to kill the beast. They would have to borrow a bull from a neighboring village—rarely a wise move for many reason—or wait for one of the calves to mature.

Saving the bull was more important than watching the intruders from her hiding place. Raiders. Nothing more than pirates.

She abandoned her hiding place and ran full tilt for the man taking aim at the bull.

The belligerent, red creature pawed the ground, head lowered, nostrils steaming, preparing to defend his territory and his harem.

Too far away. She increased her speed. Her lungs labored. Her heart pounded. Her legs strained. Her feet burned with power and speed.

She saw the IMP's finger tighten on the trigger.

"No!" she screamed.

The man barely shifted his attention to her, but his grip on the trigger eased.

Dalleena took a flying leap, knowing she must fall short.

Miraculously she collided with the man. They tumbled to the ground together. His gun flew away.

The bull charged. The ground thundered beneath Dalleena. She looked up. Enormous horns filled her vision. The tips gleamed sharply.

She thought nothing. Said nothing. Only stared in horror at approaching death.

All around her, she heard shouts and screams of panic and warning.

The shooter tried to scramble from beneath her.

And then those monstrous horns scooped her up and sent her flying over the top of the bull's head.

She landed hard. Something snapped. Something else crunched.

Black stars crowded her vision. She could not breathe. She could not move.

Pain filled her being. Fiery lances shot through her with each attempted breath. Death. Release.

If she died now, would Konner know that her last thought was of him?

"Something is wrong," Konner said as he jumped out of the lander's hatch.

Loki had parked the vessel three klicks from *Rover*, well away from IMP patrols.

"Of course something is wrong," Loki said as he joined Konner on the ground. "Our home is swarming with IMPs."

They watched the enemy prowl around the village. Few strayed more than a single kilometer from the cluster of their comrades.

"Dalleena is not here." Konner made a rapid circuit of the lander, searching with all of his senses for sight, sound, smell, or *feel* of Dalleena anywhere in the vicinity.

"She would be here if she could." Kim placed a soothing hand upon his shoulder.

"Konner, you only spent one night with the woman. Maybe she's had second thoughts." Loki shrugged his shoulders.

Konner pinned him with a glare.

"Okay, maybe she is special to you. But any one of a hundred things could occupy her right now, including spying on the IMPs. Maybe she's just late."

"No. I know she's in trouble. I know it here." Konner pounded his gut with a fist. "And I know it here," he said more softly, open palm atop his heart.

"Trust your instincts," Kim agreed. He paused in the hatchway long enough to assist Kat down. The force bracelets still limited her movements.

"Well, if we're going to help your lady, shouldn't you remove these?" Kat held up her hands.

"Your word of honor as an O'Hara that you will not try to escape." Loki planted fists on his hips.

"My word of honor as an officer of the Imperial Military Police that my duty is to escape and warn my superiors of your threat to the stability of the Empire." She assumed a posture as arrogant as Loki's even with the force bracelets inhibiting her arms.

"The bracelets stay." Loki insisted.

"I wish I had Dalleena's tracking talent. Then I could find her," Konner said. He set off toward the fields beside the village. She was supposed to have watched the IMP intruders from a safe distance.

(*Listen to your heart,*) Irythros said into his head.

Konner stopped short. He paid no attention to his siblings as they plowed into his back.

"Speak plainly, Irythros," he commanded.

(*Be still. Listen.*)

"Basic technique for working magic," Kim whispered into his ear.

"You heard him?" Konner did not think anyone could overhear a private conversation with a dragon. Unless the dragon wished.

"That was more than just one dragon talking. I still have a minor connection to Iianthe. Through him, I heard them all speak." Kim shrugged as if listening to dragons was an everyday occurrence. For Kim and his Tambootie, it might be.

Kat came up beside them and rolled her eyes. "More mumbo jumbo. Why not use the sensors to isolate groups of people. Surely the natives have had enough separation from humanity to have a slight DNA variance."

"Tech doesn't solve every problem," Konner nearly shouted at her. "The locals are as human as you and I. Three hundred years isn't enough for genetic drift."

"Don't be so bushie defensive," Kat snarled. "I didn't intend it to be an insult."

"We have to do something with the king stone, Konner." Loki placed a reassuring hand on his shoulder. "Soon. Probably before we can look for Dalleena. This is the first place the IMPs will look for it, as soon as they realize we've left the ship."

A moment of panic grabbed Konner. He had to find Dalleena. But the entire future of this planet depended upon keeping the king stone out of IMP hands.

Why hadn't he just smashed it?

Because it was alive and he could no more kill the crystal than he could murder a human.

"You may have to choose between saving the king stone and saving Dalleena," Loki reminded him.

"I'll scout the village." Konner checked the position of the sun. Still plenty of daylight. "You three transfer the stone to *Rover* and recharge the fuel cells. I'll be back in an hour. Then we'll look for a place to secrete the stone."

"What kind of place. I'll review the maps . . ." Kim said.

"I'll know the place when I see it." Konner stalked off. A plan nudged his brain. But he couldn't do anything about it until he knew Dalleena was safe.

He began walking.

"Take me with you, Konner." Kat hurried to catch him.

"Why? So you can escape?"

She answered him with silence.

"You stay here where our brothers can keep you out of trouble."

"Define trouble."

"Mari Kathleen O'Hara Talbot." He turned his back on her and kept walking.

The distance to the village had never seemed longer. Before the circle of huts came into view, Konner angled south to keep small hills between him and the intruders. Then he crawled through tall grasses to the edge of the plowed fields.

The moment he dropped to all fours, he heard/sensed frantic movement off to his left. He risked a peek above the tasseled tips of the wild grass. Five uniformed IMPs carried something away from the bull's pasture. Medic Lotski forged ahead of them speaking rapidly into her comm unit.

Konner wished he were closer. At this distance he could not identify the injured person. Too many people crowded around the inert figure to determine clothing, size, or coloring.

A terrible feeling gripped his gut.

He crawled closer, using the distraction of a serious injury or illness among the IMPs to move faster than he would if armed patrols still swept the area.

He noted a number of natives bound with force bracelets and crude rope on the far side of the fire. Taneeo among them. Yaaccob, the village elder from the neighboring community hunched in the middle of the group, working silently at his rope bindings.

Konner watched the IMPs carry the limp figure into the largest cabin, the one he shared with Loki. The home he had invited Dalleena into last night. As the men carrying the burden maneuvered through the narrow doorway, Konner caught a glimpse of dark leather trousers, the legs stuffed into crude boots. Above the waist, he saw a white homespun shirt and leather vest.

His heart leaped to his throat.

Dalleena!

CHAPTER 32

M ARTIN FORTESQUE faced his mother.
In person.

No hiding behind a computer-enhanced vid screen. He had to do this in person.

"Mother . . ."

"I told you to call me Melinda." She continued working at the stack of messages on her personal desktop. The entire surface was nothing more than a compressed vid screen that allowed her touch point corrections. A miniature electronic pencil dangled from her subdued earrings. She detached it from the molecular adhesive of the gold jewelry and highlighted something on her desk, then returned the tool to its resting place. "You are nearly grown now. Soon I will train you to help me run the corporation. In business circles we must appear as equals even though I will always hold a controlling share of stock and votes on the board of directors."

"Mother, will you look at me when I speak?" Martin couldn't keep the childish waver out of his voice.

Something in his tone must have startled her, for she looked up sharply, narrowing her eyes to look directly at him. And only at him.

Perhaps she had a scrap of motherly emotion in her after all.

Before she reverted to corporate coldness, Martin plunged forward with his planned speech.

"Mother, I need access to systems beyond my tutorials."

"Why? So you can interfere with my shipping manifests again?"

"No." That was strictly true. Martin had no intention of messing with shipping *manifests*. "It's for a school project. I need to do some research."

"Such as?" Melinda touched a corner of her screen.

Martin had no doubt his full curriculum spread before her in minute detail.

He had to make this sound good.

"I . . . ah . . . I'm doing a report on the changes in shipping lanes since the advent of the armed conflict with the Kree." The only other sentient beings humanity had encountered since entering space had proved belligerent in territorial disputes. So far, those had been few and far between. However, the GTE had taken pains to stay out of sectors now claimed by the winged creatures.

Most of the population went about their lives as if the Kree did not exist and nothing barred the expansion of the almighty GTE. Those who lived near the border prepared for all-out war. Corporations that built their fortunes on interstellar trade had to be aware of the constantly changing boundaries and currencies.

"An admirable project, Martin. I shall review it when you are finished. Our business will benefit from such a study." Melinda made an adjustment to Martin's curriculum. "You are now free to use the system. But if I discover you tampering with anything, there will be repercussions."

Martin backed out of his mother's office as rapidly as he could and still remain upright. The moment the door whispered closed, he turned and ran back to his own suite.

Time had grown short. He had to remove port restrictions for *Martin* Konner O'Hara quickly. (And hadn't he and his friends had a time hacking his father's full name out of an obscure database on an even more obscure bush world.) Those port restrictions were the only things keeping Martin's father from coming to claim him. He was certain of it.

"Martin." Melinda's voice chimed through his personal chip embedded behind his ear.

"Yes, Mother?" He had no doubt she could hear him through hidden comm ports in the palace corridor.

"I have ordered you a new suit for your birthday. Be available for a fitting at seventeen hundred hours."

"Why do I need a new suit? I have six that still fit very well."

"We have an important appointment on your birthday. You must look your best."

"What appointment." Martin knew. But he had to play along as if his mother was as omnipotent as she pretended.

"An appointment that will ensure our future together. Never forget that you are my only child and heir." Melinda disconnected with a slight popping sound.

Martin was left with a vacancy between his ears from the absence of sound.

Come and get me, Dad. Please come and get me soon. We can't let her win this one.

(*South.*) A dragon voice spoke directly to Kim.

"Iianthe, greetings," he said. He peered at the cloud cover seeking the only purple-tipped dragon in the nimbus. No mistaking the deep, sonorous tones of his old friend.

(*What you seek is to the south.*)

"Loki, I think we are heading back toward the volcano," Kim told his brother. They stood beside *Rover*, waiting for Konner.

"More magic and hoodoo voodoo?" Kat asked sarcastically. She lounged against the shuttle as if she had no cares. But she worked at the force bracelets continuously. Her wrists looked like raw meat.

Kim spotted a flash of sunlight on a transparent wing. "Maybe we should let her ride the dragon who guides us." Kim looked at her levelly, with a half smile.

She blanched but returned his gaze with courage. Her chin lifted just a little in defiance.

For a moment Kim was proud of her. He just wished she recognized the family connection and cooperated more.

But if she capitulated too easily, would she be a true O'Hara?

"Loki! Kim! They have Dalleena. She's hurt. Bad." Konner pelted toward them, gasping for breath between words. "They've also captured Taneeo and about two dozen men from the other village.

A series of sharp feedback squeals brought him up short. He whirled around to face the direction he had come from.

Flashes of red pain filled Kim's vision. He felt the hot burst of energy against his skin and his thick skull. A need to bellow, paw the ground, and charge filled his being.

Then nothing. A great emptiness spread outward from Kim's navel.

"St. Bridget, they've killed the bull." Kim's mouth hung agape.

"Are you certain they shot the bull?" Konner started toward the pasture, then stopped short.

What could any of them do? Why would the IMPs intentionally kill a living animal? Supposedly they considered all life sacred. Civilized members of the GTE did not eat meat because they refused to take a life. Any life.

"How civilized are the Marines among your crew?" Kim turned slowly to face his sister.

Kat shrugged. "Many are bush born. Sergeants Duggan and Brewster are barely civilized."

Bushies ate meat in order to survive. The GTE demanded nearly all of their grain, fruits, and vegetables as payment for protection, medicines, and technology among the far-flung worlds. Bushies lived as exploited colonists. They could not enter the GTE as full members with voting rights or self-rule until they industrialized, gave up their uncivilized dietary habits, and domed their cities.

How could these IMPs appreciate the value of a single bull beyond a meal for the troops?

"They won't get away with this," Kim vowed.

"You can't stop them," Kat reminded them.

"I can make them pay."

"How? You have only a few weapons and fewer numbers," Kat continued.

"We have the king stone," Konner said. His voice was cold. For the first time that Kim could remember, his brother sounded mean.

Then Konner looked back toward the village. His face crumpled with despair. "I have to go to her."

"As much as we hate the IMPs," Loki said, placing a hand upon Konner's shoulder. "They have better medics, equipment, and medicines than we do. They won't let her die. Lotski is one of the good guys. She won't let a patient die."

"But what if it's the plague?" Konner balanced on the balls of his feet, ready to run toward Dalleena.

"We sowed the entire area quite liberally with selenium this summer," Kim reminded him. "The bioengineered virus is now inert. You found the cure, Konner. You know we eliminated the plague."

"What if . . ."

"No. Do not think about it. We have work to do. You have to tell us what to do with the king stone."

"He could give it back," Kat offered.

None of the brothers listened to her.

"Without the king stone, *Jupiter*'s orbit will decay and the ship will crash. Your people are stranded here, Kat. They invaded and lost. They have to learn to live among us on our terms. We can't let any of you leave. The GTE must never be allowed to pollute our home," Kim told her.

Konner stepped into *Rover*. "The dragons say we need to go south. Let's fly."

Kim placed his hands on Kat's shoulders and pushed her to follow Konner.

"Irythros spoke to you?" Kim asked Konner as they settled into their familiar places in the cockpit.

"The entire nimbus told me to find what I seek in the south."

"I got the same message. Do you think they mean for us to return to the volcano?"

"The strange magnetics would certainly help hide the crystals," Loki agreed. He gave Kat's force bracelets one more check before taking his place in the pilot's chair.

The cockpit only had three chairs. The brothers had never anticipated needing a fourth. So Loki placed their sister on the deck and restrained her with various cables crossed around her chest and hooked to the bulkhead of the cockpit. In a moment of compassion, Kim placed a cushion from the lounge behind her back and neck. She sighed in relief but said nothing.

"I have something better in mind than that haunted volcano." Konner looked smug.

"Do I dare ask what?" Kim asked as Loki sent the shuttle forward into takeoff.

"A place to hide us as well as the entire crystal array."

"Are you thinking what I think you are thinking?" Loki looked both pleased and pained. He shook his head and set course due south.

"The cloaking I developed for both *Rover* and *Sirius* is nothing more than a confusion field," Konner explained.

"Like those nearly invisible dragons?" Kat asked. "I should have guessed. They warp light rays defying the eye to look anywhere but at them, at the same time they challenge you to look nowhere else. Damn. Now I know where you hid your ship in orbit. I looked right at it and forgot I'd seen it." She hit her forehead with both palms.

She grimaced and eased her hands back into her lap.

Kat would be looking to steal the key to the bracelets at every turn. Being an O'Hara, she'd likely find it.

Kim reminded himself to keep a closer eye on her.

"If you are using the entire crystal array, then we need a roughly circular place," Loki mused, biting his lip in thought.

Kim took his eyes off Kat long enough to load maps and surveys onto his screens.

"If we were riding dragonback, we could fly lower, spot the place with our eyes," Konner said as he leaned over to check Kim's charts.

"There." Konner pointed to the top of one of the foothills to the Southern Mountains. A pass through the chain of peaks ran close by.

"Far enough east and north of the volcano that the volcano's EMF won't mask it from sensors," Loki objected.

"I don't need EMF to hide us. That's the right place. I can feel it." Konner sounded triumphant.

Kim felt a nod of agreement in the back of his mind from the dragons.

Loki shrugged and corrected course. The land beneath them began to rise as they neared the mountains, leaving the river plains behind.

"I'm willing to bet that when we get there, we find a confluence of ley lines," Kim said. He couldn't help but smile. With ley lines under his feet and Tambootie trees in the nearby woods, he could experiment with magic to his heart's content. Who knew what powers he would develop, pass on to his children. Perhaps even teach Hestiia to share in the powers.

"Ley lines?" Kat sat up straighter against the bulkhead. Her improvised crash harness strained against her shoulders.

"Think of theoretical transactional gravitons," Konner offered.

Kat's emerald-green eyes did not light with recognition.

"A web of energy that holds the universe together," Kim explained. "King stones use the lines of the web to maintain contact with the mother stone and facilitate faster-than-light communications. Ley lines are similar, but on a planetary basis. We don't know if they are connected to the gravitons or not. I suspect that we tap into them for energy to fuel our psi powers. The number and consistency of the lines here augment our talents more than anywhere else." Even more so with a good dose of Tambootie. Kim dug in his pocket seeking a scrap of a leaf, anything to help him think straight.

He came up empty. His hands began to shake and his head ached. He clenched his fists and bit the inside of his cheeks to cover his aching need for more of the drug.

Kat slumped against the bulkhead where she sat. "More magic. You three are really giving in to bush madness."

"We don't see it as madness, Kat," Kim said quietly. "We see it as salvation for ourselves, the family, maybe even for the entire GTE. The exploitation of people and resources has got to stop. We won't let it come here."

"The emperor is trying," Kat replied defensively. "He has introduced legislation to allow bush planets membership in the GTE without doming and industrializing."

"But he hasn't succeeded in reversing the mind-set of six hundred billion people," Konner added.

"Not even a majority of the six thousand members of Parliament," Loki finished.

"When I can see a transactional graviton, or ley line, or whatever and feel the energy coursing through my body, then I might begin to listen to you." She set her face, O'Hara stubbornness written all over it.

"A confluence of ley lines coming right up!" Kim laughed to cover his trembling voice. A neat clearing, almost perfectly circular came into view. He drank in the sight, knowing he had come home.

Tambootie trees filled the nearby woods.

CHAPTER 33

✦ ━ · ━ ✦ · ━ ✦

KONNER GUIDED the king stone into a hole a meter and a half deeper than he was tall. He and his brothers had used the laser pulse from *Rover* to define the hole. Then counter-grav equipment purloined from the IMP lander lifted the chunk of dirt in a solid heap. It lay to the side of the hole, ready for deposit around the king stone once Konner had the stone anchored in position.

Now Loki held the shuttle in a tight hover directly above the center of the hole. Kim kept the cables wrapped around the crystal from tangling. At least he tried. His movements seemed clumsier than usual. The blue crystal spun frequently and Loki had to raise the stone higher while Kim untangled it.

Kat sat at the edge of the clearing, worrying her force bracelets. A frown drew deep lines beside her mouth and between her brows.

"A little to the left, Konner," Kat called out.

"Quiet. I can see where it has to go," Konner spat back at her. But he edged the cable a little to the left.

The crystal ceased dropping. "Another meter, Kim."

"We're out of cable," he called back, over the roar of VTOL jets Loki used to keep the shuttle in place.

"Damn!" Konner jumped down into the hole. He wrapped his arms around the stone. The weight of the thing shook his balance.

"I need your help, Kat."

"Not on your life, O'Hara."

"I'll take the bracelets off you."

"Promise?" She stood up and crossed the distance at a near run. Her face brightened.

"No, Konner. Keep her restrained. I'll come down." Kim looked as if he'd jump the eight meters from the shuttle to the ground.

"Kim, you'll break your neck. Where will she go if she tries to escape? She'd need a week or more to get back to the village on foot."

Just then, the stone jerked upward out of his arms. Kim waved frantically. The shuttle's nose jerked up and so did the king stone.

Konner stumbled. His nose crashed into the packed dirt on the side of the hole. Then the rest of his face followed.

"One of my last memories of you is with grime smudged all over your face from the fire at the household compound. You haven't grown up much in the last twenty years," Kat chuckled. She winced as she braced herself to jump into the hole beside him.

Once on his level she sobered. "You smiled at me and took my hand as we ran away from the noise and confusion. Your teeth showed bright against the dirt. I thought that everything would be all right just because you smiled for me, Konner. You don't smile enough."

"You pulled your hand out of mine, Katie. Why? I followed you, but lost you in the darkness. Why, Katie? We could have both gotten away if you'd just stayed with me."

She looked away a moment while she fished a handkerchief out of her front pocket. Her movements were awkward. The pain must have been incredible.

"I forgot Kim's teddy bear. I knew he wouldn't sleep without it." She swiped at the dirt on his face with the handkerchief. It came away filthy.

"Let me get those bracelets off you." He avoided the emotional moment by retrieving the electronic key from his inside vest pocket. He slapped both pockets. Both were flat and empty.

"Looking for this?" Kat held up the black remote.

"Yes." Konner grabbed it back. "How?" he asked as he pointed the gadget at the electrode between her wrists. A brief buzz from the bracelets and the wrist circles snapped open at the electrode.

"I picked your pocket between wiping your face and distracting you with poignant memories." Her half smile came back.

Konner returned it. Then he waved at Kim.

The shuttle lowered once more, and with it the king stone.

Konner wrapped his arms about the giant crystal. Kat did the same on the opposite size. Together they balanced it while Kim cut the cable from above. With feet braced, they both lowered the crystal until it rested firmly in the depression filled with fiber optics at the bottom of the hole.

The flat bottom nestled into the dirt as if coming home. For the first time in hours the strident wail of the crystal separated from its family shifted to a more harmonious note.

"It's happy here," Kat said. She looked surprised.

"It will be happier when I restore the array." Konner kicked some additional dirt against the base of the stone and stamped it down.

"Why do I think it won't move, even without bracing?" Kat did not assist in planting the crystal.

"Because your psychic talent is kicking in and you can hear it sing."

She shook her head and clambered out of the hole.

Konner followed her. They watched as Loki lifted the pile of dirt with the counter-grav and dumped it back into the hole. It mounded slightly. Konner wondered if he should tamp it down, make the excavation less visible.

Kat moved to board *Rover* the moment Loki settled the shuttle on the far side of the clearing.

"Now where?" she asked.

"You stay here." Konner left the mound of dirt. Rain would settle it better than he could and a storm was building off to the east. He smelled the cold moisture.

Both Kat and Kim looked surprised.

"I have to go to Dalleena." Konner took a deep breath to control the anxiety that had not left him since seeing his lover carried into the hut by the IMPs. Limp. Unresponsive. Bleeding.

"Kim, you and Loki need to start removing the central array of driver and directional crystals from *Jupiter*. I'm going after Dalleena. Taking Kat with us is too risky. She'll have too many opportunities to reveal our plans to the IMPs. We can't take a chance on anyone finding this place before I finish the confusion field or all personnel are evacuated and the landers deactivated."

"I have a wife, too, Konner. I need to check that Hestiia is okay."

"You'd know if she wasn't." The two brothers stared at each other in a moment of understanding. "The last we heard she was whole and hale. Dalleena isn't."

"We'll need help with the crystals. Hestiia, Raaskan, and a few others, I think," Kim replied hastily. "We stop long enough to pick them up."

Konner nodded and boarded the shuttle, pushing Kat aside.

She tumbled onto her backside. "And what am I supposed to do while you are gone?" Kat asked. She hadn't gotten up from her ignominious position. "I'll be all alone! I might be attacked by wild animals. Or wilder natives. I'll get cold and hungry. I'll be alone!"

Konner flipped a serviceable iron knife so that the blade tip embedded in the ground half a meter from her hand. A blade he'd forged and polished himself. He'd even bound it with strips of sinew to a section of deer antler for a hilt. Kat would never understand what a precious gift he gave her.

"Learn to use this for defense. For cutting bracken for a bed. For digging roots to eat. I recommend the bulb of the yellow flowering plant beside the creek. Fire is optional, if you can figure out how to start one by striking sparks off the knife blade with a rock. Use the knife for cutting branches to build a lean-to. Vines make very good twine. The presence of the king stone will probably protect you from wild animals bigger than you are. I'd advise you not to leave the clearing until one of us returns for you, though. There are bandits in these hills, Gypsies, too—the locals call them Rovers. They don't have the same sense of honor as we do."

"You're abandoning me again. I should have known."

"Stranding for a few hours. Not abandoning," Kim clarified for her. "We'll be back. We keep our promises."

"You didn't twenty years ago."

"You'll never know how much trouble we went through to go back for you and find you gone. Presumed dead," Konner said bitterly.

"And what am I supposed to do while you go off adventuring?"

"Think about circles." Konner slapped the hatch control. It irised shut slowly. He did not turn away from her penetrating gaze until several layers of cerama/metal separated them. Still he felt the green fire sparking from her eyes, stripping him to his soul, and finding him wanting.

Guilt slammed him in his face. In his worry for Dalleena and the fate of the planet he had forgotten his primary goal: to gain custody of his son.

Time leaked away from everything he held dear.

Kim gathered Hestiia into his arms the moment he cleared the hatch of *Rover*. He clung to her a long time while Loki and Konner barked orders to the villagers. His wife fit tightly against him, her dark curls just reaching his chin.

"Beloved," Hestiia whispered. She tried to draw away from him. He tucked her closer. "Beloved, I have dire news."

"It does not matter. I have you in my arms. All is well," he replied, trying to believe his own words.

"Taneeo has betrayed us."

Kim stilled in diappointment. "I guessed he would, but I did not want to believe it. He is our friend. We saved him from Hanassa. I thought he was stronger," he said sadly. Lumbird bumps rose on his skin. A sour taste began in the back of his throat.

"Taneeo led two dozen men, some from our village, some from Yaaccob's village. They returned weapons and comm units to the Others," Raaskan added. Carefully he related what he had seen.

A chill ran up Kim's spine.

"Taneeo is not Taneeo," Pryth said as she surged through the crowd toward Kim and his brothers.

"I agree, he's not been himself since . . . But I thought he had overcome Hanassa's pressure. I thought his will was stronger."

"Another is now Taneeo." The old woman turned and parted a way through the crowd as a ship through water. Hardened warriors, children, and matriarchs shifted to allow her easy passage.

"At least we know who now hosts Hanassa," Konner said quietly.

As one, the villagers crossed their wrists, right over left, and flapped their hands.

Silence hung over them like a heavy cloud.

"We don't have time to deal with this," Loki said. He began pacing in front of *Rover*'s hatch. "We need to get the crystals from *Jupiter* and get back to Kat before she finds a way to escape."

"After dark I will take a group of females to rescue our people from the Others." Hestiia straightened away from Kim. "We will deal with their treachery." A hard glint came into her eyes.

Her fierceness almost frightened Kim.

"I sure would not like to be Taneeo at about sunset," Konner muttered.

His brothers nodded.

"Let Pryth lead the women. I want you with me," Kim insisted to his wife. "I do not want to take a chance that you might be captured," he said more quietly, for her ears alone.

"It is my place as the wife of a Stargod to lead . . ."

Kim stopped her protest with a finger across her lips. "I need you with me. I trust you to help. Not all of our people have the . . . ability to assist us." Many of the villagers would be so frightened of flying in *Rover* they would be useless in retrieving the crystals.

"Right," Loki said. "Raaskan, Poolie, you two come with us." He pointed to several others who had proved themselves more adaptable to change than others.

"I'm staying here. I'll see to Dalleena," Konner said firmly.

"Fine. Whatever." Loki jumped aboard *Rover*, ushering half a dozen villagers into the cabin.

"Loki, Konner, are we sure we want to do this?" Kim hesitated to move to the lander. The sight of his wife, their friends, all they had to lose could not soothe his conscience. "We are going to strand three hundred people on this planet. Separate them from their friends and families, put an end to all of their hopes and dreams."

"It's not the same, Kim," Loki barked. His face flushed with anger. Or was it guilt?

"It is the same. We are going to imprison these people against their will."

"They would do the same to us," Konner reminded him.

"Does that make it right?" Kim began to shake.

"No." Konner said. "It does not make it right. But we have to weigh the welfare of our people against what would happen if we do not do this."

"They are invaders," Loki insisted. "Humans resisted the Kree when they invaded Earth. We have the same right here on our home."

"I go on the record as having serious reservations against this." Kim clenched his teeth to keep his chin from trembling.

"Fine. You record it later. Let's get this show on the road!" Loki dismissed the problem by marching forward to *Rover*'s cockpit.

"We will find a way to make it right, Kim," Hestiia whispered. "After we ensure the safety of our people."

"I certainly hope so." Kim reluctantly climbed into the lander.

CHAPTER 34

CHAOS. LANDERS, shuttles, jolly boats, and fighters fled *Jupiter's* launch bay and scattered in all directions. Some headed for the ocean directly beneath the ship's decaying orbit. Others sought a more hospitable landing place.

At least some of the scout ships must be seeking the king stone. Loki did not believe they would find it.

He slid *Rover* into the loading bay just as the doors began their slow slide closed. Kim squeezed in behind him with the lander.

Waiting for bay doors to close, force fields to reestablish, and atmosphere to fill seemed to take forever.

In the meantime, lines of IMP personnel formed in the corridor beyond. Their strident voices leaked through the sealed hatch. Fists pounded upon the bulkhead demanding entrance. Tension crawled along Loki's spine like a thousand itching bugs.

"Why the panic exodus?" Kim asked over the comm. "The orbit should not be decaying yet."

"Did you notice some slowing in the spin?" Loki replied. "Something other than normal gravitational pull is already affecting this ship. At this rate, they'll be lucky to get everyone off, even using escape pods. The fact that we have one of the landers and Konner ditched another means more trips back and forth, using up more fuel, and twice the panic."

And military discipline had broken down. Severely. Why wasn't the infamous Commander Amanda Leonard commanding an orderly escape? Where was the captain of *Jupiter* anyway?

"While they run to and fro without thinking, we can move in with minimal interference." Kim sounded defeated already. His guilty conscience must really be bothering him.

Or was it the Tambootie he had stuffed in his pockets before liftoff? The kid definitely needed a long treatment with gamma blockers.

Loki did not have the luxury of a conscience or an addiction. As the eldest, he was responsible for the family's safety and their success.

"Let the droids refuel," Loki told Raaskan. "After that, no one but us gets aboard these two ships. And keep an eye on Kim. Don't let him do too much. Think about his orders before you do anything."

"I shall lead the foraging party for the red crystals," Raaskan said quietly. "I have memorized the plans. Stargod Kim should remain here to help guard the ships."

Loki nodded agreement. Under the influence of so much Tambootie, Kim might bond with the directional crystals and take off on some lumbird-brained excursion of his own.

"What about the people pounding on the doors?" Hestiia asked. She looked as if she wanted to throw the hatch open, or maybe grab a spear and run all of the IMPs through.

Part of Loki wanted to give in to the pleas of the people waiting outside the doors and give them a ride back to the planet. He did not dare. They had other means of escape. *Jupiter* should not crash for several weeks yet. Possibly months or even years. Plenty of time to strip the ship of everything usable.

Except the spin had already begun to slow. Momentum should have kept it going for weeks. Why weren't the techs making corrections manually?

Raaskan relayed the orders to his small band of warriors. Each was armed with iron knives, clubs, and/or iron tipped spears. They looked a fearsome bunch. More fearsome than fearful, he hoped. Bringing them along had been a calculated risk. They'd never encountered null g before. They'd never seen a spaceship.

But they were survivors one and all. And they obeyed the Stargods with unflinching loyalty.

Kim grabbed two antigrav cargo sleds from the racks along the bulkhead. Raaskan relieved him of the burden. Hestiia and Poolie each grabbed two more. Loki took the last two and parceled them out among the villagers. That left four men, including the two brawny blacksmith apprentices to guard the shuttle and the lander. And Kim. Enough.

Gravity remained here in the outer section of the ship, not as heavy as the last trip. Enough to make the antigrav sleds necessary.

Kim directed four men from his crew to begin loading the sleds with the small red directional crystals from the nearest rabbit hole. One hundred forty-four of the small red stones would take time to load, but should offer no great challenge.

"I'll stay here and supervise. Can you get the drivers?" Kim asked. His eyes looked bloodshot and he moved sluggishly.

"Twelve greens shouldn't present a problem. Getting from here to the crystal room and back again will be the problem. Konner insisted we need the drivers from the midship array. They are a fraction bigger than the aft and bow circles. How do we keep the evacuees from breaking in here and stopping us?"

"Give me two minutes at the sensor terminal." Kim grinned, more sarcastic than humorous. He nibbled on a leaf of the Tambootie. Then he nearly skipped toward the computer terminal near the hatch into the corridor as if no more than normal g pressed upon him.

Loki shook his head at the immediate change in his brother. He vowed to himself that as soon as they returned dirtside, he'd get Kim those gamma blockers.

"Can you hack your way into bridge controls from here?" Loki asked Kim. Meant for recording quartermaster manifests, the terminal had limited access to the primary systems.

"Doubtful. But I can screw up a lot of signals. Anyone bothering to look at screens will see that the bay doors are damaged and the bay is empty and open to vacuum." Kim began working away at the touch screen.

Within a few moments, the line of desperate people fled the corridor, seeking another escape. Loki heard cries of dismay. They pushed and shoved each other ruthlessly. One small woman had trouble turning and moving with the flow. A heavy duffel bag on her shoulder already overbalanced her.

"Out of my way, SB," a squarely built man with a blind justice insignia on the collar and cuff of his black uniform snarled. He had a prow of a nose beneath black hair and beady eyes. "I'll have your stripes for blocking my way. I'm the judge. I ordered this evacuation. Now everyone out of my way. No one gets off this boat until I do." He shoved the woman viciously, slamming her into a bulkhead.

Her head smacked against the cerama/metal walls. The judge did not even look back at her. Blood trickled down the side of her face.

The crowd ignored her. They stepped around her. One slight man tromped on her sprawled legs trying to get out of the way of a bigger man.

Loki bit his lip. He gulped hard. She needed help. He should go to her. He didn't have time. *She* was not his responsibility.

Hestiia prodded his back. "We have to get going. She is the enemy. Not our concern," she said.

"I can't just leave her."

Loki's stomach sank. He had to obey his conscience after all.

• ——◆—— •

Kat looked up at the thick cloud cover. A raindrop plopped onto her cheek. Then another struck her eye. She blinked rapidly to clear her vision.

"Nacring Nebulae!" she cursed. "First they abandon me. Then they kidnap me. Now they've stranded me in the middle of the bush in the middle of a rainstorm with only a primitive iron knife."

She turned slowly, trying to get her bearings. Which way led back to the village where her crewmates had landed?

Thick clouds obscured the sun's position. She'd never find north without help.

"I don't dare strike out on my own." She almost wept. "I don't even know which direction to go, even if I knew which direction to take."

She clenched her fist around the hilt of the weapon. The chunk of horn hacked from some poor animal warmed under her touch, seemed to mold to her grip. She stared at it a moment.

"Well, if you want to work, best we get started." She clamped her mouth shut on the last words. "What am I doing, talking to an inanimate object. A knife, by St. Bridget. A bloody *knife*."

The barbaric weapon did not answer her. Of course it wouldn't. She hadn't expected it to. She just needed to hear the sound of her own voice to convince herself she wasn't dreaming. That wasn't stepping over the line into insanity.

Was it?

Insanity? She'd invoked a saint she had not thought about since early childhood. Governor Talbot—Dad—had followed a different faith from her birth mother. She no longer believed in saints and miracles, or dragons and unicorns. She believed in her own hard work and intelligence.

Surely she could tame one wild clearing in the middle of nowhere long enough to give herself shelter and some food.

Her stomach growled. "Why didn't I bother with lunch before those barbarians invaded my ship?" she moaned.

(*Because you were too excited at the prospect of meeting your family to eat.*)

"Who said that?" Kat turned rapidly, scanning the clearing for intruders. She kept her knife at the ready. It balanced easily in her hand. She saw no one to use the weapon on. Not even a small rodent that might become dinner.

Then she shuddered at her primitive thoughts. No matter how desperate, she would not succumb to killing an animal, taking a life, merely to serve her noisy stomach. Maybe if she missed a meal or two a few of the extra inches on her hips would dissolve.

(*You must eat to keep your energy and your mind at peak functioning.*)

"Who is hiding in the bushes?" she demanded. She charged a large clump of greenery slashing with the knife. She bounced against flimsy branches. Her weapon embedded in the trunk. As she wrenched it free, she kept looking over her shoulder for the speaker.

A low chuckle came from behind her.

She whipped around, brandishing the knife. Nothing. No one. He had sounded so close.

Who?

Maybe she was going insane. People stranded on bush planets did that.

Maybe she was only hungry. Konner had said something about the bulb of a plant with yellow flowers, down by the creek.

Where in the frocking black hole was the creek?

(*Listen.*)

Sound advice. Her brain must be working properly and her imagination only put voice to it. A bright tenor voice. Too high to be one of her brothers. Too slow and drawling to be one of her shipmates.

She stood still and listened to the clearing. Birds chirping. Insects buzzing. Wind and rain. Grass growing. Trees reaching out with gratitude for the moisture . . .

"Stop that!"

Another low chuckle.

Then she heard it, beneath the other sounds, a soft ripple of water, faster than the dripping rain, gentler than the wind. She headed toward the sound.

Her nose worked in wonder. Gone was the citrus smell that permeated ships and domed cities. Green growth, falling leaves, sap from a softer wood, and the faint musk of an animal in rut flooded her senses. And over it all she inhaled the clean scent of vibrant life.

Her skin prickled from the cooler air. She rubbed her arms for warmth. The ground beneath her feet became spongy and descended at a gentle angle. Kat pushed aside drooping ferns. One of the fronds sliced her palm. She jumped back startled. Then she stared in fascinated horror at the drops of blood welling up from the wound.

A string of curses escaped her.

(*Suck it,*) the voice in the back of her mind suggested.

She knew she should. Enzymes in her own saliva would begin the clotting and healing process. But the thought of tasting blood sent waves of revulsion through her. All of them knotted in her stomach.

If only she had a med kit she could spray the wound with a cooling gel that would clean and disinfect as well as seal it. Cool. She needed something cold to slow the bleeding. Then pressure and elevation.

(*The creek.*) This time the voice coaxed as if dealing with a small child.

In the bush she was an infant.

Not quite an infant. She'd taken shore leave on bush planets before. She'd aced three advanced survival courses. St. Bridget, she'd been born and raised in the bush. She knew what to do.

Always before, she'd had the option of an emergency beacon and extraction if she became overwhelmed, or hurt, or ill. Not here. Not now. She had to think and act in her own defense.

"The creek it is. I just hope I don't get infected with some exotic bacteria that causes my flesh to rot and slough off, leaving me a living skeleton."

(*Hardly.*)

She was getting used to the voice now.

Avoiding the ferns and placing her feet carefully, she descended a few more steps to find a wide pool fed by a small waterfall and draining by a narrow defile into another steeper fall. She plunged her hand into the pond. Cool water soothed the slight burn of the wound. After a few moments she lifted it free of the gently lapping water. Several moments passed and only a few beads of blood appeared. Satisfied, she looked for something to press against the wound.

All she could find was her trouser leg. Dared she risk getting her hand dirty again on her grubby uniform? Captain Leonard was finicky about uniforms. Kat followed her example and never allowed anything to mar the sharp crease on her trousers or the grime to show. Instantly, she felt grubby and itchy. The rain did nothing to cleanse her of the sensations. Surely kidnap and stranding in the bush offered an adequate excuse for a less than pristine uniform.

She pressed her palm against her thigh. What was one more stain? Still she wanted a bath and a clean uniform. NOW.

"I'm as bad as a dome breather," she admonished herself. "This isn't building a shelter or providing me with fuel."

She looked for yellow flowers. Three stalks of them to her left drooped under the weight of the rain. A few thrusts of the knife loosened the soil at their base. She tugged them free. Sure enough a fat bulb grew at the end of each plant.

She shook off loose dirt. Too much remained. Back to the pool. She had to kneel in the muck at the edge, further staining her uniform. After swishing the knife and vegetation in the water, some splotches of soil and rotting vegetation clung to both. Nothing for it but to use her hands to scrub.

A little pressure from her fingers cleared off any remaining debris. She let her hands linger in the soothing water. Not as cold as she expected. The feeder creek looked like it cascaded straight down the nearest mountain glacier. It should numb her skin by now.

"Hot springs?" she asked the air.

No answering voice, just a sensation of a nod of agreement.

She'd have to remember the hot spring when the rain chilled her to the bone.

"A fire. Konner said I could start a fire by sparking a rock off the knife blade." If there was any wood dry enough to burn.

Cautiously, she broke a path back to the clearing, being careful to avoid the fronds of the plant she named saber ferns. Beneath some of the taller shrubs she spotted small twigs and branches that had broken off in an earlier season. These she gathered. By the time she made one full circuit of the clearing, she had an armload of bigger branches.

"Now if only I can remember the formation for the most efficient fire."
She'd aced the classes on survival. As she'd aced all of her classes and graduated a year early. So why had what she had learned about fires slid out of her
brain like hot grease poured down a drain?

"What good was it to finish at the top of two classes and be denied assignment for years?" she muttered the old grief. Flying admin touch screens for
four years while training on every vessel in the fleet and earning graduate
degrees did not advance her career. Space time alone granted promotions.
Well, she had some space time now and look where it got her. Stranded on a
bush planet by her own flesh and blood.

"I'll get you for this, Brothers O'Hara. One way or another I'll see all
three of you mind-wiped or dead." Resolutely, she set about stacking her
wood. When she ran out of fuel, she sat back on her heels and admired her
construct. Text book construction. But would it work?

(*May I light this for you?*)

Kat looked up and stared straight into the swirling eyes of a red-tipped
dragon, steam trailing from its nostrils, teeth longer than her knife blade
dripping with saliva.

She fainted.

CHAPTER 35

LOKI GRABBED THE LATCH. He had to help the trampled crew woman. The rest of the mission had to wait. Hestiia followed him into the corridor, right on his heels. She stared about anxiously as Loki stooped to touch the stranger's neck.

Her pulse beat strong, if a little too fast. Her eyelids fluttered.

"Let me help you up," he said quietly, hoping for a soothing tone. He checked her insignia and name tag at the same time.

She opened her eyes and gasped. Her eyes threatened to roll up in another faint.

"I won't hurt you. My word of honor," Loki protested. He grasped her elbow and lifted her.

She scrambled to pull away from him.

"SB Lee, compose yourself," he ordered.

She nodded at his authoritative tone, blinking her almond-shaped eyes rapidly and chewing on her thick lower lip. Then her expression brightened.

A lone straggler hastened down the corridor, checking monitors every ten paces. He had a duffel matching SB Lee's slung over his shoulder.

Lee shrugged off Loki's helping hand and rushed to the newcomer's side. Jabbering explanations, they turned away from Loki and Hestiia. They seemed more interested in finding an escape vessel than reporting the presence of intruders.

Loki breathed a sigh of relief.

When the IMP couple disappeared around the curve, Loki led his troops toward the center of the ship.

They made good progress in the outer level. As they climbed, gravity lessened. At first the bushies smiled and bounded from corridor to corridor. They hopped and rebounded, delighted with the lessening gravity.

The next set of stairs upward gave them all fits until Loki got behind and pushed everyone and the sleds up. Then the fun began. All seven of Loki's charges began bouncing off bulkheads, ceilings, decks. They abandoned their sleds in order to experiment with the novelty of micro gravity.

Normally reserved and thoughtful, Hestiia turned a double somersault in midair. She quickly learned that she could increase her speed by grasping her knees and tucking her head.

Poolie walked delicately upside down. She took small, mincing steps and managed to maintain her orientation.

Niveean, a stout and seasoned warrior, lost his lunch in a cross corridor.

Loki stood back and watched for several minutes. As much as he wanted to rush to finish his job, he knew his helpers needed time to learn to move without the anchor of gravity and the orientation of a horizon. A few moments of play now might save them an hour of mishaps later when the sleds were laden with precious crystals.

Two dozen IMPs jogged toward them. At fifteen meters' distance, they stopped abruptly and brought their weapons to bear. Counter-grav equipment gave them stability in the .3g sector.

Loki gulped.

"State your business, bushie," the sergeant spat. His voice sounded a lot like one of his weapons would when he pulled the trigger.

"We're crew, in native disguise. Deep cover. We're salvaging for dirtside survival. Commander Leonard's orders," Loki returned. He refrained from saluting.

"Command code?"

Loki spat back the data stream he'd gleaned from Kat's mind. The one that opened the launch bay doors.

The sergeant nodded abruptly and signaled his men forward. They pushed past Loki and his natives, weapons shouldered.

At least some semblance of military discipline remained, even if it was lax. Leonard should have changed the command codes.

"You'll never be experts, but I think you can manage in null g now." Loki called his group together. "Follow me, move cautiously. Remember the bounce is strong. Keep your movements small and slow."

They had a few mishaps on the journey inward. The sleds did not want to move straight, especially up stairs. Niveean never did find a firm orientation and retched three more times before they reached the crystal room. He continued to plow forward, a small measure of the courage bred into him by centuries of warfare. A warrior endured pain and privation in order to protect his honor and those he held dear.

The chaos of the IMPs fleeing a sinking ship looked organized compared

to the mess in the crystal room. Six techs flew, literally, from crystal to terminal to workbench and back again. They rebounded expertly into proper tra-
jectories, grasping familiar handholds to brake or redirect their flight. Fiber
optics, cables, and tools trailed in their wake, presenting hazards to the unwary. One woman worked frantically at a terminal trying to become the king
stone for this array. The expression on her face showed the strain of thinking
and entering commands at speeds beyond normal human capability.

Hestiia watched them with her mouth half open. Awe brightened her
countenance.

Twelve beautifully clear, green crystals dominated the room, each a meter
high, bigger around than a blacksmith's well-muscled upper arm, and sharply
faceted. The bright glow of life had burned low in their cores. Unless their
connection to a king stone was restored soon, they would die. Loki had to get
them back to the clearing quickly and reconnect them as a family.

"If you are trying to stabilize *Jupiter*'s orbit, your job is futile," Loki announced to the techs.

"Fearsome Kahli!" one exclaimed. "It's him again."

"The O'Hara," stated another.

"Stinking bushie!"

At the last insult, anger burned Loki's cheeks. Every one of the men and
women in their ugly khaki coveralls had the short, compact stature of civils,
civilized citizens of the GTE. Sonic bathers. *Dome breathers.*

"I'll have you know that I bathe every day in real water with soap," he
replied coldly. He could not give in to the temper that demanded he lash out
with fists and feet. Too much depended upon getting the crystals safely back
to the clearing.

Loki moved to the first driver crystal. Konner had disconnected them.
The stones would not lash out with burning energy if disturbed. He twisted
the first one and lifted it out of its socket. Tens of meters of fiber-optic cable
attached to it tangled between the stone and its designated computer interface.

"Stop that. You're killing the ship!" A tech tried to pull the green crystal
from Loki's grasp.

"That is the idea, odiferous civil. This ship will crash and you and your
mates will be stranded dirtside forever," he snarled. He jerked to his left, pulling the stone away from the tech. The abrupt movement sent him spinning.

Niveean stopped Loki with a strong hand.

The tech hit the bulkhead. His head slammed against the unforgiving
walls with a sickening thud.

"Techs, take care of your buddy. Time for you to join the rest of the rats
fleeing this ship," Loki ordered.

If a person could scuttle in null g, the techs managed to give that appearance as they hastened to take one of their own to the nearest medical facility.

Loki gently placed the crystal on the sled. The fiber optics tangled and coiled around his feet.

"May I assist?" Hestiia asked. Even before he could answer, she began separating the fiber optics at the source.

In a remarkably short time, Hestiia had untangled the cables as if working with a very fragile yarn.

The woman at the terminal continued her futile task, never looking up. Every micron of her attention belonged to her task.

Would she even notice when her green crystals left the array and she had nothing left to command?

"This is for your own good, ma'am." Loki pressed two fingers hard against her jugular vein until her head lolled forward. Before she could recover consciousness, he lifted her from her chair and placed her outside the room, slumped against a bulkhead.

Then he exhaled sharply. Followed by a deep inhale. He felt better. His mind cleared of the red mist of anger.

"Hestiia, you and Poolie work on the cables . . . er . . . ropes." He had to remember to use vocabulary they understood, though they learned fast. Faster than some civils. "Men, you free the crystals, carefully wrap the ropes around each one and load it onto a sled."

They obeyed without question and treated the crystals with care and respect; more so than many civils would have.

"Well done, my friends. Now we have to get them back to the launch bay. Avoid contact with any of the . . ." How to describe the IMPs? "The Others. These stones are very valuable. They will help defend the Stargods and our people in the weeks to come."

They all nodded solemnly. Hestiia and Poolie both placed a hand flat against their bellies in an instinctive protective gesture. Time to get them back into gravity. Too much time in null g during gestation kept babies from developing correctly.

The corridors seemed more crowded on the return journey. Perhaps because Loki tried to avoid contact. He feared an overzealous Marine might try to retrieve the crystals. Niveean, the warrior, became their lookout. He directed them into shadowy hiding places Loki never would have considered viable.

They had just crept out from one such alcove beside the hatch they needed to take them back to the launch bay when a woman in a bright suit of fashionable cut stepped in front of them. Her blonde hair looked as if she'd combed it with her fists. Creases marred the sharp tailoring of her trousers. Scuffs showed on her dainty boots.

She pointed a needle pistol at Loki's eyes.

"Hello, Cyndi," Loki gulped.

"Bastard bushie. Why are you trying to kill me?"

CHAPTER 36

✦ —— · —— ✦ —— · —— ✦

(*IRYTHROS.*)

"Is that a name?" Kat mumbled. She kept her eyes closed, not wanting to acknowledge that she had fainted or why.

(*Yes.*)

A pregnant pause. The voice waited for a reply.

"Kat Talbot, Lieutenant JG assigned to IMP Cruiser *Jupiter.* Helmsman."

More silence.

"Not enough? Yeah. Mari Kathleen Talbot."

(*O'Hara.*)

"O'Hara by birth, not by choice." Kat opened one eye warily. She still saw the dragon. Immense. Shimmery in the fading light. Red outlined its horns and wing veins. It blinked a translucent membrane over the red-and-silver eyes. The swirling pupil opened wide, drawing her into unknown realms of thought and imagination.

She slammed her eyes shut against the invitation to trust her soul to this creature's scrutiny.

A sense of hurt and embarrassment spread outward from the back of her neck.

"Sorry, critter, but my thoughts are my own. You may not have them."

The dragon lowered its head. In acceptance? Or to skewer her with the spiraled horn on its forehead?

She scrambled backward rather than take a chance. She found the knife still clutched in her left fist.

Konner had said she could defend herself against animals bigger than herself with it. She snorted in derision. The knife would prove useless against this beast.

"What do you want from me?" She sat up straight. The dragon did not come any closer. Rolling to her knees and then her feet, she kept the knife ready. She figured the half-furled wings would be vulnerable. If she damaged one, the beast would not be able to take wing and follow her through the underbrush.

Provided she could get away before it flamed her. The smoke kept curling from its nostrils in mute reminder that it liked to eat its meals cooked.

"What do you want from me?" she repeated.

(*To help.*)

Puzzled, Kat stared at him, braving those hypnotic eyes. "Why?"

(*You are of the blood of the Stargods. You need help. I must aid you.*)

That made no sense at all.

"I am not even certain I believe you exist. Why should I ask for help?" Dismissing the beast as an obvious hallucination—prolonged exposure to the alien air must have made her feverish—Kat knelt before her pile of brush, picked up a nearby rock and struck it against her blade.

A feeble spark died before jumping onto the kindling.

(*Allow me to light the fire, please.*)

"Go away. You do not exist."

A sharp prod to her back brought her to her feet, swinging the blade.

The dragon had lowered the tip of its spiral horn level with her chest. (*I exist!*)

"Okay, okay, I believe you."

(*No, you do not.*)

"Well . . . I can barely see you, and then only in certain lights. All the science I know proves that dragons cannot exist in this dimension within the physical laws of the universe.

(*If you ride on my back and see the ley lines, will you believe?*)

"Now I know you are a product of my imagination."

(*You said this to Stargod Konner.*)

"But . . ."

(*Come. Mount. I will show you.*) The dragon crouched down and extended its foreleg.

Kat gulped. Then she squared her shoulders, anchored the knife inside her belt, grasped one spinal horn, and heaved herself aboard. The dragon did not wait for her to settle her butt before it bounded three steps across the clearing, flapped its giant wings, and leaped above the trees. Chill wind and rain rushed past them. The ground and trees fell away. A cloud enveloped them in thick mist.

She swallowed, trying to keep her stomach and its slight contents in place. She clung to the horn in front of her with both hands. Another horn braced her back. She clamped her knees tightly against the dragon's back. Through the insulated cloth of her uniform she felt the animal's muscles ripple as it worked the wide wings. She risked a look at the translucent marvels of flight.

Fascination overcame her fear. In her mind, she saw the air currents vector across the wings. The beast would not tumble from its flight path unless injured. She was as safe here as in any craft built by the Imperial Military.

Maybe safer.

Then she gloried in the sensation of freedom. How often had she dreamed of flying without a craft surrounding her?

"Which direction?" she shouted over the rush of air in her face.

(South and east.)

"Why there?"

(Because it does not rain in the desert.)

"No rain. No clouds. We can see the ground."

(And the ley lines.)

"What exactly are ley lines?"

(Life.)

"What is that supposed to mean?"

The dragon banked into a wide circle, moving farther east than south. If her sense of direction was correct. Up here, shrouded in mist, nothing seemed real. She'd lost her horizon and landmarks.

"Why are we changing direction?"

(To avoid the place of Hanassa.)

"I've heard that name somewhere."

(Your brothers.)

She could not remember in what context she had heard the name, only that she had. Painstakingly, she dredged up every word of her conversations with her brothers. Nope. No mention of Hanassa.

"Why do we have to avoid this place?"

(Evil. Can you not feel it? Can you not hear it?)

Then she sensed a vibration that might be a pinging in her ears. The sound of a distress beacon.

Adrenaline shot through her. "We have to help them."

(Hanassa lies. Never believe anything that comes from Hanassa.)

"Is Hanassa a man or a place?" A burning sensation on her right shoulder drew her attention. The distress beacon broadcast to all of her senses, demanding she come to it.

(Both.)

"But the beacon . . ."

(Is false.)

"The second beacon. Why are there two? I thought the bounty was for only one."

A mental shrug from Irythros. Good thing only his mind responded. If he'd rotated his massive shoulders, she might lose her grip.

They burst clear of the clouds. Bright sunshine pelted her eyes. She closed them tightly, then opened them slowly, getting used to the change in light by degrees.

Jagged mountain peaks tipped with snow stretched from left to right in a broken chain. They seemed close enough to touch, yet so far away as to be unreachable, even on dragon back. She tried to pick out a pass through them. Faint traces of trails showed possibilities, all too rugged for any but the most intrepid traveler.

Her uniform had not been designed for high-altitude open air flight. The cold settled into her bones and would not let go. Her fingers and toes grew numb. Her teeth began to chatter.

The cold squeezed her bladder.

Did Irythros increase his speed?

She hoped so. She did not know how much longer she could endure without losing her grip upon his horn.

Without a chrono, Kat had no way of determining the passage of time. Flight across the mountain range could have taken digital hours or mere femtos.

Then, quite suddenly, with no warning at all, the mountains fell behind and a vast desert opened before them. Irythros shed altitude. The air temperature warmed. As they dropped closer to the scrubby plateau, Kat forgot her physical discomfort. She forgot her need to relieve herself.

"Hundreds of square klicks of nothing but a few low shrubs, rocks, and dust."

(*Look more closely.*) Irythros skimmed the surface.

She caught a glimpse of movement. A lizard scurried beneath them, frantically seeking shelter from the huge predator. It finally crouched in the shadows cast by a cluster of rocks.

"So there is life in the desert. It isn't empty."

(*Look more closely.*) Irythros surged upward and stabilized about one hundred meters higher. He flew a lazy circle.

Kat peered down. "What am I supposed to see?"

No answer.

She checked the horizon. Mountains on three sides, in the distance she caught glimpses of a deep river valley emptying into the sea. A magnificent landscape. But then hundreds of bush planets had awe-inspiring vistas.

(*Look deeper.*)

"Beneath the soil? Are there subterranean streams?"

(*Deeper into your self. Look with your other sight.*)

The hot desert air penetrated the synthetic fabric of Kat's uniform. She began to perspire. Sweat dripped into her eyes. The salty moisture stung. She dared not lift a hand from her grip of the horn to dash it away. She blinked it away and wiped her cheeks on her shoulder as best she could.

When she looked again, her eyes detected an altered spectrum. Reds shifted toward blue, greens toward yellow, and the light slanted in from an angle at odds with the westering sun. She blinked again to clear her eyes of salt.

Colors became prisms. Individual drops of moisture became crystals.

And then she saw it. Them.

A giant web of blue energy. Random lines crossed, merged, veered off in new directions. No uniformity or symmetry. Just pulsating life.

"I believe," Kat breathed.

(*First you must touch a ley line and understand.*)

"It's getting late. Maybe another day."

(*Now.*) Irythros shed the last hundred meters of altitude with a stomach-jolting dive.

Kat clung to the spinal horn with all her might. Acceleration flung her against the horn at her back with the force of at least two gs. Not so bad a pressure in an enclosed craft. Dangerous in the open, with no buffer from the wind that tore at her hair and ground her face with grit.

Blessedly, the dive lasted only a few femtos. Kat alighted from the dragon with shaking knees. "May a Denobian muscle-cat develop a taste for your flesh," she cursed. Then added a few more in three languages.

Irythros glared at her, unappreciative of her creativity.

"And may the fleas of a thousand camels infest your lair," she added for good measure.

The dragon's skin rippled the length of his entire back, as if it itched.

(*Find your ley line and learn it,*) he snapped and turned his tail toward her. It thrashed the ground in agitation.

She skipped away from him. Only when she was out of reach of the lethally spiked tail did she look around and assess the landscape.

"As soon as I find one of those ley lines, we can leave?"

A sense of agreement, but no words formed in the back of her mind.

Kat heaved a sigh of resignation and walked a little farther away. Her soft ship boots scuffed the loose red dirt. The light breeze picked up the loose grains and swirled them away. Heat baked the chill of flight from her bones and flushed her skin.

She wouldn't last long out here without water, skin protectors, and a hat. Best she get on with this. Stalling and denial would not get her out of the desert.

A deep breath inward and she allowed her eyes to unfocus. Nothing. Maybe if she let some sweat drip into her eyes again, she could let the fractured sight line reveal the energy beneath the ground.

Nothing. Another deep breath of the hot dry air. She almost coughed out the grit that permeated everything. Her exhalation went on and on. She couldn't get rid of enough tainted carbon dioxide. When she thought her lungs would collapse, her body shuddered and jerked and took in a huge gulp of fresh air. It still tasted of dirt but seemed to fill every crevice of her being with . . . clarity.

Blue lines jumped into view. Some fat, others skinny. Farther apart than she'd expected from her first glimpse from one hundred meters up.

Now what?

(*You must take the energy into yourself and understand it.*)

Kat took another deep breath, this time for courage. Was she about to be electrocuted? Torn apart by antimatter? Sucked into another dimension?

Well, if the lines killed her, she'd likely die more quickly and with less pain than from exposure in the desert.

She picked out a particularly fat line about one hundred meters to her left. As she approached it, she noticed that if she followed it back toward where the dragon crouched it met two more lines, forming a kind of pool or knot. Instinctively, she headed for the junction.

Irythros nodded as if in approval.

Keeping her eyes slightly unfocused and her breathing deep and even, she stretched forth her left foot, letting her toes brush the silvery blue that wanted to elude her, like mercury released in null g. A tiny jolt crept up her leg as far as her knee. She jerked her foot away. Not exactly a jolt, more like a thrill. Enticing. Probably dangerous.

She checked out the dragon again. He had not budged.

"Again?"

No response from the dragon.

This time Kat placed her left foot fully inside the pool. Tingles slid up her limb, climbing higher with each breath. When it reached her heart, gravity seemed to disappear. If she lifted her arms just so, she might truly fly. Alongside the dragon rather than atop him.

Addicting. She brought her other foot into the circle of arcane power.

The world tilted, colors shifted.

Her senses opened. A cacophony of insects buzzing, wind sighing, burrowing animals digging, the dragon's innards boiling, ready to flame something. She heard it all, became a part of it all, shared the life of each entity. Suddenly she knew what it meant to be a dragon and breathe fire upon a fresh kill and savor the rich flavor of broiled meat. She understood a mouse's need to dig a deep burrow to hide from the elements and predators. She became the air with a deep urge to flow from here to there to balance air pressure. Massing moisture buoyed her.

She had purpose. Life had meaning if only she reached out and grasped it.

Her mind opened and she knew how to reach out telepathically, to equalize weight and mass and lift anything with her mind. If she thought about the future, she could catch glimpses of possibilities. . . .

Like a king stone reaching out to its mother stone, Kat extended her senses upward, outward. She brushed past *Jupiter*, acknowledged *Sirius*, and sped onward, seeking something familiar. A home. Mum?

She conjured an image from memory of a woman nearing forty Earth Standard Years, taller than mid-height but nowhere near as tall as her oldest teenage son. Her features took on care lines from worry. Kat gave the woman her own nose and chin but softer eyes that lighted with love whenever she looked upon her four children. She had to have red hair, like each of her off-spring, but with gray hints at the temples.

With the image came the brush of a mind. Just a hint. Nothing more than knowing that the woman existed, alone, frightened, worried, and . . . obsessed.

Her obsession turned inward. Grew malignant. Shifted focus. The need to amass more money outweighed the purpose for that money. She would never have enough wealth to go in search of her daughter. That quest might end in failure. She'd failed at so much already. The need to make more and more money was something she never failed at.

Abruptly Kat dropped out of the trance. She swayed as her mind plummeted back into her body. For one hundred too-rapid heartbeats reality took on the pallor of the unreal.

When she thought about the enormity of her mental journey, Kat stumbled.

She caught her balance on Irythros' muzzle. Then she straightened, more sure of herself and what she had to do than she had been in many years.

She blinked, puzzled by the uncertain light. While she had been . . . elsewhere, day had turned to night. Stars shone brightly in the skies, alien constellations teased her mind with mythical creatures and heroic figures behind them.

"How long was I gone?"

(*Not long. Day turns to night quickly here.*)

"Thank you, Irythros." She caressed the soft fur of his muzzle gently. "Now I know what my brothers call magic and why it works. I do not agree with the life path they have chosen, but I understand it."

(*Then we can return.*)

"Will you take me to my people?"

(*Of course. Where else would we go?*)

CHAPTER 37

STRANGE FACES CROWDED around Dalleena. They drifted in and out of her field of vision. The sounds of their senseless jabbering left her bewildered, uncertain, frightened. So intense. So rapid in their dialogues.

Desperately, she tried to get a sense of place. The light was wrong. Yellow-ish. Harsh. Her eyes did not want to open to confront it.

She let go of her need to know for a moment. If she could just relax and let her senses take in the flood of information, she could sort it out later.

A vague recollection of flying soothed her. She had flown with Stargod Konner. He had shown her the wonders of her world from the inside of his magic dragon. Not magic, she reminded herself. A machine. A very compli-cated machine.

One day, perhaps, he would allow her to control it, to feel the rush of air beneath the wings and the speed of flying across the vast ocean in a few hours. Fishing boats needed many months to do the same and rarely under-took the perilous journey to the other side of the world.

She wanted to fly again. In the machine called *Rover* and in Konner's arms. The wonders of the last two days flooded her with warmth. She felt herself smile and sigh contentedly.

The barrage of voices quieted. Good. They confused her so that she could not think, could not sort through what her senses told her.

Another long space of time. She thought she slept. The light changed. Dimmed. No longer harsh, just . . . different. Finally, she opened her eyes.

Starlight glimmered beyond the window. She knew where she was now. The cabin of the Stargods. The bed she had shared with Konner last night. Where was he now?

Beyond the curtain that separated the two rooms of the cabin, she heard a murmur of voices. He must be there, talking with his brother Loki. Too many voices. One feminine. Kim and Hestiia must have joined Konner as well.

Why had he left her alone?

She tried sitting up. Pain lashed across her middle. Her breath caught and she cried out.

Memory returned. The bull. The intruder with the gun. The bull charging. The wide horns filling her vision. Flying through the air. Landing heavily, too heavily, hearing something snap. Something else crunched.

If she did not move, she could breathe through the pain. Every muscle stilled. A gnawing ache persisted.

Then true fear assailed her. The IMPs controlled the village. Konner and his brothers had gone to steal something very important from the intruder's ship, far up in the sky, near the blanket of the night sky.

She wanted to cry with loneliness and pain. She dared not. Until she knew the extent of her injuries and her status with the Others, she had to remain strong. And silent. Listening and watching.

Stillness was good. She could control the pain and her breathing if she remained motionless.

A shadow blotted out the stars for a moment. She held her breath. Then a familiar scent wafted across her face. Her heart warmed.

"Konner," she breathed.

"Dalleena, sweetheart." His lips whispered across hers.

"Are we safe?" She barely heard her own voice.

"Not completely. What happened? Are you ill?"

"Hurt. The bull." She gasped for air. Her chest did not want to expand far enough to let her bring enough in. "One of the *Others* was going to shoot him. I could not let him. Ruin village if lose bull. I tackled. Bull charged." Each phrase came out more broken than the last.

Stillness, she reminded herself. After several long moments she could breathe almost normally again.

Konner hushed her with a hand over her mouth. He made a brief but thorough examination of her body with gentle hands.

"Gored?" he asked.

"Broken ribs. Don't know what else."

She sensed his nod more than saw it. "Immobility cast across your belly. Head?" His fingers found the bindings on her brow.

She tried to shake her head no, but it hurt too much, all the way down her spine to the backs of her legs and up over the top of her skull into her eyes.

He must have felt her wince.

"Concussion. Painkillers. Can you be quiet if I help you out of here?"

No! Her mind and body protested the thought of moving. But she had to trust Konner. The Stargod must know what was best for her.

As long as he remained by her side, she could endure anything. She hoped.

"Yes." She breathed deeply, preparing herself for the sharp onslaught of pain.

He ripped something from her wrist. Just a tiny prick of discomfort compared to the thought of actually moving her body. A few drops of moisture trickled across her hand. Then he removed a patch from her temple. It came off with a sucking sound. She winced again as several hairs tore free with the patch.

A quiet chirp, like a baby bird, began. The soft voices on the other side of the curtain ceased.

Dalleena felt them listening.

Konner hurriedly replaced the patch. The bird ceased chirping.

"I'd better check on that," a female voice said.

Konner faded away from Dalleena. One of the yellowish lights glowed brighter, closer. It appeared around the edge of the silvery curtain that separated the two rooms of the cabin. The too-steady light reminded her of an overlarge fish eye glowing in the depths of the Great Bay at midnight on the dark of the moon.

Soft footfalls behind the light explained the slight bobbing motion the eye made. Still it did not flicker like a normal candle or oil lantern. Dalleena studied the area illuminated by the eye, memorizing the placement of the few articles of furniture and the baskets of clothes and tools. Konner was neater than his brother, but still not overly concerned with the clutter that blocked direct pathways. Some of the baskets showed signs of having been pushed hastily aside to clear a broader path.

Of the person behind the light, she could see nothing.

Dalleena lay still, barely daring to breathe as gentle hands probed the patch on her temple and then ran down her arm.

"What have you done, silly girl?" The woman shook her head as she laid the light down on top of the machine beside Dalleena. The new position of the light allowed greater visibility. Words flew rapidly from the woman's tongue. Dalleena had to listen carefully and sort them through several times to make sense of them.

"If you are awake enough to rip out your IV, I guess you don't need it anymore." The woman stared at the transparent snake in her hand. Instead of a head, it had a long metal tongue at the end. A tongue that was so sharply pointed it could easily penetrate flesh. Moisture dripped from it onto the floor.

"You'll feel the lack of pain meds, but I think we can leave this out. You'll be able to eat and drink in the morning. Then we'll get a real ultrasound unit from *Jupiter* to hasten the healing." The woman set aside the snake.

"How about another session with the US?" The woman sat on a stool beside the bed. She retrieved a small device from her pocket. With a quick flick of the woman's hand, Dalleena's shirt fell open. She placed the small device upon Dalleena's ribs, right at the sorest point. Something thick and hard lay between the device and her skin.

The immobility cast?

After several long moments the woman sighed and lifted the device. "Enough for now. That should speed the healing and let you move a little easier. But you have to leave the monitor alone for now." She pressed the temple patch tighter against Dalleena's skin. "Now go to sleep. That is the best medicine for broken bones and a bump on the head."

The woman left as quietly as she had come, taking the light with her.

"She woke up and ripped out her IV. Must have panicked. You know primitives. They fear anything they haven't seen before," the woman explained to her unseen companions.

When their soft murmurs resumed, Konner eased back beside Dalleena. Where had he hidden? The light had been powerful enough to eliminate all but the darkest recesses of the room.

He fumbled with the machine attached to the patch by a stiff string. Then he removed the patch again. The bird remained asleep.

"Not a sound," he breathed.

She nodded her consent. Then he gently helped her to roll to her side and drop her feet to the dirt floor. Her body was on fire with pain. She kept moving, knowing if she flopped back upon the bed she would never get up again. The effort made her hold her breath against crying out.

Tears pricked her eyelids. She clamped them shut while she breathed heavily.

Konner sat beside her. She leaned into him, grateful for the support of his body. He draped one arm around her hips, placing her own arm around his.

"Together," he breathed and stood, carrying her with him.

She wasn't ready. Agony sent her head spinning. She had to close her eyes again to maintain her balance. But she was up. The worst was over.

She hoped.

One step at a time, halting for her to catch her breath with each one, they walked to the curtain. Konner breathed deeply, three times. Then he gently eased the silvery material aside.

Dalleena nearly stepped back into the darkness at the sight of a blonde woman and two men, all in the mud-colored uniforms of the Others, sitting on stools of curious construction around a small table. They held flat things in their hands, like leaves but sturdier, covered in bright colors and designs. Surely they must look up from their intense study of the leaves and see Konner and herself.

As if she had commanded it, the blonde woman looked up and stared right at them.

Dalleena held her breath.

Konner kept his body between her and the intruders and kept walking, slowly, quietly.

The woman returned her gaze to her leaves. Her eyes did not focus upon Konner and Dalleena.

Dalleena held her breath until they passed through yet another of the silvery curtains. The night was warm and the intruders had not closed the door that Loki had installed just days before. He had been proud of his accomplishment, showing the others how the door would keep out the cold, wind, and rain better than blankets woven of red cow fur.

Outside, Dalleena breathed short gasps of the humid air. The intense pain of getting out of the bed faded to sharp aches. She breathed again, shallowly. The air was heavy with recent rain and more to come. It smelled wet, clean, better than the closeness of the cabin. Clouds obscured the stars. Rain would fall again by dawn. She and Konner had to be far away long before then.

How? Already her knees wanted to buckle from the strain of walking through the pain and the dizziness from the lump on the back of her head. Konner kept her upright and moving. Konner showed her the way through the sleepy patrols around the perimeter of the village. Konner gave her the strength and courage to keep moving when all she wanted was to fall upon the ground and sleep until the ache went away.

Finally they reached Petram, the huge boulder that had refused to be moved from the middle of the fields.

Gratefully, Dalleena leaned against the rock. The cool surface soothed her sweating body. She hoped she wasn't feverish from her injuries.

Konner scanned the skies and restlessly paced around Dalleena and the rock. She was afraid the sentries would see his movement, a darker shadow in the night.

"Konner, you have to know. Taneeo betrayed you. He . . ."

"I know. Raaskan told us. Pryth led a band of women to rescue the men. We will question Taneeo later."

"Then your people are safe from the Others?"

"For now. But they are not safe from Pryth." He almost chuckled.

"Now what?" Dalleena whispered. She doubted she could walk much farther without more rest, and nourishment. And more rest.

"We wait." They still spoke in hushed tones mindful of how sound carried on the still night air.

Dalleena was more than willing to wait. Not move. Just exist. She shifted against the rock and started to slide to a sitting position.

"Don't." Konner was beside her before she could do more than bend her knees. "If you go down, we'll have a s'murghin' difficult time getting you back up. We won't have a lot of time once things start happening."

"Like what?" She had to keep talking, keep him talking in order to stay awake. Her entire body felt too heavy to remain upright. And her torso ached. The pain reached all the way up her spine to her head and then darted between her eyes.

A refreshing breeze wafted across her face. It became a wind.

"Our transport just arrived," Konner said.

She felt the smile in his voice.

Dalleena dared move her eyes beyond the dim outline of his face. A larger shadow directly behind him blotted out the rest of the darkness.

"Oh," she moaned. "I do not think I can climb atop a dragon."

"You have to, Dalleena. This is the only way I can get you to safety."

CHAPTER 38

"CYNDI, HONEY," Loki pleaded with the irate woman before him. "You know I would never deliberately hurt you."

"Do I?" she snarled at him. "Now answer my question. Why are you doing this?"

"It's a long story. One that will sound better around a campfire with a good dinner inside you." Five months ago, Loki had scorned the evening ritual. At this moment in time, he wanted nothing more than to be in the middle of one.

"Campfire? *Campfire!*" she shouted. "You expect *me* to contaminate myself with smoke, and meat, and . . . and *unscrubbed* air?" Lucinda Baines, daughter of a planetary governor, granddaughter of an Imperial Senator, and great-niece to a previous emperor, shuddered with genuine fear. Her attention wavered and her grip on the needle pistol loosened.

Niveean, the silent warrior, pushed off the bulkhead to his left and slammed into Cyndi. Startled, Cyndi did not begin to struggle until they slid toward the deck.

Loki grabbed the loose pistol and tossed it to Hestiia. "Don't use it unless you have to, to save the crystals. Get the crystals to Kim," he commanded. He lunged into the fray, heavily and clumsily.

Hestiia, Poolie, and the others grabbed the sleds and disappeared down the last hatch.

Cyndi kicked and tore at Niveean. She twisted herself on top of him. Each movement became slower in the heavier g. The big man kept his arms around her in a wrestler's hug.

Loki fell short of his target. With his head in the middle of Cyndi's back he locked his arms around her legs. She kicked back, connecting hard with his upper thigh. The heel of her fashionable shoes gouged his flesh. He gritted his teeth and hung on. When he knew his grip was firm, he flung his legs wide, encircling hers. They tumbled backward, Niveean on top of both.

She heaved against Loki. He pressed harder.

Niveean scrambled to his knees and then to his feet. He grabbed the jamb around the hatchway. His breath came in short sharp pants.

Then Loki pressed their limbs together in an odd parody of a lovers' embrace.

Loki rolled, keeping his arms around Cyndi. The open hatch downward toward the launch bay was at his elbow. "Duck," he screamed in her ear and swung his feet into the opening.

She barely obeyed him in time. The top of the hatchway scraped her flying hair close to her scalp. With a little yelp of surprise, or indignation, he couldn't tell which, she complied.

They fell heavily.

Still locked together, they slid down to the lowest level of the ship. The extreme gravity—less than when Loki had left the launch bay an hour ago—grabbed hold of them. They landed heavily on a pile of tarps and rolled.

To their right, Kim was helping his wife and Poolie steer the sleds into the launch bay. The corridor was otherwise empty.

"Loki, we don't have the time or resources to tend a hostage," Kim warned him.

"This one we have to take extra special care of," Loki grunted. Slowly, he disentangled himself from Cyndi.

"Who?" Kim asked. Then his eyes widened as he saw Cyndi's face.

"I believe you two have met," Loki said as he assisted Cyndi to her feet. He kept one hand firmly locked on her wrist. His grip must be painful to her, but she said nothing, only glared at him.

"A few years ago," Kim admitted. He turned his back on them and pushed Poolie and the second sled ahead of him into the bay.

"You owe that man your life," Loki reminded her. "Remember that and stay out of trouble."

"I owe you and your brothers nothing, Mathew Kameron O'Hara. You sabotaged this ship. You endanger my life now. Mine and everyone's aboard this ship." She hung back, bracing her feet wide.

"I always knew that life with you would never be easy," he grunted. Before she could reply, he slung her over his shoulder, clamped his arms around her legs, and lurched into the launch bay.

"Put me down, you barbarian."

"Quiet." He swatted her bottom. "There was a time when you liked being mauled by this barbarian."

"Never again!"

He did not care. He had better things to do with his life than cater to this spoiled dome breather.

(*Iianthe,*) the dragon announced his name.

A niggle of disappointment crawled up Konner's spine. He had come to think of Irythros as his personal dragon. Iianthe seemed more attached to Hestiia and Kim. Konner had to remind himself that no one "owned" a dragon. Wild creatures, they belonged only to themselves and to this planet. They assisted and advised humans as their whims and sense of honor dictated. Humans had little if anything to do with the decision.

"Konner." He bowed slightly to the purple-tipped dragon. "Give him your name, Dalleena. Dragon protocol."

She wheezed something that approximated her name. Konner did not like her labored breathing or how heavily she leaned against him.

"Sweetheart, we have to leave," he urged her forward. She shuffled her feet heavily. "It's for the best, Dalleena, no matter how much it hurts. I could not have gotten you away from the IMPs tomorrow."

She nodded her mute agreement and trudged the few remaining steps to the huge beast who waited for them.

Then the significance of the dragon name penetrated through Konner's worry about Dalleena.

"Iianthe?" Konner peered more closely at the purple-tipped dragon crouched in the middle of the field. "I expected Irythros." Where was the red-tip? They had planned for him to meet Konner and Dalleena.

(*Elsewhere,*) Iianthe responded to Konner's unspoken question.

"Welcome, Iianthe," Konner bowed again to the dragon. "May we ride upon your back to the place of safety?" He did not have time to debate with the dragon. He needed help getting Dalleena away *now*.

(*Yes.*) The deep bronze bell of Iianthe's voice reverberated on the back of Konner's tongue and at the base of his spine. (*Irythros sends greetings and a warning. You must beware of the one you trust. The one who does not smell correctly; the one who still speaks to the stars.*)

"And who might that be?" Typical cryptic dragon speech. Konner had no more time or patience for it. Why couldn't they just come out and say what was on their minds?

Iianthe did not reply.

Sighing heavily, Konner reverted to the purpose of this meeting. "If you speak of Taneeo, then we know of his betrayal. Pryth deals with him now. My lady is injured. Can you crouch lower to make climbing easier for her?"

(*You must carry her.*) With that pronouncement, Iianthe spread out, bringing his belly into contact with the ground and his left foreleg lower.

"I worry that our combined weight will damage you." Konner eyed the makeshift staircase of the dragon's limbs.

(*Do not.*) The dragon made himself flatter yet.

"Easy, love. This is going to hurt, but only for a little." He scooped Dalleena into his arms.

She groaned and her head fell against his shoulder. Before he could think twice about his actions, he hastened along Iianthe's foreleg to his shoulder. He had to shift Dalleena's weight to grasp a neck horn for balance as he heaved her upward between two spinal horns. She came awake again with a pain-filled gasp. She clutched her middle with crossed arms.

"Hey, you!" an IMP guard hailed them from the village compound. He brought his weapon to bear.

Konner scrambled up behind her. "Now, Iianthe." He slapped the dragon's side.

Iianthe took five steps, working his wings frantically.

A blast of energy shot from the IMP's weapon.

"Fool, you could kill her!" Lotski, the medic, cried. She clung to the guard's arm, tugging at his rifle.

Iianthe took three more long strides. His wing action seemed slower. He still did not have enough momentum or lift to fly.

Konner tried hunkering lower. Dalleena groaned as he pressed against her back. Her injuries would not allow her to bend.

Another bolt of energy slid past them. Voices rose in disagreement.

At last, after lumbering across three fields, Iianthe lifted in flight. Konner breathed a sigh of relief. Dalleena slumped against him.

And a low moan filtered into the back of Konner's mind.

"Iianthe? How fare you?"

(*Not well. I must land.*) With that pronouncement, he dropped rapidly below the tree line, onto a small knoll beside a tributary river. They had covered less than fifteen klicks' distance from the village

Konner dropped to the moss-covered rock. He let his hands roam over the dragon's hide, seeking the source of injury. He did not get far before he noticed the left wing drooping, only half folded. A little more investigation showed a deep burn where the lower wing bone met the spine.

"How can I help you?" he asked, careful to keep his hand off the injury.

(*Remove your lady from my back, Stargod Konner.*)

"Down is easier than up," Dalleena attempted a grin. She fell more than climbed down into Konner's arms. The jolt sent her groaning again.

Konner cradled her close to his heart. Tears smarted in his eyes. Disaster piled on complication. He bit back his own cries of frustration and disappointment.

Somehow they must make the best of this awful situation.

Before he could voice his thoughts, a soft silvery light emanated from the dragon's hide.

Konner blinked. The light grew to engulf him. It brightened until he had to close his eyes. Even through closed eyelids, the light nearly blinded him. He turned his back to the dragon's light, still protecting Dalleena in his arms.

With the light there came a hum. Unlike the song of the dragongate, this music tickled his mind with elusive harmonies and tunes.

Finally, the glare around them softened and receded. He opened his eyes and turned back to face the dragon. He nearly dropped Dalleena in surprise.

"Iianthe?" he asked of the black cat that crouched before him. No ordinary cat, this one had wings. One of them drooped.

(*Who else?*)

"You transformed into a flywacket. Never thought I'd live to see it happen." According to Hestiia, only a purple-tipped dragon could perform this miracle.

(*See and believe.*)

"Oh, I believe. Now what?"

(*We rest. Dalleena and I must huddle together for a time. You should build a fire, fish, bathe, refresh yourself.*)

"Never question a dragon." Konner shrugged and set Dalleena down beside the black cat. She draped an arm around the solid feline body. They leaned together, supporting each other.

The hum intensified and grew louder.

"Ultrasound," Konner murmured. "The original ultrasound for healing was a cat's purr."

No comment from either patient.

Konner set about his chores. Fire. Food. Bath. Sleep. Morning would determine if they could continue their journey. For now they were hidden from the IMPs.

CHAPTER 39

◆——•—◆—•——◆

"WHERE IS EVERYBODY?" Loki asked as he stomped down the ramp from *Rover.* "We need to get started on building our defenses against the IMPs. We need plans and tools and Konner."

Kim had already disembarked from the stolen lander. He had an arm around Hestiia's waist and seemed oblivious to all else.

"What?" Kim asked, lifting his gaze from his wife.

"Konner. Kat. Where are they?" Loki knew a moment of panic. He suppressed it. If he showed weakness, they'd never get anything done. His people would doubt his wisdom.

All his troops looked about, puzzled by the emptiness of the clearing.

"Someone started to build a fire," Raaskan offered.

"Probably Kat. Konner knows how to build a better fire than that." Loki kicked at the pile of branches. It toppled easily. Lights from the two vessels illuminated the clearing but did not penetrate the tree line beyond.

"What do we do with the crystals?" Poolie asked. Like Kim and Hestiia, she and Raaskan clung to each other as if they had been parted for years instead of hours.

"Is this what you brought me to?" Cyndi whined from the hatchway. "There isn't even a building or a road, or other people or . . . or . . ." She bit her lip and turned her head away.

Loki caught a glint of moisture in her eyes.

"Sorry. Life is primitive out here in the bush. We survive by our wits and make what we need." Loki had no sympathy for her. Why had he ever believed himself in love with this spoiled dome breather?

"Primitive? Primitive implies rudimentary amenities. This is barbaric!" Cyndi's voice became shrill.

Loki blocked out the stream of invective that followed. "Stay aboard the shuttle, Cyndi. You'll only get dirty if you try to interfere." He might just deck her himself if she kept up her complaints.

Wisely, she retreated with a pout and an angry glint in her eye. The last time Loki had seen that expression on her face, he'd made love to her to soothe her mood. His aggression had excited her and her mood changed rapidly.

He'd not resort to that method of appeasing her again.

"What do we do with the crystals?" he asked Kim.

"Konner knows where he wants them placed," his brother replied.

"Can we not duplicate the distances on the mother ship?" Hestiia asked. Her ability to learn new vocabulary and make associations never ceased to amaze Loki.

"I know the specs for *Sirius*'s crystal array. But that's a star drive. St. Bridget only knows if Konner needs the same ratios for a confusion field." Loki shook his head and began pacing off distances.

"He's created a confusion field around *Sirius* with our crystal array," Kim reminded him.

"Then let's break out the laser sight on the needle rifle. That will give us distances to the picometer. Something to do while we wait. Save time once Konner gets here."

"I'll build a proper fire," Hestiia said. She disengaged from Kim's embrace with a quick kiss to his cheek. She and Poolie cleared away the ineptly piled wood and began anew with a wad of dried moss and ferns. By the time the first crystal rested beside a small cairn of rocks marking its eventual resting place, the women had a fire blazing and something cooking over it.

The rain showers held off.

"How are we going to bury these things?" Loki looked up from his measuring of the last driver.

"We'll think of something." Kim shrugged.

"We can dig," Raaskan said.

"With what? All our tools are in the village, half a continent away."

Everyone sobered a few moments.

"We fly," Hestiia replied blithely. "We can bring our villagers here at the same time."

"We'll need three trips with both vessels for that." Loki marked the place for the next crystal with three small rocks. Niveean carried a green over to him. "We're running low on fuel cells again and no way to recharge them."

"We have sunlight," Kim suggested.

"That will take weeks, if we ever see the sun again," Loki protested as a raindrop plopped onto his nose.

A roaring wind accompanied the rain. All of them ducked into the open hatches of the shuttle and the lander. The feeble light from the drowning fire and the portable illuminators revealed a ghostly silhouette descending from the heavens. All of the locals crossed their wrists and flapped their hands.

Loki felt an unreasonable urge to mimic the ancient ward against the bloodthirsty demon Simurgh. Kim crossed himself, murmuring silent prayers.

"You mangy traitor! I'll feed you to an Anubian blood worm." Another string of curses, in a language Loki did not recognize, as Kat's husky voice split the air.

Unceremoniously, the dragon thudded to the ground. Kat's spine must have jarred, for she bit off the last diatribe. Then the dragon rippled his back and extended his wing. Kat slid from her perch and landed in the soft dirt directly above the buried king stone.

"Oh!" She rubbed her abused bottom. With her legs splayed and her hair drenched she did not look happy. Or comfortable. "You promised to take me back to my own people," Kat spat at the dragon.

(*What are your people other than blood kin?*)

"I don't claim them. I don't like them or their way of life. I belong with His Majesty's Imperial Military Police."

The dragon looked down his long nose at her. For a moment the spiral horn on his forehead looked as if it would lift Kat off her feet and toss her into the air.

Loki smothered a smile.

Kim had a sudden coughing fit and had to turn his back. He snaked out an arm to keep Hestiia from running out to assist Kat to her feet.

(*Irythros,*) the dragon announced his name.

"Welcome, Irythros. Loki here."

"You didn't welcome me!" Kat protested.

"You, baby sister, are a pain in the ass. What happened, Kat? Did the dragon foil your escape plans?"

She did not deign to answer.

"May I come in? I'm cold and wet, sunburned, and I have a headache," she spat through gritted teeth.

"Survival often depends upon the hospitality of others. By custom we honor your request for shelter. May you return the favor to others so benighted." Loki bowed to her in the same manner he had witnessed Raaskan greet newcomers to the village.

She muttered something that sounded like, "Extremely unlikely." To put it politely.

"Your word of honor as an officer in His Imperial Majesty's Military that you will honor the custom of hospitality." Loki braced his feet and stood firmly in the hatchway. He kept reminding himself that they all had to learn to live together on this planet.

"Lieutenant Talbot!" Cyndi pushed past Loki and ran to help Kat to her feet. "At last, a civilized person. Tell these people to return me to the ship immediately. I shall perish in the cold and the damp. Who knows what bacteria lurk in this filthy air!" she gushed.

Kat shook off the helping hand and stiffly got her feet under her. She shot the dragon a malevolent look. "I suggest you keep your thoughts and words to yourself, Ms. Baines. Return to the ship is dangerous at the moment and unlikely to help the situation."

Cyndi stared at her, mouth agape.

Loki racked his brain trying to remember why he ever thought Cyndi attractive let alone the most beautiful and desirable woman in the galaxy. Thoughts of Paola Sanchez jumped to his mind's eye. Determined, energetic, independent, her stark beauty held much more appeal at the moment.

Cyndi dominated by manipulating people, like Mum. Paola led.

The dragon took off in a huff, leaving behind a flurry of windblown debris that cascaded over Kat and Cyndi. Dragons were big enough and powerful enough they did not have to hide their emotions or cater to the whims of others.

Loki wished he were a dragon at that moment. Or had the respect proffered to them.

"Your word of honor, Kat," he reminded them all of the reason for the delay.

Kat returned his glare for a long moment before firming her shoulders and thrusting out her chin. "My word of honor. I will honor the custom of hospitality and deny it to no one who asks properly for shelter in my abode."

"Full of loopholes but good enough for now. You'll learn the value of honor and hospitality and a bunch of other qualities alien to civils of the GTE." Loki turned his back on the women and retreated deeper into the shuttle.

"Qualities totally alien to the O'Hara brothers who have broken nearly every law honored by civilized humans since time began," Kat retorted.

Loki froze. The weight of his crimes came crashing down upon his shoulders. He wanted to justify his actions, blame them on others who had cheated him. The truth was, he enjoyed the danger and excitement of defying the law, always one jump ahead of arrest.

Suddenly he needed to punch someone and did not like himself very much for the thought. How could he lead this ragtag group of refugees when he could not properly exhibit the qualities he professed?

—◆—

Konner drifted slowly to the surface of his meditation. A bird chirped a tentative inquiry.

A soft glow of predawn light shimmered around the edges of Konner's awareness. A gentle shaft of warmth struck his back. Then all of the birds came alive with songs of greeting to the sunrise.

Konner heaved a deep sigh of release and opened his eyes. He looked around before moving. Nothing but the birds and a slight breeze filtered through to this grassy creekside. He might be the only person alive on the entire planet.

Except that his heart ached for the one missing. Best let her continue resting until she awoke naturally. The healing magic of a cat's purr needed time. Even the more intense ultrasound treatments of modern medicine needed hours to show an effect.

The muted roar of Iianthe's throat rumbles ceased abruptly.

"Wake up, Konner," Dalleena whispered. Her hand touched his shoulder.

He scrambled to his feet and encircled her with his arms, needing to protect her from whatever had roused her. "What's wrong," he asked quietly.

"They come."

There was only one "they" that would make her eyes go wide with alarm. IMPs.

"How far away?"

"Not far."

"Can you travel? Is that still sore?" Konner asked, exploring the bump on the back of her head with his fingers. She winced but stayed within the circle of his embrace. He peered at the spot, not daring to touch it. He wished Kim were here. His brother could hasten the healing started by Iianthe.

(*I cannot fly today,*) the dragon announced. His mental voice sounded as hushed as Konner's and Dalleena's whispers, as if he feared alerting the approaching soldiers.

"We must hide," Konner decided. IMP officers used hostages as bargaining tools. Their captain must be desperate to regain the king stone by now. If they had to, would Loki and Kim trade it for Konner's safety?

He did not intend to give them the opportunity.

"We have to get to the clearing. I have to leave today to get to my son in time." He wanted to shout and pound things with his fists. No time.

Muted voices came from a spot due west, a few hundred meters away.

"Can you climb?" He shoved Dalleena toward the tallest tree he could see.

She stretched one arm above her head. Grimaced. Nodded hesitantly, then shook her head. She looked as if she might cry.

(*To me,*) Iianthe called.

Shafts of sunlight seemed to concentrate upon the mossy rock where the flywacket crouched. Surely the IMPs must see the blinding explosion of light. Konner whirled Dalleena around so that both of their backs were to the transforming dragon. She clutched her middle from the abrupt motion. When the glare dissolved, Konner peered over his shoulder.

(*Your enemies see only the sunrise.*)

Konner hoped that was so. True civils like Pettigrew had probably never observed a sunrise. Looking east they might mistake Iianthe's shedding of light as nothing more dangerous.

(*To me,*) Iianthe repeated. He lifted his good wing a little.

"I hope this works." He and Dalleena slipped beneath the wing. They lay flat upon the cushion of moss.

(*Do not move,*) Iianthe admonished them. (*Color and movement betray the hunted.*)

"What about your purple-tips?" Konner asked as quietly as he could.

(*Inconsequential.*)

The voices came closer.

"Heat sensors indicate the quarry has . . . I can't find them anywhere, Lieutenant Commander M'Berra," a female voice said. "Must be something wrong with the handheld. All I see is one block of heat half a klick square."

Konner wished he could see through Iianthe's wing. He needed to read body language as well as vocal tones to judge the degree of danger.

"People cannot just disappear into thin air," replied the deep bass voice of *Jupiter*'s second-in-command.

Iianthe's skin rippled in sympathetic vibration. His own voice had much the same timbre.

"Begging the Commander's pardon, but the O'Haras have been known to do that on any number of occasions," the woman with the sensor corrected her superior officer.

"Tricks," M'Berra insisted. "Smoke and mirrors. Now where are they? This is the place they hid just a few femtos ago."

"Sensors can't find . . ."

"To hell with the sensors. Use the eyes and the nose God gave you. Use your hands to feel every micrometer within a square klick. Now spread out, all of you, and find the two escaped prisoners."

CHAPTER 40

◆——·——◆——·——◆

KAT LAY MOTIONLESS in the hammock slung across a corner in the body of the lander. Somehow, she had to get out of here. She could salvage this mission and save many lives with a little luck and more skill.

Half a dozen bushies snored in other hammocks around her. She was boxed in. Big warriors slept to each side of her, more between her and the hatch. The slightest movement would set the portable beds to swinging and awake the occupant. No easy escape.

She'd graduated top of her class in "Escape from Hostile Territory." But she'd never had to actually do it before. She had no doubt that the bushies who guarded her would kill her if they caught her. They were not bound by the conventions of civilization.

Holding her breath, she rolled out of the hammock, keeping one hand on the mesh to prevent the bars at head and foot from knocking into something and making a noise. Her knees bent, absorbing her weight. Did the others hear her soft landing?

She counted to one hundred. The man next to her snored a little louder, mumbled something, and heaved himself over. His hammock careened back and forth. Kat dropped to her knees to avoid being hit in the back and thus awakening the man.

Eventually the hammock swings slowed. Kat crawled around and beneath the other hammocks toward the cockpit. Once clear of the sleeping men, she eased to her feet. The cold cerama/metal decks reminded her that the season changed toward autumn and winter. Loki had taken away her boots and socks. The soft synthleather wasn't much protection in the bush, but better than bare feet. She shivered in the cold morning air.

Someone moved behind her. She froze in place. Barely daring to breathe, she peeked over her shoulder. The guard nearest the hatch scratched, then settled back into sleep. Predawn light filtered through the portholes. Everyone would wake soon. Except perhaps Lucinda Baines. The diplomatic attaché had a different circadian rhythm than anyone else. Kat had found the woman prowling *Jupiter* at odd hours, no matter which shift had just ended.

Kat crossed the last open space on tiptoe as rapidly as she dared. Silently, she moved aside the curtain that separated the cabin from the cockpit. Loki lay sprawled against the control panels, his hand firmly on the interface that locked all pilot controls.

Through the windscreen she saw a burly warrior prowling around the lander and the shuttle. He carried a spear and an iron sword as long as her arm.

A new plan glimmered in her mind. She'd bet a month's pay that Kim did not guard the cockpit of the shuttle as well as Loki guarded this one. He'd not separate from his wife so readily.

One micrometer at a time, she eased away from the cockpit. Down on her knees again, she crawled back the way she had come to the small hatch giving access to the engines and the all-important fuel cells.

The hatch opened on noiseless hinges. Kat dropped into the belly of the lander just as two of the guards dropped out of their hammocks, scratching and yawning. She eased the portal shut, letting it latch only as the men began speaking.

If they questioned the extra noise, she did not hear. The emergency lights did not come on. She bit back curses as she stubbed her toes on protruding equipment. Where was the switch? SBs handled this sort of thing, not officers. Still she should have memorized the layout of every micrometer of the vessel. It was her job to know about light switches and such.

Blindly, she reached to her left. The bulkhead was blank. She moved her hand around. Still nothing. But then she was left-handed. Most people, including designers used their right hand. Her fingers met the recessed plate on the first try to the right. Soft red light flooded the cramped compartment.

A quick scan showed the fuel cells right where they should be, along the two exterior bulkheads. Six to a side. A cubed meter each in size. Paired. The ship would operate under reduced power if some of the cells were damaged or empty, but only if the operating cells were paired with an equally fueled one on the opposite side.

Kat knew precisely how to disable the lander. Quickly, she yanked connecting cables from all the cells. She opened others at random, letting the energy held under pressure dissipate.

Sometimes in combat a cell took too many hits and absorbed the energy directly into the storage coils. Crews needed to get rid of it before it exploded. She opened the jettison port.

Then she unbolted two of them on the same side and heaved them out beneath the lander. She heard the casings crack as the two cells hit the ground.

As a final desecration she crawled backward through one of the jettison tubes, pulling a cell behind her. This one she cradled in her arms as she dropped to the ground. Bulky and awkward, it nearly toppled her. She braced her feet and gritted her teeth. A pebble pressed against the soft skin on her sole. She felt a bruise forming and needed to hop and curse and get rid of the offending rock that felt as big as a boulder.

Somehow she managed to carry the fuel cell across the clearing to the shuttle. She expected the watchman to shout an alarm at any moment.

Now for the tricky part. She hid herself and her purloined treasure behind one of the wheel struts. Not a great hiding place for long. Clouds obscured the sunrise. Tall trees and adjacent hills ringing the clearing would keep it dark here until the sun was well above them. She prayed that she had enough time.

One by one the locals trooped out of the two vessels, including the gloomy Lucinda Baines. That surprised Kat. Dared she leave the diplomatic attaché to the not so tender mercies of the brothers O'Hara? No matter. Kat would be back soon with reinforcements. Besides, Ms. Baines seemed to have a prior acquaintance with Loki. If she had survived his friendship before, she would again.

The moment the last occupant of the shuttle stumbled toward the remnants of last night's cooking fire, Kat sneaked aboard with the fuel cell. She coaxed the hatch closed and dashed for the cockpit.

"Controls keyed to O'Hara DNA," Kim had said yesterday. She laid her hand flat upon the lock.

"Retina scan," a voice from her past demanded. She almost choked with tears at the sound of her mother's voice. Then Kat remembered how the woman had abandoned her. Their moment of communion in the desert had sickened Kat from first contact with Mum's obsessed mind.

"Override. Emergency," she barked in as deep a voice as she could muster.

"Emergency password," Mum's voice replied in an equally gruff tone.

"St. Bridget and all the angels," Kat cursed.

"Password accepted." The engines roared to life.

Kat almost laughed. Mum's archaic religion was not popular in the GTE. No civil would think to invoke a saint for a password. She scanned the screens quickly. She didn't have time for more. Already her brothers and their lethally armed guards dashed toward the shuttle. She set the VTOL jets and lifted off.

"Well," Cyndi huffed. "She could have at least taken me with her."

"Oh, shut up," Loki retorted.

"Do you know who you are talking to?" she fumed. Hands on hips, hair disheveled from sleep, she almost looked like a woman worthy of this planet.

Then Loki noticed how her makeup had smeared, darkening her eyes and blurring her mouth. She'd be a lot prettier without the enhancement.

"I know precisely who you are," Loki said with a calmness he did not expect. "You are my prisoner. A hostage. Rank means nothing here. You have to earn respect—not be born to it."

Cyndi narrowed her eyes in deep concentration. Loki had always feared that expression. He never knew if the result of her intense thinking bout would produce brilliance or trouble. Trouble for him. Trouble for her father. Trouble for the universe.

He no longer cared. Fear of losing her love had always made him succumb to her moods. Now he knew deep in his gut that she had never truly loved him. She loved the adventure of an affair with an outlaw. She loved outwitting her father and his security. She loved manipulating people. Just like Mum.

"Kim, are the fuel cells repairable?" he called to his brother rather than waste any more time with Cyndi.

S'murghit, he should have put the force bracelets back on Kat. Restrained both her hands and her feet with the blasted things. But he'd spent a few sleepless nights in jail cells wearing the electronic shackles until Mum either organized a rescue or bailed him out. He hated the thought of doing that to another human being. Especially his sister.

"I think Kat made more of a mess than actual damage," Kim said. He stood up from his close examination of the cracked casings. "A little cerama/metal caulk ought to repair the exterior." He headed for the hatch.

"What about the energy that's leaking out?" Loki racked his brain for a solution. "Where is Konner when we need him most?"

"He should have been back here before us," Kim said. He reached under the pilot's seat for the emergency repair kit.

"I'm getting worried," Loki admitted.

"Well, we have plenty to worry about. The caulk is nearly used up in this kit. Not enough to fix more than one or two cells." Kim emerged from the hatchway shaking his head. "Maybe some of the local moss will fill the cracks."

"Raaskan," Loki called to the people gathered near the fire. "We need to explore and forage. We're going to be stuck here for a while."

Raaskan nodded, then began a conversation with the other warriors accompanied by many pointing gestures.

"I'm not going anywhere until I get a shower," Cyndi announced.

Hestiia looked at her with contempt. "Bathe in the creek."

"You mean with . . . with water! Fish crap in that water." She stared aghast at Hestiia. When that evoked no response, she tried logic. "Water is inefficient, barbaric, and probably contaminated. I need a sonic cleansing. You all do." Cyndi wrinkled her nose. "I've never smelled anyone so . . . offensive."

Hestiia looked as if she would slap the GTE diplomatic attaché. Cyndi deserved it, but violence would not settle the issue.

Rain dropped on the top of Loki's head. Cyndi screeched and ran for the interior of the lander. Hestiia shrugged and returned to reheating last night's leftovers. Kim muttered and cursed as he scrounged around the cockpit for tools and caulk. The warriors spread out and disappeared in pairs behind the tree line.

"Now what?" Kim asked.

"When Konner gets back, tell him to start building a still. I think we're going to need it." Loki pulled a toolbox from the lander and dumped the contents on the ground. "Bathing the coils in alcohol might enhance the effects of sunlight in recharging the cells."

"What are you going to do?" Kim eyed the discarded tools as if they might hold the answers to all of their problems.

"I'm going to collect some of the fruit of the Tambootie and make some dragon wine."

CHAPTER 41

◆——•——◆——•——◆

"WHERE ARE YOU, Martin Konner O'Hara?" Martin Fortesque slammed his fist against his Lazy-former®. The cushions absorbed the impact and eased none of his frustration. The vid screen remained quiet, unable to answer his question.

"Marty, I found it!" Bruce Geralds popped onto the screen almost as if summoned. He sounded breathless and a little frightened.

"Found what?" Martin sat straighter. He peered into the screen as if he could penetrate the pixels to delve across space and time directly into Bruce's terminal.

"The will."

"My grandparents' will?"

"Yes," Bruce breathed. He looked over his shoulder as if afraid of being observed. "I'll shoot it to you directly . . . and file a copy with the local courts." His eyes refused to look directly at the screen.

"What is it, Bruce?" Even as he spoke a document appeared in the lower right corner of his screen.

"Read it. Then destroy your file. I've secured the official copy where your mother can't find it."

Bruce disappeared.

"Scaramouch, enhance document." The screen enlarged the document enough so that Martin could read the fine print from his chair.

"Where as . . . wherefore . . ." he skimmed the legalese looking for the core of the document.

"'Everything to daughter Melinda Georgina Fortesque.' No surprise there."

The next paragraph jumped out at Martin. He began to chill. His mother's police record followed. Embezzlement, blackmail, conspiracy to falsely accuse another for a fatal accident involving loading equipment at spacedock. Sale of a controlled substance on the black market. Smuggling of said controlled substance. Any other person would have spent a number of years in prison undergoing psychological rehab, possibly even a mind-wipe.

Obviously Melinda's parents had bought her suspended sentences and paroles.

Since taking over Fortesque Industries, Melinda had been a model of propriety. No whisper of scandal ever attached to her for long. Record of her crimes had been scrubbed from local courts—and probably from GTE jurisdiction as well.

"Principal and seat on board of directors to be held in trust until her thirtieth birthday or her marriage," Martin read the last sentence.

His mother had married Konner O'Hara within two months of her parents' death.

Martin scrubbed the will from his files as well as any record of having received a document from Bruce.

Slowly, almost reluctantly he called up the minority report of the accident that had killed Melinda's parents.

"Evidence suggests the explosion was caused by external weapons fired from a small independent merchant vessel."

He began to shake uncontrollably.

"You murdered your parents. You hired a Sam Eyeam to do it for you. All you ever wanted was control of the corporation. Nothing else. Not even me."

Konner tried frantically to think of a way to distract the IMPs long enough for Dalleena and him to run away. But where would they run to? How could they run with her ribs still paining her?

She seemed to have fallen asleep. He hated to awaken her for any reason until she healed.

He was about to give himself up and hope the enemy would settle for him, without looking further for her. Then the skies opened up. Huge drops of water pelted the IMPs.

M'Berra cursed in a dialect full of fluid syllables Konner did not recognize. His tech screeched something about drowning. The scattered footsteps of the rest of the squad returned.

"We're screwed, Lieutenant Commander." Was that Ross Duggan's voice? "The changing air pressure and temperature is fouling up all our readings, sir. The rain and cold are dulling our own senses. We need better gear to do more than exist in this climate."

"We are Marines deployed with the Imperial Military Police, Sergeant. A little rain should not deter us."

"The crew are not acclimatized, sir," Corporal Paola Sanchez interjected. "In our haste to recover Lieutenant Lotski's patient, we left most of our foul weather gear behind."

Konner almost laughed out loud at how his new allies sabotaged their own people.

"With your permission, sir, I'd like to take the men back to our landers and equip them with rain and cold weather gear," Duggan said. "The quarry cannot go far in this weather. The female is severely injured. Lieutenant Lotski was surprised she could even walk beyond the hut."

"We'll find them faster with rain gear and shields for the tech equipment," Sanchez finished.

"Very well. Sergeant, recall the crew and return to the lander in close formation. No strays. I'll take the point."

More rustling and stamping and uncomfortable mutters. Then a few moments of silence.

"Wherever you are, get out now. I figure you've got one half a metric hour at the most to disappear into thin air," Duggan whispered. Then his footfalls retreated.

Konner waited. He counted one hundred heartbeats. He was about to speak to Iianthe when the dragon lifted his wing. Konner crawled out from beneath its shelter. Immediately, the rain drenched him. He shivered and clutched his arms close against his body.

"We need a better hiding place," he said.

(*Help comes.*)

"My brothers?" Hope remained dormant. The IMPs would hear the shuttle and open fire with the heavy guns aboard their lander.

(*Irythros!*) a second dragon voice chimed in. This one was brighter, higher in pitch, and more enthusiastic.

"Konner here." He looked up into the pelting rain against the gray sky. He saw no shimmering form outlined in red. He saw nothing but more gray clouds dumping more cold rain on his face, clinging to his eyelashes and dripping in chilly runnels down his back.

The sound of a large splash blended in with the rain dropping into the creek. Konner peered in that direction. Only a few meters away and he still could not see much detail.

The splashing continued. Eventually, Konner detected a pattern in how the water cascaded around a bulky form.

"Are you here to take Dalleena and me to safety, Irythros?" he asked, still peering through the rain.

(*Yes. I love flying against the weather.*) He almost chortled.

Konner was reminded of a puppy he'd had as a kid. All feet and ears, the dog had much more enthusiasm than sense.

(*Awaken your lady, Konner,*) Iianthe said politely. His deep bronze bell of a voice sounded much more mature. Perhaps his pain added weight to his years.

All of their problems seemed trivial compared to getting Dalleena to safety where she could mend in peace and quiet.

And what of his appointment with his son, Martin. He needed to leave today if he was going to make it to Aurora on time. He prayed the shuttle had enough fuel to get him back to *Sirius* and the crystals had finished growing. Would his brothers ever forgive him for deserting them at this terrible time?

In short order he managed to hoist a reluctant Dalleena aboard Irythros' back. She seemed more alert this morning and moved with more ease. But she still walked stiffly and cautiously.

"What about you, Iianthe? How will you fare, grounded and alone?"

(*I am not without defenses, Stargod Konner. Go. Keep your lady safe. I respect her courage and your dedication to those you love.*) A curl of steam snaked out of the dragon's nostrils.

"Farewell, friend. Take care. I hope our next meeting is less fraught with danger."

(*Danger will always follow you, Stargod Konner. Take care that you defeat your enemies with honor.*)

Now what did that mean?

Konner did not have time to reflect on it. Irythros pranced down the creek, splashing through the rain until he had enough momentum and lift for takeoff.

He flapped his wings vigorously until they were secreted among the thick clouds. The air was a little drier up here. But not much. Thoroughly soaked and chilled, Konner clung to Dalleena and the dragon for warmth. He clenched his teeth so they did not chatter.

Soon Dalleena began to shudder violently in the cold. Konner wrapped his arms tighter around her, letting her draw what little warmth she could from his body. He clamped his knees tighter against the dragon's back, hoping for a smooth flight and gentle landing.

(*Understood,*) Irythros said. He sounded more sober and mature than Konner remembered. Had he curbed his youthful energy out of concern?

Konner sensed more than felt the land rising beneath them. He presumed they headed south, toward the clearing. The clouds and the cold deadened all of his other senses.

And then they lost altitude abruptly. Dalleena swallowed a yelp of surprise. Or was it dismay.

Konner's stomach flipped and his balance distorted. He dropped one arm from around Dalleena to clutch the dragon's spinal horn. The clouds stayed with them until they were barely fifty meters above ground. Irythros circled lazily. Dalleena spotted a fire and pointed it out to Konner. The stolen IMP lander came into view. He made out Loki's and Kim's red hair among a scattering of people.

As promised, Irythros landed slowly, gently, working his wings to cushion them.

"Where's the shuttle?" Konner shouted to Loki before Irythros had fully settled.

Loki's face looked grim. Kim's looked just as bad. They told him in blunt terms of Kat's escape, her sabotage, and her theft of the shuttle. They had few rations and were far from help. The IMPs would come and find them as soon as Kat revealed their hiding place.

Even if Konner could get the lander up and running he wasn't sure he could get past his own booby traps aboard *Sirius* with any vessel other than *Rover.*

"Forgive me, Martin. I think I'm going to miss your court date and our one chance to be together."

CHAPTER 42

KAT PARKED THE SHUTTLE out of sight and weapons range of the camp. No sense in being shot down by her own people in a notorious smuggler's vessel before she could explain herself.

"Where is Captain Leonard?" she asked the first guard she encountered on the perimeter of the village.

Her feet ached from wearing the too thin and too large boots she'd found thrown into a locker aboard the shuttle.

The guard shrugged and gestured with his head toward the cluster of cabins and huts. Kat proceeded. She asked everyone she met where to find their captain. No one knew.

"Captain is still aboard *Jupiter*. She's vowing to remain aboard until we find the crystals or until the ship's orbit decays beyond repair," Josh Kohler, the navigator, said. "M'Berra's out chasing an injured native kidnapped by one of the outlaws. Guess that puts me in charge as senior officer."

"What about Pettigrew?" Kat did not like to think about the self-righteous Marine in charge of the mission. They needed level heads and careful plans to capture her brothers and reclaim the king stone.

"Lotski has him doped up and pumped full of antibiotics. She's ordered bed rest until she's certain his wounds do not infect."

"Wounds from what?"

"He claims that a dragon dropped him onto ancient razor wire soon after first landing." Kohler worked his cheek muscles to keep from laughing out loud.

Kat did not see the humor in the situation. She knew from personal experience just how big and dangerous a dragon could be.

"The man is delusional." Kohler sobered. "But then we all knew that before this mission. Can't have him charging into the fray and possibly damaging one or more of the crystals in his enthusiasm."

"He'd likely do that."

"Yeah. Pettigrew wants revenge. Been raving about it for hours. Word from the latest batch of refugees is that the enemy sneaked back aboard *Jupiter* with a bunch of bushies. All armed to the teeth. They killed a bunch of people who opposed them and stole the rest of the crystal array."

Kat's knees grew weak. She did not want to believe the three men she had met capable of the atrocity of murder. Bad enough that they deprived animals of life to feed themselves. But to kill another *human!*

Somehow, the legendary exploits of her brothers did not match the image she now had of them.

"I know where the O'Haras are hiding," Kat blurted out before she had time to rethink her plans. "But we have to move fast if we are to capture them and recover the crystal array."

"I think we need a superior officer, Kat," Josh refused to look her in the eye.

In that moment she knew he'd never move much higher than navigator. He was good at that job, but he did not have the self-confidence and initiative of an officer of the line.

Kat had no intentions of letting this man hold her back just because he outranked her by one degree and had two years' seniority on her.

"Fine. I'll fetch M'Berra. Where did he go?"

"That way," Kohler pointed vaguely to the south and west. "He took a squad out before dawn, as soon as Lotski discovered her patient missing."

"Dalleena, Konner's lady. The middle brother hadn't returned to the hiding place as of two hours ago. I bet he stayed behind to grab her. He's the only one who could correct the sabotage I left behind. We'll leave Konner to M'Berra. Our first officer will keep the man busy and away from the clearing. Best to strike the others while they are divided. They have Ms. Baines." She hoped the last statement would spur Kohler to action. He'd been watching the diplomatic attaché with lustful eyes for weeks.

"My orders are to secure this compound at all costs. Unless M'Berra counters his own orders, or Captain Leonard tells me otherwise, I and the people under my command will stay here and prevent the locals or the O'Haras from stealing the stores or burning the place down." Kohler bit his lip and refused to look Kat in the eye.

"Very well. I'll get Captain Leonard's orders to move out. Where's communications?"

"Uh . . . James is missing. His escape vessel must have landed in a different sector. Our communications are rudimentary, just what Brewster could cannibalize from a lander that's out of action. Some local bacteria is eating away at the cerama/metal."

Kat did not like what she was hearing. Not one little bit. Disorganization, lack of leadership. Fear. Why had they all evacuated? The ship should still be manageable, even without the king stone.

"We'll need a mechanical genius to get that lander in the air again."

"Just don't let Konner O'Hara near it," she muttered. "Any other vessel that comes within hailing distance will have to be dunked in the saltwater bay to kill the bio-gunk in the upper atmosphere. Otherwise, we'll lose them all." She captured Kohler's gaze with her own until he nodded. "Permission to contact Captain Leonard aboard *Jupiter*, sir." She saluted smartly. At least she'd make it look like she proceeded through proper channels.

"Permission granted, Lieutenant Talbot." Kohler returned her salute. He stepped back and began scanning the horizon with a FarSight® sensory visor. The infrared detectors would reveal more than his eyes peering through the gloomy clouds. At least the rain had let up a little down here in the valley.

Kat sloshed through mud churned by too many boots toward the largest hut in the center of the village. A mess sergeant had managed to boil up some grains for a cereal breakfast.

He shook his head and grumbled. "First salvage trip back to *Jupiter,* I want the hydroponics tanks and all of the food stores. First priority. No questions." He pinned Kat with his gaze. "Growing food in the dirt is most inefficient. If these grains had been tanked, I could feed twice as many people on half the amount. This planet needs civilizing. Fast."

"I'll do what I can," Kat replied. She grabbed the next bowl of mush and chowed down. No telling when she'd eat again and she'd had nothing since last night's meal of roasted vegetables—she had refused the rabbit so proudly caught by one of Loki's warriors.

From the chow line, she made her way to the largest hut. She figured she'd find communications there.

A harried Sergeant Brewster sat at a collapsible table with six handheld communicators and pieces of the lander's more elaborate system configured to beam data among them. Eight other noncoms crowded around her with demands to contact this person, that officer, a love interest.

"Silence!" Kat cut through the jumble of people with the authority of her rank, her training, and her superior height.

"Communication with *Jupiter* has to take priority," she announced.

The noncoms met this demand with loud protests and indignation.

"We can sort out units after we recover the crystals. I know you are missing friends, people you care deeply about. We can only hope they have landed in friendly territory. But we have no hope of reuniting any of you until we get those crystals back. Now disperse and see to your gear." She leveled a stern gaze at each of them.

They snapped to attention, saluted smartly, turned, and departed on a quick march.

The sergeant heaved a sigh of relief. "Thank you, Lieutenant," he said re-aligning some of the handhelds. "Maintenance has been slack on the landers. We've been too peaceful for too long. There are parts missing. Weird atmospheric fluctuations and a lack of satellites are interfering with communications. I think that green layer in the upper atmosphere is creating havoc."

"Are the missing parts a lack of maintenance or sabotage?"

"Your guess is as good as mine. First landing party had all their comms and weapons stolen by the locals the first night, then returned—inoperative. I vote for sabotage."

"Can you reach *Jupiter*?"

"Sometimes. But even if I can get through, there is no guarantee the captain will answer." He began fiddling with and adjusting his units.

"Why wouldn't a comm officer answer a hail from the surface?"

"Captain's the only one left aboard. Who knows what she's doing to maintain orbit. Might be too busy to answer."

"Keep trying to reach her. If she answers, tell her I'm on my way up with the captured smuggler's shuttle *Rover*." Kat took off at a run for her brother's vessel. She could not allow mud and drizzle and discomfort to slow her down.

"Take a squad with you," Josh Kohler called as she hastened away. "Start salvaging what you can."

Kat grunted a noncommittal reply as she ran.

The shuttle was fast. Faster than any lander designed by a GTE engineer. Almost as fast as a two-man scout, or even one of the new cyber-fighters where the controls were linked to the pilot's brain synapses. Commands happened as fast as thought. Still, the trip took hours. Far too long.

With the dragons at his beck and call, Konner could easily have eluded M'Berra's squad and returned to the clearing. A few more hours would see the crystals connected and buried. The confusion field would snap into place soon after.

When *Jupiter* finally came into view, Kat shook her head in dismay. The cruiser was a mess. It listed at an odd angle, half pointed toward the planet below. It no longer spun to generate gravity. The troops had fled the ship with too much haste to secure bay doors. Only a few lights showed in those open bays. It looked dead.

She had less time to save the ship than she thought.

Kat prayed that Captain Leonard had kept enough power generating to provide atmosphere.

She docked without challenge. In the back of the shuttle she found an EVA suit that fit remarkably well. Her uniform EVA had to be custom tailored to her tall frame.

Atmosphere did not register on the suit until she found the bridge. The first air lock did not want to close behind her. She slammed the panel with her fist. Sparks flew. Her faceplate instantly polarized and her helmet light dimmed. After a few moments her vision cleared and she found the door closed.

Another fist to another control brought air into the lock. When it reached point zero five atmospheres, Kat dared release her faceplate. And wished she hadn't. The air smelled stale, as if the scrubbers were overtaxed or only working at half capacity.

Another few moments brought the pressure up and the inner door creaked open slowly.

Lieutenant Commander Amanda Leonard swung her chair to face the door, a needle pistol in her hand. A huge bruise covered the right side of her face and swelled that eye closed. Her upper lip curled in a sneer.

"So you've come to finish the job your brothers started," she snarled and tightened her finger on the pistol.

CHAPTER 43

✦ —— · —— ✦ —— · —— ✦

"MASTER MARTIN." His Super Snooper, enhanced with the latest features thanks to his friend Gerald, appeared on the screen in front of the graph Martin was building showing shipping lanes of the Galactic Free Market.

"What?" Martin replied querulously. He almost had enough data to put this portion of the program into the hologram star map he and Bruce and Jane were composing.

"I have detected activation of the rescue beacon assigned to Melinda Fortesque's agent-at-large, Sam Eyeam."

"Where?" Martin sat forward eagerly. He sent his graphs into the background. The Sam Eyeam could be anywhere in the known galaxy. But Martin was willing to bet that Melinda had sent him in search of Konner O'Hara, to keep him from returning to Aurora in time for the custody hearing.

"Unknown. The signal is faint and irregular."

"Guess."

"Star charts do not extend to the location suggested."

What to do? "My dad needs help. I know it."

"May I suggest, Master Martin, extrapolation from the merchant charts."

"Yes!" He'd designed the project to show anomalies in the ever-changing borders among the GTE, the Free Merchants, and the Kree Empire.

A three-dimensional swirl of colored lights appeared in the far corner of the room. The hologram had swelled since the last time he'd set it into motion. GTE solar systems appeared in blue, the Free Merchant stars in green, and the enemy empire in red. Known jump points flashed yellow. The chart nearly filled the room. Even then, the vast distances between stars were hardly representative.

As he examined the troubled borders, several stars changed color, from red to green, green to red, and blue gobbled up three from each. Aurora changed from blue to green and back again in less than one digital minute. Melinda frequently used the threat to withdraw from the GTE as leverage in negotiating trade concessions or waivers in the judicial system. Martin had no idea what today's switch involved.

He hoped his mother's threats did not have anything to do with the custody hearing coming up in just a few days. Or worse, the arrest and conviction of Konner O'Hara.

"Scaramouch, show me the beacon."

"Insufficient data."

"Extrapolate."

"Insufficient power."

"What?" Martin pulled up a diagnostic. Sure enough, the huge mapping program and holographic display had eaten up almost all of his spare memory and speed.

Dared he ask Melinda for a few upgrades?

No. "Melinda can't be involved in this in any way," he muttered to himself.

He called Bruce and Jane. Neither one had a solution.

Martin paced the room. He wandered through the hologram, watching the changes in colors, looking at how the jump points connected star systems in seemingly random patterns.

Crystal drives made jumps possible, bridging the light-years. Crystals made near instantaneous communications between the planets possible. Crystals . . .

"Scaramouch, locate souvenir crystal from camp." The icon of two fencers moved back and forth across the screen.

Two years ago Konner had given him a tiny crystal, a miniature of a king stone. "My dad said it would be a tangible reminder of our friendship."

Perhaps it was something more.

Experiments on integrating crystals into computer components had drifted through the scientific journals several times over the last decade. Always the government had classified such experiments as top secret and made the growth of miniature crystals illegal.

Martin did not question how Konner O'Hara had come by such a thing.

"Your crystal is secreted inside your personal terminal." The computer's voice sounded almost animated.

Of course. Martin had been hiding childhood treasures in there for years. He'd cleaned it all out last year on his birthday, feeling too old for such things. But he'd left the crystal there. It was more than just a memento from a favorite camp counselor.

He yanked open the wall panel revealing the guts of the machine. He remembered now that he had hidden the crystal, about the length of his palm, here, because this was one place Melinda would not search, one place his tutors and companions had no need to access. Konner and his unique gift were parts of his life he had always needed to keep separate and secret from his mother and her flunkies.

He reached deep into the recess, fumbling around for the cool, glassy feel of the faceted crystal. He brushed his knuckles against . . . could it be? . . . a Klip. Cautiously he drew out the thumbnail-sized clamp. It remained attached to one wire. The primary wire.

Melinda was tapping into his programs. At the same time, she drained memory and power from his system to severely limit his capabilities.

Anywhere else in the GTE this little device would be illegal. So was murder.

Melinda had gotten away with both here on Aurora where she owned everything.

Not anymore.

With cold determination, Martin slipped the clamp off the primary wire. Nothing changed overtly. No alarms beeped and no surge of power changed the holographic display. He dropped the Klip back into its hidey-hole.

Then he retrieved the crystal. He dredged up from memory the last report he'd read on crystal experimentation. If he placed it between the processor and the Q drive, connected to both by fiber optics . . .

Where would he get nitrogen to bathe the crystal?

No, this was not a crystal star drive. The mini crystal would not be a monopole seeking an opposite pole in an array of crystals. This was a single king stone that wanted to be connected to a mother stone.

He connected it to the communications port where it could tap into whatever theoretical energy bigger king stones used to connect to the rest of the universe.

Instantly the hologram of a star map began filling in details. New stars and jump points appeared. Star systems Martin had not charted became blue, green, or red.

The entire thing shifted and rotated to a new alignment.

"North!" Martin chortled. "My crystal is now galactic north."

And then the jump points changed. Some remained stable and yellow. New ones wandered, taking on paler colors. Some became so intense they changed to orange.

Martin noticed very pale lines of white connecting the jump points to their destinations.

And at the core of it all remained a huge blank spot with no jump points entering or leaving. It stood strategically bordered by all three political entities.

"Scaramouch, what is this hole?" Martin asked his computer.

"Define hole?" the computer replied.

"This area without any stars." He circled the dimensions of the hole. It was big enough to contain fifteen or twenty star systems, but none showed.

"Unknown. No charts exist for that area."

"Scaramouch, correlate the distress beacon with this area." Martin tapped his foot anxiously while he waited for the computer to make calculations. It seemed to take an inordinate amount of time.

Finally a tiny violet light blinked at him from an area of the hole farthest away from Earth. But only a few jumps from Aurora.

"Scaramouch, highlight jump points into this area."

"All known jump points shown." The area remained free of entry.

"Scaramouch, calculate probability of a black hole in this area."

"Insufficient data," the computer replied.

"Martin?" Melinda Fortesque appeared on the vid screen. "I need you in my office immediately." She did not sound happy.

"What is it, Melinda?" he asked, careful not to call her "Mother."

"Stop questioning my orders and come here," she snapped. Her image disappeared so quickly he almost heard the pixels pop.

"Uh-oh, she sounds mad. Really, really mad. She must have discovered the Klip is now disconnected." Martin hastened from the residential wing to Melinda's office. He paused at her door long enough to straighten his rumpled shirt and trousers and run his fingers through his hair.

His mind spun with lies. He plastered a blank expression of supposed innocence upon his face.

Melinda, of course, was impeccably groomed, wearing one of her expensive suits. This one had a longish skirt rather than her usual trousers. Who did she intend to impress? Certainly not Martin.

"What is this?" Melinda thrust a handheld screen at Martin without preamble.

The harbormaster's calendar lay before him, the date of Martin's last birthday highlighted. And a week later the date of Konner O'Hara's banishment from Aurora stood out in bold red letters.

"Looks like a calendar." Martin shrugged and returned the screen to his mother's desk. He bit his cheeks rather than ask her about the Klip.

Maybe she hadn't discovered it yet.

"Do not feign ignorance with me, Martin. Your computer's telltales are all over that entry." She tapped the entry regarding Konner.

Martin opted for silence. He tried to keep his face bland and his eyes level. He'd learned the art of a masterful stare from the best. His mother.

"You moved the entry," she accused.

He maintained his silence.

"I have to respect your perseverance, if not your actions. Do you know who this man is?"

"Yes, Mother, I do."

She returned his silence. He knew he could not out-stubborn her in this mood.

"Martin Konner O'Hara is my father. You cannot keep me away from him after my fourteenth birthday."

"Yes, I can. He will not arrive in time for your birthday. He will never arrive in Aurora. My latest intelligence says that he is dead. Killed in a battle with the Imperial Military Police five months ago. I have just received a copy of his official death certificate on file with the GTE. Any man appearing with his name is an obvious imposter and will be arrested and extradited immediately."

Martin swallowed the sob that threatened to escape his throat. He had to blink back hot tears.

Rather than show emotion in his mother's presence, he turned and marched back to his own quarters. He slumped into his Lazy-former®. Black despair threatened to drag him deeper and deeper into himself until he disappeared completely.

"If your father is dead, Master Martin, why would Sam Eyeam activate the beacon?" the Super Snooper asked.

"Scaramouch, trace agent Sam Eeyam's movements over the past three months and display in purple on the hologram."

"How did you know the O'Haras are my brothers, Captain?" Kat asked. She kept her attention on Leonard's eyes, knowing they would signal any change in her intent to fire before her finger reacted. In minimal g, could she avoid a spray of needles aimed at her face?

"I had the displeasure of meeting one of your brothers. The family resemblance is remarkable, Lieutenant Talbot. No wonder you are obsessed with finding them. The one who stole the king stone did this to me." Amanda Leonard gestured with her free hand to the bruise that marred her face. The fingers of that hand were swollen and hung limp, as if she had broken them. "He stunned me in the face, then kicked me." Her words began to slur.

"I think you have a concussion, Captain. You've been breathing bad air, too. May I relieve you of the weight of that weapon?" Kat asked blandly. She crept forward, wincing at the clank of the boots of her EVA suit.

"No, you may not." Leonard steadied her grip on the pistol.

"We can still recover the king stone, sir. If we act fast."

"I will not desert my ship, Lieutenant."

"I am not asking you to, sir. But the others will not act without your orders. It's chaos down there. We need you to take command and restore order."

"Chaos. Rats deserting a sinking ship. It's all Judge Balinakas' fault. He ordered the evacuation while I was unconscious. He took the crystal techs away from their terminals at gunpoint. He caused the panic. Ever since the day I came aboard as captain he has challenged my authority. Just because he has served aboard *Jupiter* since her commissioning does not give him authority over *my* crew. Only over judiciary . . ." Her words trailed off.

Good. Her animosity diverted her attention from Kat and her brothers. "Would you like to prove your superior ability to the judge, Captain?"

Amanda Leonard's eyes brightened a bit and she looked at Kat with a glimmer of hope.

"Sign an order, sir. I know where the smugglers are hiding. I watched where they buried the king stone. We can retrieve it along with the rest of the crystal array. But I need your authority to command the Marines." Kat bent over Leonard, fixing her with her gaze. When she had the captain's complete attention, she folded her hand around the pistol and pulled it free. She breathed easier.

So did the captain. "Your eyes are different from your brother's. His are blue. Midnight blue. I almost lost my soul looking too deeply into his eyes."

"The orders, Captain. I need you to sign the orders."

"Very well. Take every Marine, lander, and piece of equipment you can scrounge." She whipped out a handheld and scribbled with a new electronic pencil from her earring.

"Sir, this puts Lieutenant Pettigrew in charge of the mission." Kat gulped back her dismay. "I'm the only one who knows . . ."

"You are too close to the situation, Lieutenant. If you give the orders, you might jeopardize the mission in a misguided attempt to spare your brothers."

"I assure you, Captain. I have no love for any man or woman with the name O'Hara. They abandoned me when I was a child. They left me without a backward glance." That was not exactly true. A flash of heat flushed her face as she remembered the moments of laughter and reminiscence with her brothers during yesterday's adventures.

Then she remembered the incredible experience of reaching out through the universe and touching her mother's thoughts; of feeling bound to everything and everyone. Especially her family.

But she did not want to be bound to the woman whose obsession to recover her daughter had become an excuse for gaining wealth that would never be used.

"Pettigrew is in charge. He outranks you."

"What about M'Berra. He's your second-in-command. He should lead."

"M'Berra needs to remain at that rustic headquarters and coordinate everything. Pettigrew leads the mission to retrieve the crystals. You will obey him, Kat. I'm depending upon you to behave yourself and obey."

"Yes, sir." Kat snapped a salute.

"Take a hydroponics tank back with you and as much food as the droids can carry. You're all going to be very hungry if you fail."

"I won't fail, sir."

"I have my doubts, Kat. Do this for me."

"Captain . . . ?"

"I intend to sail my ship back home with the O'Haras as my prisoners and Judge Balinakas in chains, or go down with it in flames."

"Not if you keep breathing bad air with a concussion. Sorry, sir." Kat slammed her fist into Amanda Leonard's jaw. As the captain slumped into unconsciousness, Kat slung her over her shoulder and tromped back to the shuttle *Rover.*

"We need you dirtside more than you need to remain aboard a sinking ship, Captain."

CHAPTER 44

"THEY COME," Dalleena called to Konner and the others. She stood at the edge of the clearing, facing north, her right arm extended palm out. In her left hand she clutched the small ultrasound device Kim had given her. She did not need the healing machine much now.

"Where? How many?" Konner poked his head out of one of the many holes in the ground.

"How long?" Loki asked. He and Irythros, the red-tipped dragon, dug yet more holes opposite Dalleena's post.

So many holes for so many crystals. Everything counted in twelves, the crystals, the holes, the distances that separated them. She did not pretend to understand the why and where of Konner's operation. She knew only that he considered it important and the others followed his directions.

"Landers lifting now. Thirty, no fifty people."

"Your talents are getting more precise," Konner said as he vaulted out of a hole. He still carried the intriguing weapon that shot fine ropes over long distances.

She could think of many times such a tool would have aided her in rescuing lost ones. Especially sheep and small children who tended to get into awkward places where adults could not fit.

Konner came up beside her. He rested a hand comfortably upon her shoulder, as if it belonged there. As if each of them was incomplete without the other.

"This place . . ." She shrugged at her lack of understanding. Perhaps the crystals made her tracking sense keener. She knew without thinking that fifty hearts beat against her palm.

Konner's hand tightened. Fifty minds brushed against hers. The fifty minds separated, became individuals. She shared fifty different emotions. One stood out from the others, determined, focused, single-minded.

"They are angry and afraid," she said. The pressure of that anger made it hard to breathe. Perhaps this refinement of her talent was not for the better.

"Fifty troops, that's two landers." Loki joined them at the perimeter of the clearing.

"Four," Dalleena corrected him. "They plan to leave with the crystals."

"The confusion field anywhere near ready?" Loki asked.

"No. I need another full day, even if you and Irythros finish the digging and placement of the directionals," Konner replied.

"The Others will be here in two, perhaps three hours. The leader pushes them hard. He . . . she seeks vengeance." The force of the personality swamped Dalleena's senses.

She swallowed hard, trying desperately to reclaim her sense of self.

"Your sister."

"Kat," Konner said at the same moment.

Sadness swept from brother to brother, then through Dalleena. With her talent engaged and heightened she became a part of their anguish.

"We will have to fight our own sister. Mum will kill us." Konner choked.

"Do not think about it, Konner." Dalleena dropped her seeking hand to wrap it around Konner's where he clutched her shoulder with desperate fingers. She felt her skin bruising beneath his grip.

"We cannot engage them here." A note of panic crept into Konner's voice.

Dalleena's chest felt as if an iron band squeezed it. She needed to sever her physical contact with him in order to keep breathing. Yet she could not. He needed her. She knew with absolute certainty that he would break something in his mind if she removed his hand from her shoulder, her hand from his, his mind and emotions from contact with hers.

"We have strategic advantage here. They will have to come at us uphill, over rough terrain," Loki countered.

"If we fight them here, I will have to kill one of them." Konner's words came out, barely above a whisper.

Dalleena could not breathe. She saw the man he meant, Lieutenant Pettigrew. For three very long heartbeats she relived with Konner the vision of the man turning into a skeleton, of a bright tunnel swirling, drawing them in, like the dragongate, but without a destination.

Was that what it was like to die? She shuddered.

Loki stared into Konner's eyes for a long moment. Then he nodded as they came to a silent agreement.

"They can't land four vessels here and Kat knows it. Two were a tight fit." Loki began to pace.

Kim joined them, Hestiia close on his heels, as if one could not act without the other. "Perhaps one of us should go up with Irythros and scout."

"I don't think that will be necessary. Dalleena is following them," Konner said.

"If I were Kat, I'd land at the foot of this hill and hike up," Loki said. He picked up a stick and began drawing a rough map of the area in the loose dirt. The brothers called Raaskan and Niveean over to consult.

Dalleena tuned out their conversation and listened to the emotions of the Others. The similarity of Kat's thought patterns and emotions to Konner's frightened her. She tried to block out the leader, Kat. She raised her hand again, seeking the practical information of speed and direction.

"Six small vessels, two men each, approach very fast. They are surrounded with energy. Dangerous energy," she called to them. "Fighters with weapons charged." The alien words invaded her mind and heightened her fear.

Konner went rigid. The image of the bright tunnel swirling, faster and faster, pulled her closer and closer toward death. A death she/he/they would inflict? Or a death they would suffer?

She had to break free of this man. Now. Forever. She could not live with this terrible knowledge.

"Heads up," Loki whispered into his comm. He spotted movement through the tall ferns and scrub. The intruders came. Right on schedule.

He watched from the vantage point of a tall tree. The only reasonable path from the flats to the clearing lay within his view. He hoped that Kat would not take the unreasonable route over cliffs and dead-end ravines. If she had skilled rock climbers among her Marines, she might be able to reach the clearing unobserved.

Loki had gladly left Cyndi gagged with duct tape and bound to a tree half a klick before the clearing. The IMPs would have to rescue her. Her protests and demands ought to slow the IMPs further and alert anyone left in the clearing.

Loki's few warriors had a chance to pick off the intruders one by one as they negotiated obstacles, natural ones and those created within the last two hours.

"See them," Raaskan confirmed. "Pettigrew leads." A long pause. "Taneeo guides him." The last came out on a hiss.

"Expected that," Loki muttered. One more piece of evidence that Hanassa's spirit had taken over Taneeo's body. Hanassa had gone to great lengths to remove the Stargods from the land of the Coros. He hadn't given up, even in death.

Where was Kat, if not up front? He sought a different vantage point. A rock outcropping offered him clear line of sight of Raaskan's position. Unfortunately, it also gave Pettigrew the slanting line of sight to Loki. He stayed prone, shielding his eyes against the westering sun filtering through the cloud cover, searching for the tall female and whatever company she might lead.

Thank St. Bridget, Pettigrew kept his eyes focused straight ahead. He prodded Taneeo with a sharp finger every few meters and barked questions. He should have kept scouts ranging ahead and placed himself in the middle of the column for his own protection, but the cocky lieutenant had to lead. He probably saw this as his one chance at promotion.

But Pettigrew had to get past Loki and his warriors first.

The Marines all wore helmets and battle armor that hid hair color, complexion, and gender. At this distance he could distinguish few features other than relative height.

Where was Kat?

Raaskan popped up behind the last private in line. A knotted vine twisted about the throat left the hapless Marine choking. A quick snap of Raaskan's powerful arms and his victim's head lolled limply on his neck.

Unbearable pressure built within Loki's chest, robbing him of breath. The cords along his nape burned and ached. He had to close his eyes and concentrate upon Pettigrew. If he watched the grisly work of his warriors, he'd share the deaths. His orders to render the IMPs unconscious whenever possible had not registered with the locals.

Tribal warfare had been their way of life for generations.

Fifty meters farther along the path Hestiia took out a straggler with a well-placed arrow—again to the vulnerable throat.

Loki was prepared for this death. With his feet braced and his hands locked behind his neck, he kept his focus on Pettigrew and Taneeo. The slight priest seemed to know the path better than Loki's own warriors.

About every one hundred heartbeats Loki scanned the area for signs of his sister and a squad of specialized bush troops. Nothing.

Surely he should be able to find her. If not with his eyes, then he must seek her with his mind and his heart.

Three deep breaths. His mind cleared of the confusion of dying men. Consciously, he blocked out his awareness of each of his own troops. He filtered through the company of determined soldiers. Seeking, always seeking, something familiar.

A whisper of thought brushed against him. He honed in on the pattern of logic that could only be Kat. Behind him. Close. Getting closer.

"Freeze, Loki, or I blast you from here to kingdom come." Kat stood at his feet, braced against a tree with ten men behind her. All of them held stunner rifles, fully charged and aimed at his heart.

· —◆— ·

Large rocks crashed down hills and through brush. Their fall echoed around the clearing. A cloud of dust drifted through the trees.

(*Trouble,*) Irythros called.

Konner peered through the brush toward the path. Niveean and the two blacksmith's apprentices jumped up and down in triumph. The rockfall continued beneath their feet. They had fulfilled their part of the ambush and levered a boulder into the path of the approaching IMPs.

Konner bowed his head a moment, praying that no person stood in the path of that rock and the others it released as it plummeted downward.

He caught a flash of bright light on the periphery of his senses. Quickly he rolled to his right.

Fighters whizzed past the clearing. An energy bolt singed the saber fern to his left. The next blast fired across the top of the clearing as if engaging more fighters rather than enemies on the ground.

Then Konner caught a flash of a dragon wing and a wild chuckle from Irythros.

(*They waste their ammunition on what they cannot see and will never catch.*)

Konner shook his head. The dragon did not take this battle seriously.

He should.

The clearing was a mess. Piles of loose dirt littered the place along with uprooted ferns, shrubs, and grasses. Konner had to expand the open area by nearly five acres to accommodate his measurements. One crystal lay within feet of the edge of the pool. The hot spring there fed extra energy to the crystal. The stone, in turn added heat to the water. All of the crystals drew power from the iron and nitrogen in the soil, shooting energy back and forth among themselves and the king stone.

At last the stones had stopped singing their unharmonious wail in the back of his mind. They waited now in tense silence for the connections that would make them a family again.

At their urging he'd finished the hard work of placement and connection twelve hours ahead of schedule.

Now he just had to establish the programming of the confusion field and bury a small handheld computer within a force field beside the king stone. This would be easier if he had access to the database aboard the shuttle. But Kat had stolen that.

(*You must leave the clearing. The fighters leave. They have no more ammunition or fuel. But the Others come. Quickly,*) Irythros said. His tone sounded very insistent.

"Not yet," Konner replied. "Dalleena, can you see anything?"

"Just dust." She stood on the opposite side of the clearing, keeping acres of land between them.

He did not understand her coolness. Or her silence. He did not have time to wonder.

"Just a few more moments and I can engage the field." He ran back to the center and the king stone. He dropped into the deep hole.

"Konner!" Dalleena called. "Konner, help me!"

He could not ignore the plea.

(*Stay hidden.*)

"St. Bridget help me, I can't." Before Irythros could counter the argument, Konner nearly flew up the crude ladder from the depths of the hole.

Taneeo held Dalleena from behind, a knife at her throat. Fifteen armed IMPs ranged behind them, Pettigrew at the fore.

Konner still had the unconnected handheld in his pocket. No time to finish the last few commands. No time to keep the IMPs out of their hiding place.

No time to save anyone.

Konner's gaze was drawn to the strange object suspended upon a thong and hanging around the priest's neck.

The second distress beacon. How had he gotten it from the freelance merchant with the good teeth?

A feral grin spread over the traitor's face. "Any move from you or the dragon and I kill her where she stands," he snarled.

"I see you have returned from the dead to terrorize innocents again, Hanassa."

CHAPTER 45

◆———•———◆———•———◆

"PSST!" KIM signaled Loki. From his vantage point on a ledge below his brother, he could not see if Loki heard him or not. Or if Kat heard and would send her shock troops after him.

He counted one hundred heartbeats. He heard only the muffled sounds of strident conversation above him.

"I can do this," he told himself.

Slowly, he breathed in and out three times, clearing his mind. When he felt disembodied, he pictured in his mind exactly where Loki should drop off the top of the rock outcropping. Dangle here, drop there. Avoid this rotten foothold. Take this less obvious one. Then he sent the images to his brother.

Behind him, he heard the confused thrashing of the IMPs freeing themselves from the rockfall. He had to leave the mop-up to his people. Hestiia and Raaskan would dispose of as many as they could.

Best if Kim did not know how many or where. He forced himself to think in terms of obstacles removed rather than people.

He was just about to give up on Loki and concentrate on diverting Kat, when his brother rolled down the rock face. He slipped dangerous meters, then grabbed a tree growing horizontally out from the cliff. He swung there for many long moments until he balanced and added his other hand to firm his grasp.

Shots buzzed in Loki's wake. Kat's red head appeared above them. "I'm not finished with you yet!" she shouted and fired her stunner blindly.

Kim ducked back into the shrubbery to avoid the shot.

Loki laughed. The landscape picked up his mocking and reverberated it up and down, back and forth until it lost meaning and direction.

More shots followed. Kat let loose a string of curses and epithets that would have earned her one of Mum's frowns of disappointment.

At last, Kat and her squad retreated from the edge of the rocks.

Now, Kim urged Loki with his mind. *Before she finds a way around.* He sent mental images of a likely route of descent rather than exact words.

You sure about this?

Kim felt Loki's uncertainty.

As certain as I am that your sister will be upon us before you get down here if you do not hurry.

Loki let go of his branch and dropped one and a half meters to a narrow ledge. He teetered on the edge.

Kim braced himself to break his brother's fall.

Loki found his balance and dropped to all fours. Clinging to the ledge by his fingertips, he proceeded downward.

Kim kept urging speed. Loki took his time, testing each hand and foothold before committing his full weight to any of them.

Kim heard the clatter of ten armed and armored people winding downward by a circuitous path.

Then he saw Kat drop over the top and grab the same tree Loki had.

Kim inhaled sharply, willing Kat to use both hands to climb down and leave her weapon holstered.

She did. But she moved faster than her older brother, showing more recklessness than Loki ever had.

At last Loki dropped the last few meters. Kim braced his feet against a tree trunk and grabbed Loki to keep him from tripping and rolling on the rough ground.

"Where?" Loki asked, panting. He glanced over his shoulder at the uniformed figure still working her way down the cliff face.

Kim pointed out their path. "Shuttle," he mouthed. The hair on his nape tingled. Kat was very near.

Loki's eyes brightened and he grinned without mirth. "Comeuppance," he mouthed.

At least Kim thought that was his word. A few obscenities would fit the same syllables.

A shot burned above their heads. It severed a tree limb and dropped it in their path. Wild shouts and more fluent curses from Kat followed the bolt of energy.

Kim pelted through ferns and bracken, slid on mud and tripped across a roaring creek. Loki followed close on his heels.

Scratched, bruised, and filthy, they emerged from the tree line onto the flatter surface of a fertile plateau. Before them waited their own shuttle *Rover*, its cerama/metal hull dulled by a layer of green. Beyond it rested three landers.

More shots.

No time to disable the landers.

They ran faster, diving into *Rover*'s open hatch. Kim slapped it closed while Loki scrambled for the cockpit. "Break out the weapons, Kim," he called over the roar of the engines.

Before Kim could belt in and take command of his screens, they rolled toward the sea.

The cliff edge came too soon. Not enough lift beneath the wings. Below them treacherous rocks played peek a boo with the crashing waves. Gravity pulled them down into the teeth of the broken shore.

At the last minute, Loki fired the VTOL jets and lifted. A cannon pulse blast rocked them. They dipped lower, losing the little bit of altitude they had gained.

"She's got a lander up already," Loki cursed under his breath.

"And she's shooting to kill." Kim locked his own tiny blaster onto the looming target of the military vessel. It gained on them by the millisecond. The next shot would be at point-blank range.

He fired.

The energy burst in front of the cockpit windscreen. The pilot did not falter. The lander kept coming.

"I've got nothing to match that thing."

"I'm not sure I can outrun it," Loki admitted. "She's one hell of a pilot, matching me move for move in a bigger and clumsier craft."

They skimmed the surface of the waves and bounced up again. The lander could not match the maneuvers. It did not need to. Kat bullied forward.

(*You need a bath*,) Irythros reminded them.

"So we do." Loki slowed abruptly and plunged *Rover* into the waves.

Hanassa! Dalleena swallowed. Felt the knife scrape her throat. The priest's muscles shifted. The tip of the knife pricked her skin. She winced and started. Warm liquid trickled down her neck.

"I will not be a sacrifice to your perversion," she whispered. Anger fueled by fear sent jolts of energy through her veins.

Silently, she contracted her abdomen and shoulders, testing the level of pain lingering from her injuries.

"Irythros warned me against you, Hanassa."

"Irythros!" the man spat. "A child among dragons. A meddler who breaks the law and reveals secrets!" He pressed the knife a little closer against Dalleena's neck. She winced and prepared herself for pain.

"What will you gain by taking a life?" Konner asked the IMP casually. His attention seemed to focus upon the man beside the priest rather than the man with the knife.

"I do not take a life," the IMP replied, equally casual.

"You employ the assassin. By your own laws, that makes you an accessory before the fact. Punishable by five years imprisoned rehabilitation after a mind-wipe."

"What about the twenty men you and your brothers killed?" Heat rose in the man's voice. "You are as guilty as the men who unleashed an avalanche of boulders."

Out of the corner of her eye, Dalleena saw the man lift a black box of a weapon. A stunner, Konner had called it. At the same time, he moved forward.

The priest did not like that. He shoved Dalleena forward, elbowing the IMP aside. He stumbled and fought for balance. A blast of red light shot from the stunner into the shrubbery. Well away from Konner.

Konner lunged.

Dalleena rammed her elbow into the priest's gut. Then she stomped upon his bare foot. As he doubled over, she whirled and slammed the heel of her hand against his jaw and her knee into his groin.

Her ribs protested. She clenched her jaw against the pain.

Hanassa thudded upon the ground, rolled to his knees, and bounced upward.

"It will take more than your puny efforts to fell me," Hanassa snarled. Gone were all traces of the priest's mild tenor voice, replaced by a deeper, harsher baritone. His body was bulkier than the man she had found suffering from a severe beating. Had he done that to himself?

She did not wait for an answer. Her foot swept across the back of his knees, and she turned and ran for the creek.

Heavy footsteps pounded after her. Booted feet that crashed through the underbrush.

"Stop or we shoot!" the IMP called.

"Shoot her and you die!" Konner replied. Sounds of a struggle.

The pool came into view. Dalleena angled southward and uphill. A tangle of calubra ferns slowed her down. She pushed them aside, vaulting over them. Pain lashed her ribs with each harsh breath. She tripped and rolled upon landing. The ferns loosed their pungent perfume. A sedating aphrodisiac.

Holding her breath, she jumped up and climbed the hill. A new, sharper pain began in her side. Breathing came hard. Her legs grew heavy.

Then miraculously, Konner was beside her. He braced her with an arm about her waist. Running became easier. His strength guided her back toward the sound of the cascade of water. After a long, dry summer, boulders formed a damp ford across the upper creek.

Konner leaped to the top of the first boulder. She grabbed his wrist with both hands. She clambered up beside him.

"We have to get outside the field," he said when she faltered. "I'll activate it with them in and us out. They shouldn't be able to follow." He bounded across a gap to the next boulder.

She followed more cautiously, afraid to imitate his leap and jar her abused bones upon landing. She slipped at the edge. He held her hand tightly, keeping her from falling over the cascade and landing upon a pile of broken rocks below.

"Stop," the IMP leader yelled. He managed to shinny up the first boulder on his own.

Someone behind him fired one of the stunners.

Moss sizzled at their feet.

Konner halted and raised his hands. Dalleena did the same. They turned slowly to face their pursuers.

"I have no quarrel with you, Lieutenant Pettigrew," Konner said.

"But I have a very large one with you," the IMP replied. He rose from his crouch upon the first boulder. "You have broken the law many times and resisted lawful arrest. You have sabotaged an Imperial vessel. And now you flee again. Judge Balinakas will dish out many long sentences to you and your brothers."

"We do not have to live with this animosity. We can share this planet in peace," Dalleena offered.

"I have no intention of allowing you to strand me in this godforsaken wilderness, O'Hara. Where is the king stone?"

"Practically under your nose."

Pettigrew looked down. So did the IMPs behind him.

A cold wind blasted Dalleena in the face. A thunderous beating of wings. She brought her right palm up and jerked her head right and left.

Irythros burst from the cloud cover. He screeched. The IMPs grasped their ears in pain.

Dalleena wanted to hunker down and cover her head. Konner remained standing. So she did, too.

A stream of flame ejected from the dragon's mouth. It brushed the top of Pettigrew's head, singeing his hair.

The lieutenant screeched to match the dragon. He bent so far over he fell into the creek, deep here near the cascade. How deep?

The IMPs let loose a volley of shots.

Konner jumped into the water. He flailed about, dove. Surfaced. Gasped. Dove again.

Dalleena peered into the churning water, scanning with her palm as well as her eyes. She couldn't sense anything.

The IMPs stood, rooted in place, exchanging worried glances. Hanassa danced around them in glee.

"Help him!" Dalleena screamed.

Konner surfaced again, flung water out of his eyes. Then once more he kicked up and back and plunged back into the water.

Favoring her ribs with one arm clutched across her midriff, Dalleena slipped into the water. Only a little deeper than Konner was tall. She felt about with toes and hands and senses.

Nothing but more water, sand, and a few slippery green things.

The current gently wove around her.

She dropped below the surface, caught a glimpse of a white foot to her right. She grabbed. It kicked. She came up with a firm grasp of Konner's ankle.

"They can't swim in armor with field kits on their backs." he choked out. "No time to undress." The agony on his face mimicked what she had seen when she shared his vision.

Two IMPs struggled out of their heavy packs while their comrades unfastened shin guards and breastplates. They still had arm, back, and thigh armor to remove. They'd never get into the water in time to help their lieutenant.

"You are not responsible if he dies, Konner," she called to him as he dove once more.

"Yes, he is!" exclaimed Hanassa. He jumped up and down on the bank, brandishing his knife toward anyone who tried to enter the water. "Konner O'Hara alone determines if the petti-man lives or dies."

Dalleena went under once more. When she could hold her breath no longer, she gave up. Clinging to one of the rocks while gulping long draughts of air, her right palm began to tingle. Then she spotted him.

"Konner!" She did not wait for him but swam a few strokes to her left, toward the opposite bank. She tugged on a limp white hand drifting above a tree snag.

Konner splashed right behind her. He plunged deeper.

Dalleena tried to clear branches and roots. The man beyond the visible arm remained stuck.

"Help us," she called to the IMPs. "We can still save him."

Hanassa drove his knife into the throat of the first man who tried climbing onto the ford of boulders.

The remaining IMPs felled him with a concentrated blast of stunners.

Not enough. Hanassa twitched and moaned, then rolled to his knees and crawled into the underbrush, still alive, still able to menace them all.

CHAPTER 46

K AT BIT HER LIP. Did she dare plunge the lander into the bay in pursuit of her brothers? She'd watched Loki and Konner closely when they executed this maneuver. She knew she could duplicate it. Was it worth the risk? Perhaps she should hover and monitor, waiting for them to emerge.

On the other hand, the lander needed a bath to clean off the growing green gunk.

"Go after them!" her Marine sergeant urged. "We can shoot them underwater."

"Efficiency?" Kat snapped at him.

He ran numbers through the weapons array. "Saline content of the water will dissipate the focus by twenty-three point six percent."

"Intensity?"

"I'm not a data tech," the sergeant protested.

Kat glanced at the data. "Fifteen point zero two percent drop." Close enough.

She aimed the craft into the water. She had to slow to a near stall to allow the transition of pressure to hit the hull gradually. Sensors distorted the moment she hit the water.

The ten men with her were combat troops, not pilots or techs. They understood weapons. She had to fly (drive) the lander and interpret the data.

"Look for this symbol in the data stream." She pointed to the glyph that represented the cerama/metal alloy common to any hull that could be exposed to the high radiation of space or intense heat of reentry. The same specs protected them from water seepage from increasing pressure.

The sergeant gulped and nodded. "Starboard. Seven point three degrees."

"How far ahead?"

"Sixty meters to firing range. Sixty-five. Seventy."

"Damn."

"Port. Twenty-five degrees."

"Can't. There's an outcropping between us." Kat steered around it. By the time she cleared the pile of jagged rock, she'd lost contact with her quarry. Frantically, she searched the water ahead and her sensors for the tiniest glimpse of a man-made object.

"Something big on the ocean floor," the sergeant said excitedly.

"Show me?"

He pointed to the sensor screen. Sure enough a long and dense object glowed with the distinctive glyphs of cerama/metal.

"That's one of the landers the O'Haras stole." Disappointed and frustrated, she steered for it. "Suit up, Sergeant. You and two others are going to fly that thing back to base."

"I'm no pilot."

"You are now. You know how to fire the engines, rock it a bit to get it off the bottom and aim for camp."

"How about if I take this one back to base and you maneuver that one off the bottom?"

"Fine." Alone, Kat would not have to report to anyone. Alone with a lander, she could take her revenge without the restrictions of GTE military protocol.

"The controls are yours, Sergeant. I'll retrieve the lost one."

Konner fought the white vortex. His mind swirled ever deeper into the whiteness. He clung to Dalleena's last words to him. "You are not responsible."

His heart wanted to protest. Of course he was responsible. Pettigrew had chased Konner and become a victim of the chase.

His logical engineer's brain scoffed.

A violent, mechanical roar tugged him back toward reality.

He blinked rapidly. Outlines appeared before his eyes. Then color began to fill in the blank spaces.

"Dalleena?" he called.

A muffled grunt.

"Dalleena, where are you?"

"Here," she croaked, less than a meter from him.

"How do you fare?" He swam the single stroke from his side of the snag. Her face looked pale. Tight lines drew her mouth down and furrowed her brow. He stroked the lines with a delicate finger. They did not fade.

"I tracked him and lost him," she muttered.

"You are not responsible."

"Neither are you," she said. Then she shivered.

"You're chilling. We have to get out of the water."

"We have to retrieve the body."

"Leave it for the IMPs."

"Tracker's code. I *have* to bring him back to his people for proper burial."

"Later." He tried dragging her away from the snag. She resisted. The glare she shot him should have sizzled his hair. "Very well."

Without the press of time to save a living man making his movements clumsy and ineffectual, Konner freed Pettigrew's trapped foot with only two more dives beneath the surface.

The mechanical roar became a pulsing weapon. Konner looked shoreward. The IMPs crouched low, weapons drawn and aimed at *Rover* hovering above them.

A red electronic charge skimmed the edge of *Rover*'s nose.

"Damn it, Loki, not now!" Konner grabbed two handfuls of moss and tore them free of one of the rocks. The moss that chinked gaps in cabin walls, lined baby diapers, and served as a fire starter. "Stuff this into your ears. Tight. Follow me. And hurry."

He pulled himself up onto the ford, pausing only to grab Dalleena's wrist and haul her up. She choked off a scream.

Still holding her hand, he ran as fast as he could for the opposite shore.

"St. Bridget and all the angels, save me!" Kat stared at the sunken lander through the faceplate of her EVA suit. The long vehicle tilted on the edge of a trench. If it had touched down three meters farther, it would have plunged thousands of fathoms deeper, well beyond her reach, possibly beyond hull tolerances.

"You say something, Lieutenant?" the sergeant asked over the comm unit.

"Nothing worth repeating. Stay close, Sarge."

"Will do. Easier keeping this hunk of bolts in one place than swimming to the surface."

"Until the currents get you," Kat subvocalized. No need scaring the man into doing something stupid.

Kat half swam/half walked the twenty meters to the rear air lock of the lander. Her heavy magnetic boots dragged her down to the sandy bottom. The water felt as thick as soy pudding. Her suit kept beeping alarms, not liking the pressure she endured at this depth.

She punched in the codes to work the air lock. The keypad responded sluggishly. She checked her air supply. At this rate she'd be breathing water by the time the chamber pressurized to equal that of the ocean bottom.

"We're sinking!"

"Give her a little juice, Sergeant Brewster," Kat ordered. She fought to keep her voice calm.

A blast of water swirled around her. She braced herself against the air lock, desperate to keep her feet. A hasty glance over her shoulder showed the other lander swaying back and forth, creating its own current.

Her lander rocked in response.

A flood of curses spilled out of Kat's mouth.

Then the air lock opened. The change in pressure rocked the lander again. Kat held her breath, praying it did not tip over into the trench.

A few rocks back and forth, then it settled into the sand. Was it a fraction farther forward?

"Don't go anywhere just yet, Brewster. Gotta make sure I can get this baby off the bottom." She stepped into the air lock and closed it behind her.

Agonizing moments passed before the automatic system flushed out the water, replacing it with air. Her wrist monitor looked stuck in the hazard position. Finally, the numbers crept upward showing breathable atmosphere.

"You still there, Brewster?"

"Barely. I'm really uncomfortable at these controls, Lieutenant."

"Can you fly an air car? Take your girl out on a date back home?"

"Yeah." He sounded hesitant.

"Real hot shot, I bet. Show off for the ladies."

"Yeah." His voice brightened.

"Same thing. This is just a bigger vessel, a little clumsier, a lot more powerful."

"You make it sound easy, Lieutenant."

"'Cause it is. Now stick around until I give you leave. I want this thing off the bottom before I see your tail in the viewscreen."

Kat opened her faceplate. The air tasted stale and salty. She hadn't much time.

Edging forward on the slightly tilted deck, she stayed near the outer bulkhead as much as possible, keeping the lander balanced. "So far so good," she breathed as she neared the cockpit.

Her third step toward the middle of the craft sent shivers through the hull. She grabbed the nearest handhold, riding out the rocking of the hull. When the lander finally settled, the deck tilted forward at least five additional degrees.

She gulped and waited.

"You okay, Kat? That thing looks mighty unstable."

"Yeah, Kent. Give me a few more moments. I think I can get to the copilot's seat without any more disturbance. Firing up the engines could shift the balance." Before she lost her courage, Kat slid into the nearest chair. She unlocked the legs and scooted along the rail that ran along the deck at the base of the circle of terminals.

Halfway to the viewscreen she found systems control. A quick check showed the essentials working, navigation, weapons, environmentals, hull integrity, and fuel. When Konner had ditched the vehicle, he'd set it to go through automatic shutdown at some point after launch. The family mechanic couldn't kill a machine any more than he could kill a king stone.

Kat fully intended to take advantage of her brother's weakness.

She breathed a little easier as she ran through ignition. A comforting rumble answered her commands. Ever conscious of her precarious position, she edged her chair further along the rail. She came to command position and looked out the viewscreen. The trench yawned before her.

A behemouth swam across her bow. It flipped its tail twice and shot upward. The crush of water pressed downward against the nose of her vessel. She tilted farther forward and slid . . .

"Sonics, now," Loki ordered Kim.

His little brother reached for the red interface on his screen in the upper right-hand corner. Out of the way of any casual brush of his fingers.

"No. Wait!" Loki stayed the command with a tight grip on Kim's shoulder. "That's Konner and Dalleena down there."

"IMPs taking aim at them." Kim hesitated, his index finger one micro above the screen. "I've got to down the IMPs."

"If Konner and Dalleena fall off the ford, they'll either drown or break their necks going over the cascade."

"If the IMPs shoot them, they face the same choice."

"Two more femtos and they'll be on firm ground."

"Damn, there's Taneeo and his knife. He's going to kill one of the IMPs." Kim dropped his finger onto the blinking red interface.

Muffled echoes of the piercing blast of sound penetrated the hull. Annoying. Almost painful.

The figures below doubled over in pain, hands holding ears, grimaces of agony on their faces.

Loki could not find Konner among them, or on the opposite bank.

CHAPTER 47

KONNER DOVE BEHIND the upended roots of a huge fallen tree. The tangled roots, rocks, and mud, with infant ferns growing in the middle stood between him and *Rover*. Dalleena crawled behind him, burrowing deep into the leaf litter that collected between the root ball and the tree trunk.

He mounded more of the plant debris around their heads as he lay on top of her, shielding her head with his body.

Less than a heartbeat later his ears rang with the harsh pulses of a highly illegal sonic weapon. Every hair on his body felt as if it stood on end. His teeth ached. Tears streamed down his face.

"I love you, Dalleena," he whispered, fighting to stay conscious.

"Loving you can be very dangerous, Stargod Konner O'Hara."

Kim counted each IMP as he fell victim to the sonic blast. Taneeo fell last, his wickedly curved knife still clutched in his hand.

When the traitor's body stopped twitching, Kim breathed a sigh of relief. But he left his hand upon the sonics trigger.

The moment Taneeo succumbed, Loki signaled Kim to cease firing.

The silence after the sonic blast seemed to echo around Kim's head. Unnatural. Surreal. How much hearing had he lost? How much had the IMPs lost after the full exposure?

"Where's Konner?" Loki's eyes were wide, nearly bulging out of their sockets.

Kim searched with his eyes and every other sense he could muster. He saw fifteen IMPs and Taneeo all lying unconscious at the edge of the pool. Konner remained elusive.

"I have to land this thing, quick. We have to find them." Loki sounded as frantic as Kim felt.

Loki moved *Rover* into the center of the clearing and dropped to the ground. Not the smoothest of landings. Kim hardly noticed. They ignored Cyndi, still gagged and bound, slumping against the tree where they'd left her hours ago. The sonics had silenced her, too.

Together, Kim and Loki pelted down the narrow path toward the creek.

"Konner!" Kim yelled across the water.

Taneeo moaned and twitched. Loki pulled a set of force bracelets out of his pocket and slapped them on the little priest. "What's this?" he held up the missing second beacon. Ungently, he yanked it away from Taneeo, snapping the leather thong that suspended it.

The strained leather did not leave so much as a mark on the traitor. Loki felt along the man's neck.

"*St. Bridget!* Hide toughening, exoskeleton forming. He's turning into a dragon. Just like Hanassa."

Kim examined the man's neck and torso. His fingers met hard cartilage becoming as dense as bone.

"We'll have to make another trip back to the volcano and destroy that beacon, too," Kim muttered.

He pulled a length of vine away from the shrub it nearly choked. Viciously, he twisted it into convenient lengths, ignoring how it looped back upon his hands and arms, trying to snare him. Bloody welts appeared beneath its thorns. Devil's vine the locals called it, with good reason.

He used it to bind the wrists and ankles of all of the IMPs. The thorny weed gouged any skin it contacted, wrapping easily where Kim guided it. If one believed the locals, the plant was almost sentient. Kim had a hard time keeping it from tangling his own hands. The IMPs would not break free easily.

"Konner!" Loki called again.

"Here," came a strangled voice.

"Can you handle these guys?" Loki asked.

Kim nodded grimly. "We can dump them a few kilometers from their camp after dark. Make them walk back." He twisted a length of vine securely on the last of the IMPs. Then he yanked off their boots. All fifteen of them began to stir and moan.

· —◆— ·

Loki leaped from slippery rock to jagged boulder across the ford without care for his own bare feet.

He landed on the opposite muddy creek bank clumsily, sliding to his knees. Irythros had been digging here and left a mess. Desperate to find his brother, he regained his footing with only two backward slides toward the water. Behind him he heard the groans of recovering IMPs. Ahead of him, only silence.

"Konner!" he yelled again.

Was that a soft whimper ahead and to his right?

"Konner, get your sorry ass out of whatever hole you crawled into."

"Do we have to?" The voice was weak. No, soft. Like an intimate whisper.

"Where are you?" Loki began peering under bushes and around the massive root ball of a fallen forest giant.

"Ow." Konner's protest was followed by a soft, feminine giggle. "Get off my foot, Loki."

Loki looked closer at the mound of leaf litter and plant debris filling the triangle between the root ball and the place where the tree trunk met the ground. He found a foot. Big and callused. Konner. Then a second foot, smaller and booted. Dalleena.

"Do I need to leave you two alone? If so, then make it quick. We've got a clearing full of IMPs and our sister on the way in a lander."

"Coming," Konner said. He sighed heavily. "Dalleena and I have the rest of our lives to be together."

"Well, I'm glad that's settled." Loki's sigh sounded relieved, as if he'd been waiting a long time for Konner to find a life mate.

"How did you manage?" Loki asked. He spoke louder than normal and mouthed his words carefully.

Konner pulled the wads of moss out of his ears. Dalleena did the same. "I'll have to analyze this more thoroughly. It does more than fill chinks in the cabins and insulate against the cold."

"It lines baby diapers, too. Quite absorbent," Dalleena added with a glint of mischief in her eyes.

Konner kissed her again, needing to linger. Other matters pressed upon his conscience.

"I have to activate the confusion field before Kat arrives." Konner crawled out from his hidey-hole, followed closely by Dalleena. He kissed her palm the moment she stood upright, then captured her hand in both of his. He did not want to break the contact, as if their skin had bonded as well as their hearts and minds.

"We need to get across the creek first." Loki moved toward the water, keeping his back to his brother, giving the couple a moment more of privacy.

"I want to be well inside the field when you close it. Who knows what happens to someone caught in the boundary when it snaps into place."

Konner lingered only a moment longer. He grabbed another quick kiss from Dalleena and followed his brother quickly.

The moment they dropped from the last boulder of the ford onto the ground, Konner pulled a handheld from his pocket. He peered closely at the screen a moment and logged in a few more codes.

"Are we ready for this?"

Loki and Kim nodded.

Konner tapped the screen three times.

"I don't see anything different," Loki said. He turned in a full circle, examining everything.

"My sense of anything beyond the circle is dulled." Dalleena scanned the entire area with her hand extended in tracking mode.

"That's the beauty of this cloaking," Konner chortled. "No one sees the field. But if anyone without O'Hara DNA tries to penetrate from either direction, they get pushed back, misdirected, deluded into believing they move forward instead of in a circle around our private enclave."

"How do we open it?" Kim asked. He monitored the pulse of one of the IMPs who remained still long after his fellows twitched and squirmed for release.

"Harmonics." Konner grinned. "All we have to do is hum Mum's favorite lullaby and we will match the resonance of the crystals."

A lander moved up the hillside. It looked perfectly clear to Konner, but the roar of its engines seemed slightly removed, more distant than it should. He doubted it was a lingering aftereffect from the sonics.

"Loki, Konner, and Kim O'Hara, where are you," Kat called to them from the lander's exterior speakers. She circled the area, never quite steering directly above them.

Konner walked back to the shuttle and opened a frequency to his sister. "Lose something, Kat?"

Loki and Kim stayed close upon his heels. Dalleena squeezed in as well. Konner pulled her into his lap at his customary terminal.

"Yes, I lost you three. Open the field and let me land."

"Sorry, little sister. We can't trust you," Konner said.

"I'll find you eventually. You know that. The dragon showed me how to use my latent psi powers. I'll penetrate the field one way or another."

"Probably too late to save *Jupiter*, Kat," Konner said.

"We'll see about that. You have to come out of the clearing soon to go rescue your son, Konner. I'll be waiting."

"It's too late for that, Kat. I can't reach Aurora in time to gain legal custody."

"Since when has legality stopped you?"

A slow smile spread across Konner's face. "I think I have a plan."

EPILOGUE

✦━━•━━◆━━•━━✦

"YOU SEE, MARTIN? Konner O'Hara did not arrive at the custody hearing. He is dead. You are well rid of him," Melinda Fortesque said brightly. She paused long enough to pat Martin on the shoulder. "Now that there is no question of where you belong, I have authorized an increase in your allowance as well as a lump sum as a birthday present. You may purchase that jet pedcycle you have lusted after for so long." Then she marched down the palace corridor. Clearly the custody hearing had taken too much time away from her busy schedule.

"Even if Dad lives, he can't get me now," Martin muttered. He hung his head and scuffed his feet, reluctant to retreat into the privacy of his own suite. He did not care if the servants, toadies, petitioners, and corporate employees saw him cry. He did not care that his mother knew of his intense disappointment.

A question niggled at his brain. "If my dad is dead, then why bother with the formality of a custody hearing?" He scooted into his room and activated Super Snooper.

"Status on the distress beacon?" he demanded before the icon figure fully formed.

"The signal has ceased," Super Snooper replied.

"What about agent Sam Eyeam?"

"He has not responded to your mother's hails."

"What about tracing his movements? Scaramouch, display star map hologram with Sam Eyeam's last known movements."

The map came up. A scattered series of purple lights flashed. The last one faded and disappeared at the edge of the vacant anomaly.

Martin's heart skipped a beat.

"Show area suspected to contain the beacon."

The entire anomaly lit up in a violet haze.

"I think I'll have to find the jump point into the hole in space by myself." Martin made a brief detour into his bank account. Sure enough, Melinda had deposited a huge amount of money; more than enough to buy two jet pedcycles, with all the accessories.

"Super Snooper, find out which ships in port are available for charter, and a pilot who can be bribed into silence. Make a conference call to Bruce and Jane Q, they'll want to be a part of this. Then open a new account in the commodities market. We have to make a bit more money for this project."

THE DRAGON'S REVENGE

This book is for Karen, Deb, Connie, Mike B., Bob, Mike M., Eric, Sheila, and Di Anne, the friends from "Digging Deeper" who reinvigorate my writing and keep me going when the books muddle in the middle.

PROLOGUE

◆━━━•━◆━•━━━◆

*T*HE NIMBUS OF DRAGONS *has found a way to eliminate the foreign ship that orbits our home. We manipulated forces as a group that would elude any single one of us. Together, we have ensured the safety of our nimbus and those we protect. No more foreigners will plague us with their machines and their diseases. The rest of their vices we can manipulate or eliminate as we did their ship.*

A dragon dream is a powerful tool, and a dangerous one. We all agreed that this one must be given. Only if we all agree will we use one.

If only eliminating the threat of the Krakatrice were just as easy. The snake monsters are resilient and more resistant to manipulation. Perhaps we should pit the humans against our enemy since we may not kill them ourselves. All life is sacred.

One of us has gone rogue. We have no way of controlling the one called Hanassa. The purple-tipped dragon has developed a taste for human blood, human power, and living within a human body. He changes bodies at will until he finds a host strong enough of body and weak enough of will to destroy or imprison him. The dragon nimbus is out of options. We may not destroy one of our own any more than we may destroy the Krakatrice.

There is one among the humans who needs our help. Which of us shall we dispatch to guide her in finding what she truly quests for and not what others tell her she must quest for? We have promised the God of All that we would aid the humans. We have promised to maintain the unity among every living thing in the universe. The Krakatrice add nothing to the unity. The one called Hanassa threatens unity with his every breath.

CHAPTER 1

LIEUTENANT KAT TALBOT, Imperial Military Police, wrestled the massive hydroponics tank through the listing shuttle bay doors. The six-meter-by-two-meter apparatus weighed nothing in zero G, but its bulk and mass were awkward. She couldn't see around it and kept bumping into bulkheads. Commander Amanda Leonard, captain of this derelict ship, had chosen Kat because of her bushie height and strength as well as her experience in and affinity for zero G, more than anyone else among the scattered crew.

Since *Jupiter* had stopped spinning two months ago, gravity had evaporated aboard. Atmosphere had leaked away before that. Unless Kat could find and replace the stolen crystal array and get the ship operational again, all she could do was salvage as much as possible.

She paused in her struggles. The air in her EVA suit tasted stale. "Nothing for it but to get this thing aboard a lander so I can fire up some atmosphere," she grunted.

A flicker of movement off to her left made her stop and look around. Nothing.

She shivered. Just her imagination running wild. Ghost ships were notorious for evoking atavistic fears. *Jupiter* was very much a ghost ship. Derelict and drifting in space.

Nine months ago, the three outlawed O'Hara brothers had stolen the crystal array from *Jupiter*. Without the star drive the ship was doomed, her crew stranded in the back of beyond.

For nine months she'd been salvaging essentials for survival and still life dirtside resembled a tribal hunter-gatherer society more than civilization.

"How long, Kat?" Lieutenant Commander Jetang M'Berra called over her helmet comm.

"Ten minutes," she panted. She'd spent too much time dirtside breathing real air. Getting used to recycled oxygen mixtures again would take time.

The hydroponics tank tilted and jammed in the partially open hatch. No power to open the doors further.

"*S'murghit!*" she borrowed an epithet from the planetary locals. "You could have made this easier by assigning me an extra crewman." She didn't care if M'Berra heard that comment or not. She didn't care if Commander Amanda Leonard heard it either.

Her superior officers had gotten too used to her initiative as well as her bushie height and muscle mass for doing their dirty work.

"My sensors read you are running low on air, Kat," M'Berra advised her. "You have less than ten minutes to get that tank aboard a lander and fire up life support."

"Acknowledged." No wonder her air tasted stale. Her EVA suit's monitors hadn't operated properly in months. But the suit worked. That was more than she could say for most of the high-tech equipment they'd salvaged.

She heaved and levered the tank free of the obstruction. A gentle shove sent it gliding toward the open bay doors of a lander.

She wished for her more maneuverable and sleeker fighter. But she needed the extra cargo space and fuel efficiency in a lander.

"Kat, what did you do in med bay?" M'Berra's voice contained an edge of worry.

"Didn't go near the place," Kat grunted as she shoved the tank into the hold of the lander. It was a small lie. She'd passed the med bay on a private errand to her own quarters, but M'berra didn't need to know that. Besides, she hadn't actually gone into that med bay.

She climbed in after the hydroponics tank and closed the hatch. Still eight minutes to spare on her suit air. She reached the cockpit and keyed in comm system and life support before settling into the pilot's seat.

"What's wrong in med bay?" she asked. Good thing she'd set the entire lander's systems on standby before going after the tank and her own personal memento. She'd have air and heat before her suit emptied.

"Get out now, Kat." M'Berra didn't mask the anxiety in his voice.

"Can't. I need two more minutes to fire up all systems."

"Don't wait!"

"What's wrong?"

M'Berra's panic was contagious. Kat skipped the usual safety protocol in favor of faster engine ignition. Life support would come on faster that way, too.

"Something sparked in med bay. The volatile chemicals . . ."

"No air to support a spark," Kat reassured herself and M'Berra.

That flicker of movement had been in the direction of med bay at the center of the ship.

"Still some air in med bay. It's sealed better than the rest of the ship. A spark. Kat, the whole ship is going to blow with you in it."

"Not if I can help it."

In the background she heard a dull roar. Something flashed on the periphery of her vision.

Without thinking, she tapped an override sequence into her interface. Before she could inhale one last gulp of rancid artificial air, she launched out of the shuttle bay.

The explosion rushed through the confined passageways seeking an exit and expansion. The force behind it propelled Kat's lander through the open bay doors faster than safety dictated. Her tail fins nicked the edge.

More flashes of light sent her adrenaline surging. With a teeth-grinding screech she broke free. A hard bank to starboard brought her looping around the mass of the space cruiser and back within view of the planet below.

Large chunks of cerama/metal hull followed her and greeted her. Another sharp veer, this time to port. A flying mass just barely missed hurtling into her viewscreen.

Was one of those chunks a fighter headed dirtside?

No way to tell. No time to think.

Kat exhaled and realized she had nothing left to inhale. Quickly she ripped off her helmet and gasped the first faint traces of atmosphere generated by the lander.

"What did you do to my ship?" Commander Leonard's voice screamed through the ship comm. "We saw the explosion from here, Talbot. What did you do? I'll court-martial you here and now."

"A lot of good that will do you, Capt'n Leonard, sir," Kat grumbled. "We're three sectors off the star charts and no way to communicate with civilization."

Friction from the planetary upper atmosphere began to glow around the nose of the lander. Kat hit the control to extend the rudimentary wings to slow her descent. She overrode the command just as quickly to avoid having the wings torn off by another burning chunk of debris that flashed past her.

"Simurgh take you, Konner O'Hara, and both your brothers. Once again, you've destroyed my home," she cried. Unwanted tears touched her eyes. She blinked them away and concentrated on keeping her trajectory shallow. Kat's curse, while not exactly accurate, reflected the emotions welling in her chest.

Somehow the outlawed brothers had something to do with that stray spark. They had to have. Just as they had stolen the crystal array. They had given the ship and its crew a death sentence, stranding them on the primitive planet below, without possible communication with the rest of the galaxy.

Atmospheric stresses screamed through the lander.

"M'Berra, this lander steers like a garbage scow. I'm having trouble keeping to flight plan." She turned as tightly as the ship allowed, trying to bring the big vessel back to the proper coordinates. Three G's of pressure pushed her against her restraints and flattened her face. At the end of the tight turn, Kat breathed heavily. Sweat dotted her brow. She checked her sensors.

Chunks of *Jupiter* still fell around her, just a small percentage of the ship. The explosion had directed most of the debris out of orbit and away from the planet.

As the stray pieces hit the upper atmosphere and encountered friction, they became various sized fireballs, shedding bits in their wakes. The westering sun added red brightness to the mass.

"Report, Lieutenant Talbot," Commander Leonard barked over the comm unit. "How much of the ship is lost? Can we make it spaceworthy once we reclaim the crystal array from those thieving O'Hara brothers?"

Kat grimaced and dodged another piece of glowing debris from the once-proud vessel. She checked her rear visual screen. "Not much left, sir." She flashed the sensor view of the scene to ground communications.

Commander Leonard wasn't going to like it at all.

"Salvage?" Leonard said. Her voice lost none of its bite.

"Unknown," Kat spat back. In the last nine months her captain had lost her sense of reality in her obsession over restoring *Jupiter* and, with it, her command.

Kat pictured Amanda Leonard in the back of her mind as she had last seen *Jupiter*'s captain: a black patch over her left eye, pacing Base Camp with the comm pressed closely against her face, her uncovered eye looking black and sunken from lack of sleep. The uniform she insisted upon wearing was clean and pressed, but it hung on her wasted figure. More than lack of sleep and poor appetite ate at Leonard's once buxom and robust body.

"Not good enough, Talbot. I need a clearer picture. I need evidence to condemn the O'Hara brothers for sabotaging my ship," Leonard sneered. As if she didn't have enough evidence already.

To convict, first they had to capture the outlaws.

At the moment Loki, Konner, and Kim O'Hara, though outlaws, virtually owned the planet except for Base Camp.

What's more, the locals revered them as Stargods.

"May a Denubian muscle-cat scratch the balls off all three of the O'Hara brothers," Leonard cursed. "They cost me an eye and now they've cost me my ship."

Kat smiled. She'd wished similar fates for the O'Hara's—as well as their infamous Mum—many times herself. She'd sought revenge upon them for twenty years, long before their sabotage had stranded the crew of the *Jupiter* on this forgotten planet three jumps beyond nowhere.

She fingered the bracelet of braided hair she had retrieved from her own quarters on this trip. The detour had cost her time and air. But she was glad now that she had this last memento of her mother and the family she had lost at the age of seven.

"Get that hydro tank back here, Talbot, then report to me. Directly to me. Not to First Officer M'Berra, not to your buddies in the flight pool, and definitely not to any enlisted personnel."

"Yes, sir," Kat replied in her briskest military voice. If she'd been face-to-face with the captain, she'd have snapped a salute. She discommed and returned her focus to her sensor screens.

Pieces of *Jupiter,* large and small—too many big ones—descended toward the surface at a steep angle. Cerama/metal flared brightly against atmospheric friction. Kat's viewscreen darkened automatically. The afterimage of flames streaking across the sky lingered on her retinas.

"I will never forget this," she said to herself through gritted teeth. "Nor will I forgive you, O'Hara brothers, for causing this."

"What is happening, Talbot?" the captain's voice demanded through the comm unit.

"What you see is what you get, Captain," Kat muttered.

"Will any of it hit Base Camp? Do we need to seek shelter?" Leonard continued her barrage of questions.

"Looks like most of the larger pieces are east of you," Kat reassured her captain.

Silence from Leonard.

"Captain, you still there?" Kat dreaded silence from her commanding officer more than she would a string of curses.

Proximity alarms blared. A sensor array flew directly toward Kat. She banked the lander to port and barely missed the aerial.

Her path took her into the backwash from a larger glowing piece. She fought the shuddering controls of her lander.

"*Dregging* stupid computer interfaces!" She cut off her complaint to punch in a new command before she collided with the next piece of debris.

Something large and hard smashed into her starboard wing. The lander careened off at an odd angle, north over the uncharted ocean rather than back to Base Camp.

"*S'murghit!* The starboard proximity alarm is gone." No maintenance and few spare parts these last nine months in the land of the Coros had caused the breakdown of more than one plane. Kat was lucky they had enough fuel cells operating to get this lander back with the precious hydroponics tank. None of the crew knew how to grow food in dirt. Few wanted to experiment with the distasteful and unknown medium.

She fought the lander for control. It shuddered and listed more with each maneuver. Finally, in frustration, she kicked at the underside of the control panel.

The plane righted and resumed the last course she had commanded.

"Lieutenant Talbot, your recording has lost resolution," Commander Leonard yelled. "Your sensors are facing directly into the sun. I can see the sunset with my own eyes. I don't need to see a recording of it."

"Correcting now, Captain," Kat replied. She said some more things, but not out loud. *I just hope that M'Berra is with you, Amanda, to keep you calm. Hard enough to convince the troops you are sane under normal circumstances.*

Amanda Leonard wasn't sane. That didn't matter, though. She commanded the Marine contingent. They followed her with blind, almost worshipful loyalty. They delighted in punishing any infraction of the rules or suggested slur against their captain.

The ocean receded behind Kat. She spotted a small port city on the primary continent north and east of the small land mass where they'd set up Base Camp. Gray-black-red desert stretched endlessly ahead of her.

Kat fought to return to her proper flight path. The ship resisted. It shuddered and vibrated right through to her bones. A crack appeared beneath her feet and widened with every attempt to turn the lander.

"Talbot, I'm still not getting coherent pictures of the breakup of *my* ship," Leonard said. She sounded frantic. "I see a heck of a lot of desert beneath you and not much else."

"I've lost navigation. Sensors going fast," Kat reported. She gulped back her momentary panic. She could do this. She could land the vessel safely. She'd just be delayed getting the tank back to Base Camp. M'Berra would send someone after her.

If he had enough fuel cells.

If he could find anyone brave enough to fly across the uncharted ocean after dark.

If he survived the crash . . .

She switched to real-time view out the windscreen rather than trust the sensor-transmitted image.

A network of spidery, silver-blue lines showed just beneath the surface of the desert. Kat had seen them once before. She'd used the power in the lines to extend her senses and perceptions.

Her lander plummeted. She fought to get some air under the wings, get the nose up, fight the gravity that pulled at her and her craft.

"Transmit your coordinates, Kat. Tell me what you need to land safely," Lieutenant Commander M'Berra's deep voice came over the comm. He broadcast an aura of calm.

"You got the evidence to convict the O'Haras of sabotage, treason, and murder. Use it," Kat demanded. If she accomplished nothing else in this life, she had to know the tyranny of the O'Haras would end.

"Talbot, you do not sound reasonable." M'Berra always sounded calm and reasonable.

"I'm going to crash unless I can conjure up a lot of magic. Promise me to use the evidence to convict the O'Haras."

"Eject, Talbot," M'Berra ordered. "Eject."

Kat pushed on the manual eject button. The canopy remained closed, her seat intact.

CHAPTER 2

✦ —— · —— ✦ —— · —— ✦

LUCINDA BAINES, Cyndi to her few friends, granddaughter of an emperor, daughter of a planetary governor, and niece to a galactic senator, shifted uneasily from foot to foot. She watched carefully as Kim O'Hara, the youngest brother, performed his arcane ritual to allow her through the force field.

No matter how many times she watched each of the three brothers, her captors, she could not figure out the process for opening the way into or out of the family clearing.

"Loki is going to be very upset that I let you in to use the hot spring pool," Kim said grimly as he gestured Cyndi through the barrier.

"I wouldn't give a microgram of stardust for your brother's opinion," Cyndi replied haughtily.

Two years ago she did. Then she'd cherished her engagement to Loki, the oldest O'Hara brother. Legally, he was Matthew Kameron O'Hara, but no one called him that without getting a black eye and bloody nose.

Since then she'd seen how inconsiderate, self-centered, and amoral he was.

That was why she'd broken her engagement to him and secretly married a nephew of the emperor. Then she'd thought perhaps she should tell Loki to his face about her altered plans.

But he and his brothers had sabotaged *Jupiter,* her unofficial transport back to Earth, and had stranded her and the entire crew on this benighted planet.

"I have to admit, I understand your need for a real bath in the hot spring," Kim said. He nodded his head toward the path to the bathing pool. His bright red hair clubbed back into a queue and scraggly beard reminded her too much of Loki. She looked away from him.

"The hot spring will be pure luxury after a winter of sponging off with a bucket of cold seawater." Cyndi shuddered. Not that water could truly cleanse a person. She needed a sonic shower. Nothing else was civilized.

When would these people—namely the three O'Hara brothers—learn that their so-called freedom wasn't worth the inconvenience of primitive living! Any life outside the Galactic Terran Empire was no life at all.

But the hot spring would feel good. Besides, it gave her an excuse to get into the clearing alone.

Kim closed the portal into the clearing and left.

All Cyndi could see was a slight distortion in the landscape if she peered too closely directly into the force field. She reached a tentative hand to check its integrity. Her palm met a burning wall of energy.

Good. She checked the confines of the forest clearing for any signs of habitation.

For once, all of the family—the three brothers and the two wives—had decamped from the clearing. She'd watched Konner, the middle brother, and his local wife Dalleena take off in a hurry toward the shuttle *Rover* about an hour ago. Loki was out fishing with the village men, Kim and his wife Hestiia had been in the village this morning. Cyndi hadn't seen Hestiia since, but the woman was hugely pregnant—positively indecent of the woman to show herself in public in her condition—and wouldn't walk uphill for an hour to get to the clearing alone. So if Kim was working in the village, his wife was there, too.

She didn't bother checking the lean-to where Taneeo the priest lay comatose. He hadn't so much as blinked his eyes without prompting let alone spoken or moved in the nine months Cyndi had lived—been held captive more like—in the nearby village.

Cyndi couldn't remember what Taneeo had looked like when conscious and vigorous.

Initially, he had sided with the Imperial Military Police from *Jupiter* against the O'Hara brothers. Then, in the battle for the crystal array, the priest had been injured in some manner. Cyndi had endured most of the battle tied to a tree and gagged, bait to lure the IMPs farther uphill.

Once the IMPs lost the battle and Konner O'Hara closed the force field, the Imperial troops had retreated to Base Camp and left Taneeo with the O'Hara brothers.

They had no use for the man now that he was comatose.

Satisfied that no one eavesdropped, Cyndi pulled out a handheld communicator. "Are you there?" she whispered. She heard only static.

"Psst. Are you there? It's nearly sunset, the time you said to call."

"What . . . who . . . Oh, yeah, Lady Cyndi," a rough voice issued from the communicator with a yawn.

Cyndi shuddered as she imagined her contact stretching and scratching in indelicate places.

"What am I supposed to do to the power cells?" Cyndi crept toward the open half acre the O'Haras had designated as the "power farm." The spare fuel cells sat in orderly rows with maximum exposure to sunlight; they were filled with dragon wine distilled from a local berry. The berry was inedible, and she assumed the liquor was too, at least based on the stench.

She wrinkled her nose and placed one dainty foot next to the first cell.

"Do you see a seam along the top?" her contact asked.

"Yes," she replied hesitantly. Not much of a seam, more like a long dent in the casing.

"Run your fingernail along the seam and press hard."

Cyndi stared at her broken nails and jagged cuticles. Once upon a time her manicure had been impeccable, with nails all the same length, beautifully shaped and painted in delightful colors to match her pretty outfits. Using them to open a fuel cell couldn't hurt them much more than any other of the disgusting chores the locals forced her to perform. Not at all suitable for the wife of one of the Imperial heirs to have to clean *fish*.

She placed the outside edge of her right thumbnail in the groove at the top of the cell and ran it the full length of the meter square top.

"Nothing's happening," she cried into the handheld.

"Press harder. You've got to get the fuel cells open. If you don't, they win. If they win, they'll never let us leave. We'll be stranded here all of our lives, all of our children's lives. They'll register themselves as sole owners of this planet and close it to all outside influence."

"If you say so." Cyndi repeated the operation on the fuel cell, pressing as hard as she could without straining her arm. She hated the look of all the muscles she'd developed working for her keep. If she never washed a dish, peeled a tuber, or carried a water bucket again, she'd be happy.

The groove widened. She reported her success to her contact.

"That's good, Lady Cyndi. Now do it again. You have to make the groove wide enough to stick your fingers in it and pry it open."

Cyndi tried again and again. Finally, she could push the tips of her fingers into the crack and pull it apart.

The lid of the fuel cell slid open. A nauseating red-and-yellow mist whooshed out at her as the pressure released and the fuel dissipated.

Cyndi laughed.

"How many cells they got?" her contact at Base Camp asked.

"A full dozen." She counted the blocks.

"They only need four in that shuttle of theirs. You've got to open some more cells or the brothers'll be flying outta here tomorrow."

"We can't have that," Cyndi agreed.

"My commander wants to know if you can steal one of the recharged cells and put it where one of our flyboys can pick it up."

They'd tried to find the clearing many times. Cyndi had heard them fly over. But the force field that kept nonfamily out also cloaked the clearing from observation.

Cyndi looked askance at the heavy blocks. "I don't think so. The path down to the village is pretty rough and these things are too heavy for me to carry alone."

"Just a thought. If we had those extra cells, we might be able to locate the brothers' ship in orbit and call for help. You'd be one of the first ones evacuated."

Cyndi sighed in disappointment. She so wanted to go home and claim her rightful place at court.

"Maybe I can get some help next trip up here." She mentally checked off which of the men in the village she could convince how important she was so they would help her betray their Stargods. Not a single one came to mind. Men on this planet married early and remained faithful. What kind of civilization was that?

She had two more of the cells open and reclosed when she heard someone singing. Hestiia, Kim's wife. She sang all the time in a husky voice. One of the few decent voices in the village that, with some training, might serve some smoky jazz joint on the edge of civilization where the clientele had little taste and no exposure to better.

Cyndi straightened from her chore and stepped away from the power farm. She listened more closely.

No, it wasn't Hestiia. The voice was deeper, raspier. And it sang a sad dirge, not the happy little ditties Hestiia favored.

Cyndi crept the two dozen paces to the central fire pit. From there she followed the sound of the mournful song that sounded as if the singer's heart would break.

At the edge of the clearing, nearly half a kilometer away, she stopped short of the lean-to where Taneeo lived. He lay unmoving as always, eyes staring directly at her as if he knew what she had been up to.

The singing continued in his accusatory tone. But he did not move his mouth. He still stared into nothing.

Help me, someone whispered into the back of her mind. *Help me cast off the demon who possesses me.*

Cyndi tried to step away from the lean-to.

Taneeo's unwavering gaze kept her rooted to the spot.

Please, help me. The words came separately from the tune. Both sounded as if they came from the same voice.

Cyndi's knees shook.

"I . . . I don't know what you want."

Taneeo's clawlike hand snaked out and grabbed hers.

Blackness swirled through her mind, clouding her vision and upsetting her balance. She locked her knees and fought to remain upright. All the while she pulled desperately on her arm, trying to free it from Taneeo's firm grip.

He shouldn't have that much strength after nine months in a coma.

Jolts of electric energy coursed from his hand to hers, up into her shoulders and down the other arm.

For one brief moment she knew everything about Taneeo: how he'd apprenticed under another priest named Hanassa; how Hanassa had used his priestly power to satisfy his bloodlust; how Hanassa had enslaved Taneeo.

She relived in a flash the scene where Loki and his brothers had freed Taneeo and killed Hanassa in the tunnels beneath the blown-out volcano.

And then—nothing. No memory of the months that followed, of the coming of the IMPs, or of the battle for the crystal array. Nothing.

She had to grit her teeth to keep from crying out.

Just as suddenly as the alien feelings engulfed her, they disappeared.

Taneeo's hand relaxed. He fell back upon his pallet, eyes closed, body limp, and memories contained in his own body.

She jerked free of his grasp but had to cling to a tree for several moments to regain her balance and her composure.

"What just happened?"

Silence. Even the singing had ceased.

Heart racing and mind whirling, she ran headlong toward the place where Kim had let her into the clearing. She bounced off the force field with a stinging jolt. Desperate to escape, she pounded on the invisible barrier until her hands ached and burning pain lanced up her arm.

Crying and desperate for the company of another human, another *sane* human she ran down the path to the hot spring. The force field ended just beyond the pool, making it very private for the O'Hara family. It also trapped Cyndi in with Taneeo and that strange swirling blackness of the mind.

Hestiia looked up from where she sat at the edge of the pool dangling her feet in the water. "That's no way to get a bath. The water won't hurt you," she said lightly. She levered her bulky body off a rock and shed her leather wrap. Totally nude and unembarrassed, she waded into the pool between two small waterfalls and began splashing the water over her uniformly tanned body.

"Was that you singing?" Cyndi asked, still looking over her shoulder toward the clearing and Taneeo. He knew what she'd done to the fuel cells. He'd tell Loki.

"Of course I was singing. Who else?" Hestiia replied in that aggravating drawl that took forever to pronounce just a few words.

"I don't know. I thought maybe Taneeo had awakened."

"I wish he would," Hestiia said as she splashed warm water over her gravid body. "Will you wash my back? I can't quite reach anymore."

Bleakly, Cyndi shed her threadbare clothing and boots, resigned to the fact that she would have to wait a while longer to finish her job of sabotage.

And for explanations.

Hanassa hovered over the collapsed figure of Taneeo, one clawed foot embedded in the man's brain. Long had he fought to regain total control over the body. Long had he struggled to keep his get from throwing him out completely.

The tight confines of the lean-to kept Hanassa from fully stretching his purple-tipped wings, even though his spirit body remained small and silvery; as he had been in the flesh before he invaded his first human. That person had only been two years of age, the same as Hanassa at the time. That conquest had been easy. The child had been weak, on the brink of death, without a fully formed identity. Hanassa's dragon strength had flooded the body and allowed it to heal.

Dragon strength had given Hanassa power within the human community. Dragon cunning had given him control over the lives of many. Dragon appetites had made pitiful humans quake in terror of him.

Let the dragon nimbus keep their winged bodies and their rules and their traditions.

Hanassa made his own rules and traditions among humans.

Until the Stargods came and ruined everything. They had finally managed to kill Hanassa's human body, but not his spirit. He had taken over the body of Taneeo without the Stargods suspecting. He had dwelled among them for many moons without their noticing.

But Taneeo was stronger in will and mind than Hanassa had suspected. He fought Hanassa every day. Even after the Stargods had nearly killed him again with their weapon of murderous sound, Taneeo had continued to fight Hanassa's control, until he finally lapsed into a coma rather than accept defeat.

Hanassa needed another body.

He thought he had to wait for one of his own get to happen by. Only one of his own blood would provide the unique combinations of compatibility of mind and flesh.

But now he knew differently. The woman Lucinda had shown herself strangely vulnerable to his presence. And strangely resistant at the same time.

How close did she have to be to accept him? Physically touching? Within the confines of the clearing? Or anywhere on the planet?

CHAPTER 3

✦ —— · —— ✦ —— · —— ✦

"TWO POINTS TO STARBOARD," Loki O'Hara, sometimes known as Stargod Loki, called to the rudder man and the oarsmen behind him. The sound of the waves crashing over the rocks nearly drowned his words. He dug his paddle deep into the next trough. The little fishing boat responded. His companions must have heard him.

The next wave pushed the boat sideways to port.

Loki could see his youngest brother, Kim, waving frantically to him from the shore. The setting sun turned his dark red hair into a halo of fire. Early summer and his usually fair skin was already deeply tanned. He'd shed his shirt in favor of a leather vest. He wore that and knickers—like the locals; only the locals called the men's pants trews.

"*Starboard,* you muscle-bound sulfur worm!" Kim's words drifted to Loki. "Paddle starboard."

"I'm going to starboard, my starboard, you brain-deprived lumbird," Loki called back. A big grin split his face as salt water sprayed over him, further soaking his sweat-drenched shirt. He sank his paddle deep and corrected course around a pillar of water-carved volcanic rock.

Yaakke, Kim's brother-in-law, acted as rudder man on this fishing venture. He muttered something incomprehensible to their two comrades in the boat.

None of them seemed to appreciate the grand adventure of pitting wits and muscle against the sea.

Loki fended off the rock to port with his paddle. He caught a glimpse of a clear path to the cobbled beach.

"Come on, men. We're close and I smell dinner cooking!"

Submerged portions of the jumble of broken volcanic rock scraped the bottom of the boat.

Loki bit his cheeks. "Stay afloat. Just a little longer," he pleaded with the boat and whatever gods might listen.

They had lost three boats and six men over the course of the winter. His people needed the small catch flopping in the bottom of the boat. They'd lost more people to disease and cold than to the sea.

"Simurgh take every last one of the Imperial Military Police. If they hadn't stolen our stores and confiscated our village as their Base Camp, we'd have had enough to get us through," Loki grumbled a familiar litany as he dragged his paddle through the water. A few more strokes, a couple of good waves to push them landward . . .

The boat scraped bottom. Pebbly bottom this time. They'd made it home with minimal damage to the last boat and no loss of men.

Loki jumped into the surf to drag the boat higher onto the beach. Frigid salt water soaked him to his thighs. His calloused bare feet barely felt the rounded rocks.

Kim waded toward him to help.

Yaakke and the other men leaped free and added their strength to the task.

"What troubles you, little brother?" Loki grunted while tugging on the bowsprit. "Your face is nearly as long as this boat."

"Pryth. She's taken ill."

Loki gulped. Not Pryth, the ancient Rover woman, midwife, and bard. Sometimes Loki thought the old wisewoman was all that held the villagers together. His own leadership qualities seemed minuscule compared to hers, his status as a Stargod notwithstanding.

"Can't you do anything to help Pryth?" Loki asked Kim. "You're the healer in the family."

"Not alone. I need you and Konner to support the spell," Kim replied. He gave one last tug and the boat was high enough for the villagers to begin unloading the fish.

"Where is Konner?" Loki looked around at the gathered villagers. Light and dark hair, tanned and pale, they all wore combinations of leather and woven red cow wool. None of them had the red hair and deep blue eyes of Loki and his brothers.

"Konner's favored dragon, Irythros, commandeered him and Dalleena. *Jupiter* exploded," Kim said. "The dragon is flaming debris in the atmosphere to minimize damage when it falls." He began walking up the cliff path to the plateau and the village.

"Good, they aren't wasting fuel in *Rover?*" Loki shouted as he followed Kim.

"Why fly a shuttle when you have your own pet dragon?" Kim turned a big grin on Loki.

"I gather that other dragons are also flaming debris, but without passengers," Loki asked.

The villagers began unloading and cleaning the fish. They were better at it than any of the three brothers. They wouldn't waste a bit, turning innards into bait.

"Konner and his wife seem joined at the hip to that red-tipped monster Irythros." Loki sighed, almost jealous. Kim and Hestiia communicated often with Iianthe, the purple-tipped dragon. Konner and Dalleena had Irythros. No dragon had come forward to befriend Loki, or his lover across the sea, Paola.

But he had *Rover.* He'd rather control the shuttle than be a passive passenger on a dragon any day. He just couldn't take the shuttle up often enough to suit himself and, therefore, saw very little of Paola.

Efforts to manufacture enough fuel for *Rover* so they could return to their mother ship *Sirius* and depart this primitive planet had proved slower and more difficult than expected. But then, accomplishing anything on a world that had just barely embraced iron-age technology was slow and difficult.

A wave of homesickness engulfed Loki as completely as the waves in the cove had nearly capsized the fishing boat. He hadn't seen Mum in almost two years; hadn't had boots or new clothes in a year; hadn't eaten a meal that didn't taste of smoke and copper, or listened to recorded music, or . . .

He swallowed the despair that threatened to swamp him.

Soon. He and his brothers would leave the land of the Coros soon.

Kim stopped Loki with a hand as soon as they were out of earshot of the locals. "Now that *Jupiter* is gone and the IMPs can't divulge the coordinates of this planet to the civilized world, perhaps it's time to make peace with them."

"Never," Loki spat.

"They have antibiotics, medical equipment, a trained medic. Our magic may not be enough to help Pryth. Pryth may not have enough skills to help Hestiia when she delivers our baby. We need their help. We need to expand our gene pool . . ."

"We need to get off this planet without interference from IMPs. We do that and we don't have to worry about the gene pool," Loki shouted. His face grew hot and his hands itched to hit something.

Qwarlian swamp slime for brains! he thought, being careful not to project telepathically to his receptive brother.

A year ago, when the brothers happened upon this hard-to-find planet while running from the IMP cruiser, none of them had considered that magic, a.k.a. psychic powers, might work or that dragons were real. This planet had shown them otherwise.

He took a deep breath for calm that never quite reached his hands. "You know that now that *Jupiter* is gone the IMPs will try to steal *Sirius,*" Loki surmised. "Kat Talbot has the right DNA to break into the ship and override command locks. All she has to do is figure out how we cloaked the ship and hack through the programming. She's smart enough to do it. In fact, I'm surprised she hasn't done it already."

"We are going to have to learn to live with the IMPs eventually, Loki," Kim said, altogether too calm and rational.

"No, we don't. *We*—you, me, and Konner—are leaving as soon as we have enough fuel." Loki pressed forward, angry at his brother for bringing up the forbidden topic. Again. "I'm packed and ready to go as soon as Konner finishes up on the fuel cells."

"I am not leaving my wife and child, Loki. Konner and Dalleena are coming back as soon as they get his son away from his first wife. We and our people have to live with the IMPs. I will not abandon them or betray them."

"Will you keep Cyndi Baines here, too? We can't take her with us. You know she'll blab everything to everyone she meets if she ever sees civilization again. You want to live with that woman?" Loki sneered.

Kim blanched.

Loki chuckled.

"I can't see why you ever thought yourself in love with Cyndi, Loki." Kim shook his head. "Nor can I imagine who was stupid enough to make her a diplomatic attaché. She's the most undiplomatic person alive."

"Cyndi got her appointment because she's related to royalty. I fell in love with the idea of stealing her precious self right out from under the nose of her important and officious father. Why she hopped aboard *Jupiter* rather than a luxury liner for a quick trip home, I can't begin to guess."

Loki turned and stared at his brother. "We have to leave here soon, Kim. We have to report back to Mum. We have to help Konner retrieve his son. You have to come with us." He tried to force his brother's compliance with a mental probe.

The power bounced back to him, stabbing him between the eyes, instantly generating a fierce headache. He stumbled and pressed a hand over his eyes, blocking the light of the suddenly too bright sun. He reached his other hand to steady himself against whatever rock or shrubbery was nearby.

Kim grabbed hold of Loki's arm and held him upright.

"Will you at least consider an expedition to steal some drugs from the IMPs?" Kim asked.

"I have no problem with stealing from the enemy. Why don't we kidnap their medic Lotski while we're at it," Loki tried to smile around the pain in his head. He was always up for an adventure. Well, almost always. Right now he wanted only a cold cloth over his eyes and complete darkness.

Kim pressed his hands to Loki's temples.

The pain faded.

"Remember this next time you try to manipulate me with magic, Loki."

"I'll remember."

CHAPTER 4

(USE THE LEY LINES,) a calm voice whispered into the back of Kat's mind. *(Find their power and make it your own.)*

"Yeah, right. Want to tell me how to do that?" she sneered at the invisible voice.

(Remember.)

"Remember what?" Last time she had seen the spiderweb of blue power lines beneath the surface of the land, a dragon had guided her to place her feet atop a junction of two lines. She could not do that now. She was still several hundred meters above the rapidly approaching ground.

The lander nosed down.

"Ley lines." She closed her eyes and thought about how the power had tingled up her legs, along her spine, then into her mind. She pulled on the memory and forced the nose of the lander up with all of the considerable strength in her arms and shoulders and will.

Her shoulders ached. Her face ached. And her head ached when she finally got the nose up.

"I shouldn't have been able to do that!" Had her psychic powers actually overridden the laws of physics?

Nonsense. Loki O'Hara had filled her head with nonsense. No one had enough psychic power to force an out-of-control aircraft to break the laws of physics and defy gravity.

With enough air under her wings to glide, she took a deep breath and a quick look around. She was low, too low. No wonder the cockpit wouldn't eject, she didn't have enough altitude for a parachute to open or a jetpack to engage.

Breathing deeply, half wondering if she were already dead and only dreaming, she guided the fighter down in large swoops, first starboard then port, shedding altitude gracefully and gradually. The setting sun cast long shadows, disguising the true height of obstacles in her path. She took a chance and selected what appeared to be an almost level landing field. Her VTOL jets were history and unable to steady her drop.

She had to do this the old-fashioned way, by the seat of her pants. Very few pilots in His Majesty's fleet knew how. She was glad her father and brother had taught her more tricks than the official manual allowed.

The lander bounced and kicked and rolled over the rough desert floor. Kat rolled and bounced and kicked all over her seat, despite the tight safety harness. The hydroponics tank broke free of its restraints and slid forward, blocking access to the hold from the cockpit.

Finally, the cumbersome lander came to an abrupt halt, nose crumpled against a rock, one wheel off the ground. The other tire was slashed to ribbons by the rocky ground. Both struts were mangled.

Shaken and shaking, Kat released her harness. She tested her limbs and head for obvious injury. No bleeding, a few aches and bruises.

"I've survived worse in simulation," she muttered. But in simulation she'd always had a cup of hot coffee and a medic awaiting her.

Out here in the desert she had only herself for comfort and solace.

"Saint Bridget, I hope Brewster packed the emergency kit to regulation before I took off." She pulled out the bin from beneath her seat. It felt suspiciously light.

"Simurgh take his hide!" No water, no food. Only a basic first aid kit.

The thought of being without water suddenly made Kat extremely thirsty. Her throat thickened and tasted sour. She wanted a long cool drink now. *Right now.*

"Now what am I supposed to do?" Kat wondered out loud. Commander Leonard did not know if she'd survived or gone up in a fireball. The captain would be unlikely to cannibalize three planes to get one in the air to search for Kat. She had not passed any sign of civilization beyond the coastline a thousand klicks west. The rest of the continent was largely unmapped.

"Lesson number one in Advanced Bush Survival, look for water." Kat shoved at the cockpit. It remained clamped into place. Muttering enough curses to exhaust her extensive vocabulary, she banged on override switches, released manual clamps, and finally heaved with her back pressed into the canopy. It gave with a sudden jerk that threw her off balance and flailing into the control panel.

A blast of desert heat rose up from the gray-green sands. She almost ducked back beneath the smoke-colored canopy. But this was desert; without a cloud cover, the land would lose heat rapidly the moment the sun dropped below the horizon. She guessed she had about a half hour for a preliminary search, then back to the plane for shelter.

Kat made the awkward climb out of the cockpit, cursing that she couldn't get past the hydro tank to exit through the main hatch in the hold. It now weighed half a metric ton in full gravity, well beyond her capacity to shove it aside without mechanical help.

She jumped onto the wing, checking the area for specific landmarks in case she got turned around and lost sight of the plane. The sun made a fiery ball due west. She wouldn't find a much better landmark than that. It turned the area under her aircraft into an inky morass.

An inky morass that moved and slithered.

Kat scrambled back up the wing toward the cockpit in a hurry. She fished an emergency light out of the kit and shone it down into the shadows.

Hundreds of black snakes covered the ground. Thick ones. Skinny ones. Long ones. Short ones. All moving. Wedge-shaped heads with venom pits and viper heat sensors lifted and tasted the air with rapidly moving forked tongues of blood red.

And then one particular dark knot lifted to become a giant snake. Bigger than the biggest snake she had ever heard about. Its head was bigger than hers.

As the monster rose up to stare her in the eye, it fluttered six pairs of black bat wings.

She could not run from it. She could not climb high enough to get away from it. She could not hide from it.

"Yaakke!" Loki called to his friend from the path. "Join me in the bathing pool." A good soak in the hot springs ought to loosen some of the tight muscles in Loki's shoulders and ease the remnants of his migraine.

"Never try to read someone who can backlash the probe," he reminded himself. Kim was a talented healer, but even he couldn't cure everything. The tight and tired muscles in his neck and shoulders only aggravated the psychic pain of the backlash.

Maneuvering the fishing boat was hard work. Satisfying work. He deserved a soak in the pool.

The only work he'd rather do was outsmarting customs patrols with a high-profit black market cargo in the hold of *Sirius*.

"Thank you, Stargod Loki. My wife appreciates me more when I wash the stink of fish off my skin before I come home to her," Yaakke announced as he caught up with Loki and Kim on the path to the village. The man might be Kim's brother-in-law, but he still deferred to them as if they truly were gods and not just men.

"Enjoy your bath. I'm going to check on Pryth." Kim hastened ahead of them to the plateau and the village.

Loki and Yaakke proceeded more slowly, bypassing the village for a second uphill path that skirted a cliff, wound around a few ravines, and leveled out near the family clearing. Loki hummed a few phrases of his mother's favorite lullaby, but to a lively march tempo and touched the force field surrounding the clearing. The programming responded to the harmonic vibrations of the tune and his DNA to open a portal.

"I do not see how you do that. How you know when the barrier is up and when it is down?" Yaakke shook his head.

"Magic," Loki replied with a huge grin. He loved having control over the secret to the force field. He loved the amazement he created in the locals.

A screech that made the hairs on his arms rise sent Loki running toward the bathing pool. He grabbed an ax from the woodpile as he passed.

Another bone-chilling feminine cry. Shudders ran up and down his spine. He hurried his pace down the path, careening into trees and undergrowth as he rounded each bend.

He had nightmare visions of Hestiia going into premature labor and Kim being in the village, nearly an hour away.

"Yaakke, check on Taneeo. Make sure he's still in a trance." Another nightmare. The village priest's body had been taken over by a rogue dragon last autumn. Now he lay comatose, capable of moving if led, capable of eating if fed, otherwise Taneeo's young body seemed empty of mind and soul.

Loki and his brothers knew that the spirit of Hanassa had possessed Taneeo, had ruled his body for months until the battle for the crystal array. A sonic blast from *Rover* had felled the enemy and disrupted Hanassa's control over Taneeo's body.

Disrupted but had not ousted.

If the alien spirit of Hanassa should rise again in him, there was no telling how much murder and mayhem would follow.

"Stop it this instant, you silly child!" another feminine voice commanded, followed by a resounding slap.

Loki came to a heel-skidding halt one layer of shrubbery away from the bathing pool. The second voice, calm and musical, belonged to Hestiia, Kim's wife and Yaakke's sister. The strident screecher could only be Cyndi, Lucinda Baines.

"The bane of my existence," Loki moaned.

"What's wrong now?" he called out. He needed to stay back from the natural hot spring while the women made use of it. Hestiia was not terribly body conscious, but Cyndi certainly was. No sense borrowing trouble.

"What's wrong?" Cyndi stormed through the brush. A damp tunic in her favorite deep teal clung to her body, outlining her lush figure.

A year ago, Loki would have nearly fainted with desire at the sight of her body. Since coming to this planet he had no interest in this spoiled socialite.

"I'll tell you what's wrong. A fish tried to eat me in that cursed water." She shuddered. "How can you expect me to get truly clean without a sonic shower? My hair is a mess. My skin feels like cerama/metal. I have no makeup or proper shampoo. Not even a decent hydroponic diet. I'm certain my body is withering into premature old age open to every disease imaginable without the proper nutrients."

Loki had to turn his back on the woman before she saw him chuckling. Actually, her skin glowed and her hair gleamed from the natural cleaners of water and a soapy root. The lack of makeup allowed her natural beauty to shine through the mask of sophistication. She'd put on a little weight, replacing sharp planes and angles in her figure with natural curves. But she would never see that. She would never accept life in the bush, despite the evidence of how she thrived.

"How dare you turn away from me, Mathew Kameron O'Hara?" Cyndi grabbed his arm and spun him around.

Loki cringed at her use of his full name. No one called him that—not even Mum.

She trembled with anger. Or was it more? Cyndi was arrogant and spoiled, but she usually had more control over her emotions. She could strip a soul to the bone with a sarcastic tongue. But anger? Fear? Not the Cyndi he had once loved.

"Eric Findlatter will have you mind-wiped for such an insult to his wife!" Cyndi continued. Instantly she clapped her hand over her mouth as if to take back the words.

"Eric Findlatter?" Cold washed through Loki at the name. "Nephew to the emperor? Mostly likely among the heirs to be elected next emperor by the GTE Parliament? That Eric Findlatter? And you married him without telling me?"

Anger flooded him after the cold dread. Boiling hot anger that turned his vision red and made his hands itch to hit someone.

Cyndi straightened and assumed a regal post. "Of course. I wouldn't settle for anyone less."

"Meaning me."

"Especially you, you filthy outlaw."

"I am tired of baby-sitting this woman. Her hysterics accomplish nothing," Hestiia snarled. She waddled up the slight slope from the pool. She'd draped a long sarong around her body, covering the bulk of her pregnancy and her engorged breasts. She pressed her left hand against the small of her back as she moved. She moved very slowly.

Loki did not think she could get much bigger. No wonder Kim was anxious for her.

"Hysterics?" Cyndi screamed. She didn't seem to have any other volume to her speech lately. "Hysterical is what I should be after Taneeo tried to invade my mind and fill me with darkness. I'll show you hysterical." She launched herself at Hestiia, fingers extended like dragon talons.

"No," Loki said firmly as he grabbed Cyndi about the waist. "Have you lost your mind, Cyndi? Attacking a pregnant woman is frowned upon in domed cities. Here, it will get you burned at the stake. New life is precious. Nothing and no one endangers it! Not even the wife of an Imperial heir."

He took a deep calming breath. "Now what is this about Taneeo?"

"Unhand me," Cyndi ordered. She continued to squirm and kick. Her fingers remained extended, ready to scratch whatever she could reach.

"Stop it!" Loki turned her to face him with a hard twist.

"You can't do this to me!"

Loki slapped her.

Instantly Lucinda Baines sobered. She grew rigid. Her eyes turned icy.

Loki knew a moment of fear. Then she shoved herself away from him.

"I'll kill you for that, Matthew Kameron O'Hara. I've had enough of you. I never want to see you again."

"Good. Because I don't want to have to see you again either. You are banned from the hot spring and this clearing. If I could, I'd exile you from the village, I would, but that's not up to me." He marched back to the circle of lean-tos and cabins in the clearing.

"Yaakke, take her back to the village. Now."

"Gladly. Maybe I can talk some sense into the primitives. You won't be a god to them when I get done. You'll be their next sacrifice." Cyndi's voice turned deadly cold.

"The happiest day of my life will be the day I leave you behind on this planet while I enjoy the freedom of space." Loki took a deep breath for calm.

A moment of panic crossed Cyndi's face. She looked almost vulnerable. For half a femto Loki considered softening his edict. What had she said about Taneeo?

Then he remembered how she had betrayed him—marrying another without so much as a good-bye to him first. And not just any other man, an Imperial heir. A man who could push through Parliament a Bill of Attainder, the hated edict that could condemn an individual to incarceration and mind-wipe without trial or other due process of law.

"You can't leave me behind," she whispered. "You have to take me with you, Loki. I'll die if you leave me here. I'll shrivel up into an old woman and die. Alone. Filthy and starving. Do you want that on your conscience, Loki O'Hara?"

"We all die sooner or later." He shrugged and leaned casually against a tree. At least he hoped his stance was casual. His nerves felt as tightly strung as one of Hestiia's bowstrings.

He suddenly wished he had Hestiia's bow and her expertise with it to use on the coming raid against Base Camp.

Maybe he should take Cyndi along instead and let the IMPs deal with her hysterics and pouting demands. *S'murghit,* he would do just that.

"Why did you hop aboard *Jupiter* for transport, Cyndi?" Loki asked, suddenly exhausted from the day's exertions and trying to figure her out. "You could afford faster and more comfortable ships. Did you manipulate them to come find me and my brothers? Did you want to watch them arrest me, mind-wipe me, and throw me in prison?"

"I do not have to explain my actions to you," she said haughtily. She tried to fix him with a withering gaze.

He yawned and looked away.

"May I escort you, Lady Cyndi, to the village?" Yaakke asked. He sounded meek, totally unlike his forthright, adventure-seeking normal self.

From the vacuous look in his soft brown eyes, he was in for quite an adventure.

"If she tries to escape, let her. I'm done with her," Loki called after them.

"This primitive barbarian has more manners than you, Loki." Cyndi stalked toward the portal. Loki hummed, making the lullaby into a dirge, to let her through.

"You have made a formidable enemy, brother Loki," Hestiia said quietly. "I hope the backlash of her hatred does not destroy more than herself."

"Me, too. Did she say anything about Taneeo to you?"

CHAPTER 5

◆—·—◆—·—◆

(*I DO NOT LIKE this place, Stargod Konner,*) Irythos said into Konner's mind.

"I don't like it either, Irythros," Konner replied to the red-tipped dragon as they flew tight circles around the crash site of a large chunk of debris from *Jupiter.*

Dalleena, Konner's wife, clung tightly to him from behind. They were both wedged between two of the dragon's red spinal horns, but they were also both aware of their altitude and the very long fall should they slip off Irythros' broad back. Each hair acted like a crystal or mirror deflecting light and casual glances around the dragon.

Glass globules littered the impact crater below them. The heat from the ship's reentry had melted sand into glass. A tall column of dust rose high into the atmosphere.

"We must land, no matter how much we dislike this place. We have to see what we can salvage. There might be an intact fuel cell or two."

"This place reminds me of the volcano crater," Dalleena whispered. "The place where the IMPs tried to capture you." Her eyes grew wide with wonder. She never showed fear, even if she felt it.

That was only one of the reasons Konner loved this woman from a primitive planet. She embraced new experiences.

Many of her people cowered in fear at the least hint of change. The IMPs and a lot of politicians in the Galactic Terran Empire had the same attitude; anything different had to be bad.

"At least you did not have to listen to the crystal array scream in agony as the ship exploded. The crystals are safe." She hugged him. After only nine months together her vocabulary nearly matched his own, even if she did maintain the slow drawl of the locals.

"The crystals seem quite happy maintaining a confusion field around our clearing," Konner replied absently. He didn't want to remember how the king stone had screamed in his mind when he removed it from *Jupiter.* All of the crystals had protested disruption of their harmonic unity until he built a new home for them beneath the clearing and gave them the task of protecting his family.

He'd had to disable the crystal star drive aboard *Jupiter.* If any of the IMPs left this planet, ever, they would be obligated by law to reveal the location of a pristine planet ripe for colonization and exploitation. The incredible beauty of the place, the culture of the natives, everything they valued would be destroyed under the onslaught of droves of new people, mechanization, pollution. And for what? To feed a bloated empire that valued industry and money more than people.

He focused on the tailpiece of *Jupiter* where it stuck above the impact crater.

"I wish we'd seen this piece soon enough to flame it into smaller pieces," Konner muttered. He did not like the amount of dust reaching toward the jet stream. It could cause all kinds of climatic damage in the next year.

(If we land, we must leave as the sun touches the horizon,) Irythros said ominously.

Konner checked the level of the sun. It lacked only a few degrees to the deadline imposed by the dragon.

"Perhaps we should return another day, when we have more time," Dalleena suggested. She bit her lip as she watched the sand. "Salvage will not get up and walk away on its own."

The lengthening shadows moved as if a wind scattered them.

The only wind Konner could find was from Irythros' passage through the air as he circled.

An eerie sensation crawled up his back, like a chill or a dozen tiny snakes slithering over his skin.

"We can come back when the crater has cooled," Konner said. He didn't want to know what awaited him down there tonight.

The eerie feeling intensified. He suddenly knew he was needed elsewhere. Where?

(Home,) Irythros said.

"Not home. Somewhere else. Somewhere close." The crawling along Konner's spine made him want to twitch and scratch. He forced himself to still his body and breathe deeply.

Something to the north and west tugged at his senses.

Dalleena's right arm shot up, level with her shoulder, palm out. She rotated her body slowly, tracking something lost and in trouble. "There." She pointed northwest.

A scream rent the air. Konner felt the distress behind it like a knife along his spine. The crawling sensations ceased, replaced with a sharper, scarier feeling. He was surprised he didn't start bleeding.

Irythros thrust his massive translucent wings downward, once, twice, a third time. They rose a hundred meters in the air and shot forward.

Konner clung more tightly to the red spinal horn in front of him, and clamped his knees against the dragon. Dalleena wrapped her left arm around his waist, her right hand remained extended over his shoulder. Her tracking talent was fully engaged.

"Who?" Konner asked.

Neither Dalleena nor Irythros answered.

"Anyone we know?"

Dalleena nodded her head against his back.

"Kat," he said flatly. He'd seen an Imperial Military Police lander gliding out of control amongst the debris. Only his sister Kat Talbot or his brother Loki had the skill and spirit to risk maneuvering among the flaming chunks so closely.

Who else would be out in this dangerous desert so close to sunset?

"Kat?" Dalleena sounded as if she tasted the name on the wind. "Kat is there, but she is not the one who screamed."

"I'd hate to be on the receiving end of her temper if I was foolish enough to attack her. She may have been adopted and raised by Governor Talbot when she was seven, but she has all the stubbornness and ferocity of an O'Hara," Konner said. He dug his knees into the dragon's side, urging him to more speed.

Irythros snaked his long neck back to glare at him. Dragons flew at the speed they determined, not at any urging from a mere human.

Konner sighed and hunkered down, making his position on the dragon's back more aerodynamic. Dalleena bent with him.

Very shortly, another crash site came into view. An Imperial lander lay canted to one side, supported on the broken strut of one wheel. The stubby wings on the cigar-shaped vessel looked partially retracted. One dipped into the rocky ground, the other stuck up at a twisted angle.

A few more wing flaps from Irythros and Konner saw a figure balanced precariously upon the thrusting wing. The setting sun caught the red of her hair and turned it into a corona of flame.

"Kat," he said again.

His sister held a stun pistol out in front of her and blasted away at something moving around the lander. Long tendrils snaked up out of a dark mass and struck out at the gun. Kat blasted it.

It screamed in pain, almost in a human voice.

Konner heard the electronic pulse of the gun and watched the tip of the tentacle, or snake head, explode in a spray of red gore against the black mass.

Deep inside the moving shadow, red eye-shine blinked and twisted, constantly moving. Constantly watching for an opening in Kat's defenses.

Another downward thrust of Irythros' powerful wings and Konner knew that a thousand snakes besieged his estranged sister. One of them crept up behind her.

"Flame, now, Irythros," he called.

The dragon obliged, shooting a long tendril of fire into the midst of the snake pile beneath the wing with pinpoint accuracy.

"Good shot, Irythros. I couldn't have done better myself!" Kat called as she loosed another blast. That stream of energy seared the coil of snakes moving behind her.

"Need some help, Kat?" Konner asked belatedly.

"Is that you, Konner?" She shot another beast trying to climb over the wing of her downed lander.

"Who else would be riding Irythros in the middle of nowhere?"

"Dalleena might. Or I will." Kat hopped atop the nose of the aircraft, shooting snake after snake. Some of the monsters withered and died on the spot. Others—the biggest ones—merely jerked out of the way and continued their siege.

Her gun dribbled less and less energy with each shot.

Irythros blasted the center of the mass.

The odor of burning meat and fried venom rose up, nearly choking Konner.

Kat doubled over, coughing.

A particularly large black snake with a head the size of Konner's two fists combined sneaked up behind her.

"Behind you, Kat," Konner called, wishing he had a weapon of his own.

Dalleena peered over his shoulder. "That's the matriarch, Irythros. Kill her and the entire coil dies," she called.

The dragon obliged with another stream of flame at the wedge-shaped head and darting tongue. The fire swept past Kat's feet, nearly igniting her flight suit. Kat jumped onto the other wing, away from the shooting fire just as it scorched her ankles.

"Shite!" she yelled.

The mother snake reared back and away. She hissed and bared her fangs. But she dropped back into the coil.

Another viper wrapped itself around Kat's good ankle. It lifted its head and prepared to plunge fangs into her calf.

"Keep flaming the mother snake," Konner called. He crawled up the dragon's back to balance on his head. Before he could reconsider he jumped atop the nose of the lander and stomped on the tail of the attacking snake. He held his breath as he stretched across the aircraft and grabbed for the head just behind the eyes. He wrenched the beast away from his sister.

The snake twisted and fought. It spat venom. It hissed. Its red eyes blinked and looked at him with malevolent intelligence.

Kat reached into the open cockpit. She came up with a tube of wound sealant. She sprayed it into the snake's face.

In a single heartbeat, the beast went limp. Its eyes closed. The fangs withdrew.

Konner threw it as far out into the now dark desert as he could.

The mother snake detached from the coil and slithered after her wounded knight.

In seconds it was over. Kat sagged with relief. Konner draped an arm around her shoulder, as much for his own need to know they both had survived as to offer her comfort.

"Is it safe for you to land, Irythros?" Konner called.

Without answering, the dragon circled once and touched down lightly a short distance from the IMP craft.

(There is room for one more upon my back, if you wish a ride, Kat O'Hara,) the dragon suggested.

"I am not an O'Hara!" Kat spat.

Konner remained silent for a moment at the false insult.

"We lost you when you were seven, Kat. But we are still family. Will you accept our hospitality for a short time?"

"Will you return me to Base Camp?"

Irythros blinked. His multicolored swirling eyes glowed a shielded white when he opened them again. *(If that is what you desire in your heart of hearts.)*

"What is that supposed to mean?" Kat asked. She tested her weight upon her burned ankle. It nearly crumpled beneath her.

Konner put his arm about her waist and held her up. "Never expect a direct answer from a dragon. But think about what he says deep in the night when you have only yourself to answer to. You'll find truth there." Konner remembered some of his other encounters with dragons. They exhibited wisdom with each carefully chosen telepathic word and each action. They'd saved his butt more than once.

"I don't expect to find truth with you or your brothers. You are outlaws, smugglers, saboteurs," Kat spat. She tried to pull away from his supporting arm.

He held her tighter, knowing she'd crumple if he didn't.

"That may be. But we are still your brothers. Let me help you, Kat. I promise we'll let you go back to Base Camp."

"Why would I believe you?"

"Because I have a dragon and my lady to answer to if I break this promise."

"I'll believe the dragon when I walk into Base Camp. But not you, Martin Konner O'Hara. I'll never trust an O'Hara again."

"Then you will have to learn to trust yourself as well as your brothers. For you are an O'Hara by birth. We never deliberately abandoned you when Governor Mitchell firebombed our home, Kat. You have my solemn oath for that."

Kat snorted.

Konner continued to beg her with his eyes to reconsider. Maybe she could learn to believe and trust him if she ever spent any time with her brothers, rather than cerama bonding herself to Base Camp. In the nine months since the IMPs had landed she'd spent perhaps ten hours in the company of her family.

Prior to that the O'Haras had not seen their prodigal sister in twenty years. Nor had they known for certain that she lived.

But she, apparently, had made it her mission in life to find out all she could about her missing family. She'd tracked them to the weird jump point that led to this planet with the intention of arresting them. The Imperial judicial cruiser *Jupiter* had a judge and attorneys aboard, all the facilities for bringing captured outlaws to trial. They even had mind-wipe equipment for carrying out sentences.

He drew a deep breath. "Got any fuel cells aboard the lander?"

"All of them are nearly spent," she returned. Her saucy air told him that she was pleased to deny him even one fuel cell.

But she allowed him to lift her free of the plane and she leaned heavily upon him as they climbed aboard the dragon.

CHAPTER 6

MARTIN FORTESQUE PACED the VIP salon at the Aurora Space-port. A hologram of the landing facility in the wall mimicked a window. It remained empty of any craft, large or small. The shuttle from the orbiting space station was late. Three hours ago his best friend Bruce Geralds had called to say that he, Jane Quenton, and Kurt Giovanni had arrived. They'd be down as soon as they cleared customs. The trip should only take an hour. What was keeping his friends?

They'd been planning this reunion for nine months, ever since Martin's fourteenth birthday. All their parents had agreed to allow the four to meet on Aurora rather than go to summer camp.

Melinda Fortesque, Martin's mother and owner of Aurora, had denied Martin the right to attend the camp where the four teenagers had met every year for eight years. Melinda didn't want her son to leave Aurora at all.

At last, a small transport came into view. It circled twice before finding an approach vector and landing. It rolled to a stop beside an awning protecting a private entrance. Not his friends.

Then a woman stepped out from the awning to greet the three men and two women who disembarked from the shuttle.

Martin would never mistake the woman's blond hair, trim figure, and stylish suit that cost a year's salary for most of the workers on Aurora.

Melinda Fortesque.

His mother, sole stock holder, president, and CEO of Fortesque Enterprises, the corporation that owned and operated Planet Aurora.

"Melinda, you had better not have interfered with a visit from my friends," Martin growled. "If you've ruined our plans, I'll find a way to ruin yours."

Never before in his fourteen and three quarter years had he been as angry with his mother as he was now. Nor as frightened of her.

He pulled out his handheld and called up the latest bit of information he'd dug out of Earth Archives. It was still there. Melinda had not managed to steal it from him. Yet.

If he showed this to a judge on any planet belonging to the Galactic Terran Empire, combined with other bits and pieces he and his friends had gathered, Melinda would end up in prison, mind-wiped, and rehabilitated over a long period.

But at the first indication of trouble with GTE law, Melinda would transfer membership of Aurora from the empire to the Galactic Free Market—or the black market as some referred to the loose alliance of planets. She'd done it before for economic advantage. She'd do it again for legal safety. In the GFM, she did not have to obey any law but her own.

But markets were fewer and trade profits were lower within the GFM.

Money always dictated Melinda's moves.

If Melinda would not allow Martin off planet to attend the most exclusive summer camp in known space, then she would not even consider allowing him to go where he could present damning evidence to the authorities.

He needed his friends' help for that.

Until they landed safely, and then departed safely, he had to hope his mother had no idea he knew so much about her.

At long last a shuttle appeared in the distance.

Martin breathed a sigh of relief as it taxied into position outside his waiting area.

"Marty! You've grown." First off the shuttle, Jane Q—as opposed to Jane Zelany, her roommate at summer camp—rushed to hug him.

"So have you, squirt. But I'm still taller than you." Martin returned her hug while extending his hand to Bruce and Kurt.

"Not taller by much, flagpole." Jane put him at arm's length to survey him more closely. "Something's different." She frowned.

"Two years' difference," Martin hedged. "You gave up braids for curls."

"Like it?" Jane pirouetted showing off her cap of loose brown hair that bobbed with every move. She highlighted the rather plain color with subtle red-and-blue streaks.

"Yeah. I like the dress, too." Martin admired her legs, which he'd never noticed before, even when she wore shorts. At summer camp they were all just buddies; gender never played into their schemes and daydreams.

"There is something else different about you, pal." Kurt Giovanni peered over the top of his spectacles—purely an affectation. Implants at the age of two had cured his myopia. Always the tallest and skinniest, he topped Martin by only a few centimeters now.

Martin exchanged a glance with squarely built Bruce. He disguised his true weight and form with flowering particolored shirts and baggy panta-loons.

"Not here, *mes amies*. We'll talk later in a more secure location." Bruce took charge of them and herded them away from the mass of people exiting the shuttle.

Martin had divulged a few bits of information about his plans to Bruce under strict oath of secrecy. Even among Kurt and Jane.

Luggage trolleys began appearing on the far side of the waiting area. One man came out of the hidden recess with the trunks and suitcases. He stood squarely in front of a massive pile. Tall with light brown hair and medium coloring, he could pass for any bushie who'd had the rough edges honed off and pasted on a veneer of civilization. His stance and alert awareness defined him as a bodyguard. Bushies had more muscle mass than civils and therefore tended to drift into security work. Martin had put up with his fair share of private security personnel over the years. His own lurked in a dark corner to the right. He easily spotted them in any crowd.

Kurt made his way over to the bodyguard and the assorted luggage. "Sorry guys, my dad insisted he come with me." Kurt shrugged and began sorting his soft sided fold-up and duffel from the three trunks.

"Why?" Martin asked. He surveyed the area as warily as the bodyguard.

"Dad's up for reelection this year." As Prime Minister of Neuvo Italia, Giovanni Padre commanded almost as much power as Melinda, but not nearly the wealth. "He's made some enemies. His political advisers suggested that taking me out was a good way to force him to drop out of the election." Kurt shouldered his own bags.

"Have there been attempts on your life?" Martin asked. This could put a big crimp in their plans.

Kurt shrugged again.

"Only one," Jane said. She handed Martin two large suitcases and flagged down a skycap for an antigrav trolley to manage her trunks. She certainly had changed since her days of showing up for three Standard Months at camp with only a backpack.

"What happened?" Martin added the suitcases to the trolley. He wanted his hands free if things got messy. He didn't trust his bodyguard—Melinda had selected him and signed his paychecks, not Martin.

"Bomb in the limo that takes me to school. Good thing I decided to take my ped-cycle that day." Kurt half grinned. His eyes told a different story; one of fear. His casual traveling suit looked two sizes too big rather than his usual saggy off-the-rack outfits, like he hadn't been eating much.

"The good news is that the bodyguard is also a rated pilot. We don't have to hire another one," Kurt whispered as he tried to put on a bright face.

"What's your rating?" Martin asked the guard. This was all just too coin-cidental.

"Ace solo on everything up to fifty million tons. And call me Quinn."
The bodyguard remained alert, only briefly making eye contact with Martin.

"License?" Martin wasn't taking the man's word. He already had his handheld ready to search six databases for the man's identity and credentials.

Quinn fished in his inside jacket pocket, still keeping his eyes on the moving crowd. He handed a smart, synthleather wallet to Martin.

Martin flipped it open to find the man's ID and license up front. "He's a
Sam Eyeam," he told his friends. Part private investigator, part bodyguard,
part freelance agent and courier, the coveted SE license exams were tough to
pass, tougher to find an administrator for the test. Only the best became SE
(officially Security Executive but the nickname from an old children's book
was more popular). The best of the best commanded huge salaries and bonuses for "delicate" work for the politicians and corporate executives that ran
the Galactic Terran Empire. Some SEs were known to move outside the law
as often as in.

Bruce nodded with an "I-told-you-so" grin.

Jane rolled up her eyes and snatched the wallet away from Martin.

Martin's handheld beeped. Three pages of credentials, references, and ré-
sumé scrolled past him. Full name: Adam Jonathan Quinnsellia.

"Why'd you quit being the emperor's private pilot, Quinn?" Martin asked
suspiciously.

"His Majesty got his own licenses and didn't need me anymore. I decided
I could make more money freelancing than flying for the major liners."

Martin refrained from commenting on that. The story was just a little too
pat.

"May I suggest we get out of here," Quinn stated. "We are too noticeable
in this crowd." He shouldered the last bag and gestured them through the
hidden door into the bowels of the spaceport. "Inform your driver to meet us
at entrance D12," he said quietly to Martin as they trundled past baggage
handlers and runway guides. Servobots scanned and read luggage tags, rout-
ing them to various waiting areas.

"Some Earth diplomats came through the space station just after we did,"
Kurt said. "They had to clear customs and get their private transport well
away before they'd let us out of customs. That's why we were late."

"Any idea who they are?" Bruce asked Martin.

"I watched my mother meet them. Figured they had to be important for
her to come all the way out here. Usually dippos and distributors have to go
to her."

"I have heard rumors that the daughter of a planetary governor and a judicial cruiser are missing," Quinn added. "The daughter is a diplomatic attaché
and she hitched a ride on the cruiser for a fast trip home. Rumor also places
her in frequent romantic company with the emperor's nephew."

Martin raised his eyebrows. Maybe this guy's presence wasn't such a coincidence after all. "Don't see why they need to talk to Melinda about missing personnel," Martin shrugged. Maybe they had something to do with Bruce's father, another Sam Eyeam. Also missing.

Quinn ushered the four teenagers into the armored flitter that would take them to Martin's home for their reunion. The bodyguard took one look at Martin's regular pilot and guard. After a whispered discussion and exchange of credentials, Quinn dismissed them. Then he took the controls of the craft. Once they were in the air, he fiddled with the communications ports. A band of static emerged from the speaker.

"Now that we have some privacy, you kids care to tell me what this is all about?"

Martin looked at Bruce. Bruce looked at Jane. Jane looked at Kurt. Kurt looked at Martin.

Since no one else seemed interested in spilling the truth, Martin decided he had to be the one.

"We are mounting a search for my father. A search my mother will go to some lengths to stop."

"Fair enough. Now tell me how you expect to do this. I am at your disposal. My loyalty is to Kurt. His father paid me very well to keep him off planet and safe until after the election. This sounds as good a project as any to do that."

"I'll pay you, too, to keep your mouth shut and keep my mother from following us," Martin added.

Life was suddenly looking brighter than the overcast day portended.

(Be careful what you wish for,) a voice said into the back of his mind. A voice that might have been his conscience but did not sound like it.

CHAPTER 7

+—·—◆—·—+

KIM O'HARA SAT in the cockpit of *Rover,* the family shuttle. He watched through the magnified viewscreen as Yaakke waited patiently on Cyndi. He fetched a hot drink for her, refilled her trencher with fish stew, and spoke attentively to her throughout the long evening.

The rest of the villagers went about their routines, finally settling in to a session of quiet storytelling. Without Pryth, their midwife, bard, and matriarch, to lead them in spirited song and dance, their mood was subdued and cautious.

Cyndi listened politely, then moved off to the women's quarters, a cave set into the soaring cliff.

Yaakke's gaze followed her with longing. Then he returned to the evening's activities. But his eyes kept straying back to the entrance of Cyndi's cave.

Kim shook off his speculation on what had happened between Hestiia's brother and the village hostage.

He had a chore tonight. A chore which neither of his brothers would approve.

Loki was nowhere in sight. Konner and Dalleena had not yet returned. He had time and privacy to break every rule his family adhered to.

For Hestiia, his wife, and Pryth, the midwife, he had to do the unthinkable.

He fingered the comm unit.

Before he could talk himself out of his plan, he keyed in a common IMP frequency. "*Rover* to Base Camp, come in please. Over." His signal seemed to take forever before the diagrams showed it had bounced off his mother ship *Sirius* and returned to ground.

A lot of dead air was his only response. He changed frequencies three more times before he found a static-interrupted voice at the other end. "This is Base Camp. Identify yourself. Over."

Kim couldn't tell if he had contacted a male or female, someone in authority or just someone playing around with the comm units.

"This is Mark Kimmer O'Hara." He gulped, then proceeded with precious information. "Citizenship number Alpha George Cat Zero niner eight two seven Omega Prime niner eight two seven." If any of the IMPs got off the planet, they could cancel his citizenship knowing that number. Without the number they had no power over him. "I want to strike a deal."

Did they have any databases left to show that his number was legal?

"O'Hara? This is Captain Amanda Leonard. What kind of deal? Will you take us off planet? Will you reconnect your king stone and allow us to communicate with home?"

"Baby steps, Commander Leonard." He wouldn't give the woman the honor of calling her captain. She had no ship left to captain. Only her rank and name identified her now. And she would not have her rank long when her corps of followers had to hunker down and start working for survival.

Kim had never truly approved of stranding the IMPs in Coronnan. That amounted to imprisonment under conditions worse than what the IMPs would do to the three brothers if they were captured and returned to the GTE. But he recognized the necessity of keeping the GTE out of Coronnan. The exploitive policies would pollute and ruin the ecology. The GTE would totally destroy the unique and beautiful culture of the people. Hestiia's people.

His people.

If any of the IMPs ever returned to the GTE, they must by law reveal the location of this planet.

"What do you mean by baby steps?" Leonard nearly screamed.

Kim instinctively reared away from the shuttle's speaker. "I mean, Commander Leonard, we start learning to live together with small concessions to each other."

"Who said we agreed to live together?" The former captain sounded nearly hysterical.

"Mr. O'Hara," a deep voice injected into the conversation. "This is Lieutenant Commander Jetang M'Berra, First Officer of the Imperial Military Police Judicial Cruiser *Jupiter*. What do you propose?"

Kim wished he could see what was going on at Base Camp—the village he had helped build last year. He'd left communications on voice only. He could not take a chance that Leonard or M'Berra would recognize the landscape around *Rover* in the background of the messages. If they found the shuttle, then Kat could break into it and fly it up to *Sirius*. Giving any one of the IMPs access to the mother ship would destroy everything he and his brothers had fought for. Giving Kat access to anything in their lives meant instant danger to their persons as well as their liberty.

"Lieutenant Commander M'Berra, I have a hostage that you want very badly. You have a medic with drugs and knowledge that I need. Can we talk a trade?"

"I will settle for nothing less than your complete surrender, O'Hara," Leonard screeched in the background.

"Consider this, M'Berra." Kim gave up trying to reason with Amanda Leonard. The stress of losing her ship and surviving a winter on a primitive planet had obviously unhinged her mind. "In the optimistic view that you might get off this planet and back to civilization, think of the report Diplomatic Attaché Lucinda Baines will be giving her father, a planetary governor." Kim almost chuckled at the look that must be crossing the big African's face.

"We will get off this planet, O'Hara. And when we do, you will be grateful to come with us." Menace dripped from M'Berra's tone.

"Now why would we do that, M'Berra?" Kim asked, not at all intimidated. "We know how to survive on this planet. We know how to plant grain, fish the seas, and hunt for food. We know how to build shelters that keep out the cold wind and rain. You should know that. You lived in my house all winter. Now it's past time to start planting grains and vegetables, to repair winter damage to houses. Have you done that?"

"If you are so successful, why do you need a medic and medicines?" M'Berra asked coldly.

Kim almost choked out the painful confession that Hestiia was eight months pregnant and not doing well, that their midwife had taken sick, and that Lucinda Baines was a pain in the ass. He wasn't about to reveal his vulnerability.

"Winter brings aches and pains and chills and fevers to my people. I have over fifty locals to tend. They depend upon me and my brothers. We are their Stargods," he said instead.

"Barbarians!" Amanda Leonard called. Her voice sounded muffled, as if M'Berra had removed her from proximity of the comm unit.

"Think about your options, M'Berra, and get back to me on this frequency at midnight." Kim discommed and sat back in his chair in the cockpit of the shuttle. For so many years *Rover* and *Sirius* had been his home. Now he could not imagine living with recycled air, tanked food, and cramped quarters. He could not imagine living without Hestiia.

He'd go on Loki's raid if he had to. But he'd rather do this peacefully. He did not want this world to dissolve into civil war between the "civilized" few who needed to go home and the bushie many who embraced life on this planet.

That had happened once before, three hundred years ago among the first human colonists. Scientists had unleashed a bioengineered plague as a way to settle the dispute and reduced the population to the barbaric stone age. The plague went dormant for a few decades at a time and then bloomed with new intensity.

Kim and his brothers had found a cure. The locals had honored them as Stargods because of that. They had no guarantees they could help should something more disastrous erupt from a new war. Kim would not risk his wife and child, nor the villagers who depended upon him as their Stargod.

Kat limped painfully as she climbed off the dragon. She *would* walk the two hundred meters to Base Camp. In the dark. Alone.

"Sorry I can't help you, Kat," Konner said. At least he had the decency to sound regretful. "I risk capture by your friends."

"You cannot risk capture, but I can," Dalleena said. "I'm just a dumb bushie who came to her aid. Wait for me. I *will* be back in an hour." She slid off the dragon and landed easily.

She paused at the dragon's head and stroked his muzzle. "Will you wait for me, Irythros?"

(As long as we safely can.)

"Will you keep my man safe?"

(As safe as he will allow.)

Kat heard a definite chuckle behind the monster's telepathic voice.

Within a few seconds Dalleena had an arm around Kat's waist and a shoulder under her arm. She was nearly as tall as Kat, only a decimeter or two shorter than Konner. The position must have been uncomfortable for her.

"Dalleena, you don't have to . . ."

"Yes, I do. You are family."

"I don't claim . . ."

"You are family." That stated, she began walking, dragging Kat along with her.

Kat had to admit walking was easier with her sister-in-law as a crutch. Much easier. Almost too easy.

"Can you see in the dark, Dalleena?" Kat asked when they had traversed only a few meters.

"No. But my tracking talent guides me along the easiest course."

"More magic," Kat replied with a modicum of disgust. She'd had a few strange experiences on this lonely planet. Not enough to convince her of her brother's claims of psychic powers beyond imagining.

The fact that she had fought off giant serpents and ridden on the back of a mammalian dragon that appeared nearly invisible, except for his red spinal horns and wingveins and -tips, was not enough to convince her that on this planet magic worked.

(You will learn soon enough the extent of your own power,) Irythros spoke into the back of Kat's mind. There were other voices accompanying his bright tenor, deeper voices, more melodic voices, an entire choir of voices.

Kat stumbled under the onslaught of alien thoughts inside her head.

Dalleena kept walking, as if she had not heard the dragon's prophecy.

They covered nearly the first hundred meters to Base Camp slowly but relatively smoothly. Just as the torchlight—electric illumes had worn out moons ago—around the cluster of cabins became visible in the gloom, Dalleena stopped short. Kat stepped awkwardly upon her burned ankle. Fiery pain shot up her calf into her thigh. The leg wanted to crumple.

She dropped her grip on Dalleena and sank to the ground, grateful to get her weight off that leg.

Dalleena still did not move.

"What is it?" Kat whispered. As much as she needed to sit, she wanted more to be back at camp with Medic Lotski spraying cooling sealant on her wound. She'd used up the scant supply in her med kit deflecting the snakes.

"Th . . . there." Dalleena pointed hesitantly toward a darker lump against the dark meadow, then turned her palm up in that direction.

Kat peered into the darkness, barely able to discern the shape let alone the substance against the backlighting from the torches. "It looks like a rock to me."

Then the lump moved.

Both women yipped and skipped, or scooted, back a pace.

The lump lifted one end, extending a tail. Then it rocked forward and stretched, revealing a head.

"It's just a cat," Dalleena sighed. She sounded a bit chagrined by her earlier fear.

"Biggest cat I've ever seen," Kat said on a long exhalation. "Almost as big as a Denobian muscle-cat, and they are reputed to be huge, closer to a lion than a cat."

The cat wandered closer, stropped Dalleena's ankles, then butted its head against Kat's hand and purred.

She obliged it with scritch behind the ears. "Do you have a name, kitty?" she asked. The purr soothed her frazzled nerves. Knotted muscles relaxed. She wanted to gather the animal into her lap but didn't quite dare. Would the beast even fit? It must weigh eleven kilos at least.

(Gentian.) The beast spoke into her mind just as the dragon did.

Kat yipped and scooted again.

The cat followed her, insisting upon more scritches and pets. It even tried to climb into her lap, sprawling awkwardly across her legs.

"We cannot stay here, Kat. I have to get you to your people and return to Konner."

"Tell that to Gentian," she replied a little breathlessly. Something strange was happening.

"Shoo." Dalleena pushed the animal off Kat's lap and helped her to her feet again.

Gentian's eyes glowed in the dark. He looked particularly sullen as he shook and ruffled wings.

"Wings? The cat has wings?" Kat choked.

Dalleena crossed her wrists, right over left, and flapped them.

Kat didn't have time to puzzle out the origin or meaning of that particular superstition.

"Y . . . you have been honored, Lady Kat," Dalleena stammered.

"Honored? By a cat?"

"A cat with wings. A flywacket. Such creatures are rare. They bestow their affections on very few humans."

"We stumbled over it. It purred."

"He gave you his name."

"I was just getting used to dragons who speak telepathically and insist upon names," Kat moaned.

"You must introduce yourself. It is the proper protocol." She spoke the words carefully, as if still uncertain of the vocabulary. "Gentian, I am Dalleena Farseer, a Tracker, mate to Stargod Konner."

Kat sighed heavily. She waited a long moment. The winged cat just kept looking at her. Expectantly?

"Gentian, I am Mari Kathleen O'Hara Talbot. Pleased to meet you."

Gentian meowed and detached himself from Kat. He ambled forward three steps then stopped to look back over his shoulder. *(Are you coming or not?)*

"I think we are supposed to follow him," Kat said. "I just hope he takes me to Base Camp. I really need a medic right now."

"Gentian knows that. I've heard rumors that flywackets begin their lives as purple-tipped dragons. One of a set of twins, but there can only be one purple-tip in the nimbus at a time. So the redundant twin must become a flywacket. They know everything the dragons know."

"And what one dragon knows, they all know," Kat finished. "This world gets weirder every day. I really wish I could go home."

(Be careful what you wish for.)

CHAPTER 8

CYNDI WAITED IMPATIENTLY at the top of the steep path to the cove. She pretended to watch the phosphorescent waves crashing around the broken volcanic rock. Every once in a while she glanced over her shoulder toward the evening gathering around the village's central fire pit. The voices had become subdued as more and more people drifted toward their huts or caves and their beds. Someone sang a quiet ballad in a fine tenor. She thought the voice belonged to Yaakke. She hadn't paid much attention to him until today.

Now he presented her best opportunity for recruiting an ally to her cause.

The village fell into silence. Even the waves seemed quiet at slack tide.

Then she caught the whisper of a footstep behind her. She turned slowly, a gentle smile upon her face.

"You should be abed," Yaakke said. His tone was gentle but wary.

"I don't get many moments alone."

"Alone?" he asked as if the comment was alien to him. In the communal atmosphere of village life he'd probably never developed the concept of privacy.

Another reason Cyndi so desperately wanted to go home. No one here ever left her alone with her thoughts, or bathed in private. They wouldn't even allow her to launder her undergarments without ten other women marveling over elastic and silk and counter-levering.

"I cherish moments when I can watch the waves by myself," she replied simply. She sidled closer to him until they nearly touched. The hairs on her arms fluffed under the heat of his proximity.

He did not back away.

"Alone is not safe," he said. He watched the shadows for signs of predatory animals or marauding humans. But his eyes returned to her often. In the dim backlighting from the dying fire and few torches she caught glimmers of movement from the patrolling guards. They passed through and around the village silently.

Star-frags, she wasn't as alone as she thought.

"I feel safe with you organizing village defenses." She touched his arm with one finger.

He smiled at her and locked his gaze on hers. "I am second to the headman. Protecting you is my job."

Was there a slight emphasis on the word "you?"

Emboldened by his attention, Cyndi placed her palm against his chest. He'd definitely puffed it out a little.

"No one would dare attack this village with you in charge."

"Thank you, Lady Cyndi. I am proud to serve my village. The village gives us all life, purpose, security."

Give me a break! Cyndi thought. *The village is a political unit, and needs to run politically. No one serves unless they are angling for more power.*

"You should be headman," she whispered drawing tiny, sensuous circles on his chest.

"I have not the age or experience . . ."

"But you have the talent, the wisdom, the," she paused for a deep breath, "the strength." She let her hand move in larger circles, cupping his bicep firmly.

His hand captured hers. "My time will come."

"Not soon enough. I could help you become headman."

He pushed her away. "I do not need a woman's help. I will not betray Raaskan, a good man and trusted friend. Go back to the women's quarters, Lady Cyndi. I will go back to my wife and child."

He pushed her toward the upper cliff and the series of small caves where most of the village dwelled communally. She felt the heat of his anger in his tone and his touch.

"Now how am I supposed to steal those fuel cells!" she fumed.

Simmering at her failure to seduce this . . . this *primitive,* Cyndi marched back to her uncomfortable pallet more determined than ever to find a way to escape these people and their Stargods. She would do anything to help the IMPs get off this planet with Loki and his brothers in custody—preferably bound with force bracelets at hand, ankle, and neck.

· ———◆——— ·

Hanassa fluttered around the village on ghostly wings. He watched in amazement as people looked directly at him and did not see him.

Strange that he had not thought to separate from Taneeo before. This afternoon he had found that he could move about the clearing and still keep a tendril of his mind connected to the man's body. Now he ventured farther, still maintaining his hold on Taneeo.

The villagers continued to ignore him, not even stopping to shiver when he brushed past them. Anger boiled in him.

He would change their disrespect for him to terror and awe when he found another body. The right body. Someone with the potential to take control and gain power.

Then he saw her. The woman who had come with the IMPs. The woman who had become vulnerable to his touch for a moment. With her compelling beauty and ruthless ambition, she would make an admirable host.

He watched as her temper loosed her control over her will. She, too, had been rejected. She knew what Hanassa felt.

She was vulnerable!

He loosed his hold upon Taneeo and prepared to sink into the woman's body.

Martin angrily threw Kurt's suitcase on the large bed in a medium-sized guest suite of his mother's palace. Then he moved into the living room where Kurt sprawled on a long Lazy-former®. His long arms and legs dangled over the furniture as if it couldn't shift to accommodate his entire body.

As usual, Melinda had done her best to isolate Martin from his friends, from the world of Aurora, from the galaxy, and from his quest to find his father. She had housed his guests and Kurt's bodyguard in suites at the far end of the wing most distant from Martin's own rooms.

They were also in a separate wing from the Earth dippos Melinda had met at the spaceport.

Jane had the corner suite across the hall from here and Bruce the one immediately to the east—at the end of the corridor and thus theoretically marginally more vulnerable than this one.

Quinn had made the decision on who slept where once the rooms were designated. The bodyguard now prowled about with various devices looking for hidden monitoring equipment and points of vulnerability. He had already put overrides on the locks.

"We'll be private here. House guards and monitors can't open those doors without Kurt's or my permission and the password you four agreed upon," he assured them. "And, Kurt, don't open the door to anyone without that password even if the voice sounds like one of you friends or me."

"I have to call my dad," Kurt said. He fished in his pockets for his handheld.

Martin politely turned his back, an illusion of giving his friend privacy.

He could have left. But he knew that the moment he stepped into the hallway his mother would summon him away from his friends. He didn't dare disobey.

Someone pounded loudly upon the door.

Martin looked to Quinn for permission to open it.

The bodyguard nodded, indicating that his equipment recognized the person demanding entry with a second loud round of knocks. Then Quinn moved into the bedroom, still concentrating on his equipment.

"Password?" Martin whispered into the sensor at the doorjamb.

"Crystal blue quantum six to the sixth power," came an anxious reply from Jane.

Martin opened the door.

"Have you heard the news?" she asked.

"My mom says the search for the missing dippo is really heating up," Bruce added, right on her heels.

"My mom says the same thing," Jane hastened to give her version before Bruce could trump her scoop. "Eric the worthless Findlatter just announced his betrothal to Lucinda Baines, the missing dippo. The emperor has asked the Imperial Military Police to aid in the search for her and for the missing judicial cruiser."

"Seems the last anyone saw of Ms. Baines, she hopped a ride back to Earth aboard *Jupiter*. Now they are both missing." Bruce barely let Jane finish before adding his own two credits of information. "And *Jupiter* is reported to be hunting three unnamed outlaw brothers. The news is speculating that the only outlaws on the official hunt list are named O'Hara."

Martin forgot to breathe. O'Hara. "My dad?" he asked on a whisper, hoping Quinn didn't hear. "My dad has brothers?"

"My dad just confirmed the same thing," Kurt added, closing his handheld. "*And* he says that there is some mysterious connection between the O'Haras and your mother, Marty."

"A big connection. Like me."

"Something I should know?" Quinn wandered back into the living room. His eyes looked vague as if he'd been in deep concentration, not noticing anything else that went on around him.

Martin wondered if it was an act. Could anyone be that fine an actor?

Melinda could.

He decided to hold back the trust he had been on the brink of giving the bodyguard. He needed to know more. To do that, he needed to search several databases only his personal computer could access. That computer was back in his own suite where Melinda could find and track him.

CHAPTER 9

"KONNER!" SEVEN-YEAR-OLD KATIE O'Hara screamed for her brother.

Mum had taken four-year-old Kim, the youngest, to the landing strip. Loki, at fourteen the oldest brother, prepped a shuttle for them to escape.

Twelve-year-old Konner had been assigned to watch over Katie. She'd left him here just a moment ago while she ran back into their burning house.

"Konner, where are you?" she whimpered, hugging Kim's teddy bear Murphy that she had rescued from the flames. Smoke made her eyes water more than the frightened tears she already shed.

Maybe she'd left her brother in the west courtyard. She couldn't tell where she was anymore. The smoke was too thick, the night too dark. Maybe she'd gotten turned around.

"Konner!" she yelled again. She darted from one corner of the courtyard to the other. Her breath came in panicky gulps. No way out. No sign of Konner.

The fire crackling around the windowpanes of the family home reached long tendrils upward. Katie watched it, wondering if she dared go back in to try to thread her way around to the other courtyard. Maybe Konner was in the house, searching for her. She buried her face in Murphy's fur. Her little brother wouldn't sleep without it. Especially in a strange bed as the family made their escape from the men who had set fire to the house.

An explosion erupted from the center of the house. The blast knocked Katie into the courtyard wall. She hit her head with a smacking sound. Black stars burst before her eyes.

Then there was nothing but blackness.

"Konner?" Kat awoke with a start. She lay absolutely still until she figured out where and when she was. Her eyes remained sealed shut with the aftermath of sleep and a gummy film. Her chest felt heavy. She had as much trouble drawing a deep breath as she did that terrible night nearly twenty years ago when smoke had filled her lungs and the family had abandoned her.

A deep rumble in her ear chased away the last of the dream fog. "I am not seven years old and alone. I am twenty-seven. I have a career in the Imperial Military Police. I am Kat Talbot, foster daughter of a planetary governor." She repeated the familiar litany over and over, banishing the ghosts and nightmares of her childhood.

Then she opened her eyes. A huge black cat perched upon her chest, staring unblinking into her eyes. He must weigh twelve kilos.

(You went home,) the flywacket whispered into her mind.

"That is not home. It is only a memory of a nightmare," she insisted to the cat.

Gentian's eyes crossed while looking at her. His velvet-green eyes begged her to confide the truth to him.

She had spoken the truth. She had. Benedict Talbot was her dad. His two daughters were her sisters. They were family. Their home was her home.

The cat shook his head and heaved himself off her chest and off her bed.

Or was it a bed? Kat looked around for the first time since awakening. She lay on a cot in a dimly lit cabin. Ranks of vials on a crude shelf, a medical monitor in the corner, and baskets on the floor filled with clean bandages revealed her location. "Lotski's med cabin," she muttered.

Kat's ankle began to ache. It felt hot and swollen where the dragon's flame had scorched it.

Medical Officer Chaney Lotski poked her head around the door curtain. "Oh, good, you're awake. Sorry to leave you so long. We had a lost crewman wander in. He's so starved and dehydrated he's incoherent." The lieutenant babbled on as she fussed with some of the vials on the tilted shelf.

"Who is he?" Kat asked, hoping conversation would take her mind off the burning ache that shot up her calf to her knee.

"Funny, I thought I knew everyone aboard. I didn't recognize him," Lotski replied. She selected one of the little gourds strewn among the vials and bottles.

"There were three hundred assorted crew and judicial personnel aboard the *Jupiter*. Judiciary tended to keep to themselves. Same with the Marines," Kat replied.

"But Judicials tend to have more ailments in space—mostly boredom—than anyone else. And the Marines are always getting hurt doing excercises in heavy grav. They all trooped through my office at one time or another. I should know this guy."

"How do you know he's one of ours? The locals are human, and without a uniform . . ."

"His teeth are too good for him to be a local. Ah, well, we'll sort it out as soon as he's absorbed some fluid and nutrition. Looks like he walked a long way. His boots are worn through and his feet are badly bruised and cut beneath the holes. Now let's look at this. How did you get a burn this deep on your ankle? Fall into a bonfire?"

"Something like that." Kat didn't want to explain her adventures to Lotski. No one sane would believe that she had ridden on the back of a nearly invisible dragon with crystal fur that directed the eye around it, and yet challenged the watcher to look for him among the clouds and mists.

The one other time she had ridden dragonback seemed more like a half-remembered dream than reality. Irythros had taken her to an open area and shown her the ley lines. Using them, Kat had reached out with her senses, far beyond this star system, all the way across the galaxy to her mother. For a brief moment, she had tapped into Mum's thoughts, her *obsessions,* and flinched away in disgust in less than a heartbeat.

Lotski touched Kat's burn with a tentative finger.

Kat jerked her leg away from the delicate probe.

"Hurts a bit, I see," Lotski said. "I have to clean it and apply an ointment, then I'll bandage it."

"Can't you just spray a sealant on it?" Kat propped herself up on her elbows to survey the supplies. She peered into the gloom, looking for the familiar can of universal first aid remedy.

"Sorry. Ran out of it weeks ago. Our crew have had to learn to use live fire and cook over it since we ran out of fuel for the burners and lights. They aren't familiar with how flames reach out for victims." The medic chuckled at the image of sentient fire.

Kat kept her mouth shut. On this planet the green flames just might be sentient, like the dragons and her flywacket.

Where was the beast anyway?

A quiet purr told her the cat was beneath her cot, hiding in the shadows. He would not leave her alone with this talkative woman.

"This is an ointment some of the local women swear by for everything from burns to diaper rash—not that we need that yet—and insect bites. It goes on quite cool and should feel good on the burn."

"Whatever. Just do something so I can walk back to my bunk." Kat lay back on the cot.

"Oh, you won't be walking for a day or two. That burn is quite deep. I'll keep you here with our mystery crewman. You are my only two patients for the moment. You're lucky; I can fetch and carry for both of you."

"Great." Kat turned her head away from the medic and dangled her hand over the side of the cot. Gentian butted his head into her palm. She scratched his ears.

I want to be alone, Gentian, she thought. *Away from other humans.*

(We know. But now you can solve the mystery of the stranger and prevent him from doing any harm to you and yours.)

This mental conversation took some getting used to.

By "me and mine" do you mean what's left of the crew?

(And others.)

My outlaw brothers.

(And their families.)

A rush of air, like wind in the treetops, told Loki that the dragon Irythros returned long before he could see the beast.

"About time you showed up," Loki growled as Konner and Dalleena walked the short distance from their landing place at the edge of the village.

"We got delayed by a coil of black vipers in the desert," Konner growled back at him.

"Vipers? Do you suppose that is what keeps the city from expanding beyond its walls?" Loki turned away from his preparations to raid Base Camp with new interest.

They'd discovered several small port cities on the big continent. All of them huddled behind protective walls, preferring crowds, housing shortages, and inadequate sewage systems to venturing beyond those walls after sunset. Yet no one in any of those cities spoke of what they feared.

"Could be the vipers that keep them confined," Konner said on a shrug. "The beasts are aggressive. Huge. Seem to be nocturnal. And they are led by a matriarch who can direct their actions." He pulled Dalleena close to his side, as if drawing comfort from her presence. For the past nine months he rarely allowed more than a meter of space to get between them.

"We'll do another recon after we finish the current project," Loki said with a big smile. "I'm looking forward to expanding the trade network and opening up those ports. We need to advance this planet to provide surplus food for us to sell on the black market back home. Trade is the best way." He sheathed a hunting knife at his hip, grabbed a sledgehammer and a spear. Then he surveyed his crew of handpicked village warriors.

Yaakke was missing. Loki shuddered at the thought that he lingered with Cyndi.

"What are you up to?" Konner asked. He and Dalleena retreated one step.

"Pryth is sick," Kim said flatly. His eyes looked bleak. "And Hestiia does not thrive with this pregnancy. We need to liberate medical supplies from Base Camp." He looked grim, hefting a spear.

Loki knew his little brother had never enjoyed brawls as Loki did. Kim was the first among them to refuse to eat meat because a carnivorous diet deprived animals of life; always the first to suggest compromise; always the last to pick up a weapon to defend himself and his loved ones.

"We might even need to bring back the medic," Loki added. He gestured for his crew to gather around the family shuttle *Rover*.

Konner and Dalleena exchanged a strange look.

"What?" Loki demanded.

"Not tonight," Konner replied quietly.

"Why not? We're ready. *Rover* has enough fuel for the trip, even though three of the cells up at the power farm seem to be duds. They have no fuel at all . . ."

"We ran into Kat in the desert. She got hurt and we returned her to Base Camp," Dalleena said hastily.

"And?" Loki stared at her, uncertain how to respond; his mind still on the problem of the fuel cells. They'd been nearly full this morning. What had happened to them?

"While I waited for Dalleena to return from delivering Kat, I prowled the perimeter of the camp," Konner added, more slowly "A lost crewman wandered in. He was in really bad shape, starving, dehydrated, raving."

"What was he raving about?" Kim dropped his spear and suddenly took an interest in something beyond Hestiia's health.

"Cannibals. Lotski couldn't get him sedated fast enough, though. The crew heard him. They are jumpy, doubled the watch. If we go in tonight, even using magic, it's suicide."

"Cannibals?" the village headman Raaskan asked. He and his fellow warriors all crossed their wrists and flapped their hands in a ward against evil. "The man has been west of the mountains. No one returns from there alive."

"I do not think this man was a member of the crew," Dalleena whispered.

A superstitious shiver ran up Loki's spine. "Who is he, then? We are the only outsiders on this planet other than the IMPs."

"The Sam Eyeam we met last autumn, across the ocean. The one with fine teeth," Dalleena explained.

"The one who had my ex-wife's distress beacon broadcasting our location to the IMPs," Konner finished.

CHAPTER 10

KAT WATCHED through slitted eyes as Medic Lotski helped one of her corpsmen carry the stranger into the medical cabin.

Lotski tried to be quiet and not disturb Kat's slumber, but the new patient thrashed and moaned and screamed in delirium.

He fought some internal demon. Each jerking movement threatened to dislodge the IV that dumped precious liquid and nutrients into his system.

Kat opened her eyes further, trying to find something familiar in the man's features. The light from the oil lamp was too dim. Just another man, tall for a civil, barely medium height for a bushie, with shaggy hair that hung too long against his shoulders. His beard appeared to be streaked with blond, or possibly gray. If he had indeed met with cannibals, the trauma could have induced a premature stripping of color from his hair.

Civilized men shaved regularly and kept their hair trimmed above their ears. Most of the crew that had found their way to Base Camp after escaping from *Jupiter* nine months ago, had managed to keep up that indicator of civilization. Her brothers and this stranger had not.

Eventually, Lotski finished fussing over her patient and withdrew to the fire in the common area at the center of the Base Camp. The night was mild and many of the crew gathered around the fire pit for a last cup of herbal tea and a bit of gossip. Kat wished she could join them. Being stuck with a raving stranger bothered her.

The fact that he was a stranger bothered her more.

"Get away, you devils!" the stranger screamed. He punched at imaginary enemies. His thrashings tangled his IV.

The machine let off a quiet beep of alarm. Medic Chaney Lotski did not respond. She'd had a long hard day after a longer and harder nine months. Setting off a plasma cannon beside her ear might not wake her.

Kat thought the alarm should have been louder. They had seemed to shriek the last time she heard one. Apparently, the solar batteries of the machine had not fully recharged.

"I'll kill you all before I let you eat me," the stranger said. He thrashed again.

Still Lotski did not appear in the doorway.

What if the man died because of the tangled IV? Kat had to do something. She couldn't allow him to die.

Gritting her teeth against the pain in her ankle, she swung her legs over the edge of the cot. One test of her weight upon her foot sent jolts of pain and weakness up her entire leg. Dizziness spun her perceptions. Too like losing control of the lander and spiraling toward the ground.

Kat did not like losing control.

"Stand back or I'll shoot!" The stranger sat bolt upright, eyes wide open, arms flailing. "Where am I? Darkness. Oh, so dark. What hell have they dropped me into? Good Lord save me. Somebody, please help me."

Kat dropped to her knees and crawled over to the second cot. "Wake up, Mister," Kat ordered in her best military voice. "That's an order."

The stranger continued to moan and pray, still trapped in his nightmare.

"It's okay." Tentatively she touched his back.

He slammed his fist into her jaw. "Women are the worst. Most vicious. Most hungry." He tried to hit her again.

She scuttled away from him. "Settle down, soldier."

Gentian mewed quietly. He stropped Kat's legs where she sat on the floor. His purr rumbled through her. Then the large cat hopped onto the stranger's bed, still purring. He stepped into the man's lap, circling and butting his head into his chest.

Gradually, the patient ceased his raving. He breathed deeply and closed his eyes. "So scared," he murmured. A tear leaked from the corner of his eye. "So many of them. So scared." He trembled all over.

"Easy now," Kat whispered, suddenly uncomfortable with a man's tears. But she rubbed his back, kneading the strong muscles of his shoulders and the leanness of his waist.

With her free hand she untangled the IV and anchored the pole in the packed dirt floor.

"Sorry," he whispered and laid his head upon her shoulder. "Not manly to cry."

And then he nodded off. Kat shifted gently until she leaned against the wall at the head of the bed. She raised her dangling legs to rest beside his. Then she settled in for a long vigil with a stranger in her arms.

Eventually she, too, slept.

The Krakatrice, the venomous snakes, are our cousins. Still, they menace us as well as the humans. They keep the desert from blooming with their hatred of water. They have built dams to divert streams out of their territory. They have joined together to shift air masses so that no rain falls where they live. They have fed upon or driven off the game that we would hunt. Our numbers cannot increase, nor can we dwell in the lands across the seas as long as the Krakatrice thrive.

Now we must find a way to equip the humans with weapons that will end the predation of our cousins the Krakatrice. We may not kill one of our own.

At the same time we must direct the humans toward Hanassa so that they can negate his influence. We may not kill one of our own, no matter how much damage he inflicts; no matter how much he threatens our existence.

Konner pulled Dalleena back from the hasty conference his brothers convened with the village warriors. "Let's walk patrol," he said quietly.

"What troubles you?" Dalleena held her right hand out, palm up, seeking danger better than her eyes or Konner's handheld could.

"I do not like this business of the fuel cells. They are not duds. I checked them myself, thoroughly, before setting them out to recharge. Sunshine and dragon wine have worked well enough to bring them up to full capacity, even if it has taken a long time."

"What emptied them?" Dalleena stopped her prowl of the perimeter of the village to face him. She kept her left hand on his arm.

Konner mimicked the contact. This way they could sense each other's body language without visual clues and without him resorting to probing her mind—his least effective psi power.

Since their marriage—little more than pledging themselves to each other before their gathered friends and family—they had become attuned to each other, rarely needing to speak other than the most complicated thoughts.

As the tension in his body rose, she tightened her grip, reminding him to gather calm in order to think clearly.

"I don't know. And I don't have time to walk up the hill to check the cells before my brothers call us back to the conference."

"Then you must bring the cells here, where we have the light of many torches reflecting off cave walls, almost as good as daylight for your inspection." She grinned.

He kissed her lightly and ran his fingers through her long dark hair. She knew him well. They had truly become two halves of a whole that was bigger and better than either one of them alone.

"Let's find a few Tambootie leaves. I need some help in levitating the cells."

"Right behind us. I can smell them. The sap is running strong now."

"Those trees do have a rather pungent perfume." He wrinkled his nose at the aromatic scent in the warm summer night air.

Within a few moments they had plucked two fat leaves dripping with essential oils and taken a fresh torch into one of the smallest caves. Konner had to crawl into the low opening and sit with his back against the far wall. He folded his long legs to make room for Dalleena beside him and the two cells to nestle before them.

He licked the oil from the green leaf with pink veins. Warmth and energy surged from his mouth throughout his body and into his mind. Before he could hesitate and ruin his concentration with doubt, he closed his eyes and breathed deeply, gathering his mental powers.

Dalleena placed her hands upon his thigh, adding her physical strength to his as he had taught her.

Bit by bit, he pictured in his mind two fuel cells, each a cubic meter, one bursting with energy, the other spent and lifeless. Then he built the image of the gray cerama/metal cubes resting between himself and his wife on the rough dirt and rock floor of the cave.

One more deep breath to center himself and he opened his eyes.

The two cells rested upon the cave floor, a few centimeters apart with only a bare half meter between their tops and the ceiling.

Konner ran his hands over the full cell, sensing the energy within waiting to be tapped. All it needed was a few fiber optics connecting it to an engine and the direction to activate. It felt normal, like every other fuel cell he had ever worked with.

Then he shifted his hands to the other cube. His fingers felt the roughness along the top seam. He bent over to peer more closely.

Dalleena moved the torch a fraction, giving him a better, unshadowed view.

His eyes confirmed what his hands had told him.

"Someone opened the cell and released the pressurized energy. But they didn't close it properly."

"Who would do such a thing?"

"Who could gain access to the clearing to do such a thing?"

"Could your sister Kat levitate it out and then back?"

"I don't know." Konner looked into Dalleena's pained eyes. They reflected his own distress. "Would she, though? She would more likely keep the full cells for her own use."

"Kat is straightforward, honest in her hatred, honorable as are you and your brothers." Dalleena confirmed Konner's own assessment of his sister.

But he had not known her for nearly twenty years. He did not understand the people and events who had shaped her during those years.

"Let us look closer to home before we condemn my sister."

"How close? Hestiia does not want Kim to leave with you and Loki. Kim does not want to leave, though you and Loki both insist he must."

"I hate to think it, but they are the most logical suspects. No one else could enter the clearing without our knowledge and supervision." Konner closed his eyes. "I won't think that of my brother and his wife. I won't."

Something strange on the wind disturbed Hanassa. He lifted his attention from the Cyndi-woman's less-than-orderly mind to sniff the air.

What ruffled his dragon senses? An emotion rather than a scent. An emotion strong enough to reach across long distances.

A mind more vulnerable than the Cyndi-woman. A mind in distress.

"Later, my lovely," he whispered to Cyndi.

She did not hear him. Or, if she did, she ignored him, locked in her own obsessive anger.

He flew upward, seeking that other. Now that he knew he could separate from Taneeo and live in spirit form for a time, he needed to investigate and find the best candidate to host him.

A chuckle rumbled up from his belly. Yes, this might be fun. He'd sample many before he chose the best. And while he sampled, he would wreak havoc among the humans.

He might even try to temporarily give some courage to the flywacket. But only temporarily. He wanted a human body, not a miniaturized and transfigured dragon body.

CHAPTER 11

MARTIN CHECKED THE READINGS on his handheld. Two meters ahead of him, a security sensor read body heat and movement. Anyone or anything generating more heat than a servobot, or moving more than half a meter above ground would be recorded. Melinda's flunkies monitored everything in the palace except Melinda's office and private quarters. She could alert them to record there, too, but that required her voice and thumbprint override.

On top of that, Melinda and her crew moved the sensors every day.

Finding ways around them had become a daily exercise for Martin.

He did not want Melinda to know where he and his friends were every femto of the day. Especially since she had lodged them in the far guest wing, kilometers of corridors and staircases away from Martin.

He ducked directly beneath one of the sensors, trusting that his black leather pants and dark skin shirt, both woven with deflection threads, would mask his body heat. In this position, with the sensor angled toward the other side of the corridor, security should not be able to detect his movement.

A servobot came along, sweeping the edge of the corridor. It bumped against his feet, backed up, and scooted around him. Martin held his breath, praying that nothing internal to the machine reported the obstacle back to security.

Hopefully, the thing was programmed to ignore stationary pedestals and free-standing art. Melinda indulged in new decorations in binges. She hadn't bought any new artwork in almost a year. Time for things to start showing up in different places again and new ones filling odd gaps.

Melinda never discarded anything. Art she no longer wanted in the palace ended up in warehouses or servants' quarters until she craved change once more.

Martin dropped to his belly and scooted along in the wake of the servobot. Within a few meters he found the next space of dead air beneath a sensor on the opposite wall. He slid upright, back against the wall. So far so good. No blips in the sensors that his handheld could detect.

Just a few more meters and then he could round a corner into the guest wing. Melinda hadn't updated security there quite so recently. He could bypass it all with one loop of fiber optic cables.

"Martin, there you are," Melinda called out from the opposite end of the guest wing where she had lodged the Earth dignitaries.

"Melinda." Martin stood stock-still, wondering what lie he could come up with to mask his movements.

"I see you are on your way to visit your friends. I just saw them in the pool. That Quinn gentleman is most charming and Kurt Giovanni has wonderful manners. I must commend him to his father."

Martin nodded, not knowing what to say. He shuffled his feet awkwardly.

Melinda checked her chrono that sufficed as a handheld. She removed an electronic pencil from her earring and tapped something into it. Then she returned the pencil to her ear jewelry where it attached with a molecular bond.

"While I have you, perhaps it is time to introduce you to your new bodyguard and driver," Melinda said brightly.

Something was up; she was giving Martin her full attention.

"What happened to Miles and Jim?" Martin asked. He hadn't really liked the pair, but he'd sort of gotten used to them, knew their weaknesses.

"I decided they were more useful elsewhere." Her eyes narrowed. They had left Martin in Quinn's care yesterday without her permission.

Two men, nearly identical in height, breadth, and dark suits marched into view. They moved in step and swung their arms in time to their synchronized movements.

Ex-military, Martin decided. Or mercenaries. Not to be trusted.

"Martin, meet John and Karl." Melinda nodded to the two men as one, not differentiating between them. "Until this mess with the Earth diplomats is cleared up, I want these men with you at all times. All times."

"But, Melinda, I had hoped for some time alone with my friends. I haven't seen them in over two years." Martin hated that he sounded like a little kid whining.

"I'm sure we can dispense with the dippos by tomorrow. Then you can have some privacy back."

"I don't see what threat they can pose to us, Melinda." He almost called her "mother" just to annoy her.

"They seem to think I should know something about this missing judicial

cruiser and their passenger. I don't and that bothers me." She paused a moment tapping her toe and her fingertip against the chrono.

"They have nothing to do with us, do they?" Martin tried for wide-eyed
innocence.

"Not that I know of. But I'd better find out what they suspect quickly. Martin, return to your room and that map of yours. See if you can plot where that
ship disappeared and where it might have gone. I'll begin researching that
girl—their passenger. Lucinda Baines. Does the name mean anything to you?"

"Baines?" Martin had to think a moment. Melinda must be running scared
if she included her son in her plans and research. "Didn't a Carolyn McArthur
marry a planetary governor named Baines, reuniting the former royal house
with a cadet branch, thus forming a possible dynasty?" he recited a history
lesson, and gossip that Jane had given him.

"Ye . . . es," Melinda said. Now she tapped her teeth with her fingernail, a
true sign of her agitation.

"But our current emperor's father won the election in Parliament and proceeded to begin major reforms in the bureaucracy. The Baines faction couldn't
skim off nearly as much in profit from taxes as they had."

"Sounds like Lady Lucinda is off somewhere planning a *coup d'etat*. I heard
her name linked romantically to Eric Findlatter, the emperor's nephew."

"I need to know more about this woman. Go do some research and report
back to me before dinner."

"But my friends . . ."

"Will still be here when you finish. More incentive for you to get right on
it and stop testing the new security upgrades."

"You knew what I was doing?"

"Of course I knew. And you did very well. Security shows you still in your
room. If I had not spotted you with my own eyes, you might have defeated
the system completely. We can't allow that. I'll fire a few layabouts in the
monitoring room and demote some others. That ought to bring them up to
speed in plugging the holes."

"Yes, Melinda."

"And thank you, Martin. Now I know where the weaknesses in the system
are. We will make a formidable team." She turned abruptly and headed back
to her own wing, doubtless to figure some way to use the ambitious Lucinda
Baines. By dinnertime, Melinda would likely know the woman's shoe size,
color preference, and the names of her last six lovers.

"Don't suppose I could postpone that research until after a swim with my
friends," Martin mused.

"No," his guards, jailers, replied in unison. They each grabbed one of his
elbows and marched him back to his own quarters.

"Searcher, this is Jester, come in, please," Loki whispered into his handheld. He watched his screen anxiously for any flicker that might indicate a response.

With Konner and Dalleena off on some private errand—probably more lovemaking—and Kim checking Pryth, now was the best time for Loki to contact his own lover.

He hugged the cliff face near the path to the beach. A freshening breeze nearly blew him back into the heart of the village.

After interminable moments the screen on his handheld went from gray to black and then brightened enough to reveal the shadowy outline of Paola Sanchez, formerly a corporal in His Majesty's Imperial Military Police.

"Searcher here," came her crisp reply. The static of distance and a lack of satellites created a delay between the movements of her lips and his hearing the words.

"Searcher, I have new intel on the monster in your backyard," Loki said. He couldn't help the smile that crept across his face. Short and stocky, with dark hair, and an authoritative air, Paola represented everything he disliked in a woman. But she was the best lover he had ever been with. Cyndi's wild moans and thrashing paled in comparison to Paola's intensity and true passion.

"Is this just another excuse to drag me back to Coronnan for a face-to-face debriefing?" she asked with a big smile.

"I wish," Loki replied on a sigh.

"Then you have honestly found someone who will talk about the monster I'm chasing?"

"More than that. Konner and Dalleena encountered a coil of huge black snakes. Very venomous, very aggressive. Dalleena said the dominant matriarch had a head as big as a man's and a tongue as long as an arm. She also has six pairs of batlike wings. The rest of the snakes are ground huggers."

Paola let out an extended curse that taxed even Loki's vocabulary and imagination.

"That's the best intel I've had in six months. No one in the port city seems to know why they can't stray beyond the wall after dark. Digger—er, Ross Duggan—up north is having similar problems in his city. I think I need to come there and talk directly to Konner and Dalleena," Paola finished.

"Want me to bring the shuttle to pick you up?"

"Yeah. Unless you've got a dragon handy."

"They don't answer my calls like they do my brothers'."

"Probably 'cause they know you don't want to stay here. They love this planet."

"As do you and your Amazons, and Digger and his troop of rogue Marines."

Nine months ago, when Loki and his brothers began the plot to trap the

IMPs on this planet, they had found unexpected allies among the first landing parties. Paola, a corporal with ten years' experience, would never rise higher in the ranks because of her bush origins. She had gladly sided with Loki, after bedding him, for the chance to command her own troops. Thirty other women from *Jupiter* had joined her for similar reasons.

Ross Duggan, or Digger, had been an IMP sergeant with a grudge against GTE politics. He'd sided with the O'Haras for the opportunity to earn more money in order to free his family from indentured servitude. Now he commanded his own troops north of Paola in a different port city hoping to carve out some land and a place to bring his family once Loki sold some surplus produce on the black market and purchased the Duggans' indenture.

"Yeah, I love this place, bush backwater that it is. When can I expect you?"

"I'm on my way. Dawn your time." The port city on the big continent was close to a thousand klicks east and another thousand north of Coronnan.

"Good. I can catch an hour of sleep. Searcher out."

The handheld went dark again.

Loki sighed on a smile. He did that a lot when he talked to Paola. He needed Paola's vibrancy to remind him that not everything about his life was one dismal trial after another.

He hadn't used the shuttle to raid Base Camp, so he might as well use it to consult with the chief Amazon on the big continent. He stepped away from the shadows that hid him.

"Wasting fuel again?" Konner asked. He stood between Loki and the shuttle, hands on hips, feet firmly planted.

"Why aren't you making love to your wife? Back in the clearing," Loki replied. He'd not get around his brother easily, judging by the deep frown on his face.

"It's not a waste of fuel, if we can defeat the monster serpents and expand the port," Loki continued his defense. "We need a thriving port city to increase trade. Can't do that if the snakes keep everyone behind walls." They'd known for months that some monster preyed upon the populace; they just had not seen or heard about the nature of the beast.

"Agreed. But we need fuel to get back to *Sirius*. Someone sabotaged three of our cells. We haven't got any fuel to spare. If you haven't forgotten, I need to get back to Aurora to claim my son."

"I haven't forgotten. What good is claiming your son if we haven't got enough of an economy on this planet to support ourselves?"

"Later. You aren't going to take the shuttle again."

"Try and stop me." Loki pushed past Konner.

"I've rekeyed the ignition in order to keep Kat from stealing *Rover*. It only responds to my DNA now. Either I approve the mission or the shuttle goes nowhere."

CHAPTER 12

"SINCE WE AREN'T GOING raiding tonight, I propose you two assist me in a healing spell," Kim said to his two brothers. He had several hours until midnight when M'Berra might return his call.

Since he was the tallest of the three—by three centimeters over Konner and five over Loki—he did his best to command them by staring down at them. They each outweighed him by several kilos—most of it muscle—so if it ever came down to a physical fight among them, Kim would, and usually did, lose.

They shouldn't have to exchange blows to cooperate on this chore. Their fights were usually just an opportunity to vent anger and frustration at problems they couldn't easily solve. At the end of these bouts, all three of them came up laughing.

"For the good of the family and this village we have to try to heal Pryth," he urged.

"Do you know how to do this?" Loki asked. He stood with his fists on his hips and his feet braced for a fight. But then he was always braced for a fight.

"None of us have done this before, but we have to try. We are running out of options," Kim insisted.

"This won't be like the last time," Konner reminded them.

"Last time with Raaskan, a seven-metric-ton rock dropped on him," Loki reminded him. "After Konner levitated it off him, we had to push bones back into alignment and stop internal bleeding. What do we do with Pryth? We don't even know what is making her sick."

"She has all of the classic symptoms of pneumonia," Kim said. "We have to clear her lungs of fluid and bring her fever down."

"The locals swear by willow bark tea for fever," Konner mused. "I've seen it work. But how do we drain fluid from the lungs? Bringing it up might gag her. Or if we do it wrong, we could drown."

"A little bit at a time?" Kim suggested.

His brothers remained silent, shaking their heads.

"Too dangerous," Loki finally decided.

"We have to try! This village, my wife, depend too much on Pryth. We have to try!" Kim cried.

"Maybe we should read up on this before . . ."

"I have read up on this. We are running out of time. Pryth is so weak she might die tonight if we do nothing."

"If she's that weak, maybe we should leave well enough alone. What if she dies under our hands?" Loki said.

All three brothers shuddered. Each had a memory of another person dying either by their hand or by their negligence. None of them wanted a repeat performance of their spirits trying to follow another into death.

"If we don't do something, then who will deliver my baby? Who will know what to do if Hes has trouble delivering? Are either of you willing to take the chance that my wife and son might die in childbirth without Pryth?" Panic edged Kim's voice.

Both Konner and Loki looked at the ground.

"With or without you, I have to try to heal Pryth." Kim turned his back on his brothers and walked slowly toward the round hut where Pryth lay coughing and moaning, her life slipping away a little bit at a time.

As he walked, he left his mind open, "listening" for some kind of emotional reaction from his brothers. Telepathy was Loki's primary talent. Konner moved objects with his mind—the heavier the better. The first talent to manifest in Kim was precognition. He'd never have found the weird jump point to this planet without it. That weird jump point had been their only escape from the pursuing Judicial Crusier *Jupiter.* Commander Leonard had to break off the chase and go off on other errands and then come back several months later before her helmsman, Kat, had found the same jump point.

After the brothers had landed in this isolated system, Kim had discovered an ability to speed healing in others. He did not know how he did it, it just happened. Now he had to try to make the talent work on demand.

He'd studied hard over the last year to expand all of his talents and add new ones. Control over his talents increased daily. Except when he needed to heal. It either happened or it didn't. Even when he ate the addictive Tamboo-tie leaves.

He reached inside his pocket for the fat leaves he always kept at hand. He licked the oil off the pink-and-green veins. Then he nibbled on the succulent flesh of a leaf. A surge of adrenaline filled his body. He looked out upon the night with new clarity. Vague shadows in the distance jumped into view as clearly defined objects.

Then he heard the shuffle of feet behind him and mental grunts of agreement. His brothers had come to his aid after all.

Some of Kim's hesitation and fear evaporated.

They squeezed into Pryth's round hut one by one. The old woman with gray streaking her Rover-dark hair lay propped up against a makeshift bolster made up of a wolf hide draped over a basket filled with aromatic herbs and leaves. A small fire smoldered in the central hearth. More green smoke— born of the copper sulfate impregnated in the firewood—filled the room than escaped the hole in the conical roof. The smoke smelled sweet and astringent at the same time. Someone, probably Pryth, had sprinkled herbs over the coals.

Kim's sinuses cleared upon his first full breath inside the hut. The smoke might be doing some good for the patient, but not enough.

He handed the remaining Tambootie leaf to his brothers. Loki tore it in half and eagerly stuffed his portion into his mouth. Konner ate his more delicately, taking only as much as he needed to open his mind and his talent.

Kim felt their hands brush against his in rapport.

A coughing spasm racked Pryth's body. She leaned forward, hacking and choking until she could barely draw breath. Sweat poured off her brow. She shivered all the same.

The old woman began to gag. Alarmed, Kim knelt beside her. Instinctively, he reached into her mouth and pinched a wad of phlegm between his fingers. Slowly he drew out a long rope of greenish slime. He cast it into the fire. The flames sputtered and stank of garbage left out too long in the sun.

"Is that all you are going to do?" Loki snarled. "You could do that without us. It's disgusting." He turned to exit.

"We need to do more, Loki. She needs magic as well as mundane cures. Without antibiotics, we have to find a way to kill the bacteria infecting her body."

"Pryth packs moss into open wounds to prevent infection. Maybe if we made an infusion with the moss and some willow bark," Konner suggested.

"After we try this. I'm getting some ideas," Kim said. He sat cross-legged on the packed-dirt floor. His rump turned cold almost immediately from the winter chill that had soaked into it. Summer heat had not yet had time to warm it, despite the fire.

No wonder half the village had contracted various forms of the disease that had felled Pryth.

Kim concentrated on breathing. His brothers sank to the floor on either side of him. Each placed a hand upon his shoulder. They matched their breaths to his.

In on three counts, hold three, exhale on the same three counts. "Breathe deep, exhale deeper. Purge your body of foreign thoughts, alien impurities. Breathe," Kim chanted.

Gradually, the three minds merged into one. Their talents and strength combined.

The world retreated from Kim's awareness. He knew only his breath and the power he inhaled. His vision tilted slightly and colors took on strange casts, as if the spectrum shifted slightly to the left toward ultraviolet.

A web of silvery-blue lines beneath the ground jumped into view.

Shadows retreated. He looked more deeply into himself and saw the essence of Pryth, saw the rampant infection that had invaded her body. He watched her will to live fade.

Panicked, he almost lost his trance. Konner squeezed his shoulder, reaffirming the strength his brothers gave him.

One more deep breath and Kim concentrated on the red aura that surrounded Pryth, flowed in and out of her with her labored breathing. He reached out to touch the symbolic fire of infection. It burned his fingertips. He jerked his hand away, shaking it to dispel the heat.

Fortified with knowledge of the aura's nature he reached again and twined the fiery-red coils around his fingers and drew them away, as he had the phlegm. A section of red broke free of Pryth. Kim cast the pulsing red light into the hearth.

Sickly yellow-and-black smoke roiled up from the embers. It stank of rotten flesh, old sweat, and stale air.

Pryth heaved a sigh of relief. Then she began coughing again.

Kim sagged with exhaustion.

"I can't do anymore," he choked out.

"You have to," Konner urged him. "You have to get more of the infection out. Concentrate on her lungs."

"Use the ley lines," Pryth whispered.

"How?" Kim leaned forward eager for new knowledge.

Her answer was lost in another coughing spasm.

Kim took several more deep breaths. He thought he heard a rattle in his own lungs. Loki squeezed Kim's shoulder with both of his hands.

A little bit of strength trickled through Kim. He needed more of the Tambootie leaves.

He had no more with him. To leave to fetch more would break the trance. He might never achieve this level again.

Resolutely, he reached again to grasp the pulsing red aura of infection in the region of Pryth's lungs. The infection pushed his hand back. He pressed harder. His arm and shoulder ached as if he'd carried his own weight and more a long distance.

Loki supported Kim's overly heavy arm with his hand.

Kim tried again, feeling the strength drain out of him with every passing breath. At last he grasped a wad of the red light. It burned his palms.

"Hold on. The pain is not real," Konner whispered. He was sweating with the effort of maintaining the trance.

"Hold it tight and pull," Loki coached. His words came out on panting breaths.

Kim closed his fist and his eyes. He pulled. He had to lean back to extend the length of his retraction. In his mind he saw the infection drain out of Pryth. When he had as much as he could hold, he cast the long rope of it into the fire.

Rancid smoke filled his lungs. He coughed it out. Coughed again and again.

"Saint Bridget and all the angels," Loki breathed. "You've done it."

Kim sagged and coughed again, too weary to move. The pressure in his chest increased and he coughed again, and again. And again, until he could not breathe.

"Shite!" Konner exploded. "He's taken the disease into himself."

"You . . . must . . . take . . . it . . . out of him, now, before it spreads," Pryth whispered.

"I can barely lift my arms," Konner breathed. "I already worked magic tonight with the fuel cells. I've nothing left to give."

"Do it now," Kim whispered, afraid if he spoke aloud he'd cough again and never stop.

"We have to try together." Loki sounded as weary as Konner, almost as tired as Kim.

Kim felt his brothers each reach a hand to his chest and draw it away.

"Got it!" Konner said. Some of his fatigue had left his voice.

"Not all of it." Kim collapsed onto the cold floor, grateful that it leeched some of the fever heat from his face.

Then Pryth lifted a shaking hand and touched his chest, just above his heart.

The fever and pressure left him.

Kim opened his eyes. The fever pulsed again, raw and angry around Pryth.

"I cannot let you die for me," she whispered. She collapsed into unconsciousness.

CHAPTER 13

A VERY FAINT NOISE at the door to his private suite awakened Martin. He had not slept well, knowing his two new guards camped in his bedroom while he stretched out on the Lazy-former® in the main room. This latest intrusion on his rest sent his adrenaline rushing. He bounced out of his recliner and behind the chair without thought. The Lazy-former® shifted back to a standard upright position. He fished an illegal stunner from the folds of the furniture.

Before he could breathe again, a portion of the door slid back. The tall silhouette of a muscular man appeared, backlit by the lights in the corridor.

"Master Martin, we need to talk privately," Quinn whispered.

Martin remained still, listening to his heartbeat.

"You have no reason to trust me yet, Master Martin. I understand. I am here to help. But we need to talk where there is no chance of being overheard." Quinn took one step into Martin's living room. The door slid shut behind him. Only a residual glow from the solar collectors around the bioglass windows distinguished one shadow from another.

Martin crept out from his hiding place, keeping low, working his way around and behind Quinn.

"I offer you my word as an officer in His Majesty's private service, and as a Sam Eyeam, I have come to help you, Master Martin."

"Not a word more," Martin whispered, pressing the stunner against Quinn's jugular. He had to stand on tiptoe and reach awkwardly to keep the weapon in place. "Out the windows into the walled garden." He pushed the Sam Eyeam toward the exit.

Ten steps for Quinn. Fifteen for Martin's shorter legs. He grabbed a robe and threw it over his shoulders as he went. He didn't want to get caught in only his underwear.

Martin pressed his hand against the sensor beside the long window. It slid open noiselessly. No one else could open this door. Not even his mother. Once outside in the garden, open to the night air within the city's dome, he closed the door by pressing against a second sensor that answered only to his palm print and DNA. Then he touched a third sensor. A faint static hummed and echoed around the small green space, fifteen meters to a side, within a tall brick wall. Grass and exotic flowering shrubs filled the space. Martin tended them himself rather than allow a gardener inside his security.

"We can talk now," Martin said. He kept the stunner aimed at Quinn's chest.

"That is some serious security," Quinn said. He glanced at his handheld and turned a tight circle, aiming it at the entire garden including upward toward the atmosphere dome three thousand meters up.

"My mother's people designed the security for her. I tweaked it so that even her stuff can't penetrate it. Another static field around the bedroom door alerts me if the guards in there stir."

"I'm guessing you have reason to be so paranoid."

Martin nodded, unable to voice his biggest fear. "Why are you here?" he asked instead.

"I need to know more about this quest to find your father. Why does your mother object so strongly to you going?"

"Melinda Fortesque sent a Sam Eyeam after him with an assassin's retainer and a locator beacon."

Quinn turned another tight circle that aimed his handheld at every possible shrub where Melinda could have secreted listening devices.

"Even the spy satellites can't see us," Martin advised him.

"Your mother owns the entire planet, including all of the industries and support businesses. Why does she need spy satellites?"

"Melinda doesn't trust anyone. And neither do I."

"My next logical question would be 'Who is your father?'"

Martin thought about it a moment. So Quinn had not overheard his earlier conversation.

What further harm could he do this mission by telling? If Melinda sent Quinn to spy on Martin, then the Sam Eyeam would tell her everything anyway. The name meant only a little more trouble.

"Martin Konner O'Hara."

Quinn whistled softly. "Curiouser and curiouser."

"What is that supposed to mean?"

"Only that we have bit off a lot more trouble than we can chew if we get caught. You and your mother aren't the only ones searching for that man and his brothers. There is a hefty reward for their capture."

"Brothers." For the second time that day he'd heard brothers associated with Konner O'Hara. For three years Martin and Konner had met each summer at camp. Konner acted as favored counselor to Jane, Kurt, and Bruce as well. In all their long talks, Konner had never suggested that he might have a personal reason for befriending Martin. He had never mentioned his family or his history.

Martin had to discover much of that on his own.

"I have uncles?" Hope made Martin's voice squeak. "I have a family besides Melinda?"

"Yeah. Most of them are outlaws. But at this point, I'm guessing living on the run with the O'Hara brothers would be safer than angering your mother."

Another long pause while Martin thought about that piece of information. His mind raced and his heart sang.

"How did you find out your father's name, Martin?" Quinn asked. He still spoke softly. He probably didn't trust Martin's security fully.

That was okay. Martin didn't dare fully trust it either.

"Kurt found Melinda's marriage license on Meditcue II. So far we have no trace of an annulment or divorce."

"How'd he find that?"

"Bruce's father, Bruce Geralds, Sr., is also a Sam Eyeam. He deleted the record of the marriage. Kurt went looking for files that had been deleted on obscure bush planets."

"You kids have access to some kind of major software genius. Galactic Free Market?"

"Four heads are better than one. We do it ourselves."

"What else do you know?"

Suddenly liking this strange man, Martin decided to trust him. For now. He wouldn't grow up like his mother, afraid of everyone, with secrets she dared not expose to the light of day. Quinn had said he was one of the emperor's private agents. If so, he could get the information to the proper authorities and maybe . . . just maybe free Martin from Melinda.

Besides, once Quinn knew what Martin knew, his life was in as much danger from Melinda as any of her enemies, including Martin—her only child and heir.

"We found a dissenting report concerning the accident that killed my grandparents sixteen years ago. It said the ship did not blow up from an internal malfunction. Someone fired upon it. My grandparents were murdered. But the official report that was accepted as the 'true' cause of their deaths holds that the explosion was an accident. The dissenting report was suppressed. Very difficult to find."

"I've read the report."

"Is that why you came? A little late."

"I was sent for another reason, one that I cannot tell you at this moment, but one that is to your advantage. Getting Melinda out of the way can only help all parties concerned. Including your father."

"Did you know that Melinda hired a Sam Eyeam just before the 'accident'? Did you know she paid him more than double the annual salary of the average worker on Aurora? Only one small armed merchant vessel left Aurora on the same day as the accident. That vessel was the only one that could have fired upon my grandparents' cruiser just before they reached the jump point."

"I suspected as much, but I have no proof."

"I do."

"Will you share?"

"When we find my father and both of us are safe."

"Without the proof, neither of you will ever be safe."

"I know."

"Do you have any idea which Sam Eyeam your mother hired?"

Martin clamped his mouth shut and crossed his arms. That was one piece of information he could not allow free of his handheld—which he'd triple encrypted and keyed to his DNA.

"Fine. We'll deal with that later. Now I've cleared it with your mother to take you four kids on a tour of one of her industrial complexes day after tomorrow, the one that makes rides for amusement planets. What she does not know is that the air car I will fly is spaceworthy. We'll use it to dock with the vessel I have in orbit."

"How'd you manage that?" Excitement lit Martin's veins. He was going to get free. Day after tomorrow, he'd be free!

"Never mind. Let's just say it pays to be prepared for any emergency. I always plan an escape route before I commit to a mission. That's how we Sam Eyeams stay alive."

Just before dawn Kim crept up the path to the clearing. If M'Berra had returned his call, Kim had slept through it.

All he wanted was to crawl into bed, pull Hestiia close, and sleep for a week. Defeat as well as exhaustion weighed heavily on his spirit. How could Pryth waste all of his efforts to save her life?

Now the village would be lucky if she lived two more days.

He didn't know how they would cope without the old wisewoman.

And he'd lost his chance to compromise with the IMPs and gain access to the medic and medicine.

He neared the barrier and hummed his mother's favorite lullaby. A shimmer in the air showed him the portal. He stepped through to the seven-acre haven that sheltered Kim and his brothers, Hestiia, Dalleena, and Taneeo in rough cabins and lean-tos. A confusion field generated by the stolen crystal array from *Jupiter* kept the clearing invisible to the outside world.

Faint light from an oil lamp showed beneath the door to the one-room hut he shared with Hes. He paused a moment, wishing he could go to her right away. He needed to place his hand on her swelling belly and feel the life growing within. Sometimes he thought he could communicate with his son this way. Other times he rejoiced in just feeling the strong heartbeat.

Tonight he needed reassurance that Hes and the baby lived. But different duties called him first.

He tiptoed to the rough lean-to on the far side of the clearing. The crude shelter butted right up against the tree that marked the edge of the clearing and the beginning of the force field.

"Taneeo, it's Kim." He rattled the chains of beads hanging over one end of the lean-to.

The man inside remained quiet. Kim had not expected an answer, but politeness required he speak. In nine months, Taneeo had not uttered a word. When prompted, he would eat and drink if someone brought sustenance to his mouth. He could even walk after a fashion if someone held his hand and led him to the latrine or the hot springs for a bath. His eyes refused to focus. As far as Kim could tell, the former priest of the village had no thoughts of his own.

The spirit of the rogue dragon, Hanassa, had possessed Taneeo's mind and body. But Taneeo had proved himself stronger than the dragon. Still, the battle between them had left Taneeo witless, near catatonic.

Kim ducked into the shelter. Taneeo's eyes were closed. In sleep?

Kim did not know if his friend had truly slept in the last nine months or merely feigned it so that the O'Hara clan would leave him alone.

Kim ran his hands swiftly over Taneeo's slight arms and legs. The skin was smooth now, without trace of the exoskeleton he'd grown to accommodate the dragon. "That's an improvement," Kim said under his breath. Then he checked his patient's neck and spine. These, too, showed no trace of the hard cartilage.

"Physically, the spirit of Hanassa has departed, Taneeo. He no longer controls your body. But where has the rogue purple-tip dragon gone? He has to have a body, preferably one that carries his DNA. Which of his bastards does he haunt now?"

"A woman," Taneeo croaked. He turned intelligent eyes to his friend.

"Taneeo?" Kim stared at the man in surprise.

The priest nodded and swallowed deeply.

Kim offered him the nearby jug of water. He needed to prop Taneeo up and hold the vessel to his lips. The priest drank greedily, holding the liquid in his mouth for several seconds before swallowing.

"What happened? What brought you out of the catatonic trance?" Kim asked eagerly.

"Someone. Someone tempted Hanassa away."

"Who?"

"I do not know. You asked me a question. What question did you ask me?"

"Never mind about that. Let me help you up. You need to regain strength and mobility. I'll rouse Hestiia and we'll get you some food."

"I need to . . . ah . . ."

"Yes, that first. Then food. Would you like to sit by the fire?"

"Yes. That would be nice. What question did you ask me?"

"I don't remember."

CHAPTER 14

◆—·—◆—·—◆

"TIME AND TIDE wait for no man. Let's get that boat in the water!" Loki shouted. False dawn barely glimmered along the edge of the horizon far out in the bay. Too restless to stay abed any longer, he rattled the bead chains in front of every hut and cave in the village.

"The weather's fine, the tide is right, and the fish are running!" He marched around and around the central fire pit to the tune of sleepy grumbles and more than a few curses.

On his third circuit, he broadened his path to include the festival pylon, three slender trees stripped of branches and bark tilted into a narrow tripod. Every major event in village life took place at the pylon: marriages, funerals, harvest, planting, first presentation of babies.

After the villagers had fled the IMPs who now command their old home, they had migrated to the base of the cliff where the Stargods fortified and concealed their clearing. Pryth had demanded the pylon's erection before anyone selected a cave or cooked a meal. The pylon meant home more than meals and places to rest a head. On their journey they'd eaten and slept many places without a pylon. This was home. That meant a pylon first, food and sleep later.

Now Pryth lay dying.

Loki refused to think on that.

He looked around to see what was keeping the men from joining him for a day of pitting his mind and muscles against the sea and the fish.

The first shaft of sunlight glinted off the crystalline hide of a dragon parked on his haunches between the path up to the clearing and the path down to the cove.

Loki arrested his neat frantic progress through the village. He gulped in startlement. "Um . . . Loki here." He barely remembered the dragon protocol of introduction.

(Iianthe.) The voice rang through Loki's mind like the deep tolling of an ominous bell.

"Iianthe? The purple-tip?" A second shaft of sunlight revealed a hint of deep purple along the outlines of the dragon and in the series of horns marching from his forehead down his back to his tail.

(You needed me. I came.)

"I did? Um . . . I do?" He hadn't remembered calling a dragon.

(Come. The desert continent is a long way from here.)

"Yeah. Right. Paola and the snakes."

(You need to see the Krakatrice to understand their menace.)

"Krakatrice? Why do you call them that?" Loki modified his urgent steps to a casual stroll as he aimed for the dragon's side. Excitement gathered in his belly. He'd never ridden a dragon alone before. Never had one at his beck and call before. This was almost as thrilling as pushing *Rover* to its limits and evading hostile fire.

(Krakatrice is their name for themselves.)

"And what is the dragons' name for themselves?" Loki climbed up Iianthe's shoulder. He noted that the last vestige of silver had grown out of his short fur. This dragon had matured well in the last year. Iianthe wasn't full size yet, from what he'd heard, but still more than large enough to fly him to the big continent and back without tiring.

(You could not pronounce our word.)

"May I at least hear your word for dragons?"

A mental chuckle tickled the back of Loki's mind. The dragon rose up on all fours and began running and flapping his wings in preparation for flight. As his feet lifted free of the ground, Iianthe loosed a mighty roar/screech/ bellow that nearly shattered Loki's eardrums and certainly woke everyone in the village. A dribble of flame accompanied the dragon speech.

(That is our word for dragon,) Iianthe said. He sounded smug.

Loki ran the sound through his mind. "You're right, I couldn't pronounce it. I presume the bit of flame is part of the speech?"

(Of course.) Iianthe gained altitude and circled around to the east, flying directly into the rising sun.

Two hours later the coastline of the big continent came into view.

"You've been strangely quiet this trip, Iianthe," Loki said over the roar of wind in his ears. He looked all around him, noting the lack of islands, shoals, and reefs between here and the shore. Shipping would be a breeze, pun fully intended, if they could just open up those ports to the hinterland and its mineral resources.

Unfortunately, the deposits of ore were in the hills three-to-five-days'

walk from the port city. The Krakatrice had made travel impossible. No
one caught in the desert without the protection of stout walls survived the
night.

*(Your mind is preoccupied with thoughts of your lady and the problems of fighting
the Krakatrice.)*

"Well, thanks," Loki replied slightly affronted. This dragon seemed altogether too free with mind reading.

(Think on this next time you use your talent to read a mind.)

Loki stuttered and stammered a moment. "You don't like me very much,
do you, Iianthe?"

(Like. Dislike. Two sides of the same Tambootie tree.)

Neither of them said a thing for several wing flaps that drew them ever
closer to land.

"Tambootie tree. Poison and blessing."

*(When two are alike, they see in the other what they do not like about themselves.
Rather than admit the flaw, it is easier to despise it in the other twofold.)*

Loki and the dragon chuckled together.

"So we are both arrogant, adventurous, and asinine."

(Responsible, reverent, and reasonable—upon occasion.)

Another laugh between them.

(Your lady awaits). Iianthe banked and descended, gliding on the air currents that took him closer and closer to the jumble of tightly packed buildings
inside a three-point-five-meter-high wall that described a crescent along a
small bay.

From this elevation the city looked like a waxing moon. Loki saw signs of
construction of a new wall a kilometer outside the original.

Iianthe took a low pass above the city. All eyes turned upward in fear, then
awe at the sight. One feminine figure ran through the gate of the new wall
out toward an empty plain.

The dragon aimed for the woman and settled in front of her. He had to
run the last hundred meters, digging his talons deep into the dirt and raising
his wings high to slow his momentum.

Loki jumped free of the dragon's back even before Iianthe come to a complete stop.

He gathered Paola Sanchez into a tight hug and swung her around in joyful greeting. "Jaysus, I've missed you." Then he kissed her soundly.

She kissed him back. They lingered together for many long moments,
oblivious to the crowd growing around them.

(Ahem.)

Loki couldn't ignore the dragon clearing his throat. He wondered how
much flame had accompanied the sound.

(You have things to see and learn. Bring your lady,) Iianthe commanded.

"Today I am at your service, Iianthe." Loki described a sweeping bow, then scooped Paola up into his arms, deposited her on the dragon's back, and clambered up behind her.

"Loki? What is going on?" she asked inspecting the dragon with her eyes while she slapped her hips in search of the stun pistol and dagger she usually wore.

(You will not need weapons today. I will protect you.)

Paola shook her head. Her thick dark braid swung across her back.

"Kind of takes a little getting used to," Loki said, tugging the braid with affection.

"That was the dragon talking to me?"

"Not just any dragon. This is Iianthe, the only purple-tipped dragon in the nimbus. There can only be one purple-tip at a time. Say hello to him and give him your name. Dragons are big on names."

"Hello, Iianthe. I am Paola Sanchez, leader of the Amazon troops."

(Greetings, Paola Sanchez. Iianthe here. Hold tight. We have much to do before the sun sets.) Without further warning Iianthe took six running steps, sweeping his wings strongly to build lift and speed.

Loki barely got his butt settled between two spinal horns before they were airborne. He wrapped one arm around Paola in front of him and clung to a purple horn with the other.

A vast landscape of terrible beauty unrolled beneath them.

"I love this place," Paola said quietly. "I've been on a dozen bush worlds and three civilized ones, but none of them compare to this place for sheer majesty."

Loki could only shrug his shoulders. Most places were the same to him. He liked this planet better than most, but home to him was aboard *Sirius* flying the vast distances between stars.

Within one hundred klicks of the port city, Iianthe brought them to a rough landing beside a shallow ravine. He rippled his back in invitation for his passengers to debark.

"What are we supposed to see and learn here?" Loki asked. He peered uneasily at the near barren gray-green dirt spotted with volcanic rocks of black and dark red. An occasional low and spiky shrub struggled to survive in the lee of those boulders.

(Dig.) Iianthe commanded.

"In case you didn't notice, we didn't bring any tools," Loki said. Hands on hips he stared defiantly at the dragon.

"In case you didn't notice, the temperature is near forty-five degrees centigrade," Paola added. "We didn't pack any water. Working in this heat could kill us."

(Dig.) Iianthe demonstrated by scratching the dirt with one huge paw, talons fully extended. He had a hole nearly a meter deep and two long at the head of the ravine by the time Loki and Paola managed to do more than scratch the surface. He looked as if he were trying to extend the ravine.

"Uh, Loki, the soil here is different than on the surface," Paola said, holding two handfuls, one the ubiquitous gray-green, the other darker and richer.

"It feels different, too. It's damp." Loki dug with more enthusiasm. "Kim should be the one you brought here, Iianthe. He's the professor who knows about dirt and planting and such."

(He would not come.)

"You're right. He won't leave Hestiia any longer than he has to until she gives birth." Loki dug some more.

(Step back!) Iianthe commanded.

Loki and Paola scrambled for the sides of the ravine and climbed out just as Iianthe pulled aside one last clump of dirt.

A trickle of water burst free, beneath one of the rocks. The tiny rivulet grew to a sizable stream as Loki watched, jaw hanging open.

"Where did that come from?" he asked no one in particular. "If there is this much water beneath the surface, why is this place a desert?"

(The Krakatrice. They cannot live near water. Over the centuries they have moved mountains to cover all the water on this continent.)

"I need a pump and a fire hose. We can take seawater and spray the bloody snakes to keep them away from the city!" Paola chortled.

(Not enough.) Iianthe shook his mighty head. *(The matriarch can survive water. You must kill the matriarch in order to subdue the rest. Come, there is more.)*

Once more Loki and Paola climbed atop the dragon's back and flew deeper into the desert.

Once they were fully airborne, Loki suffered a moment of dizzy disorientation. He had to cling tightly to Paola and the dragon to keep his balance. Closing his eyes helped.

When he opened them again, he noticed how the terrain below them changed. A great basin fell away from the surrounding broken and lumpy ground.

"Is that water?" Loki pointed toward a distant glint of silver against the gray-green background. She shook her head as if she, too, emerged from a few heartbeats of upset.

(Yes.)

In moments the dragon landed beside a small lake. Loki and Paolo dismounted slowly, cautiously.

"Must be spring fed to survive the dirt movement of the Krakatrice," Paolo scuffed the dirt with her boots. A small cloud of dust rose up.

"Barely enough water to support six low shrubs let alone any game," Loki mused. "Is this a meteor impact crater?"

(Look at the location. See what was a long time ago.)

Loki looked up toward the cliffs that defined a rough circle around the tiny lake. A full klick away in all directions. Cliffs that suddenly grew a lot closer.

And the entire basin filled with water.

"Run! We're going to drown."

CHAPTER 15

KAT AWOKE RESTED and aware. She only suffered a fuzzy transition between sleep and reality when she came out of *the* nightmare. This morning her body wanted to linger with the stranger's arms wrapped around her and his head upon her breast.

Sometime during the night she had scooched down and stretched out. The two of them had shared the narrow cot quite well, comfortable with the implied intimacy.

A stir of activity outside the med cabin convinced her she should not be found mussed and drowsy with an unknown man. If he'd been an officer from *Jupiter,* even a noncom, no one would have thought twice about her choice. A few moments of memorizing his face with her fingertips had revealed to her that this man had not come to the planet aboard *Jupiter.* Three hundred men and women trapped together on a midsized spaceship for months at a time were not too many for her to recognize everyone on sight.

She tested her weight on the injured ankle. It held, even if it did shoot lances of fire upward. After splashing water on her face from a basin and tidying her uniform, she limped out to join the mess crew at the cooking fire.

Today she needed to corner Commander Leonard about negotiating with her brothers. Konner had rescued her. He'd kept his promise to her. A niggle of family loyalty had crept into her thoughts during the night.

Surely they could find some compromise so that Loki, Konner, and Kim would allow Kat to get a message off to IMP Central for a rescue ship. Perhaps if the O'Haras declared themselves a free and sovereign planet of the Galactic Free Market they could avoid judicial punishment. They might also avoid droves of land-hungry colonists. But they'd never keep everyone out. Progress and contact with the rest of the galaxy were a given.

The mess chief handed her a mug of something that resembled coffee in both flavor and texture. They might call it coffee, but it did not give her the satisfying jolt of the real thing. This roasted root brew was all they had. They'd run out of the coffee beans four months ago. The hydroponics tanks were too small to waste precious space on coffee bushes.

And she'd lost the last tank that might have given them a little leeway in what they grew. Chances of salvaging the tank and the crashed lander were slim. They just did not have enough active fuel cells.

"Welcome back to the land of the living," Commander Leonard said. She smiled brightly and saluted the mess crew with her own mug of hot coffee. For once, she'd left off the dramatic black patch over her left eye. She kept her left lid closed though. The skin around the socket had lost the bruised look. All trace of broken bones around the damaged eye seemed healed.

Kat looked closely into Amanda Leonard's right eye, searching for signs of the harridan who had screamed at her over the comm unit to track *Jupiter*'s explosive demise. Today Commander Leonard looked sane and cheerful, ready and eager to tackle the chores of the day. The captain opened her left eye briefly, then squinted as light penetrated. The blue iris did not track properly and the pupil seemed unnaturally dilated in the morning sunshine.

"It's good to be back," Kat replied cautiously. She looked around suspiciously and found Lieutenant Commander M'Berra hovering close by, as if he didn't want to get too far from Leonard should she begin raving again.

"I look forward to your report, Kat. I think I'll go out with the foragers today. We need . . . things. Time to get to know our new home. Do you have any recommendations where I should start?"

Kat looked down at the shorter woman in surprise. Her captain had not left Base Camp once in the nine months they'd been here. She had not eaten native foods. She had insisted upon strict military discipline, patrols, and watches. And she wore the black patch like a badge of honor—a reminder to one and all that the O'Hara brothers who had wounded her were their enemy. Judicial protocol no longer seemed enough for her. She wanted revenge.

"Perhaps you should get to know the locals in the next village. If we make friends there, they can help us survive. They might even lead us to the O'Haras. It's only a three-hour hike," Kat said. That was a three-hour hike for her, with her long legs and boundless energy—when she didn't have a deep burn on her ankle. For Leonard, the walk would take closer to four or five, especially since she still wore soft ship boots with barely any protective sole.

"The locals. Yes. I have visited them. Perhaps we should renew our acquaintance before we conscript them to plow and plant for us."

"Renew your acquaintance, sir? Conscript?" Kat asked, startled. That sounded very much like a plot to enslave the locals. A plot that had been hatching in Leonard's brain for many months. When had she become acquainted with them in the first place?

"Certainly. Oh, and call me H . . . Amanda, Kat. We have to forge a new society now that *Jupiter* is gone. *My* Marines will help." The captain turned abruptly and ambled over to inspect the hydroponics tanks.

"What happened yesterday while I was gone?" Kat asked the air.

"Nothing unusual," M'Berra replied. He stretched and scratched as he yawned. "I need coffee."

Medic Lotski emerged from M'Berra's cabin. She looked sleep tousled and relaxed for the first time in weeks.

"Nice to see I wasn't the only one who shared a cot last night," Kat murmured.

Gentian emerged from the med cabin. He stretched forward to his full (and considerable) length on his front paws, with his rear and tail high. His talons dug deeply into the packed dirt. Then he slung forward, lowering his back, nose reaching for the sky while he stretched his back legs. This gymnastic maneuver complete he opened his mouth in a huge yawn, revealing very long and sharp teeth. More teeth than any normal cat had a right to have.

Kat watched in horror as the tips of his blue/black wings escaped their protective folds of skin. She didn't know why she had to keep the true nature of this beast secret, but she did.

"What in the nine hells of Perdition's rings is that?" Amanda Leonard screeched and pointed at the cat.

Gentian's wing tips disappeared and the cat slung to the ground, ears flat against his head, and his nose working overtime.

"He's just a cat who followed me home last night," Kat said. She moved to stand between Gentian and the captain.

"Get out of here! No cats on my ship. No cats, ever, of any kind." Both of Leonard's eyes grew wild, riveted upon the cat. She began to pull at her neat black hair.

M'Berra moved faster than Kat thought possible for a human. He grabbed the captain by the shoulders and shook her. "Snap out of it, Amanda," he commanded in his deep voice that reverberated down Kat's spine.

Sanity returned to Leonard's eyes. She slumped beneath M'Berra's grasp. "My God, what did I do this time?" she whispered. Her left eye closed once more.

"I can't cover for you much longer, Amanda," M'Berra warned. "Let Cheney Lotski treat you."

Kat noted that the medic had worked her way around the campfire behind their captain. She held a hypo spray discreetly behind her back. She came up on Amanda's left, her blind side. How many times had this happened in the last nine months? Kat knew the captain had become increasingly erratic. Now she showed many symptoms of true insanity.

Without the commander, even as a figurehead, the crew had not a chance in the universe to unite and capture the O'Hara brothers' ship *Sirius* to get back to civilization.

Yet, all these months that the crew had been awaiting Amanda Leonard's orders to mount an expedition to capture the three brothers and gain access to *Sirius,* the captain had delayed, stalled, and prevaricated because if she ever did get back to civilization she would no longer have the O'Haras to blame for everything that had gone wrong in her life.

Nor would Kat.

Kat's breath came in short sharp pants. Her chest constricted. She had trouble swallowing that realization.

"No one is going to track down those men unless I lead them," Kat said under her breath. "I'm the only one who can find them. I've got to make plans now."

Would they believe her offer of compromise? Would they even accept her as a legitimate negotiator for *Jupiter*'s captain and crew?

Hanassa withdrew reluctantly from the Amanda woman. She had accepted his strength and insight without much struggle. But he could only push her so far before the black man and the medic drugged her body senseless. Perhaps Amanda Leonard was not the proper person to host his body.

He decided he'd like to be a woman this time. Their bodies responded to external stimulation with so much more awareness than a man's. Sex within one of them might prove very interesting and much more satisfying than the quick release granted to males.

He needed to look around some more, though. The Cyndi body still seemed the most likely person to help him regain control of this world. Not only did she have the cunning to succeed, the Stargods held her hostage. Hanassa wanted proximity to the three brothers.

They were first on his list to be sacrificed to the god Simurgh. He could almost taste their blood, sweetened by revenge.

"Why are you packing for an extended overland journey when there are aircraft of varying configurations sitting in the next meadow?" the stranger asked Kat. He scratched idly at the bandages where his IVs had penetrated his skin.

Kat looked up from stashing extra socks between other essential items in a survival pack. "Who are you and what business is it of yours?" she snarled at him.

She'd hoped to keep this reconnaissance mission secret from M'Berra and Leonard. But if the stranger knew, then everyone at Base Camp knew.

"Bruce Geralds, Senior." He held out his right hand in greeting while leaning heavily on a crude walking stick with the other.

"Nice to meet you, Geralds. Lieutenant JG Kat Talbot." Kat went back to finding a place for one more pair of clean underwear without shaking his hand.

"Thought you'd be more friendly after we slept together," Geralds said with a smirk.

"We did not . . . well, I guess we did. But that does not make us lovers, or friends, or buddies." She stood up and hefted the weight of the pack. Eighteen kilos. Too heavy. What could she toss?

"Your journey is my business because you are going after the O'Hara brothers. So am I."

"You aren't going anywhere real soon. I saw how cut up your feet are." Kat sank cross-legged to the packed-dirt floor of the cabin she shared with three other women. Resolutely, she began pulling everything out of the pack and inspecting it. Silently, she sorted the contents into three piles: essential, needful, and desirable. Unfortunately, the only thing that fell into the final category was the clean underwear which weighed nearly nothing.

One item at the bottom of the pack had to go with her, just as the braided hair bracelet she wore would always go with her.

"I was hired by Melinda Fortesque to retrieve her husband, Martin Konner O'Hara, in time for their son's fourteenth birthday," Geralds said quietly. "I've missed the due date, but the least I can do is take the man back to his wife so she knows he's not dead."

"Melinda Fortesque? The woman everyone in the galaxy loves to hate?"

"One and the same."

"I thought they were divorced, or the marriage was annulled or something." Kat tried to remember Loki's precise words when he told her they had a nephew.

He'd said that Konner had a son . . . nothing more. Now Konner claimed he'd married Dalleena. Kat had never questioned the legality of that union until now.

"No divorce. No annulment, according to Melinda Fortesque. She paid me very well to find the man she loves. I pride myself on completing my missions."

"You're a Sam Eyeam," Kat said flatly.

He nodded briefly.

"Where's your ship?"

"A dragon blasted my shuttle with fire. Destroyed it completely."

"What about your ship? A shuttle can't withstand a jump, doesn't have enough room inside for a crystal drive to take you through jump."

"I hid my solo merchant vessel behind the moon."

"I'd have found it when I scanned for the *Sirius* from *Jupiter*'s orbit,"

"No, you wouldn't. I stole some technology from Konner O'Hara. *Son and Heir* is shielded with a confusion field."

"Just like Kim's clearing, and the *Sirius*," Kat mused. "Come on." She sprang up in one smooth motion. "If you know the technology, then you know how to find a similar field and break through it." She grabbed her pack and his free hand and started marching.

"What's the hurry? You've waited nine months." He dug in his heels and refused to follow her. He had enough strength to keep her from dragging him.

"We are going to take a fighter five hundred klicks south of here. If we don't leave today, some other pilot will make an excuse to fly and use up our dwindling fuel."

"May I walk on my own to the fighter? Slowly?"

"Yes, of course." Her own ankle did not want to hurry either. "I'd better take some more supplies. We might be gone a couple of days."

"Good idea."

"You never said where you have been for nine months and why you came back raving about cannibals." Kat slowed her pace to match his painful hobble across Base Camp to the hydroponics tanks.

"Konner's pet dragon knocked me out and flew me to the extreme west of this island continent. He dumped me with a tribe of wanderers who call themselves Rovers." He clamped his mouth shut and refused to say more.

"How long have you been walking?" She slowed even more.

"Too long." He jerked his hand out of hers.

"Okay, I won't press you. But you have to talk about it sometime. If not to me, then to Lotski or M'Berra. Or maybe even one of the dragons. You'd be surprised at the wisdom behind their cryptic words."

Irythros had pulled memories from Kat that shifted her entire perspective. Mum and Kat's brothers were not to blame for abandoning her. But if she released her anger toward them, then she had to shift the blame to someone else.

Herself.

"Let's get moving before M'Berra stops us." She forged ahead, leaving Geralds to catch up as best he could.

"You aren't going anywhere today, Kat Talbot." M'Berra stepped squarely between Kat and the food supplies. His black skin gleamed in the spring sunshine. He glared at her. "We mount this expedition as a team, with plans and backup. I've locked up the fuel supplies for all of the aircraft. No one goes off on their own. Even you, Kat."

"I was only going to do reconnaissance," she protested.

"Not alone and not without backup."

"But . . ."

"No buts. I am in charge now and we are going to do this right. I have my own plans for the O'Hara brothers. Now get your butt back to the med cabin. Neither of you are cleared for any activity until Lotski gives the okay."

Kat hesitated. Frantically, she sought an argument to convince her senior officer.

"Move it, Kat, or I'll carry you back to your bed and lock you in."

CHAPTER 16

✦ —— · —— ✦ —— · —— ✦

"WHAT KIND OF SUMMER vacation is this? Your mom said you had homework. *Homework!*" Bruce exploded into Martin's suite followed closely by Jane, Kurt, and, of course, Quinn. They all looked damp, as if just emerging from the pool.

"Melinda never takes a vacation and doesn't see why I need one," Martin explained as he fiddled with the programming of his pet project.

Machine language marched across the holo screen in an arcane order that only Martin understood.

Kurt stared openmouthed at the symbols. "What in the name of the Holy Mother is that?"

Martin closed the programming window, then stood up from his Lazy-former®. "Scaramouch, show latest shipping route map," he told his personal computer.

"Scaramouch?" Quinn lifted one eyebrow in query.

"Personal hero," Bruce replied. His mouth worked as he suppressed a giggle. "Marty'd be a rated fencing champ in foil and epeé if Melinda ever let him off planet long enough to compete."

Martin smiled, too. He hadn't had much to laugh about these last nine months. Ever since he'd discovered just how long Bruce's father had worked for Melinda and how much he got paid. No wonder a Sam Eyeam had enough money to send Bruce to the most exclusive summer camp in the empire.

He turned his attention back to the holo screen where his friends stood silently while two fencing figures moved back and forth across it. Their blades thrust, parried, riposted, parried again, back and forth, back and forth. Quinn stepped closer and examined the silent images.

"Did you program this?" he asked Martin.

"Yes," the boy replied.

"I can't fault their technique, or yours." Quinn shook his head in amazement. "I would enjoy a bout with you, Master Martin, if we have time."

"Melinda will give us time. She postponed our tour of the amusement park factory."

"Indefinitely," Jane Q groused. "Do you think she suspects something?"

Martin glared at her. Despite all his security devices, he never knew when and if his mother would hack through them. Nothing in the palace was safe from her scrutiny.

"What is taking so long?" Quinn asked. He began pacing in front of the fencers, mimicking their moves with precision.

"The program is huge, constantly updating data. I had to pull memory and power from every system in the palace—except Melinda's."

At last one of the figures on the screen stabbed his opponent. Realistic blood burst upon the scene as the defeated fencer collapsed. The drops of blood spattered outward, spread, flashed, and became the stars in a three-dimensional, if not proportionally accurate, map of known space. Some of the stars remained red, others turned green or blue. The vast majority remained white.

Quinn walked through the map examining configurations. "Earth," he said pointing to the blue star at the center of the holograph.

Martin nodded.

"So the other blues are GTE." He continued examining the points of light. "That would make GFM green and the Kree Empire red."

"White is uninhabitable or no known valuable resource," Martin added.

They all watched as a group of stars changed from blue to red.

"I guess the war with the Kree is heating up in that sector." Quinn shook his head.

The stars in question flashed green, then blue, and back to red.

"I haven't accessed the map in a few weeks. The data is catching up. That cluster is the Murgatroyd Alliance. Each of the four star systems has a jump point and inhabitable planets. They change hands an average of three times a year," Martin explained. Then he slouched in his Lazy-former® and waited for his friends and Quinn to finish their inspection.

"What are we looking for?" Bruce asked. He traced a chain of green stars that seemed to penetrate GTE space. He whistled in amazement as another star, much closer to Earth, changed from blue to green. The war with the Kree wasn't the only war the GTE had to fight.

"There is a blank spot here," Quinn said pointing to the anomaly Martin had found when he first constructed the map. "It seems a logical extension to explore this area from adjoining sectors."

"What about jump points?" Jane Q asked, spinning around and watching everything in amazement.

"Scaramouch, show last known position of the O'Hara distress beacon," Martin called out.

An orange light appeared dead center in the anomaly.

Quinn whistled again.

"Two beacons were recorded broadcasting from that area. Both ceased to function within a few weeks of each other," Martin explained.

"How did they get in there?" Kurt asked. "That's a lot of empty space in between."

"A lot of unmapped space," Quinn corrected. "A lot of maps were lost three hundred years ago when the old republic collapsed. A lot of human colonies got lost at the same time. We haven't found half of them yet. I wonder . . ." He continued walking around and around the area.

All of them remained silent for several moments, puzzling out a number of questions. While they did, Martin noted that Aurora blinked from blue to green. His mother must be having fun with the diplomatic envoys from Earth.

"Scaramouch, show jump points," Quinn said. The bodyguard kept returning to the blank anomaly, tracing lines from other star systems toward the blinking light of the distress beacon.

Nothing happened.

Martin repeated the order. "The computer is locked on my voice print only."

"Good security. Won't keep a dedicated hacker out, though."

"It will slow them down long enough for the system to alert me to the attempt."

While they spoke, a number of purple lights began blinking. Delicate trails of violet mist connected them in an intricate web.

Jane traced one of the trails, eyes wide in awe at the amount of space the jump point had to fold between one end and the other.

At the edge of the vacant anomaly, a violet smudge wandered randomly around the sector.

Quinn's gaze riveted on the smudge.

"That isn't supposed to happen." He pointed at the weird jump point.

"Scientists haven't been able to explain the physics of jump points, let alone their existence, since the Kree first used them to invade Earth over five hundred years ago," Martin explained. "Why can't there be an unstable jump point? Why can't there be an entire sector that's been lost to human exploration because the jump point wanders and doesn't show on normal sensors very well?"

"How'd you program your system to find that thing?" Quinn took out his handheld and began making calculations.

"When you eliminate the impossible—like getting a beacon deep into that area without a jump point—what remains, no matter how improbable, must be the truth." Martin smiled.

The program shimmered. Melinda's holo image appeared in the middle of it, clear enough that she looked to be standing there.

"Martin. You will transfer this program to my system immediately," his mother said blandly. "I need to explain some things to my guests."

She disappeared as abruptly as she had appeared.

"Not even a please or thank you?" Quinn asked.

"Melinda gave up manners years ago. Have you got enough data to navigate to the area of the wandering jump point?"

"No. The program is huge. I'd like to copy it to my ship."

"Sorry. It won't copy. I don't know why." Martin did know why, but he could not explain that now. "It transfers in one lump or not all, erasing all trace of itself at its previous location." But the transfers to backup were always incomplete.

"How much time do you have before your mom returns?" Kurt asked. He, too, tapped data into his handheld.

Bruce and Jane whipped out their own instruments.

The door slid open. Melinda stood there, impatiently tapping her foot. "Martin, I know you want to show off for your friends. But I need this program now." She turned away and marched back toward her own quarters.

"She'll want to start seeing it download into her system by the time she gets back to her office."

"Damn. That's not enough time. I need more information." Quinn ran his hands across his scalp, leaving the straight brown hair standing on end in an unruly mass. He suddenly looked vulnerable . . . and more likable.

"I think I've got most of the important stuff memorized. But I've got to start transferring it now. Keep recording as long as possible." Martin moved to the wall controls and reluctantly punched in the codes to send the map to his mother.

Kat lay fuming on the cot in the med cabin. M'Berra had ordered restraints to keep Kat from taking off on her own. The first officer from *Jupiter* didn't trust her. With good cause. She had no intention of remaining in camp any longer than it would take her to find a way out of the webbed fabric straps holding her wrists to the cot.

If put to the choice, she wasn't sure she could choose between the welfare of her crew or the freedom of her brothers. All she truly wanted was a chance to get back to civilization.

At the moment it looked as if she might have to do that all on her own.

Even Gentian had deserted her. The flywacket had curled up against Bruce Geralds' feet and started purring.

Kat worried the straps with her mind as well as friction against the smooth metal cot frame. Once she'd opened electronic force bracelets with her mind. That time, Loki O'Hara had used the criminal restraints on her to keep her from blocking his and his brothers' sabotage of *Jupiter*.

How had she done it? She stopped wiggling for a moment to think. Her mind whirled with a dozen images of that long day sitting in the passageway near the shuttle bays and cargo holds of *Jupiter*. The gravity had been uncomfortably heavy in the outer reaches of the spinning ship. She and Loki had talked quietly about their childhood together before the disaster that had separated them. Kim had sat with them, nursing a numb leg—she had shot him with a stunner. Konner had spent that time stealing the king stone from the crystal array. Without the king stone the ship's power grid went berserk, orbit had decayed, communications had been severed.

Later, Loki had stolen the rest of the array for some unknown purpose, further disrupting the ship's power. Discipline had broken down when Judge Balinakas had ordered evacuation, overriding commander Leonard's attempts to keep the ship working. He'd used the short time the captain had been unconscious as a result of a fight with Konner O'Hara—the fight that had cost her the use of her left eye—to assume control. The rivalry between the judicial personnel and ship's crew had plagued Leonard ever since she took command of the judicial cruiser. Balinakas had triumphed at that moment, but not totally.

He and his people—lawyers, clerks, and anthropologists—had never found their way to Base Camp to fully assume command over the crew. The Marines—the enforcement arm of both the ship's crew and the judiciary—had pledged their undying loyalty to Amanda Leonard. Now she had no one to answer to for her insanity other than Jetang M'Berra.

And Kat.

How had Kat managed to open the force bracelets? Why had strips of conductive plastic linked by an electrode responded to her wishes.

Somehow she must have found the precise frequency of the electronic key and then hummed it.

These straps had no electronics. Instead they were woven with spider silk that molded and clung to the skin, and fastened with a molecular bond. They needed a special solvent to open them for reuse. Or a sharp blade. Kat had neither.

In most tasks she had become ambidextrous, but her choice of dominant hand was always the left. Kat took a deep breath and turned her eyes and her mind to the left strap. She concentrated on the nearly invisible overlap and bond.

The longer she stared at the strap the deeper became a pain between her eyes.

(*Use the ley lines,*) the disembodied voice came into the back of her head. (*Ley lines power your magic as the omniscium powers crystals.*)

That was a new thought. Kat knew that omniscium was the key ingredient in the bath for forming the crystal matrix for star drives. But she did not realize that the elusive element also powered them.

Crystals had to be tuned. So, perhaps, did the ley lines. She lay still a moment and tried to open her senses to the "tune" of the mysterious silver-blue lines.

She heard only a faint disharmonic buzz between her ears. Not a buzz. Gentian's loud purr. It was out of harmony with Kat's inner senses.

"Mbbrt?" Gentian woke up with a start. The constant dull roar of his purring ceased abruptly. The big black cat yawned and stretched. Then he jumped off of Geralds' cot and ambled over to Kat's. He butted his head against Kat's fingers for an ear scratch.

"Sorry, Gentian. The fingers don't work right."

The cat reached up and sniffed the straps. He licked Kat's fingertips gently and sniffed some more. The tips of his wings protruded a tiny bit.

Satisfied he knew what to do, Gentian started gnawing at the webbing where it looped around the metal frame of the cot.

"Smart cat," Geralds whispered.

Kat watched the flywacket work at the tough fabric rather than reply.

Geralds sat up and inspected his feet. "What the . . . ?"

Kat watched him twist into new contortions to see his soles. "Care to share the strange phenomena?"

"The cuts are healed." He swung his legs over the side of the cot and tested his weight on his bare feet. "Some of them were quite deep and needed stitches. Now they are closed without traces of scarring. And the stitches fell out."

He bounced up and down on tiptoe then took three dancing steps toward Kat.

"What kind of miracle did your medic work?"

A strange sense of satisfaction radiated out from Gentian, engulfing Kat in goodwill.

Did you have something to do with that? she asked Gentian.

(*Ultrasonic waves,*) the flywacket replied.

Of course. The original U.S. healing unit was based upon a cat's purr.

"What are you two smiling at?" Geralds asked.

"Nothing important," Kat replied.

Gentian reached up and touched her nose with his. An image of the webbing dissolving flashed through her mind.

"How?"

He showed her again.

She concentrated.

"You want some help with those restraints?" Geralds bent over her.

"I think I have it." With the words came the thought. The strap flopped open.

"Uh . . . uh . . ." Geralds stammered. "How? How did you do that?" He backed away from her, hands at his sides. He looked ready to flee on his newly healed bare feet.

"Magic," she whispered. She tried it again with her right hand. The straps remained firm. Gentian slid under the cot and gnawed on it a bit. His drool coated the bond.

Kat tried concentrating on the strap again. She visualized the bond dissolving—as if the flywacket's saliva was a solvent. The restraint opened.

With a sigh of relief she sat up and worked her ankles free. "Don't suppose you could spare a few of those sonorous purrs on my ankle, Gentian?"

(Later. You need to leave here. Now.)

"Right. It's broad daylight. I suspect M'Berra has posted an armed guard."

The flywacket shook himself all over and poked his nose out the door. He scooted backward at twice the speed, seeking the safety of the shadows beneath Kat's cot.

Kat felt her companion's broadcast of alarm as a cold vibration up her spine. The fine hairs stood on end and her teeth ached from clenching.

Consciously, she relaxed her jaw and approached the doorway. She flattened herself beside the opening and peered out.

Amanda Leonard stood near the center of the village with a long whip in her hand. She snapped the flayed tip against the ground in agitation. Before her stood twenty locals in a loose clump. They faced her proudly, defiance written all over their faces.

"You will obey me," Leonard snarled. "I am master here and I command you to plow and plant my fields." The whip in her hand snaked out and lashed the arm of the nearest local.

Three Marines behind the locals shifted their stun rifles, pointedly removing the safeties.

"We obey only the Stargods and our consciences," a heavily muscled man of middle years said quietly. He did not even look at the welt on his arm. His comrades nodded in agreement.

"Then you will die." Leonard replied, equally calm and quiet. She raised her arm, preparing the whip.

"Stand down, Commander Leonard," Kat commanded. She marched out from the protection of the med cabin. "Slavery and corporal punishment went out with the dark ages. You have broken about six major GTE laws in the last two minutes." She grabbed Leonard's wrist, controlling the captain's grip on the whip.

Kat's fingers sought the pressure point just below Leonard's thumb that would force her superior officer to open her hand.

"All life is sacred. We don't eat meat because it takes a life, even the life of a mere animal. Just to threaten death is punishable by mind-wipe," she added for emphasis.

"We make our own laws here, Lieutenant Talbot. Now you stand down or face the consequences." A Marine pressed his stun rifle against Kat's jugular.

CHAPTER 17

L OKI GRABBED PAOLA'S hand and lunged for the first foothold he could find. Together, they scrambled to the top of the cliff. Panting and bewildered, Loki searched for a trace of Iianthe, or the desert that had been here a few heartbeats before.

Wild cattle with their spreading horns and shaggy red coats ambled toward them across a verdant plain. Deer and a myriad variety of game dotted the landscape, grazing contentedly.

"Um, Loki," Paola gulped.

He turned around and saw the entire basin filled with clear water. What had been a cliff was now the defining edge of an inland sea.

All of the animals suddenly froze in place. Individuals lifted their muzzles to sniff the air. Some silent communication spread among them. Herds scattered in the blink of an eye. Only the cattle remained. The big bull turned and took a defensive stance while his ladies bunched together, taking turns drinking.

A huge cat—bigger than any wolf or gray cave bear Loki had seen in the land of the Coros—with yellow fur spotted with gray splotches slunk toward the water, alert, wary, predatory. It opened its mouth, revealing saber like teeth as long as Loki's forearm.

He and Paola each reached for daggers and stun guns.

(That will not be necessary,) Iianthe chuckled in the back of Loki's mind.

The lush landscape disappeared in the blink of an eye.

Loki stumbled to his knees. Paola kept her feet but had to extend her arms to find a new balance.

"What happened? We were somewhere else and then back here. What happened, Iianthe!" Loki demanded.

(I gave you a dragon dream of what was; what the Krakatrice have destroyed.)

"A dream?" Loki cocked his head and stared at the dragon, puzzled.

"No dream. I was there. I smelled the water and the grass and the animal musk. That bull was ready to mate. I could smell him five klicks away and so could every cow in the herd," Paola insisted.

(Thus is the power of a dragon dream. We do not give them lightly. The entire nimbus agreed that you needed to see what was in order to understand the true menace of the Krakatrice.)

"Okay, we saw what happens when you deprive a continent of water. Take me back to the city. It's time I organized my ladies into an offensive," Paola said.

"Wait." Loki held up his hand signaling a moment of quiet while he thought. "All animals need water to survive. How do the snakes continue without water?"

(They derive moisture from their prey.)

"But there isn't any prey left!"

Silence from the dragon for many long heartbeats.

(Come. You will see and understand.)

"I want some answers, Iianthe," Loki said. He remained in place, hands on hips, determined to be just as stubborn as the dragon.

(I have not the words. I must show you.)

Fuming, Loki and Paola climbed aboard once more. Iianthe took his time launching into the air and flying south and west. Not so very far, into another huge basin, this time without a lake at the center.

Instead, a tall finger of rock and soil poked up toward the heavens. Around the finger, the matriarch of the Krakatrice coiled her entire length. Her head rested atop the edifice, her tail at its base. She looked about her, a true monarch surveying her queendom.

Loki whistled. "She must be thirty meters long!"

"Wh . . . what is that on the ground?" Paola asked. She closed her eyes and gulped.

Loki looked more closely at the black tangle of snakes surrounding the matriarch's throne. He saw the glisten of white bone and bloody flesh. The Krakatrice had found prey.

Then he spotted a faint trace of silver wing and a blue horn. He gagged. "Jaysus, they've caught a young dragon."

(When our nestlings first learn to fly, they are vulnerable outside the nest,) Iianthe said. His mental voice choked on a sob.

"Those are big snakes. One dragonet will not fill their bellies for long," Paola pointed out. She sounded frightened.

Loki had never seen or heard of anything that could break through her courage. He held her more tightly until he could feel her heartbeat against his own chest. He tried to find comfort for them both in this little sign that they both lived.

(We guard our young carefully. But the matriarch is clever. She can fly. She seduces the young with adventure. She pushes them to fly beyond their strength to return home. Then she strikes. Our numbers grow thin because fewer and fewer of our young mature.)

"Oh, my God!" Paola gasped and turned her face away.

"What?" Loki searched for the source of her distress. He clamped his hand on his dagger, knowing full well the long knife would provide small and inadequate defense against the monsters below.

"Th . . . there." She pointed at the edge of the tangle of snakes without looking.

Loki gagged again as he watched the matriarch strangle with her tail one of the larger snakes. A bevy of her young slithered over the fallen elder and began devouring it.

(After a battle, no matter how many you kill, you will never find the corpse of a Krakatrice.)

"They can't keep this up for long. There aren't enough dragons to feed them for long. They can't cannibalize themselves without endangering their numbers. What then?" Horror began to eat away at Loki's insides. He had a feeling he knew what Iianthe would answer.

(Tomorrow night they will grow hungry again. They will attack the city. Your three-and-one-half-meter walls will not be high enough to keep them out for long.)

"Take me home, I have Amazons and defenses to organize. I think I can devise a manual pump. But a fire hose eludes me. Any idea how to kill the matriarch?" Paola said.

(If I knew I would not be allowed to tell you. Dragons may not kill one of their own.)

"The Krakatrice are not dragons," Loki insisted.

(They are our cousins. We have promised the God of All never to kill one of our own.)

"Then take me home, too. I have to settle the problem of the IMPs before I can divert more resources to help Paola and her Amazons. But I'll set Konner and Kim on the problem of the pump and fire hose. Will you take them to Paola, Iianthe?"

A mental nod of agreement. *(Knowledge is your best weapon. Use what I have shown you today wisely.)*

•———◆——— •

Cyndi marched restlessly around the festival pylon. She walked east to west. This was the path the primitives danced during their mating ritual in the early spring.

Cyndi wasn't in the mood to find a mate. She had one waiting for her back home. She thought longingly of her gentle Eric. He didn't have a lot of ambition or political acumen, but he loved her.

Right now she needed some of that quiet love, a soft touch of reassurance, and a listening ear. More than she needed a bath and clean clothes. She'd had more than enough "adventure" to last a lifetime.

She couldn't be sure, but she thought she'd seen a dragon this morning. A big one with royal purple on its wing veins and spinal horns. Only that colored outline had told her she wasn't imagining the shimmering light distortion.

"So, it's true. They do exist," she muttered as she walked.

Dimly, she was aware that the other women watched her warily as they went about their chores. The men had all left at dawn to go fishing.

Gods, she hated fish! But these people knew nothing about combining plants properly for a complete protein. She'd been forced to eat fish just to survive this last winter.

But thinking about slimy, disgusting, and foul fish didn't give her any clues as to how to use a dragon to get home.

They communicated telepathically. They flew high, higher than the human eye could see. Could they tap into the king stone aboard *Sirius* in orbit and get a message home to Eric?

She wiped away a tear of loneliness.

Eric would move the entire force of the empire to find her, once he knew where to look. She knew it in her heart.

So how did she convince a dragon to come to her aid?

If you can hear me, please talk to me, she thought as loud and as hard as she could.

Silence greeted her.

Now she couldn't suppress the tears she had not shed for nine months.

"Why do you resist me, Kat?" Amanda Leonard asked.

Kat stared back at her former captain. Once more, restraints held her to her cot. This time force bracelets immobilized her limbs rather than simple surgical tape. She forced herself to relax. As soon as Amanda left, Kat would break free. Until she had privacy, she needed to appear docile.

But she would not give this woman the satisfaction of an answer to her ridiculous questions.

Instead, she reached out with her mind to Gentian who cowered in the far corner, beyond Geralds' cot and out of sight of Amanda. Kat sent him reassuring thoughts. She wished she knew why her flywacket feared Amanda, and Amanda disliked—almost to the point of fear—Gentian.

"You know that I am destined to rule this planet." Amanda caressed Kat's face with a horny fingernail.

When had Amanda's fingernails grown so long? When had they become so strong and ugly?

"Interesting. Judge Balinakas thinks he's gong to rule the planet from his stronghold," Geralds remarked. He reclined on his cot, hands behind his head, and studied Amanda through slitted eyes. No force bracelets for him. But then he had not defied Amanda.

"Judge Balinakas!" Amanda screeched. "That bastard has tried to usurp my authority since the day I took command of *Jupiter*. He never acknowledged that a mere judge is an inferior creature to a *captain*."

Kat bit her cheeks rather than laugh. The judicial branch of the crew aboard a judicial cruiser was supposed to be a self-contained unit. Judge, attorneys—prosecution and defense—clerks, recorders, and even two anthropologists to protect the cultural integrity of outlying planets, dealt with criminals after the Marines captured them. The ship's crew ran the ship. In theory, lines of authority never crossed. Judge Balinakas challenged those lines on a daily basis.

"Balinakas had no right to order evacuation after Konner O'Hara stole the king stone. He has no right to claim any part of this planet as his own. It is mine. All mine." Amanda advanced upon Geralds, claws extended as if to scratch him to death.

"You were in med bay, incapacitated and unable to issue orders," Kat reminded Amanda. "M'Berra was dirtside trying to capture the O'Haras. The judge had the right to evacuate his own people with a contingent of Marines for protection. The rest of the crew panicked and followed the Marines out the door." She kept her voice calm and matter-of-fact.

"Another reason to bring Konner O'Hara and his brothers to my justice. You must lead me to them, Kat." Amanda sat on Kat's cot and ran one hand affectionately through Kat's tangled curls.

"My brothers will face justice eventually." IMP justice, not Amanda's. But Kat would not say that right now. Her life depended upon keeping this woman reasonable and calm.

"We were friends once, Kat. My pretty Kat," Amanda crooned. "You obeyed my orders willingly until Konner O'Hara and his brothers stole your affections."

Kat raised her eyebrows at that. "You were my commanding officer. Of course I obeyed. And I have no affection for the biological family that abandoned me as a child. Governor Talbot and his daughters are my family."

"Remember that. I'll release you when you agree to lead me to Konner O'Hara. I know you know how to find him. I will have my revenge against him for the loss of my eye and the loss of my ship." Amanda stood up and began prowling the cabin restlessly. She picked up vials and instruments at random, abandoning them in different places for some new shiny toy.

"Your eye seems quite recovered," Geralds said from his cot.

"What do you know about it?" Amanda screeched. All traces of calm fled. She arched her taloned fingers menacingly.

"I observe that you have abandoned the patch and that your eye tracks correctly, even if the pupil is misshapen and enlarged," he replied.

"Define misshapen!" Amanda demanded. Her voice descended into reasonable tones once more. But she scrunched her hair with strong hands as if ready to begin tearing it out.

Kat looked a little more closely at Amanda's eyes as the captain passed her cot in her increasingly erratic circuits of the cabin.

Both her pupils had turned into vertical oblongs—much like Gentian's. Her once pale blue eyes had darkened into the same rich purple as the flywacket's.

CHAPTER 18

KIM PROPPED PRYTH HIGHER on her makeshift bolster and offered her a cup of water liberally laced with willow bark and stewed moss. Her skin was hot to the touch, dry and crackly like fallen leaves in a drought.

The old woman turned her head away. "Let me die," she whispered.

"I can't." Kim pressed the water on his patient until she took a tiny sip. "We need you, Pryth. You have to get better. I don't know how this village would survive without you." He didn't add his fears for Hestiia's health and the safe delivery of their baby.

Guilt that he had not been able to heal her kept him at her side every moment that Hestiia did not need him. He'd moved his wife into the big cave here in the village so that she would not be alone if she went into labor.

"Another will rise to take my place. 'Tis always the way." She paused to cough weakly. She no longer had the strength to raise the fluid in her lungs that gradually drowned her.

"No one can take your place. No one has your wisdom and experience." Kim tried again to get her to take a sip.

She closed her eyes and drowsed in his arms.

Slowly, he placed her back against the bolster to let her rest in peace.

Her breathing grew louder and raspier. The labored sounds filled the round hut and pressed against Kim's sanity. The close confines amplified the noise.

Desperate to relieve Pryth of the killing disease, he threw a new handful of aromatic herbs onto the fire. The astringent smell barely masked the rancid odors of sickness and smoke.

He wanted to cough. Didn't dare, lest it rouse the old woman from her much needed rest.

She opened her mouth and coughed long and hard. Her lungs rattled and a gagging sound came from her throat.

Kim rushed to lift her higher and ease the pressures on her chest.

Spasms racked her. Her wasted body lay heavily against him.

He cradled her against his chest trying to impart some of his own strength to her.

At last she quieted.

Kim had to check to make certain she still breathed. Her chest rose and fell shallowly.

He was about to help her lay down again when she turned her big dark eyes on him. The pupils dilated more than usual in the dim room. The black irises seemed to fill the entire space available, even the whites.

Yet there was a strange awareness and intelligence there.

"Hestiia knows everything that I know. Let her grow. Love her enough to allow her the freedom to explore and expand her limits. The flywacket was once hers. She has the ear of the dragons." The old woman's voice took on the overtones of many voices speaking from the past.

"Don't talk, Pryth. You must rest and conserve your strength."

"I must pass on the mantle of my office. Bring Hestiia to me."

She collapsed, unconscious. Each intake of breath sounded loud, like a bell already tolling her death.

Kim crawled out of the hut and nearly ran to where Hestiia basked in the sunshine beside the central fire pit. She had chosen to sit upon a broad rock that seemed to fit her swollen bottom perfectly.

"Pryth has asked for you, Hes. She has something important to tell you. But you can't go in there. We can't take a chance that you will catch her pneumonia."

"I must go to her." Hestiia levered and heaved herself off the low rock. Her belly seemed to have swollen overnight.

"You are too near your time. It's too dangerous."

"This is more important than the risk." Hestiia turned stubborn eyes upon him.

He tried to stare her down.

Within moments he capitulated and offered his wife his arm. She placed it around her waist to better support her in her rapid waddle across the village center.

"You'll have to help me," she said quietly at the door to Pryth's round hut.

"Are you sure you want to go in there, Hes?"

"I have to. The life of the village depends upon this."

"Upon what?"

"Women's secrets. Women's knowledge. Women's wisdom." Once again she gave him that stubborn look.

He knew better than to fight it. Carefully, he helped her bend over through the low doorway. Once inside, she dropped to her knees beside the pallet. She placed one hand over Pryth's eyes and the other over her mouth.

The room seemed lighter, less smoky than before. Almost as if the stench of impending death no longer lingered here.

A shaft of sunlight broke through the smoke hole and bathed the two women in an eerie glow.

Kim wanted to back away in atavistic fear.

"You may stay, husband. But you must never repeat what you see, or hear, or feel to any other male. I keep you here because I need your help," Hes whispered.

Instinctively, Kim placed his hand upon her shoulder, imbuing her with whatever strength he could, much as his brothers had given of themselves during the aborted healing spell.

Guilt flooded him again.

Hestiia gave him an impatient glare. "There is no time to indulge in selfish emotions." She sounded a lot like Pryth in that moment.

Kim clamped down on his emotions and tried to concentrate on giving his wife whatever help he could.

Hestiia began to chant in low somber tones.

Kim could not catch the words or even the language. He leaned closer, trying to commit the syllables to memory. They eluded him like mercury globules floating in zero G.

Then the light shifted once more. The sun moved on. The glow around Pryth faded.

A deep aura of bright white and yellow surrounded and filled Hestiia.

Kim almost yanked his hand away, afraid of the eerie light burning his hand as well as his psyche.

Hestiia's chant turned joyful, raising from sonorous tones to a bright song. She lifted her hands from Pryth and raised them high, glorying in this arcane ritual.

Slowly, her aura dimmed to the normal layers of energies Kim detected around every living thing if he tried. He didn't have to work at seeing the pulsing orange, green, and brown of Hestiia's life.

She lowered her hands and her head. Her lips kept moving.

Kim realized that she chanted the prayer for the dead.

Pryth lay quiet, peaceful, and unmoving. Her eyes stared at Hestiia and Kim in love and blessing.

And then she was gone. From one eye blink to the next her life passed into another realm that Kim could not reach.

He braced himself for the terrible experience he had endured when another man had died at his hands many years ago. He'd felt echoes of it before, when others had passed away near him. The need to guide the loosed soul into the beyond remained dormant now. The need to follow that soul did not rise.

He breathed a sigh of relief.

Hestiia slumped against him in exhaustion.

"What happened, love?" he asked, gently caressing away the lines of fatigue on her face.

"She has passed to me the mantle of leadership and wisdom. Everything she knew is now mine, to help me build upon my own experience to guide this village. Everything she learned from her mentor and her mentor before that going back countless generations is mine to tap if I need it." She opened her eyes. They glowed strangely, the pupils huge, as if she still absorbed information through them and they could not open wide enough to accommodate the data.

"This is really strange." Kim's voice shook.

"This is the way of life. The way of women. Come. Help me up. We must prepare her pyre and mourn her properly. But she is not truly gone. She lives in our hearts."

Hestiia clutched her belly as she rose to her feet.

"The baby?"

"Will be fine. Come. We must give the sad news to the village. Tonight we will mourn her death and celebrate her life."

CHAPTER 19

"PRYTH WAS OLD, Konner. Well past the time for her to join her ancestors," Dalleena said quietly.

Konner did his best to ignore her and the sorrowful activity at the center of the village. If he had to dwell on the old wisewoman's death, he'd do it privately, not by gathering wood for her pyre and chanting her ballads and tales with the others.

He blanked his mind to all but the numbers piling up on his handheld. This fuel cell, the one he'd brought to the village last night remained full. The empty one was gone.

Who would steal an empty fuel cell?

"I think, that with the nine remaining cells, I have enough fuel for one trip to *Sirius*," he said by way of reply to his wife. He reached up from his crouched position to hold Dalleena's hand. "I've got things aboard the mother ship I can use for a pump and fire hose for Paola's Amazons. Once aboard *Sirius* I can properly recharge the fuel cells. But then I have to go. I have to find my son."

"You must not forget your duties to the dead, Konner."

"And what about my duties to the living on the big continent and to my living son?" He could not look at her. The image of Martin, as he'd seen him last, two and one-half Terran years ago, tall for his age with chestnut-brown hair and vivid blue eyes. A softness about his nose and chin reminded Konner of Melinda, but not much else did. In intelligence, vivacity, posture, and stubbornness, Martin was all O'Hara.

Konner's heart ached with emptiness. Even if Dalleena announced right now that she carried his baby, he would always miss Martin, his firstborn. A child he had been forbidden to raise. A child left in the greedy and manipulative clutches of his mother.

Melinda had cheated Konner out of their prenuptial agreement and one million Adols. The Auroran currency was the most stable in the galaxy. She'd cheated Konner out of Martin's life. She had cheated when she bribed a port employee to implant one of Konner's own patented locator beacons aboard *Sirius* and then sold the unique frequency of that beacon to the IMPs.

He had to get Martin away from that woman, even if he had to kidnap the boy.

And yet he hated to leave this place. Hated the thought of abandoning his friends and neighbors, *his people* to the mercies of the IMPs trapped here and the Krakatrice that tyrannized the big continent.

"You will come with me when I leave?" Konner asked.

"Try to leave me behind, Stargod Konner." Dalleena bent to kiss him.

He rose up with her in his arms.

"It's time," Loki said softly. He'd looked worn and weary since he'd returned from his adventures with Paola and Iianthe, just a few hours ago.

Konner and Kim had had to greet him with the news of Pryth's death during his absence.

He stood at the base of the festival pylon. Hestiia and Poolie, wife of the headman Raaskan, both heavily pregnant, draped vines laden with flowers from the junction at the top of the pylon. Three represented the fertility of the season, the unchanging cycle of birth, life, death: Maiden, Mother, and Crone.

The women seemed strangely calm and accepting of Pryth's passing. More so than Kim did.

"We gather to celebrate the life of one we loved," Taneeo placed a stick on the pyre where Pryth's body lay covered by a wolf pelt. The priest had made a remarkable recovery in the last day.

Except for a hollowness about his eyes and the fragile air of one just risen from a sickbed, Konner would not know from looking at Taneeo that he had lain in a coma for many months, possessed by an alien spirit.

Konner joined Loki and Kim at the base of the pylon, the place of honor to observe the funeral. The villagers expected their Stargods to preside over the ceremony. They'd done this too many times over the winter.

Beginning with Taneeo, each person in the village spoke in turn. "Thank you, Pryth, for your gift of sanity when mine fled," the young priest said and bowed his head. He placed a stick upon the pyre.

"Thank you for curing my child of the croup." That speaker also laid a stick on the pyre.

"Thank you for the love charm." A young man and his bride held hands as they added a bit of wood.

"Thank you . . ."

They all had a reason to thank Pryth for the giving of many gifts when she lived. She'd not be forgotten soon. They each had a reason to share in the grief.

"Thank you for accepting me as I am, and not trying to make me into a clone of someone else." Even Cyndi added a bit to the ritual.

Loki nodded to her with respect as she passed the brothers and moved into the shadows, out of the heart of the village.

"Thank you for making a joke out of my first hunt, which I believed to be a disaster. Now we remember the joy of the campfire rather than the empty bellies," a young warrior said. A chuckle went round the group.

"Thank you for making me a silly hat so that I would feel beautiful at the harvest festival," a scarred woman said as she slipped her hand into that of her husband.

Their mood lightened as they remembered the good times, the laughter, the joy of Pryth's life.

Konner's turn came last. What could he say? He'd known the old woman for less than a year. Others had already thanked Pryth for her courage and her wisdom. What he remembered most about her was the way she pranced about an evening campfire, reciting the legends and history of her people. "Thank you for the gift of song," he said quietly.

"Amen, so be it," Loki and Kim echoed.

Someone broke out a flute and began one of Pryth's favorite tunes, a sprightly march that accompanied the story of how the Stargods had rescued the villagers from Hanassa's sacrificial altar and then led them to a new life. A man took up a drum and added rhythm. A young couple began to dance about the pylon. Headman Raaskan broke out the last keg of beer left from happier and more prosperous times.

They all laughed and danced and celebrated the good things about the woman they had lost.

Almost as an afterthought, as the sun lowered toward night, Taneeo shoved a torch into the pyre.

As the first flames reached greedily for the next layer of branches, Hestiia placed both hands against her swollen belly. Her face turned pale and she bit her lip. "Out of death comes life," she whispered.

The women gathered around her, including Dalleena, hastily urging her toward the nearest cave. They shouted with joy. Kim trailed behind them, lost, anxious, shouting orders that they ignored. At the mouth of the largest cave, where several families dwelled in modest comfort, two women, one of them Yaakke's wife, turned and stopped Kim from entering.

Yaakke seemed to be missing. He, too, had disappeared into the shadows, along with Cyndi right after saying his bit and adding a bit of fuel to the pyre.

"This is women's work," the women said. "Go find something else to do." They backed into the cave and dropped the leather curtain in front of it.

"But . . . but . . ."

"Come, my friend. Let us drink to the birth of your son!" Raaskan clapped Kim on the shoulder and handed him a mug of beer.

"But . . ." Kim looked over his shoulder toward the cave. The men pushed him toward the keg where all the men gathered.

"What can you do that they can't?" Konner asked his brother. "They have a lot more experience with this than we do."

"Experience?" A strange look came over Kim's face. Then buried his expression in the act of taking a long drink. "Yeah, experience."

"Where's Loki?" Konner asked.

No one answered.

"I've read all the medical texts. I know what has to be done," Kim muttered. "I should be there. Experience or no."

"You will be in the way of women who have delivered hundreds of babies." Konner gently prodded his brother in the back. He wondered when it would be Kim's turn to ease Konner away from a birth. "Birth is one of the great mysteries of womanhood. They would be uncomfortable with you in their midst," he advised Kim.

"What if something goes wrong? Hestiia has already miscarried once. I don't know if we could bear to lose another child."

"Think about the positives. We have enough fuel to reach *Sirius*. In a few weeks we'll be telling Mum about her grandchild. I'll be telling Martin about his new cousin."

Inside the cave Hestiia screamed in pain. Poolie came rushing out, face lined with worry. She hurried as much as she could to her own hut where she gathered a bundle of supplies.

"I'm not waiting for her to die," Kim announced. "We're taking *Rover* to get the medic. I don't care if we have to kidnap her. Lotski is coming back to save my wife." He marched resolutely toward the shuttle.

Konner hastened in his wake, unable to deny his brother this small comfort. Even though it meant waiting another week or four to refuel again. He'd figure out something to cobble together a pump and fire hose for Paola.

He'd waited nine months to rescue his son. What difference could a few more weeks make?

But he wished he knew who had sabotaged the fuel cells and then stolen the empty one. That could delay him even longer if the thief got smart and struck again.

———◆———

Kat made a point of limping heavily as a Marine escorted her back to the med cabin from the latrine. She wanted them to underestimate her until she was ready to make a break.

Sergeant Kent Brewster, Kat's friend and the man who had kept their equipment running longer than anyone dared hope, stood at the edge of the camp with an armload of lily bulbs ready to be roasted for supper. An armed Marine stood next to him. Brewster paused and offered an arm for Kat to lean on. The guard prodded him forward with the butt of his stun rifle.

Brewster stumbled out of Kat's reach. He recovered clumsily, dropping half of the lilies. He shrugged at Kat and grinned on one side of his mouth. The other side seemed bruised and painful. He, too, had been forced to comply with Commander Leonard's new regime.

"Where is M'Berra?" Kat asked casually, within Brewster's hearing.

"Occupied," her Marine barked.

Brewster shook his head slightly.

So the second-in-command had opposed Leonard and found himself imprisoned or coerced.

What had happened to Leonard to make her snap? Her insanity had been growing for months. The explosion of *Jupiter* must have been the last straw.

But that didn't explain the changes in her eyes and horny hands.

"I never would have thought she'd become a despot," Kat muttered. "*My* captain was always fair and observed the rules and regs meticulously. Slavery is not legal, moral, or ethical."

"Shut your yap, or I'll shut it for you." The Marine prodded her with the muzzle of his stun rifle.

Kat marched forward, her mind numb. She knew she had to do something to end this. She *should* do something. But what?

Inside the med cabin, Gentian cowered beneath Kat's cot. Geralds appeared to be sleeping. Her heart warmed at the thought of Gentian climbing into her lap and working his healing purrs. She'd only been with the creature a day and she already felt a part of him, lost when he didn't follow her out on the simple errand of a trip to the latrine. She'd really used the excuse to scout the progress of Amanda and her slaves. Gentian's sensitive nose and ears would have given her more information than her own limited senses.

Leonard's whip cut through the air with a teeth-grating snap. A man moaned.

"Work harder, every last dregging one of you, or you'll feel more of this," Leonard commanded, as she cracked the whip again. She sounded almost reasonable. "I need these fields cleared, plowed, and planted by sunset." Not a reasonable order.

The Marine clasped the force bracelets around Kat's wrists and ankles. Then he shut the door firmly behind him as he exited. "We'll feed you at sunset if you behave yourself," he growled.

She heard him latch it with the simple loop of rope around a peg.

"Presumptive of him to think that lock and those bracelets will keep you in," Geralds commented. He slid his hands behind his head and surveyed the cabin. A casual observer might think him nonchalant.

Kat saw the tension in his back and legs. He was ready to fly off the cot and into action in a heartbeat.

She found a note in the back of her throat and hummed it. Her mind pictured the force bracelets opening. They fell away from her hands and feet. This was easy compared to the medical restraints.

Amazing how easy this magic stuff came to her now that she didn't fight it. Now that she had Gentian's senses and perceptions linked to her own.

"Now what do we do?" Kat prowled the cabin, searching for answers as much as an escape. Gentian dogged her heels. But he kept his ideas to himself.

"What do you mean 'we'?" Geralds asked.

"You are as much a prisoner as I am. Don't you want out? Aren't you afraid Leonard will enslave you, too? You are a stranger to her with little or no value but the muscles in your back."

"I've done enough running for a while. I think I need to sleep some more. At least until dark."

Kat peered out the tiny window in the back wall. She watched the locals trudge through the fields dragging a plow, two men acting as draft animals while a third guided the plow. Five more men, with an armed guard, approached the far meadow beyond the wetlands. They carried ropes and stalked the wild cattle. A new bull had moved in and taken over the herd since last autumn. Brewster had shot the old bull after it charged him and Dallenna. Dallenna had been seriously hurt by the charging animal. Brewster—as usual—had avoided injury. Nothing seemed to touch that man.

Where was he?

"Leonard has close to one hundred men loyal to her. They are all heavily armed and eager for a fight," Kat muttered.

Gentian flashed her an image of every weapons stash in Base Camp. She instantly knew by smell who carried fully charged weapons and who had empty ones just for show. Recharging them had proved just as difficult as keeping any of the other equipment running. But those weapons had priority with Amanda Leonard. Gentian had seen fuel cells stolen from fighters and landers hooked up to spare weapons.

Grateful for the information, Kat reached down and scritched Gentian's ears.

"I wouldn't want to tackle those Marines in the *daylight*." Did Geralds put extra emphasis on the last word?

"Neither would I. I wonder if they are going to break some more taboos by killing and eating one of the cows." The previous bull had made several fine meals for the crew who rapidly lost all their inhibitions about eating meat. They seemed also to have lost their belief in the GTE law never to take a life, any life, even the life of an animal for food.

"If they eat a heavy meal full of meat they will be sleepy and sluggish," Geralds commented.

"So they will," Kat replied. The beginning of an idea tickled her mind.

She sank back onto her cot, checked to make certain her backpack was beneath it and stretched out. Gentian jumped into her lap. He didn't purr. He didn't make a sound. He just quivered in fear.

"We'll think of something, Gentian. I promise."

They both fell asleep.

CHAPTER 20

KIM FELT THE SUN set behind the mountains at his back. The rhythm of day shifting into night settled into his bones. His hearing sharpened as his eyesight closed down in the reduced light. He heard a few frogs croak in the wetlands south of Base Camp—nowhere near as many frogs as a year ago.

Last year, too many frogs had carried a plague. But Konner had seeded the swamp with selenium to neutralize the bioengineered disease. Another reason the locals had named the three brothers Stargods.

Now Kim and his brothers had to live up to their expectations and the responsibility.

Crickets joined the gentle chorus and a night bird added syncopation. Kim's heart beat in rhythm with the land. He shifted to a more comfortable position, lying prone at the edge of a rise just west of Base Camp.

At the back of his mind, a knot of worry threatened his need to meld with the planet. He knew Hestiia labored long and hard. The faint disquiet in his gut became a roiling cramp.

He clenched his teeth and breathed slowly, desperately trying to master the pain in himself and in his wife.

All his focus had to remain on liberating Medic Lotski and as many medical supplies as he and his brothers could. He hoped the ten warriors along with his brothers would be enough manpower.

Commander Leonard had one hundred Marines.

"Look!" Loki pointed toward the fields near the wetlands. "They're driving *our* villagers with stun weapons and whips." He gnashed his teeth.

"Are you saying only we can enslave those people?" Konner asked with wry amusement.

"No, I am saying that after we went to the trouble of liberating them, no one has the right to enslave our people," Loki reiterated.

"They have my father," Yaakke said. He half rose from his crouched position in the long meadow grasses. He'd inserted himself into the pack of men after the funeral. Kim didn't know how he'd occupied himself during the ceremony.

"Not for long." Kim pulled Hestiia's brother back down into hiding. "But it won't help our cause if they catch you, too. We have to think this through. There are more of them than of us. And they are better armed."

"But we are meaner," Loki said. A hard glint came into his eyes devoid of the mischief he usually exhibited before a brawl.

"I wouldn't count on that," Konner said. He pointed to the woman who drove the slaves with a whip. "That's Amanda Leonard. She has several grudges against me—and us."

"This could be a trap to lure us in," Kim mused. "Kat knows that we will feel honor bound to rescue our people." Trap or no, he had to get into camp tonight and get the medic out. Hes needed help from a professional, not just the accumulated experience of several women of childbearing age. He had trouble believing Pryth had transferred her wisdom to Hestiia, even though he'd witnessed the magical ritual and given the women enough of his bodily strength to complete the procedure.

"I don't think Kat would . . ."

"Wouldn't she?" Loki returned. "Last time I saw our sister, after the battle for the crystal array in the autumn, she had all the weapons of a lander loaded and ready to kill the three of us, if she could find us." Finally, he let loose his old familiar grin of mischief, eager for a fight.

"No, you aren't thinking what I think you're thinking." Konner's face also split in a big smile.

"Give our baby sister some comeuppance?" Loki was enjoying this too much, not focusing on the real problem of the enslaved locals and the need to take the medic back to the village.

"Chances are that Chaney Lotski will be in the med cabin," Kim changed the subject.

"*Our* cabin," Loki growled.

"So how do we get in?" Kim nibbled on a bit of Tambootie, willing the drug to enhance his night vision.

"We need to work around the perimeter to the east," Konner whispered. "Approach from the back."

"Patrols are heaviest there," Kim reminded him. As he spoke, he watched an armed Marine pace the east end of the village. He held his stun rifle restlessly, more than ready to shoot something.

"They are expecting an attack from the coastal village, to liberate the slaves," Loki surmised. "I would."

"How about the north end, from the river?" Kim watched one man leaning against a tree by the boat launch.

"Possible." Loki held his hand out to Kim for a bit of the Tambootie.

Kim gave him a leaf fragment, regretting immediately he had not brought more. He always needed more. Each dose had to be larger than the last to gain the same effect.

"Then again," Loki mused as he nibbled, "maybe we should just walk right in through the front door." He rose from his prone position to a crouch. Obscured by the long meadow grass, he dashed toward the end of the line of slaves.

Kim shrugged and followed. Why not? He and his brothers were as ragged and dirty as the exhausted men who trudged in from the fields.

"The rest of you stay put until the time is right. Keep *Rover* safe at all costs," Kim whispered to their gathered men.

"I doubt those arrogant Marines know every one of their slaves on sight," Konner whispered.

"They might even feed us," Loki said, now in line behind the last slave.

"Do not count on the bitch doing anything for our well-being. She is worse than Hanassa," said Yaaccob, the village headman and father to Hestiia and Yaakke, two places up the line from Loki and Kim.

"Hanassa?" Kim asked. He kept his head down as a guard wandered the length of the line of twenty-five, now twenty-nine, slaves. "Is it possible?" he whispered to his brothers once the guard had passed on.

"Anything is possible," Loki replied. "But my money is now on Cyndi as the dragon's host."

"Neither woman is of Hanassa's blood," Yaaccob reminded them.

"Is that required?" Kim asked. He wished Iianthe, the purple-tip dragon was around to answer some questions.

(You have but to ask,) a deep and melodic voice came into the back of his head.

"Does Hanassa need a body of his own lineage to transfer his spirit?" Kim asked subvocally.

(Trust no one who has touched the one we cannot name, or been touched by him.) An angry flurry of wings signaled the end of the conversation.

The wind from his passage swirled about them, gathering dust and dried leaves in its wake.

The entire line of slaves ducked and covered their heads with their arms. All of the guards scanned the skies with rifles aimed upward.

"When you decide to piss off a dragon, you do it in spades," Loki whistled through his teeth.

"I did not realize Iianthe was so near. I should have felt his presence in my mind," Kim said.

"Get back in line, all of you!" snapped the nearest guard.

Amanda Leonard snapped her whip to emphasize the order.

"Gather around the fire. All of you," she said, most pleasantly. "I have a little surprise for you."

"I don't like surprises," Kim muttered.

"Silence!" barked the guard. "You will listen and obey our beloved captain."

Kim grimaced. The Marine's eyes burned with the light of fanaticism. They'd have a hard time breaking the captain's hold on her followers.

"Bring out the women," Amanda Leonard ordered quite loudly, as if she wanted everyone within a kilometer's distance to hear and understand what she intended.

A growl of pained anger rose from the throats of twenty-five enslaved men.

"Silence!" Leonard cracked her whip. An older man slumped in the middle of the line, clutching his naked chest.

Kim stepped toward him. His hands ached to touch and heal the red welt running diagonal across the man's chest. Blood oozed from the top end of the wound. Kim's entire torso burned in sympathetic agony.

"Stay put," Loki hissed. He held Kim back with a fierce grip upon his elbow. "She'll recognize you."

"But . . ."

"Not yet. We have to think, have to come up with a plan."

"Where's Kat?" Konner asked.

"Haven't seen her," Kim replied. Scanning the Base Camp inhabitants gave him something to do other than fretting over the wounded man he dared not help.

"I can't find Lotski either," Loki said.

"We need Lotski. Hestiia can't last much longer. She's been in labor for hours. I don't know how to use my magic to help her."

Just then, three armed Marines led out seven local women, all stripped to the waist, wearing nothing but their summer sarongs slung about their hips. They kept their eyes lowered, away from their husbands, brothers, and fathers among the male slaves. One young woman, barely sixteen, trembled and blushed in shame.

"I understand that when my people first landed here, that you primitive barbarians enticed them with food, strong drink, and promises of sex." Amanda Leonard began pacing. She coiled her whip and tapped her leg with the handle in rhythm with her steps.

Kim blanched at the reminder of the subterfuge he and his brothers had concocted in order to strand the three hundred crew members on this planet, so they could never, ever reveal its location to the Galactic Terran Empire. They could not risk that the GTE would leave the planet unpolluted or politically free.

Civilization and its conveniences carried a price.

"If my people are to be believed, and they always tell the truth," Leonard continued her pronouncements and her prowl. Behind her, an entire squad of Marines smirked at her statement, giving the lie to her words.

"None of them got lucky that night." Leonard whirled to face the slaves. Her eyes accused them of betrayal. "Not one of them got lucky. So tonight they will. With your women. While you watch."

"That is enough." The door to the big cabin flew open with a bang. Kat stalked out. Her eyes blazed greener than the green bonfire. Her long strides gobbled up the space between herself and her captain.

"Stand down, Lieutenant," Leonard barked.

"No. I renounce your authority to give illegal orders." She took a deep breath and speared the commander with the icy fire of her gaze. "I deny your sanity. I refuse to obey you, Commander Amanda Leonard. I, Lieutenant JG Mari Kathleen O'Hara Talbot order all those who still honor the laws and ideals of His Majesty's Imperial Military Police and the Galactic Terran Empire to lay down their weapons and lock you up until a rescue ship arrives or your wits and morals return."

As one, fifty stun rifles locked and loaded. As one, all fifty turned their aim toward Kat.

CHAPTER 21

"GENTIAN, YOU WANT to provide a distraction that will allow us to get out of here?" Kat asked. She tried to keep her eye on all of the Marines. There were too many of them.

(No,) Gentian squeaked. He scooted farther into the shadows.

"Please. I really need some help."

The flywacket sighed.

Kat sensed his fear. Finally, he emerged from the med cabin, body low, ears flat against his head, tail twitching nervously, Kat's pack in his mouth. One step outside he spread his magnificent black feathered wings, let loose a yowl, and launched himself into the air.

The pack dropped neatly at Kat's feet. The flywacket knew how much she treasured the item in the bottom.

The slave women dropped to the ground shrieking.

"Plague bringer!" Yaaccob, the village elder, shouted. "Shoot the plague bringer." He dove for the nearest Marine, trying to wrestle the stun rifle from his hands. He smiled hugely. "You must shoot the plague bringer!"

"What is happening here?" Amanda Leonard commanded. She sounded almost like her old self, rather than the insane despot she had become.

"I did not just see that." Geralds hugged himself in the doorway. "I have seen some mighty weird things since landing on this planet, but that takes the stardust."

His comments went unnoticed in the chaos that followed. Kat noted that the slave men all seemed to have engaged Marines in close combat, trying to take control of the weapons.

"That's a good enough distraction for me," Kat said. She grabbed her pack and then Geralds by the arm and ran toward the nearest aircraft south of Base Camp.

"Where's Lotski?" A voice rang out. It sounded very much like one of her brothers. Kim by the tenor quality.

"I should have known those three would be involved in this," she grumbled.

"Those three? The O'Haras?" Geralds stopped dead in his track. "If Konner is there . . ."

"We've got to get out of here. Capturing Konner is no good unless we are free to leave the planet." She yanked him into a stumbling jog. Not that she was sure she'd let anyone capture Konner. He and Dalleena had rescued her from the snake monsters. Then he had kept his promise to deliver her back to Base Camp.

She owed Konner.

Besides, Geralds hadn't earned her trust even if he was a dregging attractive man.

Ahead lay the shadowed mounds of several small aircraft at rest. Kat jumped into the first, a one-man fighter that could almost accommodate a second small person crouched behind the pilot's seat. She slammed her palm against the manual override and hit the ignition.

A red light blinked in silence. The engines remained dead. She tried the ignition again. The red light blinked faster—almost louder.

"No fuel!" she screamed at the inanimate machine.

"M'Berra said he'd locked up the fuel cells to keep you grounded," Geralds reminded her.

Kat let loose a string of curses she didn't realize she knew. And would never knowingly use in mixed company.

Geralds chuckled from the ground outside the cockpit. "I admire your independent spirit. But that won't fuel the plane."

"With me, Kat," Konner called. He let loose an indiscriminate spray of stunner fire.

Kat scrambled out of the fighter. "Have you got a dragon?" she asked, taking the stun pistol he offered and blanketing Base Camp with energy bolts.

"Better, I've got *Rover,* the shuttle."

"Got room for two more?" she asked. Then she threw herself onto the ground, just beneath return fire from the Marines.

"We'll manage." Konner shot a wide blast and sprinted away from Base Camp.

Kat followed. She shoved Geralds hard to make him keep up with her.

She thought she saw a glimmer of a blue ley line in the moonlight. Desperate to get free of Amanda Leonard and her fanatical followers, Kat veered her path to stand upon the line. Then she turned and fired blindly four times.

Four Marines slumped to the ground.

She grinned and continued to run after her brother and Geralds.

Angry shouts and curses and the pounding of heavy feet against the land erupted behind her. Many booted feet. She risked a glance over her shoulder. Kim followed her, shooting at a phalanx of pursuing Marines, Amanda Leonard in the lead.

He, too, sought to stand upon the ley line for his next shot.

Kat watched as three blasts in a row from Kim's gun hit the captain square in the chest. Amanda Leonard should have fallen unconscious with the first.

She kept plowing forward, her whip in her hand and a murderous gleam in her eyes.

Kat shuddered in fear and disbelief.

Then Loki roared through the squad of uniformed men and women, the familiar figure of Medic Chaney Lotski thrown over his shoulder. Jetang M'Berra ran hot on their heels, also firing a weapon into the midst of their shipmates—now enemies.

Three natives armed with clubs and spears guarded the open hatch of the family shuttle. Kat did not question their presence; she dove onto the deck, then scrambled as far into the cabin as she could to make way for the others.

Gentian swooped in and landed beside Kat. He did his best to hide behind her along with the pack she had forgotten while trying to start the fighter.

One by one, Geralds and her brothers followed. Konner had the shuttle fired up and rolling before Loki threw his prisoner onto the deck and hopped aboard. M'Berra came last, still laying down cover fire while the natives took their places in the shuttle.

Kat slapped the hatch control before M'Berra had his feet all the way in. The portal irised closed, slowly. Too slowly.

A stunner blast shot through the partial opening. One of the natives slumped to the deck.

The engines roared louder. The shuttle lifted off, leaving Amanda Leonard and her faithful followers jumping, screaming, and shooting uselessly at the cerama/metal hull.

"I guess this makes you one of us again," Kim said with a grin. "An outlaw on the run from the IMPs."

"I guess it does." Kat sank onto the cushioned bench of the cabin. All her hopes and dreams for military advancement, her happy, *civilized* life had just gone up in smoke.

If she ever got back to civilization and the people she called friends and family.

For good or ill, she was stuck with the brothers she had disowned for twenty years.

"I guess I'm back in the family again. For good or ill."

We have concerns about the flywacket who must prove himself. His courage lacks conviction. He reacts only when prodded by the one he must guide. He does not take action on his own. The one he must guide does not seek his advice. She follows her own path. We must make certain she stays on the correct one now that she has found it. We know now that the flywacket will not push her; he will not fulfill his destiny. Should we recall him now or later? Later might be too late.

Hanassa screamed curses long and fluently at the retreating glow from the shuttle's engines. The voice of his host body sounded harsh, cracking from overuse.

"Simurgh take you all. I will find you. I will follow you and I will kill you one and all!"

His body suddenly grew faint from hunger. Only blood would satisfy the dragon within.

He turned and examined the Marines who had failed to recapture Kat and the brothers.

"One of you will die."

They backed away, bringing their useless guns to bear.

"You failed me. I will have blood. Only blood will pay for your betrayal."

The mind of the one he possessed tried to claw her way through him, trying to put a halt to the bloodlust that drove him.

He recognized the logic behind her demand.

"Bring me a slave," Hanassa ordered the contingent of Marines. "For every day that Lieutenant Talbot remains at large, a slave will die. By day after tomorrow the natives will bring me all three of the Stargods and their treacherous sister and be glad to sacrifice them to me."

"We could send a fighter after them. Shoot them down," a corporal offered.

"Do not waste the fuel. The natives will bring the offenders to me."

The three men who stood closest to her smiled and their eyes lit with enthusiasm for the plan.

The others melted into the shadows.

Hanassa returned to Base Camp and retreated into the med cabin, the largest and finest of all the structures left behind by the O'Hara brothers. This building was now his home. From here he would rule.

But first he had to put Amanda's body to bed while he went hunting for a way to get closer to his enemies.

CHAPTER 22

"KEEP YOUR BACK turned to me while you watch the door, Bruce," Martin instructed his friend.

"I don't see why," Bruce grumbled. "We're friends. We're not supposed to have secrets from each other."

"Believe me, you do not want to know what I'm doing if Melinda ever gets hold of you." Martin sank his right arm up to the elbow into the guts of his computer. He'd had to put the entire system to sleep, including the systems he'd borrowed memory and power from, for this surgical operation. Otherwise, Melinda could monitor his activities too easily.

The wall panel lay at his feet. The bottom of the secret compartment was deep. He had only recently grown tall enough to reach it without a step stool.

He groped with his fingers, feeling for the treasure he'd secreted here months ago.

"That's another thing, Marty. You never call her 'Mom' or 'Mother.' You always use her name, like she was your sister or an impersonal guardian." Bruce shifted anxiously from foot to foot, gaze riveted on the door.

"Her rules. No reminder that she has blood or emotional ties to me. That would make her vulnerable through me. She also likes to thinks she is younger and therefore more attractive than the mother of a teenager."

Ah, there. His fingers brushed against the cool blue crystal he sought. A faint tingling progressed up his hand to his arm and shoulder. Suddenly, his eyes found a new focus as if seeing the crystal nestled into its bed of fiber optics as well as the scene in his room.

Dizzy for a moment, he lost his grip upon the crystal and grabbed something else. He withdrew a palm-sized clamp.

"Is that what I think it is?" Bruce whistled and grabbed the device.

"Yes. It's an illegal Klip. Melinda put it on my computer to drain power and monitor everything I do."

"Then how did you keep our correspondence secret?" Bruce examined the Klip closely, memorizing its construction.

Martin smiled and reached again into the wall compartment. "Will you get back to the door?"

"You mean you've got more in there than just this?" Bruce's eyes went wide with awe. He shook his head. "This is amazing. You've got a mind to match your m . . ."

Martin glared at his friend as he grasped the blue crystal—even more illegal than the Klip.

Bruce docilely returned to his vigil at the doorway. He slipped the Klip into his pocket and seemed to forget it.

Martin grabbed the crystal and yanked it free of its fiber optic connections. Without this, the star map only reached half its true potential. He didn't need the map anymore. He had the proximity coordinates of the wandering jump point firmly in his mind.

"Will you hurry up, Marty," Bruce said. He continued to peer into the hallway looking for potential intruders. "Jane and Kurt are waiting for us. We'll miss the best part of the factory tour. I really want to see how they program the virtual reality scenes into the rides without requiring headgear."

Bruce turned around again.

Martin slipped the crystal into his pocket. It was about as big around and as long as his index finger. He had to keep his hand around it to disguise the telltale shape in his formfitting synthleather slacks interlaced with heat deflector threads. They made his long legs look even longer and, he hoped, gave the illusion that he was taller than he already was.

Bruce always opted for the baggy pantaloons, which made his square body seem bulkier. But the drapes and folds of fabric could hide a myriad of secret pockets and gadgets.

Martin needed to find a better place to secrete the crystal—a gift from his father, Konner O'Hara. He rubbed it idly.

His focus shifted again. The room seemed to tilt to the left and colors took on new depth and brightness.

He stumbled, not certain where the floor truly was or which way was up.

Bruce jumped to hold his arm and keep him upright. "You feeling all right, Marty? You look kind of pale. Maybe we should postpone the tour of the factory."

"No. We have to go today. It's the only time Melinda will let me out of the palace without her. She's tied up with those dippos from Earth. We *have* to go today." He couldn't tolerate another day of being his mother's prisoner. In another day she might figure out just how incomplete the star map appeared on her system and come looking for answers.

They took two steps together, Martin leaning heavily on Bruce. Either the world righted or he got used to the strange slant to his perceptions. Then he shook himself free of his friend's support and marched to the hallway. They'd meet Quinn and the others at the side entrance near the garages. Just a short distance, then he could sit and think about the crystal and what it did to him. What the miniature king stone did to his computer. Did it have something to do with the way a full-sized king stone reacted with the rest of a crystal array to power spaceships and take them through jump points?

He almost giggled at the thought of flying through a jump point wearing nothing but an EVA suit and the little crystal that warmed to his touch and seemed to snuggle into his hand. Crystals were monopoles—no north or south to their magnetism, just their own internal forces. Perhaps he was a monopole, too. Separate, they were lost. Together, they were a family.

"Where are you going, Master Martin?" An armed security guard at the side door jerked Martin out of his strange looping thoughts and back to reality.

"My mother authorized a field trip to the amusement park factory." Melinda might not like being reminded that Martin was her son, but it never hurt to keep that in the front of any conversation with her employees.

"My orders say that trip was canceled. Ms. Fortesque wants you to join her for lunch with her guests from Earth. I'll just escort you to the formal dining room. Your friends are free to take the tour without you if they choose, or they may dine in the family parlor." The guard grabbed Martin by the elbow and propelled him back down the corridor the way they had come.

CHAPTER 23

"**W**HO ARE YOU REALLY, Sam Eyeam?" Konner asked the stranger who had followed Kat so faithfully into *Rover;* the man who had brought one of Melinda Fortesque's beacons to this planet and then disappeared. He almost did not recognize the man with his scraggly beard and hair. He'd know those straight white teeth, those perceptive hazel eyes, and that blade of a nose anywhere, though.

Konner made an adjustment to their altitude. The extra bodies in *Rover* made their flight home slow and ponderous. Too slow. The IMPs could probably fuel up one of their fighters and get it airborne before *Rover* landed and cloaked.

The Sam Eyeam shrugged. "I am who I am. I do what I do."

Kat almost doubled over in laughter at that answer. But her mirth carried the edge of hysteria. She held the flywacket too tightly, almost crushing the big cat with both arms wrapped around it. The flywacket didn't seem to object.

"What's the joke, baby sister?" Konner asked, only slightly pleased at the emergence of her sense of humor. He wanted answers before they reached the village at the base of the cliff. Answers to questions and solutions to dilemmas.

"You might as well tell him, Bruce. If he can't pry the answers out of you, he'll turn Loki loose on your mind with his telepathy," Kat said. She sounded as if she only half believed her words.

"Take over the controls, Loki," Konner said. "And don't deviate from the flight plan. We can dispatch a dragon later to check on Paola and her Amazons." As soon as his older brother transferred the operation of the shuttle to his station, Konner swung his chair around to face his sister and the Sam Eyeam in the cockpit of the shuttle.

"There is no such thing as telepathy," the stranger said quietly.

Konner and Kat both cocked their left eyebrows at him.

"But on this planet, with flying cats and dragons and such, maybe . . ." His words drifted off as Konner and Kat continued to gaze at him fixedly.

"You mean . . . ?" he choked.

"Yes," Konner replied quietly. "Psi powers work here. Maybe not elsewhere, but on this planet they do."

"It's the ley lines," Kat added.

"My name is Bruce Geralds, Sr.," the Sam Eyeam gulped. "I was hired by your wife to find you and bring you back to Aurora for Martin's fourteenth birthday. We missed the date."

"Melinda Fortesque is my ex-wife. Dalleena Farseer is my wife," Konner corrected the man. Did Geralds truly believe the story he spouted? Had he memorized it at Melinda's command? If he believed it, he was too gullible to be a successful Sam Eyeam. But then, maybe that was why Melinda hired him, because he believed her lies and she could manipulate him.

"Not according to Ms. Fortesque," Geralds replied. "And not according to GTE law. In fact, by my reckoning you are a bigamist and the only way to straighten this out is to return to Aurora with me." Geralds grinned.

Konner's stomach sank abruptly. He knew Melinda's tricks. Why was she working so hard to get him back when she had gone to great lengths to get rid of him?

"Actually, Ms. Fortesque is guilty of lying to you." Konner leaned back, assuming an act of casual confidence he did not feel. Melinda was up to something and he did not trust her or her Sam Eyeam. "I have copies of the annulment papers, all properly signed and sealed."

"Then that makes Martin illegitimate and any claim you might have on him null and void," Geralds returned with a smile that did not reach his eyes.

"On certain worlds in the Galactic Free Market, that might be correct," Kim interjected. Leave it to the family professor to come up with the facts. "In the GTE, if the child is conceived within the bounds of a legal marriage, even if that marriage is later annulled, then the child is legitimate and both parents have claim to custody until settled irrevocably in court."

"And that court date has passed." Konner swung his chair back to his console. He did not want to think about it. If he concentrated on one thing at a time, he could hold off the bad thoughts that threatened his sanity. If he concentrated upon Dalleena, the future had hope. A future he planned to share with his son.

"While this conversation is very interesting, it does nothing to save the people Amanda Leonard enslaved on this planet," Jetang M'Berra said. His black skin gleamed with perspiration. "Nor does it explain why you kidnapped Chaney." He and the medic knelt beside the wounded Raaskan on the floor. She tested pulse and temperature and read off numbers to M'Berra who stayed within touching distance of her at all times. Her blonde fairness made an interesting contrast to his nearly blue-black skin and hair.

"We came specifically to persuade Dr. Lotski to come with us. My wife is in labor after a difficult pregnancy," Kim said. He held his hand across his middle as if he shared the birthing pains. Knowing Kim, he just might.

"Sheesh! I haven't delivered a baby since medical school. I'm a military medic not an OBGYN," Lotski protested. Still she crept closer to the cockpit. "What have you got in the way of medical databases?" She and Kim dissolved into a conversation about swollen ankles and back pain.

"I need to go back," M'Berra insisted. "Now that I know Chaney is safe, I need to do something about Amanda Leonard. I need to liberate her slaves and lock her up with reinforced force bracelets."

"You can't do anything behind a locked and guarded door," Konner reminded him. "Which is where her Marines will put you once you return."

"But . . ."

"Our villagers will be safe for a while. Most of them escaped in the fray created by the flywacket." Konner tried to keep the worry out of his voice. "Smart of Yaaccob to use that old superstition about flywackets being connected to the plague we cured. Now they know Gentian had nothing to do with the disease. But they created quite a diversion."

In the midst of the fray, Konner had whispered to Yaaccob that all from the village would be welcome in the south.

If they could find a way to feed them. If the villagers could travel five hundred klicks on foot.

The weight of responsibility pressed heavily against his mind. At this rate he'd never get away long enough to untangle the skein of lies Melinda had woven around their son Martin. He'd never regain custody of the boy within or outside the law.

He needed to use the Sam Eyeam, Bruce Geralds, to get to Martin, but how?

If only he had four pairs of fully charged fuel cells, he'd grab Dalleena and fly back to *Sirius* alone. With the mother ship he could get to Aurora in about four jumps, a little over a week's travel.

Without the fuel cells he was stranded, and they'd just used up most of their remaining reserves on this latest crazy mission.

* —◆— *

Cyndi gasped for breath. Her lungs resisted life-giving air.

The pressure on her chest increased.

"Get off of me," she ordered. She had no breath to scream.

Setting her mind, she thrashed her arms at whatever tried to crush the life from her.

Her blows hit only cold night air.

She smelled sulfur over the salt that permeated the air of this coastal village.

Something hot breathed on her neck. *Do not resist me.* The words sounded raspy, nearly as breathless as she.

"No man rapes me," she said or thought with all of the formidable determination her father had instilled in her.

I have need of your body.

"So do I." With a tremendous heave, she rolled to her side. The pressure moved to her back. But that allowed her to grab some air.

Harder on both of us this way.

"I have no intention of making this easy for you or any other."

Why couldn't she hit the man? Why didn't she recognize his voice? After nine months in this filthy village she knew every one of the natives by their voice, their posture, their *smell.*

This assailant was a stranger.

How had he gotten past the guards? She could have sworn the warriors who prowled the perimeter by night could see in the dark. She'd never been able to sneak past them. And she had become an expert at eluding the best security systems in the galaxy when she thought she loved Loki. She'd managed to meet him in the most obscure and the most obvious places without detection.

You are weak. You grow weaker.

"Never!"

A sharp stab to the back of her neck felt like a medical probe. She twisted and shrugged and rammed backward with her elbow.

She met only air. Hot, rancid air.

Give in to me. I need your body.

"The seven rings of hell around Perdition take you," she screamed.

Cyndi got her knees under her and reared back. The pressure fell away. She panted for breath, head down, hands resting upon the floor of the cave where she slept with five other women.

Somehow she'd managed to roll all the way to the back of the cave. A little niche beneath a sandstone ledge offered her refuge. She squeezed in, confident that no one could reach her there.

Why hadn't anyone responded to her screams? In the dim glow from the fire outside she discerned the shapes of five other women where they sprawled awkwardly upon their mats in the areas each had staked out as her own. One snored.

Still they all remained deeply asleep.

They cannot help you. They cannot hear you.

The pressure came back, this time atop her skull. Her temples screamed with pain. Her eyes felt as if they would bulge out.

"You cannot have me." She rammed her head against the ledge above her. The pain felt almost good in contrast to the pressure.

Cease! I cannot use your body if you damage the skull.

"I will kill myself before I let you have me. I will smash my skull so badly my brains will leak out. You." Bang. "Will." Bang. "Not." Bang. "Have me," she breathed in relief as the pressure evaporated, leaving her with a monstrous headache.

She closed her eyes and fought to manage the new pain. If she concentrated just so, she could imagine the pain and bruises liquefying and draining out of her body and mind.

Some time later she came to her senses with a dull roar in her ears and a new, warm pressure upon her chest. She opened her eyes.

Daylight streamed into the cave. The other women stretched and yawned and prepared to start a new day.

Cyndi lay upon her own mat near the back of the cave, her meager possessions strewn about her. Her head ached and she felt a lump on her forehead that must have bruised into an ugly purple and black.

Then she became aware of a huge black cat sitting and purring upon her chest.

(You had need of me.) The cat levered itself off her chest, stretched and yawned, in mimicry of the humans who shared the cave.

Then it sauntered toward the entrance. Each of the women sharing the cave paused to scratch its ears. But it kept moving toward the cave mouth and the open air. At the arched opening it spread glossy feathered wings and took off.

Cyndi held her breath a moment, watching the magnificent animal.

"This place is getting to me. The nightmares are getting weirder. Or I am going insane. I have to find a way to leave. Soon. With or without Loki O'Hara. I don't care who wins possession of this place anymore. I want out. I want my husband who appreciates who and what I am."

CHAPTER 24

MARTIN DRAGGED HIS feet. The guard, a new man he did not know, hauled him along mercilessly.

Halfway to the cross corridor that led to Melinda's wing, Martin willed his knees to collapse. The guard merely stooped long enough to hoist him up with both hands.

But that gave Martin the chance to stick his left hand into his pocket and finger the blue crystal. Could he stash the thing somewhere along the way for later retrieval?

If Melinda found the treasure, she'd surely confiscate it and find some way to punish Martin for possessing it. That would not keep Melinda from using it—if she figured out what it could do.

Damn! He wished the guard had not been so diligent, had not recognized Martin.

The guard's hands went slack; he stared off into space. After a moment he touched the comm port embedded in his skull behind his left ear. Everyone who worked for Melinda had one so she could communicate with anyone at any time. Even Martin had a port, though Melinda rarely used it. She preferred to speak through a holo image on his computer.

"Master Martin did not pass my post, sir," the guard said. "I have not see him." Still staring blankly, the man returned the way they had come.

Martin touched his own port to monitor communications. All the while he kept his other hand on the blue crystal.

"The boy must still be mucking about in his room," the authoritative voice of the security chief came over the comm system. "Roger, you are closest. Go see what he's up to. The boss is getting a bit antsy."

Martin didn't wait for a reply from Roger. He took off down the corridor at a run. Not quite understanding what was happening, he kept his hand on the miniature king stone and willed himself invisible. He slid to a halt outside the family parlor.

He'd guessed right. His friends were dining there, discussing how to spend the afternoon since Melinda had hijacked their plans.

"Good, you are all here," he panted as he nearly careened into the door-jamb.

Jane and Kurt looked around the room anxiously, their eyes never lighting on Martin.

Quinn squinted and stared at Martin, not quite focusing his eyes.

Bruce looked out the window, staring as blankly as the guard.

Belatedly, Martin released his death grip on the crystal while keeping his hand in his pocket.

His three friends and Quinn finally looked at him in bewilderment. Before they could voice their questions, he blurted out orders right and left.

"We have to go now. I mean right now. If we aren't halfway to orbit within ten digital minutes, Melinda will find us. But right now all is chaos and they aren't looking in the garage."

Quinn threw down his serviette and jumped up. He punched data into his handheld. "No time to gather our luggage, time to move. Good thing I already stashed Jane's extra trunk with emergency provisions."

Jane grinned at Martin mischievously. All of her extra baggage did more than just serve her vanity.

Martin wanted to kiss her. Not now. They didn't have time for anything, let alone the explanations he'd have to give afterward.

"We'll take the servants' tunnel to the kitchen and then to the garage. Come on. Stop staring and get moving. Time for questions later." Quinn bounded for the exit on the other side of the dining parlor.

Martin followed Quinn through a doorway hidden within the rich wall paneling. He returned his hand to the crystal, praying that his new discovery worked as well with groups as himself.

"No one say a word and keep your steps quiet," he whispered.

"What . . ." Kurt began a protest.

"Shush," Martin commanded. "Later," he mouthed.

They hurried down the tunnel, letting the slight downslope speed their steps.

Martin wanted to run. He didn't trust the crystal to keep them invisible. He didn't dare hope that he might finally break free of Melinda's grasp.

But running would make noise and make it harder to keep the group together.

He forced himself to breathe calmly and evenly.

A waiter passed them bearing a laden tray with the second entrée. He looked at them curiously then passed on, too well trained to question his employer's son.

Inwardly, Martin cursed. He gripped the crystal tighter. *Concentrate,* he told himself. *Concentrate on the entire group being invisible.*

Giles, the family butler, strode purposefully up the tunnel.

Martin held his breath. This man was an old and loyal retainer. He reported everything to Melinda as part of his job.

Concentrate, concentrate. Martin forced himself to look where he placed his feet and not into Giles' eyes. He forced himself to think about being elsewhere with his friends and not in the tunnels.

Black stars burst before his vision.

Still he could not draw a breath. He had to concentrate.

Giles passed on and turned right into the connecting tunnel to Melinda's wing.

Martin released the breath he'd held too long. He gasped and bent over, hands on his knees while his lungs spasmed.

"Easy, Marty. Breathe," Bruce whispered. He grabbed Martin's arm and propelled him forward.

Jane and Kurt kept looking around in puzzlement. They both opened their mouths to ask questions.

Quinn pressed his index finger to his lips, signaling absolute quiet.

They moved on.

Servitors dashed about the kitchen, clanging trays, cursing each other and tripping over their own feet. The normal organized chaos of mealtime for a demanding employer.

Martin had spent far too many free moments ensconced in the cheerful warmth of these rooms when no one bothered to take notice of him, except the servants. He knew the most likely path through here without triggering inquiries.

He continued to stroke the crystal, but trusted more in the busyness of the place to pass through unnoticed.

At last they slipped into the garage. Six small air cars rested on mounts near the front. Melinda's huge limousine, and Martin's smaller, older one were parked nearer the rear.

All of the mechanics, driver, and maintenance people had gone to lunch.

Quinn waved the group over to a midsized boxy-looking vehicle that would seat six comfortably but not attract attention in traffic as the flashier limos would.

"It looks different," Martin whispered to Quinn. "Modified for orbital travel?" An extra layer of cerama/metal encased the vehicle, painted a modest gray to match the original van body. New seals about the windows and a bulky "something" attached to the undercarriage betrayed the true nature of the changes to a careful observer like Martin.

A passing glance showed a bulky passenger vehicle, nothing unusual.

The bodyguard shushed him and nodded.

Silently, they all settled into the van. Martin took the seat beside Quinn, the only licensed driver in the group. Martin drove frequently with his tutors because no one on Aurora would think of arresting him. This time they wanted anonymity, not the token police force watching for a teenage driver.

Jane and Bruce took the middle seat. Kurt happily stretched out his long legs on the rear seat well below window level. He'd learned how to maintain a low profile after the assassination attempt on his home planet.

Quinn fiddled with something below the dash. When he finally raised his head, a big grin split his face. "That should give us some privacy. I've disabled the GPS as well as the tracking device your mother had secreted here as soon as I asked permission to use this air van."

The bodyguard touched a couple of interfaces on the dash and the engines purred to life. He signaled for the garage door to open. It remained firmly shut.

Martin whipped out his handheld and keyed in an override. The door remained stubbornly closed.

"Try this, I found it somewhere, I don't remember where," Bruce said handing the Klip to Martin over the top of the seat.

Martin grinned and applied the clamp to a set of controls beneath the dash. Then he tried the override code again.

The door rose sluggishly.

A mechanic wandered in, wiping his mouth with his sleeve. A woman behind him, also in green mechanic overalls, yawned widely. She looked up and pointed toward the van. A questioning look crossed her face.

Her companion pressed his comm port and spoke urgently.

Martin did not need to hear his words to understand that he notified security of the breach in protocol. No one had scheduled the van for use today.

Quinn stepped on the accelerator and launched the vehicle out of the garage with the door only half open.

An alarm sounded inside the palace.

Sirens blared on the airways outside.

"Hang on tight. This is going to be close," Quinn said through gritted teeth. He pulled back on the controls and sent the van upward the moment the tail cleared the garage. Then a sharp ninety-degree turn left, another turn sixty degrees right.

Martin keyed his handheld to close the garage door. Then he tapped in Melinda's override code. No one would be opening that door soon.

The palace fell away behind them. Martin did not even take a last look at his home. His thoughts were all on the future and getting away.

Quinn pushed the air van higher and higher. He squeaked through heavy traffic above, below, and in front of them. Atmospheric forces screamed around them.

He pushed them higher yet.

A black air car with flashing red-and-white lights came up beside them, an unmarked police vehicle. "Descend and park. Repeat, descend and park, by order of the Aurora City Police," a voice broadcast through the interior comm system as well as loudspeakers outside.

Quinn put the van into a sharp dive. The police followed at a more leisurely pace. Then Quinn pulled out and accelerated upward once more.

Caught unaware, the police continued on their downward path for nearly a full digital minute before recovering. They sped up in full hot pursuit.

An energy pulse zinged past Quinn's side of the vehicle. He grinned tightly and swerved crazily, all the time pushing them closer and closer to orbital altitude.

Another shot sizzled along the roof.

Martin smelled burning cerama/metal and heard the hiss of escaping air. "We aren't going to make it, are we?"

"Never say never, Martin. I still have a few tricks up my sleeve." Quinn put the van through a couple more wild swings. "There should be a tube of caulk beneath your seat. Seal that leak before the atmosphere gets any thinner."

The police fell back.

Another shot pierced the rear window. Quinn sent the van into a wild dive.

The police car zoomed closer.

Quinn jammed controls upward and to the right.

A sharp jolt from the rear rocked them hard. Martin's safety restraints bit into his shoulders as he fell forward and to the side.

The van careened downward, out of control.

Martin shook his head and looked around. He had to grip the seat hard with both hands to keep himself from launching toward the windshield.

Quinn lay slumped forward, limp and unconscious, eyes closed. A bruise was already forming on his forehead.

Martin shook the man, pushing him back against the seat, away from the steering column. His head flopped backward. No response.

CHAPTER 25

M OVEMENT STIRRED AROUND the entrance to the largest cave. Kim lifted his attention from the dying flames of the communal fire. He didn't dare hope that Hestiia's long labor was finally over.

The sun had risen over the bay an hour ago. Pryth's pyre smoldered. By tonight, it might be reduced to ash so that they could cast the remains to the four winds.

The villagers milled around, sharing breakfast, completing small chores, lingering while they all awaited news of a new life added to the village. Kim's brothers and Kat sat with him upon rocks placed conveniently to the fire for them. Kat yawned and looked longingly at the ground, as if she'd like to stretch out and fall asleep right there.

M'Berra and Geralds had found beds somewhere and gone off to them hours ago.

Loki jumped up and paced, unaware that people passed back and forth across the entrance to the big cave with some speed and urgency.

At last Chaney Lotski ducked out of the cave entrance and wandered toward them. Her eyes looked sunken and hollow with fatigue and her already pale skin seemed almost translucent in the early light.

But a grin split her face when she saw Kim. "Congratulations, Mark Kimmer O'Hara. You are the father of a healthy baby girl," she said, offering her hand.

Kim took it numbly. "A girl?" He gulped in shock. "We were sure it was a boy."

"Disappointed, little brother?" Konner asked. Then he jumped up and slapped Kim's back with enthusiasm. "I have a niece. Did you hear that everybody? I have a niece!"

Kat and Loki joined him in jumping up and down with excitement.

Slowly the fog lifted from Kim's mind. "A girl. It's a girl!" he shouted. Then he sobered. "Hestiia. What about Hes? Is she okay?" He anxiously searched Lotski's face for a clue.

"She will be fine." Lotski became serious. She seemed weighed down with responsibility. "She lost a lot of blood. She's weak and tired. But she's nursing. That will help slow the blood loss. The women here know more about childbirth than I do. If they hadn't come up with special herbs and moss to pack the bleeding, we might have lost her."

She took a deep breath and closed her eyes, heavy with fatigue. "Herbal remedies or not, I don't want her out of bed for three days and she shouldn't even think about another child for a couple of years. She needs to fully recover. And if that means celibacy to prevent another pregnancy, then so be it."

"I can't even think about that. As long as Hes is okay, I'll do anything, anything to keep her that way."

"It's what you don't do that's more important."

"Can I see her?" Kim started walking with long purposeful strides toward the cave before he had an answer.

"If the ladies have finished cleaning up and will let you in. But don't stay too long. Hestiia needs her rest."

Kim hesitated at the cave mouth.

Poolie, as wife of the headman and therefore in a position of authority among the women, beckoned him in. Hugely pregnant herself, she rubbed under her belly in ever larger circles, as if soothing her own early labor pains. She held a finger to her lips, then pointed to the still, pale face of Hestiia beneath a mountain of sleeping furs on a pallet near the center of the cave.

Kim crept close to his wife and knelt beside her. A lump of emotion clogged his throat and his hands trembled. One of the other women twitched the edge of the furs aside to reveal a wrinkled pink lump cradled in the crook of Hestiia's arm.

"My daughter?" he breathed.

"Our daughter," Hestiia whispered. She raised a tired arm and caressed his face with one finger.

He caught her hand in his and kissed her palm. "She is beautiful, as light and fragile as the air." He didn't quite dare touch the little thing that opened vague blue eyes to stare at him. The pink fuzz on top of her head looked like it might turn red later, maybe blond. He didn't care.

"Then we must call her Ariel." Hestiia smiled as she gently uncovered the baby for Kim's inspection. "But remember that the wind can be a formidable force. Remember the storm last Solstice?" A bit of a smile touched her lips.

"Just like her mother," Kim agreed. He counted ten perfect fingers and ten wrinkled toes. Two arms. Two legs. A head atop a long skinny body. What more was necessary?

"Ariel she is. But she is also Pryth. She will carry both names," he decided. The memory of the old wisewoman passing the mantle of experience and responsibility to Hestiia lingered in his mind.

"Yes. Thank you." Tears filled Hestiia's eyes. "'Tis right and fitting that we honor our friend and mentor."

"Get some rest, love. I'll be right outside." Kim bent to kiss his wife on the brow.

Her eyes closed. Immediately, her breathing took on the slow steady rhythm of sleep.

Kim sat and watched her a long time, unwilling to accept even the little separation of leaving the cave.

"You know, Kim's going to be even more reluctant to leave this place with us when we return to civilization," Loki said quietly.

Kat stared at her oldest brother aghast. "How can you even think about separating them at a time like this!" She placed her clenched fists on her hips and stared at Loki, chin set as stubbornly as she knew how.

"We can't leave him behind," Loki protested. He matched her posture with equal belligerence.

"Now, now, don't fight. We just got reunited," Konner stepped between them.

"If anyone leaves this planet, it will be me," Kat insisted. She had a brief mental image of herself leading Loki in force bracelets off an IMP rescue ship. She shook her head.

No, she would not do that to her brothers. She had grown past the need for revenge. But she'd still like to slug all three of them for the twenty years of separation.

Well, maybe not Kim. He had been little more than a baby when the family broke up. And now he was a new father.

She couldn't help grinning. For twenty years she had been the adopted daughter, accepted and loved but just slightly outside the family dynamic in Governor Benedict Talbot's household. Now she had more family than she knew how to manage.

"Look, we can't settle the issue of who goes and who stays until we get the fuel cells recharged again," Konner said. The middle brother, the neutral one who always found ways to mediate among his siblings. Just as he had twenty years ago. "I'm as anxious to get back to civilization to claim my son as you are to get back to your lives. But we have to settle the problem of Hanassa and what he's doing to the people here. We have to find a way to kill the Krakatrice on the big continent."

Kat took a deep breath to settle herself. "We are all tired and jumpy. Any decision we make now will be based on flawed judgment. Let's get some sleep." She stretched her back. Then she yawned. It grew to encompass her entire body. And just kept growing until she thought her jaw would crack and she'd never be able to open her eyes again.

"Sleep sounds good. I'll take you up to the clearing and get you settled." Konner yawned, too.

An emptiness settled in Kat's belly that could only be filled with sleep. Sleep and something else.

"Where's Gentian?" she asked.

Konner shrugged.

"I saw him skulking around near dawn," Loki offered. "But not since."

Kat's emptiness became a knot of anxiety. She called the flywacket with her mind. He did not reply and he did not appear.

"He'll turn up when he's ready." Konner shrugged and led the way to the uphill path.

"Somehow, I don't think so." Kat shivered with a new loneliness.

The flywacket has gone into hiding. We cannot find him. We cannot recall him to the nimbus if we cannot find him. He may have his uses yet. But he has abandoned his chosen one. She will flounder without his guidance. We have no other to send to the aid of the humans. We dare not allow any more of our numbers to be corrupted by them. Their taint is potentially more damaging than the one we may not name gone rogue, or the threat of the Krakatrice to our way of life. The humans must blunder their own way now. We may not interfere further. The nimbus has decided.

CHAPTER 26

◆——·——◆——·——◆

WITH THE GOOD NEWS that both Hestiia and baby Ariel would thrive, the village moved, as one, to go about their day. The men downed the last of their tay, a hot herbal infusion that sort of tasted like tea, and headed for the cove.

Loki held Yaakke back from the group headed down to the fishing boat. The tide was nearly full, and it was time to negotiate the treacherous cove and bring back food for the village.

"You don't seem yourself lately, my friend," Loki said. He didn't quite know how else to ask the man about his gloomy mood and how his eyes followed Cyndi wherever she went.

"I am more myself now than a few days ago." Yaakke looked affronted. At the same time he would not meet Loki's gaze.

"Has Cyndi done something . . . ?"

"She insulted my honor and the traditions of the Coros."

Loki breathed a little easier. "Then you are not likely to succumb to her seduction. I wanted to warn you."

"I lusted after the woman. She is beautiful." Yaakke flashed Loki a wide grin. "But no more. I have seen her kind before. She uses men and then discards them. We do not allow women like her to live among us. We tolerate Lady Cyndi only because she is a prisoner of the Stargods."

At least the man knew in his head the dangers he faced. But had his heart caught up with the logic?

Loki didn't think so, not the way Yaakke searched the village for a glimpse of a bright blond head that wasn't there.

Loki let the man go off to his fishing. Then he went in search of the woman who had been missing for several hours. Who knew what mischief she was up to now.

He found her hiding a short distance west of the village. She sat in a pool of sunshine in the center of a lovely copse. Two empty leather buckets lay upon their sides at her feet. Eventually, she'd have to fill those buckets in the creek three meters away. But the longer she idled here, the fewer trips she could make before someone else did the job.

"Where'd you get that bruise, Cyndi?" Loki stood behind the woman he had once loved. Even from here he could see the black-and-purple mark on her temple and the swelling lump beneath it.

"I tripped. Not that it's any of your business." She did not look at him, continuing to bask like a cat.

"What did you trip over? Your conscience?"

She turned a malevolent glare upon him.

Loki shrugged it off.

"As much as I dislike you, you are my responsibility. I need to know if someone hit you." Loki sat on the grass beside her, his back against a sapling Tambootie tree. Proximity to the tree of magic might elevate his ability to pry secrets from her mind.

"You would not believe me if I told you." The sarcasm and contempt left her face. She hunched in upon herself.

"You look almost vulnerable. What happened, Cyndi?" He couldn't allow himself to sympathize with her. That way lay disaster. He deliberately pulled an image of Paola into his mind. A small secret smile began in the middle of his belly and moved upward.

She looked upward as if counting the leaves in the tree canopy above.

"You must have realized by this time that life on this planet is weird," Loki said quietly. "I've seen some pretty strange things since I came here, including dragons and flywackets. I've done stranger things. Things that you'd call magic and disbelieve until you thought deeply about it. I don't believe half of it yet myself."

"Have you seen any ghosts?" she asked, almost casually.

He caught a whiff of intensity in her posture.

"Sort of. There was man called Hanassa. Three times my brothers and I killed him. Twice he returned to plague us. And this third time . . ." Loki shook his head, not willing to voice to an outsider what they suspected Hanassa capable of. Last night's battle with Amanda Leonard was too reminiscent of their previous encounters with Hanassa.

"Hanassa." She rolled the name around her mouth as if tasting it. "What did he look like?"

"Middling height and coloring. Stocky. Vibrant. Very intense eyes."

"Did . . . did he have something to do with Taneeo?"

"Taneeo was his apprentice for a while. Then his slave. Then . . ." Loki clamped his mouth shut.

"Taneeo was in a coma. Now he's not. Did Hanassa do something to his mind?"

Loki gulped. "Yes."

"Did the ghost of Hanassa take possession of Taneeo's mind?" Cyndi rolled to her knees and stared fiercely into Loki's eyes.

For a few heartbeats her face took on the wild intensity that reminded Loki of Hanassa. Her mild blue eyes glowed and flared. Did he catch a glimpse of red in there?

"Did he?" she repeated. "Tell me, Loki. I need to know."

"Yes."

"How?"

"You wouldn't . . ."

"Try me."

"In the dragon nimbus, there are red-tipped, blue-tipped, green-tipped dragons, and maybe some other colors I haven't seen yet. But there can only be one purple-tipped dragon at a time. Purple-tips are always born twins. In this latest generation three purple-tips were born. The nimbus refuses to kill one of their own. Two of the purples had to become something else. Iianthe remains a dragon. Gentian shrank into a flywacket—a large black cat with wings."

Cyndi nodded at that, as if she'd sent the critter.

"Hanassa possessed the body of an ailing human boy child about two years of age. He grew up looking and acting like a human, he became a priest. But he was filled with anger at no longer being a dragon. He began forcing the Coros into war and took blood sacrifices. He enslaved many people until my brothers and I ended Hanassa's life."

"No wonder the locals worship you as a god."

"I am not a god. Merely a man with the technology to solve a few of their problems. But I'm running out of supplies and ideas." The problem of the Krakatrice hung heavy in his gut.

If anyone could handle those monsters, it was Paola. But he feared for her.

"When you killed Hanassa . . ."

Loki shuddered at the memories her words conjured. He'd pulled the trigger on a needle rifle and shot Hanassa. More than a little bit of himself had died at that moment. He'd tried to follow his enemy into death. Never again would he kill, man or animal.

"When you killed Hanassa, he didn't stay dead, did he?"

"We think—we think his spirit invaded Taneeo. He was physically weakened by months of privation and injured. Vulnerable." Taneeo had caught more than a few of the poisoned needles in the rifle spray. His body had taken a long time to recover, and when it did . . .

"We think Taneeo's will was stronger than Hanassa's. He fell into the coma because he fought Hanassa's possession of him."

"But Taneeo is awake now, showing no signs of inner struggle."

"That is correct."

"So where did the spirit of Hanassa go?" Her chin trembled as if she already knew.

Could this truly be Cyndi speaking? The woman Loki had known would never have accepted any of this discussion as more than horror stories, the product of an overactive imagination.

"Possibly into the body of Commander Amanda Leonard."

"You battled her last night. No, don't deny it. I heard the talk around the fire."

"Yes. Kim shot her four times, square in the chest with a fully charged stunner. The energy in *one* of those shots should have knocked her unconscious. Possibly stopped her heart. She kept right on following us. Never missed a step."

"Afterward, what happened to Amanda?"

"We fled. I don't know. Where is this going, Cyndi? What does this have to do with the bruise on your forehead?"

"I had a bizarre nightmare in the middle of the night. I think Hanassa tried to take me. But I wouldn't let him. He fled when I threatened to kill myself rather than give in to his pressure."

"Cyndi, I don't know if I should believe you. Or if I should lock you in force bracelets until we know that slippery bastard hasn't invaded you." Loki sat up straighter.

"I'm clean, Loki. Believe me, I forced the bastard out. When I woke up this morning, the flywacket was on my chest purring. And then he flew away. I thought I was going insane until you told me about . . . about purple-tipped dragons." She sank back down in her half recline.

"The flywacket belongs to Kat."

"Who cares?"

"You should."

"Loki, you have to promise me, that when you leave this planet, you will take me with you. You can't leave me here. You can't take a chance that I will succumb to Hanassa."

"I can't promise anything. Right now we don't have enough fuel to leave. You wouldn't happen to know anything about some sabotaged fuel cells, would you?"

"If you won't take me with you, then be warned, I will do everything I can to escape to Base Camp and help the IMPs get off this miserable rock."

"Go ahead. But believe me, if Hanassa is in Amanda Leonard's body, he isn't going anywhere. He's bound to this miserable rock by more than a lack of fuel."

How did he know that? He shook his head clear of the strange notions that kept invading his thoughts—like he'd touched more of a dragon than just its back when he rode one and experienced a dragon dream.

Loki climbed to his feet and returned to the village. His insides quivered and his hands shook. For the first time since the night he and Mum had escaped their burning home with Konner and Kim, he was scared. Truly frightened that his wits, his audacity, and his strength would not prevail over his foes: supernatural, monstrous, or human.

CHAPTER 27

◆——·——◆——·——◆

"CAPTAIN?" one of the Marines addressed Hanassa.

He remembered to salute the man. Strange how cooperative the mind of his host had become. Especially when that mind realized that Hanassa's dragon strength had partially repaired the damaged left eye. Eventually, he would fully repair it, but such work took time and energy he did not have at the moment.

"Report," Hanassa barked. Amanda continued to supply him with the proper vocabulary.

"Captain, the village is empty. All of the natives have deserted." The Marine stood at full attention.

Hanassa sensed the fear, the loyalty, and the courage that kept the man in front of her and so rigid his body nearly hummed when the breeze struck him.

He wanted to lash out at the bearer of bad news. Amanda gripped his will and held tight. *Use his fear, do not abuse it,* she whispered.

"Explain," Hanassa spat. He began to pace, unable to contain the energy that wanted to lash out and draw blood.

"During the night they all slipped away. We have only two dozen men as slaves." The words came out clipped. The Marine's face glistened with a sheen of sweat.

"Two dozen? That is barely enough to work the fields," Hanassa's anger flared again. He needed blood to calm himself.

His stomach roiled in revulsion. This Amanda person had a stronger influence on him than he thought.

If we kill any of those slaves, then we will lose them all. We will not have enough to work the fields and feed us. If we and our men starve to death, we will not have a base of power to achieve total control of the planet.

Amanda also had logic.

"Do you still wish me to select a sacrifice?" the Marine asked.

"Select one man for flogging. Send the rest into the fields. And keep a careful watch on them all. Oh, and, Sergeant?"

"Yes, Captain?" The man sagged with relief.

"After I have drawn blood with the whip, I will need . . . I will need two of my men to come to my cabin."

"For punishment, Captain?" He went rigid again.

"Not exactly." Hanassa allowed himself a wicked smile. "Though by the time I am sated, they may believe it to be so."

"Very well, Captain." The man saluted and backed off.

You are learning. Between the two of us we should go far. Now listen carefully while I show you how to field strip and recharge a stunner.

Late in the afternoon, Kat helped move Hestiia back to the family clearing. She carried the new baby while Kim carried Hestiia. She marveled at the tiny scrap of life in her arms and wondered if she'd ever have the courage to form a lasting bond with a man so that she, too, could have children.

She heaved a sigh of relief as she settled the baby next to her sister-in-law.

But she couldn't settle herself. She wandered randomly through the environs of the family clearing. About every tenth step she glanced over to the main cabin where Hestiia slept.

But the baby didn't sleep. She apparently didn't like the move and refused to nurse or sleep.

Kim walked his own path around the clearing, crooning to the tiny baby he carried, trying to keep her quiet while his wife slept.

A soft pinkish-blond fuzz crowned the baby's head and her eyes were the unfocused blue of a newborn. Hard to tell yet if she would grow into the family's bright red cap of curls or the midnight-blue eyes of her father and uncles.

Undoubtedly, she'd inherit the pale skin and cursed tendency to freckle.

Kat let her mind wander at will along with her feet. If she concentrated too hard on how to deal with Amanda Leonard, then all she could think about was the terrible injustice of enslaving the natives. She wondered if she could have prevented her captain's slide into insanity if she'd noticed the signs in time.

But then Jetang M'Berra had noticed the signs and covered for Amanda, tried to mitigate her actions for months.

She'd done it again, dwelled on the past rather than solutions. So she wan-

dered and called to her flywacket. Since his disappearance the morning of
Ariel's birth, the flying cat had not returned to Kat's side and had not communicated with her.

She missed him terribly. Not until he was gone had she realized just how
lonely she was. She might have found her family, but she was not yet one of
them, did not share growing up with them, did not agree with them. She
considered herself a civil. Her brothers disdained her culture and clung desperately to their bush origins. She had been taught to scorn them with equal
fervor.

And then there was the little matter of their crimes against the GTE,
transporting contraband, nonpayment of customs duties, escape from various
jails, fleeing arrest, assault upon a judicial cruiser, and others, she was sure.
They must answer for them eventually.

If they ever got off this planet.

Gentian come to me, please, she called. *I miss you.*

"Konner?" She paused by his "power farm," the array of fuel cells set out
to collect solar energy augmented by brandy distilled from the Tambootie
berries. The still burbled happily off in the woods somewhere, converting the
toxic fruit to something the cells could use to recharge. "Konner, how did
you know to call Gentian a flywacket?"

"Gentian? He's returned from the dragon nimbus?" Konner looked up
from his endless fussing with the cells.

"You've met my flywacket before?"

"He belonged to Hestiia when we first arrived. Then he disappeared. The
dragons said something about him not being worthy due to cowardice."

"Hestiia didn't miss him?" She'd only had the beast at her side one full day
and she felt empty without him.

"Hestiia had Kim by that time." Konner grinned.

Kat had to match his expression. Their younger brother seemed to have
found his soul mate, his other half, in Hestiia. He still stared blissfully at his
daughter as he carried her around the clearing. He pointed out the wonders of
the world to her as he walked and bounced. The baby seemed oddly alert and
content for a newborn. No wonder Kim vowed never to return to civilization. He'd found a home here on this isolated planet beyond the back of beyond.

"You, too, seemed to have found happiness, Konner."

"Yeah, I have. I never thought I'd find a woman as comfortable around
machines as I am, least of all on a primitive planet. Dalleena and I are better
suited than I dreamed possible. She's coming with me when I leave here to
find my son." He returned to his work.

The clearing seemed strangely empty without the bustle of a dozen people.
Loki was in the village trying to cobble together some kind of pump and fire
hose. Dalleena was in the village helping Lotski, M'Berra, and Geralds settle

in to village life. They weren't family, so they did not get to live in the clearing.

Kat strolled by the lean-to she had claimed. It was well chinked with moss to keep out drafts and piled with furs for comfort. Still, she had not slept well, missing Gentian. And possibly Bruce Geralds.

She returned to her pacing and her thinking.

At the center of the clearing, where she and Konner had buried the king stone from *Jupiter* last autumn, she stopped abruptly. Something was wrong.

"Konner?"

Her brother barely looked up from his fuel cells.

"Konner, what happened to the ley lines that used to cross here?" Her steps had not been as random as she thought. Without realizing it, she had traced the path of the mysterious silver-blue lines.

"Ley lines?" He stood and brushed his hands against his buckskin trousers. "I placed the crystals according to predetermined ratios. Blue king stone at the center, surrounded by twelve green drivers, then one hundred forty-four red directionals at the rim of the force field. The ley lines had nothing to do with it."

"Oh, yeah?" She took a deep breath and allowed her eyes to lose focus. Three straight lines of magical power slid into her vision. Then she plotted the lines on a graph only she could see. "Three lines should converge and form a pool of power right where the king stone stands. There's a hole in the web where you dug."

"I can't see the lines from this angle." Konner paced a circle around where Kat stood. The disturbance in the dirt had settled beneath winter rains. It hardly showed at all.

And yet power filled Kat like an electrical current. She felt as if she were the energy flowing along fiber optics to the concentric circles of crystals that powered the confusion field around the clearing.

"Take a deep breath, Konner," Kim advised, coming closer. He cradled the now sleeping baby in one arm. He, too, pointed out the three lines with his free hand. Each gesture came to an abrupt stop short of the crossing point, directly beneath Kat's feet.

"Both of you, breathe deep and slow," Kim continued. He drew in a long breath himself.

Kat mimicked his rhythm, the world seemed to shift slightly to the left, colors intensified, her vision sharpened, then blurred as halos appeared around her brothers' heads and each object within the clearing. Strange how Kim's aura was bright yellow and green, the baby's only mild shades of blue and green, so pale they were almost white. She must be too young for definition.

Konner pulsed bright orange.

Kat held out her hand to see what colors she emanated. She saw only a layer of white.

She looked at the ley lines. Now she could see that the main lines had shot out small tendrils toward the junction point, repairing themselves.

"Do you see that?" Kat explained the phenomenon to her brothers. "I guess this means we should always look before we dig."

She thought back to the time last autumn when the dragon Irythros had flown her to the desert south of here to show her the ley lines and teach her how to use them. She had used the power to reach outward, to travel along the theoretical transactional gravitons, like a king stone seeking its mother crystal. Kat had sought her own mother and not liked what she had seen when she found a woman obsessed with amassing more and more wealth and power in order to find her daughter. But she'd never have enough. Never allow herself to have enough because if she tried to find Kat and failed she could not live with herself.

So why was Kat filled with the same kind of power now? The ley lines did not yet reach the spot where she stood, right over the king stone. She sent her vision diving down. Blades of grass and weeds, individual grains of dirt, tiny rocks, fat worms, all peeled back, layer after layer as she delved deeper and deeper. Down a full meter to the apex of the giant blue crystal.

Deeper yet she dove, down the two-meter length of the stone to the nest of fiber optics that spread outward to connect to the twelve green driver crystals, each one meter in length, and the one hundred forty-four red directional crystals, each only half a meter in length. The entire family of crystals hummed happily in harmony gathering nitrogen and other elements from the planet to fuel themselves. They spat energy outward in a dome to enclose the clearing in a shield that opened only to a combination of O'Hara DNA and music.

Kat withdrew with a jerk. She flailed for balance, totally disoriented from her rapid withdrawal of communion with the crystals.

"Breathe, Kat. Breathe deep. Don't panic. Crystal thrall is like that." Konner steadied her with words and physical strength.

"Konner, what did you use in the crystal baths to regrow the damaged array aboard *Sirius?*" She knew, but she needed confirmation.

"Our starter kit was outdated and useless. But we found a veritable soup of every known element and mineral in a creek spilling out of the blown-out volcano," Konner explained.

Both brothers eyed her warily.

"You found omniscium in the creek?" Impossible but they must have. The key ingredient to crystal growth for star travel was only found in gas giant planets and hard to mine. It turned to vapor upon contact with atmosphere.

"Yes, we found trace amounts of omniscium. Enough to complete a crystal bath," Kim confirmed. He wrapped both of his hands around the baby, cuddling her close. For warmth? Security?

"Do you still have the equipment to test for omniscium?" Kat began to tremble all over with the magnitude of her theory. She deliberately stepped away from proximity with the king stone and avoided touching any of the ley lines.

"I've got a gas chromatograph."

"Will it test dirt? With a probe?"

"I can adjust it."

"Then test the ley lines. I think we are dealing with rivers of omniscium. I think your theoretical transactional gravitons, the web of energy that holds the universe together and conspires to keep everything in place, are also rivers of omniscium. I think this planet is riddled with the stuff and that is why dragons are real and magic works."

The beginning place is in danger, the place where the web of ley lines begins and ends. These human invaders are smarter than we thought. We cannot allow them to proceed. We cannot allow this knowledge to spread. The one who harbors Hanassa can use this knowledge to wreak greater damage than all the others combined. That one has no conscience, no consideration for anything but violence and subjugation.

CHAPTER 28

$\blacklozenge$ — $\cdot$ — $\blacklozenge$ — $\cdot$ — $\blacklozenge$

MARTIN PLACED HIS HANDS flat on the steering controls of the van. Rapidly he touched in new commands. His stomach trembled and his teeth chattered in fear. Quinn was unconscious. Quinn, their only hope to escape Melinda.

"Drag Quinn into the back seat," he yelled at anyone who might hear. Crashing from this elevation was worse than getting caught. He didn't intend to do either.

"Someone get him out of my way." He scooted as far right as he could, trying to get a firmer grip on the column with its touch pad. Quinn's heavy body slumped against his shoulder, interfering with Martin's control.

Sluggishly, the van leveled out. He nosed it upward a notch. They were deep into the tangled grid of working class domiciles. Martin knew how to lose the police hot on his tail. But he had to have fine control of the screens.

Pressure on Martin's shoulder eased.

"Help me, Bruce. You, too, Kurt," Jane ordered.

Quinn moaned.

"He's alive!" Jane cried. "Come on, guys, help me move him. We've got to treat that wound and Marty's got to drive."

Somehow his friends hoisted Quinn into the center seat. The man rolled his head and half opened his eyes. But he did not hold onto consciousness long.

Martin settled into the driver's place with ease. Now he could fly this thing the way Quinn had meant to. Maybe better. He knew this city. Quinn did not.

His body still shook with shock and nervousness. But he had a plan. He could do this. With help. They just had to stay free and alive until Quinn came to.

Bruce climbed over the seat and took the navigator's place beside him. He didn't know the city either, but he could look out for obstacles, like new constructions creating box ends.

Martin banked hard left, down into an alleyway, then hard right through a tunnel made by two buildings that had grown together by a skyway that expanded into more apartments.

"Barrier on the left-hand alleyway," Bruce warned.

Martin swung right and down.

The more maneuverable police car followed him, gained on him. "Jonesy must have hired some new officers. These guys know what they are doing," Martin muttered.

"Marty, I don't think that's a police vehicle," Kurt said, hesitating on the last words.

"He's right," Jane added. "Auroran police would never fire on a vehicle with you in it, Marty. You are too valuable to Melinda."

"Or too much of a liability," Martin said.

"I think it's the guys sent after me. They're trying to kill me and don't care about collateral damage," Kurt said. He slunk down deeper into his seat.

"Everyone gets out of this alive if I have anything to say about it," Martin said through gritted teeth. He sent the van into a steep climb, out of the maze. As he came level with the roofs of the dwelling complexes, his engines nearly stalled and he twisted into a tight spiral around the buildings. Within a few blocks he'd put a fair amount of insulated building foam between him and his pursuers. Their sensors should be mightily dusted. If they were using standard police equipment.

But what if they were hired assassins out to get Kurt?

Or Martin?

Or Quinn?

A few more twists and he came up behind the unmarked car.

"Hang on to Quinn," he called back to his comrades.

With a deep breath and a mumbled prayer he shot forward. His front end slammed against the black car. Their pursuer lurched and twisted, loosing altitude rapidly.

Martin shot upward, seeking orbital elevations. "We still losing air through the places those bastards shot us?"

"I sealed those that didn't self heal," Kurt replied. He pressed his hand against the three previous holes. "That's the good thing about the insulation foam between the normal hull and cerama/metal."

"Get my handheld out of my pocket, Bruce." Martin shifted his hips a little to give his friend better access.

"You could have worn pantaloons, buddy. These synthleather breeches are too tight," Bruce complained.

"Pantaloons don't attract the girls, though." Martin flashed a cheeky grin at Jane.

A few more mumbled protests and Bruce squeezed the device free. Martin placed his thumb on the screen to activate it.

"Punch in the following code to open the atmosphere dome." He spewed a string of numbers and letters, almost faster than Bruce could tap them in. The code should dissolve as fast as it entered the computer so no one could copy it. Unless they had an eidetic memory. Bruce probably did.

"Wow, how'd you get that code? Only the flight controllers at the orbital station are supposed to have it." Kurt craned his neck to watch the slightly cloudy distortion of the force field dissolve.

"Same place I got the Klip. I stole it from Melinda."

"You have your father's instincts," Quinn mumbled. "Let me take over from here." He tried to sit up, groaned, and flopped back with his head in Jane's lap.

"Just tell me how to find your ship, Quinn," Martin said. He and Bruce exchanged grins. In a similar situation either of them might have preferred to rest their heads in Jane's lap. She'd grown up a lot in the last two years. For the better.

"You mean, you haven't figured it out yet?" Quinn asked. He still slurred his words.

"Good thing that you had your safety harness on. You banged your head, probably got concussed, but you didn't crash through the windshield," Jane said. She stroked the man's straight hair lovingly. A dreamy look crossed her face.

Martin frowned. His face grew hot and his hands clenched on the drive panel. He forced himself to concentrate on the puzzle of where a Sam Eyeam could hide a ship in a closely patrolled planetary system.

He'd have to have brought the ship to the Aurora system ahead of time, abandoned it while he returned to escort Kurt here. That meant several weeks had passed without being able to monitor the ship. Several weeks for patrols to accidentally stumble upon it.

"You hid it in plain sight, piggybacked to that derelict military cruiser in high orbit. Melinda leaves the cruiser there as a reminder to IMP officials of what she can do if anyone interferes with her absolute control over Aurora," Martin chortled.

"And conveniently near the jump point," Quinn added. He had better color in his face, but his eyes still looked glassy.

Martin set a course for the cruiser.

"I don't suppose any of you four have ever piloted a ship through jump?"

Quinn asked. He struggled to sit up again. With a gentle push from Jane he made it this time though he held his head between both hands and kept his eyes closed.

"I know the theory for putting a ship in line with a jump point," Kurt said.

"Marty, here, is the only one of us who has ever driven anything," Bruce said grudgingly. "My mom insists I wait until I'm of age. If my dad were home more often, he'd teach me, though."

Martin refused to mention that Bruce's father had gone missing about the same time as the IMP judicial cruiser carrying an Earth diplomatic attaché in the same quadrant where the O'Hara brothers had disappeared. Bruce's father had a long history of employment with Melinda. He was probably responsible for a number of questionable projects.

"I've sat beside my mom's pilot when we went through a jump," Jane added. "I tried to keep my eyes open to see what jump really is, but I couldn't."

"Great—that means I'm going to have to do it on my own. I can't talk you through it. Not until one of you has had a *lot* more experience," Quinn moaned.

"Jane, there should be a first aid kit under your seat. See if there's a pain blocker in there," Martin said to hide his nervousness. Jumps were dangerous, and they'd be going through them fast, probably with Melinda's military on their tail to compound the dangers. As soon as they broke free of the cruiser, her people would spot the ship and pursue.

"Quinn, how did you know to park your ship here?" Martin asked. The timing was all wrong for him to have done it *after* Kurt's dad hired him.

"If I told you, I'd have to mind-wipe all four of you, and that would defeat the purpose of the mission."

"You're still working for the emperor. Only his private Sam Eyeam would have the authority to do that."

"I thought he was working for my dad," Kurt protested.

That statement met silence all around.

"You want me to give evidence against Melinda so you can break her control over Aurora." Martin didn't know if he should feel dirty, depressed, or elated. Maybe he just felt used. Manipulated by the emperor as badly as he had been by his mother.

He had the evidence to condemn Melinda. A lot of people would be hurt if that evidence ever became public. Including his friends. Would he ever use it?

"Believe what you want. Just dock with my ship so we can get out of here. Safely."

"Will I ever be safe again, Quinn?"

"I'm going to work very hard to make certain that all four of you remain safe." He placed a neural pain blocker against the back of his head and closed his eyes as well as the conversation.

· ◆ ·

"What do you mean, the ley lines are rivers of omniscium?" Loki burst through the clearing's barrier heedless of Bruce Geralds who followed him. All thoughts of a long soak in the hot spring fled in the wake of this exciting new development.

"Just what I said," Kat replied. "But it's only a theory."

"Your theory sounds plausible to me." Loki let a smile crease his face. "This could mean our salvation. We could buy seats in Parliament as well as our citizenship. We could change GTE policies if we control this much omniscium."

"But we won't," Kim said quietly. "If we let the GTE, the GFM, or the Kree know about the omniscium, then we open this place to destruction far faster than farming and industrialization would. A vote in Parliament won't change policy fast enough to save this planet from pollution, overpopulation, and any number of other ills inherent to the GTE."

"Believe it or not, the galaxy needs fresh food more than it needs more star drive crystals," Konner added. He pulled three gadgets out of the jumble of equipment around the power farm.

"But . . . but . . ." Loki protested. He knew his brother was right. But the wealth, the power, the *control* they would gain. No one would dare outlaw them again. They'd be free to go anywhere in the galaxy they chose. Even Cyndi would have to respect him—not that he cared anymore what she thought.

"We're going into war with the Kree. We are going to need more ships, that means more crystals. The GTE really needs this planet," Kat said. She lifted her chin in typical O'Hara stubbornness.

Loki wanted to object to her argument, just because he could not allow himself to agree with her. But he did agree with her.

"We don't have the equipment to mine omniscium, even if we agreed to do it," Kim said with a degree of finality.

"We don't even have enough fuel for *Rover* to get back to *Sirius,* so we can't market the stuff," Konner added. He stuck probes from his gadgets into three different places in the clearing. Then he whipped out a handheld and studied it.

"You are recharging the fuel cells," Kat countered. "You'll have enough fuel in a few weeks."

"It's taken me all winter to get that much and we wasted half of it rescuing you last night." Konner lifted his chin in stubbornness to equal his sister's.

"We are headed into summer, greater solar power to recharge the cells, more fruits and berries to distill. We'll have enough fuel in no time," Loki soothed. He couldn't help but rub his hands together in glee. "And I have some ideas about mining. Didn't the omniscium turn to a salt in the creek? If we can channel a ley line into a water source . . ."

"And poison the entire watershed of that creek?" Kim asked. "We don't know how toxic omniscium is in large amounts. No one has ever found enough in a single concentration to find out."

"Base Camp has a forge," Geralds offered. "If we depose Amanda Leonard long enough to get access to the forge, we could make pipes to stick into the ley line junctions and funnel it into the water. Or vats of water if you insist."

"No," Kim and Konner said together. They both looked at the handheld and whistled.

Loki grabbed the device and watched numbers pile up next to an obscure glyph he guessed represented omniscium. This find grew by orders of magnitude with each passing moment.

"Will pottery seal tight enough to contain the salt?" Loki asked the group. He moved closer to Kat. Geralds followed him. The three of them lined up against Konner and Kim.

Kat picked up one of the dozen water jugs resting near the path to the hot spring and the creek, ready for filling the next time someone went in that direction. "One beaker of omniscium salt this size would fill the baths for fifteen crystal arrays."

"No one leaves this planet, or comes back to it except Konner and Loki. We will not contaminate the land or the culture with outside influences," Kim reiterated.

"We agreed on this, Loki," Konner said. "The location of this planet must remain secret to protect the people as well as our resources."

"We can't keep this place a secret if we start marketing omniscium in large quantities," Kim added. "I won't have my daughter exposed to GTE influences." He cooed at the baby as she began to fuss.

"We can keep it secret," Loki insisted. "It's all in the marketing. We only release a little bit at a time, food and omniscium." Desperation fueled his mind with new ideas, new possibilities.

"The three of us vote as a family, as we always have," Kim said.

"Kat is family, too," Loki reminded them.

"So are Dalleena and Hestiia, and the new baby," Konner countered.

Control of the situation began slipping out of Loki's hands.

"Mum also must be consulted on something this big." Surely Mum would agree with Loki. Mum would do anything to regain her citizenship, anything to regain her daughter. And her vote outweighed all the others combined.

At the moment Loki had Kat and Mum. That had to be enough to overrule his two bush-blind brothers.

"Mum cannot be consulted. She's too far away and we don't have the resources to set up communications," Konner said, almost with glee. He thought he had control of the question.

"I know how to contact Mum. I can show you how, Loki, with the king stone and the ley lines," Kat whispered.

Loki felt a smile and a plan growing in the back of his mind.

"Why don't we discuss this after we depose Amanda and gain access to our forge again." He had to stall. In the meantime, he and Kat and Geralds could begin experimenting with mining techniques and long-distance telepathy.

CHAPTER 29

"UH, QUINN, I'VE NEVER docked a van to an orbiting vessel before," Martin said hesitantly. The ramshackle solo vessel looked like a piece of mismatched junk thrown together with no regard for aesthetics. He was surprised any of the parts fit together well enough to maintain a seal. It looked to be just another piece of the derelict cruiser it perched under.

Quinn held his head in his hands and moaned.

The lack of gravity made Martin fight to maintain a horizon. His upside-down view of their world made the air car drift at unexpected angles. The darkness, barely alleviated by the van's headlights, didn't help matters.

"He's in pretty bad shape, Marty. Can't you figure it out?" Jane asked. She continued to stroke the bodyguard's hair and murmur soothing nonsense at him.

"Line up your headlights to the docking clamps, just like parking in a garage," Quinn said. His words slurred and his face looked pale. That concussion was probably more serious than he wanted to let on. But at least he was conscious.

Martin gulped and did his best to follow orders. Every time he'd parked an air car—a much smaller and more maneuverable air car—he'd had attendants guiding him and gravity anchoring him. He didn't like the proximity of the belly of the ship against the side of the van. He'd have to scrape the cerama/metal sides of both to line up with the clamps.

"I don't think this thing is going to fit. The clamps look too far apart." Martin slowed as much as possible, creeping forward one centimeter at a time. He had to fight the controls to keep the van in a straight line.

The van scraped the hull. He cringed and backed off a few centimeters.

"You can't hurt the hull with a van," Quinn said. "Unless you care about returning the van to your mother in pristine condition, go ahead and scrape. Just park the damn thing."

"Consider this learning under fire," Bruce added.

"That helps a lot, Bruce," Martin ground out. "Fire won't burn in vacuum and that's what we've got outside. And I think we are running out of air inside. This van was modified for suborbital travel, not built for it."

He eased forward a bit more and felt the docking clamp lock on to the front of the van. Martin breathed deeply. Perspiration drenched his back and brow worse than at the end of an extended fencing bout.

"Are you aligned properly for the air lock to secure tightly?" Kurt asked. He scanned the extending portal skeptically.

Tears prickled Martin's eyes. What if he had failed and they all died in the air lock because he had done a sloppy job? His mother would kill him for damaging the van . . .

She would murder him anyway for trying to escape her net of control. She'd murdered her parents. Or at least she had hired the assassin and then bribed the investigators to declare the incident a tragic accident. She had cheated Martin's father out of a prenuptial agreement. She had deprived Martin of a family and a normal home life, all so that she could manipulate and control everything and everyone around her.

Why hadn't she just arranged for Konner's death once she had confirmed her pregnancy?

Because Konner O'Hara had family who would ask questions.

If Martin and his friends died escaping her, she could blame it all on Giovanni political enemies from Nuevo Italia. Had she arranged that, too, to cover her tracks?

"What's the seal readout?" Quinn asked. His eyes still did not track properly.

"Where do I find the display?" Martin asked, jerked from his self-defeating loop of dismal thoughts.

"On the portal's arm, just outside your window."

Martin found the red display of digital numbers. "Does eighty-nine percent sound right?"

"Good enough if we hurry." Quinn handed Martin his handheld. "You'll have to authorize the lock to accept five bodies without EVA suits. Code sixteen alpha, twenty-three gamma, delta, delta, beta."

Martin tapped in the code. The portal creaked and shifted ominously.

"Okay, open the doors and scramble." Quinn didn't look as if he could move, let alone scramble.

Somehow, they dragged him into the air lock, closed the van doors, and engaged atmosphere. A lot of air leaked out of the faulty seal.

At last the inner door opened and they all stumbled gasping and careening into a storage bay onboard the saucer-shaped vessel.

"Help me to the bridge." Quinn looked as if he was about to vomit. But he held it in as he grasped a handhold and reached for the next. "We've got to get moving before Melinda figures out where we are."

"Flight control sensors will lock on as soon as we engage engines," Martin warned. He gulped, too. He hadn't much experience in free fall and still had trouble finding his horizon.

"You don't look like you can stay conscious long enough to get us through jump," Jane said. She planted herself directly in front of Quinn.

Martin had often seen that stubborn expression on her face at summer camp. Usually when she opposed Kurt's plans for some new mischief with the computers, or Bruce's practical jokes, or Martin's solo hikes deep into the wilderness. Rarely had any one of them won an argument with Jane when she put on her "den mother" face.

"All I have to do is get us to the jump. The ship's computers do the rest." Quinn plowed forward, pushing Jane aside. In null G, she floated to the opposite side of the bay before she found another handhold.

"We'll have to remember that move," Bruce whispered to Martin. In the echoey bay, Jane had to hear it.

She "hmpfed" and followed Quinn and the boys through a maze of gangways to the bridge, a bubble of viewscreens somewhere in the midsection of the ship.

"Anchor yourselves." Quinn sounded more alert. At least he did not slur his words. He followed his own orders, pulling his safety harness over his shoulders and anchoring it to the center of his seat before the pilot screens.

Martin took the copilot's seat, assuming he had a right to it after driving the van this far. His three friends pulled down "jump" seats from various parts of the bulkheads and strapped in as well. They all tried looking over Quinn's shoulders to watch how he took the vessel out of sleep mode and into full power.

"Jettisoning the van from the portal," Quinn said.

Martin scanned his screens and saw an icon drifting away from the ship. Jane peered out the porthole nearest her and nodded. One less encumbrance from Martin's past.

"Does this ship have a name?" Martin asked. He tapped a duplicate pattern to Quinn's on his blank screen. If he could just do it one more time, he'd have it memorized.

"All ships have names and ID codes. We are sailing aboard the *Margaret Kristine*."

"Who is she named for?"

"You'll have to ask the emperor that. It was his ship before I bought it. I kept the name because I like it."

"What's that blinking yellow light over my head?" Kurt asked. He strained against his harness to see the beacon better.

"Jump warning," Quinn muttered.

"Already?" Bruce gulped. "We haven't even disengaged from the derelict yet."

"Then that red light flashing on the comm board is normal, too," Jane said. Her voice quaked a little.

Martin jerked his attention away from Quinn's screens to his own.

"Quinn, someone is trying to signal you. I bet it is flight control on the orbital station."

"Ignore it. We'll be out of here before they can send someone out to see what's going on." As he spoke, the ship moved. Acceleration gave them limited gravity.

A klaxon blared three times. Martin wanted to hold his ears and close his eyes against the noise. He didn't dare. He needed to say awake and alert. He had to make sure Quinn did, too.

"Entering jump," Quinn warned.

Reality blurred and dissolved.

Motion seemed to cease.

Time stopped.

Martin lost contact with his body.

And then they were into the jump. Martin looked down upon his inert body from somewhere . . . somewhen else. Time became a meaningless measure of existence.

Jane screamed. Kurt slipped his harness and dove through low G to shake Quinn's slumped form.

The klaxon sounded a proximity alert. "Unknown ship approaching," ship's computer said in a sweet, lilting feminine voice. "Proximity alert. Prepare for crash."

After a second lonely night of sleeping in the clearing alone, without Bruce Geralds at her side, Kat joined her brothers Kim and Konner as they marshaled every available hand and headed back to clear a new field in the village.

Kat toted rock after rock out of the west field until her back felt as if it would split in two and her hands were a swollen mess of cuts.

Her brothers expected a wave of refugees from near Base Camp. They needed several more acres cleared and planted before they arrived. The season had already progressed too far into summer for them to expect a full crop. Hopefully, they'd harvest enough to get them all through the next winter.

Food took precedence over mining omniscium.

Kat mopped sweat off her brow with her sleeve. The remnants of her uniform looked as tattered and filthy as the clothing of everyone else in this village. She'd carried her fair share of rocks from the field to the borders where skilled stoneworkers piled them into low walls. Eventually, the walls would separate the various fields and keep the livestock from munching new crops.

She plopped down upon a good-sized boulder, one too big to carry, and took a swig of water from a nearby bucket. She'd seen others take brief rests here.

Everyone in the village and the clearing had been drafted to help—even the protesting and disdainful Lucinda Baines. Taneeo, the village priest, had told her that she would not eat unless she worked. The village would not survive without the crops.

Even the Stargods—the three O'Hara brothers—added their backs to the heavy labor.

Kat's shoulders and legs ached from the unaccustomed work. Her back itched where perspiration had dripped and dried.

Trying to look casual, Kat made her way to the festival pylon at the center of the village. She leaned against it, letting the poles support her weight. The three poles lashed together into a tripod and anchored deep in the ground marked more than the middle of the living area. It marked the junction of three ley lines.

She had some serious experimentation and research to do before Loki's plans for mining went any further.

Kat breathed deeply as Kim had showed her: in on three counts, hold three, exhale on three. She felt the now-familiar shift in orientation and spectrum. Power tingled in her feet, up her body, and into her mind. Her perspective shifted from inside her body to up above the top of the pylon. She looked down upon her body and up into the heavens. With just a little stretch she could reach . . . reach out to Gentian.

Her mind zeroed in on her errant flywacket directly into his body. The gray-green desert around him/them looked frighteningly familiar. Gentian clawed and twisted at something metallic and mechanical. Too close. She couldn't discern what the thing was from five centimeters' distance.

Forcibly, Kat removed herself from Gentian's mind and watched him from a slight distance. The metal "thing" resolved into the hydroponics tank inside the lander she'd had to abandon after *Jupiter* crashed. Gentian worked at freeing pumps and hoses from the innards of the contraption.

Kat chuckled. Gentian wasn't truly a coward, he just disagreed with nimbus definitions of courageous acts. Right now, he defied the nimbus to help Paola with a kind of weapon to defend the port city.

Loki would be glad when Kat told him.

She shifted her mental reaching upward. Up . . . up to the saucer-shaped *Sirius*. She drew its deep silence and patience into herself, understood the nuances of the sleeping crystal array, and listened to the computer running maintenance diagnostics.

For a femto of a second she flitted through the fiber optics to the computers. She became the ship, attuned to the crystal array.

She could now fly this ship no matter what booby traps and safety protocols Konner had installed.

Communication with Mum, or possibly even Kat's adopted father, Governor Talbot, should be an easy jump from here. Dad would not know how to respond to a telepathic call, might not even receive it. But Mum . . . all four of her children had psi powers. She probably did, too. For that matter, both Kat's blood parents probably had strong psi factors for their children to manifest their talents so strongly.

All she had to do was find the transactional graviton the king stone used to contact its mother stone. That web of energy should be a mere extension of the ley line she stood upon.

There. She grabbed hold of the energy with her metaphysical hand and began tracing it back toward Earth's moon and the crystal factory in orbit around it.

(Go back,) a deep voice, that might have been many voices, echoed in her mind. *(Do not venture beyond the realm of dragons.)*

"I have to," she told them. "Since you won't return Gentian to me, I want to talk to my mother," she lied. She did not *want* to talk to the obsessive woman her mother had become, but she needed to know how, to show Loki.

(You speak the truth only when you say you miss your flywacket. For the rest: You can lie to your brothers. You can lie to the stranger, the Sam Eyeam you want as a lover. You can lie to yourself. But you cannot lie to us.)

"Oh, yeah?" she sneered silently.

She sensed an equally private chuckle from the voices.

"Please let me do this. I need to know if I can talk to my Mum this way."

(Not until you have found your true home and know what you want from your mother and your brothers.)

"But . . ."

She fell abruptly back into her body. Her senses reeled and her stomach rebelled.

"Let's get you a cool drink and some shade," Bruce Geralds said. He took Kat's elbow and led her off to the nearest cave. "You should know better than to work out in the sun without a hat."

(You should know better than to deal with dragons before you are ready.)

CHAPTER 30

THE SUN SET upon the village at the base of the cliff. Weary workers trooped back into their caves and huts eager for a hot meal and sleep. Kim wanted nothing more than a soak in the hot spring and the chance to hold his wife and daughter in his arms again. But he had duties to this village and the one that Amanda Leonard had enslaved.

"Iianthe?" Kim called the purple-tip dragon with his mind as well as his voice. "Iianthe, we need to know what Amanda is up to. We need to know how the other villagers fare. But they are far away and we cannot fly to them right now. Can you help us?"

His mind and ears remained empty of any dragon presence.

"Maybe Irythros will answer me," Konner offered.

"Try. Irythros is more adventurous and eager to please than Iianthe. My dragon is serious and all too aware of his status as the only purple-tip in the nimbus." Kim sipped the herbal infusion the local women called tay. It tasted nuttier and sweeter than real tea. Still, it refreshed him and kept him occupied while the old women who had not been in the fields finished preparing the communal pot of stew.

Konner turned on his sitting rock and faced the bay. His brow furrowed in concentration.

"All I get is emptiness." He turned back to face the evening bonfire, shaking his head. "It's like they are all occupied with something else."

"You both look as if you have a headache," Kat said, joining them. Her own face looked pale and her eyes squinted as if the campfire was too bright.

"Try some tay," Kim offered her a cup and the pottery jug filled with the hot brew. "What have you been doing to share our headache—besides working twice as hard as anyone else out in the bright sun?"

"Trying to contact Gentian. I really miss my flywacket. His purr cures any number of ailments, including headaches." She sipped at the tay, grimaced at the strange taste, then sipped again. A little of the strain eased from her face but not her hunched shoulders and scrunched neck muscles. "I stood at the festival pylon and reached out with my mind. I found him trying to dismantle the abandoned hydroponics tank for a pump and hoses. He's helping Paola without permission from the nimbus."

"Speaking of working too hard," Loki joined them. He carried a larger mug that smelled of beer. "What are we going to do about Ms. Lucinda Baines?" He folded his legs and sank onto his own rock. "I don't think she carried more than two handfuls of pebbles all day."

"Let her go hungry," Konner muttered. He stretched his back. He'd spent the day wrestling a pair of oxen into a yoke and then plowing. His ability to lift heavy objects with his mind should have made the job easier. Psi powers drained more energy from the body than hard physical work.

Only the Tambootie eased the burden. Konner rarely indulged in the drug.

Kim had a hard time fighting his constant need to lick the oils from the leaves and then chew them, even when he wasn't working magic.

The old women and young children passed plates of stew around to one and all. Kim ate hungrily, barely noticing the chunks of fish that had gone into the mix. The men had not had a chance to hunt today. He and his brothers had eased their refusal to eat meat enough to consider fish edible. The addition of shellfish from the shore made a nice change in their diet.

Yaakke picked up a reed flute and began playing a lilting ballad about a lover lost at sea. One of the women picked up the tune in a husky alto. A tenor voice added harmony.

And then, miracle of miracles, Cyndi added her clear soprano. She sang the sweet lyrics with passion while the village as a group hummed along in a quiet resonance until the last poignant chorus where the dragons returned the lost sailor to his lover.

Loki sat with his mouth open in wonder. "She actually joined the group!"

"I wish I could sing as well as she does," Kat said around a yawn. "Might ease the long lonely nights aboard ship."

"Did she sing while aboard *Jupiter?*" Loki asked.

"Once. She got a little tipsy during a poker game. She sang as she cleaned us all out of chips. I could have sworn she cheated, but I never figured out how."

"I thought if we gave Cyndi enough freedom, she might try to escape to Base Camp," Loki muttered. "Now she seems to be fitting in a bit, she might prove an asset. Our people do love their music."

"I don't think we need to worry about Cyndi harboring Hanassa's spirit.

Amanda Leonard's insanity and attempt to enslave the locals is more typical of the rogue dragon than Cyndi singing love ballads," Kim said.

"I agree," Loki said quietly. Then he related Cyndi's strange dream.

"Sounds like Hanassa tried to gain a foothold here to work mischief against us," Kim admitted.

"We need a spy at Base Camp, but I wouldn't ask anyone to volunteer for that dangerous job," Konner said.

"*S'murghit*, we need to find out what is happening at Base Camp." Kim slammed his cup against his sitting rock, sloshing tay on the ground and onto his buckskin breeches. Just one more stain among many.

Kat's head jerked up. She stared at the rising moon in intense concentration. All traces of the earlier headache vanished from her expression and posture.

"What is it?" Kim whispered.

"Gentian," she breathed. "He's coming back." Her shoulders relaxed and a smile crossed her face. "He's certainly a chatterbox tonight."

"What's he saying?" Kim asked. He hoped that Gentian had messages from the dragons.

"Right now he's flooding my mind with images of his hunt. Yuck, I didn't need to know the fine details of gutting a squirrel." She grimaced as if the images had left a bad taste in her mouth.

"Wait a minute." She held up her hand to hold off Loki's sarcastic comment. "Paola now has the parts to make a pump and hose to fight off the snakes." She paused another moment while she listened. "He saw a line of people walking this way from the big river—I think they are the slaves who escaped from Amanda. They are weary but safe, about a week's walk from here."

"How many?" Kim asked. He whipped out a handheld and began plotting the number of acres they would need to feed additional mouths.

"Gentian doesn't think in numbers," Kat replied. She stood up, eyes still on the moon.

A shadow crossed the pale surface. Villages stood to look as well. Some of them crossed themselves in superstitious fear. Many more crossed their wrists and flapped their hands in a ward against Simurgh, the bloodthirsty demon dragon they used to worship.

"There he is," Kat sighed in relief. Then her face and body stiffened.

"What, Kat?" Kim asked. He did not dare imagine what new worry replaced his sister's joy at the return of her flywacket.

"Amanda and her Marines have fired up the forge. They are making weapons to replace their stunners. Lethal weapons. This time they mean to kill all those who resist."

•———◆——•

"Solo merchant vessel, this is Imperial Military Police Cruiser *Hercules*. Identify yourself," a crisp male voice announced over Quinn's comm system.

Martin sank back into his body from the jump with a stomach lurching jolt. He shook his head to clear it.

Jane shook Quinn's shoulder to rouse him.

"What do we do?" Bruce whispered, as if the vessel outside could hear them.

Martin slapped the comm unit. "*Hercules,* this is Imperial Scout *Margaret Kristine,* piloted by Adam Jonathan Quinnsellia," Martin said in his deepest voice. Was that how Quinn would introduce himself?

"State the nature of your mission, Pilot Quinnsellia."

"I'm on a private mission for His Imperial Majesty."

"Not enough info, Quinnsellia. You could be anybody trying to bluff your way past this blockade."

Aurora blockaded? Martin's head spun with questions. No time for speculation. He had to convince this IMP cruiser that they were on a legitimate mission or risk being sent back to Aurora and Melinda's wrath.

"Secrecy code," Quinn mumbled. "Alpha, alpha, alpha, one, one, one, zeta, two, quantum, three."

Martin repeated the code out loud to the IMP cruiser.

"Good hunting, Agent Quinnsellia," the voice from *Hercules* replied. "Let us know if you find any trace of the *Jupiter* in your travels. Politics are heating up over the loss of that ship and the dippo they carried as a passenger. His Majesty, in particular, wants that ship found."

"Will do," Martin replied. He shut off the comm link and stared at the pilot's screens. "Now how do I get this thing underway?"

Quinn touched a few places on his screen. "You have control. Steer by the touch screen."

Martin placed one finger on the dark rectangle at the center of his controls. An icon of the ship appeared on the viewscreen along with a glyph representing the IMP cruiser.

"Now ease your way around the other ship. Very light touch," Quinn directed. His eyes crossed and he looked close to losing consciousness again.

Martin complied. The icon careened a long way toward starboard.

"You having problems, Quinnsellia?" The voice from the IMP cruiser overrode Martin's cut off of the comm system.

"Too broad a stroke. This isn't a VR game. Little movements," Quinn advised.

"Let me do that," Jane eased into position next to Martin. She placed her smaller fingers on the screen and barely moved them. The icon of the ship straightened up and moved slowly around the cruiser. "You talk to the man and make it sound like you really are Quinn."

"Um . . . *Hercules,* that last jump was rough," Martin said. "Left me a little dazed at first. I'm okay now."

"You flying solo? Sounds like you need some help. I'll gladly lend you a navigator."

"Don't let him. He just wants to monitor my mission," Quinn protested. "IMPs don't like the fact that His Majesty employs solo agents."

Martin nodded and returned his attention to the comm. "If I let your navigator aboard, I'd have to mind-wipe him. That would defeat the purpose of his presence. Thanks for the offer anyway, *Hercules. Margaret Kristine* out."

This time Quinn turned off the comm unit and added a few extra commands. "He won't override that again."

"You look better, but still shaky, Quinn," Jane said, as she steered the ship into space beyond the IMP.

"Can you navigate us to the next jump?" Quinn asked. He posted coordinates on the upper left-hand corner of Martin's screen. Their current position appeared in the upper right-hand corner.

"I think so." Jane bumped Martin with her hip, indicating he should move.

He scooted out of the chair and let her take his place. She settled comfortably, never letting up her control of the steering. "Just a matter of watching the numbers until they match. I've worked similar exercises at home manipulating robotic arms for virtual dissections in biology."

"I've worked robotic arms when I rebuilt my dad's home security system," Kurt chimed in. "If I could shadow Jane's moves for a little while, I'm sure I could spell her."

Good idea." Quinn tumbled out of his own chair so that Kurt could take it. "I'll be in my quarters with the med kit. Holler if you run into any problems bigger than space dust. The galley is fully stocked, help yourselves. Oh, and Martin, why don't you see if you can load your star map into my system."

"The only copy is on Melinda's computer."

"Is it?"

Martin fingered the blue crystal in his pocket and wondered the same thing.

CHAPTER 31

K AT HELD GENTIAN close in her lap, cherishing their togetherness. After everyone had eaten, she had slipped away and now sat on the ground overlooking the cove at slack tide. She blanked her mind a moment, trying to center herself. Maybe then she could figure out what was important, where she belonged, who to trust.

Amanda Leonard, her *captain,* had gone insane and now apparently hosted an alien spirit. The brothers she had blamed for abandoning her twenty years ago now seemed honest men, victims of a corrupt judicial system. Her own thoughts and perceptions had gone awry, affected more by new psi powers that gave her information without hard evidence.

She communicated with a flying cat more readily than she did Bruce Geralds, an attractive man she considered a potential lover.

She had some sorting out to do.

"Will you spy for me again, Gentian?" she asked quietly, stroking the silky fur around his ears.

(*I am afraid. But I must or my nimbus will take me away from you. I do not know how they will punish me for cowardice.*)

"It is okay to be afraid, my friend." Kat continued her loving caress of the flywacket, reassuring him and herself of their bond. "I am often afraid. My duty is stronger than my fear, though. I need you to help me stop Amanda from doing more damage to herself and the people around her."

(*Your brothers will do it. You must remain safe, so that I may remain safe.*)

"My brothers need you to spy for us as well. The dragons do not respond to our request for aid. You alone can travel the distance between here and Base Camp and back again safely. You alone can help us. I need you to help me put my world in order. I have many new emotions and situations to sort through. I need to take care of Amanda and the world I came from before I can accept my brothers as family."

(For you I will do this thing, though I do not like it. I fear the spirit that moves your Amanda.)

"We all fear her. And I promise that when I leave this place for good, I will take you with me. I will protect you from the nimbus. I will keep you safe."

The flywacket settled deeper into her lap with a sigh. Kat thought the conversation ended. Then her companion spoke again.

(My nimbus may not allow you to protect me from them.)

"Your nimbus has never run up against Mari Kathleen O'Hara Talbot before." Kat laughed a little and ruffled his ears with rough affection.

They both yawned hugely, reminding them that a very long day was nearing an end.

Her brothers prepared to climb the hill to return to their wives and their beds. The villagers wound down their celebration of a hard day's work successfully completed. Their songs had dwindled away along with their chatter. A few women nursed mugs of hot drinks and men finished off their beers, as one by one they sought their night's rest.

Teenagers patrolled the perimeter of the village, taking the first watch.

She heard a hesitant step behind her and stiffened her back, prepared to defend herself.

"Don't go back up the hill tonight, Kat," Bruce Geralds said quietly. He wrapped his arms around her shoulders.

Kat leaned back a little, welcoming his warmth. Sleeping snuggled against him, waking with him close would be nice.

"Bruce, I'm not ready for a relationship. I've just found my family after a twenty-year search. They aren't the monsters I believed them to be. They aren't angels either. Until I figure out what they are, and what I want from them, I can't really accept them as family. It's all too new. I've too many emotions to sort through to risk an entanglement."

"I'm not asking for a long-term commitment, Kat—unless we never get off this rock. For now, I just don't want to sleep alone." He kissed the back of her neck.

Tingles of pleasure radiated down Kat's spine and through her shoulders. She basked a moment within his caress.

Gentian jumped off her lap and began circling her. He made a point of coming between her and Geralds.

"I guess that damn cat has a voice in this matter." He broke contact with Kat.

"I guess he does. Maybe later, Bruce. Just not tonight." She stood and brushed off her crumpled and filthy uniform. "We might be able to find a few moments of privacy tomorrow in the hot spring." She lifted her eyebrows in speculation. She realized she needed more from him than just sex if she were ever to truly trust him.

"I'll hold you to that. I haven't had a proper bath in months."

"None of us have." She laughed, too. "We all smell a little musky and ripe. But if we all do, then we don't offend anyone."

"Kat, what are we going to do about the omniscium? We can't just leave it. The GTE needs it. With the money from it, I could break free of Melinda Fortesque. Konner could buy custody of his son. You could buy yourself three promotions." He stood beside her and looked her squarely in the eyes by the light of a cloud-covered moon.

"Not very likely. The emperor is trying to reinstitute merit promotions. If we ever get back, I'll have one heck of a lot of explaining to do." Something about his last statement bothered her. Her thoughts scattered as he kissed her full on the mouth.

"All nice speculation. I'll dream about it in my cold lonely bed. I'll dream of you, too." He pushed her away and walked back toward the jumble of caves and huts.

"What did he mean by breaking free of Melinda Fortesque?"

Gentian did not have an opinion. She stropped her ankles and butted his head against her so that she stumbled toward the path uphill to the clearing.

"Ready for bed, Kat?" Konner asked. He carried a small lantern that burned fish oil. It stank.

So did she.

"Can I get a bath tonight?" she asked, moving close to her brother's side and the circle of inviting light.

"Maybe in the morning, when the light is better."

Loki and Kim joined them. Companionably, they all climbed the hill together. For the space of an hour Kat felt almost as if she belonged with them, almost as if she were a part of the family and not an outsider.

How long could it last?

"Why would you have to buy custody of your son if Melinda sent Geralds to bring you back to become a family again?" she asked quietly. "Why would you have to buy custody if you are still married to her as she claims?"

"Melinda is full of lies. Our marriage was annulled, and our prenuptial agreement destroyed—except for my carefully guarded copy," Konner said bitterly. "Melinda no more wants a family than she wants to share control of Aurora with anyone. She's blinded Geralds with stardust."

"Or maybe he's lying to get on your good side, Kat," Loki added.

"Or to get into my bed."

"Be careful, baby sister. Don't let your emotions blind you to people's faults," Konner warned.

"Use your magic to see who tells the truth and who lies," Kim added. "I'll show you how to use the Tambootie tomorrow."

"Can I practice on you three, see how much of the truth you are telling me?"

They all found something else to look at rather than answer her.

That was answer enough. She turned her back on them and walked back down the hill.

"Kat, remember that trust has to be given before it can be received," Kim called after her.

She almost stopped. A deep ache in her heart kept her moving back to the village and a lonely bed in the women's dormitory.

Noon sunshine sparkled on the water of the bathing pool. Kat stood in the pool at the base of the falls. Warm water swirled about her legs while a cool splash from the falls refreshed her face. For the first time in months she felt truly clean. Her clothes lay out on rocks, equally clean and drying in the summer sunshine.

Bruce Geralds swam lazy circles around her. His clothes were spread out next to hers.

He probably expected physical intimacies from her special invitation to enjoy the family hot spring.

She intended a different kind of intimacy—probes into his memories of his time before he showed up at Base Camp.

"Don't hunch your shoulders," Geralds whispered in her ear as he came up behind her. He grabbed her at the base of her neck and began massaging twenty years of knotted muscles.

Her head lolled forward accepting his closeness.

The current around her legs changed. She realized that he stood behind her, feet braced in the mud, while he gently pulled her body backward into a float.

She dug her toes into the soft streambed.

"Let me work on your neck for a while." She eased away from him enough to turn him so that he faced away from the bank on the clearing side of the pool. The force field ended just beyond the stream.

Kat now knew that Konner had had to make the force field quite large to accommodate the full crystal array in proper proportions. The king stone resided in the middle of the clearing with twelve green drivers in a circle at a specified distance. One hundred forty-four red directionals stood out from there in another circle, spaced proportionally. Every measurement came down to an exact ratio of twelve to one.

The whole encompassed enough land for a large garden, the hut, and this pool, with acres of trees to shade and shelter it.

With strong hands, she worked on the cords of Geralds' neck, then spread out to his shoulders and back. He had firm, lean muscles, a long body, and not much body hair. He seemed a perfect compromise between the short, compact body of the civilized planets and the taller, leaner body of the bush planets. Genetic manipulation had determined the differences many generations ago.

She liked his body. She wanted to like the man inside.

"There's an ugly scar here." She ran her fingertips diagonally down his back from right shoulder to left hip. "You should have Lotski look at it. Maybe she has something to reduce it."

"It's old. Too late for cosmetic repair." He moved her hands back up to his shoulders.

"How'd you get it?" She wanted to ask why he hadn't been able to get medical help soon enough to seal the wound without the ridge of thickened flesh.

"Accident. Too near an exploding ship in space. I had enough air and sense to climb into an EVA suit until the authorities picked out my life signs among all the debris."

"Still . . ." Any inhabited planet connected to the trade routes had decent medical care. He'd only have the scar if he had been in hiding after the accident with nothing more than rudimentary first aid.

Why would he have to hide? Unless he caused the accident.

"Leave it, Kat. It's history. Let's talk about something important. Like the omniscium."

"What's to talk about?" Kat returned her attention to the tightening cords of his neck. "We can't do anything until we figure out how to mine it. Then we have to figure out how to get it and us off this planet."

"I got a peek at the stash of fuel cells at Base Camp. Lots of partials, few full. I think if we put all of them in one of the fighters, you and I can get back to my ship." Geralds turned to face her, placing his hands upon her shoulders. His thumbs traced her jaw in a gentle caress.

"What about my brothers?" A chill ran up Kat's legs that had nothing to do with the currents in the pool.

"Let them fend for themselves. They'll recharge some cells eventually. But you and I can be free. Once we've sold a single beaker of omniscium, we can come back here. We can build a palace in the west and rule our own kingdom." He twirled in the water to face her, grabbing her about the waist in his enthusiasm.

"I—ah—thought cannibals lived in the west; that it was truly barbaric over there." She backed up through the tight whirlpool he had created with his move. Her balance was off as well as her ideas about controlling this conversation. "You had nightmares of cannibals."

"Only in the mountains between here and there."

"You had to walk through their territory to get to Base Camp. How did you survive?" Kat tried to put winsome admiration into her expression. She'd never been very good at flirting. She liked her relationships honest and open.

"I guess I'm too ornery to eat. They captured me in a blind pit. Left me there for a day and a night." His face fell and his enthusiasm faded. "I just barely escaped when they pulled me out. They chased me for days."

"Why? They must be desperate for food if they have resorted to eating other humans."

"On the contrary. They eat humans in a very solemn ritual. It's a rite of passage and a way of honoring an enemy they respect for his prowess in battle." He gulped and turned his face away.

"I'm sorry you had to go through that. No wonder you had nightmares."

"That part isn't important. I escaped," he said firmly. "What matters is that Judge Balinakas and his entire judiciary crew managed to get their escape pods to land together on a river near the far west coast of this continent. They've set up their own little city already, gotten the locals to build for them, organized crops and trade and communications . . . everything. The land is incredibly lush, full of everything, including mineral deposits. We could settle there, make it our base for mining and selling omniscium. We wouldn't have to put up with Amanda Leonard or her megalomaniac ideas." His face lit up again and he hugged her tight.

"Judge Balinakas won't accept rivals to his power," Kat hedged.

"Then we'll make our home someplace else. Someplace new and untouched. This planet is practically empty. Plenty of room for separate kingdoms. Please say yes. Say you'll join me."

"What about your wife and children?"

"Who ever said . . ." He did not deny that he already had a family. "I'll divorce her as soon as we get back to civilization. But I'll bring my son here. I want Bruce, Jr. with me. He's my son and heir."

"Just like the name of your ship."

Kat pointedly removed his hands from her waist and stepped back toward shore.

"Sorry, Bruce. I don't think I can desert my brothers. The omniscium belongs to the entire family. I can't and won't go it alone." She waded back to the embankment and began to dress in her nearly dry clothing.

"I trust my brothers more than I trust you," she said to herself and suddenly felt a lot better.

CHAPTER 32

KIM AND HESTIIA, perched upon their usual sitting rock, watching Medic Chaney Lotski progress through the village with half a dozen young women trailing after her. All of them wore flowers in their hair, in strings around their necks, wrists, and ankles. Chaney carried more flowers.

Jetang M'Berra and Taneeo awaited her at the festival pylon.

"I am glad we can celebrate a new marriage after so many have died," Hes murmured. She snuggled her face next to their sleeping daughter in her arms.

"We also celebrate new life. We present Ariel to the world today," Kim added. He draped an arm about them. Warmth born of love and pride blossomed in his belly. Today was the first day his wife and daughter had ventured out of the clearing since he'd carried them up there over a week ago, the day after Ariel's birth.

Taneeo evoked promises from Chaney and Jetang. To work together as one, to trust each other, to love each other, to support each other in times of trial, and rejoice together during good times.

Kim looked deeply into Hestiia's eyes, reliving the moment Taneeo had spoken the same words over them. His heart swelled. "I love you," he whispered to her.

She smiled up at him and leaned in a little closer. "You are my life," she replied.

"Marrying you was the best thing I ever did."

They gloried within their own private world a moment.

And then the gathered village erupted in shouts of joy and applause as M'Berra bent his tall African frame to kiss his petite blonde bride.

"I'm glad they did this," Kat said plunking herself down on the rock next to Kim and Hestiia. Gentian stropped her ankles and wove a purring path between and around the two rocks.

"Military authorities frown upon marriage between officers. They don't mind if they sleep together, but they don't want them committed. Too much work to make sure they are posted together." She frowned slightly.

"Is there someone you regret not committing to?" Hestiia asked quietly, almost shyly.

"Not me. I've yet to meet a man I can respect, trust, and like enough to commit to." Kat kept looking down at the pack she had placed at her feet.

Kim allowed her the space to follow through whatever deep thoughts troubled her.

"I want you to have something, Kim." Kat finally reached into the pack. She lifted her face and made certain she met and matched his gaze. Then she placed something soft and furry in his lap.

He looked down in surprise.

"What?"

"The reason I ran back into the house while it was burning," Kat almost choked on the words.

Kim couldn't tell what strong emotion welled up within her.

"Murphy!" His own fragmented memories brought tears to his eyes. He fondled the very threadbare green teddy bear.

"He was mine before I gave him to you the day you were born. Konner had him before me, and Loki before that. He's old enough maybe Mum or Dad had him originally. I really wanted to be a responsible big sister and pass it on properly."

"I used to sleep with him," Kim gasped. He'd only been four when Mum fled the family compound with her three boys. Kat—Katie then—had run back into the house and become lost.

"You . . . you risked your life to bring me my teddy bear."

"Mum forgot him. I heard you crying for him. I couldn't leave him behind. He's one of the family."

"The only family you had for a long time."

Kat nodded, swallowing deeply. Still, two tears trickled down her cheeks.

"He kept me company until Governor Mitchell's storm troopers found me. They fed me and then threw me into a cell. Mitchell didn't last long. He was too much a tyrant even for a bush planet. Governor Talbot replaced him within a month or two. He found me in the prison and rescued me and Murphy. Talbot adopted me, raised, and educated me as if I were one of his own."

"You needed Murphy then. You've kept him safe all these years. Maybe you should keep him."

"That's okay. I think Ariel needs him now." Kat reached over to caress the baby's cheek.

For the first time Kim noticed the bracelet of braided hair on her right wrist.

"Is that what I think it is?"

"Mum's. She made it from locks of each of our hair." She touched the fairest of the four strands. "That's Loki, he was almost strawberry blond as a kid."

"This dark chestnut has to be Konner's."

"Actually that's yours. You got brighter as you grew. This bright one is Konner's. He got darker as he matured."

"Then this flaming one must be yours." Kim caressed the silky strands.

"And this one, almost identical but a little lighter is Mum's. That makes the dark brown one our dad's. Did Mum ever find him? He disappeared just weeks before we had to flee."

"I don't know that Mum ever looked for Dad," Kim said sadly. "I would have liked to have known him."

"He was a great pilot. He started to teach me how to fly just before he left."

"You were, what, seven?"

"Yeah."

They shared a big grin.

"Can I come back to the clearing? I'd like to get to know my brothers, and my niece, and my sisters-in-law."

"You trust us enough?"

"I trust you with my life."

"But not your secrets," Hestiia added.

"In time, Hes. Give her time. We've been apart a long time."

"I've been lonely a long time. I didn't realize that until . . . Gentian invaded my life. He showed me how much I need my family."

"Then, welcome, Sister. Welcome home." Kim hugged her close, unable to check the tears of joy that flooded his eyes. His sense of completeness expanded and redoubled.

"I don't see why he did it." Cyndi watched the simple wedding between the tall African and the properly civil-sized medic. She didn't want to admit that this bush ceremony actually moved her more than an expensive legal union with all the trappings of gowns and flowers and lavish reception back home. "M'Berra could have gone places, but no, he had to throw away his career to be with her," she continued her litany of complaint.

She shuddered to think how close she had come, two years ago, to throwing away her own career, her place at court, and any chance of inheriting money from her parents when she had the opportunity to marry Loki.

She might well have already thrown away everything in boarding *Jupiter.* She reminded herself that she wanted to personally supervise Loki's arrest, trial, and punishment. In truth, she had the stupid, romantic, foolish need to do the right thing and break off her engagement to Loki in person. Her conscience had gotten her stranded here.

"Love is blind," Geralds finished the thought for her.

"Thank the stars I shredded the veil of inappropriate love before I made the same mistake."

"Did you?" he asked coming up behind her. He stood so close she could feel his body heat. "Just why did you hop a ride aboard *Jupiter*? Did you know that Captain Leonard was chasing the O'Hara brothers? Had you ferreted out the information that Kat Talbot is really their long lost sister?"

Cyndi gulped in horror that this man might have read her mind.

"Imagine the nerve of M'Berra, asking Loki to stand up for him." Cyndi decided to changed the subject rather than venture into the space debris of her true motives. "Can you imagine the nerve, the audacity of asking a known outlaw to be his best man? He should have asked you, or the headman. What's his name? Raaskan?"

"You don't know that I'm any better than Loki." Geralds smirked.

Cyndi almost imagined him laughing at her. He wouldn't dare. He still had prospects of a life back in civilization.

"You have to be better than Loki. More law-abiding. Anyone would be better than Loki."

"Except his brothers."

"I think his brothers have more honor than he does."

"Strange word, 'honor.'"

More shattering asteroids in that statement.

"You'd think that Chaney Lotski would have enough sense to ask me to be her maid of honor rather than Kat Talbot. I have more status, and I no longer have the taint of O'Hara associations." Cyndi wanted to give the medic a piece of her mind. She took two steps toward the knot of celebrants beginning to dance around the festival pylon.

"I think I know how to get you and me off this barbaric planet," Geralds said quietly.

Cyndi froze in place.

"Is that an invitation to go with you?"

"Could be. Can you help me steal some fuel cells from the O'Haras?"

"I have one already. I could have had two, but I couldn't lift one of them. So I took the lighter one and hid it."

"Right idea. Wrong fuel cell. You stole an empty one. We need six to get one of the fighters from Base Camp up to my ship."

"Fighters only require two."

"Two that are properly charged from the crystal array, under pressure. The patch job Konner has set up isn't enough. I'm not taking off with less than two sets of backups."

"The fighters are at Base Camp. How do we get ourselves and six fuel cells back there?"

"We get Captain Leonard to come here with one."

Cyndi fought the urge to run away screaming. The nightmare of fighting off the creature that Leonard had become frightened her more than losing her place at court.

"I think I can get into the clearing to steal the cells," Geralds continued. "But I need you to distract Loki while I cart them outside the force field."

"Plenty of places to hide them." She knew that for certain. No one had found the cell she'd stolen—even if it was empty. "But how do we get Leonard to fly one of the fighters here?"

"We call her and offer her the one thing she wants most—the heads of the O'Hara brothers on a plate."

CHAPTER 33

❖ — · — ❖ — · — ❖

KAT WATCHED CAREFULLY as Chaney Lotski deftly wove a series of knots in a torn fishnet.

"Where'd you learn to do that?" Kat asked. She looked at the hopeless tangle in her own net.

"My own version of surgeon's knots." Chaney shrugged and smiled. She glowed in the summer sunshine. Marriage to Jetang M'Berra seemed to agree with her.

The big black man planed the outside edges of a new boat with a primitive tool. His bare back glistened with sweat as he concentrated on the task. The sweet scent of freshly worked wood drifted on the morning breeze.

"You two certainly seem happy." Kat needed to explore the topic of leaving with these potential allies.

"Never thought I'd be glad to land in the bush again," M'Berra laughed. He rested on his bare heels, knees in the dirt, one hand possessively on the boat.

"I always wanted to retire to the bush, just didn't think it would be this soon," Chaney added. Her hands flew as she continued working her net.

"Will you stay here when we have enough fuel to leave?" Kat shifted uneasily. Her brothers would certainly object if they knew she discussed the possibility of anyone leaving their precious planet and spreading the news of its existence.

"We've talked about it, Kat." M'Berra ran his hands up and down the length of the boat looking for uneven places that might eventually leak. "Frankly, we both feel we've come to a dead end in the military."

"Surely you are up for a promotion. Maybe your own ship . . ."

"I'm bush. The only way I can get my own ship is to steal one and become a pirate or smuggler. Like your brothers. You'll run into the same prejudice if you go back, Kat. You can only rise so far, then the inbred nobles will put impossible barriers around promotions. Here I can be my own man, make my own decisions. Own my own land." He dropped the plane and picked up a bag of wet sand and began rubbing an imperfection his fingers had found.

"If you want to own land, why did you join the IMP service?" Kat just didn't understand this.

"On Meditcue II all the land is owned by two families. The rest of us worked for them. My only chance at an education was to join the military. My only chance to learn a skill other than farming or fishing was to join the military. Now it's time to move on and do something else."

"What about you, Chaney? Why do you want to retire to the bush?"

"Because everything I learned in medical school points toward a basic incompatibility of the human body with overcrowded domed cities, canned air, and bioengineered tank food. We're setting ourselves up for either some serious mutation or vulnerability to new diseases created by those overcrowded domed cities, canned air, and bioengineered tank food. The answer to the salvation of our bodies is here in the bush with fresh air, natural food, and space to be human." She smiled at M'Berra with love and longing.

"We've decided to raise our children here. The GTE and the IMPs be damned," M'Berra said, still concentrating on sanding the boat.

"We want our children free of GTE restrictions, pollution, and exploitation." Chaney touched her belly with tender fingers. "We agree with your brothers, Kat. This planet must be kept secret from the rest of the world. You might as well accept the fact that you will live out the rest of your days here."

"Not if I can help it." Kat threw her tangled fishnet aside and stalked away.

A week passed, then two. Kat watched the skies impatiently. She and her brothers heard sporadic reports from Paola Sanchez on the continent. The Amazons had killed many of the black snakes, but the matriarch eluded them. Construction of the second wall outside the port city grew slowly. The workers kept having to rebuild what the snakes knocked down during their nightly attacks. The pump worked to keep the snakes at bay, but the water also damaged the mud-brick walls.

Kat paced the clearing and the village. She completed the chores assigned to her while she thought and fretted. She had decisions to make and could find no answers to her questions.

Gentian frequently flew over Base Camp and reported back to her. Each time she had to spend an hour or more cuddling him to calm his fearful quivers and his need to run and hide.

Each day she ground her teeth in frustration as Amanda Leonard and her Marines ranged farther and farther afield on slave hunts. They captured large contingents of men and women who worked the fields a few days and then managed to escape.

"Amanda doesn't have the power of religious fear to keep her slaves in awe and afraid. The natives know that most of the Marines carry empty weapons. They no longer have the power to recharge them," Loki mused.

Then he told Kat how Hanassa as a priest of Simurgh had maintained absolute control over vast tracts of the lush river valley. The former purple-tip dragon had threatened retribution on the entire populace from their god Simurgh. The awesome terror of a dragon attack forced the Coros to give themselves as slaves and sacrifices.

Until the O'Hara brothers landed in search of raw materials to repair their ship. In outrage, they deposed Hanassa. The Coros named the three red-haired brothers Stargods and followed them instead. Kim had invented a kind and gentle religion modified from his mother's beliefs for the locals.

"No wonder almost half of Amanda's original crew has deserted," Kat gasped. "Only the core of one hundred bloodthirsty Marines puts up with Amanda/Hanassa's harsh regime that breaks every law of the GTE and the Imperial Military Police."

Kat didn't report that Amanda kept her Marines enthralled with sex and vicious punishments. She didn't want to think how far her honorable captain had sunk in her quest for power.

Gentian reported that Amanda and her Marines weren't having a lot of luck forging proper weapons. They didn't have the secrets of working with iron that Konner had discovered.

And then Amanda managed to capture and enslave a true blacksmith. He and his apprentices turned out blade after blade of strong steel. Swords. Daggers. Spear tips. Arrowheads.

Kat clenched her fists and cursed at the stories she heard of Amanda killing and torturing any who defied her.

Then the first refugees arrived at the village of the Stargods at the base of the cliff. The time had come to find safe homes for them. Either that or attack and kill Amanda Leonard.

The dragons remained strangely quiet.

On the night of the full moon, Kat waited until Loki patrolled the far side of the clearing with his back to the portal. Then she crept out and sneaked halfway down the path to the village. Gentian followed her on silent cat feet. But she felt his distress at her new plan to stop Amanda. She halted at a large outcropping of rock that provided a clear view of the valley below.

"Gentian, please help me. I need a dragon tonight," she said as she settled cross-legged on the rock.

(This is too dangerous. To you and your brothers.)

"But our cause is worth fighting for. It is worth the risk to free this place of Hanassa, or Amanda, or whoever tyrannizes the people." She petted the flywacket with long strokes from ears to tail. "Only when we are free of Hanassa can I leave this planet with good conscience. I'll take you with me. I promised. I always keep my promises."

He leaned into her hand. But his tail remained fat and bristled like a sea brush—a prickly animal that floated into fish traps and pricked the unwary with its poisonous spines.

"Gentian, if you ever want to redeem yourself in the eyes of the nimbus, you must help me. This is an act of bravery. Please help me call a dragon."

Gentian drew away from her, ears flat, tail now tucked tightly around him. *(If I must.)*

"You must."

(Why do humans have to lie to each other?)

"Because honesty is sometimes more dangerous than those lies."

Loki paced the clearing as part of his evening watch. He'd spent the last two weeks impatiently observing everyone; trying to find solutions to impossible situations.

Cyndi avoided him, always looking the other way when they passed in the village. She was up to something. He knew it. He just couldn't figure out what.

Over these last two weeks, no one had come up with a good idea on how to mine the omniscium, or power up the fuel cells faster. Loki's temper grew shorter than usual.

And so he paced, and thought, and paced some more.

He knew what he had to do, the one thing he had vowed never to do again. He had to kill Amanda, the host for Hanassa, a worse enemy to this world than the GTE, the GFM, and the Kree combined. Then he had to find a way to take out the matriarch of the Krakatrice to stabilize the rest of this planet.

Then maybe his brothers would see reason about mining the ley lines and getting off this rock in the middle of nowhere.

Resigned to his decision, he wearily crawled into his bunk in one of the lean-tos scattered about the clearing. During the coldest months, they had all crowded into the single cabin. Now in early summer only Kim and Hestiia slept there—when Ariel allowed them to sleep at all.

The roll of sleeping furs cushioned his body. He stretched and turned onto his side, ready to welcome a few hours of sleep.

"Loki," Kat hissed, barely audibly.

"What?" He was instantly awake, fearing . . . he did not know what. Mostly he feared his own memories of the time he had to pull the trigger on a needle rifle aimed at the heart of the man they had known as Hanassa.

Every night when he closed his eyes, he relived that awful moment as his soul tried to wrench free of his body and follow Hanassa into death.

"Come with me," Kat whispered urgently. "I finally convinced a dragon to take me to Base Camp. But she won't take me alone. She said it's too dangerous."

"You defecting?" Loki pulled his boots back on.

"Usurping. I'm going to take command of Base Camp and get the forge working properly." She held up one of Kim's readers.

Loki knew the thing was stuffed with books and data. This one probably had Konner's notes on working iron.

"Then what?" Loki stuffed his knife back into his belt and sorted through the essential supplies he always kept near to hand.

"We start mining. I think if we combine all the fuel cells from Base Camp and here we can get one of the fighters to Geralds' ship *Son and Heir.* Then the three of us can return to civilization with the first load of omniscium."

"I figured you wouldn't leave the spy behind." Loki didn't trust the man who asked too many personal questions of others and never revealed a thing about himself. Kat spent altogether too much time with the Sam Eyeam. But she repulsed his touch and kept him at arm's length. And she never allowed him into the clearing, not even to use the hot spring.

"Bruce is an innocent, trapped here by mistake." She wouldn't meet Loki's gaze. A sure sign she hid something.

"We're all trapped here by mistake. One mistake after another." Loki crawled out of his lean-to and stood beside his sister. "We take *Sirius,* not Geralds' ship. I will command it, not him."

"What about Kim and Konner? We have to leave *Sirius* for them, if they ever get enough fuel to fly *Rover* again."

"We'll come back for them later. But I will not let Geralds take command. I command or we do not go." He set his jaw.

Kat set hers. They stared at each other a long moment in silent stubbornness.

CHAPTER 34

✦ —— · —— ✦ —— · —— ✦

"ALL RIGHT. We take *Sirius*. But we leave a coded message so Kim and Konner can find and break into *Son and Heir*," Kat said meekly.

Loki nodded his acceptance.

"Which dragon came to you?" he asked.

"A different one. The female. She calls herself Irisey."

"Is she big enough to carry three adults?"

"Irythros carried Konner, Dalleena, and me and he's only a juvenile. Irisey is fully grown—mother to both Irythros and Iianthe, and mighty proud of it." She grinned hugely.

"What about Gentian? Is he coming, too."

"He . . . he's too afraid." She wouldn't meet his gaze. Which meant she wasn't telling the whole truth.

Loki was almost willing to bet a fully charged fuel cell that Gentian disapproved of Kat's plans. He decided he'd be leery and watchful. He couldn't pull Kat's secrets from her mind, but he knew her well enough now to know she was up to something very sneaky.

They tiptoed to the barrier by the light of a setting moon and the glowing embers of the central campfire.

"Where's the dragon?" Loki asked quietly the moment they cleared the barrier. Bodies might not be able to penetrate the confusion field, but sound did.

"In the village, keeping Bruce from bolting. The last time he flew with a dragon, Irythros dumped him on the extreme western coast. It took him months to walk to Base Camp."

"He doesn't talk about his experience there." That bothered Loki. He'd grown used to communal adventure stories around the campfire each evening.

"He doesn't want to think about it," Kat said quietly. She knew more. Loki knew that by the tightness of her mouth and the way her shoulders reached for her ears.

A few paces farther and Loki lit a small lamp to guide their way. In recent weeks he'd noticed a marked improvement in his night vision, but he was reluctant to reveal that to Kat.

"Do you think the dragon would swing over to the big continent and pick up Paola?" Loki asked. He hadn't seen his lover in weeks and he missed her terribly. He also wanted a firsthand account of her attempts to deal with the snake monster. "We could use her strategic thinking."

"You will have to ask Irisey yourself."

They descended the last switchback in silence, aware how easily sound carried. No need to wake the villagers tonight. In the dim starlight, Loki caught a whisper of glow off a translucent dragon wing.

"She's gorgeous," he gasped in awe. In his mind he traced the curve of the wing back to the body. The size of the beast staggered him.

A faint chuckle brushed across his mind.

"Good evening, Irisey, Loki here," he introduced himself to the dragon on a whisper.

(Good evening, Loki. I am Irisey, matriarch of the nimbus.) Her lilting voice danced across his mind.

He bowed slightly, feeling himself in the presence of true majesty. Cyndi could learn a lot from this lady dragon.

"We've got to get going, before someone misses us," Kat hissed in his ear.

"Introduce yourself," he hissed back. "Dragon protocol."

"We've already met," Kat pouted.

"In person, or only in your mind? Do it, baby sister. We want to keep the nimbus happy and pleased with us."

Kat glowered at him a moment.

He met her stubbornness with his own.

"Irisey, I am Kat Talbot," she said. But she did not bow, she kept her shoulders straight, her spine stiff, and her chin up. She approached the dragon, equal to equal.

Maybe they were.

A flicker of prescient vision rocked Loki's balance. For a single heartbeat he saw his sister as a matriarch presiding over a brood of children; power radiated from her aura, and ease with that power as if long accustomed to it.

He reached out and braced himself. His hand brushed the dragon's muzzle.

(Easy, Loki. The time is not yet for your sister to step into that role. Many dangers await your entire family before that can happen.)

Loki nodded and gulped. "She has a lot of growing up to do first."

"Who does?" Kat asked.

A flash of mental agreement crossed Loki's mind from the dragon.

"Cyndi," he lied. But it was the truth.

Kat scrambled atop the dragon. Loki followed as soon as she settled between two spinal horns. He took a long moment to caress the dragon's crystal fur.

"Your wing tips and spinal horns are iridescent?" he asked quietly.

(All colors, and yet no color at all.)

"Where is Bruce?" Kat asked, querulous and cranky. "What are we waiting for?"

(An other.)

At that moment Bruce appeared out of the darkness. He held the hand of someone . . . someone with bright blonde hair.

"Cyndi," Loki breathed. "Why did he drag her along?"

(She is needed.)

"For what?"

(To remind you of what you fight for and against.)

"Enigmatic as usual," Loki muttered.

Cyndi followed Bruce eagerly until she spotted their transport. "You can't expect me to believe this isn't a nightmare," she protested, her voice rising into the now familiar whine. "Another nightmare." She stared at Loki.

He didn't know how to ease her misgivings. Her last encounter with a dragon had been Hanassa trying to force his spirit into her body.

"It'll be fun," Geralds cajoled her, unaware of her fears. "Think of it as sneaking out of your father's house to meet your friends and riding in a really sporty flitter."

"But . . . but I'm hardly dressed for an adventure." She waved her hand vaguely at her usual tunic and leggings.

"Don't worry about it, Cyndi. We don't have dress codes on this planet," Loki said flatly.

"Obviously. People still eat *meat* here. And they wear animal leather. And they bathe in," shudder, "water."

"Just get onboard. The dragon won't fly without you," Loki ordered. "We have important things to do."

"Like what?" Cyndi stood rock still, hands on hips, mouth set to disagree with whatever they planned.

"Like saving this planet from degenerating into civil war that will plunge it back into the stone age."

"Bruce?" Kat gestured toward the man.

Gleefully, he lifted Cyndi off her feet and threw her over his shoulder. She squealed and kicked him. He swatted her bottom. She cried out again.

A cry of alarm rose from the village.

Geralds climbed partway up the dragon's leg, then plunked Cyndi behind Loki.

"Hold on tight, little lady," Geralds said as he positioned himself behind Cyndi. Spinal horns braced them fore and aft. Cyndi squirmed restlessly.

"I don't have to obey any mere dragon. And I don't have to obey you, Loki," Cyndi pouted.

"Just what I need, two women in sour moods. Irisey, may I please leave one or both of them behind?"

(No.) The dragon took three lumbering steps toward the cliff, flapping her wings.

"Do I have to touch it?" Cyndi held her hands away from the spinal horn.

"You do unless you want to fall off onto the rocks in the cove," Loki replied. He gritted his teeth, forcing himself to watch as they approached the drop off. Would Irisey have enough air beneath her wings to fly? Or would she plummet onto the jagged beach, impaling her passengers?

Cyndi yelped and grabbed Loki fiercely around the waist. She buried her face into his back.

Sounds of alarm died away behind them.

Irisey took one last step off the cliff . . . and flew.

Loki breathed easier. He did his best to ignore the warmth that spread along his ribs from Cyndi's grip.

He threw his head back and let the wind play with his hair and beard. He opened himself to the chill air and savored the contrast between the cold penetrating his bones and the warmth of the woman clinging so desperately to his back.

In an amazingly short period of time, the dragon had flown along the coast and swung inward at the great river. Just a few wing flaps later she circled Base Camp. The watch fires glowed in the darkness along with two or three oil lanterns leading toward the latrine.

Irisey circled and banked a second time, selecting a landing place just south of the camp, away from the tilled and planted fields. She came down gracefully, running the last few steps to shed speed.

Kat dropped off the dragon's back before she came to a complete stop. "My thanks, Irisey." This time Kat bowed to the dragon.

Irisey dipped her head until the long spiral horn growing from her forehead nearly touched Kat's chest. Kat grabbed the tip and rubbed it gently.

Some private communication passed between them.

Loki strained to listen while Geralds helped a shaking Cyndi onto the ground, then supported her for several steps until she got her land legs again.

At last Loki slid down Irisey's haunch and faced his sister. "What was that all about?"

"Stand clear," Kat called.

Loki moved away from the dragon. Irisey's fur shimmered in the starlight and then . . . she disappeared. He heard her steps and wing flaps, but saw nothing of her form.

"I should be used to that by now." He wiped sweat from his brow, not liking his reaction to the mysterious dragon. "What's the plan, Kat?" he asked firmly.

Kat whipped out a needle pistol and aimed it at Loki's heart. "The plan is that you surrender to me and I turn you over to Her Majesty, Queen Amanda."

CHAPTER 35

M ARTIN CHECKED the sensor monitor in the lounge aboard *Margaret Kristine* for occupants. He knew his companions had all stayed on the bridge. Still, he had to be certain before he called up his star map. Quinn already suspected that Martin had done something special to his computer back home to create the massive program and maintain it.

Seeing the glyphs indicating four warm bodies on the bridge, Martin withdrew the miniature blue crystal from his pocket. The facets sparkled in the artificial light of the lounge. It grew warm in his hand. He fancied it hummed at a special frequency in harmony with his own brain synapses.

He stared at it several long moments, enthralled.

"Martin, have you found coordinates for the jump point yet?" Quinn asked over the intercom.

Martin shook himself free of the crystal's enchanting voice. "Working on it," he called back.

Carefully, he opened a panel on the bulkhead and inserted the crystal into a nest of fiber optics that ran to the central computer. "Star map, please," he whispered to the crystal.

Instantly, the air swirled and sparkled in the middle of the lounge. Pinpoints of red, blue, and green light burst forth from the swirling hologram.

Martin walked through the three-dimensional map to stand before the anomalous blank space and waited for the program to settle. It drew new data from the central computer and updated.

Aurora blinked from blue to green to red three times before it returned to a steady blue. Melinda had been busy in the last two weeks since Martin had escaped her clutches. Six green lights belonging to the Galactic Free Market switched to the blue of the Galactic Terran Empire in the immediate environs of Aurora.

Melinda *had* been busy for the Terran government to forcibly retake those six key systems in Melinda's trading empire. She must have pissed off the diplomatic envoys significantly for them to use that leverage. Melinda would have a hard time making much profit off those planets now that the GTE controlled their economy and tariffs.

Finally the lights stopped blinking and changing with updated information.

"Display jump points, please," Martin requested.

Purple lights popped into place in a seemingly random pattern. Martin blinked. The ship and the map seemed to tilt slightly to the left. If he looked at it just so . . .

Gone. He'd lost his brief glimpse into the pattern of jump point placement. No one had ever been able to determine where the jump points were until someone stumbled upon one and then charted its entry and exit points. Jump points always appeared either near a star system or near another jump point. He wondered why scientists had considered the wandering jump point near the *Margaret Kristine*'s current location the only dead end in the known galaxy.

"What's taking so long?" Bruce asked from the bridge. "We've been sitting out here for three days looking for the frigging jump point. I want to find it *now*."

"Just a femto. The map isn't as complete as it was back home." That was a lie, but Martin hadn't let any of them see it during their voyage to this point. He needed to keep the secret of the crystal, and the fact that it retained the entire massive program within its depths, just a little longer.

While he spoke, the pale lavender light indicating their wandering jump point came into view. He had to look carefully to make certain he truly saw it rather than imagined the pale pinpoint of light.

"Coordinates of jump point, please," he requested.

Strings of numbers appeared above or below every jump point except the one he watched.

Martin sighed in disappointment. Maybe he did imagine that pale lavender smudge.

"Crystal, please show me where the wanderer is at this moment."

Three strings of numbers appeared around the smudge.

"Quinn, this doesn't make any sense."

"Nothing about that jump point makes sense," Quinn said from the other side of the lounge.

Martin jumped back from peering at the smudge of light. "I didn't hear you come in," he gasped.

"I didn't intend for you to hear me. I wondered why you were so secretive about this map." He strode heavily to the open bulkhead panel and the crystal interface. A low whistle escaped his pursed lips at sight of the blue crystal.

"Don't touch it," Martin warned.

"I have no intention of touching it. I know what a full-sized king stone can do to a man who tries to disconnect it abruptly or incorrectly. I imagine this little guy can deliver quite a jolt." Quinn fingered the still bruised lump near his right temple.

"You need to see this, Quinn." Martin coaxed Quinn away from the crystal over to the jump point coordinates.

Quinn bent his tall frame to peer at the numbers. "Does it mean that it will be at each of those points or that it has been there?"

"Your guess is as good as mine."

"Why don't you ask it."

"I didn't program it to do that."

"You didn't program it to do this." Quinn swept his hand around the room indicating the map that filled the lounge and spread into three gangways.

"Computer, explain the imprecise numbers at the wanderer."

Silence.

"*Margaret Kristine,* please explain the three coordinates given for the wanderer," Quinn asked.

Silence.

"I think it must be where the jump point has *been*. It has no way of plotting the future, only past data. Kurt, bring yourself and your math genius down here," Martin ordered.

In moments Kurt's big feet and lanky frame clanked into the lounge.

Quinn quietly closed the bulkhead panel before Kurt reached the last step.

"I see you got it up and running," Kurt said. He pulled out his handheld. "What do you need?"

"Look at these three coordinates and extrapolate a pattern."

Kurt punched numbers and formulae into his handheld. "Time interval?"

"Unknown."

Kurt shrugged and kept playing with numbers and formulae. Finally, he held up the mini computer. "According to this, the next time it appears it will be here." He pointed to the string of coordinates. "When that will be I have no idea."

"Good enough for me." Quinn shrugged. "I'll get us there. Martin, you do some refining on the sensors. This thing may not register normal energy fluxes. Whose turn is it to cook? We might as well get comfortable. We could be in for a long wait."

"About time you came to your senses, Kat," Cyndi said, arching her back and stretching her arms over her head. "I'm glad you came on board with Bruce's plan. Maybe now we can get something done about getting off this hunk of rock and back to civilization."

"We work on Her Majesty's timeline now," Kat replied. She fought to keep her tone level and her mind blank. She really did not want Loki rummaging around her thoughts with his telepathy. "Everybody march. We're late for our appointment with Queen Amanda."

"I can't believe the dragons went along with this plan, Kat," Loki said quietly. He had his hands in the air in surrender, but his eyes twitched as if a dozen plans ran through his mind at once.

"The dragons don't know everything," Kat replied, still forcing her mind to remain blank. Those eye twitches could be her brother's attempt to probe her mind as Irisey had probed her heart.

"Your heart isn't in this, Kat," Loki said. His voice took on a peculiar lilting quality, as if he tried to lull her suspicions. Or plant ideas in her head.

"I always knew you had a mercenary heart, Kat," Bruce Geralds chortled. "Queen Amanda will be much more open to mining the omniscium than your hidebound brothers. We'll be rich in no time. Richer than Melinda Fortesque." He hugged her briefly and began the short trek to Base Camp.

Queen Amanda, indeed. Kat almost snorted. Amanda Leonard's new title grated on Kat's nerves. But she had to go through with the plan. This was the only way she could hope to get close enough to the woman to subdue her. And if necessary, she'd kill her captain. Civilized people never took a life, not even animals for food. But Amanda had stepped way over the line of civilization. She had violated every moral and ethical code Kat could remember. Amanda's punishment—if she ever came to trial—would be imprisonment and mind-wipe. By any other words, death of the soul and personality if not the body.

"Konner and Kim will come after me," Loki continued his litany of advice.

"No, they won't. Kim won't leave Hestiia and the baby for more than a few hours and Konner won't use the fuel to come get you in the _Rover_."

"The dragons . . ."

"Obey me."

Loki slumped his shoulders. Kat hated to see him looking so defeated. But she couldn't trust him to stay that way. Her oldest brother was resourceful if nothing else.

"Walk." She prodded his back with the needle pistol.

Loki took a few slow steps. "No comment from you, Cyndi?"

"I will go along with any plan to get me home and see you punished, Loki." She tossed her head and walked ahead of them. She greeted the Marines as old friends and made her way to the central fire pit and a cup of something hot.

Bruce joined her. Two armed guards stepped forward from the perimeter of their patrols. They took up positions on either side of Loki and matched him step for step into Base Camp.

Kat sighed gratefully that neither of them was Kent Brewster, the one Marine who might see through her facade—or glare at her in true disappointment. He'd be easier to recruit to her plan if he did not gain wrong first impressions.

"Kat, you know that the person wearing Amanda Leonard's body is no longer the captain you respected and admired. You do not owe her any kind of loyalty," Loki said.

"I don't want to talk about it with you, Loki." She jabbed the muzzle of her needle pistol sharply into his back.

Loki stumbled to his knees.

"Open your hands before you stand," Kat ordered. "You won't be flinging dirt in my eyes."

Loki obeyed her, shaking his head. "Who taught you to fight dirty, Kat? I thought you were a law-abiding officer in His Majesty's military."

"Never mind. Now stand up and walk, hands up, palms empty." She nudged his backside with her boot.

"Well, well, well. The prodigal lieutenant returns," Amanda said.

Her voice slithered over Kat and nearly made her shudder in revulsion. Kat suppressed her involuntary reaction.

"I've brought you a prisoner, Your Majesty, just as I promised. Konner O'Hara is now at your mercy."

Loki looked at her sharply, lowering his brows in puzzlement. He opened his mouth to say something.

Kat cuffed him alongside the head with the butt of her pistol. "Keep your mouth shut and show some respect for Her Majesty," she growled. Kat wanted to scream into his mind to trust her. She didn't dare. Amanda might overhear the telepathic communication. Kat had no idea what powers Amanda had acquired since coming to this place. For all Kat knew, her former captain could have as many magical skills and talents as all four O'Haras combined.

"Take Mr. Konner O'Hara to the new prison cell I built just for him. It's as close to sensory deprivation as I could make it, given the primitive technology and limited resources," Amanda purred. "I am so going to love hearing you scream when the darkness and silence press against your brain."

"How . . . ?" Kat started.

"Never mind how I contrived the cell. I have another one for you."

"Majesty . . . I . . ."

"You deserve punishment for running away from me, Kat. You should

know better than to defy me." Amanda caressed Kat's cheek with an extremely long fingernail that had begun to curve downward, like a talon.

Three more Marines appeared out of the darkness. Two of them each
grabbed Kat by an elbow. The third cut the air menacingly with a primitive
sword.

"You won't be in your cell as long as your brother, Kat. I do reward people
who bring me presents. But punishment always comes first."

CHAPTER 36

◆━━ ·━━ ◆ ━━· ━━◆

KONNER WOKE UP in the dead of night. Something nagged at his mind. He rolled over and ran his hands lightly over Dalleena's body. She breathed evenly, resting comfortably.

Satisfied that she was not the source of his disquiet, he slid from beneath their sleeping furs and peered out of their lean-to.

The campfire embers glowed, ready to be stoked into brightness with fresh tinder and wood. The surrounding trees and shrubbery rustled faintly in the night breeze.

He listened closely. Perhaps the baby?

Even Ariel, the two-week-old infant, slept quietly for a change.

Pressure in his mind sent Konner prowling around the perimeter of their clearing. He knew there was something wrong, something out of place. What?

Finally, he checked the other lean-tos. Taneeo had moved back to the village once he'd freed himself of Hanassa's possession. That left two more sleeping places.

"Loki," Konner whispered outside his brother's shelter. "Loki?" he said a little louder.

He rapped upon the side of the structure and crouched to peer inside. The sleeping furs lay in disarray. Both Loki and his boots were gone.

Konner stood up in alarm. He searched the clearing with all of his senses. Maybe Loki had just stepped out to the latrine. Maybe, but not likely. He would not have bothered with his boots for such a mundane errand.

"Kat?" Konner stepped over to his sister's lean-to. He skipped politeness and peered in as soon as he spoke. Her bed looked undisturbed, or neatly made up. Her boots were missing, too.

Where could they have gone?

Konner stoked the fire for light and searched the clearing one more time. The pressure in his mind increased.

Wake up, a voice nagged him. He listened more closely. *Wake up and pay attention.*

Some of the pressure decreased, as if the speaker paused to draw breath.

Traitor. Kat betrayed us.

Not so much words as an impression of guns and Marines and Kat and Amanda together.

"Loki?" Konner asked the pressure in his mind.

The only reply was a vague sense of assent.

"Let me get Kim. He's better at this than I am." Konner ran the few steps to the one-room cabin Kim shared with Hestiia and the baby.

Abandoning politeness, he crashed through the doorway. He paused only a moment to orient himself and then felt his way to the far wall. "Kim," he whispered as he shook his brother's shoulder.

"Jaysus, I just got to sleep," Kim mumbled.

Ariel whimpered in her basket beside the bed. Kim picked her up and stumbled toward the doorway, a patch of slightly lighter darkness than the dim interior. He aimed for the central fire pit, holding Ariel against his shoulder, patting her back and murmuring soothing words.

"Now what is so all-fired important you had to wake me," he demanded querulously. "I swear I haven't slept more than ten minutes all night between a fussing baby and Hestiia's restlessness.

"Loki's in trouble. He says Kat betrayed him to Amanda."

Kim swung around to face the lean-tos.

"They're both gone. Took their boots."

"How?"

"There is this pressure in my mind. When I stopped to listen to it, Loki contacted me telepathically. You're better at this than I am."

"Not on no sleep. I need Tambootie to concentrate."

"You need that drug for everything."

"Do you want to clear up this mess tonight or not?"

"Okay. You get Ariel settled and I'll find you some fresh leaves." Fortunately, Konner did not have to go more than a few steps beyond the edge of the clearing. The first rays of dawn showed the distinctive umbrella outline of the deciduous tree with aromatic bark and toxic sap. The green leaves grew fat with pink veins. The moment he touched the first one, it dripped oil onto the back of his hand. It tingled immediately.

Before he could stop himself he licked the essential oils off the leaf.

His mind brightened. Every object in the clearing took on auras, highlighting their silhouettes. He wanted to study each rock and blade of grass, delving into the secrets contained in those subdued coronas of living light.

Another lick of Tambootie oil. Just one more. Well, maybe another a well.

Suddenly the pressure in his mind eased and became coherent communication.

They locked me in the fuel bay of a lander. Strapped me down so I can't move more than my eyelids. Insulated the hull so I can't hear anything. No light. Makes it easier to concentrate.

"Loki, we'll get you out."

No! The word sounded loud inside Konner's skull.

They think I am you. As long as Amanda is under that delusion, we have leverage. She hates us all, but you more than any of us.

"How did she get the impression you are me?"

Kat . . . Oh, Saint Bridget. She deliberately misled Amanda. She's laid a trap of her own. But Amanda decided to punish her before rewarding her. Kat's locked in another lander.

"How did you get to Base Camp?" Konner tried to fume over the misuse of his precious fuel.

The female dragon, Irisey.

"If the dragons cooperated, then they have to agree with Kat. She didn't betray us, she used us to further her own stupid plan. Was Gentian with her?"

No.

Kat, how stupid can you get? Konner asked himself as much as his absent sister. *Couldn't you have confided in me?* Of all three brothers, Kat seemed to have bonded most closely with Konner. They had sat for hours these last few weeks just talking. He had rescued her from the snake monster.

She blamed him for abandoning her at the burning house back home when she was seven.

"Have you got some of those leaves for me?" Kim asked. He'd stopped long enough to put on his trousers.

Konner still wandered the clearing in his underwear. Strangely, with the Tambootie coursing through his system he did not need clothing for warmth.

He handed Kim a fistful of leaves. His hand nearly burned with the power they gave him.

Briefly, he outlined the situation to Kim as his younger brother licked and nibbled his Tambootie.

"Can you get out of your restraints, Loki?" Kim asked. His eyes crossed as he focused on something inside him. He stared blankly into the now burning central fire.

That's Konner's talent.

"And telepathy is yours, but he heard you. Now concentrate, both of you."

"Loki, you must have seen the restraints when they put you in there. What do they look like?" Konner asked. He dragged his thoughts away from the need for more Tambootie. The drug would help him blot out his disappointment in Kat.

He concentrated on the fire and what needed to be done.

Sticky webbing from med supplies.

"Good, they aren't force bracelets. Now picture the webbing in minute detail in your mind." Konner waited a moment to allow Loki to get the image firmly fixed.

The trail of Loki's thoughts, like a brightness in Konner's mind faded. He hadn't known it was there or what it looked like until it was gone.

"Once you can see it clearly in your mind, think about the stickiness dissolving. Watch each molecule of glue separating and becoming inert."

I can't.

"You can. Concentrate. Forget about talking to me. Forget everything but the webbing. Watch it dissolve." Konner waited a few more moments. "Now, the two layers that overlap are no longer sticking together. All you have to do is lift your wrists and the restraints will fall away."

A few more moments passed. The fire burned down. Kim added more fuel.

When it flared up again, Konner thought he saw a holo image within the flames of Loki lying in the darkness fighting the webbing.

In a few moments the restraints flew off Loki's wrists and legs. Nearly sobbing with relief, Loki released the head and throat bands.

"He's free," Konner breathed.

"Loki, you have to get out of there quickly. Dawn is just breaking." Had only a few moments passed? Konner felt as if he'd been staring at the fire for hours.

Where?

"Get to the village at the confluence of the river and the bay. Hide there. We'll come to pick you up."

What about Kat?

"I think we have to leave her to Amanda's not so tender mercies for a while."

"Ask him to steal a fuel cell or two," Kim prompted. He already nibbled on more Tambootie, as if the first dose had worn off and dropped him out of rapport with Loki.

Konner began to shiver. His own dose of Tambootie grew thin in his blood. He conveyed Kim's message quickly and received a tentative reply.

Then his hands began to shake and his stomach revolted. He dashed to the nearest bush and vomited up the shreds of the leaves he didn't remember eating.

· ——◆—— ·

"Try it now, Kurt," Martin called from under a control panel on the bridge of *Margaret Kristine*.

"No change in any of the sensor readings," Kurt called back.

"Maybe if you up the UV sensitivity," Jane said. She stood behind Kurt, watching his screens as closely as he did.

"We've tried UV, how about tachyon emissions?" Bruce offered. He swiveled idly in the copilot's chair.

"These instruments can't go any higher on either read," Martin spat, disgusted with the whole process.

"Martin, there is something else you have not tried," Quinn said quietly. He watched the viewscreen directly in front of them at the real-time display, as if he'd get to see a jump point open.

As far as Martin knew, no one had actually seen a jump point. They appeared as energy fluxes in the data stream.

"What?" Jane, Bruce, and Kurt all asked at the same time.

So much for keeping the illegal miniature king stone secret.

Martin scooted out from his supine position beneath the panel. He had to stand up to fish the crystal out of his pocket. Maybe Bruce had a point in wearing pantaloons. But he couldn't change clothes now; they had only the limited luggage Quinn had stashed in the van ahead of time—mostly changes of underwear and personal hygiene items.

He tried to keep the crystal in his palm, hidden from the others as it emerged from its hiding place.

Jane was on him in a flash, opening his hand. "By Gaia, its beautiful. Perfect," she gasped. She stroked the crystal as if it were a living being.

Perhaps it was.

Quinn swung around in his chair to observe the scene.

Kurt and Bruce reached simultaneously to grab the thing from Martin for closer examination. A spark lashed from the crystal to their fingers.

Instinctively, Martin closed his finger around it protectively.

"Acts just like a real king stone, too," Quinn remarked. A half smile quirked his mouth. "It seems that Martin here is attuned to the crystal. I'm surprised it doesn't hum."

"It does. It's in harmony with your crystal drive." Martin didn't know what else to say.

"All crystals are monopoles. They seek a crystal family to complete them, just as a bipolar magnet is attracted to its opposite," Quinn said casually.

"Where'd you get it?" Bruce asked. He kept his hands safely in his voluminous pockets as he peered at the little bits of blue light that were visible between Martin's fingers.

"My dad. Two summers ago."

"Where'd he get it?" Bruce acted offended that their favorite camp counselor hadn't honored each of them with something similar.

"Why didn't it reject Jane?" Kurt asked.

"She only touched it, she didn't try to take possession of it."

"It burned my fingers a little," Jane added trying to mollify her comrades. She shook her finger as if to emphasize the crystal's reaction to her.

"Enough speculation. Plug that into the computer matrix before we lose the jump point," Quinn ordered.

Grateful for the excuse to avoid further discussion of the crystal, Martin slid back beneath the panel. He fished around for a suitable nest of fiber optics to accept the crystal. At last he found a place deep into the sensor wiring.

"No map this time. Just a look at where the jump point is," he whispered to the crystal as he attached three fiber optics to it.

"Nothing happening to the sensor array," Kurt called back to him, a little too loudly, as if the panel and bulkhead muffled more sound now that Martin had the crystal in hand.

"King stones like multiples of twelve," Quinn reminded him.

"I know. I've studied crystal drives intensively since I started using this," Martin muttered, not caring if anyone heard him.

The next thee connections came easy. Then he had to seriously look for the next five. The last was the most elusive of all.

"I've used up all the fiber optics, and I still need one more," he complained.

Look deeper, someone said.

Martin thought the deep voice might be Quinn's. Yet it didn't sound exactly like the Imperial agent. Who could tell for certain halfway between the bulkhead and the hull?

"I am looking deeper." Blindly, he reached above his head and grabbed whatever came to hand.

Three fiber optic cables broke free of their connections. Which one was best? They all looked great. Two of the ones already connected came from secondary systems.

Martin sighed and began rearranging.

As he touched the final cable to the crystal, before he had firmly attached it to the facet, the miniature king stone began to glow. Flames seemed to shoot from the deep heart out along the cables. Quickly, he finished the last connection and nestled the crystal into a safe niche.

Jubilant music burst upon his ears.

"Are all the crystals singing?" Jane asked.

Martin clawed his way free of the dim bulkhead and blinked in the sudden brightness of the bridge. More than the usual change of contrast brightness. Every screen sparkled with new light.

"Wow," Quinn said, leaning back in his chair to take it all in. "That is some enhancement. Don't suppose I could persuade you to leave that crystal onboard?"

"Not on your life. My dad will need it when we find him. More than you," Martin said. He turned a full circle, trying to take in all of the new data that blazed across the screens.

"Jump point coordinates on screen!" Kurt nearly jumped up and down with excitement.

"Strap in, now!" Quinn called. "It's practically on top of us."

Martin fumbled for the nearest seat and found Jane already there. The klaxon blared its three-note warning. The ship tilted. Martin slid across the floor, flailing for balance. He slammed into Bruce in the other chair. He landed flat on his back on the deck.

The klaxon sounded again.

"So soon?" Less than twenty seconds had passed between warning and jump.

Martin grabbed whatever was handy. One hand wrapped around the support column of the copilot's seat. The other lay flat upon the deck, clawing at the cerama/metal for purchase. He stretched a foot to brace against the same place as his left hand.

The deck thinned to transparency, then disappeared. Martin held his breath. The ship dissolved. Only his mind kept the killing vacuum of space at bay.

CHAPTER 37

✦━•━✦━•━✦

"**Y**OUR MAJESTY." Bruce Geralds bowed low before Amanda. Cyndi made a graceful curtsy, worthy of a ball gown, tiara, and the emperor's palace. She kept her eyes carefully lowered, all the while scoping out Amanda's body language and expression.

"We have information of great benefit to you," Geralds continued the moment Amanda waved him upright. He explained the significance of the ley lines and the amount of wealth that could be gained from mining it.

"Treasure?" Amanda's eyes brightened a moment. "I have no need of treasure. I require power." That voice was huskier and raspier than the voice Cyndi remembered from onboard *Jupiter*.

Then Amanda went silent a moment and her eyes cleared, willing to listen once more.

"Treasure is power," Cyndi reminded the former captain. Something had changed about the woman's eyes and posture. She sat hunched forward, as if her back hurt. She opened both eyes wide, yet her lids seemed hooded, leaving shadows upon Amanda's face. Cyndi could not capture her gaze, no matter how hard she tried.

Would she, Cyndi, show the same hardening of the skin, the talon nails, and the hunched posture if she had given it to the spirit of Hanassa?

Would she exhibit the same insanity and cruelty? She swallowed deeply, trying to rid her mouth of a bad taste. She, the granddaughter of a previous emperor, wife to an heir of the current emperor, and daughter of a planetary governor would never allow her body and posture to become so ugly. Power also lay in beauty, if one knew how to use it.

"Explain how treasure can be power. Treasure is the useless accumulation of pretty objects that have value only to the frivolous."

"May I?" Cyndi asked, gesturing toward the camp stool beside Amanda. Amanda glared in hostility.

Cyndi returned her stare with equal stubbornness.

Finally, Amanda nodded. Cyndi smiled to herself. Information was also power and she had a lot of it. She had to remember that the entity that now inhabited Amanda's body was still primitive. It did not have the sophistication and education that Cyndi did. It had bits and pieces of Amanda's technical knowledge, maybe a few of her memories, but not the understanding of how to use it.

She seated herself and settled her back against the big cabin before speaking. "On other worlds, money governs every action. Those with money can buy treasure. They can also buy people, influence, prestige, status. They can buy votes in Parliament."

"Money buys transportation to and from planets throughout the galaxy," Bruce added. "Money buys safety from those who have the power of coercion and blackmail."

Both Cyndi and Amanda glared at him.

"Go away, silly man," Amanda ordered. "I have no use for you at the moment."

Geralds blustered.

"Men have only one use. I do not need servicing at the moment," Amanda said mildly.

A great guffaw rose from the armed Marines waiting in attendance.

"Don't worry, you'll get your chance soon enough. She's insatiable," one of the Marines called. That met with another round of laughter.

Geralds stalked off.

"Now tell me how to gain access to this treasure you allude to but do not address directly," Amanda said in a raspy tone that implied intimacy.

"The O'Haras speak of a web of energy beneath the ground," Cyndi tried to visualize what Geralds had explained to her. She still didn't understand how the planet could be filled with omniscium. The most valuable element in the galaxy had only been found in uninhabitable gas giants.

"The ley lines. Yes, I know about them."

"They are made up of omniscium. That's an element that powers our starships." Not exactly true but close enough. She didn't know how to explain about crystals and star drives. She barely understood the basic principles herself. "A very small amount commands large sums of money outside this planet."

"If I control this omniscium, then people will come to me? They will worship and attend me as I deserve?"

"Ye . . . es."

Amanda fell silent a moment. "If people from afar will worship me, then I will have no need to cater to dragon needs for plentiful food and clean water," she mused.

"With our technology, we can clean the air and water of any pollution generated from mining the omniscium. We can grow food in tanks, no need to preserve the land." Cyndi imagined a domed city replacing the hovels of Base Camp. She smiled.

"Go away. I must think on this. This is information I can use."

A Marine grabbed Cyndi by the elbow and dragged her off to the other side of Base Camp. They left her nowhere near where Geralds prowled with two more Marines watching his every move.

Loki carefully placed his purloined fuel cell in the hollow of a tree and sank down gratefully beside it. He mopped perspiration from his brow with the back of his arm.

"Steal a fuel cell or two, Konner says," he muttered. The power source was nearly a meter cubed and weighed about thirty kilos.

The missing fuel cells from the power farm had been empty, easy for the thief to carry. Anyone who visited the clearing could have taken it.

Getting out of Base Camp in the sleepy hour before dawn was easy. Carrying a fully powered fuel cell five klicks before breakfast was a different proposition altogether.

"Speaking of breakfast . . ." He reached over and yanked a fading flower out of the ground. Dirt clung damply to the fat bulb at its base. He gathered his energy a moment before taking the plant to the nearest stream to wash it. This close to the braided delta of islands fresh water was the least of his problems.

He ate the bulb raw, then went searching for another. This time of year they were plentiful, not as nutritious as in the autumn but still sweet and tasty.

Eventually, he left the fuel cell in its hiding place and proceeded toward the village at the confluence of the river and the Great Bay. He stepped cautiously, mindful of the various swamps and how easily he left a trail in the damp ground.

Less than half of the village's one hundred families had found their way to the new habitat five hundred klicks to the south. He did not know if the remainder had shifted allegiance to the newcomers. They'd done it before to survive. They'd do it again. Survival mattered more to them than honor or freedom.

At the edge of the lines of huts and substantial houses, Loki paused to reconnoiter. The one street and many lanes seemed deserted. He looked and sniffed for smoke from cooking fires and communal gathering points. The air remained fresh and clean. Even the midden smelled stale and old.

If the villagers had not gone south, where had they gone? Surely the few slaves he'd seen at Base Camp were not the only ones left?

Then he heard the one sound that could chill him to the bones. Marines cocking stun rifles.

Loki did his best to fade into the tree line without betraying his presence.

Still facing the village he spotted two armed men, wearing heat-vision VR gear, as they emerged from a side lane. They marched purposefully toward his hiding place. Two more men joined them from the opposite side of the street.

Loki turned and ran. He hopped over fallen logs, skirted sharp saber ferns, dodged the biggest trees he could find, anything to put distance and obstacles between himself and the enemy.

Every hundred meters or so he paused behind a tall everblue to catch his breath and listen. The four men plodded on, relentlessly. They moved like robots on autopilot.

He wondered if Amanda had stolen their minds as well as their integrity.

He took off again and again. He didn't remember jumping two creeks or splashing through shallow channels of the river. Then he abruptly came to a very broad and deep arm of the river, sluggish at full tide, just before ebbing. A few meters to the west he spotted a causeway to the next island. He dashed across it and dove behind a broad cairn of tumbled boulders.

The ground beneath him tingled against his skin. He must have landed flush upon a ley line.

"Saint Bridget, make me invisible," he willed and closed his eyes. Maybe if he could not see his pursuers, they could not see him.

Kim, where in the saint's name are you? He broadcast the mental call on a wide band, using only the image of his youngest brother to drive his message rather than a direction.

Konner, are you out there?

The entire island seemed to vibrate with the rhythm of his words. Power surged through his body. He had to look down to make certain he did not float above his hiding place.

Opening his eyes, he knew where the four Marines had lost his trail. He watched them in his mind as they wandered aimlessly all around his island, never quite noticing the causeway.

And then he looked, really looked at where he lay. The land pulsed with silvery-blue light. He bathed in the glow from the merging ley lines. A deep well, or lake of power engulfed him.

(Welcome to the beginning place,) the dragons shouted at him.

He had to cover his ears to protect himself from the cacophony of their mingled voices.

Colors assaulted his eyes from the grass and rocks and dirt. The bay and the sky became as intensely blue as the power beneath him. He watched sap rising in the surrounding trees and heard worms and bugs burrowing beneath him.

"We're coming. Delays finding active fuel cells and pairing them up in the bay," Kim's voice and mind bounced off the rock and the well of ley lines. It echoed against the sky and the bay.

About time, Loki complained. He had to step off the pool. Too much power, too many sensations. He hadn't had time or practice to assimilate it all.

A mighty roar defended him. He looked up, expecting to see the entire nimbus of dragons spitting flame at him.

He saw only a swirl of energy far up in the sky, at the edge of the solar system, and a tiny ship jumping through the center.

Konner, Kim, jump point just opened. I have no idea who is coming to plague us now.

CHAPTER 38

"KONNER," DALLEENA SAID through the comm system. Konner opened a frequency to match hers. "What, Dalleena?" She sounded anxious. She wouldn't contact him on an open line while he was flying unless something terrible had happened.

"A jump point opened." Her voice shook. The last time her tracking sense had pinpointed the jump, Amanda Leonard and her IMPs aboard *Jupiter* had descended upon the planet.

"They're right," Kim said quietly. "Sensors just picked it up."

"We're on it, Dalleena. We'll contact the new ship and find out who they are." He hoped. Running everything on reduced power to conserve fuel also reduced their signal strength.

"Do we really want to tell strangers who we are and where we are?" Kim asked.

"Not really. Can you get any readings on what kind of ship?"

"Too far out."

The ship is small, Loki whispered into Konner's mind.

"Loki, I hope you aren't doped up on Tambootie. That stuff is addictive and toxic." Even as Konner spoke, he remembered both the revulsion of his reaction to the leaves and craved the wondrous power that surged through him.

No Tambootie on this island. I have found the beginning place. It is the tenth wonder of the universe and all ours.

"What?"

The confluence of all the ley lines. I can't imagine the amount of omniscium in this pool. Enough to create a million crystal arrays and then some.

"Loki, you are coming through as clearly as if you were sitting right next to me," Konner shivered at the amount of power behind his brother's psychic talent.

I feel as if I could fly with dragons!

"Well, don't try," Kim ordered.

"You hearing him, too?" Konner asked.

"Clear and clean."

I sense five people aboard the new ship.

"Some kind of IMP scout?" Konner asked.

They do not taste of officialdom, but I sense authority in at least one of them.

"Dalleena, can you sense anything about the people or the ship?" Konner opened the comm line again.

"They are too far away." Dalleena's voice was less clear and more distant than Loki's mental contact. That must be some pool of ley lines he had found.

(It is the center of the universe!)

Was that every dragon in the nimbus shouting?

Hanassa prowled Base Camp while Amanda gave him information. In the hour since Lucinda Baines had told him about the value of the ley lines, he had learned the basic principles of the star drives, about the extent of the GTE, about their new war with creatures called the Kree—winged beings not so different from dragons.

For the first time since assuming his first human body, he felt the urge to grow wings and fly.

Amanda inserted a memory.

A much younger Amanda encased in a flight suit barking commands into a helmet comm. Soaring above the atmosphere in a small fighter. Twisting and turning to avoid enemy fire. Laser cannons pulsing around her as she dodged the pirate ship with its cargo of food and medical supplies stolen from a relief convoy.

Her mind melded seamlessly with each new command that sent the tiny ship in a tight spiral around the enemy. Too close for them to aim. Just far enough away from the hull to drop a pulse torpedo into its engines. Then accelerating away, fighting six, maybe seven G's.

An explosion behind her.

Glorious triumph as her comrades back on the cruiser shouted success.

"I do not need the clumsy limitations of dragon wings. I shall fly again as you flew, Amanda," Hanassa whispered to himself and his otherself.

We need to help destroy the Kree. They are kin to the dragons. They must fall to our power as the dragons will fall once we make this planet unlivable for them. Without the dragons to protect them, the O'Hara brothers will succumb to our power as well.

"Yes, we must destroy the dragons and all their kin. We will mine the omniscium. Then the galaxy will bow to us as a god." A secret smile played over Hanassa's face. He knew just how to accomplish all of his goals at once.

We need Kat. She is the key. She has knowledge we do not.

"Kat is an O'Hara."

Then we destroy her after she releases the knowledge we need.

"Why do people keep running away from me? I want only the best for them," Amanda Leonard said quietly into the darkness that surrounded Kat.

Kat kept her mouth shut. No matter what she said, Amanda would find fault and lengthen the punishment. During the long night Kat had conceived and abandoned countless plans for escape. If she ran away now, she'd never again get close enough to Amanda to overthrow her.

"Your brother Konner ran away before I could exact his proper punishment. He does not love justice. But you did not run away from me, Kat. You know justice and love it as I do." Amanda ran her long fingers through Kat's tangled curls. "You could have run away, but you stayed because you know I am right. You know that I am the only one who can make this land the shining center of my empire. You want to stand by my side when the galaxy bows to me and my power."

Kat had managed to loosen her restraints enough to nod. She did and felt Amanda's talons—there was no other word to describe those horny fingernails—scrape her scalp. She cringed beneath the brief but fierce pain.

"People learn through pain, Kat. You know that and I know that. You shall be my chancellor, my chief adviser. I trust you to mete out the punishments I declare." Gently Amanda loosened the strap across Kat's forehead and the one around her neck. "Your Mr. Geralds tells me that there is a treasure trove of omniscium beneath the surface of this land. He wants to mine it to sell across the galaxy. I have plans, too."

Kat nodded again. Her throat went drier than it had been. Bruce seemed quite capable of selling his loyalty to the highest bidder. What more could she expect from a Sam Eyeam?

She'd kept him at arm's length for weeks because she didn't trust him. Her instincts had proved right.

"I have been studying Konner's notes on blacksmithing, the ones you so thoughtfully brought me. I captured a blacksmith, but he knows only copper and bronze. The few good pieces of iron he turned out were happy accidents. Now I can force him to work properly in iron. Before the day is out, I will have pipes to channel the omniscium into the river. There I shall capture it in its salt form. I shall allow you to join in the celebration." Amanda opened an exit hatch. Blessed daylight flooded the fuel bay.

Kat had to blink rapidly against the sudden transition from absolute darkness to dim sunlight.

"You need to rest here a little longer. I need you strong. Learn from this, Kat."

The hatch slammed shut again.

Kat saw stars and afterimages as her retinas shifted once more to darkness. She cursed long and fluently.

"Where am I?" Martin asked the universe. If he had a body, he thought he'd be floating in open space far beyond anything known. He should panic. But he couldn't. The space around him was too beautiful. Distant glowing stars and nebulas against a blacker-than-black background, energy fluxes, and transactional gravitons pulsed around him in every color imaginable, and some quite beyond his imagination.

(Welcome, child of the Stargods.)

"Who said that?"

(We welcome you.)

"But who are you?"

(We are what we are. Who are you?)

That required some thought. He had trouble remembering anything beyond the vast starscape around him.

"I am Martin Fortesque-O'Hara," he proclaimed.

(You are who you want to be.)

"Am I?"

(A wise question from a child. You have much to learn, many to meet, and experience to gain. You have come to the right place to find answers to your questions.)

"I don't think I know enough to ask those kinds of questions."

(You will.)

Abruptly, Martin fell through time and space and lurched back into his body. His bones ached. His eyes ached. He thought he was going to throw up from the abrupt transition from the vision world to reality.

Or was his vision real and his body but an illusion?

No, an illusion wouldn't hurt this much.

Slowly, he opened his eyes to find the deck solid, and hard, beneath him. He wiggled his toes and fingers, grateful they were still attached to his body. Then he looked around. His friends seemed safe, if a little dazed.

"Was that jump longer than normal?" Bruce asked. His hands shook as he tried to adjust his screens.

"Seemed like it lasted a week," Jane replied. She wrapped her arms around herself, shivering, though the temperature on the bridge was a perfect twenty-one degrees Celsius.

"Chronometers read that jump lasted seven-point-three-six seconds," Kurt said. "Within normal parameters." His glasses hung askew from one ear and his perfect politician's son's hair stuck out at odd angles.

"Time is distorted in jump," Martin croaked. "Chronometers are useless. That jump could have lasted seven-and-one-half seconds, or an hour. We'll never know for certain until chronos record how long they were stopped."

How did he know that? An hour seemed about the right amount of time that Martin had hung in space conversing with . . . the universe was as good a term as any.

"I need some water." Martin rolled to his knees and consulted his body before moving further. Nothing seemed broken or ill, just out of sync with reality.

"You okay, kid?" Quinn asked. "You weren't strapped in, and that was a rough jump."

"Nothing wrong with me now," Martin replied. To prove his statement, to them if not himself, he bounced to his feet and slid down the railing of the gangway to the galley.

Later, he'd ask if anyone else had weird experiences during that jump. Much later. When he had time to think about what really happened and what he imagined.

· ——◆—— ·

Danger, danger, danger. These foolish humans do not realize that iron is scarce and copper plentiful for a reason. Iron and power combined are volatile. Iron will be the death of our home. And the humans, led by Hanassa, will be our undoing.

Hanassa should know this. He should remember our lessons. But he left the nimbus when quite young. Perhaps he never learned that iron and power are poison; just as he never learned honor, dignity, and the value of promises kept.

CHAPTER 39

K AT AWOKE TO WATER dribbling across her face. She opened her mouth to capture a few drops of the precious moisture.

Not enough. Not nearly enough to satisfy her thirst. The air in the dark fuel bay had gone stale hours ago. The sun must be high or waning. It beat down on her prison mercilessly.

She ached all over from hours trapped in the same position. Lights danced before her eyes in tantalizing illusion that freedom lay just beyond her reach.

Sweat dripped off her face. She ran her tongue around her mouth as far as it would reach to reabsorb as much as she could.

Another stream of cool water hit her upper lip.

"Is it raining out?" Her voice sounded weak and raspy and loud to her own numbed ears.

(Soon. It takes time to convince the air to move from there to here.)

"Gentian?" she asked with new hope.

(Yes.)

Kat lifted her head a little. A tiny sliver of light shone at her feet, near the hatch to the cabin of the lander. Amanda had exited by a closer hatch. It remained sealed.

"How did you get in?"

(Through the main entrance.)

An image of the central cabin of the lander appeared in Kat's head. She barely recognized it stripped of seats and webbing for securing crew and cargo.

(You must come. Now.) Gentian began ripping at the sticky webbing with teeth and claws. He found the overlap and pulled. With a ripping sound, Kat's left hand came free of the restraints.

She reached and quickly dispatched the one on her right wrist, then the one around her waist.

By this time the trickle of light around the hatch had allowed her eyes to adjust. She could just barely see the outlines of fuel cells and her flywacket.

Careful of the low ceiling she sat up and dispatched her ankle straps. Blood rushed into her limbs with sharp prickles. Her head ached and every joint felt inflamed.

(You must leave this place. Now. The air is bad.) Gentian spat.

His drool hit her hand and she wondered if that was the life-giving moisture she had drunk so greedily. Her mouth and body were so parched she didn't care.

"Water," she croaked.

Gentian made his way to the hatch leading back up into the main cabin. He began digging at the lower edge with his talons.

Kat crawled after him and reached her heavy arm up to the latch. She barely had enough strength to pull the lever down. It protested with a loud groan of metal rusted in place. Impossible. The alloys couldn't rust. Maybe Amanda had coated the device with something caustic to seal her prison.

Gentian leaped at the hatch, snagged the latch, and combined his weight with Kat's. Together, they pulled the portal open. It swung inward. Kat fell backward, banging her head on a spent fuel cell. Better a minor cracked head than a bashed-in face. That hatch was heavy.

Rubbing the hurt with both hands, she managed to right herself and drag her body up the two steps to the main cabin. A hasty glance around showed the place had been stripped of all supplies and anything that could be used in Base Camp. Her footsteps echoed hollowly in the bare vessel. Even the pilot's emergency kit was gone from the cockpit.

She stumbled out of the lander into cloudy daylight in search of water. Even that hazy light was too bright. Everything appeared as white on white afterimages with fuzzy outlines. She squinted and blinked rapidly, willing her vision to adjust and her headache to go away.

(Get water,) Gentian urged her from the safety of the lander.

"Come with me."

(If the one you call Amanda sees us together, she will murder us both.)

"And if she sees only one of us?"

(She will accept your escape.)

"What if she spots you?"

(Then my existence will cease. I will not earn another opportunity to atone for my cowardice.)

"Then stay hidden. And thank you for helping me. I think you are very brave. Fear is a good thing if it keeps you safe." She stumbled toward the center of camp and the jug of water kept beside the fire pit. She drank greedily at first. Then she slowed down and allowed the water to linger in her mouth, bathing the parched tissues and restoring some of her equilibrium.

"About time you figured out how to escape," Amanda said sharply behind Kat.

"I gave up waiting for you to decide when to end my punishment. I am of no use to you dehydrated, starving, and ill from heat prostration," Kat snapped back. She didn't care if she antagonized the woman. All she wanted was water, a light meal, and a hat with a wide brim to shield her eyes.

"Your timing is perfect, Kat," Amanda gazed at the northwest corner of Base Camp and the abandoned forge. Only it wasn't abandoned anymore. A stout man alternately worked the bellows and hammered at a sheet of red-hot metal. Nearby lay a circular clay mold about fifteen centimeters in diameter and a full two meters in length.

As Kat watched the blacksmith shouted something and two young assistants carried the long mold and rested it across two sawhorses and poured several jugs of water onto the clay. The blacksmith transferred the sheet of iron to the mold with tongs. A sharp sizzle and steam rose up when the two met. Then, with other tools Kat could not identify, he shaped the metal around the mold to make a piece of pipe.

Amanda jumped up and down, clapping her hands with joy. "I've done it," she crowed. "I've made the first length of pipe. Tomorrow, we begin mining the omniscium."

Kat glared at the woman out of the corner of her eye. Amanda had not done any of the work, but she took the credit for fashioning the iron treasure.

Something outside Kat prompted her to ask the question no one had yet put forth. "Why wouldn't a copper or bronze pipe work as well? Much easier to work with, and copper is much more readily available."

"Not enough strength. The omniscium will corrode copper."

"How do we know that? No one has ever found omniscium in large enough quantities to test it against various substances. I think gas giant miners use glass or cerama/metal to capture the elusive elements."

"We can't make fires hot enough to burn all the impurities out of sand to make good glass. All we can get is something quite useless, too brittle. Trust me, Kat. I know that iron serves *me* best."

A great chill ran through Kat's overheated body. The world tilted and all the bright green of early summer seemed to shrivel and turn brown before her eyes.

She forced herself to breathe deeply and ignore the prescient vision. If it came true, Amanda could turn the entire planet into a barren prison.

· ——◆—— ·

Loki peered over the top of his rock barricade to scout for any sign of *Rover*. One of the IMPs stared directly at him through his heat-seeking VR gear. The cursed soldier stood less than ten meters away.

The soldier fired his lethal needle rifle.

Three neurotoxic needles scraped Loki's scalp. The top of his head instantly grew numb.

Loki pressed himself flat upon the ground, soaking up the power of the ley line lake.

"Saint Bridget, I wish I were anywhere but here." In his mind he saw himself standing next to Paola. He added the details of the black-and-red boulders surrounded by gray-green sand on the continental desert. Why not a battle with the snake monsters, too. Killing monsters had to be easier than avoiding IMPs with heat-seeking VR gear.

He imagined himself there two heartbeats before he had lifted his head.

His perspective shifted ninety degrees. White sparkles filled his vision. He lost contact with his body for one heartbeat—did his heart actually stop beating?

Then heat and grit blasted his face. A mighty roar filled his ears.

And Paola's strong arm wrapped around his waist.

"Take the stunner," she shouted at him.

All around them other women in tattered IMP uniforms fought off a tangle of big—extremely big—black snakes with stunners, bows and arrows, lances, and clubs. Another contingent worked furiously cranking a hand pump that sprayed the snakes and the sand before them with seawater. The women let loose long ululations of victory each time a serpent succumbed to their attack.

The Amazons held their ground against the oozing advance.

Behind the coil of slithering black muscle, a giant serpent, fully as big around as a pulse torpedo and too long to measure, rose up a full four meters. Six pairs of bat wings fluttered along her back. The matriarch roared protests of anger and pain.

Too stunned to object, Loki took the gun from Paola and fired into the open mouth of a snake. It swallowed the burst of energy, gulped, opened its red eyes wide in surprise, and fell backward.

Sweat poured off Loki's brow as he fired again. This time his blast took a smaller snake directly in its venom gland. Poison exploded in all directions.

Everyone, including the snakes, hit the dirt and covered eyes, ears, and mouths until the spray subsided.

The pump workers cranked harder and directed their spray upon the Amazons. The venom sizzled a femto in contact with seawater and then diluted and washed free.

"Dangerous move, Loki," Paola snarled as she slung an arrow into a bow as long as she was tall. "But thanks for the diversion. Now we know that the venom is toxic to them as well."

Even before she finished speaking, she loosed an arrow. It arched high and flew long.

Loki almost lost track of it against the glare from the dying sun at his back.

And, miraculously, he watched it descend directly into the sagging red pouch beneath the open jaw of the matriarch.

"Hit the dirt!" Paola screamed.

Loki didn't wait for the venom to explode. He suspected a single drop on the skin could eat away at flesh like acid. Grabbing Paola by the hand, he imagined them back in the pool of ley lines. He felt himself drawing in the awesome power.

Again, his perspective shifted ninety degrees. He saw a myriad of white stars. His feet hit the ground and he fired the stunner directly into the heart of the IMP who took aim at where he had hidden moments before.

"What the hell just happened?" Paola demanded, blinking. She shifted her feet, fighting for balance, lost the battle and sank to the ground, legs neatly folded, head in hands, bow discarded.

"I'm not exactly certain." Heat and disorientation rose from deep within Loki. He needed to sit.

But first he needed to make sure the IMP was unconscious and any other enemies far away.

Then he saw the mangled remains of one of the snakes wrapped around his leg. More than just a stunner blast had turned the viper's body inside out and scattered bits of it around the lake of power.

He took one tentative step away from the gore and crumpled to the ground. His bare feet ached and stung. He took one glance at the monster venom burning the flesh around his anklebone and lost his battle to remain conscious.

CHAPTER 40

K IM SCANNED THE GROUND anxiously from *Rover*'s cockpit. He and Konner had heard nothing from Loki for over an hour. He didn't like the shiver at his nape that told him something was wrong.

"There!" He pointed at a red blob on his heat sensor panel. "Just beyond the causeway between two islands."

"I know the place," Konner replied and shifted direction slightly to port. "Hestiia led us across that causeway on foot the day we landed. Too bad we didn't know about ley lines and psi powers back then."

Kim switched his attention between the heat seeker and real-time views out the windscreen. The heat sensors left him with afterimages too similar to the symbols he saw during a prescient vision. But he needed the accuracy of those sensors to find his brother.

"Brace yourself. This landing could be a bit rough," Konner warned. He toggled the VTOL jets to set the shuttle down as close to the causeway as possible, without damaging the natural bridge.

The moment Konner gave the all clear, Kim threw off his safety harness and dashed for the exit at the center of the vessel. It irised open too slowly. He jumped clear before the portal completed the cycle and lowered the steps.

Loki sat in a lopsided huddle with his left foot dangling in a nearby creek. Paola stood in the creek, bathing his foot. Her round face looked tired with care lines radiating out from her eyes and below her mouth. An ominous yellow tinge marred her near perfect olive skin.

"What?" Kim asked, sliding into the creek beside Paola. He lifted Loki's foot in both of his hands and examined the wound.

"I'll bring the med kit," Konner called from a few steps away and dashed back to *Rover*.

"I think I got all the venom off," Paola said. Her voice shook. "But fresh water doesn't neutralize it anywhere near as well as seawater."

Kim had never seen or heard anything faze the Amazon before.

"Is the snake still around?" Kim asked. He looked anxiously at the water and nearby banks, not eager to be bitten himself.

"Sort of," Loki whispered. His face looked paler than Paola's. Kim thought he must be in terrible pain.

"What is that supposed to mean?"

"I killed it," Loki said. "I killed it with magic."

Kim gulped. "How?" he asked as he checked Loki's eyes for signs of vacancy, and his aura for leakage into death.

"I . . . I'm not sure how, but I willed myself into the middle of Paola's battle with the serpents. *On the other continent.*" He gulped and closed his eyes. "Then I willed us back here. But the snake was coiled around my ankle. It . . . it . . . turned itself inside out and exploded in transport." Loki gagged and held a hand over his mouth.

"By Saint Bridget, that's not possible," Kim breathed. If he could master that spell, a lot of their problems with fuel would vanish.

"I am afraid that it is possible," Paola replied. "One femto I'm in the battle of my life with fifteen of my ladies. The next femto Loki is beside me. We shot a few times. Took out a few more snakes, then he and I are back here with snake gore scattered all over the island."

She shivered and climbed out of the creek. She sat beside Loki and gently eased his head into her lap.

"I've got to get back to my ladies, Loki," she said softly. "I have to see if we took out the matriarch and how many of my Amazons are hurt. Please send me back."

"Can't." Loki's teeth chattered. "Too weak." His eyes rolled up in his head.

"I don't think any of us should try magical transport until we figure out what went wrong with the snake," Konner said, handing Kim the med kit. "I took a quick look around. That snake wasn't killed by any weapon I know of." He shook his head and looked more pale and worried than Paola.

"We'll worry about the transport later. Right now, Loki's foot is a mess."

It had swollen to about three times normal size and the venom had eaten into the muscle nearly to the bone before Paola was able to get it all washed out. Dead skin and muscle sloughed off in chunks.

"I don't have enough Tambootie with me to heal it." Grief and pain and guilt ate away at Kim. He should have thought ahead and brought a basketful of leaves. He couldn't see any of the trees in the immediate vicinity.

What could he do?

"The pool of ley lines," Loki said weakly. He'd barely regained consciousness. The pain must be incredible.

"The what?" Paola asked.

Kim squinted slightly and looked at the ground through his peripheral vision. Hundreds of silvery-blue rivers of power poured into the island. Their brightness nearly blinded him.

Then he saw it. A great lake of converged ley lines.

His jaw dropped in awe. "This truly is the beginning place," he whispered.

"The center of the universe," Konner added. He dropped the med kit and ran to the center of the pool. "This is the well. This is where all the transactional gravitons begin their web that holds the universe together!" he shouted. He raised his arms and turned circles in homage to the power.

"Help me carry Loki over there," Kim called.

Reluctantly, Konner returned to the creek. Together, he and Kim lifted Loki. The vast amount of power emanating from the land gave them strength beyond measure. Kim felt as if he could have tossed his oldest brother into the center of the well. But that would have been uncomfortable for Loki who groaned in pain at every movement.

They set him down behind the tumble of boulders.

"Check the IMP, Paola. Make sure he doesn't rouse and cause trouble," Konner said.

"Already done," the Amazon replied. She paused long enough to test the fallen soldier's pulse and the twisted vines she'd used to bind his hands and feet. "This devil's vine is a powerful restraint. It twines on its own and every movement by the prisoner makes the thorns jab deeper. Almost as good as force bracelets."

"Bloodthirsty wench," Kim muttered.

"That's what I love about her," Loki whispered. He tried to grin, but it turned into a grimace.

Kim returned the grin. Hestiia could be as fierce as any woman on the planet. As could Dalleena. "Looks like we've all found fitting partners," he said.

"Except Kat." Loki frowned. "Amanda still has her."

"We'll worry about our sister when I've fixed this." Kim looked more closely at Loki's wound, trying to figure out what needed to be done.

He took three deep breaths, exhaling each fully. With each intake he pulled power from the ground through his system, just as the dragons had taught him.

Eldritch light pulsed around him, encapsulating all three brothers in the magic of healing.

Kim's head seemed to disconnect from his body, feeling lighter than air. From this new perspective above his body, he looked more deeply into Loki. He saw damaged blood vessels.

With a thought he reconnected them.

He added fiber to the absent muscle, tendons, and ligaments from other parts of Loki's body. He took bits and pieces from the strong shoulders and back. Loki would reforge those areas quickly.

With only a tiny bit of the power available to him, he encouraged bonding and regrowth at one hundred times the speed normal to a body.

As they watched, the swelling reduced and the wound closed. Loki's facial color improved, though he still looked pale and exhausted.

Now for the skin. Kim needed to find seven layers the size of his fist to cover the raw flesh.

His strength flagged. The healing faltered and the glow surrounding him diminished. No matter how much power Kim drew from the ground, he needed his own strength to use it.

He dropped to his knees, still holding Loki's foot. His neck did not want to hold his head up and his eyes closed of their own volition.

Konner placed his hand upon Kim's shoulder. For an instant they shared memories, emotions, and energy.

Kim stared at his bother, fully understanding him for the first time.

"That should do you for the finishing touches," Konner said. He looked as if he'd wilt, or fall over in a strong breeze.

"Take him, Paola. Feed him," Kim ordered.

Fully restored, he began the delicate job of building up tissue in layers to cover the gaping wound.

He funneled more power into his eyes and his hands. Blue light grew out of his fingers. With infinite care he molded and wove the power into the wound, forcing new skin to grow from the inside out.

At last he laid Loki's foot down as gently as possible. "I can't think of anything else to do. I don't know if it will even work," he said on a sigh.

"Loki has been telling me about the miracles you three can work. I only half believed. Now I know," Paola said. She examined the injury with a critical eye. "Not even a scar. We've never been able to save anyone if the venom gets below the skin." She folded her legs and sat beside Loki's head. She smoothed sweat-dampened hair off his brow.

Loki leaned into her caress and kissed her palm.

"You should probably stay off that foot for a couple of days," Konner added. He didn't seemed inclined to move from his spot a few feet to Kim's left.

"I can't sit idly by while Amanda has our sister. It's my responsibility to look out for all of you." Loki struggled to sit up, despite Paola's restraining hand on his chest. "And I don't think we should allow Amanda to mine the omniscium."

"That's a change of tune," Konner said.

Kim was too tired to talk. But he, too, was surprised by Loki's decision. Loki rarely if ever changed his mind once he took a position.

"This pool has to be protected," Loki insisted. "I saw some things in transit between here and the continent and back again. I didn't understand them then, just thought it was part of the . . . spell for lack of another word. This well of power is connected to the transactional gravitons. It might not be the center of the universe. There are probably hundreds of such wells scattered about the galaxies, maybe thousands. But disturbing any one of them could disrupt the entire web of energy."

"Mining here could begin the unraveling of the web," Konner mused. "I'd never thought about it before, but that sense of oneness with the universe we achieve when we work . . . magic for lack of another word . . . is because of the omniscium in the ley lines. It's connected to the web."

"You three are the Stargods. Can't you just declare this a holy spot?" Paola asked.

"That will work with the locals, but not with Amanda. The spirit of Hanassa that has possessed her doesn't respect us or anything holy. He . . . it . . . only respects his own personal power" Kim said.

"Loki is right. We have to stop Amanda before she mines," he added. "We need a plan. And we need the transportation spell. But do we dare use it before Loki figures out what he did and how he did it?"

"It's too risky." Konner shook his head and pointed to the pieces of snake that had begun to stink.

"I've got to get back to my Amazons," Paola insisted.

"We need help," Loki said. He tried to get his legs under him, then thought better of it. He sank back against Paola's strong body. "You have to do this without me."

"We need to bring our warriors here," Kim said. We need to take back our land and our villages from the IMPs.

How could they without fuel; without the transportation spell? How could they defeat Amanda and save the planet without killing *people?*

And they had to do it all before the new ship arrived and complicated things.

CHAPTER 41

◆——·—◆—·——◆

THE PROXIMITY ALARMS blared suddenly. The *Margaret Kristine* shuddered and veered sharply down, relative to the artificial gravity field.

"Pulse cannons, port and starboard!" Quinn yelled.

Viewscreens showed a dense asteroid field dead ahead and closing fast.

Bruce called up the tiny weapon to port. Martin took starboard. "Just like in the games! Better than steering. I like gross movements over minute any day," Bruce chortled. He blasted three small chunks of debris before he finished speaking.

"Only this is for real," Quinn reminded him. "One of those gets by you and I can't steer around it, we are all dead, exposed to vacuum. It's not a pretty or comfortable way to die."

Martin held back his own shout of triumph as he nudged aside an asteroid at least three kilometers long and two wide. The enhanced sensors showed it a miner's dream of minerals and ores.

Quinn veered sharply to port before Martin had time to think. He blasted the detritus of an exploded planetoid in every direction as quickly as he could swivel and aim the little cannon.

The next hour passed in a blur of concentration, aim, fire, aim again. Martin wished fervently that he had the crystal in his pocket and not nestled among the sensors. Maybe it enhanced his screens to give him time to aim properly. Maybe he only thought it helped.

At long last he loosed a big sigh of relief. He couldn't see any more asteroids or planetary debris in their path. Their route toward the inner planets of this system had been circuitous at best.

"I estimate travel time to the second planet roughly fifteen hours at reduced speed with sensors running at full capacity," Quinn said. He yawned hugely. "Wake me if anything strange comes our way." He stood and stretched.

Martin made a brief sensor scan. Two hours later he hit the comm unit. "Uh, Quinn, I think I see something strange."

"What?" Quinn's voice sounded groggy.

"Cerama/metal. Megatons of it spread between here and . . . and the orbit of the second planet," Martin replied. He continued staring at his screens in wonder. He'd never seen anything like it, even in simulation.

"Approximately fifty thousand megatons," Kurt corrected. He perched his useless glasses atop his head and looked more closely at his screens. "That's almost enough for a small cruiser." He whistled at the end of his sentence, a clear sign that the numbers presented an awesome picture.

Quinn appeared in the cockpit a femto later, hair mussed and eyes heavy. He swung into his chair and scrutinized his own screens. "Saints preserve us, that could be a judicial cruiser." He ran some hurried calculations.

"Kurt, get a reading on that big chunk." Bruce pointed to an object on the front screen that displayed real-time views of their path.

"I don't like the looks of this," Jane whispered. She sat firmly in her jump seat staring wide-eyed at the front screen. "Those dippos on Aurora were looking for a missing judicial cruiser and its passenger, a planetary governor's daughter."

"So was the ship just outside Aurora's jump point." Martin chilled in memory of the scare the ship had given them.

"I've got a signature signal from the black box," Kurt said.

"Run it through my screen," Quinn ordered. He pulled up another screen.

"Registry marks that frequency as the *Jupiter,* the ship that's missing," he said quietly. "We've got to retrieve the black box."

"Any chance we can crack the box and find out what happened?" Martin asked. "The crew might have made it to the second planet. It's habitable."

"But there aren't any signs of civilization coming from there," Bruce protested. "No signals, no pollution, and definitely no doming. How would they survive?"

"The black box has to go back to GTE authorities. They are the only ones with the codes to crack it," Quinn said, his face stern.

A big grin spread over Martin's face. "When has a lack of codes ever stopped us? And we've got the mini king stone to help. Besides, this is an uncharted system. Who's to say that the GTE and their IMPs have jurisdiction?"

"If the IMPs are here, then they have jurisdiction. That makes opening the box illegal . . ." Quinn said.

"Like I said. When has that ever stopped us?"

"Your father is an O'Hara. He and his brothers have been redefining 'legal' for twenty years." Quinn shook his head and took a bearing on the black box.

"How would they survive?" Bruce asked again.

Martin shrugged. "They have to be alive. My dad's down, there, I know it."

"Don't get your hopes up" Quinn advised. "Have any of you ever seen an undeveloped planet?"

"Our summer camp was on a bush planet," Jane said. "It was pretty primitive."

"Summer camp with food shipped in, or fields already planted for harvesting, shelters, and plumbing; all that is luxury compared to what we are likely to find on the second planet from this star. Better think about what we need to take dirtside." Quinn set his jaw and went about retrieving the back box.

Martin sent out a broad signal, hoping against hope someone had salvaged basic communications from *Jupiter.*

Within an hour, they had homed in on the black box.

Kurt spent a long time concentrating with the robotic arm at an air lock in the belly of the ship. Martin watched him work in real time through a porthole. Kurt reached out and grabbed the box three times only to have it slip out of the claws. The fourth time he managed to retract the arm, with the box firmly clutched, into an air lock.

Martin waited impatiently while the air lock cycled through and allowed him entrance. He pounced on the black box a femto later. He ran his hands over the solid cube, one meter square, seeking a seam or the source of the signal.

"Quinn?" he asked through the comm. "Have you ever seen the inside of one of these?"

"No. And no one I know has. Not even the emperor. IMPs keep the workings top secret to avoid sabotage."

Martin walked around the thing. It offered no clues.

"Let's get it up onto the bridge. I need proximity to the mini king stone." He tried lifting the box by himself. He couldn't budge it.

"Maybe it's magnetic and stuck to the hull," Kurt offered. He pushed his glasses further up his long nose and scrutinized the box.

"Or it's extremely heavy," Bruce joined them. "Let me try. I've been lifting weights in heavy gravity back home."

Martin and Kurt looked at him skeptically. Bruce had always been the lazy one, more content to read about exercise than actually do it. He rarely swam at camp because that meant revealing his pudgy body to the scrutiny of counselors and girls.

"Hey, I can disguise a lot of muscle under these pantaloons!"

"Yeah, right." Kurt adjusted his glasses on his nose and peered through them as if examining a bug.

"So I'll prove it!" Bruce crouched down and wrapped his arms around the box. Using the thick muscles in his thighs he heaved upward, grunting and moaning.

The cube shifted a few centimeters, then plunked back into place.

"Well, he did move it more than we did," Martin said with a shrug.

"This requires some creative thinking," Bruce said, surveying the cargo hold. His eyes brightened and he grabbed an antigrav sled. "I'll shift it, you two cram the sled under it. You should have thought of this in the first place."

"Didn't think we'd find one on a private vessel." Kurt looked mystified. "What would Quinn need an antigrav sled for?"

"Shifting heavy objects when he's alone." Bruce crouched down again.

"Why doesn't he just turn off the artificial gravity?" Kurt replied.

"We can do that?" Bruce stood up again without moving the box.

"But gravity takes over again as soon as we reach the bridge," Martin said.

"So we turn it off there, too."

"Reducing gravity to ten percent of normal," Quinn called through the comm. He chuckled. "Took you long enough to figure it out."

Within a few femtos Martin felt the tension leave his face and the weight of gravity leave his shoulders. He shuffled one step forward and nearly lifted himself across the hold.

Bruce jumped up and turned a somersault in the air.

Kurt frowned and shook his head at the frivolity.

Martin returned to the box and hoisted it to his shoulder. Cautiously, he proceeded up the gangway and onto the bridge.

With the box securely in place next to the bulkhead where the miniature king stone presided, he set about examining it more thoroughly.

"Mind if I get some weight back?" Quinn asked. "I really prefer to navigate with better control of my hands than this."

"Sure," Martin replied absently. He turned his entire focus onto the box. A faint pressure nagged at the back of his neck.

"I almost hear something," Jane said. She slid onto the deck and put her ear up to the box. Then she took it away, shaking her head.

"The king stone is humming," Martin said. Once Jane had brought his attention to the sound, he realized the source of the pressure. The vibrations changed pitch. "I think the king stone is trying to talk to the box."

The pitch changed again, became louder. The box responded with a major third down from the king stone.

The king stone adjusted its note again, this time pulling harmony from the primary crystal array and matching the box with a major fifth chord.

Quinn spun around in his chair and stared at the box. "Is there anything that stone can't do?"

"I don't hear anything," Bruce said. He assumed a posture and expression of affront.

"I'm attuned to the primary array. Martin is attuned to the miniature. When you have your own ship, you'll develop your own empathy with your crystals," Quinn explained.

The box let forth with another note, complementary to the crystal but up a major third. Then the crystal found the right response. The box split open along an invisible seam right around the center.

Martin jumped on the box and pried it open. Inside he found a holographic replay system. He pressed the start button.

A map of the *Jupiter* displayed itself in the air above the black box. Onboard sensors noted two human heat sources.

Martin tracked the two bodies. One exited in a solo scout craft. The other continued to move awkwardly to a different bay and a large troop or cargo lander.

An explosion of light and sound burst along the gangways of the ship.

"Get out of there, Kat. Get out now," a man's deep voice screamed. Then silence.

The system played the same explosion and vocal command over and over.

"What happened to them?" Jane asked.

"Three hundred people aboard that ship. Some of them had to survive." Quinn pounded his fist against his thigh.

"I hope my dad was dirtside when that happened." Martin blinked back tears. "Two people aboard. Only two people. That meant the rest evacuated. Right?"

"Let's hope they were all dirtside when the ship blew. Otherwise they are all dead, including the planetary governor's daughter. The GTE will move heaven and earth to find her," Quinn added.

CHAPTER 42

K AT WATCHED the captive blacksmith with awe. He heated and
pounded the iron into a sheet ready to wrap around a clay mold. She
matched the blacksmith's actions to the words on the reader she had stolen
from Kim. At the very end of Konner's notes she saw a reference to purifying
the coal until the smoke billowed nearly clear. Otherwise the fire couldn't
raise enough heat to burn impurities out of the iron. The resulting metal
would be too brittle to withstand ordinary stresses.

The smoke from the forge looked oily and yellow.

How much stress would the pipe undergo in channeling the omniscium?

The secret smile on the blacksmith's face told Kat that he knew he forged
an inferior product. Why did Amanda let him get away with it?

Did she even know?

Amanda hovered around the forge, urging the smith to hurry. Her own
impatience doomed her pet project before it fully started.

"Wonderful day, love," Geralds said, snaking his arms about Kat's waist.

She started within his embrace. She'd been so intent upon the forge, she
hadn't noticed his approach. A dangerous lapse, considering her plans.

"Jumpy today, aren't you, love." Geralds tightened his grip on her, pulling
her back against his chest. He nuzzled her hair.

Kat resisted the urge to slam her elbow into his gut. She had to make him
believe she agreed with Amanda about the slavery and the exploitation of all
the planet's resources, including people.

"Amanda, I'm not certain iron will work. It's so impure. Copper or bronze,
now . . ."

"No!" Amanda screeched.

Everyone at the forge froze in place.

Amanda looked around, wild-eyed, fists clenched, and shoulders hunched.

Then quite suddenly her posture softened, a bit of the old, logical, and reasonable captain peeked through her expression. "Believe me, Kat, I know that iron is the only metal that is proper. Trust me. All will work out in the end."

"Something feels wrong."

"Don't you want to provide the GTE with the means to destroy the Kree? Have you switched loyalties since you found your *outlaw* family, Kat?"

"No. I still respect the GTE. I want them to win the war with the Kree. But I'm not certain this is the way."

"The Kree must be destroyed!" Amanda's eyes turned black and she nearly tore her hair in desperation. "The Kree cannot be allowed to prevail. They must be destroyed once and for all."

As all dragons must be destroyed.

Kat wasn't sure whether she truly heard that last statement or not. She needed to stop this mining operation until she had a chance to think it through, maybe consult Irisey or one of the other dragons. Gentian would know if he hadn't disappeared again.

She made to close the reader and back away from the project.

"Let me see that." Geralds grabbed the reader away from her. "The smith is doing it wrong," he said quietly.

"Careful," Kat warned him. "I'm not sure we should . . ."

"Kat, I need the money from the omniscium. I need to buy the safety of my wife and son from Melinda Fortesque."

Kat raised her eyebrows at him. He truly did look desperate.

He stared at her long and hard for a moment, then his posture slackened a bit as he finally relented. "Melinda Fortesque held my pregnant wife hostage with a needle pistol at her head until I agreed to do . . . some very bad things for her. Then she held exposure of those deeds over my head for sixteen years." He gulped, keeping silent a moment as he mastered the strong emotions playing across his face.

Then he straightened out of his loop of bad memories. "Money is the only thing that Melinda understands. But with money I can hide my wife and son so that she can never find them, or me again."

"There has to be another way . . ."

"No. There isn't. Captain Leonard, I'd like to try my hand at pounding the iron." He held the reader out to Amanda. "Someone other than one lone blacksmith, who just happens to be a slave with no vested interest in the project, needs to know how to do this."

Amanda calculated something in her head while she looked Geralds up and down.

"You may proceed."

Geralds spoke slowly and distinctly to the smith. Either he had figured out that the local dialect was a lingering drawl, or he thought the man stupid. Then Geralds pulled the heavy hammer out of the man's hands.

The smith backed off, hands at his sides. He still had that secret smile on his face.

Kat was willing to bet Geralds' first or second blow would shatter the iron. Blame for the disaster would fall on the Sam Eyeam's shoulders and not the slave's.

But Geralds consulted the reader and dumped a half bucket of water onto the greasy looking coals.

"What are you doing to my fire!" Amanda demanded.

"Purifying the coal so that it will burn hotter," Kat explained.

"Help him," Amanda commanded.

Kat backed up, unwilling to assist in this project that felt more and more wrong with each consideration.

A Marine leveled a stunner at Kat.

She shrugged and worked the bellows under the coals. The smoke billowed up dark and oily. Another dose of water and air cleared the forge of the stench of burning salt. One more dose made the smoke clear and white. The coals glowed green, just like every other fire on the planet.

Konner's notes had said the copper sulfate wouldn't hurt the forging, just the salt and other minerals found in sea coal.

"I need to reheat the iron before pounding it again," Geralds said.

The smith scowled and backed away. "Might as well start over with new slag," he said in his rough accent.

"That will take too long. We have to get these pipes made," Amanda ordered. She paced around and around the forge, wringing her hands.

The old Amanda, before Konner O'Hara sabotaged *Jupiter,* before Amanda went insane and became vulnerable to the ravaging spirit of Hanassa, never reacted so nervously.

Geralds gestured the smith to reheat the metal.

Reluctantly, the big man grabbed the flattened iron with a pair of tongs and thrust the piece into the fire.

Kat kept working the bellows, keeping the fire hotter than before.

Amanda continued to pace and shout and speak nonsense words to the sky.

Kat owed this Amanda no loyalty.

Hanassa, what do you want of us? She projected her thoughts outward, wondering who, if anyone, she would contact.

Amanda jerked her head up and stopped pacing. She looked all around her, eyes narrowed.

Who dares speak? a thick masculine voice hissed back at Kat. She fought to keep her body and expression passive.

Another dragon, Kat replied. She averted her eyes from Amanda, pretending only to monitor the fire. *One who wishes to see an end to your tyranny.*

The iron glowed white hot now. The smith removed it from the coals and began pounding and folding it again. This time the iron looked brighter, resisted the hammer more. This time it would make a good length of pipe.

"I will see all of the dragons dead before I let you harm me. I will rule you all," Hanassa/Amanda said aloud and projected telepathically.

Watch your back, Hanassa. Your death comes from behind, above, below, and face on. You will give up this mad plan or die.

Never! I am immortal!

"We'll see about that," Kat muttered.

"Captain!" Sergeant Kent Brewster ran toward the forge from the center of the village. He'd retreated to playing with the comms rather than come under Amanda's too close scrutiny. "Captain, a ship has answered our distress signal. A ship, Captain. We're going to be rescued," the sergeant crowed. He did a little victory dance.

"Get that pipe ready. We've got some mining to do before the ship arrives," Amanda snarled. "I don't want anyone but me claiming the rights to the omniscium."

"We share the profits," Geralds insisted. He approached Amanda with clenched fists. "You promised, Captain."

"Lock this man up," she ordered the Marines that always hovered around her. "No one gets the omniscium but me. Kill the newcomers when they land and take possession of their ship."

CHAPTER 43

L OKI STARED AT the magnificent pool of blue at his feet. "Come back a femto," he called to his brothers.

"We need to get back to the village, start making plans," Konner protested.

"Just wait a bit while I think something through." Loki couldn't take his eyes off the well of ley lines. "If this omniscium is so powerful, if it fuels our psi talents by remote contact, why can't it refuel one of the cells?"

"What?" Konner's eyes lost focus.

Loki didn't need to read his mind to know that Konner ran calculations and physics probabilities through his head.

"Well, let's test it." Ever practical, Paola started in the direction where Loki had stashed the fuel cell he stole from the IMPs.

Loki followed her, dragging his feet. The moment he stepped off the well onto normal ground, heaviness returned to his body. In contrast, his mind was lighter and freer than ever before. He felt as if he'd just awoken from a long night's sleep filled with vivid dreams and had not yet coordinated his mind and body with reality. His ankle still ached, like the last few days of a sprain, but it supported him well enough.

His perspective was off, though, and he had to place each foot carefully. Before he'd reached the causeway, Paola had returned with the half full fuel cell in her strong arms. Kim and Konner relieved her of the awkward and heavy burden. They toted it back to the well and placed the cube in the center.

Loki considered following them. Then he decided that if he touched the well again, he might not ever leave.

Within moments, Konner had one of his testing and monitoring gadgets out and pointed at the fuel cell. "I don't believe it." He shook his head, tapped the instrument, then peered closely at the fuel cell.

"It's regenerating! I've got to figure out how." Kim nearly danced across the well of power.

"Come on, Paola, let's get the rest of the cells from *Rover* and get them charged." Loki took her arm as if escorting her to a ball.

"Then can you take me back. I've got to find out about my ladies, and those snakes. There was venom flying everywhere when we left. I can't believe I took out the matriarch with a single arrow." She tripped alongside him.

Loki kissed her temple. "I can believe you did it. You are the finest warrior of your entire army of Amazons."

She paused a moment to snuggle up to him. "Now that you can recharge the cells, will you come visit me?"

"As often as I can. But with a fully fueled *Rover,* Konner's going to want to leave. He has to go to his son."

"I'm staying here." Paola stopped, hands on hips in a defiant pose. A pose that showed off her magnificent proportions and her stubborn pride.

"I know you are. You give me reason to come back as often as I can." He kissed her again. Never would he try to tame her. He had dealt with a "tame" Cyndi and learned to despise her. He wanted Paola just the way she was. He wanted a regular lover who demanded no commitment from him; who had no more use for hearth and home than he did.

"I love you, Loki O'Hara." Paola rose up on tiptoe to kiss him. "And don't you dare take that as any kind of commitment."

"I won't." He kissed her back. "Let's get those fuel cells charged so we can get on with our lives.

"Good plan. So, if we've taken out the snake monsters, what's our first move in expanding the port?"

"Building boats."

"No timber near the port."

"Farther north on the continent?"

"What about cutting it here in Coronnan and transporting it to the big continent for building?" Paola grabbed a nearly empty fuel cell from *Rover*'s interior and handed it to Loki.

"Easier to build the boats here and sail them across. That will establish connections between the two." Loki set the meter-square cube on the ground and took the second cell from Paola.

She jumped down from the fuel bay and hefted the first cell into her arms before replying. "The people here are fearful of the water beyond the bay. Will they take the risk of sailing beyond it?"

"If one of us goes with them."

"Not Konner. He's too anxious to head out and see his son. Kim's fearful of leaving Hestiia and the baby until they both get stronger. That leaves you, and I know you are as anxious to leave as anyone."

They began walking.

"Not much sense in working to establish markets for our produce until we have a surplus and a port to lift off from."

They nearly tripped over the now conscious and struggling body of the restrained IMP.

"And we have to take care of Amanda and her pet Marines before this place can grow."

"All before the new ship arrives."

"Let's get to work." Loki increased his pace, determined to finish what he started.

"I'll kill Captain Leonard for you," Paola said quietly. "I know how you feel about taking a human life."

Loki's insides chilled. For half a femto he relived the time he had shot Hanassa with a needle rifle. He'd died a little bit inside himself and needed to follow the tyrant into death. Only Kim and Konner had pulled him back.

"It's my job to secure this planet. I'll do it." All of the euphoria from the well of ley lines and discovering how to refuel the shuttle drained out of him. "But I'd rather capture Amanda Leonard and let the dragons punish her. Maybe they can free your captain of Hanassa's possession."

"If it works. But I will never go back to taking orders from anyone, not Amanda Leonard, and not you, Loki O'Hara."

The Krakatrice are subdued. Another matriarch will rise, in time. Until then we must break their earth dams and begin the water flowing again. Only water will contain them. Only water will restore the land to life. We need that land to grow and expand our nimbus.

Our Stargods recognize the importance of the beginning place. They have not yet eliminated the danger. They must work quickly or all will be lost. Removing the menace of the Krakatrice was a minor battle compared to what they face now.

"I'm getting a signal from the planet!" Martin cried out to his companions. They'd scattered about the ship for food and rest. Except for him and Quinn who rarely needed to rest or eat.

Jane, Bruce, and Kurt scrambled up the gangway to peer over his shoulder.

Quinn kept a close watch on the debris field, both real time and computer enhanced.

Martin took the mini speaker out of his ear and turned on the full comm system.

"This is Lieutenant JG MK Talbot of His Majesty's Imperial Military Police. Please identify yourself." A woman's voice came through the static and background interference.

"That's a pretty weak signal. Let me boost it." Bruce took over Martin's place and began fiddling with the interface.

"Captain Adam Jonathan Quinnsellia of the *Margaret Kristine,* at your service Lieutenant Talbot," Quinn announced. "We are happy to find someone alive down there."

"You found the remains of *Jupiter,* then. We are happy that someone found us." Lieutenant Talbot's voice was a little clearer, but not much.

"What's she using for a comm, a handheld?" Bruce scratched his head and fiddled some more.

"We've been down here for nine Terran months. We only have one comm unit left with any power," she explained. Then she gave them landing coordinates. "What's your ETA?"

Martin checked the chrono and the nav plot. "Twenty hours," he replied.

Quinn looked at him strangely.

Martin placed his hand over the speaker to muffle his words. "Give us a chance to scout the place before we land," Martin whispered.

Quinn nodded his acceptance of the twelve-hour addition to their ETA.

"Strange name for a ship." Talbot's voice came in clearer than expected.

Bruce smiled and fiddled some more.

"Your signal is breaking up, Lieutenant. I'll explain when we meet in person." Quinn killed the signal.

"What?" Bruce protested. He ran his fingers over the controls again. "I was just getting through the static."

"Don't want to give too much info until we scout the situation."

"You didn't ask about Martin's dad," Jane said.

"Martin Konner O'Hara has at least seven warrants posted for his arrest," Martin explained sadly. "If we tell IMPs that we suspect he's on the planet, they'd go after him in a hurry. Any chance we have of getting him out before they bring him to trial and mind-wipe him and his brothers depends upon secrecy."

"Getting another signal," Bruce said.

"From Lieutenant Talbot?" Martin asked.

"Different location, different signature."

"Answer it, Martin. It might be from your family." Quinn said.

"What . . . what if it isn't? Maybe you should do it. Officially. In case there's trouble later." Martin couldn't explain why he was so reluctant to finally talk to Konner. His dad. He'd waited so long. If it turned out to be someone else at the other end of the comm . . . someone like Bruce's dad . . . he didn't think he could stand the disappointment.

Quinn sighed and opened the link. "Private merchanter *Margaret Kristine* here."

"Who?" the startled voice over the system was stronger and clearer than Lieutenant Talbot's.

"That sounds like him," Jane whispered.

"Not quite," Martin replied just as quietly.

Quinn spilled out his ident numbers and the name again.

"Strange name for a private merchant," the anonymous voice said.

That was the second time within the hour strangers had questioned the name of Quinn's ship.

"To whom do I have the honor of speaking?" Quinn's tone went cold and formal.

"Sorry. We're a little out of touch with protocols here. Mark Kimmer O'Hara, citizenship number Alpha George Cat Zebra niner eight two seven Omega Prime niner eight two seven."

"And your ship?"

"You don't want to know."

"That's the youngest brother," Quinn mouthed. "Very well, why did you hail me?"

"Looking for a little rescue down here. We've been stranded for over a year, running low on supplies and fuel."

Martin signaled for Quinn to cut the speaker. "Why don't I believe him?"

Quinn shrugged and turned the speaker back on. "ETA in twenty-five hours. Do you have landing coordinates?"

Martin's uncle gave them a string of numbers.

Bruce shook his head rapidly and pointed to the coordinates Lieutenant Talbot had given them. The sets of coordinates were nearly five hundred klicks apart. But the signal source from O'Hara was the landing place designated by Lieutenant Talbot.

What was going on down there?

Quinn raised his eyebrows. Then he read back the numbers deliberately transposing the first two.

"No, you don't want to land there. That will put you in the middle of the bay in about two hundred meters of water." Then the uncle read off the same set of numbers he had before.

Quinn confirmed them. "How many in your party, Mr. O'Hara? I'm a small ship, haven't got room for many."

"At least three, possibly as many as six. We just need a lift to our mother ship in orbit."

"I don't scan any ship in orbit."

Bruce did something else to the scanners. Another small ship appeared in the vicinity of the moon. "It's cloaked," he whispered.

"You probably won't find it. We're pretty good at hiding where you least expect to find us. See you when you get here. O'Hara out."

The comm went dead.

"My dad uses a cloaking field," Bruce explained. "I knew how to adjust the sensors to find it. Wonder if these people stole the program from my dad."

"More likely, your dad stole it from Konner O'Hara. I've been hearing tall tales about that man's genius for a decade. At least some of the rumors should be true," Quinn replied.

"We need detailed sensor data," Martin said. "I'm going to do some adjustments to the system. Bruce, you program that cloak into the landing shuttle. We don't want them to know we're coming until we get there."

Martin opened a bulkhead and rolled onto his back. Then he pulled himself into the guts of the ship. "Jane, hand me a light."

"Not unless you show me what you are doing."

"Only room for one in here."

"I'll look on my own when you are done."

"I want that cloaking program on the *Margaret Kristine* as well," Quinn said. "I have the feeling we are headed into a mess worse than a nest of armed Kree."

CHAPTER 44

HANASSA HAD to keep moving. Had to keep all of his people in sight at once. So much depended upon that crucial length of pipe. He could not fail now. Amanda had shown him the way. The way to eliminate all of his enemies at once.

Mundane copper or bronze would not do the job properly. The dragons would survive if he used those common metals. He could not mine the omniscium properly with copper or bronze. He would not have the glorious opportunity to save the world by opening it to the Galactic Terran Empire. He needed the doming technology.

Amanda had shown him.

Amanda was the best host he could have chosen. He graciously bowed to her expertise in this.

Iron, the pipe must be. And Kat must be the one to insert it into the conjunction of two ley lines.

Kat carried one end of the heavy iron pipe. Geralds carried the other. Two meters of silence grew between them. He'd stopped asking why she resisted Amanda's plan and had to be compelled to carry the pipe under the duress of two stunners and three needle rifles aimed at her.

During the forging and shaping of the pipe she'd clenched her jaw so tight for so long that her entire face ached and her temples throbbed.

Amanda danced around them, crowing at the triumph of the pipe and glowering at the lack of communication from the approaching ship.

"Here, here, here." She finally pointed to the ground a full klick upriver from Base Camp.

Kat gratefully dropped her end of the pipe. Why hadn't Amanda commandeered a couple of Marines with muscles to carry the blamed thing?

Because Amanda trusted no one except her Marines and had them "guarding" the precious pipe and mining operation.

"Aren't we a little close to the river?" Kat asked. "We don't know what will happen when we release the omniscium."

"We have to be close to water so the omniscium will turn into a salt," Geralds said. He dropped his end just as heavily.

The pipe began to roll toward the river.

"Stop it!" Amanda screeched. She didn't seem to have any other volume lately.

"If she's not possessed, then she is insane," Kat muttered to herself.

"Then why did you betray your brothers to come back here?"

"Because it seemed the only way to get what I want." Like Amanda/Hanassa subdued, confined, possibly even dead.

She shivered with cold dread.

"I thought you and your brothers were the ones who say there is always another way."

Kat just glared at him.

The Marine contingent brought up five slaves with shovels made from the shoulder blades of slaughtered cattle.

"Careful, just a few millimeters at a time," Amanda cautioned.

Kat allowed her eyes to cross while she studied the ground. The slaves dug at the precise center of a conjunction of two ley lines. The hub would provide a fair amount of omniscium, not nearly as much as if they had dug near the festival pylon at the center of Base Camp.

She dismissed the nagging alarm at that thought. She had other things on her mind.

If she wrestled a stunner away from one of the Marines, how much time would she have to shoot Amanda before the rest of the guards felled her with the needle rifles?

Since that plan would not work, she had to think of something else.

"The ship that's coming in, a private merchanter," she addressed Geralds. "Could Melinda Fortesque have sent another Sam Eyeam to complete your mission?"

He shrugged. "I haven't communicated with her in over nine moths. I believe both homing beacons she sent disappeared—deactivated or destroyed by Konner O'Hara. He's the only one who could figure out how to do it—since he invented them. Amanda probably believes me dead, and might send someone else. I don't know that she has leverage over anyone else like she does me."

"What crime did she force you to commit that she knows you won't disobey her orders?"

"What?" Geralds jerked away from Kat.

She had her answer. The explanation was more complex than he'd said. Melinda Fortesque—the richest woman in the galaxy—had blackmailed Bruce Geralds, Sr. into doing something heinous so that he could not betray his boss. Or risk the incriminating evidence sending him to prison and mindwipe. Otherwise, he might confess to the GTE and accuse Melinda of blackmail. Why hadn't he and his family simply disappeared into the Galactic Free Market?

Melinda Fortesque's arms were long, but not that long.

"Kat, time for the pipe," Amanda called.

"What, is she afraid the slaves will sabotage seventy-five kilos of iron?" Geralds growled.

"Probably," Kat mumbled. She crouched to lift one end of the heavy pipe. Slowly she rose, feeling the burn in her thighs and lower back. "Help me, Geralds. I can't do this alone."

"I thought you were superwoman," he replied sarcastically. "Why can't you just maneuver it into place with the power of your mind?" He stood, hands on hips, feet braced, daring her to show off her psi talents.

"Do you really want me to open that nest of Kree in front of her?" Kat set her load back down and matched his stance, stubbornness for stubbornness.

"Do it, Kat. Show us why you are so special and why I have made you my heir," Amanda said. She almost panted in anticipation.

A glimmer of an idea. If she could pull it off . . .

"Oh, come on, you don't truly believe that stuff?" Cyndi asked from the sidelines. She'd come up on them very quietly.

"You are a menace and a failure. Why do you question me?" Amanda whirled to face Cyndi.

A true daughter of politicians and diplomats, Cyndi held her ground and replied with aplomb. "I asked a simple question. No one in their *right* minds believes in this so-called magic." She kept her eyes hooded, hiding something.

Kat raised a quick probe. This close to a ley line, she had enough power to catch a glimpse of a phantom dragon digging at Cyndi's mind. She believed all right, but still felt compelled to goad Amanda for a reason. She wasn't willing to give total power to a madwoman.

"And I am not a failure. I am a highly respected diplomatic attaché and wife to an heir to the Imperial throne."

"Errand runner," Geralds muttered. "Eric Findlatter is nothing more than a flunky and never will be."

"Not a failure?" Amanda laughed loud and long. "You have failed every time you tried to sabotage the O'Hara brothers, my enemies. You failed to find a way to gain fuel for an escape. The fuel cell you stole was empty. You failed to seduce any of the natives. You bore me. Take her away and lock her up." Amanda dismissed Cyndi with a gesture and turned her back on the woman.

Two Marines dragged Cyndi away. She spluttered and resisted the entire way.

"Now, back to work. Kat, show us your talents."

Kat looked around at the expectation on everyone's faces. If she showed the possibilities of the mind to these hard-nosed military types, born and raised into a technological society, she would alter their culture forever. Was that such a bad thing?

Only if she ever intended to allow Amanda and her pet Marines to return to the GTE.

Before she could do anything about that, she needed the omniscium.

Dared she begin the mining process without further research?

Without a word she placed her feet on either side of the shallow hole dug by the local slaves. At least half of them had melted away into the underbrush while the guards were preoccupied with Cyndi, Kat, and Amanda.

Kat rested her worn boots upon the ley lines coming together beneath the hole. She closed her eyes and took three deep breaths.

When her body felt lighter and her mind clearer, she recalled the image of the pipe resting on the ground. With each new breath she pictured the heavy iron lifting free of the ground. When she knew she could reach down and grab the pipe, she raised it with her mind and sent it swinging directly at Amanda's head.

Amanda screamed.

Kat opened her eyes and watched her enemy duck and bury her head in her hands. The Marines stared in confusion at the pipe, at their commander, at Kat.

Fatigue tugged at Kat's shoulders and her mind. Her control of the pipe began to slip. It careened wildly. She let it slam into the backs of knees and then tipped it up to mow the Marines down with unplanned clips to jaws and guts.

"Enough!" Amanda ordered. She lifted one hand, palm out, and grabbed the end of the pipe. She slammed it into the ground so that the base rested directly on the hole prepared for it.

A lucky strike? Or did the dragon within her give her amazing strength?

"Prop it up and anchor it," Amanda ordered.

Three marines jumped to hold the pipe upright while kicking dirt back into the hole and stomping on it until the length of iron stood on its own.

"Cap it," Kat whispered. "Cap the pipe or we lose the omniscium to the air."

"Push it deeper, Kat," Amanda said. "Push it into the ley lines."

"Not until you cap it."

Amanda continued to glare at her.

"Or give me something to cap it."

A slave handed her a clay bowl that fit precisely over the top. She tied it in place with a length of vine. The slave scuttled away.

"Push it the last three centimeters, now. Or die. Your choice." Amanda snapped her fingers.

The full contingent of Marines leveled their rifles at Kat.

"Saint Bridget help me," she prayed on a whisper. She gulped and stepped away.

"For heaven's sake. Let's just do it." Geralds wrapped his hands around the pipe and shoved it downward twisting the bottom end of the pipe down, down into the ground.

Kat closed her eyes and with her mind fully attuned to the pipe watched it move beneath the ground. She saw in the back of her head how it pushed the dirt aside a grain at a time. With the power of the ley line where she still stood she gently displaced plants, roots, seeds, worms, and insects so that they would not be trapped in the storm of elements about to occur.

Then Geralds gave the pipe one final push, letting it penetrate the knot of silvery-blue omniscium.

A ruffle of power along her back told Kat that the pipe had done its deed. She stepped away, uncomfortable with the new sensations. One step. Then five. Then another six steps.

She felt more than herd the other scurrying around her.

"Look out!" Geralds yelled. His strong hands yanked Kat away from the pipe.

She opened her eyes to see the upright tube of iron glowing. A blue aura pulsed along the full length of the upright. The pipe swelled and the glow burned ever brighter until she had to clamp her eyes shut again to avoid burning holes in her retinas.

Then she tumbled to the ground and rolled, Geralds on top of her. His hands and body shielded her from the increasing heat.

"What is happening?" Kat demanded. "I have to see what is happening." She twisted and opened her eyes to find Marines and slaves running desperately in all directions.

The clay cap blew upward fifty meters or more. Streams and sparks of unleashed omniscium gushed up and out like a volcanic explosion. The blue-and-silver sparks seared and withered all that they touched in a growing circle.

Amanda cavorted gaily around a shooting fountain of omniscium fire.

The fire poured into the river. The water boiled and smelled of dead fish. Birds screamed, their feathers burned in mid-flight. Animals fled, awful burns boring through their flesh.

Kat scrambled to her feet, grabbed Geralds' hand, and fled the growing destruction.

CHAPTER 45

HANASSA STOOD BENEATH the fountain of blue flame shooting from the wondrous iron pipe.

"Yes!" he shouted to the sky. "The dragons cannot live on this world now. I am the only dragon left. I rule this place. *Hanassa!* I name this world Hanassa."

His skin burned. The hot, sharp pain, thrilled his brain. His female body convulsed in ecstasy.

At each place a spark burned him, new dragon hide and hard cartilage grew. His bones pushed through to form an armored exoskeleton.

"The dragons must all die. But people will thrive to worship me because people know how to protect themselves from destructive air and water. Humans are smarter than dragons."

(But are humans as wise?)

"You know nothing!" Hanassa shouted.

(Will the protective domes and false air protect them from themselves?)

"That does not matter as long as they worship me. Me, Hanassa, god of this world and the only one who controls the omniscium."

(Do you control it, or does it control you?)

·——◆——·

"Does anyone find it strange that this newcomer flies a ship named for our mother and his ident code is Mum's birth date?" Kim asked his brothers as they landed at the edge of their village.

"Coincidence?" Konner asked. "There must be millions of women in the GTE named Margaret Kristine."

"With Mum's birth date?" Kim protested. He opened the hatch to find a contingent of armed warriors led by Yaakke and M'Berra awaiting them. Dalleena had obviously roused them to action.

"Less likely a coincidence. Maybe we'd better find out if Mum sent this guy," Loki suggested.

"Only after we determine that my ex-wife did not send him. She did place the homing beacon inside *Sirius,* and sent the Sam Eyeam with a second beacon," Konner said.

"We have wasted enough time with discussions," M'Berra grumbled. "I'm more than ready to mutiny. Amanda Leonard is going down today." He stepped into the shuttle with dignity and resolve set into his face. He carried a spear and a club, much as his distant African ancestors had.

"The time has come to free my people forever from the monster Hanassa," Yaakke added. He entered the shuttle wearing a fierce expression, carrying his own spear.

A dozen other native warriors followed them.

"I want the needle rifle," M'Berra said quietly.

"The what?" Kim asked, trying for innocence. "Those are illegal."

"I know you have one. The evening storytelling session may exaggerate some things, make you three into gods. But I find them remarkably accurate on details. Where is your needle rifle?"

"Melted in the lava core at the heart of a volcano," Loki said. "I destroyed it after I shot Hanassa with it. I only wish it had killed him." His face went pale with the memory.

Kim let the tale of the needle rifle rest with that lie. He knew that Konner had personally stuffed it into the storage locker beneath the bench where M'Berra sat.

"Let's fly," Konner said grimly. He brought *Rover*'s engines up from idle to full power.

Kim slapped the hatch mechanism. He watched the faces of anxious wives and mothers and the rest of the villagers left behind as they rolled forward before the hatch fully irised closed.

Silence filled *Rover* like a living entity no one dared breach during the entire journey north to Base Camp.

Konner set the little shuttle down just east of their destination.

"Saint Bridget and all the angels, what is that?" Kim stared at the magnified screens at his station in the cockpit. Seared black ground covered everything for a square klick west and north of Base Camp.

· —◆— ·

Screams of pain. The sharp acrid smell of burning flesh and plants invaded Cyndi's mind. She dug in her heels to stop the two Marines who marched her back to Base Camp.

They loosed her and stared in wonder at the mass destruction exploding from Amanda Leonard's precious pipe.

"Oh, my God!" She, too, stared as her mind gibbered in panic. She had to run. Run away. Hide.

The Marines seemed just as shocked as she. They stood frozen in place, jaws flapping.

Then all of her training to be the perfect hostess, an effective diplomat, and a successful politician slammed into place.

"Back to Base Camp," she commanded to all of the fleeing Marines and slaves. "Grab what you can and rendezvous at the big village. Take food, water vessels, and med supplies. Quickly. Move it, soldier."

The Marines gulped, stared at her for one heartbeat, and obeyed. She followed as rapidly as she could and retain her dignity. A princess did not flee; she retreated.

Along the way she pushed and urged others into action. "Food and medical supplies. All that you can carry," she urged again and again.

About every ten meters she risked a quick look over her shoulder. The fire spread. The swath of black ash encircling the still erupting pipe grew faster than she could walk.

Taking her pride and dignity in hand she broke into a run.

The air grew hotter. It burned her lungs with every breath.

She kept running, making certain everyone still mobile continued on to the big village. At the sight of burned and blackened people writhing on the ground she had to bite her lip and continue onward. They were beyond the help of any mere mortal. Stopping to ease their pains or comfort them in their extreme would only jeopardize the retreat of those who could be saved.

She stumbled onward, weeping in pain and agony for herself and everyone else.

"God, I wish I could go home."

· —◆— ·

"Our village," Loki gulped. "It's gone. Nothing but a pile of ashes." He leaned forward, peering out the windscreen at the real-time view. "Who would do that?"

"I can't believe it." Tears crept down Konner's cheeks. "All our hard work, the fields, our homes, even the wild cattle are all incinerated. What could do this?"

"That!" Kim pointed toward the fountain of fire pouring out of the ground.

And then they saw the river, the lifeline for the land and the people. The water bubbled and steamed. Thousands of fish, boiled alive, floated on the surface.

Loki crossed himself. Somehow Mum's universal ward and invocation seemed the only appropriate response. Konner followed suit.

Kim, however crossed his wrists, right over left, and flapped his hands in the local ward against the evil demon Simurgh, the first dragon to develop a taste for human flesh.

"We've got to find out how this happened," Loki said. His jaw trembled and his hands shook on the sensor array.

"Do we dare step outside *Rover?*" Konner asked.

"Please, Stargods, please take us to see if our old village, where the river meets the bay, has also been visited by this demon of destruction," Yaakke asked. He sank to his knees in the doorway to the cabin of the shuttle.

Loki hated to see his strong, adventuresome friend reduced to abject pleading.

"The village was deserted when I was there this morning," Loki tried to console the man.

"We hope to return to our homes when the intruders are eradicated. Please. Take us there. We were all born there. Our ancestors are buried there. We worshipped in the temple we built with our own hands. Please. Let us see how far this destruction stretches."

Kim gulped and nodded.

Loki knew the fierce attachment Kim and these people had for the land. He felt it himself though he hated to admit he loved this place as much or more than he did the wandering life he hoped to return to.

"We need to see the extent of the destruction," Konner agreed.

"But what is that artificial volcano? What fuels it?" M'Berra asked. He ran a series of equations through a handheld.

Loki looked back toward the blue-and-silver fire shooting out of the ground and the bizarre figure cavorting around it, impervious to the sparks and flames that did not drown in the water or the dirt.

"I'm guessing that Amanda Leonard began her mining operation with iron pipes," Konner said. "The iron may have acted as a catalyst, turning the omniscium volatile."

"Maybe there's a reason why there is so little iron on this planet. It can't exist in the presence of omniscium," M'Berra added.

"Why didn't we know this?" Kim asked.

Kim called up any and all records in storage. Loki read them over his shoulder. Nothing. The only references to omniscium at all stated that it could only be found in gas giant planets, that it was rare and fragile with a short half-life—less than ten years. The only use found so far was in the growth bath of star drive crystals. Nothing else. Nothing about its properties or behavior in the presence of other elements except those that went into the crystal baths.

"How can something so vital to our technology remain so elusive to our scientists?" Kim asked.

Loki had to stare at the scrolling information. He couldn't bear to watch the acres of black rolling by beneath *Rover*.

"There's the village." Konner pointed to the one hundred substantial, thatched homes along a major street and several alleys.

One thing Hanassa had done for these people, perhaps the only good thing the rogue dragon had done at all, was to organize the village along straight lines.

"There are the Marines from Base Camp," Loki said on a sigh of relief. The armed men and women along with the few remaining slaves huddled together in front of the temple. He spotted Kat's mop of red curls as she paced around them, seemingly giving orders.

So far the land remained ordinary green and brown. The damage spread toward and along the river from the artificial volcano.

"Look at the ley lines," Kim nearly shouted. "The damage stops in straight lines every time it encounters another river of omniscium. It's policing itself."

"Thank whatever gods who might listen for small favors," Loki breathed. He didn't feel as if Mum's God was interested in this place right now. Otherwise He shouldn't have let it happen.

"But the destruction flows back up every stream and rivulet to the headwaters and out from there. Without the river system, the land will die," Konner pointed out.

"We have to stop it," Loki said as much to himself as to his brothers.

"We will take care of this Amanda person. You deal with the fountain of fire," Yaakke said. "Only a god can handle that."

What if we are not gods, only men? Mortal and fallible, Loki asked himself. He felt totally inadequate and did not know how to lead his people.

CHAPTER 46

"OKAY, MARTIN, this is your family, your call. Where do we land?" Quinn asked.

"I . . . I don't know. All our options look bad," Martin replied.

Jane, Bruce, and Kurt remained ominously silent. This was indeed Martin's decision.

"Let's go with the coordinates Lieutenant Talbot gave us. That seems to be the center of activity and I think they need our help," Martin said all in one breath. He prayed he was right and that the IMPs had not laid a trap for them.

"We've only made one pass . . ." Jane finally ventured.

"I know," Martin said. He couldn't look her in the eye.

"Those coordinates would have been my call, too, Martin. Had it been my choice," Quinn reassured him. He banked the small shuttle—the passenger area was not much bigger than the van—circled around the scenes of destruction, and dropped the nose for a touchdown just outside the village beside the bay.

"Should we all wear EVA suits until we know what is happening?" Martin asked.

"Sensors read normal atmosphere," Kurt put in.

"Normal atmosphere doesn't scorch everything in sight along geometrical grid lines," Bruce grumbled.

"You kids know the protocol. When it doubt, suit up. Anaphylactic shock due to alien pollens and microbes can kill you in minutes. I've got an implanted filter. You four don't." Quinn waved toward the compartment at the rear of the shuttle.

Jane dragged out five EVA suits and passed them around. In the tight confines they struggled into the bulky equipment and secured the helmets. They were now all linked by comms.

Quinn began the routine to close down controls of the shuttle. "This is keyed to me and Martin. No one else will be able to hack or jump the ignition," Quinn added as he stood and checked the cockpit. "We've been through a lot together. Remember to back each other up and we'll get through this one, too." He jerked his head into a single nod of approval to all four of them. Then he checked their seals and air supplies before donning his own EVA suit.

A morsel of pride swelled in Martin. He only hoped his own father appreciated him as much as this new friend did.

Quinn led the way as the five of them stepped out of the cabin of the shuttle.

"I thought a volcano would make more noise," Martin whispered over the comm system.

"I don't think that's a volcano," Kurt said. He moved his lanky body awkwardly in the ill-fitting EVA suit.

"Who knows what volcanoes are like on this planet." Bruce shrugged. "Every planet is different."

"But those mountains to the south are definitely volcanic," Jane protested. "They erupted along normal patterns spilling magma and ash, building through repeated eruptions and normal plate tectonic lifting."

"Quiet," Martin ordered. "I think I hear something . . . someone crying."

A high-pitched wail pierced the air and the sensors of Martin's suit.

Quinn increased his pace. Martin kept up with him. The others followed more cautiously, scouting the terrain carefully, watching Martin's and Quinn's backs, like the good friends they were.

Ash crunched under their boots. Rocks split at the barest touch. Martin guessed that the large mounds of crumbling black matter might have been trees. From the size of the mounds, this planet grew trees on a grand scale.

Heat radiated up from the seared ground. The ash billowed with each step, soon clogging their atmosphere filters.

Martin labored for each breath. Bruce and Kurt fared worse.

"Quinn, we have to shed the helmets," Martin said. Each word came out heavily. He had to pause and cough at the end of the simple sentence.

"You guys don't have filter implants." Quinn lifted his helmet free of his head, and shook his sweat-darkened hair. "I don't know if you will be able to tolerate the foreign pollens and impurities."

"An allergic reaction is better than not breathing at all." Bruce lifted his helmet free of his head.

"I have allergy meds on the ship." Kurt followed suit.

Martin and Jane exchanged looks and brief nods. Then they, too, shed their helmets. Martin inhaled deeply, got a mouthful of ash and coughed it back out.

Over it all, the sounds of someone wailing in pain and grief kept rising. They hurried forward.

Then the roar of another shuttle overhead made them all duck.

"That's one big shuttle," Bruce gasped.

"It's *Rover*. That's my dad's shuttle!" Martin jumped up and began running in the same direction as the shuttle.

"Martin, come back. We don't know . . ." Quinn called after him.

"My dad's there. I know it." Martin kept on going, marking in his mind the short track of level ground at the edge of the village where the shuttle set down using its VTOL jets.

Three tall, red-haired men and a dozen or more people armed with primitive weapons spilled out of the shuttle mere femtos after it settled to the ground. The engines continued to run. The shortest of the men began shouting orders.

Martin's heart beat so hard and so fast in his ears he had trouble hearing every word. But he understood.

"Kim, check on the well. Konner, you and M'Berra fetch Taneeo and Chaney Lotski. Tell them to bring every remedy they know and a few they haven't thought of before. I'll sort out and triage."

"Wait," Martin gasped. "Dad, wait."

All three men froze in place.

"Martin?" Konner took one step forward.

Martin skidded to a halt a hair's breath away from him. They fell into a tight hug. Martin clung to his father with all the desperation of a two-year-old and a lifetime of separation.

Tears pricked at the back of his eyes.

The piercing wail of grief and pain rose behind them.

"Dad, what can we do to help?" Martin couldn't let go of Konner, but he had to do his best to stop the awful destruction all around them.

"We?" Konner stood back a moment, keeping his hands on Martin's shoulders, also unable to let go.

His fingers dug tightly into Martin's flesh. The pain was nothing compared to the joy of seeing his father again, feeling his strength, being a part of his life once more.

Konner stared at Martin with hungry eyes.

"I ran away from Melinda. My friends helped. We've come to rescue you. What can we do to help?" Martin gushed as he pulled his dad close once more.

"You're the people aboard the *Margaret Kristine*?" The tallest and youngest came up beside Konner.

Martin guessed he was Mark Kimmer—Kim to the family.

"AJ Quinnsellia, pilot of the *Margaret Kristine,* at your service." Quinn held out his hand.

"Introductions and reunions later. We've got a crisis on our hands." A tall woman disengaged from the wailing crowd of ragged people in the village. She, too, had red hair and bore a marked resemblance to the three brothers, to Martin himself.

He wondered where she fit into the family tree. He'd never heard of a sister, even in the official records he'd stolen from Quinn's shipboard database.

"Are you okay, Kat?" all three brothers asked at once.

"For now. But we've got to get that iron pipe out of the ground *now*."

"I have a shuttle, what can I do?" Quinn stepped forward, keeping Bruce, Kurt, and Jane behind him. "I have four teenagers in my custody. I'd rather fetch the people you need from distant places than have my charges endangered by proximity to that . . . volcano."

"Good plan," Kim said. "Take the kids to the coordinates I gave you originally. Ask for Taneeo, he's the village priest and a healer. Lotski is a real medic from the IMP cruiser. Martin, tell the villagers that you are the son of Stargod Konner. They'll take care of you and your friends."

"I want to stay with my dad," Martin insisted.

Konner's fingers tightened on his shoulders once more. Neither of them dared separate right now. They might never see each other again.

"He knows?" Kim raised an eyebrow at Konner.

"He's my kid." Konner shrugged. "He's smart enough to figure it out. I presume there are no IMPs or agents of Fortesque Industries on your tail."

"None," Quinn reassured them.

"I can help you, Dad. Let me stay here." Martin's gut tightened. He had a feeling something terrible would happen to both himself and his father if he let Konner out of his sight.

"As much as I want you here with me always, I have to insist. Go with your friends. For your own safety. You will also be my representative in the village. Your family resemblance is the only way they will recognize your authority and not capture all of you and impound your shuttle. My wife Dalleena will help you. Now go." Konner gave Martin one last brief and fierce hug.

"Dad, please."

"You have to go. Martin, I can't do my job if I'm worried about you. Besides, you need to introduce yourself and your friends to the locals. They won't believe Quinn without you."

Martin turned around with a sniff. Then he straightened his shoulders and marched back to the shuttle. He had to blink back his tears. He had a mission to accomplish for his father. He'd do it. But he was coming back with Quinn and this Taneeo person. No one would stop him.

"I'm the son of a Stargod." He smiled and hastened his steps.

CHAPTER 47

"BREWSTER, YOU'RE in charge," Kat called over her shoulder as Quinn's shuttle roared off into the southern distance. Interesting coincidence. But she didn't have time to mull this over right now.

She joined Loki as he marched toward *Rover*.

"No one leaves this planet without me, and I'm taking this one hostage," Cyndi called. She stood on the top step of the temple, a needle pistol aimed at Geralds' throat.

Kat sighed in disgust.

Kat gauged the distance between herself and where the refugees crowded around the entrance to the temple with its silver bloodwood columns and carved dragon capitals.

She cursed fluently. Loki raised his eyebrow at her creativity.

"No way we can take her out from here. Too many people in the way," Loki said quietly.

"Fine," Kat yelled at the planetary governor's daughter and close kin to the emperor. "I don't care what you do to him. He's a murderer. I planned to take him back for trial and mind-wipe. Go ahead and kill him. That's one less worry." Kat turned her back on Cyndi. "I've got a planet to save." She gestured Loki back toward the shuttle.

"How dare you turn your back on me, Lieutenant!" Cyndi said as she ran for Kat, hands extended like claws. "I'll have your commission for this."

Loki didn't even try to come between the enraged woman and his sister.

Kat glared at him as she prepared herself for attack.

"Listen to me when I talk to you!" Cyndi launched herself onto Kat's back, reaching to gouge her eyes with her broken fingernails. She breathed in hysterical pants.

Today's trauma had finally broken her control over her emotions.

Kat bent double and flipped Cyndi onto the ground. In two moves she had twisted Cyndi's arm into an impossible position and planted her foot on the smaller woman's waist. "No one attacks my back." Kat dropped to plant her knee on Cyndi's chest and hold a wicked knife at her throat. The knife Konner had made and then given to Kat for defense when they were first reunited nine months ago.

"What did you mean 'you don't care' what this trollop does to me?" Geralds added his own invective to the noise and confusion. "I thought we meant something to each other, Kat."

"Here your rank and connections mean nothing, Ms. Baines," Loki said quietly. Too quietly.

Kat wouldn't want to be on the receiving end of his wrath when he spoke like that.

"Now, see here, Kat. There's no call for violence." Geralds made to grab Kat by the collar.

"Oh, what the hell." Loki planted his fist in Geralds' jaw. "I've wanted to do that for a long time."

The man went down in a spluttering rage, blood trickling from a split lip. He started to get up.

"I'd stay down and stay out of the way if I were you," Konner added with menace.

"Saint Bridget, I wish we could leave them both here," Loki muttered.

"We'll deal with them later. Brewster," Kat called to the Marine who'd tried to hide himself in the crowd.

"Brewster, get your sorry ass over here. I want force bracelets on these two and you organizing these people. Do some triage until we get a medic."

"What about . . ." Kent Brewster jerked his head toward the still armed Marines mingling with the crowd, just as confused and panicked as the locals.

"I said, you're in charge. Anyone questions that has to deal with me." She glared at the contingent of Marines.

They all nodded acceptance of her authority.

Happily, she noted that they all placed their weapons at their feet and saluted her.

"Fickle bastards," she muttered to herself. After the stunt she had pulled with the iron pipe, they probably figured she had more power than crazy Amanda. They sided with her now.

She trusted them about as far as she could throw an asteroid out of a gravity well.

"Now what is this well that so desperately needs checking?" she turned to her brothers.

"The place where all the ley lines begin and end," Loki said quietly. "It takes up almost an entire island in the delta."

Kat froze at the implications. "It's feeding that volcano," she whispered her conclusion.

"We've got to take out Amanda and cap that . . . fountain of fire. The well will wait," Loki said. "Paola, you are with me. The rest of you help the refugees and begin evacuation. Find an escape route to higher, rocky ground." Then he and his lady climbed into *Rover*.

"This chore is not yours alone," Yaakke, the warrior leader from the village, stood firm, facing Kat. "We will come with you."

"Some of you," Kat agreed. "Half of you stay with the refugees." She marched toward *Rover*.

"I'll fly," Konner said right behind her.

"Amanda is mine," M'Berra said, hopping into the shuttle.

"If I don't get her first," Kat announced through gritted teeth.

(She belongs to the dragons.) Gentian flew above and around Kat for the first time in hours.

"Where have you been, friend?" She pointed out the soaring flywacket to her brothers—the only living creature left for many square kilometers.

(You may not meddle in the affairs of dragons.) With that, the flywacket disappeared into the sky that grew as gray and black as the ash beneath their feet.

"I will meddle with whomever I choose! With or without your permission, Gentian."

Within moments Konner set *Rover* down just beyond the circle of sparks from the eruption.

"Paola and I will circle around, try to approach Amanda from the rear," Loki said. He and his Amazon slid through the fuel bay and out the belly of the vessel.

"Yaakke and I will come at her from the other side." M'Berra and the local man followed Loki out the hidden exit.

Amanda greeted Kat, Kim, and Konner with a needle rifle. Her skin had blackened from innumerable burns. Bony ridges pushed through to form a hard exoskeleton. Long talons had replaced her fingernails. Her once lustrous black hair stood up in horny spikes. A hump on her back could be vestigial wings.

"She really is turning into a dragon," Kim breathed.

"The person you knew as Amanda is no more," Yaakke, said from behind a mound of ash that had once been a tree or a wild animal, no way to tell now. "Hanassa has taken both her body and her mind."

Kat could no longer think of the figure before them as a person. It was a *thing*. Taking its life did not violate any laws, ethics, or morals among civilized people.

She stepped ahead of the others, hoping some residual of the favoritism this *thing* had shown her a few hours before might allow her to get close enough to disarm it.

"You knew what the iron would do to the omniscium, didn't you?" Kat accused. "You've never valued life, only your own power. You would willingly destroy the entire planet rather than let someone else have power over you."

"My pretty Kat, you know me so well," the thing said in a wildly fluctuating singsong. The voice had deepened to masculine tones and came out in the volume of a dull roar. "Step out of the way so I may remove the menace of these others."

"I can't let you kill my brothers." Out of the corner of her eye, Kat saw Yaakke and M'Berra and two others working around to the *thing's* back.

"But your brothers have already killed me three times. It is about time I evened the score. Pity I can only kill each of them once."

"What makes you think that?" Konner asked. He sidestepped in the opposite direction, drawing attention away from Yaakke and the others.

Kat had no idea where Kim had gotten to. She hoped he stayed out of range as long as the *thing* kept the needle rifle locked and loaded. Did Hanassa have enough of Amanda's memories to know how to use it?

For answer, the thing laid down a spread of lethally drugged needles at Kat's and Konner's feet.

Kat froze in place, hands out to the side. Konner did the same.

"We are the Stargods, Hanassa. You cannot kill us." Konner edged a little farther around the circle.

Silver-blue sparks continued to spray the ground and Hanassa, just beyond Konner's feet. Rather than burning, the thing seemed to absorb the fire, growing more and more like a dragon with each blast of heat.

"Gods? I see only one of you, and your sister who is no god. She isn't anything but a bad little soldier who thinks too much and shows off." Another round of needles flew from the rifle.

Kat dove into the powdery ash. Dozens of drugged needles sprayed over the top of her embedding harmlessly into the dust. She sweated freely, from the fire and from her own fear. How had the others fared? Where the hell were Loki and Paola?

Konner held his ground. The needles aimed at him lay in a neat pile at his feet. He'd called upon some kind of magic to shield himself.

"Saint Bridget I wish I'd thought of that." With so much omniscium loose in the ground and in the air, she should be able to draw on it for power.

Konner took a step forward. A spark landed upon his "bubble" of protection and fizzled. He took another step forward.

Hanassa fired the rifle again. "This is how you killed me the third time!" it screamed.

The needles bounced off the shielding.

Kat scrambled backward toward a discarded needle handgun. The omniscium hadn't melted the cerama/metal housing yet. The gun didn't have the range of the rifle. But in Kat's hands it should have more accuracy.

Yaakke chose that moment to dash through the rain of fire, his spear leveled at the *thing's* gut. A wild ululation erupted from his throat. "You die, Hanassa. In the name of all the Coros, I kill you!"

He lunged forward. The spearhead pierced Hanassa's side.

"And what do you think you are doing, little man?" Hanassa loosed a full volley of needles directly into the man's gut.

He fell forward, dead before the next spark burned through his flesh to his bones.

His dead weight pushed the spear deep into his quarry.

Hanassa seemed not to notice the spear or the blood that flowed from its side.

Kat choked. A terrible pain filled her gut. White light filled her vision. The silhouette of a man appeared in the center of the light. He walked calmly away from her.

Sweet longing pulled Kat in his wake. Lassitude drained her body of strength and will.

CHAPTER 48

"YAAKKE, NO!" Loki reached to stop his friend as Yaakke went down under a spray of needles. His entire body flinched in shared pain.

"You can't save him." Paola held him back with a fierce grip. "You'll only burn up as fast as he did." She clenched her jaw.

Loki had to close his eyes. He couldn't watch the horror of the blue fire eating away at the man's flesh. His gut ached and the siren song of death lured his soul away from his consciousness. He pinched his thigh hard, concentrating on his own pain rather than the silhouette of a man walking into a vast tunnel of white. Yaakke's wandering soul invited Loki to cast aside his worries and cares—permanently.

The lure was too strong. The need to guide his friend into the light, to linger, to leave behind his pain and responsibilities . . .

Paola slugged him in the gut.

The physical pain jerked him back to reality.

With each deep breath he separated himself a little further from his need to die alongside his friend.

Then he saw Kat, curled into a fetal ball, wrapped around a pistol as if she needed to fire the thing into her own belly.

"Not yet. I can't lose you yet, Kat." He grabbed her hand and wrenched the gun away from her. Then he held her hand so tightly he felt her bones though his fingers. "Come back to your family, Katie. Come back to me."

"I won't die yet," she whispered with her eyes clamped shut. "I refuse to die before I have freed this world of Hanassa." Her breathing evened and color crept into her cheeks. "Guess working magic, tapping ley lines, has awakened the family curse in me."

Loki put his arms around Kat's shoulders and helped her to stand. He handed the pistol back to her. Emotions and thoughts flowed between them. They shared the awesome emptiness of losing a friend to death. Grief became a living ache within them both.

"That is the last innocent you will kill, Hanassa," Konner said. He stalked another dozen meters toward their foe. Anger poked holes in his bubble. Sparks penetrated to his skin.

They had to act quickly. Kat broke away from Loki. She whirled, aimed, and fired at Hanassa in one smooth movement.

Loki braced himself to share the rogue dragon's death as he had a year ago, the first time he'd killed him.

Hanassa held up a horny hand, talons arched to gouge out an opponent's eyes. The entire load of needles bounced against the palm and dropped harmlessly to the ground.

"You cannot kill me, O'Hara. No one can kill me. I am Hanassa. I am immortal!"

Kim saw his chance.

Kat distracted Hanassa with her pistol.

Yaakke's spear was still embedded in Hanassa's gut. The wound bled hideously.

Kim wanted to gag on the stench of fresh blood pouring down on the burned landscape.

With a great shout of defiance, he dashed into the circle of blue fire. Ten long strides and he leaped, drawing both his legs up to chest level. He kicked out on his downward arc. Both feet connected with the iron pipe. He slapped the ground to break his fall, and rolled to his knees in one movement.

The pipe tube tilted toward the river, away from the land. Not good enough.

"My cannon?" Hanassa wailed. He had to be growing weaker. No creature could not feel the loss of so much blood. "You can't destroy my cannon." He whirled, rifle leveled toward Kim's chest.

Kim stood. Most of the rivers of fire now flew away from him, toward the river. Stray sparks burned his face and through his clothing.

He screwed up his courage and attacked the pipe with all of his weight. Searing burns took their toll upon his strength.

Konner tackled Hanassa. The rifle spewed more lethal needles as it flew from Hanassa's hands.

A needle penetrated his arm. Another caught his leg. Instant numbness. But he had to keep pushing. He had to topple Hanassa's cannon of total destruction.

Ignoring that fray, Kim leaned his entire weight against the iron pipe. The flames lessened. He kicked again. And again. And again.

The pipe broke free of the ground and landed with a thud. Long cracks grew up and down its length.

The opening to the omniscium bubbled, belched one last flame into Kim's face, and died.

Kim reared back, arms across his face. The pain ate at his sanity, his will, and his consciousness. He collapsed and rolled into a fetal ball, praying he would die and the pain would go away.

But he'd destroyed the horrible weapon. He'd ended Hanassa's plans for total destruction of the planet.

CHAPTER 49

◆—•—◆—•—◆

THE AIR SCREECHED and groaned. Kat wanted to cover her ears and eyes. She didn't have time.

"Get out of the way, Konner. I need to shoot this creature and end our misery," Kat called. Her middle brother held Hanassa in a wrestling position that unbalanced their enemy and kept its hands separated.

Konner's greater height gave him the leverage to keep Hanassa from gaining a solid foothold on the ground.

The spear stuck in Hanassa's torso waggled obscenely, threatening to overbalance them both.

Loki tackled Kat from behind. They fell to the ground together.

Kat clung to her pistol like a lifeline.

"I can't let you kill, Kat. You'll die, too. Or want to. I won't lose you now. We've come to love you. All of us have." He continued mumbling the same nonsense into her back as he pinned her to the ground with his greater height and weight.

Kat tried to throw him off. He braced himself and clung tighter.

"I have to do this." She almost wept with frustration. Perhaps Hanassa was right. Perhaps it was now more dragon than human, immune to attack with mundane weapons.

Immortal.

The gray sky turned darker. Thunder echoed around them. It rumbled on and on. It grew louder with each peal. Came closer and closer until the sound filled Kat's mind and blotted out all other thoughts.

Hanassa craned its neck away from Konner's pinning hold and stared at the growing darkness. "You have no command over me. I am no longer a dragon," it shouted.

Kat followed Hanassa's gaze. Hundreds of nearly invisible dragons hovered above them. Dragons with red wing tips and horns, blue-tipped and green-tipped dragons, and five iridescent all color/no color female dragons.

Their crystal fur refracted the weird and uncertain light beneath the ash cloud. Edges and outlines blurred together into one huge confusion field.

But only one purple-tipped dragon stood out among them. Iianthe hovered below the nimbus, smaller than his fellows, his colors brighter and more complete. All of the dragons faced Hanassa, eyes whirling in anger.

Gentian landed on the ground beside where Kat lay with her elbows braced to fire the pistol. The flywacket stood on his hind legs and placed both front paws upon her wrists.

She had to drop her arms in the dusty ash from his weight. Her body went slack and Loki eased his weight off her.

The gun dangled from her limp hands. The drive to kill drained out of her.

(Hold,) the flywacket whispered into her ear. *(Our laws prevail here. Justice is ours to exact.)*

Kat tried to formulate an argument. She dropped her head onto her arms. She had to think.

She was so tired logic deserted her.

The thunder of hundreds of wings flapping drove out all coherence.

"I've been running and fighting so long I just want it to be over. I just want to go home."

(What if you are home?)

"Go away and just let me finish this, Gentian. Then I can think."

(We can no longer tolerate the rebellion of one of our own.) The full nimbus of dragons spoke as one voice, deafening Kat's ears and mind. *(We have judged Hanassa guilty of wanton destruction of our home. Let him be exiled and his name no longer spoken among us.)*

"Never! I am not subject to your laws anymore," Hanassa proclaimed.

It wrenched free of Konner and raised a fist in defiance to the nimbus. Then it wrenched the spear out of its body and cast it aside. A fresh spate of blood flowed to the ground.

Could nothing weaken it?

"There is no place on this planet you can send me that I can't escape." Hanassa emptied the needle rifle upward into the bellies of a dozen dragons.

If any of the needles penetrated thick dragon hide and crystalline fur, the gigantic creatures did not react.

Kat covered her head and neck with her hands to protect herself from any falling projectiles.

(You need not fear the weapon of Hanassa. We have stopped this attack as we should have stopped every other attack.)

With that, Iianthe, the purple-tipped dragon, swooped down from the sky, talons extended and steam escaping his muzzle.

(This responsibility is mine,) he said sadly. His deep voice reverberated along Kat's spine.

Gentian launched himself up to join his brother as they both grabbed Hanassa by the shoulders and flew back to the gray clouds of ash that filled the sky. Hanassa flailed and twisted, screeching in protest. Its cries faded in the distance as the dragon and the flywacket disappeared.

"Where will you take Hanassa?" Kat called up to the dragons. The downdraft from hundreds of massive wings stirred square kilometers of ash into a dense miasma.

(We take the exiled one to the caldera of the volcano in the south. If ever he leaves that place, he will die.)

"What about the dragongate?" Konner asked.

(The warp in time and space will kill one of dragon blood. Neither the exiled one nor his descendants will ever leave that place by that exit.)

"A mere dragon taboo or curse will not confine Hanassa for long." Kat coughed and buried her face in her arms. When the wind of dragons passing eased, the ash still hung in the air.

"It's over, Kat," Loki said. "The dragons found a better way for us. We have to remember that there are always alternatives to violence and death."

"At the cost of our baby brother." She gulped deeply and blinked back her tears. As quickly as she could in the dense air, she made her way over to the fallen pipe. "Saint Bridget, I wish I'd known what would happen before." She kicked at the pipe. The cracks widened and it crumbled into four pieces.

Kim groaned.

Kat joined Konner and Loki in a crouch around him. She placed her fingers lightly on his neck pulse. He winced at her touch. The fluttering beat against her fingertips was faint and too rapid.

"Let me die here," Kim whispered. "I beg you. Let me die here on Kardia Hodos, the path of my heart, my home. Bury me here."

The air screeched and groaned as if the very elements along with the dragons mourned his passing.

The roar of an incoming shuttle only slightly registered with Konner.

"We've got to get him to the well. Between us, we can heal him there," he said.

"The well is reduced by almost half," Loki said. "Will that be enough power? You and I don't have the healing talent."

Konner's mind spun, refusing to alight upon any answers. He couldn't lose Kim. He couldn't watch his brother die.

Kat stood up and began looking around, as if searching for an ambulance and stretcher. "We can't let him die."

Konner looked around, too. Then he remembered the returning shuttle. Quinn had come back. Did he have Taneeo or Lotski with him? Or had he left them at the village? Martin ran toward them with a knapsack bulging with packets of herbs and a few crude surgical instruments.

Right behind him came Hestiia and Dalleena. Thank Saint Bridget and all the angels. He gathered Dalleena to him even as Hestiia threw herself across Kim's chest. Tears and wails poured from her.

Konner wished he could join her. His gut ached with the emptiness of grief. What could they do? How could they save Kim when he was so horribly burned that he wanted to die?

Dalleena's steadiness gave him the courage to begin thinking again.

"Quinn, what have you got in your shuttle that we can use as a stretcher?"

"Not much, but I've got a portable stasis unit," Quinn replied. "If we get him into suspended animation, we can get him to a hospital in less than a week."

"I'll get it!" Martin reversed course and in just a few heartbeats he leaped free of the shuttle, carrying the rolled-up metallic blankets and cryo-generator.

Konner's heart warmed with pride for his son. But he had to be the boy's father now, not just his friend and camp counselor. "I told you to stay in the village, Martin."

"I'm needed here."

"Your mother . . ."

"Has nothing to say about this. I have chosen my custodial parent."

"The courts . . ."

"Since when have you paid attention to the courts?" Martin gave him a cocky grin that reminded Konner too much of Kim at age fifteen.

"Don't let them take me away, Hes," Kim said. "Let me die here. Bury me on the island where I first saw you, Hes. Bury me in my home, Kardia Hodos." He gripped her hand with his remaining strength.

"Save him!" Hes demanded. "You must save him. No matter what it takes." Tears spilled down her face. Great sobs racked her too thin body. "Even if you must take him from me and our daughter, you must save him!"

"She's right, Loki," Konner said. "We can't let our baby brother die. If there is even a breath of a prayer that he might live, we have to get him to a hospital."

"What about the well? We can heal him there," Loki insisted.

"Gentian says no." Kat cocked her head, listening to some distant advice only she could hear. "He says that the well of life is the same as the well of death. The beginning place will only make his wounds worse."

"Martin, give me the stasis unit." Konner took the cumbersome bundle from his son. "Help your Uncle Loki roll out the blankets while I make sure the cryo-generator works."

"I'll fire up *Rover*," Kat said.

Hestiia put a delicate hand upon Konner's arm to stop him from beginning the process of taking her husband away from her and their home. Chin trembling and eyes brimming, she peeled back the metallic blanket and tucked it gently beneath Kim's chin.

He forced a tentative smile. "I love you, Hes," Kim said, voice painfully weak.

"I love you, Stargod Kim. Come back to me and our daughter." Hestiia kissed his mouth, his cheeks, and his brow in solemn farewell.

Then she rose and walked back to the shuttle, spine straight, dignity and pride keeping her moving.

Konner dashed away his own tears as he pressed the start-up sequence on the stasis unit.

Kim closed his eyes and fell into a forced cold sleep.

Martin and Dalleena slipped their hands into Konner's. He held them both tightly, praying he would never have to separate from them like this. Praying they were doing the right thing in taking Kim away from his beloved planet. Kardia Hodos he had named it.

Kardia Hodos, the pathway of the heart.

"Perhaps I should take Kim back to civilization aboard the *Margaret Kristine*," Quinn said, monitoring the controls of the cryo-generator. "I have some diplomatic clearances. Kim has a citizenship number. I can arrange for questions to be squashed," he offered as they flew the frozen bundle that was once an honorable man toward the gathering of refugees.

Kat was about to ask the next question, but Konner beat her to it. "That is another question that has to be answered before we do anything. Why is your ship named for our mother and why is the identification number the same as Mum's birthday?' He worked to keep the metallic blankets in a bubble so they didn't adhere to Kim's skin and damage him further. The rig had come without a frame.

"Your *mother!*" Quinn asked. He sounded almost accusatory.

"Yes, our Mum," Kat chimed in.

"The ship had that name when I bought it. I liked the name." Quinn closed his mouth and lowered his eyes.

Kat knew that look. The man had secrets. Well, she and her brothers had secrets, too, like mind reading.

She looked calmly at Quinn. A bright green layer of energy lay atop his aura. She peered close, seeking to unfold the physical barriers between his mind and hers.

She met a blank wall, not so much a wall as a mist. Her mental probe sped right through. But she caught a glimmer of an image. A man saying good-bye to the love of his life and their children.

"Who did you buy the ship from?" Could it be her father? Was there a way to find out if Dad still lived? Perhaps he thought them all dead. Perhaps that was why he had never come looking for them.

"That is information I cannot and will not give you." Quinn turned his head away and looked pointedly out the portal toward his own shuttle flying alongside them, piloted by Martin.

No more information leaked out of him.

Frustrated, Kat looked to Loki for help. He piloted *Rover* and kept his eyes forward. But he shrugged.

I tried several times and couldn't get into his mind. I have no idea who he is or what he is thinking.

So much for that strategy.

"I'll use Geralds' ship to take Kim back to civilization," Kat said. "I'm blood kin and can get him into any hospital, even the best military facility. That way I can concoct some story about Melinda Fortesque's brave Sam Eyeam rescuing me and dying in the process. Konner and Loki won't be endangered at all."

"Geralds?" Martin gasped over the comm unit from Quinn's shuttle. Konner had insisted he keep the comm open in case he ran into trouble. Quinn had assured him he wouldn't. "Bruce Geralds, Senior? Captain of the *Son and Heir?*"

"What do you know about Geralds?" Kat demanded. She moved to the copilot's seat and set the comm to privacy.

"His son is my best friend. He's at the village with Kurt and Jane," Martin explained to his aunt. He lowered his voice as if he knew she needed this information kept between them. "He's a criminal who needs to be brought to justice. But it will devastate my friend if he finds out."

"Let me worry about that for now. Do you have evidence?"

"Yes, Aunt Kat. In my handheld and on an encrypted database aboard the *Margaret Kristine.*"

"Keep it safe and don't let anyone else know you have it until I tell you different."

"He killed my grandparents on my mother's orders."

Kat gulped. Somehow she'd known the man couldn't be trusted. As much as she liked him, enjoyed his company, she had never let her guard down in his presence. Now she knew why.

But Melinda had coerced him into committing that crime.

So why did he stay employed by her? What other hold did she have on him to keep him from running off to the Galactic Free Market with his family?

"Coming in for a landing, folks," Loki announced. "I'll try to keep it gentle. Martin, you copy my every move one hundred meters to starboard."

"Aye, aye, Captain."

"Cheeky kid. I like him."

"So do I," Kat admitted.

"He's going to be a better pilot than I am!" Loki said as he watched Martin set down the smaller shuttle with ease.

"It's a smaller vessel than *Rover,* state of the art controls," Kat said wistfully.

"Here's the plan. We evacuate as many people as want to go south. Then Konner and I take Kim back to *Sirius* and on to the nearest medical facility. We have contacts in the GFM that aren't afraid to try something new and experimental if it will work on his wounds. Kat, you take the kids back to their parents on *Son and Heir.*"

"What about me?" Quinn asked.

"You are stranded here along with everyone else. This planet has to remain secret from the rest of civilization," Loki insisted.

"I'm taking Kim," Kat protested, ignoring Quinn's spluttering comments.

Loki jumped down to the ground at the north end of the village without replying.

"Stubborn O'Hara won't listen to anyone," Kat muttered.

"Just like you, Kat," Konner almost chuckled as she passed.

"Lieutenant Talbot," Quinn said quietly at her shoulder. "Is that Lucinda Baines, the diplomatic attaché?" He pointed toward the glaring and defiant woman sitting on the temple steps with force bracelets on her wrists and ankles.

"Yes," she replied cautiously.

"Half the galaxy is out looking for her. You need to take her back to civilization. The patrols will find the jump point near the coordinates of *Jupiter's* last transmission sooner or later. And when they do, this paradise will no longer be a secret. The devastation Hanassa caused will be nothing compared to what GTE miners will do to get that much omniscium. And if I don't return, the emperor himself will come looking for the *Margaret Kristine.*"

CHAPTER 50

—·—·——·—·—*

"STARDUST TAKE THEM ALL," Loki cursed. "I wish this mess would just go away." He stared in turn at Quinn and Cyndi across the evening gathering at the home village. They'd evacuated every warm body, injured and hale, that they could find from the region of Hanassa's omniscium canon. Quinn and Martin had worked tirelessly side by side with Konner, Kat, and Paola.

M'Berra had suffered burns from the omniscium to his arms and legs. He might lose the use of his left arm. Chaney Lotski, his wife and the only true medic, worked on him with desperation. The village women added their herbal knowledge to all of the injuries.

And Yaakke had died a hero's death. Loki wanted to choke with grief at the loss this represented to himself as well as the village.

A song in tribute to Yaakke's valiant act tickled the back of Loki's mind. By the end of the night he hoped to eulogize his friend. He wished Paola could stand at his side as he sang the song that would make a historical legend of the man. But Paola had gone back to her Amazons to clean up after the death of the matriarch Krakatrice as soon as they could spare a trip aboard *Rover*.

Jane, Kurt, and Bruce, the other three teenagers, had pitched in at the village end. For some reason, Loki hadn't bothered to think things through; he'd deliberately kept Bruce Geralds, Sr. away from his son until the last minute.

Now they all sat in shocked and exhausted silence nursing hot cups of tay and wondering what would happen next.

Did they dare trust the end of the day to be the end of the horror?

Hestiia and Ariel sat in *Rover,* quietly grieving with Kim's body, telling him of their love for him, though he lay in stasis, unable to respond. Could he hear?

Loki and his siblings, along with Martin, gathered for a private conference at the far end of the circle of firelight, close to *Rover's* parking place and the illusion of escape. "We can't leave Cyndi, Quinn, Geralds, and Martin's friends . . . and we can't let them escape," Loki continued his litany of grief. He didn't trust his former lover and he didn't know Quinn well enough to trust him—though Martin did and that spoke well of him.

"I wish I knew who Quinn had bought his ship from. If I could pry that secret from his mind, or his mouth, I'd trust him more." Kat stood up and brushed her trousers free of a few specks of dirt, as if dealing with this thorny question soiled them more than nine months of living rough on a primitive planet had.

"Quinn might swear to keep this planet a secret, but I'm not willing to take the chance. He doesn't have a vested interest in keeping this place secret. He does have a vested interest in reporting to the emperor." Kat sighed and shrugged. "I've been betrayed too often by those I thought I could trust and saved by those I knew I could not." She grinned at her brothers.

Loki hugged her. He needed to make sure she was still here, still allied with them.

"Martin likes and trusts him," Konner offered. He hugged his son as if afraid the boy would slip away forever if he didn't keep him close.

"But apparently, Quinn's got the ear of the emperor," Kat said. "Don't ask me how or in what capacity. I barely understand it myself. That opens more jump points into the unknown."

"If the ley lines here are a part of the transactional graviton web, then we can't disrupt the balance any more than we already have," Konner said. "Star travel, communications, even planetary gravities might be disrupted." He and Martin studied a handheld, trying to puzzle it all out.

"Omniscium is too valuable. The emperor couldn't ignore this source, even if Quinn swore him to secrecy," Loki added.

"What are we going to do?" Kat banged her fist against her thigh. "All of these people have connections to important people who will come looking for them eventually."

(May I help?) Gentian asked them all.

"Who said that?" Martin jumped.

"He's never spoken to me before!" Loki said as he scanned the night sky in wonder.

"Or me," Konner echoed.

Then the flywacket dove below the clouds and came to a flapping halt at

Kat's feet. He neatly tucked his wings beneath their protective flap of skin and rubbed his face against Kat's leg. She bent to scratch his ears and his purr rumbled loud and full.

Martin's jaw dropped in wonder as he, too, reached a tentative hand to pet the flywacket. Maybe he needed to make certain the beast was real.

"How can you help, my friend?" Kat asked.

(Take me with you when you leave Kardia Hodos,) Gentian begged. His eyes engaged each of them in turn.

"If that's what you wish. But we aren't certain how we can leave without the outsiders."

Loki's heart swelled to hear her refer to the others as outsiders—as if she finally felt she belonged here. With her family.

(I can give them each a dragon dream. They will each believe the story I send them, with no memory of this place.)

"A dragon dream is a powerful weapon." Loki crouched down to stare the flywacket in the eye. "Do you dare do this without the consent of the entire nimbus?" He'd had firsthand experience with one of the dreams. The image of a spotted saber cat leaping to attack him remained as vivid in his mind as if he'd actually lived through the experience.

"I've heard of dragon dreams," Kat whispered in wonder. "Irisey, the female dragon, said something about wishing she had the authority to give Amanda a dragon dream so she would banish the spirit that possessed her. But all of the dragons must agree before a dream may be given."

"How complete is a dragon dream?" Konner asked Gentian.

Hope began to lift Loki's spirits. "A dragon dream is more real than reality."

(Yes. Kardia Hodos will become to these people less than a dream, only an occasional flicker of the imagination. Ask the one called Brewster if he remembers setting a spark inside the ship that brought Kat.)

"Brewster," Loki called the sergeant over to him. He looked closely at the man's aura. Shades of innocent green looked open and vulnerable. Loki set his mind to probe the man. "When was the last time you were aboard *Jupiter?*"

"I went back once with Lieutenant Talbot right after we evacuated nine moons ago. I helped her salvage comm units and a hydroponics tank right after you stole the crystal array. Lot of good that did. Everything at Base Camp is ash." The man frowned deeply. "I sure hope a rescue ship comes soon. I don't see how any of us can survive without hydro tanks."

"You'll learn," Kat said. "You didn't go back the day *Jupiter* exploded?"

"Are you kidding? Once was enough. That ship was spooky, all empty and silent." He visibly shuddered all over.

Kat sent him back to help Taneeo and Lotski care for the frightened and wounded.

"His mind is vacant of any sense of lying," Loki said quietly as soon as Brewster was out of earshot.

(I assure you, he set the spark that destroyed the intruding ship. I watched him do it.)

"Why?" Kat asked the flywacket.

(The ship presented a danger to the nimbus. It had to die. One of its own had to perform the act.)

"And most of the debris went outward, outside the planet's gravity." Kat shook her head in wonder.

"I . . . I retrieved the black box," Martin said quietly.

The adults looked at him skeptically.

"We cracked it," he affirmed and met their gazes with confidence. "I showed a small fighter leaving the ship's schematic just before the explosion. The bigger lander left in the wake of the blast."

"Why am I not surprised that you alone in the GTE figured out how to crack a black box without the codes?" Konner hugged his son again.

"Can Brewster pilot a fighter?" Loki asked his sister.

"I coached him on flying a lander a couple of times." She shrugged. "If he's as bright as I think he is, he could figure it out, but his piloting wouldn't be pretty."

They all looked at each other in silence.

"Okay, so we give these people a dragon dream. They forget this place," Loki said with resolve.

"There is something else we have to do," Kat faced her brothers with her jaw set in O'Hara determination. "A dragon taboo won't keep Hanassa confined for long. He . . . she . . . it will find a way out of the volcano sooner rather than later."

"Any ideas?" Loki asked her. He wasn't too happy about leaving the problem in dragon hands either.

"If we had any crystals, we could set up a force field like the one around the clearing. Opposite to it, designed to keep one person in but open to all others," Konner offered. "But the only spare crystals we have are aboard Geralds' ship and we need that to get everyone off this planet who has to go."

"Crystal? Like a king stone?" Martin asked.

The adults all looked at him questioningly. Something stirred in Loki's mind. Something akin to hope.

"Will this help?" Martin fished a glowing blue stone from his pocket.

Loki gasped in wonder. "A mini king! Where'd you get that? You know they are illegal?"

"Dad gave it to me two years ago. And I know how illegal they are and how powerful."

"Where'd you get it?" Loki demanded of his younger brother.

"A very talented craftsman in the GFM." Konner shrugged. "He helped me figure out the physics of the cloaking field using that crystal."

"Will that little king stone be enough? Don't we need a bunch more crystals to complete the array?" Loki asked. He wanted to reach out and grab the magnificent stone but forced himself to keep his hands at his sides. The stone wasn't his. He wasn't attuned to it. It would reject him as assuredly as its big brothers would aboard a ship.

"There are lots of native crystals," Kat said, whipping out her handheld.

"But are they monopoles?" Konner looked over her shoulder, making adjustments to her scans.

"Martin, would you please place the mini king on the ground behind the rock you are sitting on?" Konner asked.

The boy looked at his father skeptically but obeyed. Then Konner took his own handheld over to the stone and attached some kind of probe to it.

"We have a match!" he crowed. "This little guy is so hungry for a task to complete it is already bonding with the crystal matrix in this ordinary granite."

(We must hurry,) Gentian reminded them. *(We must work your magic and mine very quickly, before the dragons find out. They do not like their judgment questioned or interference in their decisions.)*

"Then let's do it. We gather crystals at dawn." Loki sat back on his rock and relaxed, happy to have a plan for him to direct. Happy to have his family working together.

Martin stared at his king stone. It rested comfortably in his hand. In the back of his mind he heard it humming quite happily.

Through the stone, Martin was aware of every rock chip and boulder within the ancient volcano caldera as if they were living beings instead of inanimate lumps of mineral. He could explore all of the caves leading off of the bowl of this dry and dusty place. He even knew the cycle of the mysterious dragongate that overlooked the lava core deep within the blown-out mountain.

He smiled to himself as he memorized the workings of the dragongate. A jump point. Only this one was limited to locations on the planet rather than distant star systems. The dragongate also had many termini. A true jump point only had one.

"You ready to bury the king stone?" his father asked him gently. "We've got the rest of the array spread around the exterior of the mountain, including one at the opening to the dragongate." He looked around at the dirty and dusty crew of locals they had drafted for the dirty work of burying the crystals at precise intervals.

"I think so." Martin remembered all the times the king stone made him

feel special when no one truly loved him. Now he had his dad and a wonderful, if weird stepmother who could track anything on planet or off. He also
had uncles and an aunt and a cousin.

"I don't need the crystal anymore, Dad. I've got family." He didn't need
the stone anymore. But the stone needed a family of crystals to be happy.

Konner hugged him tightly. Then together they connected a handheld to
the base of the crystal with fiber optics and placed the king stone upright in
the deep hole Gentian had dug for it.

"I used to admire you, Captain Leonard," Kat said to the huddled figure before her.

Hanassa had retreated into one of the caves to nurse its hurts. The wound
in its side had scabbed over, but it must still give pain and the blood loss had
left the rogue dragon weak and resentful.

Now it hunkered into a throne carved of silver bloodwood on a dais one
hundred meters inside the labyrinth of caves. The toxins in the sap would
poison anything else that touched the raw wood. But Hanassa seemed impervious to the beautiful carving.

The only light came from Kat's torch. Hanassa didn't seem to need illumi-
nation.

Only one more thing remained to do before Kat could blast off from this
planet and return to her life and her career. She had few regrets.

Kat still hated the thought of leaving all of her shipmates stranded on this
primitive world. Fortunately, most of them, led by M'Berra's example, had
settled in and begun to forge a new life.

A brief check on Judge Balinakas' city to the far west revealed a thriving
society. They'd begun building massive government buildings and temples.
They'd even begun a campaign to tame the cannibals in the mountains.

Only Amanda's seventy-eight remaining Marines objected to being left.
M'Berra held them in a separate cave by force of arms until the force field was
in place. His useless left arm cradled in a sling served as a powerful reminder
of the crimes those Marines had committed and helped Amanda commit.
The Marines would be able to come and go from the caldera, to serve their
captain, and bring in supplies. But they were exiled from the villages. They
faced a miserable existence in this barren volcano with only one small area on
the plateau capable of growing food.

"I know you are in that body somewhere, Amanda Leonard," Kat continued. "I know that some bit of your psyche still lingers. You deserve to know
what is happening here."

Carefully, Kat outlined the purpose of the force field, a reverse of the one that protected the family clearing. This one was keyed so that Hanassa alone could not penetrate the field, others could come and go without triggering the energies bonded to the king stone and its family of native crystals.

Presumably the dragongate was similarly keyed to not allow Hanassa passage. But no one truly understood that weird exit point except the dragons. Kat had to trust Gentian's assurances that Hanassa would not leave by that portal.

"I learned a lot from you, Amanda. I learned what it means to be a good captain. I also learned how easy it is to let personal obsessions get in the way of leadership. Thank you for those lessons." She turned to go but paused at the narrow passageway to the outside. "Thank you, Captain Leonard."

"You will fail," Hanassa snarled. "You don't have the courage to put aside your personal desires and your 'love' for your family. They will always get in the way of your career. You should kill them now."

"My family will not get in my way. They will support me. They love me. You never loved anything except your ship and yourself. That got in the way of your success."

Kat left before the *thing* behind her could offer any more "advice" that she would not take.

She still hadn't decided what to do about the outstanding arrest warrants on her brothers. And her mother.

"She's right, you know," Bruce Geralds said at the cave entrance. He'd volunteered to help set the force field since he understood it well enough to steal the cloaking configuration for his own ship with a similar setup.

"How so?" Kat held back from coming too close to him. Given half a logical explanation for his actions, she just might allow her attraction to him to overcome her good judgment.

"Your brothers are still criminals. They will drag you down, keep you from getting deserved promotions." He had the decency to keep his eyes on his feet.

"And what about you? What about your criminal actions? Why did you continue to work for Melinda Fortesque? Do her dirty work. Make life miserable for my brother Konner. You lied, cheated, stole. You arranged the murder of her *parents*. What about your crimes?"

Geralds gulped and looked away. "My sister held a seat in the planetary Parliament of Enigma VI when Melinda first hired me. She's in the GTE Parliament now. She's a good politician. And an honest one. She cares about people and she won't be bribed. But her husband's family has connections." His eyes met Kat's gaze briefly then darted away again.

"What kind of connections?" she probed. Good connections could make or break a political career.

"With the pirates of Palaleeze II." He named a notorious group of raiders. They nominally held membership in the Galactic Free Market so the GTE couldn't go in and clean out the nest of murderers, slavers, and thieves.

"Ouch," Kat whispered.

"Ouch, yes. One whisper of those connections and Pat's career is dead. Her husband would be arrested and their kids taken from them. Jim's a good man. He's broken from his family. But the association is enough to send him to prison and mind-wipe."

"Melinda threatened to expose your brother-in-law if you didn't do her dirty work."

"Over and over again. She may have already ruined my family since I didn't return with Konner, dead or alive."

"If she had, then your son would have known about it, suffered for it."

"That's my only hope. That he never finds out the truth about me."

"That can't be helped, Geralds," Quinn said, coming up behind them. "We're ready to set things in motion and leave, Kat." He looked her in the eye with frank appraisal. But he still had too many secrets for Kat's liking.

"What can we do for Geralds?" Kat asked. "He was coerced. He's not likely to repeat his crimes once he's freed from Melinda."

"Will you testify against her?" Quinn asked.

"Gladly." Geralds sighed as if relieved of a heavy burden. "As long as you keep my brother-in-law's family connections a secret."

"You'll probably have to do some prison time, but I think we can plea-bargain you out of mind-wipe."

"Does Bruce have to know?"

'I can't see a way around it," Kat said. "But in bringing Melinda down, we set Martin up as her heir. He can do a lot for Bruce and your wife. That's better than staying here for the rest of your life. Letting them wonder if you are dead or alive."

Geralds gulped. "I surrender to you, Quinn, as a fellow Sam Eyeam. I trust you to treat me and my family squarely." Geralds bowed his head.

"You do know what we plan to do to you?" Kat stopped Geralds and Quinn from exiting with a tense hand on each of their arms.

"It is for the best," Geralds sighed. "I don't want to remember a lot of what happened here."

"You can make me forget this place, Mari Kathleen O'Hara Talbot," Quinn said quietly. "But I don't think I'm capable of forgetting you." He took Geralds by the elbow and led him out to the relentless sunshine and the waiting shuttles.

"Now what did he mean by that?" Kat stared after them a moment, then looked back one last time on the pitiful remains of her once proud captain. "Good-bye, Amanda. I know you will never be happy. You never could be happy even before Hanassa invaded you. But I do hope you find peace here on Kardia Hodos."

"This place is Hanassa!" Amanda insisted.

"Very well, then, you rule this volcanic crater called Hanassa. But we give a different name to the rest of this world." She turned her back on Hanassa, knowing that her captain had died inside the crabbed and twisted body.

Sadly, she joined the others for the last trip back to the family clearing and the village.

Then she could go home at last.

If home was out there, beyond the stars, then what would she call this place?

(Kardia Hodos, the pathway of the heart.)

EPILOGUE

"**D**O WHAT YOU MUST," Kat said, petting Gentian. All those who were leaving had gathered around *Rover* and Quinn's shuttle.

(You must promise to take me away with you.) Gentian leaned his considerable weight against Kat's ankles.

"I promise. You will leave with me, Gentian. You will be my companion henceforth, wherever I happen to roam."

"Let's do it," Loki ordered. "Do it now and we will all be free of the burden of this place." He looked anxiously into *Rover,* checking on Kim's stasis, ready to take off.

(But you will never be free of Kardia Hodos. This home will remain with you forever.)

Kat smiled at each of her brothers, her sisters-in-law, her niece, and her nephew. "We will come back. Each of us in our turn, if nothing else, to return Kim to his wife and daughter."

Hestiia cuddled her infant daughter close as she gave each of the family a tight hug. Then she moved off to join the villagers. She had shed her tears and now she entrusted the love of her life to his family. Her family. They'd enlarged the coding on the family clearing so that she could come and go without Kim.

(Each of you will come here in turn for your own reasons. In your own time you must make peace with this place,) Gentian continued. *(Then it will be your home forever, no matter where you roam.)*

"Amen, so be it," Kat whispered. Her family echoed her sentiment.

Gentian turned to face those selected for the dragon dream. He spread his wings and flapped them once, commanding attention.

Then, one by one, the faces of his victims went slack, their eyes vacant. As one, they turned their backs on Kardia Hodos and retreated to their assigned shuttles.

Loki and Konner dropped Kat and her two passengers aboard *Son and Heir.*

With their help Kat strapped a sleeping Geralds onto the lounge bench and Cyndi into the narrow bunk aboard *Son and Heir.*

Then her brothers departed with brief but intense hugs.

Kat blinked away her tears before these two strong men could see them. She suspected they shared her emotions, but she refused to reach out with her psi talents to eavesdrop.

She envied the diplomatic attaché the smile on her face. Whatever she dreamed pleased her.

Kat would report to her superiors in the Imperial Military Police that she and Cyndi had barely escaped the explosion of *Jupiter.* All hands were dead or missing. Geralds, already strapped into another bunk, had rescued them from certain death as their escape pod drifted in void beyond the jump point.

The nine-month delay in their return to civilization resulted from a king stone damaged in a battle with the O'Hara brothers who escaped.

Back on the planet, Hestiia grieved over Kim's injuries but fully expected her Stargod to return. Dalleena accompanied Konner along with Martin.

Kat stooped to scratch Gentian's ears just as the comm system beeped. She answered it in the gangway so as not to awaken Cyndi.

"Yes, Loki?' she asked recognizing *Sirius'* signature on the screen.

"All secure over there?" His face on the screen showed him running departure protocols on his bridge. Konner sat beside him as copilot.

"Getting there. Just tucked in my passengers. Gentian says they'll sleep for another day."

"The *Margaret Kristine* just blasted off without so much as a good-bye." Loki looked a little miffed at the impoliteness.

"Why should Quinn say good-bye when he doesn't know he's been here? He or the kids?" But he had promised to remember Kat. She was beginning to look forward to their next meeting. Not soon, but someday.

"Will they be all right, Aunt Kat?" Martin asked from the third console aboard *Sirius.*

"Gentian says so. They believe you bailed out before they left Aurora. The weeks they've been in space were just idle travel to keep Kurt away from assassins until his father is elected again. Truth drugs and electric probes shouldn't pry any different information from them."

"That's a relief. I want to call them as soon as I safely can."

"You can stay with your dad until Geralds and I can present evidence of your mother's crimes to the GTE. I have the documents from your database. I'll leave a message at the rendezvous point when Melinda is arrested and you can claim your inheritance."

Kat switched the signal to the bridge of the tiny ship and made her way there to continue the conversation as she prepared for launch.

"We'll let Mum know you're alive," Konner said. "If she agrees to see you, we'll have her leave messages at the same rendezvous."

"I'll look for it." Kat stroked the braided hair bracelet. What would Mum live for if she acknowledged that her lost daughter wasn't lost anymore? Would she know where to find the man who had sold his ship *Margaret Kristine* to Quinn? Would the family be able to find their father and finally all be together again?

"Let me know how Kim fares and when he's ready to go back home. I'd like to be on that flight." Kat shifted to the more immediate problem rather than dwell on "what ifs."

"Will do. We'll wait for you to launch, then follow you through the jump point. Good luck, baby sister."

Kat familiarized herself with the bridge controls, ran her safety checks and fired up the crystal drive. Only then did she look through her viewscreen. Two very large male dragons, one green, one blue, hovered in front of her.

How did they survive in the vacuum of space?

She paused with her hands on the controls.

Gentian slunk down in the copilot's seat as far as his safety harness would let him.

(You must return the flywacket to the nimbus,) the dragons said in chorus. *(He must answer to us for his crime of cowardice and disobedience.)*

"Cowardice?" Kat asked incredulously. "Gentian acted with more courage than the entire nimbus combined. He helped me and my family when you all would only stand back and watch!"

"Is everything okay, Kat?" Konner asked over the open comm.

"Everything will be." She glared at the image of the dragons in the viewscreen. They had not moved, but she sensed they consulted each other along a private line of thought.

(Gentian is one of us. He must remain with us.)

"Sorry, gang. He's part of my family now." Kat's heart warmed. She had a family; brothers, sisters-in-law, a nephew, and a niece. Even Murphy, the green teddy bear, had a new home and a new child to love. She swallowed a lump in her throat.

And she had Gentian. A friend and companion. She also had a place to call home, a place outside her career in the Imperial Military Police. She wasn't lonely anymore.

She reached over and reassured Gentian with a lingering caress. He leaned into her hand and purred.

(Can you guard the flywacket as we would?) the dragons asked Kat.

"I can do better. I can love him as part of my family."

(Then he is yours until he realizes that humans are less than perfect companions for kin of a dragon.)

"I trust Gentian to let me know if he's ever dissatisfied with me as a companion."

(I will love you as my own until you no longer need me. Then I will return to the nimbus if no other of your family needs me. And not before.)

When Kat looked back at the viewscreen the dragons had vanished.

"Jump point coordinates plotted in and ready for launch," she announced to her brothers.

She activated the controls and began the flight to the rest of her life.

"Kardia Hodos," she mused. "The pathway of the heart. Kim named this place correctly."